MAURICE GUEST

A Novel

Henry Handel Richardson

Skyhorse Publishing
A Herman Graf Book

To Louise

First Skyhorse edition published 2015
First published by William Heinemann 1908

Skyhorse Publishing books may be purchased in bulk at special discounts for sales promotion, corporate gifts, fund-raising, or educational purposes. Special editions can also be created to specifications. For details, contact the Special Sales Department, Skyhorse Publishing, 307 West 36th Street, 11th Floor, New York, NY 10018 or info@skyhorsepublishing.com.

Skyhorse® and Skyhorse Publishing® are registered trademarks of Skyhorse Publishing, Inc.®, a Delaware corporation.

Visit our website at www.skyhorsepublishing.com.

10 9 8 7 6 5 4 3 2 1

Library of Congress Cataloging-in-Publication Data is available on file.

Cover design by Brian Peterson

Print ISBN: 978-1-63450-507-9
Ebook ISBN: 978-1-5107-0054-3

Printed in the United States of America

PART I

S'amor non è, che dunque è quel ch'io sento?
Ma s'egli è amor, per Dio, che cosa è quale?

PETRARCH.

I

ONE noon in 189—, a young man stood in front of the new Gewandhaus in Leipzig, and watched the neat, grass-laid square, until then white and silent in the sunshine, grow dark with many figures.

The public rehearsal of the weekly concert was just over, and, from the half light of the warm-coloured hall, which for more than two hours had held them secluded, some hundreds of people hastened, with renewed anticipation, towards sunlight and street sounds. There was a medley of tongues, for many nationalities were represented in the crowd that surged through the ground-floor and out of the glass doors, and much noisy ado, for the majority was made up of young people, at an age that enjoys the sound of its own voice. In black, diverging lines they poured through the heavy swinging doors, which flapped ceaselessly to and fro, never quite closing, always opening afresh, and on descending the shallow steps, they told off into groups, where all talked at once, with lively gesticulation. A few faces had the strained look that indicates the conscientious listener; but most of these young musicians were under the influence of a stimulant more potent than wine, which manifested itself in a nervous garrulity and a nervous mirth.

They hummed like bees before a hive. Maurice Guest, who had come out among the first, lingered to watch a scene that was new to him, of which he was as yet an onlooker only. Here and there came a member of the orchestra; with violin-case or black-swathed wind-instrument in hand, he deftly threaded his way through the throng, bestowing, as he went, a hasty nod of greeting upon a colleague, a sweep of the hat on an obsequious pupil. The crowd began to disperse and to overflow in the surrounding streets. Some of the stragglers loitered to swell the group that was forming round the back entrance to the building; here the lank-haired Belgian violinist would appear, the wonders of whose technique had sent thrills of enthusiasm through his hearers, and whose close proximity would presently affect them in precisely the same way. Others again made off, not for the town, with its prosaic suggestion of work and confinement, but for the freedom of the woods that lay beyond.

Maurice Guest followed them.

It was a blowy day in early spring. Round white masses of cloud moved lightly across a deep blue sky, and the trees, still thin and naked, bent their heads and shook their branches, as if to elude the gambols of a boisterous playfellow. The sun shone vividly, with restored power, and though the clouds sometimes passed over his very face, the shadows only lasted for a moment, and each returning radiance seemed brighter than the one before. In the pure breath of the wind, as it gustily swept the earth, was a promise of things vernal, of the tender beauties of a coming spring; but there was still a keen, delightful freshness in the air, a vague reminder of frosty starlights and serene white snow—the untrodden snow of deserted, moonlit streets—that quickened the blood, and sent a craving for movement through the veins. The people who trod the broad, clean roads and the paths of the wood walked with a spring in their steps; voices were light and high, and each breath that was drawn increased the sense of buoyancy, of undiluted satisfaction. With these bursts of golden sunshine, so other than the pallid gleamings of the winter, came a fresh impulse to life; and the most insensible was dimly conscious how much had to be made up for, how much lived into such a day.

Maurice Guest walked among the mossgreen tree-trunks, each of which vied with the other in the brilliancy of its coating. He was under the sway of a twofold intoxication: great music and a day rich in promise. From the flood of melody that had broken over him, the frenzied storms of applause, he had come out, not into a lamplit darkness that would have crushed his elation back upon him and hemmed it in, but into the spacious lightness of a fair blue day, where all that he felt could expand, as a flower does in the sun.

His walk brought him to a broad stream, which flashed through the wood like a line of light. He paused on a suspension bridge, and leaning over the railing, gazed up the river into the distance, at the horizon and its trees, delicate and feathery in their nakedness against the sky. Swollen with recent rains and snows, the water came hurrying towards him— the storm-bed of the little river, which, meandering in from the country, through pleasant woods, in ever narrowing curves, ran through the town as a small stream, to be swelled again

on the outskirts by the waters of two other rivers, which joined
it at right angles. The bridge trembled at first, when other
people crossed it, on their way to the woods that lay on the
further side, but soon the last stragglers vanished, and he was
alone.

As he looked about, eager to discover beauty in the strip
of landscape that stretched before him—the line of water, its
banks of leafless trees—he was instinctively filled with a desire
for something grander, for a feature in the scene that would
answer to his mood. There, where the water appeared to end
in a clump of trees, there, should be mountains, a gently undulating line, blue with the unapproachable blue of distance,
and high enough to form a background to the view; in summer, heavy with haze, melting into the sky; in winter, lined
and edged with snow. From this, his thoughts sprang back to
the music he had heard that morning. All the vague yet eager
hopes that had run riot in his brain, for months past, seemed to
have been summed up and made clear to him, in one supreme
phrase of it, a great phrase in C major, in the concluding
movement of Beethoven's Fifth Symphony. First sounded by
the shrill sweet winds, it had suddenly been given out by the
strings, in magnificient unison, and had mounted up and on,
to the jubilant trilling of the little flutes. There was such a
courageous sincerity in this theme, such undauntable resolve;
it expressed more plainly than words what he intended his life
of the next few years to be; for he was full to the brim of
ambitious intentions, which he had never yet had a chance of
putting into practice. He felt so ready for work, so fresh and
unworn; the fervour of a deep enthusiasm was rampant in him.
What a single-minded devotion to art, he promised himself his
should be! No other fancy or interest should share his heart
with it, he vowed that to himself this day, when he stood for
the first time on historic ground, where the famous musicians
of the past had found inspiration for their immortal works.
And his thoughts spread their wings and circled above his head;
he saw himself already of these masters' craft, their art his, he
wrenching ever new secrets from them, penetrating the recesses
of their genius, becoming one of themselves. In a vision as
vivid as those that cross the brain in a sleepless night, he saw a
dark, compact multitude wait, with breath suspended, to catch
the notes that fell like raindrops from his fingers; saw himself
the all-conspicuous figure, as, with masterful gestures, he compelled the soul that lay dormant in brass and strings, to give

voice to, to interpret to the many, his subtlest emotions. And he was overcome by a tremulous compassion with himself at the idea of wielding such power over an unknown multitude, at the latent nobility of mind and aim this power implied.

Even when swinging back to the town, he had not shaken himself free of dreams. The quiet of a foreign midday lay upon the streets, and there were few discordant sounds, few passers-by, to break the chain of his thought. He had movement, silence, space. And as is usual with active-brained dreamers, he had little or no eye for the real life about him; he was not struck by the air of comfortable prosperity, of thriving content, which marked the great commercial centre, and he let pass, unnoticed, the unfamiliar details of a foreign street, the trifling yet significant incidents of foreign life. Such impressions as he received, bore the stamp of his own mood. He was sensible, for instance, in face of the picturesque houses that clustered together in the centre of the town, of the spiritual *Gemutlichkeit,* the absence of any pomp or pride in their romantic past, which characterises the old buildings of a German town. These quaint and stately houses, wedged one into the other, with their many storeys, their steeply sloping roofs and eye-like roof-windows, were still in sympathetic touch with the trivial life of the day which swarmed in and about them. He wandered leisurely along the narrow streets that ran at all angles off the Market Place, one side of which was formed by the gabled *Rathaus,* with its ground-floor row of busy little shops; and, in fancy, he peopled these streets with the renowned figures that had once walked them. He looked up at the dark old houses in which great musicians had lived, died, and been born, and he saw faces that he recognised lean out of the projecting windows, to watch the life and bustle below, to catch the last sunbeam that filtered in; he saw them take their daily walk along these very streets, in the antiquated garments of their time. They passed him by, shade-like and misanthropic, and seemed to steal down the opposite side, to avoid his too pertinent gaze. Bluff, preoccupied, his keen eyes lowered, the burly Cantor passed, as he had once done day after day, with the disciplined regularity of high genius, of the honest citizen, to his appointed work in the shadows of the organ-loft; behind him, one who had pointed to the giant with a new burst of ardour, the genial little improviser, whose triumphs had been those of this town, whose fascinating gifts, and still more fascinating personality, had made him the lion of his age. And it was only another step in this train of half-conscious thought, that, before a large-lettered poster, which stood out black and white against the reds and yellows of the circular advertisement-column, and bore the word " Siegfried," Maurice Guest should not merely be filled with the anticipation of a world of beauty still unexplored, but that the word should stand to him for a symbol, as it were, of the easeful and luxurious side of a life dedicated to art—of a world-wide fame; the society of princes, kings; the gloss of velvet; the dull glow of gold.—And again, tapering vistas opened up, through which he could peer into the future, happy in the knowledge that he stood firm in a present which made all things possible to a holy zeal, to an unhesitating grasp.

But it was growing late, and he slowly retraced his steps. In the restaurant into which he turned for dinner, he was the only customer. The principal business of the day was at an end; two waiters sat dozing in corners, and a man behind the counter, who was washing metal-topped beer-glasses, had almost the whole pile polished bright before him. Maurice Guest sat down at a table by the window; and, when he had finished his dinner and lighted a cigarette, he watched the passers-by, who crossed the pane of glass like the figures in a moving photograph.

Suddenly the door opened with an energetic click, and a lady came in, enveloped in an old-fashioned, circular cloak, and carrying on one arm a pile of paper-covered music. This, she laid on the table next that at which the young man was sitting, then took off her hat. When she had also hung up the unbecoming cloak, he saw that she was young and slight. For the rest, she seemed to bring with her, into the warm, tranquil atmosphere of the place, heavy with midday musings, a breath of wind and outdoor freshness—a suggestion that was heightened by the quick decisiveness of her movements: the briskness with which she divested herself of her wrappings, the quick smooth of the hair on either side, the business-like way in which she drew up her chair to the table and unfolded her napkin.

She seemed to be no stranger there, for, on her entrance, the younger and more active waiter had at once sprung up with officious haste, and almost before she was ready, the little table was newly spread and set, and the dinner of the day before her. She spoke to the man in a friendly way as she took her seat, and he replied with a pleased and smiling respect.

Then she began to eat, deliberately, and with an over-emphasised nicety. As she carried her soup-spoon to her lips, Maurice Guest felt that she was observing him; and throughout the meal, of which she ate but little, he was aware of a peculiarly straight and penetrating gaze. It ended by disconcerting him. Beckoning the waiter, he went through the business of paying his bill, and this done, was about to push back his chair and rise to his feet, when the man, in gathering up the money, addressed what seemed to be a question to him. Fearful lest he had made a mistake in the strange coinage, Maurice looked up apprehensively. The waiter repeated his words, but the slight nervousness that gained on the young man made him incapable of separating the syllables, which were indistinguishably blurred. He coloured, stuttered, and felt mortally uncomfortable, as, for the third time, the waiter repeated his remark, with the utmost slowness.

At this point, the girl at the adjacent table put down her knife and fork, and leaned slightly forward.

" Excuse me," she said, and smiled. " The waiter only said he thought you must be a stranger here: *der Herr ist gewiss fremd in Leipzig?* " Her rather prominent teeth were visible as she spoke.

Maurice, who understood instantly her pronunciation of the words, was not set any more at his ease by her explanation. " Thanks very much," he said, still redder than usual. " I . . . er . . . thought the fellow was saying something about the money."

" And the Saxon dialect *is* barbarous, isn't it? " she added kindly. " But perhaps you have not had much experience of it yet."

" No. I only arrived this morning."

At this, she opened her eyes wide. " Why, you are a courageous person! " she said and laughed, but did not explain what she meant, and he did not like to ask her.

A cup of coffee was set on the table before her; she held a lump of sugar in her spoon, and watched it grow brown and dissolve. " Are you going to make a long stay? " she asked, to help him over his embarrassment.

" Two years, I hope," said the young man.

" Music? " she queried further, and as he replied affirmatively: " Then the Con. of course? "—an enigmatic question that needed to be explained. " You're piano, are you not? " she went on. " I thought so. It is hardly possible to mistake the hands"—here she just glanced at her own, which, large, white, and well formed, were lying on the table. "With strings, you know, the right hand is as a rule shockingly defective."

He found the high clearness of her voice very agreeable after the deep roundnesses of German, and could have gone on listening to it. But she was brushing the crumbs from her skirt, preparatory to rising.

"Are you an old resident here?" he queried in the hope of detaining her.

"Yes, quite. I'm at the end of my second year; and don't know whether to be glad or sorry," she answered. "Time goes like a flash.—Now, look here, as one who knows the ways of the place, would you let me give you a piece of advice? Yes? —It's this. You intend to enter the Conservatorium, you say. Well, be sure you get under a good man—that's half the battle. Try and play privately to either Schwarz or Bendel. If you go in for the public examination with all the rest, the people in the *Bureau* will put you to anyone they like, and that is disastrous. Choose your own master, and beard him in his den beforehand."

"Yes . . . and you recommend? May I ask whom you are with?" he said eagerly.

"Schwarz is my master; and I couldn't wish for a better. But Bendel is good, too, in his way, and is much sought after by the Americans—you're not American, are you? No.—Well, the English colony runs the American close nowadays. We're a regular army. If you don't want to, you need hardly mix with foreigners as long as you're here. We have our clubs and balls and other social functions—and our geniuses—and our masters who speak English like natives . . . But there!— you'll soon know all about it yourself."

She nodded pleasantly and rose.

"I must be off," she said. "To-day every minute is precious. That wretched *Probe* spoils the morning, and directly it is over, I have to rush to an organ-lesson—that's why I'm here. For I can't expect a *Pension* to keep dinner hot for me till nearly three o'clock—can I? Morning rehearsals are a mistake. What?—you were there, too? Really?—after a night in the train? Well, you didn't get much, did you, for your energy? A dull aria, an overture that 'belongs in the theatre,' as they say here, an indifferently played symphony that one has heard at least a dozen times. And for us poor pianists, not a fresh dish this season. Nothing but yesterday's remains heated up again."

She laughed as she spoke, and Maurice Guest laughed, too, not being able at the moment to think of anything to say.

Getting the better of the waiter, who stood by, napkin on arm, smiling and officious, he helped her into the unbecoming cloak; then took up the parcel of music and opened the door. In his manner of doing this, there may have been a touch of over-readiness, for no sooner was she outside, than she quietly took the music from him, and, without even offering him her hand, said a friendly but curt good-bye: almost before he had time to return it, he saw her hurrying up the street, as though she had never vouchsafed him word or thought. The abruptness of the dismissal left him breathless; in his imagination, they had walked at least a strip of the street together. He stepped off the pavement into the road, that he might keep her longer in sight, and for some time he saw her head, in the close-fitting hat, bobbing along above the heads of other people.

On turning again, he found that the waiter was watching him from the window of the restaurant, and it seemed to the young man that the pale, servile face wore a malicious smile. With the feeling of disconcertion that springs from being caught in an impulsive action we have believed unobserved, Maurice spun round on his heel and took a few quick steps in the opposite direction. When once he was out of range of the window, however, he dropped his pace, and at the next corner stopped altogether. He would at least have liked to know her name. And what in all the world was he to do with himself now?

Clouds had gathered; the airy blue and whiteness of the morning had become a level sheet of grey, which wiped the colour out of everything; the wind, no longer tempered by the sun, was chilly, as it whirled down the narrow streets and freaked about the corners. There was little temptation now to linger on one's steps. But Maurice Guest was loath to return to the solitary room that stood to him for home, to shut himself up with himself, inside four walls: and turning up his coat collar, he began to walk slowly along the curved *Grimmaischestrasse*. But the streets were by this time black with people, most of whom came hurrying towards him, brisk and bustling, and gay, in spite of the prevailing dullness, at the prospect of the warm, familiar evening. He was continually obliged to step off the pavement into the road, to allow a bunch of merry, chattering girls, their cheeks coloured by the wind beneath the dark fur of their hats, or a line of gaudy-capped, thickset students, to pass him by, unbroken; and it seemed to him that he was more frequently off the pavement than on it. He began to feel disconsolate among these jovial people, who were hastening forward, with such spirit, to some end, and he had not gone far, before he turned down a side street to be out of their way. Vaguely damped by his environment, which, with the sun's retreat, had lost its charm, he gave himself up to his own thoughts, and was soon busily engaged in thinking over all that had been said by his quondam acquaintance of the dinner-table, in inventing neatly turned phrases and felicitous replies. He walked without aim, in a leisurely way down quiet streets, quickly across big thoroughfares, and paid no attention to where he was going. The falling darkness made the quaint streets look strangely alike; it gave them, too, an air of fantastic unreality: the dark old houses, marshalled in rows on either side, stood as if lost in contemplation, in the saddening dusk. The lighting of the street-lamps, which started one by one into existence, and the conflict with the fading daylight of the uneasily beating flame, that was swept from side to side in the wind like a woman's hair—these things made his surroundings seem still shadowier and less real.

He was roused from his reverie by finding himself on what was apparently the outskirts of the town. With much difficulty he made his way back, but he was still far from certain of his whereabouts, when an unexpected turn to the right brought him out on the spacious *Augustusplatz,* in front of the New Theatre. He had been in this square once already, but now its appearance was changed. The big buildings that flanked it were lit up; the file of droschkes waiting for fares, under the bare trees, formed a dotted line of lights. A double row of hanging lamps before the *Café Français* made the corner of the *Grimmaischestrasse* dazzling to the eyes; and now, too, the massive white theatre was awake as well. Lights shone from all its high windows, streamed out through the Corinthian columns and low-porched doorways. Its festive air was inviting, after his twilight wanderings, and he went across the square to it. Immediately before the theatre, early comers stood in knots and chatted; programme- and text-vendors cried and sold their wares; people came hurrying from all directions, as to a magnet; hastily they ascended the low steps and disappeared beneath the portico.

He watched until the last late-comer had vanished. Only he was left; he again was the outsider. And now, as he stood there in the deserted square, which, a moment before, had been so animated, he had a sudden sinking of the heart: he was seized by that acute sense of desolation that lies in wait for one, caught by nightfall, alone in a strange city. It stirs up a wild longing, not so much for any particular spot on earth, as for some familiar hand or voice, to take the edge off an intolerable loneliness.

He turned and walked rapidly back to the small hotel near the railway station, at which he was staying until he found lodgings. He was tired out, and for the first time became thoroughly conscious of this; but the depression that now closed in upon him, was not due to fatigue alone, and he knew it. In sane moments—such as the present—when neither excitement nor enthusiasm warped his judgment, he was under no illusion about himself; and as he strode through the darkness, he admitted that, all day long, he had been cheating himself in the usual way. He understood perfectly that it was by no means a matter of merely stretching out his hand, to pluck what he would, from this tree that waved before him; he reminded himself with some bitterness that he stood, an unheralded stranger, before a solidly compact body of things and people, on which he had not yet made any impression. It was the old story: he played at expecting a ready capitulation of the whole —gods and men—and, at the same time, was only too well aware of the laborious process that was his sole means of entry and fellowship. Again—to instance another of his mental follies—the pains he had been at to take possession of the town, to make it respond to his forced interpretation of it! In reality, it had repelled him—yes, he was chilled to the heart by the aloofness of this foreign town, to which not a single tie yet bound him.

By the light of a guttering candle, in the dingy hotel bedroom, he sat and wrote a letter, briefly announcing his safe arrival. About to close the envelope, he hesitated, and then, unfolding the sheet of paper again, added a few lines to what he had written. These cost him more trouble than all the rest.

Once more, hearty thanks to you both, my dear parents, for letting me have my own way. I hope you will never have reason to regret it. One thing, at least, I can promise you, and that is, that not a day of my time here shall be wasted or mis-

spent. You have not, I know, the same faith in me that I have myself, and this has often been a bitter thought to me. But only have patience. Something stronger than myself drove me to it, and if I am to succeed anywhere, it will be here. And I mean to succeed, if human will can do it.

He threw himself on the creaking wooden bed and tried to sleep. But his brain was active, and the street was noisy; people talked late in the adjoining room, and trod heavily in the one above. It was long after midnight before the house was still and he fell into an uneasy sleep.

Towards morning, he had a strange dream, from which he wakened in a cold sweat. Once more he was wandering through the streets, as he had done the previous day, apparently in search of something he could not find. But he did not know himself what he sought. All of a sudden, on turning a corner, he came upon a crowd of people gathered round some object in the road, and at once said to himself, this is it, here it is. He could not, however, see what it actually was, for the people, who were muttering to themselves in angry tones, strove to keep him back. At all costs, he felt, he must get nearer to the mysterious thing, and, in a spirit of bravado, he was pushing through the crowd to reach it, when a great clamour arose; every one sprang back, and fled wildly, shrieking: " Moloch, Moloch! " He did not know in the least what it meant, but the very strangeness of the word added to the horror, and he, too, fled with the rest; fled blindly, desperately, up streets and down, watched, it seemed to him, from every window by a cold, malignant eye, but never daring to turn his head, lest he should see the awful thing behind him; fled on and on, through streets that grew ever vaguer and more shadowy, till at last his feet would carry him no further: he sank down, with a loud cry, sank down, down, down, and wakened to find that he was sitting up in bed, clammy with fear, and that dawn was stealing in at the sides of the window.

II

In Maurice Guest, it might be said that the smouldering unrest of two generations burst into flame. As a young man, his father, then a poor teacher in a small provincial town, had been a prey to certain dreams and wishes, which harmonised ill with the conditions of his life. When, for example, on a mild night, he watched the moon scudding a silvery, cloud-flaked sky; when white clouds sailed swiftly, and soft spring breezes were hastening past; when, in a word, all things seemed to be making for some place, unknown, afar-off, where he was not, then he, too, was seized with a desire to be moving, to strap on a knapsack and be gone, to wander through foreign countries, to see strange cities and hear strange tongues, was unconsciously filled with the desire to taste, lighthearted, irresponsible, the joys and experiences of the *Wanderjahre,* before settling down to face the matter-of-factness of life. And as the present continually pushed the realisation of his dreams into the future, he satisfied the immediate thirst of his soul by playing the flute, and by breathing into the thin, reedy tones he drew from it, all that he dreamed of, but would never know. For he presently came to a place in his life where two paths diverged, and he was forced to make a choice between them. It was characteristic of the man that he chose the way of least resistance, and having married, more or less improvidently, he turned his back on the visions that had haunted his youth: afterwards, the cares, great and small, that came in the train of the years, drove them ever further into the background. Want of sympathy in his home-life blunted the finer edges of his nature; of a gentle and yielding disposition, he took on the commonplace colour of his surroundings. After years of unhesitating toil, it is true, the most pressing material needs died down, but the dreams and ambitions had died, too, never to come again. And as it is in the nature of things that no one is less lenient towards romantic longings than he who has suffered disappointment in them, who has failed to transmute them into reality, so, in this case, the son's first tentative leanings to a wider life, met with a more deeply-rooted, though less decisive, opposition, on the part of the father than of the mother.

But Maurice Guest had a more tenacious hold on life.

The home in which he grew up, was one of those cheerless, middle-class homes, across which never passes a breath of the great gladness, the ideal beauty of life; where thought never swings itself above the material interests of the day gone, the day to come, and existence grows as timid and trivial as the petty griefs and pleasures that intersperse it. The days drip past, one by one, like water from a spout after a rain-shower; and the dull monotony of them benumbs all wholesome temerity at its core. Maurice Guest had known days of this kind. For before the irksomeness of the school-bench was well behind him, he had begun his training as a teacher, and as soon as he had learnt how to instil his own half-digested knowledge into the minds of others, he received a small post in the school at which his father taught. The latter had, for some time, secretly cherished a wish to send the boy to study at the neighbouring university, to make a scholar of his eldest son; but the longer he waited, the more unfavourable did circumstances seem, and the idea finally died before it was born.

Maurice Guest looked back on the four years he had just come through, with bitterness; and it was only later, when he was engrossed heart and soul in congenial work, that he began to recognise, and be vaguely grateful for, the spirit of order with which they had familiarised him. At first, he could not recall them without an aversion that was almost physical: this machine-like regularity, which, in its disregard of mood and feeling, had something of a divine callousness to human stirrings; the jarring contact with automaton-like people; his inadequacy and distaste for a task that grew day by day more painful. His own knowledge was so hesitating, so uncertain, too slight for self-confidence, just too much and too fresh to allow him to generalise with the unthinking assurance that was demanded of him. Yet had anyone, he asked himself, more obstacles to overcome than he, in his efforts to set himself free? This silent, undemonstrative father, who surrounded himself with an unscalable wall of indifference; this hard-faced, careworn mother, about whose mouth the years had traced deep lines, and for whom, in the course of a single-handed battle with life, the true reality had come to be success or failure in the struggle for bread. What was art to them but an empty name, a pastime for the drones and idlers of existence? How could he set up his ambitions before them, to be bowled over like so many ninepins? When, at length, after much heart-

burning and conscientious scrupling, he was mastered by a
healthier spirit of self-assertion, which made him rebel against
the uselessness of the conflict, and doggedly resolve to put an
end to it, he was only enabled to stand firm by summoning to
his aid all the strengthening egoism, which is latent in every
more or less artistic nature. To the mother, in her honest
narrowness, the son's choice of a calling which she held to be
unfitting, was something of a tragedy. She allowed no item
of her duty to escape her, and moved about the house as usual,
sternly observant of her daily task, but her lips were com-
pressed to a thin line, and her face reflected the anger that
burnt in her heart, too deep for speech. In the months that
followed, Maurice learnt that the censure hardest to meet is
that which is never put into words, which refuses to argue or
discuss: he chafed inwardly against the unspoken opposition that
will not come out to be grappled with, and overthrown. And,
as he was only too keenly aware, there was more to be faced
than a mere determined aversion to the independence with
which he had struck out: there was, in the first place, a pardon-
ably human sense of aggrievedness that the eldest-born should
cross their plans and wishes; that, after the year-long care and
thought they had bestowed on him, he should demand fresh
efforts from them; and, again, most harassing of all and most
invulnerable, such an entire want of faith in the powers he was
yearning to test—the prophet's lot in the mean blindness of
the family—that, at times, it threatened to shake his hard-won
faith in himself.—But before the winter drew to a close he was
away.

Away!—to go out into the world and be a musician—that
was his longing and his dream. And he never came to quite
an honest understanding with himself on this point, for desire
and dream were interwoven in his mind; he could not separate
the one from the other. But when he weighed them, and
allowed them to rise up and take shape before him, it was invariably in this order that they did so. In reality, although he
himself was but vaguely conscious of the fact, it was to some
extent as means to an end, that, when his eyes had been opened
to its presence, he clutched—like a drowning man who seizes
upon a spar—clutched and held fast to his talent. But the
necessary insight into his powers had first to be gained, for it
was not one of those talents which, from the beginning, strut
their little world with the assurance of the peacock. He was, it
is true, gifted with an instinctive feeling for the value and

significance of tones—as a child he sang by ear in a small, sweet voice, which gained him the only notice he received at school, and he easily picked out his notes, and taught himself little pieces, on the old-fashioned, silk-faced piano, which had belonged to his mother as a girl, and at which, in the early days of her marriage, she had sung in a high, shrill voice, the sentimental songs of her youth. But here, for want of incentive, matters remained; Maurice was kept close at his school-books, and, boylike, he had no ambition to distinguish himself in a field so different from that in which his comrades won their spurs. It was only when, with the end of his school-days in sight, he was putting away childish things, that he seriously turned his attention to the piano and his hands. They were those of the pianist, broad, strong and supple, and the new occupation soon engrossed him deeply; he gave up all his spare time to it, and, in a few months, attained so creditable a proficiency, that he went through a course of instruction with a local teacher of music, who, scenting talent, dismissed preliminaries with the assurance of his kind, and initiated his pupil into all that is false and meretricious in the literature of the piano—the cheaply pathetic, the tinsel of transcription, the titillating melancholy of Slavonic dance-music—to leave him, but for an increased agility of finger, not a whit further forward than he had found him. Then followed months when the phantom of discontent stalked large through Maurice's life, grew, indeed, day by day more tangible, more easily defined; for there came the long, restless summer evenings, when it seemed as if a tranquil darkness would never fall and bar off the distant, the unattainable; and as he followed some flat, white country road, that was lost to sight on the horizon as a tapering line, or looked out across a stretch of low, luxuriant meadows, the very placidity of which made heart and blood throb quicker, in a sense of opposition: then the desire to have finished with the life he knew, grew almost intolerable, and only a spark was needed to set his resolve ablaze.

It was one evening when the summer had already dragged itself to a close, that Maurice walked through a drizzling rain to the neighbouring cathedral town, to attend a performance of *Elijah*. It was the first important musical experience of his life, and, carried away by the volumes of sound, he repressed his agitation so ill, that it became apparent to his neighbour, a small, wizened, old man, who was leaning forward, his hands hanging between his knees and his eyes fixed on the floor, al-

ternately shaking and nodding his head. In the interval between the parts, they exchanged a few words, halting, excited
on Maurice's part, interrogative on his companion's; when the
performance was over, they walked a part of the way together,
and found so much to say, that often, after this, when his week's
work was behind him, Maurice would cover the intervening
miles for the pleasure of a few hours' conversation with this
new friend. In a small, dark room, the air of which was
saturated with tobacco-smoke, he learned, by degrees, the story
of the old musician's life: how, some thirty years previously,
he had drifted into the midst of this provincial population,
where he found it easy to earn enough for his needs, and where
his position was below that of a dancing-master; but how, long
ago, in his youth—that youth of which he spoke with a far-
away tone in his voice, and at which he seemed to be looking
out as at a fading shore—it had been his intention to perfect
himself as a pianist. Life had been against him; when the resolve was strongest, poverty and ill-health kept him down, and
since then, with the years that passed, he had come to see that his
place would only have been among the multitude of little
talents, whose destiny it is to imitate and vulgarise the strivings
of genius, to swell the over-huge mass of mediocrity. And so,
he had chosen that his life should be a failure—a failure, that
is, in the eyes of the world; for himself, he judged otherwise.
The truth that could be extracted from words was such a
fluctuating, relative truth. Failure! success!—what *was* success, but a clinging fast, unabashed by smile or neglect, to that
better part in art, in one's self, that cannot be taken away?—
never for a thought's space being untrue to the ideal each one of
us bears in his breast; never yielding jot or tittle to the world's
opinion. That was what it meant, and he who was proudly
conscious of having succeeded thus, could well afford to regard
the lives of others as half-finished and imperfect; he alone was
at one with himself, his life alone was a harmonious whole.

To Maurice Guest, all this mattered little or not at all; it
was merely the unavoidable introduction. The chief thing was
that the old man had known the world which Maurice so desired to know; he had seen life, had lived much of his youth in
foreign lands, and had the conversation been skilfully set agoing
in this direction, he would lay a wrinkled hand on his listener's
shoulder, and tell him of this shadowy past, with short hoarse
chuckles of pleasure and reminiscence, which invariably ended
in a cough. He painted it in vivid colours, and with the un-

conscious heightening of effect that comes natural to one who
looks back upon a happy past, from which the countless pricks
and stings that make up reality have faded, leaving in their place
a sense of dreamy, unreal brightness, like that of sunset upon
distant hills. He told him of Germany, and the gay, careless
years he had spent there, working at his art, years of inspiriting,
untrammelled progress; told him of famous musicians he had
seen and known, of great theatre performances at which he had
assisted, of stirring *premières,* long since forgotten, of burning
youthful enthusiasms, of nights sleepless with holy excitement,
and days of fruitful, meditative idleness. Under the spell of
these reminiscences, he seemed to come into touch again with
life, and his eyes lit with a spark of the old fire. At moments,
he forgot his companion altogether, and gazed long and silently
before him, nodding and smiling to himself at the memories he
had stirred up in his brain, memories of things that had long
ceased to be, of people who had long been quiet and unassertive
beneath their handful of earth, but for whom alone, the brave,
fair world had once seemed to exist. Then he would lose himself among strange names, in vague histories of those who had
borne these names, and of what they had become in their subsequent journeyings towards the light, for which they had set
out, side by side, with so much ardour (and oftenest what he
had to tell was a modest mediocrity) ; but the greater number
of them had lost sight one of the other; the most inseparable
friends had, once parted, soon forgotten. And the bluish smoke
sent upwards as he talked, in clouds and spirals that mounted
rapidly and vanished, seemed to Maurice symbolic of the brief
and shadowy lives that were unrolled before him. But, after
all this, when the lights came, the piano was opened, and then,
for an hour or two, the world was forgotten in a different way.
It was here that the chief landmarks of music emerged from the
mists in which, for Maurice, they had hitherto been enveloped;
here he learned that Bach and Beethoven were giants, and
made uncertain efforts at appreciation; learnt that Gluck was
a great composer, Mozart a genius of many parts, Mendelssohn
the direct successor in this line of kings. Sonatas, symphonies,
operas, were hammered out with tremendous force and precision on the harsh, scrupulously tuned piano; and all were
dominated alike by the hoarse voice of the old man, who never
wavered, never faltered, but sang from beginning to end with
all his might. Each one of the pleasant hours spent in this
new world helped to deepen Maurice's resolution to free him-

self while there was yet time; each one gave more clearness and precision to his somewhat formless desires; for, in all that concerned his art, the nameless old musician hated his native land, with the hatred of the bigot for those who are hostile or indifferent to his faith.

With a long and hot-chased goal in sight, a goal towards which our hearts, in joyous eagerness, have already leapt out, it is astonishing how easy it becomes to make light of the last, monotonous stretch of road that remains to be travelled. Is there not, just beyond, a resting-place?—and cool, green shadows? Events and circumstances which had hitherto loomed forth gigantic, threatening to crush, now appeared to Maurice trivial and of little moment; he saw them in other proportions now, for it seemed to him that he was no longer in their midst: he stood above them and overlooked them, and, with his eyes fixed upon a starry future, he joyfully prepared himself for his new life. What is more, those around him helped him to this altered view of things. For as the present marched steadily upon the future, devouring as it went; as the departure this future contained took on the shape of a fact, the countless details of which called for attention, it began to be accepted as even the most unpalatable facts in the long run usually are, with an ungracious resignation in face of the inevitable. Thus, with all his ardour to be gone, Maurice Guest came to see the last stage of his home-life almost in a bright light, and even with a touch of melancholy, as something that was fast slipping from him, never to be there in all its entirety, exactly as it now was, again: the last calm hour of respite before he plunged into the triumphs, but also into the tossings and agitations of the future.

III

It was April, and a day such as April will sometimes bring: one of those days when the air is full of a new, mysterious fragrance, when the sunshine lies like a flood upon the earth, and high clouds hang motionless in the far-distant blue—a day at the very heels of which it would seem that summer was lurking. Maurice Guest stood at his window, both sides of which were flung open, drinking in the warm air, and gazing absently up at the stretch of sky, against which the dark roof-lines of the houses opposite stood out abruptly. His hands were in his pockets, and, to a light beat of the foot, he hummed softly to himself, but what, he could not have told: whether some fragment of melody that had lingered in a niche of his brain and now came to his lips, or whether a mere audible expression of his mood. The strong, unreal sun of the afternoon was just beginning to reach the house; it slanted in, golden, by the side of the window, and threw on the wall above the piano, a single long bar of light.

He leaned over and looked down into the street far below—still no one there! But it was only half-past four. He stretched himself long and luxuriously, as if, by doing so, he would get rid of a restlessness which arose from repressed physical energy, and also from an impatience to be more keenly conscious of life, to feel it, as it were, quicken in him, not unakin to that passionate impulse towards perfection, which, out-of-doors, was urging on the sap and loosening firm green buds: he had a day's imprisonment behind him, and all spring's magic was at work to ferment his blood. How small and close the room was! He leaned out on the sill, as far out as he could, in the sun. It was shining full down the street now, gilding the canal-like river at the foot, and throwing over the tall, dingy houses on the opposite side, a tawdry brightness, which, unlike that of the morning with its suggestion of dewy shade, only served to bring out the shabbiness of broken plaster and paintless window; a shamefaced yet aggressive shabbiness, where high-arched doorways and wide entries spoke to better days, and also to a subsequent decay, now openly admitted in the little placards which dotted them here and there, bearing the

21

bold-typed words *Garçon logis,* and dangling bravely yellow
from the windows of the cheap lodgings they proclaimed vacant.
It was very still; the hoarse voice of a fruit-seller crying his
wares in the adjoining streets, was to be heard at intervals, but
each time less distinctly, and from the distance came the faint
tones of a single piano. How different it was in the morning!
Then, if, pausing a moment from his work, he opened the
window and leaned out for a brief refreshment, what a delightful confusion of sounds met his ear! Pianos rolled noisily up
and down, ploughing one through the other, beating one against
the other, key to key, rhythm to rhythm, each in a clamorous
despair at being unable to raise its voice above the rest, at having to form part of this jumble of discord: some so near at
hand or so directly opposite that, none the less, it was occasionally possible to follow them through the persistent reiterations of
a fugue, or through some brilliant glancing *étude,* the notes
of which flew off like sparks; others, further away, of which
were audible only the convulsive treble outbursts and the toneless rumblings of the bass, now and then cut shrilly through
by the piercing sharpness of a violin, now and then, at quieter
moments, borne up and accompanied by the deep, guttural
tones of a neighbouring violoncello. This was always discovered at work upon scales, uncertain, hesitating scales on the
lower strings, and, heard suddenly, after the other instruments'
genial hubbub, it sounded like some inarticulate animal making
uncouth attempts at expression. At rare intervals there came a
lull, and then, before all burst forth again together, or fell in,
one by one, a single piano or the violin would, like a solo voice
in a symphony, bear the whole burden; or if the wind were in
the west, it would sometimes carry over with it, from the
woods on the left, the mournful notes of a French horn, which
some unskilful player had gone out to practise.

This was that new world of which he was now a part—into
which he had been so auspiciously received.

Yes, the beginning and the thousand petty disquiets that go
with beginnings, were behind him; he had made a start, and he
believed a good one—thanks to Dove. He was really grateful
to Dove. A chance acquaintance, formed on one of those early
days when he loitered, timid and unsure, about the *Bureau* of
the Conservatorium, Dove had taken him up with what struck
even the grateful new-comer as extraordinary good-nature,
going deliberately out of his way to be of service to him, meeting him at every turn with assistance and advice. It was Dove

who had helped him over the embarrassments of the examination; it was through Dove's influence that he had obtained a private interview with Schwarz, and, in Dove's opinion, Schwarz was the only master in Leipzig under whom it was worth while to study; the only one who could be relied on to give the exhaustive *technique* that was indispensable, without, in the process, destroying what was of infinitely more account, the individuality, the *temperament* of the student. This and more, Dove set forth at some length in their conversations; then, warming to his work, he would go further: would go on to speak of phrasings and interpretations; of an artistic use of the pedals, and the legitimate participation of the emotions; of the confines of absolute music as touched in the Ninth Symphony: would refer incidentally to Schopenhauer and make Wagner his authority, using terms that were new to his hearer, and, now and then, by way of emphasis, bringing his palm down flat and noiselessly upon the table.—It had not taken them long to become friends; fellow-countrymen, of the same age, with similar aims and interests, they had soon slipped into one of the easy-going friendships of youth.

A quarter to five! As the strokes from the neighbouring church-clock died away, the melody of Siegfried's horn was whistled up from the street, and looking over, Maurice saw his friend. He seized his music and went hastily down the four flights of stairs.

They crossed the river and came to newer streets. It was delightful out-of-doors. A light breeze met them as they turned, and a few ragged, fleecy clouds that it was driving up, only made the sky seem bluer. The two young men walked leisurely, laughing and talking rather loudly. Maurice Guest had already, in dress and bearing, taken on a touch of musicianly disorder, but Dove's lengthier residence had left no trace upon him; he might have stepped that day from the streets of the provincial English town to which he belonged. His well-brushed clothes sat with an easy inelegance, his tie was small, his linen clean, and the only concession he made to his surroundings, the broad-brimmed, soft felt hat, looked oddly out of place on his close-cut hair. He carried himself erectly, swinging a little on his hips.

As they went, he passed in review the important items of the day: so-and-so had strained a muscle, so-and-so had spoilt a second piano. But his particular interest centred upon that evening's *Abendunterhaltung*. A man named Schilsky, whom it was no exaggeration to call their finest, very finest violinist, was to play Vieuxtemps' Concerto in D. Dove all but smacked his lips as he spoke of it. In reply to a query from Maurice, he declared with vehemence that this Schilsky was a genius. Although so great a violinist, he could play almost every other instrument with ease; his memory had become a by-word; his compositions were already famous. At the present moment, he was said to be at work upon a symphonic poem, having for its base a new and extraordinary book, half poetry, half philosophy, a book which he, Dove, could confidently assert, would effect a revolution in human thought, but of which, just at the minute, he was unable to remember the name. Infected by his friend's enthusiasm, Maurice here recalled having, only the day before, met some one who answered to Dove's description: the genial Pole had been storming up the steps of the Conservatorium, two at a time, with wild, affrighted eyes, and a halo of dishevelled auburn hair.—Dove made no doubt that he had been seized with a sudden inspiration.

Gewandhaus and Conservatorium lay close together, in a new quarter of the town. The Conservatorium, a handsome, stone-faced building, three lofty storeys high, was just now all the more imposing in appearance as it stood alone in an unfinished street-block, and as, opposite, hoardings still shut in all that had yet been raised of the great library, which would eventually overshadow it. The severe plainness of its long front, with the unbroken lines of windows, did not fail to impress the unused beholder, who had not for very long gone daily out and in; it suggested to him the earnest, unswerving efforts, imperative on his pursuit of the ideal; an ideal which, to many, was as it were personified by the concert-house in the adjoining square: it was hither, towards this clear-limned goal, that bore him, like a magic carpet, the young enthusiast's most ambitious dream.—But in the life that swarmed about the Conservatorium, there was nothing of a tedious austerity. It was one of the briskest times of day, and the short street and the steps of the building were alive with young people of both sexes. Young men sauntered to and from the café at the corner, or stood gesticulating in animated groups. All alike were conspicuous for a rather wilful slovenliness, for smooth faces and bushy hair, while the numerous girls, with whom they paused to laugh and trifle, were, for the most part, showy in dress and loudly vivacious in manner. On the kerbstone, a knot of the latter, tittering among themselves, shot furtive

glances at Dove and Maurice as they passed. Here, a pretty,
laughing face was the centre of a little circle; there, a bevy of
girls clustered about a young man, who, his hands in his pockets,
leaned carelessly against the door-arch; and again, another,
plump and much befeathered, with a string of large pearl-
beads round her fat, white neck, had isolated herself from the
rest, to take up, on the steps, a more favourable stand. A
master who went by, a small, jovial man in a big hat, had a
word for all the girls, even a chuck of the chin for one unusually saucy face. Inside, classes were filing out of the various rooms, other classes were going in; there was a noisy
flocking up and down the broad, central staircase, a crowding
about the notice-board, a going and coming in the long, stone
corridors. The concert-hall was being lighted.

Maurice slowly made his way through the midst of all these
people, while Dove loitered, or stepped out of hearing, with
one friend after another. In a side corridor, off which, cell-
like, opened a line of rooms, they pushed a pair of double-
doors, and went in to take their lesson.

The room they entered was light and high, and contained,
besides a couple of grand pianos, a small table and a row of
wooden chairs. Schwarz stood with his back to the window,
biting his nails. He was a short, thickset man, with keen eyes,
and a hard, prominent mouth, which was rather emphasised
than concealed, by the fair, scanty tuft of hair that hung
from his chin. Upon the two new-comers, he bent a cold,
deliberate gaze, which, for some instants, he allowed to rest
chillingly on them, then as deliberately withdrew, having—
so at least it seemed to those who were its object—having,
without the tremor of an eyelid, scanned them like an open
page: it was the look, impenetrable, all-seeing, of the physician
for his patient. At the piano, a young man was playing the
Waldstein Sonata. So intent was he on what he was doing,
that his head all but touched the music standing open before
him, while his body, bent thus double, swayed vigorously from
side to side. His face was crimson, and on his forehead stood
out beads of perspiration. He had no cuffs on, and his sleeves
were a little turned back. The movement at an end, he paused,
and drawing a soiled handkerchief from his pocket, passed it
rapidly over neck and brow. In the *Adagio* which followed, he
displayed an extreme delicacy of touch—not, however, but
what this also cost him some exertion, for, previous to the
striking of each faint, soft note, his hand described a curve in

the air, the finger he was about to use, lowered, the others
slightly raised, and there was always a second of something
like suspense, before it finally sank upon the expectant note.
But suddenly, without warning, just as the last, lingering
tones were dying to the close they sought, the *Adagio* slipped
over into the limpid gaiety of the *Rondo,* and then, there was
no time more for premeditation: then his hands twinkled up
and down, joining, crossing, flying asunder, alert with little
sprightly quirks and turns, going ever more nimbly, until the
brook was a river, the allegretto a prestissimo, which flew
wildly to its end amid a shower of dazzling trills.

Schwarz stood grave and apparently impassive; from time
to time, however, when unobserved, he swept the three listeners with a rapid glance.   Maurice Guest was quite carried
away; he had never heard playing like this, and he leaned forward in his seat, and gazed full at the player, in open admiration.   But his neighbour, a pale, thin man, with one of
those engaging and not uncommon faces which, in mould of
feature, in mildness of expression, and still more in the cut
of hair and beard, bear so marked a likeness to the conventional Christ-portrait: this neighbour looked on with only a
languid interest, which seemed unable to get the upper hand
of melancholy thoughts.   Maurice, who believed his feelings
shared by all about him, was chilled by such indifference:
he only learned later, after they had become friends, that
nothing roused in Boehmer a real or lasting interest, save
what he, Boehmer, did himself.   Dove sat absorbed, as rev-
erent as if at prayer; but there were also moments when, with
his head a little on one side, he wore an anxious air, as if not
fully at one with the player's rendering; others again, after
a passage of peculiar brilliancy, when he threw at Schwarz a
humbly grateful look.   While Schwarz, the sonata over, was
busy with his pencil on the margin of the music, Dove leaned
over to Maurice and whispered behind his hand: "Fürst—our
best pianist."

Now came the turn of the others, and the master's attention wandered; he stretched himself, yawned, and sighed aloud,
then, in the search for something he could not find, turned
out on the lid of the second piano the contents of sundry
pockets.   While Dove played, he wrote as if for life in a
bulky notebook.

Maurice remarked this without being properly conscious of
it, so impressed had he been by the sonata.   The exultant

beauty of the great final theme had permeated his every fibre, inciting him, emboldening him, and, still under the sway of this little elation when his own turn to play came, he was the richer by it, and acquitted himself with unusual verve.

As the class was about to leave the room, Schwarz signed to Maurice to remain behind. For several moments, he paced the floor in silence; then he stopped suddenly short in front of the young man, and, with legs apart, one hand at his back, he said in a tone which wavered between being brutal and confidential, emphasising his words with a series of smart pencil-raps on his hearer's shoulder:

"Let me tell you something: if I were not of the opinion that you had ability, I should not detain you this evening. It is no habit of mine, mark this, to interfere with my pupils. Outside this room, most of them do not exist for me. In your case, I am making an exception, because . . ." —Maurice was here so obviously gratified that the speaker made haste to substitute: "because I should much like to know how it is that you come to me in the state you do." And without waiting for a reply: "For you know nothing, or, let us say, worse than nothing, since what you do know, you must make it your first concern to forget." He paused, and the young man's face fell so much that he prolonged the pause, to enjoy the discomfiture he had produced. "But give me time," he continued, "adequate time, and I will undertake to make something of you." He lowered his voice, and the taps became more confidential. "There is good stuff here; you have talent, great talent, and, as I have observed to-day, you are not wanting in intelligence. But," and again his voice grew harsher, his eye more piercing, "understand me, if you please, no trifling with other studies; let us have no fiddling, no composing. Who works with me, works for me alone. And a lifetime, I repeat it, a lifetime, is not long enough to master such an instrument as this!"

He brought his hand down heavily on the lid of the piano, and glared at Maurice as if he expected the latter to contradict him. Then, noisily clearing his throat, he began anew to pace the room.

As Maurice stood waiting for his dismissal, with very varied feelings, of which, however, a faint pride was uppermost; as he stood waiting, the door opened, and a girl looked in. She hesitated a moment, then entered, and going up to Schwarz, asked him something in a low voice. He nodded an assent,

nodded two or three times, and with quite another face; its
hitherto unmoved severity had given way to an indulgent
friendliness. She laid her hat and jacket on the table, and went
to the piano.

Schwarz motioned Maurice to a chair. He sat down almost
opposite her.

And now came for him one of those moments in life, which,
unlooked-for, undivined, send before them no promise of being
different, in any way, from the commonplace moments that
make up the balance of our days. No gently graduated steps
lead up to them: they are upon us with the violent abruptness
of a streak of lightning, and like this, they, too, may leave
behind them a scarry trace. What such a moment holds within
it, is something which has never existed for us before, something it has never entered our minds to go out and seek—the
corner of earth, happened on by chance, which comes most near
the Wineland of our dreams; the page, idly perhaps begun,
which brings us a new god; the face of the woman who is
to be our fate—but, whatever it may be, let it once exist for
us, and the soul responds forthwith, catching in blind haste at
the dimly missed ideal.

For one instant Maurice Guest had looked at the girl before him with unconcern, but the next it was with an intentness that soon became intensity, and feverishly grew, until he
could not tear his eyes away. The beauty, whose spell thus
bound him, was of that subtle kind which leaves many a one
cold, but, as if just for this reason, is almost always fateful
for those who feel its charm: at them is lanced its accumulated
force. The face was far from faultless; there was no regularity of feature, no perfection of line, nor was there more
than a touch of the sweet girlish freshness that gladdens like
a morning in May. The features, save for a peremptory turn
of mouth and chin, were unremarkable, and the expression
was distant, unchanging . . . but what was that to him?
This deep white skin, the purity of which was only broken
by the pale red of the lips; this dull black hair, which lay
back from the low brow in such wonderful curves, and seemed,
of itself, to fall into the loose knot on the neck—there was
something romantic, exotic about her, which was unlike anything he had ever seen: she made him think of a rare, hothouse
flower; some scentless, tropical flower, with stiff, waxen petals.
And then her eyes! So profound was their darkness that,
when they threw off their covering of heavy lid, it seemed to

his excited fancy as if they must scorch what they rested on; they looked out from the depths of their setting like those of a wild beast crouched within a cavern; they lit up about them like stars, and when they fell, they went out like stars, and her face took on the pallor of early dawn.

She was playing from memory. She gazed straight before her with far-away eyes, which only sometimes looked down at her hands, to aid them in a difficult passage. At her belt, she wore a costly yellow rose, and as she once leaned towards the treble, where both hands were at work close together, it fell to the floor. Maurice started forward, and picking it up, laid it on the piano; beneath the gaslight, it sank a shadowy gold image in the mirror-like surface. As yet she had paid no heed to him, but, at this, she turned her head, and, still continuing to play, let her eyes rest absently on him.

They sank their eyes in each other's. A thrill ran through Maurice, a quick, sharp thrill, which no sensation of his later life outdid in keenness and which, on looking back, he could always feel afresh. The colour rose to his face and his heart beat audibly, but he did not lower his eyes, and for not doing so, seemed to himself infinitely bold. A host of confused feelings bore down upon him, well-nigh blotting out the light; but, in a twinkling, all were swallowed up in an overpowering sense of gratitude, in a large, vague, happy thankfulness, which touched him almost to the point of tears. As it swelled through him and possessed him, he yearned to pour it forth, to make an offering of this gratefulness—fine tangle of her beauty and his own glad mood—and, by sustaining her look, he seemed to lay the offering at her feet. Nor would any tongue have persuaded him that she did not understand. The few seconds were eternities: when she turned away, it was as if untold hours had passed over him in a body, like a flight of birds; as if a sudden gulf had gaped between where he now was and where he had previously stood.

Dismissed curtly, with a word, he hung about the corridor in the hope of seeing her again; but the piano went on and on, unceasingly. Here, after some time, he was found by Dove, who carried him off with loud expressions of surprise.

The concert was more than half over. The main part of the hall was brightly lit and full of people: from behind, one looked across a sea of heads. On the platform at the other end, a girl in red was playing a sonata; a master sat by her side, and leant forward, at regular intervals, to turn the leaves of the music. Dove and Maurice remained standing at the back, under the gallery, among a portion of the audience which shifted continuously: those about them wandered in and out of the hall at pleasure, now inside, head in hand, critically intent, now out in the vestibule, stretching their legs, lounging in easy chat. In the pause that followed the sonata, Dove went towards the front, to join some ladies who beckoned him, and, while some one sang a noisy aria, Maurice gave himself up to his own thoughts. They all led to the same point: how he should contrive to see her again, how he should learn her name, and, beside them, everything else seemed remote, unreal; he saw the people next him as if from a distance. But in a wait that was longer than usual, he was awakened to his surroundings: a stir ran over the audience, like a gust of wind over still water; the heads in the seats before him inclined one to another, wagged and nodded; there was a gentle buzz of voices. Behind him, the doors opened and shut, letting in all who were outside: they pressed forward expectantly. On his left, a row of girls tried to start a round of applause, and tittered nervously at their failure. Schilsky had come down the platform and commenced tuning. He bent his long, thin body as he pressed his violin to his knee, and his reddish hair fell over his face. The accompanist, his hands on the keys, waited for the signal to begin.

Maurice drew a deep breath of anticipation. But the first shrill, sweet notes had hardly cut the silence, when, the door opening once more, some one entered and pushed through the standing crowd. He looked round, uneasy at the disturbance, and found that it was she: what is more, she came up to his very side. He turned away so hastily that he touched her arm, causing it to yield a little, and some moments went by before he ventured to look again. When he did, in some tremor, he saw that, without fear of discovery, he might look as long or as often as he chose. She was listening to the player with the raptness of a painted saint: her whole face listened, the tightened lips, the open nostrils, the wide, vigilant eyes. Maurice, lost in her presence, grew dizzy with the scent of her hair—that indefinable odour, which has something of the raciness in it of new-turned earth—and foolish wishes arose and jostled one another in his mind: he would have liked to plunge both hands into the dark, luxuriant mass; still better, cautiously to draw his palm down this whitest skin, which, seen so near, had a faint, satin-like sheen. The mere imagining of it set him throbbing, and the excitement in his blood was heightened by the sensuous melancholy of the violin, which, just beyond the pale of his consciousness, throbbed and languished with him under the masterful bow.

Shortly before the end of the concerto, she turned and made her way out. Maurice let a few seconds elapse, then followed. But the long white corridors stretched empty before him; there was no trace of her to be seen. As he was peering about, in places that were strange to him, a tumult of applause shook the hall, the doors flew open and the audience poured out.

Dove had joined other friends, and a number of them left the building together; every one spoke loudly and at once. But soon Maurice and Dove outstepped their companions, for these came to words over the means used by Schilsky to mount, with bravour, a certain gaudy scale of octaves, and, at every second pace, they stopped, and wheeled round with eloquent gesture. In their presence Dove had said little; now he gave rein to his feelings: his honest face glowed with enthusiasm, the names of renowned players ran off his lips like beads off a string, and, in predicting Schilsky a career still more brilliant, his voice grew husky with emotion.

Maurice listened unmoved to his friend's outpouring, and the first time Dove stopped for breath, went straight for the matter which, in his eyes, had dwarfed all others. So eager was he to learn something of her, that he even made shift to describe her; his attempt fell out lamely, and a second later he could have bitten off his tongue.

Dove had only half an ear for him.

" Eh? What? What do you say? " he asked as Maurice paused; but his thoughts were plainly elsewhere. This fact is, just at this moment, he was intent on watching some ladies: were they going to notice him or not? The bow made and returned, he brought his mind back to Maurice with a great show of interest.

Here, however, they all turned in to Seyffert's Café, and, seating themselves at a long, narrow table, waited for Schilsky, whom they intended to fête. But minutes passed, a quarter, then half of an hour, and still he did not come. To while the time, his playing of the concerto was roundly commented and discussed. There was none of the ten or twelve young men but had the complete jargon of the craft at his finger-tips; not one, too, but was rancorous and admiring in a breath, now detecting flaws as many as motes in a beam, now heaping praise. The spirited talk, flying thus helter-skelter through the gamut of opinion, went forward chiefly in German, which the foreigners of the party spoke with various accents, but glibly enough; only now and then did one of them spring over to his mother-tongue, to fetch a racy idiom or point a joke.

Not having heard a note of Schilsky's playing, Maurice did not trust himself to say much, and so was free to observe his right-hand neighbour, a young man who had entered late, and taken a vacant chair beside him. To the others present, the new-comer paid no heed, to Maurice he murmured an absent greeting, and then, having called for beer and emptied his glass at a draught, he appeared mentally to return whence he had come, or to engage without delay in some urgent train of thought. His movements were noiseless, but startlingly abrupt. Thus, after sitting quiet for a time, his head in his hands, he flung back in his seat with a sort of wildness, and began to stare fixedly at the ceiling. His face was one of those, which, as by a mystery, preserve the innocent beauty of their childhood, long after childhood is a thing of the past: delicate as the rosy lining of a great sea-shell was the colour that spread from below the forked blue veins of the temples, and it paled and came again as readily as a girl's. Girlish, too, were the limpid eyes, which, but for a trick of dropping unexpectedly, seemed always to be gazing, in thoughtful surprise, at something that was visible to them alone. As to the small, frail body, it existed only for sake of the hands: narrow hands, with long, fleshless fingers, nervous hands, that were never still.

All at once, in a momentary lull, he leant towards Maurice, and, without even looking up, asked the latter if he could recall the opening bars of the prelude to *Tristan und Isolde*. If so, there was a certain point he would like to lay before him.

"You see, it's this way, old fellow," he said confidentially. "I've come to the conclusion that if, at the end of the third bar, Wagner had——"

'Throw him out, throw him out!" cried an American who was sitting opposite them. "You might as well try to stop a comet as Krafft on Wagner."

"That's so," said another American named Ford, who, on arriving, had not been quite sober, and now, after a few glasses of beer, was exceedingly tipsy. "That's so. As I've always said, it's a disgrace to the township, a disgrace, sir. Ought to be put down. Why don't he write them himself?"

From the depths of his brown study, Krafft looked vaguely at the speakers, and checked, but not discomposed, drew out a notebook and jotted down an idea.

Meanwhile, at the far end of the table, Boehmer and a Russian violinist still harped upon the original string. And, having worked out Schilsky, they passed on to Zollinger, his master, and the Russian, who was not Zollinger's pupil, set to showing with vehemence that his "method" was a worthless one. He was barely started when a wiry American, in a high, grating voice, called Schilsky a wretched fool: why had he not gone to Berlin at Easter, as he had planned, instead of dawdling on here where he had no more to gain? At this, several of the young men laughed and looked significant. Fürst—he had proved to be a jolly little man, who, with unbuttoned vest, absorbed large quantities of beer and perspired freely—Fürst alone was of the opinion, which he expressed forcibly, in his hearty Saxon dialect, that had Schilsky left Leipzig at this particular time, he would have been a fool indeed.

"Look here, boys," he cried, pounding the table to get attention. "That's all very well, but he must have an eye to the practical side of things, too——"

"*Der biedere Sachse hoch!*" threw in Boehmer, who was Prussian, and of a more ideal cast of mind.

"—and a chance such as this, he will certainly never have again. A hundred thousand marks, if a pfennig, and a face to turn after in the street! No, he is a confounded deal wiser to stay here, and make sure of her, for that sort is as slippery as an eel."

"Krafft can tell us; he let her go; is she?—is it true?" shouted half a dozen.

Krafft looked up and winked. His reply was so gross and so witty that there was a very howl of mirth.

"*Krafft hoch, hoch Krafft!*" they cried, and roared again, until the proprietor, a mild, round-faced man, who was loath to meddle with his best customers, advanced to the middle of, the floor, where he stood smiling uneasily and rubbing his hands.

But it was growing late.

"Why the devil doesn't he come?" yawned Boehmer.

"Perhaps," said Dove, mouthing deliberately as if he had

a good thing on his tongue; "perhaps, by now, he is safe in the
arms of——"

"Jesus or Morpheus?" asked a cockney 'cellist.

"Safe in the arms of Jesus!" sang the tipsy pianist; but
he was outsung by Krafft, who, rising from his seat, gave with
dramatic gesture:

> O sink' hernieder,
> Nacht der Liebe,
> gieb Vergessen,
> dass ich lebe .   .   .

After this, with much laughter and ado, they broke up to
seek another café in the heart of the town, where the absinthe
was good and the billiard-table better, two of his friends supporting Ford, who was testily debating with himself why a
composer should compose his own works. At the first corner,
Maurice whispered a word to Dove, and, unnoticed by the
rest, slipped away. For some time, he heard the sound of
their voices down the quiet street. A member of the group,
in defiance of the night, began to sing; and then, just as one
bird is provoked by another, rose a clear, sweet voice he
recognised as Krafft's, in a song the refrain of which was
sung by all:

> Give me the Rose of Sharon,
> And a bottle of Cyprus wine!

What followed was confused, indistinct, but over and over
again he heard:

> .   .   .   the Rose of Sharon,
> .   .   .   a bottle of Cyprus wine!

until that, too, was lost in the distance.

When he reached his room, he did not light the lamp, but
crossed to the window and stood looking out into the darkness. The day's impressions, motley as the changes of a
kaleidoscope, seethed in his brain, clamoured to be recalled and
set in order; but he kept them back; he could not face the
task. He felt averse to any mental effort, in need of a repose
as absolute as the very essence of silence itself. The sky was
overcast; a wayward breeze blew coolly in upon him and
refreshed him; a few single raindrops fell. In the air a gentle
melancholy was abroad, and, as he stood there, wax for any

passing mood, it descended on him and enveloped him. He gave himself up to it, unresistingly, allowed himself to toy with it, to sink beneath it. Just, however, as he was sinking, sinking, he was roused, suddenly, as from sleep, by the vivid presentiment that something was about to happen to him: it seemed as if an important event were looming in the near distance, ready to burst in upon his life, and not only instantly, but with a monstrous crash of sound. His pulses beat more quickly, his nerves stretched, like bows. But it was very still; everything around him slept, and the streets were deserted.

A keen sense of desolation came over him; never, in his life, had he felt so utterly alone. In all this great city that spread, ocean-like, around him, not a heart was the lighter for his being there. Oh, to have some one beside him!— some one who would talk soothingly to him, of shadowy, far-off things, or, still better, be merely a sympathetic presence. He passed rapidly in review people he had known, saw their faces and heard their voices, but not one of them would do. No, he wanted a friend, the friend he had often dreamed of, whose thoughts would be his thoughts, with whom there would be no need of speech. Then his longing swelled, grew fiercer and more undefined, and a sudden burst of energy convulsed him and struggled to find vent. His breath came hard, and he stretched his arms out into the night, uncertainly, as if to grasp something he did not see; but they fell to his side again. He would have liked to sweep through the air, to feel the wind rushing dizzily through him; or to be set down before some feat that demanded the strength of a Titan—anything, no matter what, to be rid of the fever in his veins. But it beset him, again and again, only by slow degrees weakening and dying away.

A bitter moisture sprang to his eyes. Leaning his head on his arms, he endeavoured to call up her face. But it was of no use, though he strained every nerve; for some time he could see only the rose that had lain beside her on the piano, and in the troubled image that at last crowned his patience, her eyes looked out, like jewels, from a setting of golden petals.

Lying wakeful in the darkness, he saw them more clearly. Now, though, they had a bluish light, were like moons, moons that burnt. If he lit the lamp and tried to read, they got between him and the book, and danced up and down the pages, with jerky, clockwork movements, like stage fireflies.

He put the light out, and lay staring vacantly at the pale square of the window. And then, just when he was least expecting it, he saw the whole face, so close to him and so distinctly, that he started up on his elbow; and in the second or two it remained—a Medusa-face, opaquely white, with deep, unfathomable eyes—he recognised, with a shock, that his peace of mind was gone; that the sudden experience of a few hours back had given his life new meaning; that something had happened to him which could not be undone; in other words—with an incredulous gasp at his own folly—that he was head over ears in love.

Through the uneasy sleep into which he ultimately fell, she, and the yellow rose, and the Rose of Sharon—a giant flower, with monstrous crimson petals—passed and repassed, in one of those glorious tangles, which no dreamer has ever unravelled.

When he wakened, it was broad daylight, and things wore a different aspect. Not that his impression of the night had faded, but it was forced to retire behind the hard, clear affairs of the morning. He got up, full of vigour, impatient to be at work, and having breakfasted, sat down at the piano, where he remained until his hands dropped from the keys with fatigue. Throughout these hours, his mind ran chiefly on the words Schwarz had said to him, the previous evening. They rose before him in their full significance, and he leisurely chewed the honeyed cud of praise. " I will undertake to make something of you, undertake to make something of you "— his brain tore the phrase to tatters. " Something " was properly vague, as praise should be, and allowed the imagination free scope. Under the stimulus, everything came easy; he mastered a passage of bound sixths that had baffled him for days. And in this elated frame of mind, there was something almost pleasurable in the pang with which he would become conscious of a shadow in the background, a spot on his sun to make him unhappy.

Unhappy?—no: it gave a zest to his goings-out and comings-in. Through long hours of work he was borne up by an ardent hope: afterwards, he might see her. It made the streets exciting places of possible surprises. Might she not, at any moment, turn the corner and be before him? Might she not, this very instant, be going in the same direction as he, in the next street? But a very little of this pleasant dallying with

chance was enough. One morning, when the houses opposite
were ablaze with sunshine, and he had settled down to practice
with a keen relish for the obstacles to be overcome; on this
morning, within half an hour, his mood swung round to
the other extreme, and, from now on, his desire to see her
again was a burning unrest, which roused him from sleep, and
drove him out, at odd hours, no matter what he was doing.
Moodily he scoured the streets round the Conservatorium, disconcerted by his own folly, and. pricked incessantly by the
consciousness of time wasted. A companion at his side might
have dispelled the cobwebs; but Dove, his only friend, he
avoided, for the reason that Dove's unfailing good spirits
needed to be met with a similiar mood. And as for speaking
of the matter, the mere thought of the detailed explanation
that would now be necessary, did he open his lips, filled him
with dismay. When four or five days had gone by in this
manner, without result, he took to hanging about, with other
idlers, on the steps of the Conservatorium, always hoping that
she would suddenly emerge from the doors behind him, or
come towards him, a roll of music in her hand.

But she never came.

One afternoon, however, as he loitered there, he encoun-
tered his acquaintance of the very first day. He recognised
her while she was still some distance off, by her peculiar,
springy gait; at each step she rose slightly on the front part
of her foot, as if her heels were on springs. As before, she
was indifferently dressed; a small, close hat came down over
her face and hid her forehead; her skirt seemed shrunken, and
hung limp about her ankles, accentuating the straightness of
her figure. But below the brim of the hat her eyes were
as bright as ever, and took note of all that happened. On
seeing Maurice, she professed to remember him " perfectly,"
beginning to speak before she had quite come up to him.

The following day they met once more at the same place.
This time, she raised her eyebrows.

"You here again?" she said.

She disappeared inside the building; but a few minutes later
returned, and said she was going for a walk: would he come,
too?

He assented, with grateful surprise, and they set off together in the direction of the woods, as briskly as though they
were on an errand. But when they had crossed the suspension-bridge and reached the quieter paths that ran through

the *Nonne,* they simultaneously slackened their pace. The luxuriant undergrowth of shrub, which filled in, like lace-work, the spaces between the tree-trunks, was sprinkled with its first dots and pricks of green, and the afternoon was pleasant for walking—sunless and still, and just a little fragrantly damp from all the rife budding and sprouting. It was a day to further a friendship more effectually than half a dozen brighter ones; a day on which to speak out thoughts which a June sky, the indiscreet playing of full sunlight, even the rustling of the breeze in the leaves, might scare, like fish, from the surface.

When they had laughingly introduced themselves to each other, Maurice Guest's companion talked about herself, with a frankness that left nothing to be desired, and impressed the young man at her side very agreeably. Before they had gone far, he knew all about her. Her name was Madeleine Wade; she came from a small town in Leicestershire, and, except for a step-brother, stood alone in the world. For several years, she had been a teacher in a large school near London, and the position was open for her to return to, when she had completed this, the final year of her course. Then, however, she would devote herself exclusively to the teaching of music, and, with this in view, she had here taken up as many branches of study as she had time for. Besides piano, which was her chief subject, she learned singing, organ, counterpoint, and the elements of the violin.

"So much is demanded nowadays," she said in her clear soprano. "And if you want to get on, it doesn't do to be behindhand. Of course, it means hard work, but that is nothing to me—I am used to work and love it. Since I was seventeen—I am twenty-six now—I can fairly say I have never got up in the morning, without having my whole day mapped and planned before me.—So you see idlers can have no place on my list of saints."

She spoke lightly, yet with a certain under-meaning. As, however, Maurice Guest, on whom her words made a sympathetic impression, as of something strong and self-reliant—as he did not respond to it, she fell back on directness, and asked him what he had been doing when she met him, both on this day and the one before.

"I tell you candidly, I was astonished to find you there again," she said. "As a rule, new-comers are desperately earnest brooms."

His laugh was a trifle uneasy; and he answered evasively, not meaning to say much. But he had reckoned without the week of silence that lay behind him; it had been more of a strain than he knew, and his pent-up speech once set agoing could not be brought to a stop. An almost physical need of communication made itself felt in him; he spoke with a volubility that was foreign to him, began his sentences with a confidential "You see," and said things at which he himself was amazed. He related impressions, not facts, and impressions which, until now, he had not been conscious of receiving; he told unguardedly of his plans and ambitions, and even went back and touched on his home-life, dwelling with considerable bitterness on the scant sympathy he had received.

His companion looked at him curiously. She had expected a casual answer to her casual words, a surface frankness, such as she herself had shown, and, at first, she felt sceptical towards this unbidden confidence: she did not care for people who gave themselves away at a word; either they were naïve to foolishness or inordinately vain. But having listened for some time to his outpourings, she began to feel reassured; and soon she understood that he was talking thus at random, merely because he was lonely and bottled-up. Before he had finished, she was even a little gratified by his openness, and on his confiding to her what Schwarz had said to him, she smiled indulgently.

"Perhaps I took it to mean more than it actually did," said Maurice apologetically. "But anyhow it was cheering to hear it. You see, I must prove to the people at home that I was right and they were wrong. Failure was preached at me on every side. I was the only soul to believe in myself."

"And you really disliked teaching so?"

"Hated it with all my heart."

She frankly examined him. He had a pale, longish face, with thin lips, which might indicate either narrow prejudice or a fanatic tenacity. When he grew animated, he had a habit of opening his eyes very wide, and of staring straight before him. At such moments, too, he tossed back his head, with the impatient movements of a young horse. His hands and feet were good, his clothes of a provincial cut. Her fingers itched to retie the bow of his cravat for him, to pull him here and there into shape. Altogether, he made the impression upon her of being a very young man: when he coloured, or otherwise grew embarrassed, under her steady gaze, she mentally put him down for less than twenty. But he had good manners; he allowed her to pass before him, where the way grew narrow; walked on the outside of the path; made haste to draw back an obstreperous branch; and not one of these trifling conventionalities was lost on Madeleine Wade.

They had turned their steps homewards, and were drawing near the edge of the wood, when, through the tree-trunks, which here were bare and far apart, they saw two people walking arm in arm; and on turning a corner found the couple coming straight towards them, on the same path as themselves. In the full flush of his talk, Maurice Guest did not at first grasp what was about to happen. He had ended the sentence he was at, and begun another, before the truth broke on him. Then he stuttered, lost the thread of his thought, was abruptly silent; and what he had been going to say, and what, a moment before, had seemed of the utmost importance, was never said. His companion did not seem to notice his preoccupation; she gave an exclamation of what sounded like surprise, and herself looked steadily at the approaching pair. Thus they went forward to a meeting which the young man had imagined to himself in many ways, but not in this. The moment he had waited for had come; and now he wished himself miles away. Meanwhile, they walked on, in a brutal, matter-of-fact fashion, and at a fairish pace, though each step he took was an event, and his feet were as heavy and awkward as if they did not belong to him.

The other two sauntered towards them, without haste. The man she was with had his arm through hers, her hand in his left hand, while in his right he twirled a cane. They were not speaking; she looked before her, rather listlessly, with dark, indifferent eyes. To see this, to see also that she was taller and broader than he had believed, and in full daylight somewhat sallow, Maurice had first to conquer an aversion to look at all, on account of the open familiarity of their attitude. It was not like this that he had dreamt of finding her. And so it happened that when, without a word to him, his companion crossed the path and confronted the other two, he only lingered for an instant, in an agony of indecision, and then, by an impulse over which he had no control, walked on and stood out of earshot.

He drew a deep breath, like one who has escaped a danger; but almost simultaneously he bit his lip with mortification: could any power on earth make it clear to him why he had acted in this way? All his thoughts had been directed towards this moment for so long, only to take this miserable end. A string of contemptuous epithets for himself rose to his lips. But when he looked back at the group, the reason of his folly was apparent to him; at the sight of this other beside her, a sharp twinge of jealousy had run through him and disturbed his balance. He gazed ardently at her in the hope that she would look round, but it was only the man—he was caressing his slight moustache and hitting at loose stones while the girls talked—who turned, as if drawn by Maurice's stare, and looked full at him, with studied insolence. In him, Maurice recognised the violinist of the concert, but he, too, was taller than he had believed, and much younger. A mere boy, said Maurice to himself; a mere boy, with a disagreeable, dissipated face.

Madeleine Wade came hurrying to rejoin him, apologising for the delay; the meeting had, however, been fortunate, as she had had a message from Schwarz to deliver. Maurice let a few seconds elapse, then asked without preamble: "Who is that?"

His companion looked quickly at him, struck both by his tone and by his unconscious use of the singular. The air of indifference with which he was looking out across the meadow-land, told its own tale.

"Schilsky? Don't you know Schilsky? Our Joachim *in spe*?" she asked, to tease him.

Maurice Guest coloured. "Yes, I heard him play the other night," he answered in good faith. "But I didn't mean him. I meant the—the lady he was with."

The girl at his side laughed, not very heartily.

"*Et tu, Brute!*" she said. "I might have known it. It really is remarkable that though so many people don't think Louise good-looking—I have often heard her called plain—yet I never knew a man go past her without turning his head. —You want to know who and what she is? Well, that depends on whom you ask. Schwarz would tell you she was one of his most gifted pupils—but no: he always says that of his pretty girls, and some do find her pretty, you know."

"She is, indeed, very," said Maurice with warmth. "Though I think pretty is not just the word."

"No, I don't suppose it is," said Madeleine, and this time there was a note of mockery in her laugh. But Maurice did not let himself be deterred. As it seemed likely that she was going to let the subject rest here, he persisted: " But suppose I asked you—what would you say? "

She gave him a shrewd side-glance. " I think I won't tell you," she said, more gravely. " If a man has once thought a girl pretty, and all the rest of it, he's never grateful for the truth. If I said Louise was a baggage, or a minx, or some other horrid thing, you would always bear me a grudge for it, so please note, I don't say it—for we are going to be friends, I hope? "

" I hope so, too," said the young man.

They walked some distance along the unfinished end of the *Mozartstrasse,* where only a few villas stood, in newly made gardens.

" At least, I should like to know her name—her whole name. You said Louise, I think? "

She laughed outright at this. " Her name is Dufrayer, Louise Dufrayer, and she has been here studying with Schwarz for about a year and a half now. She has some talent, but is indolent to the last degree, and only works when she can't help it. Also she always has an admirer of some kind in tow. This, to-day, is her last particular friend.—Is that biographical matter enough? "

He was afraid he had made himself ridiculous in her eyes, and did not answer. They walked the rest of the way in silence. At her house-door, they paused to take leave of each other.

" Good-bye. Come and see me sometimes when you have time. We were once colleagues, you know, and are now fellow-pupils. I should be glad to help you if you ever need help."

He thanked her and promised to remember; then walked home without knowing how he did it. He had room in his brain for one thought only; he knew her name, he knew her name. He said it again and again to himself, walked in time with it, and found it as heady as wine; the mere sound of the spoken syllables seemed to bring her nearer to him, to establish a mysterious connection between them. Moreover, in itself it pleased him extraordinarily; and he was vaguely grateful to something outside himself, that it was a name he could honestly admire.

In a kind of defiant challenge to unseen powers, he doubled his arm and felt the muscles in it. Then he sat down at his piano, and, to the dismay of his landlady—for it was now late evening—practised for a couple of hours without stopping.

And the scales he sent flying up and down in the darkness had a ring of exultation in them, were like cries of triumph.

He had discovered the " Open Sesame " to his treasure. And there was time and to spare. He left everything to the future, in blind trust that it would bring him good fortune. It was enough that they were here together, inhabitants of the same town. Besides, he had formed a friendship with some one who knew her; a way would surely open up, in which he might make her aware of his presence. In the meantime, it was something to live for. Each day that dawned might be *the* day.

But little by little, like a fountain run dry, his elation subsided, and, as he lay sleepless, he had a sudden fit of jealous despair. He remembered, with a horrid distinctness, how he had seen her. Again she came towards them, at the other's side, hand in hand with him, inattentive to all but him. Now he could almost have wept at the recollection. Those clasped hands!—he could have forgiven everything else, but the thought of these remained with him and stung him. Here he lay, thinking wild and foolish things, building castles that had no earthly foundation, and all the time it was another who had the right to be with her, to walk at her side, and share her thoughts. Again he was the outsider; behind these two was a life full of detail and circumstance, of which he knew nothing. His excited brain called up pictures, imagined fiercely at words and looks, until the darkness and stillness of the room became unendurable; and he sprang up, threw on his clothing, and went out. Retracing his steps, he found the very spot where they had met. Guiltily, with a stealthy look round him, though wood and night were black as ink, he knelt down and kissed the gravel where he thought she had stood.

IV

It was through Dove's agency—Dove was always on the spot
to guide and assist his friends; to advise where the best, or
cheapest, or rarest, of anything was to be had, from second-
hand Wagner scores to hair pomade; he knew those shops
where the "half-quarters" of ham or roast-beef weighed
heavier than elsewhere, restaurants where the beer had least
froth and the cutlets were largest for the money; knew the
ins and outs of Leipzig as no other foreigner did, knew all that
went on, and the affairs of everybody, as though he went
through life garnering in just those little facts that others were
apt to overlook. Through Dove, Maurice became a paying
guest at a dinner-table kept by two maiden ladies, who eked
out their income by providing a plain meal, at a low price,
for respectable young people.

The company was made up to a large extent of English-
speaking people. There were several university students—
grave-faced, older men, with beards and spectacles—who looked
down on the young musicians, and talked, of set purpose, on
abstruse subjects. More noteworthy were two American
pianists: Ford, who could not carry a single glass of beer, and
played better when he had had more than one; and James, a
wiry, red-haired man, with an unfaltering opinion of himself,
and an iron wrist—by means of a week's practice, he could
ruin any piano. Two ladies were also present. Philadelphia
Jensen, of German-American parentage, was a student of voice-
production, under a Swedish singing master who had lately set
musical circles in a ferment, with his new and extraordinary
method: its devotees swore that, in time, it would display marvellous results; but, in the meantime, the most advanced
pupils were only emitting single notes, and the greater number
stood, every morning, before their respective mirrors, watching their mouths open and shut, fish-fashion, without produc-
ing a sound. Miss Jensen—she preferred the English pronunciation of the J—was a large, fleshy woman, with a curled
fringe and prominent eyes. Her future stage-presence was the
object of general admiration; it was whispered that she aimed
at Isolde. Loud in voice and manner, she was fond of pro-

claiming her views on all kinds of subjects, from diaphragmatic respiration, through *Ghosts,* which was being read by a bold, advanced few, down to the continental methods of regulating vice—to the intense embarrassment of those who sat next her at table. Still another American lady, Miss Martin, was studying with Bendel, the rival of Schwarz; and as she lived in the same quarter of the town as Dove and Maurice, the three of them often walked home together. For the most part, Miss Martin was in a state of tragic despair. With the frankness of her race, she admitted that she had arrived in Leipzig, expecting to astonish. In this she had been disappointed; Bendel had treated her like any other of his pupils; she was still playing Haydn and Czerny, and saw endless vistas of similar composers " back of these." Dove laid the whole blame on Bendel's method—which he denounced with eloquence—and strongly advocated her becoming a pupil of Schwarz. He himself undertook to arrange matters, and, in what seemed an incredibly short time, the change was effected. For a little, things went better; Schwarz was reported to have said that she had talent, great talent, and that he would make something of her; but soon, she was complaining anew: if there were any difference between Czerny and Bertini, Haydn and Dussek, some one might " slick up " and tell her what it was. Off the subject of her own gifts, she was a lively, affable girl, with china-blue eyes, pale flaxen hair, and coal-black eyebrows; and both young men got on well with her, in the usual superficial way. For Maurice Guest, she had the additional attraction, that he had once seen her in the street with the object of his romantic fancy.

Since the afternoon when he had heard from Madeleine Wade who this was, he had not advanced a step nearer making her acquaintance; though a couple of weeks had passed, though he now knew two people who knew her, and though his satisfaction at learning her name had immediately yielded to a hunger for more. And now, hardly a day went by, on which he did not see her. His infatuation had made him keen of scent; by following her, with due precaution, he had found out for himself in the *Brüderstrasse,* the roomy old house she lived in; had found out how she came and went. He knew her associates, knew the streets she preferred, the hour of day at which she was to be met at the Conservatorium. Far away, at the other end of one of the quiet streets that lay wide and sunny about the Gewandhaus, when, to other eyes she was a mere speck in the distance, he learned to recognise her—if only by the speed at which his heart beat—and he even gave chase to imaginary resemblances. Once he remained sitting in a tramway far beyond his destination, because he traced, in one of the passengers, a curious likeness to her, in long, wavy eyebrows that were highest in the middle of the forehead.

Thus the pale face with the heavy eyes haunted him by day and by night.

He was very happy and very unhappy, by turns—never at rest. If he imagined she had looked observantly at him as she passed, he was elated for hours after. If she did not seem to notice him, it was brought home to him anew that he was nothing to her; and once, when he had gazed too boldly, instead of turning away his eyes, as she went close by him to Schwarz's room, and she had resented the look with cold surprise, he felt as culpable as if he had insulted her. He atoned for his behaviour, the next time they met, by assuming his very humblest air; once, too, he deliberately threw himself in her way, for the mere pleasure of standing aside with the emphatic deference of a slave. Throughout this period, and particularly after an occasion such as the last, his self-consciousness was so peculiarly intensified that his surroundings ceased to exist for him—they two were the gigantic figures on a shadow background—and what he sometimes could not believe was, that such feelings as these should be seething in him, and she remain ignorant of them. He lost touch with reality, and dreamed dreams of imperceptible threads, finer than any gossamer, which could be spun from soul to soul, without the need of speech.

He heaped on her all the spiritual perfections that answered to her appearance. And he did not, for a time, observe anything to make him waver in his faith that she was whiter, stiller, and more unapproachable—of a different clay, in short, from other women. Then, however, this illusion was shattered. Late one afternoon, she came down the stairs of the house she lived in, and, pausing at the door, looked up and down the hot, empty street, shading her eyes with her hand. No one was in sight, and she was about to turn away, when, from where he was watching in a neighbouring doorway, Maurice saw the red-haired violinist come swiftly round the corner. She saw him, too, took a few, quick steps towards him, and, believing herself unseen, looked up in his face as they met; and the passionate tenderness of the look, the sudden lighting of lip and eye, racked the poor, unwilling spy for days. To suit this abrupt descent from the pedestal, he was obliged to carve a new attribute to his idol, and laboriously adapt it.

Schilsky, this insolent boy, was the thorn in his side. It was Schilsky she was oftenest to be met with; he was her companion at the most unexpected hours; and, with reluctance, Maurice had to admit to himself that she had apparently no thought to spare for anyone else. But it did not make any difference. The curious way in which he felt towards her, the strange, overwhelming effect her face had on him, took no account of outside things. Though he might never hope for a word from her; though he should learn in the coming moment that she was the other's promised wife; he could not for that reason banish her from his mind. His feelings were not to be put on and off, like clothes; he had no power over them. It was simply a case of accepting things as they were, and this he sought to do.

But his imagination made it hard for him, by throwing up pictures in which Schilsky was all-prominent. He saw him the confidant of her joys and troubles; *he* knew their origin, knew what key her day was set in. If her head ached, if she were tired or spiritless, his hand was on her brow. The smallest events in her life were an open book to him; and it was these worthless details that Maurice Guest envied him most. He kept a tight hold on his fancy, but if, as sometimes happened, it slipped control, and painted further looks of the kind he had seen exchanged between them, a kiss or an embrace, he was as wretched as if he had in reality been present.

At other times, this jealous unrest was not the bitterest drop in his cup; it was bitterer to know that she was squandering her love on one who was unworthy of it. At first, from a feeling of exaggerated delicacy, he had gone out of his way to escape hearing Schilsky's name; but this mood passed, and gave place to an undignified hankering to learn everything he could, concerning the young man. What he heard amounted to this: a talented rascal, the best violinist the Conservatorium had turned out for years, one to whom all gates would open; but—this " but " always followed, with a meaning smile and a wink of the eye: and then came the anecdotes. They had nothing heaven-scaling in them—these soiled love-stories; this perpetual impecuniosity; this inability to refuse money, no matter whose the hand that offered it; this fine art in the disregarding of established canons—and, to Maurice Guest, bred to sterner standards, they seemed unspeakably low and mean.

Hours came when he strove in vain to understand her. Ignorant of these things she could not be; was it within the limits of the possible that she could overlook them?—and he shivered lest he should be forced to think less highly of her. Ultimately, sending his mind back over what he had read and heard, drawing on his own slight experience, he came to a compromise with himself. He said that most often the best and fairest women loved men who were unworthy of them. Was it not a weakness and a strength of her sex to see good where no good was?—a kind of divine frailty, a wilful blindness, a sweet inability to discern.

At times, again, he felt almost content that Schilsky was what he was. If the day should ever come when, all barriers down, he, Maurice Guest, might be intimately associated with her life; if he should ever have the chance of proving to her what real love was, what a holy mystic thing, how far removed from a blind passing fancy; if he might serve her, be her slave, lay his hands under her feet, lead her up and on, all suffused in a sunset of tenderness: then, she would see that what she had believed to be love had been nothing but a *fata Morgana,* a mirage of the skies. And he heard himself whispering words of incredible fondness to her, saw her listening with wonder in her eyes.

At still other moments, he was ready to renounce every hope, if, by doing so, he could add jot or tittle to her happiness.

The further he spun himself into his dreams, however, and the better he learnt to know her in imagination, the harder it grew to take the first step towards realising his wishes. In those few, brief days, when he hugged her name to him as a talisman, he waited cheerfully for something to happen, something unusual, that would bring him to her notice—a dropped handkerchief, a seat vacated for her at a concert, even a timely accident. But as day after day went by, in eventless monotony, he began to cast about him for human aid. From Dove, his daily companion, Dove of the outstretched paws of continual help, he now shrank away. Miss Martin was not to be spoken to except in Dove's company. There was only one person who could assist him, if she would, and that was Madeleine Wade. He called to mind the hearty invitation she had given him, and reproached himself for not having taken advantage of it.

One afternoon, towards six o'clock, he rang the bell of her lodgings in the *Mozartstrasse.* This was a new street, the first blocks of which gave directly on the Gewandhaus square;

but, at the further end, where she lived, a phalanx of red-brick and stucco fronts looked primly across at a similar line. In the third storey of one of these houses, Madeleine Wade had a single, large room, the furniture of which was so skilfully contrived, that, by day, all traces of the room's double calling were obliterated.

As he entered, on this first occasion, she was practising at a grand piano which stood before one of the windows. She rose at once, and, having greeted him warmly, made him sit down among the comfortable cushions that lined the sofa. Then she took cups and saucers from a cupboard in the wall, and prepared tea over a spirit-lamp. He soon felt quite at home with her, and enjoyed himself so well that many such informal visits followed.

But the fact was not to be denied: it was her surroundings that attracted him, rather than she herself. True, he found her frankness delightfully " refreshing," and when he spoke of her, it was as of an " awfully good sort," " a first-class girl "; for Madeleine was invariably lively, kind and helpful. At the same time, she was without doubt a trifle too composed, too sure of herself; she had too keen an eye for human foibles; she came towards you with a perfectly natural openness, and she came all the way—there was nothing left for you to explore. And when not actually with her, it was easy to forget her; there was never a look or a smile, never a barbed word, never a sudden spontaneous gesture—the vivid translation of a thought —to stamp itself on your memory.

But it was only at the outset that he thought things like these. Madeleine Wade had been through experiences of the same kind before; and hardly a fortnight later they were calling each other by their Christian names.

When he came to her, towards evening, tired and inclined to be lonely, she seated him in a corner of the sofa, and did not ask him to say much until she had made the tea. Then, when the cups were steaming in front of them, she discussed sympathetically with him the progress of his work. She questioned him, too, about his home and family, and he read her parts of his mother's letters, which arrived without fail every Tuesday morning. She also drew from him a more detailed account of his previous life; and, in this connection, they had several animated discussions about teaching, a calling to which Madeleine looked composedly forward to returning, while Maurice, in strong superlative, declared he had rather force a flock of sheep to walk in line. She told him, too, some of the gossip the musical quarter of the town was rife with, about those in high places; and, in particular, of the bitter rivalry that had grown up with the years between Schwarz and Bendel, the chief masters of the piano. If these two met in the street, they passed each other with a stony stare; if, at an *Abendunter-haltung,* a pupil of one was to play, the other rose ostentatiously and left the hall. She also hinted that in order to obtain all you wanted at the Conservatorium, to be favoured above your fellows, it was only necessary flagrantly to bribe one of the clerks, Kleefeld by name, who was open to receive anything, being wretchedly impecunious and the father of a large family.

Finding, too, that Maurice was bent on learning German, she, who spoke the language fluently, proposed that they should read it together; and soon it became their custom to work through a few pages of *Quintus Fixlein,* a scene or two of Schiller, some lyrics of Heine. They also began to play duets, symphonies old and new, and Madeleine took care constantly to have something fresh and interesting at hand. To all this the young man brought an unbounded zeal, and, if he had had his way, they would have gone on playing or reading far into the evening.

She smiled at his eagerness. " You absorb like a sponge."

When it grew too dark to see, he confided to her that his dearest wish was to be a conductor. He was not yet clear how it could be managed, but he was sure that this was the branch of his art for which he had most aptitude.

Here she interrupted him. " Do you never write verses? "

Her question seemed to him so meaningless that he only laughed, and went on with what he was saying. For the event of his plan proving impracticable—at home they had no idea of it—he was training as a concert-player; but he intended to miss no chance that offered, of learning how to handle an orchestra.

Throughout these hours of stimulating companionship, how-ever, he did not lose sight of his original purpose in going to see Madeleine. It was only that just the right moment never seemed to come; and the name he was so anxious to hear, had not once been mentioned between them. Often, in the dusk, his lips twitched to speak it; but he feared his own awkward-ness, and her quick tongue; then, too, the subject was usually far aside from what they were talking of, and it would have made a ludicrous impression to drag it in by the hair.

But one day his patience was rewarded. He had carelessly taken up a paper-bound volume of Chopin, and was on the point of commenting upon it, for he had lately begun to understand the difference between a Litolff and a Mikuli. But it slipped from his hand, and he was obliged to crawl under the piano to pick it up; on a corner of the cover, in a big, black, scrawly writing, was the name of Marie Louise Dufrayer. He cleared his throat, laid the volume down, took it up again; then, realising that the moment had come, he put a bold face on the matter.

" I see this belongs to Miss Dufrayer," he said bluntly, and, as his companion's answer was only a careless: " Yes, Louise forgot it the last time she was here," he went on without delay: " I should like to know Miss Dufrayer, Madeleine. Do you think you could introduce me to her? "

Madeleine, who was in the act of taking down a book from her hanging shelves, turned and looked at him. He was still red in the face, from the exertion of stooping.

" Introduce you to Louise? " she queried. " Why?—why do you want to be introduced to her? "

" Oh, I don't know. For no particular reason."

She sat down at the table, opened the book, and turned the leaves.

" Oh well, I daresay I can, if you wish it, and an opportunity occurs—if you're with me some day when I meet her.—Now shall we go on with the *Jungfrau?* We were beginning the third act, I think. Here it is:

Wir waren Herzensbrüder, Waffenfreunde,
Für eine Sache hoben wir den Arm! "

But Maurice did not take the book she handed him across the table.

" Won't you give me a more definite promise than that? "

Madeleine sat back in her chair, and, folding her arms, looked thoughtfully at him.

Only a momentary silence followed his words, but, in this fraction of time, a series of impressions swept through her brain, with the continuity of a bird's flight. It was clear to her at once, that what prompted his insistence was not an ordinary curiosity, or a passing whim; in a flash, she understood that here, below the surface, something was at work in him, the existence of which she had not even suspected. She was more than annoyed with herself at her own foolish obtuseness; she had had these experiences before, and then, as now, the object of her interest had invariably been turned aside by the first pretty, silly face that came his way. The main difference was that she had been more than ordinarily drawn to Maurice Guest; and, believing it impossible, in this case, for anyone else to be sharing the field with her, she had over-indulged the hope that he sought her out for herself alone.

She endeavoured to learn more. But this time Maurice was on his guard, and the questions she put, straight though they were, only elicited the response that he had seen Miss Dufrayer shortly after arriving, and had been much struck by her.

Madeleine's brain travelled rapidly backwards. "But if I remember rightly, Maurice, we met Louise one day in the *Scheibenholz,* the first time we went for a walk together. Why didn't you stop then, and be introduced to her, if you were so anxious?"

"Why do we ever do foolish things?"

Her amazement was so patent that he made uncomfortable apology for himself. "It is ridiculous, I know," he said and coloured. "And it must seem doubly so to you. But that I should want to know her—there's nothing strange in that, is there? You, too, Madeleine, have surely admired people sometimes—some one, say, who has done a fine thing—and have felt that you must know them personally, at all costs?"

"Perhaps I have. But romantic feelings of that kind are sure to end in smoke. As a rule they've no foundation but our own wishes.—If you take my advice, Maurice, you will be content to admire Louise at a distance. Think her as pretty as you like, and imagine her to be all that's sweet and charming; but never mind about knowing her."

"But why on earth not?"

"Why, nothing will come of it."

"That depends on what you mean by nothing."

"You don't understand. I must be plainer.—Do sit down, and don't fidget so.—How long have you been here now? Nearly two months. Well, that's long enough to know something of what's going on. You must have both seen and heard that Louise has no eyes for anyone but a certain person, to put it bluntly, that she is wrapped up in Schilsky. This has been going on for over a year now, and she seems to grow more infatuated every day. When she first came to Leipzig, we were friends; she lived in this neighbourhood, and I was able to be of service to her. Now, weeks go by and I don't see her; she has broken with every one—for Louise is not a girl to do things by halves.—Introduce you? Of course I can. But suppose it done, with all pomp and ceremony, what will you get from it? I know Louise. A word or two, if her ladyship is in the mood; if not, you will be so much thin air for her. And after that, a nod if she meets you in the street—and that's all."

" It's enough."

"You're easily satisfied.—But tell me, honestly now, Maurice, what possible good can that do you? "

He moved aimlessly about the room. " Good? Must one always look for good in everything?—I can see quite well that from your point of view the whole thing must seem absurd. I expect nothing whatever from it, but I'm going to know her, and that's all about it."

Still in the same position, with folded arms, Madeleine observed him with unblinking eyes.

" And you won't bear me a grudge, if things go badly?— I mean if you are disappointed, or dissatisfied? "

He made a gesture of impatience.

"Yes, but I know Louise, and you don't."

He had picked up from the writing-table the photograph of a curate, and he stared at it as if he had no thought but to let the mild features stamp themselves on his mind. Madeleine's eyes continued to bore him through. At last, out of a silence, she said slowly: " Of course I can introduce you—it's done with a wave of the hand. But, as your friend, I think it only right to warn you what you must expect. For I can see you don't understand in the least, and are laying up a big disappointment for yourself. However, you shall have your way—if only to show you that I am right."

" Thanks, Madeleine—thanks awfully."

They settled down to read Schiller. But Maurice made one slip after another, and she let them pass uncorrected. She was annoyed with herself afresh, for having made too much of the matter, for having blown it up to a fictitious importance, when the wiser way would have been to treat it as of no consequence at all.

The next afternoon he arrived, with expectation in his face; but not on this day, nor the next, nor the next again, did she bring the subject up between them. On the fourth, however, as he was leaving, she said abruptly: " You must have patience for a little, Maurice. Louise has gone to Dresden,"

"That's why the blinds are down," he exclaimed without
thinking, then coloured furiously at his own words, and, to
smooth them over, asked: "Why has she gone? For how
long?"

But Madeleine caught him up. "*Sieh da,* some one has been
playing sentinel!" she said in raillery; and it seemed to him
that every fold in his brain was laid bare to her, before she
answered: "She has gone for a week or ten days—to visit some
friends who are staying there."

He nodded, and was about to open the door, when she added:
"But set your mind at rest—*he* is here."

Maurice looked sharply up; but a minute or two passed before the true meaning of her words broke on him. He coloured
again—a mortifying habit he had not outgrown, and one which
seemed to affect him more in the presence of Madeleine than of
anyone else.

"It's hardly a thing to joke about."

"Joke!—who is joking?" she asked, and raised her eyebrows so high that her forehead was filled with wrinkles.
"Nothing was further from my thoughts."

Maurice hesitated, and stood undecided, holding the door-
handle. Then, following an impulse, he turned and sat down
again. "Madeleine, tell me—I wouldn't ask anyone but you—
what sort of a fellow *is* this Schilsky?"

"What sort of a fellow?" She laughed sarcastically. "To
be quite truthful, Maurice, the best fiddler the Con. has turned
out for years."

"Now you're joking again. As if I didn't know that.
Every one says the same."

"You want his moral character? Well, I'll be equally candid. Or, at least, I'll give you my opinion of him. It's another superlative. Just as I consider him the best violinist, I
also hold him to be the greatest scamp in the place—and I've
no objection to use a stronger word if you like. I wouldn't
take his hand, no, not if he offered it to me. The last time
he was in this room, about six months ago, he—well, let us
say he borrowed, without a word to me, five or six marks that
were lying loose on the writing-table. Yes, it's a fact," she
repeated, complacently eyeing Maurice's dismay. "Otherwise?
—oh, otherwise, he was born, I think, with a silver spoon in
his mouth. He has one piece of luck after another. Zollinger
discovered him ten years ago, on a concert-tour—his father is
a smith in Warsaw—and brought him to Leipzig. He was a

prodigy, then, and a rich Jewish banker took him up, and paid for his education; and when he washed his hands of him in disgust, Schaefele's wife—Schaefele is head of the *Händelverein,* you know—adopted him as a son—some people say as more than a son, for, though she was nearly forty, she was perfectly crazy over him, and behaved as foolishly as any of the dozens of silly girls who have lost their hearts to him."

"I suppose they are engaged," said Maurice after a pause, speaking out of his own thoughts.

"Do you?" she asked with mild humour. "I really never asked them.—But this is just another example of his good fortune. When he has worn out every one else's patience, through his dishonest extravagance, he picks up a rich wife, who is not averse to supporting him before marriage."

Maurice looked at her reproachfully. "I wonder you care to repeat such gossip."

"It's not gossip, Maurice. Every one knows it. Louise makes no mystery of her doings—doesn't care that much what people say. While as for him—well, it's enough to know it's Schilsky. The thing is an open secret. Listen, now, and I'll tell you how it began—just to let you judge for yourself what kind of a girl you have to deal with in Louise, and how Schilsky behaves when he wants a thing, and whether such a pair think a formal engagement necessary to their happiness. When Louise came here, a year and a half ago, Schilsky was away somewhere with Zollinger, and didn't get back till a couple of months afterwards. As I said, I knew Louise pretty well at that time; she had got herself into trouble with—but that's neither here nor there. Well, my lord returns—he himself tells how it happened. It was a Thursday evening, and a Radius Commemoration was going on at the Con. He went in late, and stood at the back of the hall. Louise was there, too, just before him, and, from the first minute he saw her, he couldn't take his eyes off her—others who were by say, too, he seemed perfectly fascinated. No one can stare as rudely as Schilsky, and he ended by making her so uncomfortable that she couldn't bear it any longer, and went out of the hall. He after her, and it didn't take him an hour to find out all about her. The next evening, at an *Abend,* they were both there again—it was just like Louise to go!—and the same thing was repeated. She left again before it was over, he followed, and this time found her in one of the side corridors; and there—mind you, without a single word having passed between them!—he took her in his arms and kissed her, kissed her soundly, half a dozen times—though they had never once spoken to each other: he boasts of it to this day. That same evening——"

"Don't, Madeleine—please, don't say any more! I don't care to hear it," broke in Maurice. He had flushed to the roots of his hair, at some points of resemblance to his own case, then grown pale again, and now he waved his arm meaninglessly in the air. "He is a scoundrel, a—a——" But he recognised that he could not condemn one without the other, and stopped short.

"My dear boy, if I don't tell you, other people will. And at least you know I mean well by you. Besides," she went on, not without a touch of malice as she eyed him sitting there, spoiling the leaves of a book. "Besides, I may as well show you how you have to treat Louise, if you want to make an impression on her. You call him a scoundrel, but what of her? Believe me, Maurice," she said more seriously, "Louise is not a whit too good for him; they were made for each other. And of course he will marry her eventually, for the sake of her money"—here she paused and looked deliberately at him—"if not for her own."

This time there was no mistaking the meaning of her words. "Madeleine!"

He rose from his seat with such force that the table tilted.

But Madeleine did not falter. "I told you already, you know, that Louise doesn't care what is said about her. As soon as this unfortunate affair began, she threw up the rooms she was in at the time, and moved nearer the *Talstrasse*—where he lives. Rumour has it also that she provided herself with an accommodating landlady, who can be blind and deaf when necessary."

"How *can* you repeat such atrocious scandal?"

He stared at her, in incredulous dismay. Her words were so many arrows, the points of which remained sticking in him.

She shrugged her shoulders. "Your not believing it doesn't affect the truth of the story, Maurice. It was the talk of the place when it happened. And you may despise rumour as you will, my experience is, a report never springs up that hasn't some basis of fact to go on—however small."

He choked back, with an effort, the eloquent words that came to his lips; of what use was it to make himself still more ridiculous in her eyes? His hat had fallen to the floor; he picked it up, and brushed it on his sleeve, without knowing what he did. "Oh, well, of course, if you think that," he said as coolly as he was able, "nothing I could say would make any difference. Every one is free to his opinions, I suppose. But, all the same, I must say, Madeleine "—he grew hot in spite of himself. "You have been her friend, you say; you have known her intimately; and yet just because she . . . she cares for this fellow in such a way that she sets caring for him above being cautious—why, not one woman in a thousand would have the courage for that sort of thing! It needs courage, not to mind what people—no, what your friends— imagine, and how falsely they interpret what you do. Besides, one has only to look at her to see how absurd it is. That face and—I don't know her, Madeleine; I've never spoken to her, and never may, yet I am absolutely certain that what is said about her isn't true. So certain that— But after all, if this is what you think about . . . about it, then all I have to say is, we had better not discuss the subject again. It does no good, and we should never be of the same opinion."

Not without embarrassment, now that he had said his say, he turned to the door. But Madeleine was not in the least angry. She gave him her hand, and said, with a smile, yet gravely, too: "Agreed, Maurice! We will not speak of Louise again."

V

HE shunned Madeleine for days after this. He was morose
and unhappy, and brooded darkly over the baseness of wagging
tongues. For the first time in his life he had come into touch
with slander, that invisible Hydra, and straightway it seized
upon the one person to whom he was not indifferent. In this
mood it was a relief to him that certain three windows in the
Brüderstrasse remained closed and shuttered; with the load of
malicious gossip fresh on his mind, he chose rather not to see
her; he must first accustom himself to it, as to the scar left by
a wound.

He did not, of course, believe what Madeleine, with her
infernal frankness, had told him; but the knowledge that such
a report was abroad, depressed him unspeakably: it took colour
from the sky and light from the sun. Sometimes in these days,
as he sat at his piano, he had a sudden fit of discouragement,
which made it seem not worth while to continue playing. It
was unthinkable that she could be aware how busy scandal was
with her name, and how her careless acts were spied on and
misrepresented; and he turned over in his mind ways and means
by which she might be induced to take more thought for herself
in future.

He did not believe it; but hours of distracting uncertainty
came, none the less, when small things which his memory had
stored up made him go so far as to ask himself, what if it should
be true?—what then? But he had not courage enough to face
an answer; he put the possibility away from him, in the extreme
background of his mind, refused to let his brain piece its observations together. The mere suspicion was a blasphemy, a
blasphemy against her dignified reserve, against her sweet pale
face, her supreme disregard of those about her. Not thus
would guilt have shown itself.

Schilsky, who was the origin of all the evil, he made wide
circuits to avoid. He thought of him, at this time, with what
he believed to be a feeling of purely personal antipathy. In his
most downcast moments, he had swift and foolish visions of
publicly executing vengeance on him; but if, a moment later, he
saw the violinist's red hair or big hat before him in the street,

he turned aside as though the other had been plague-struck. Once, however, when he was going up the steps of the Conservatorium, and Schilsky, in leaping down, pushed carelessly against him, he returned the knock so rudely and swore with such downrightness that, in spite of his hurry, Schilsky stopped and fixed him, and with equal vehemence damned him for a fool of an Englishman.

His despondency spread like a weed. A furious impatience overcame him, too, at the thought of the innumerable hours he would be forced to spend at the piano, day in, day out, for months to come, before the result could be compared with the achievements even of many a fellow-student. As the private lessons Schwarz gave were too expensive for him, he decided, as a compromise, to take a course of extra lessons with Fürst, who prepared pupils for the master, and was quite willing to come to terms, in other words, who taught for what he could get.

Once a week, then, for the rest of the summer, Maurice climbed the steep, winding stair of the house in the *Brandvorwerkstrasse,* where Fürst lived with his mother. It was so dark on this stair that, in dull weather, ill-trimmed lamps burnt all day long on the different landings. To its convolutions, in its unaired corners, clung what seemed to be the stale, accumulated smells of years; and these were continually reinforced; since every day at dinner-time, the various kitchen-windows, all of which gave on the stair, were opened to let the piercing odours of cooking escape. The house, like the majority of its kind in this relatively new street, was divided into countless small lodgings; three families, with three rooms apiece, lived on each storey, and on the fifth floor, at the top of the house, the same number of rooms was let out singly. Part of the third storey was occupied by a bird-fancier; and between him and the Fürsts above waged perpetual war, one of those petty, unending wars that can only arise and be kept up when, as here, such heterogeneous elements are forced to live side by side, under one roof. The fancier, although his business was nominally in the town, had enough of his wares beside him to make his house a lively, humming kind of place, and the strife dated back to a day when, the door standing temptingly ajar, Peter, the Fürsts' lean cat, had sneaked stealthily in upon this, to him, enchanted ground, and, according to the fancier, had caused the death, from fright, of a delicate canary, although the culprit had done nothing more than sit before the cage, licking his lips. This had happened several years ago, but each party was still fertile in planning annoyances for the other, and the females did not bow when they met. On the fourth floor, next the Fürsts, lived a pale, harassed teacher, with a family which had long since outgrown its accommodation; for the wife was perpetually in childbed, and cots and cradles were the chief furniture of the house. As the critical moments of her career drew nigh, the " Frau Lehrer " complained, with an aggravated bitterness, of the unceasing music that went on behind the thin partition; and this grievance, together with the racy items of gossip left behind the midwife's annual visit, like a trail of smoke, provided her and Fürst's mother with infinite food for talk. They were thick friends again a few minutes after a scene so lively that blows seemed imminent, and they met every morning on the landing, where, with broom or child in hand, they stood gossiping by the hour.

When Maurice rang, Frau Fürst opened the door to him herself, having first cautiously examined him through the kitchen window. Drying her hands on her apron, she ushered him through the tiny entry—a place of dangers, pitch-dark as it was, and lumbered with chests and presses—into Franz's room, the " best room " of the house. Here were collected a red plush suite, which was the pride of Frau Fürst's heart, and all the round, yellowing family photographs; here, too, stood the well-used Bechstein, pile upon pile of music, a couple of music-stands, a bust of Schubert, a faded, framed diploma. For years, assuredly, the windows had never been thrown wide open; the odours of stale coffee and forgotten dinners, of stove and warmed wood, of piano, music and beeswax: all these lay as it were in streaks in the atmosphere, and made it heavy and thought-benumbing.

A willing listener was worth more than gold to Frau Fürst, and here, the first time he came, while waiting for Franz, Maurice heard in detail the history of the family. The father had been an oboist in the Gewandhaus orchestra, and had died, a few years previously, of a chill incurred after a performance of *Die Meistersinger*. At his death, it had fallen on Franz to support the family; and, thanks to Schwarz's aid and influence, Franz was able to get as many pupils as he had time to teach. It was easy to see that this, her eldest son, was the apple of Frau Fürst's eye; her other children seemed to be there only to meet his needs; his lightest wish was law. Each additional pupil that sought him out, was a fresh tribute to his genius; each one that left him, no matter after how long, was unthank-

ful and a traitor. For the nights on which his quartet met at
the house, she prepared as another woman would for a personal fête; and she watched the candles grow shorter without
a tinge of regret. When Franz played at an *Abendunterhaltung,* the family turned out in a body. Schwarz was a
god, all-powerful, on whom their welfare depended; and it was
necessary to propitiate him by a quarterly visit on a Sunday
morning, when, over wine and biscuits, she wept real and
feigned tears of gratitude.

In this hard-working, careworn woman, who was seldom to
be seen but in petticoat, bed-jacket, and heelless, felt shoes;
who, her whole life long, had been little better than a domestic
servant; in her there existed a devotion to art which had never
wavered. It would have seemed to her contrary to nature that
Franz should be anything but a musician, and it was also quite
in the order of things for them to be poor. Two younger boys,
who were still at school, gave up all their leisure time to music
—they had never in their lives tumbled round a football or
swung a bat—and Franz believed that the elder would prove a
skilful violinist. Of the little girls, one had a pure voice and
a good ear, and was to be a singer—for before this Juggernaut,
prejudice went down. Had anyone suggested to Frau Fürst
that her daughter should be a clerk, even a teacher, she would
have flung up hands of horror; but music!—that was a different
matter. It was, moreover, the single one of the arts, in which
this staunch advocate of womanliness granted her sex a share.

" Ask Franz," she said to Maurice. " Franz knows. He
will explain. All women can do is to reproduce what some one
else has thought or felt."

As an immortal example of the limits set by sex, she invariably fell back on Clara Schumann, with whom she had
more than once come into personal contact. In her youth, Frau
Fürst had had a clear soprano voice, and, to Maurice's interest, she told him how she had sometimes been sent for to
the Schumann's house in the *Inselstrasse,* to sing Robert's songs
for him.

" Clara accompanied me," she said, relating this, the great
reminiscence of her life; " and he was there, too, although I
never saw him face to face. He was too shy for that. But
he was behind a screen, and sometimes he would call: ' I must
alter that; it is too high;' or ' Quicker, quicker!' Sometimes
even ' Bravo!'"

Her motherly ambitions for Franz knew no bounds. One of

the few diversions she allowed herself was a visit to the theatre
—when Franz had tickets given to him; when one of her
favourite operas was performed; or on the anniversary of her
husband's death—and, on such occasions, she pointed out to
the younger children, the links that bound and would yet bind
them to the great house.

"That was your father's seat," she reminded them every
time. "The second row from the end. He came in at the door
to the left. And that," pointing to the conductor's raised chair,
"is where Franz will sit some day." For she dreamed of
Franz in all the glory of *Kapellmeister;* saw him swinging the
little stick that dominated the theatre—audience, singers and
players alike.

And the children, hanging over the high gallery, shuffling
their restless feet, thus had their path as clearly traced for them,
their destiny as surely sealed, as any fate-shackled heroes of
antiquity.

*   *   *   *   *

Late one afternoon about this time, Franz might have been
found together with his friends Krafft and Schilsky, at the
latter's lodging in the *Talstrasse.* He was astride a chair, over
the back of which he had folded his arms; and his chubby,
rubicund face glistened with moisture.

In the middle of the room, at the corner of a bare deal table
that was piled with loose music and manuscript, Schilsky sat
improving and correcting the tails and bodies of hastily made
notes. He was still in his nightshirt, over which he had thrown
coat and trousers; and, wide open at the neck, it exposed to
the waist a skin of the dead whiteness peculiar to red-haired
people. His face, on the other hand, was sallow and unfresh;
and the reddish rims of the eyes, and the coarsely self-indulgent
mouth, contrasted strikingly with the general youthfulness of
his appearance. He had the true musician's head: round as a
cannon-ball, with a vast, bumpy forehead, on which the soft
fluffy hair began far back, and stood out like a nimbus. His eyes
were either desperately dreamy or desperately sharp, never
normally attentive or at rest; his blunted nose and chin were
so short as to make the face look top-heavy. A carefully tended
young moustache stood straight out along his cheeks. He had
large, slender hands, and quick movements.

The air of the room was like a thin grey veiling, for all
three puffed hard at cigarettes. Without removing his from

between his teeth, Schilsky related an adventure of the night before. He spoke in jerks, with a strong lisp, and was more intent on what he was doing than on what he was saying.

"Do you think he'd budge?" he asked in a thick, spluttery way. "Not he. Till nearly two. And then I couldn't get him along. He thought it wasn't eleven, and wanted to stop at every corner. To irritate an imaginary bobby. He disputed with them, too. Heavens, what sport it was! At last I dragged him up here and got him on the sofa. Off he rolls again. So I let him lie. He didn't disturb me."

Heinrich Krafft, the hero of the episode, lay on the short, uncomfortable sofa, with the table-cover for a blanket. In answer to Schilsky, he said faintly, without opening his eyes: "Nothing would. You are an ox. When I wake this morning, with a mouth like gum arabic, he sits there as if he had not stirred all night. Then to bed, and snores till midday, through all the hellish light and noise."

Here Fürst could not resist making a little joke. He announced himself by a chuckle—like the click of a clock about to strike.

"He's got to make the most of his liberty. He doesn't often get off duty. We know, we know." He laughed tonelessly, and winked at Krafft.

Krafft quoted:

In der Woche zwier—

"Now, you fellows, shut up!" said Schilsky. It was plain that banter of this kind was not disagreeable to him; at the same time he was just at the moment too engrossed, to have more than half an ear for what was said. With his short-sighted eyes close to the paper, he was listening with all his might to some harmonies that his fingers played on the table. When, a few minutes later, he rose and stretched the stiffness from his limbs, his face, having lost its expression of rapt concentration, seemed suddenly to have grown younger. He set about dressing himself by drawing off his nightshirt over his head. At a word from him, Fürst sprang to collect utensils for making coffee. Heinrich Krafft opened his eyes and followed their movements; and the look he had for Schilsky was as warily watchful as a cat's.

Schilsky, an undeveloped Hercules—he was narrow in proportion to his height—and still naked to the waist, took some bottles from a long line of washes and perfumes that stood on the washstand, and, crossing to an elegant Venetian-glass mirror, hung beside the window, lathered his chin. It was a peculiarity of his only to be able to attend thoroughly to one thing at a time, and a string of witticisms uttered by Fürst passed unheeded. But Krafft's first words made him start.

Having watched him for some time, the latter said slowly: " I say, old fellow, are you sure it's all square about Lulu and this Dresden business? "

Razor in hand, Schilsky turned and looked at him. As he did so, he coloured, and answered with an over-anxious haste: "Of course I am. I made her go. She didn't want to."

" That's a well-known trick."

The young man scowled and thrust out his under-lip. " Do you think I'm not up to their tricks? Do you want to teach me how to manage a woman? I tell you I sent her away."

He tried to continue shaving, but was visibly uneasy. " Well, if you won't believe me," he said, with sudden anger, though neither of the others had spoken. " Now where the deuce is that letter? "

He rummaged among the music and papers on the table; in chaotic drawers; beneath dirty, fat-scaled dinner-dishes on the washstand; between door and stove, through a kind of rubbish-heap that had formed with time, of articles of dress, spoiled sheets of music-paper, soiled linen, empty bottles, and boots, countless boots, single and in pairs. When he had found what he looked for, he ran his eyes down the page, as if he were going to read it aloud. Then, however, he changed his mind; a boyish gratification overspread his face, and, tossing the letter to Krafft, he bade them read it for themselves. Fürst leaned over the end of the sofa. It was written in English, in a bold, scrawly hand, and ran, without date or heading:

My own dearest
Now only four days more—I count them morning and night.
I am good for nothing—my thoughts are always with you.
Yesterday at the Gallery I sat alone in the room where the
Madonna is, pretending enthusiasm—while the rest went to
Holbein—and read your letter over and over again. But it
made me a little unhappy too, for I soon found out that you
had written it at three different times. Is it really so hard
to write to Lulu?

Have you worked better for want of interruption?—my damned interruptions, as you called them last week when you were so angry with me. Shall you have a great deal to show me when I come home? No—don't say you will—or I shall hate Zarathustra more than I do already.

And now only till Friday. This time you will meet me— yes?—and not come to the station an hour late, as you said you did last time. If you are not there—I warn you—I shall throw myself under the train. I am writing to Grünhut. Get flowers —there is money in one of the vases on the writing-table. Oh, if you only will, we shall have such a happy evening—if only you will. And I shall never leave you again, never again.

Your own loving

L.

Fürst could not make out much of this; he was still spelling through the first paragraph when Krafft had finished. Schilsky, who had gone on dressing, kept a sharp eye on his friends— particularly on Krafft.

"Well?" he asked eagerly as the letter was laid down.

Krafft was silent, but Fürst kissed his finger-tips to a large, hanging photograph of the girl in question, and was facetious on the subject of dark, sallow women.

"And you, Heinz? What do you say?" demanded Schilsky with growing impatience.

Still Krafft did not reply, and Schilsky was mastered by a violent irritation.

"Why the devil can't you open your mouth? What's the matter with you? Have *you* anything like that to show—you Joseph, you?"

Krafft let a waxen hand drop over the side of the sofa and trail on the floor. "The letters were burned, dear boy—when you appeared." He closed his eyes and smiled, seeming to re-member something. But a moment later, he fixed Schilsky sharply, and asked: "You want my opinion, do you?"

"Of course I do," said Schilsky, and flung things about the room.

"Lulu," said Krafft with deliberation, "Lulu is getting you under her thumb."

The other sprang up, swore, and aimed a boot, which he had been vainly trying to put on the wrong foot, at a bottle that protruded from the rubbish-heap.

"Me? Me under her thumb?" he spluttered—his lips became more marked under excitement. " I should like to see her try it. You don't know me. You don't know Lulu. I am her master, I tell you. She can't call her soul her own."

"And yet," said Krafft, unmoved, " it's a fact all the same."

Schilsky applied a pair of curling tongs to his hair, at such a degree of heat that a lock frizzled, and came off in his hand. His anger redoubled. " Is it my fault that she aches like a wet-nurse? Is that what you call being under her thumb?" he cried.

Fürst tried to conciliate him and to make peace. " You're a lucky dog, old fellow, and you know you are. We all know it—in spite of occasional tantaras. But you would be still luckier if you took a friend's sound advice and got you to the registrar. Ten minutes before the registrar, and everything would be different. Then she might play up as she liked; you would be master in earnest."

" Registrar? " echoed Krafft with deep scorn. " Listen to the ape! Not if we can hinder it. When he's fool enough for that—I know him—it will be with something fresher and less faded, something with the bloom still on it."

Schilsky winced as though he had been struck. Her age— she was eight years older than he—was one of his sorest points.

" Oh, come on, now," said Fürst as he poured out the coffee. " That's hardly fair. She's not so young as she might be, it's true, but no one can hold a candle to her still. Lulu is Lulu."

" Ten minutes before the registrar," continued Krafft, meditatively shaking his head. " And for the rest of life, chains. And convention. And security, which stales. And custom, which satiates. Oh no, I am not for matrimony!"

Schilsky's ill-humour evaporated in a peal of boisterous laughter. " Yes, and tell us why, chaste Joseph, tell us why," he cried, throwing a brush at his friend. " Or go to the devil— where you're at home."

Krafft warded off the brush. " Look here," he said, " confess. Have you kissed another girl for months? Have you had a single billet-doux? "

But Schilsky only winked provokingly. Having finished laughing, he said with emphasis: " But after Lulu, they are all tame. Lulu is Lulu, and that's the beginning and end of the matter."

"Exactly my opinion," said Fürst. "And yet, boys, if I wanted to make your mouths water, I could." He closed one eye and smacked his lips. " I know of something—something young and blond . . . and dimpled . . . and round, round as a feather-pillow "—he made descriptive movements of the hand —"with a neck, boys, a neck, I say——" Here, in sheer ecstasy, he stuck fast, and could get no further.

Schilsky roared anew. "He knows ot something . . . so he does," he cried—Fürst's pronounced tastes were a standing joke among them. " Show her to us, old man, show her to us! Where are you hiding her? If she's under eighteen, she'll do—under eighteen, mind you, not a day over. Come along, I'm on for a spree. Up with you, Joseph!"

He was ready, come forth from the utter confusion around him, like a god from a cloud. He wore light grey clothes, a loosely knotted, bright blue tie, with floating ends and conspicuous white spots, and buttoned boots of brown kid. Hair and handkerchief were strongly scented.

Krafft, having been prevailed on to rise, made no further toilet than that of dipping his head in a basin of water, which stood on the tail of the grand piano. His hair emerged a mass of dripping ringlets, covetously eyed by his companions.

They walked along the streets, Schilsky between the others, whom he overtopped by head and shoulders: three young rebels out against the Philistines: three bursting charges of animal spirits.

There was to be a concert that evening at the Conservatorium, and, through vestibule and entrance-halls, which, for this reason, were unusually crowded, the young men made a kind of triumphal progress. Especially Schilsky. Not a girl, young or old, but peddled for a word or a look from him; and he was only too prodigal of insolently expressive glances, whispered greetings, and warm pressures of the hand. The open flattery and bold adoration of which he was the object mounted to his head; he felt secure in his freedom, and brimful of self-confidence; and, as the three of them walked back to the town, his exhilaration, a sheer excess of well-being, was no longer to be kept within decent bounds.

"Wait!" he cried suddenly, as they were passing the Gewandhaus. "Wait a minute! See me make that woman there take a fit."

He ran across the road to the opposite pavement, where the only person in sight, a stout, middle-aged woman, was dragging slowly along, her arms full of parcels; and, planting himself directly in front of her, so that she was forced to stop, he seized both her hands and worked them up and down.

"Now upon my soul, who would have thought of seeing you here, you baggage, you?" he cried vociferously.

The woman was speechless from amazement; her packages fell to the ground, and she gazed open-mouthed at the wild-haired lad before her, making, at the same time, vain attempts to free her hands.

"No, this really is luck," he went on, holding her fast. "Come, a kiss, my duck, just one! *Ein Küsschen in Ehren,* you know——" and, in very fact, he leaned forward and pecked at her cheek.

The blood dyed her face and she panted with rage.

"You young scoundrel!" she gasped. "You impertinent young dog! I'll give you in charge. I'll—I'll report you to the police. Let me go this instant—this very instant, do you hear?—or I'll scream for help."

The other two had come over to enjoy the fun. Schilsky turned to them with a comical air of dismay, and waved his arm. "Well I declare, if I haven't been and made a mistake!" he exclaimed, and slapped his forehead. "I'm out by I don't know how much—by twenty years, at least. No thank you, Madam, keep your kisses! You're much too old and ugly for me."

He flourished his big hat in her face, pirouetted on his heel, and the three of them went down the street, hallooing with laughter.

They had supper together at the *Bavaria,* Schilsky standing treat; for they had gone by way of the *Brüderstrasse,* where he called in to investigate the vase mentioned in the letter. Afterwards, they commenced an informal wandering from one haunt to another, now by themselves, now with stray acquaintances. Krafft, who was still enfeebled by the previous night, and who, under the best of circumstances, could not carry as much as his friends, was the first to give in. For a time, they got him about between them. Then Fürst grew obstreperous, and wanted to pour his beer on the floor as soon as it was set before him, so that they were put out of two places, in the second of which they left Krafft. But the better half of the night was over before Schilsky was comfortably drunk, and in a state to unbosom himself to a sympathetic waitress, about the hardship it was to be bound to some one older than yourself.

He shed tears of pity at his lot, and was extremely communicative. *" 'n Körper, scha-age Ihnen, 'n Körper!"* but old, old, a *" halb'sch Jahr'und'rt"* older than he was, and desperately jealous.

"It's too bad; such a nice young man as you are," said the *Mamsell,* who, herself not very sober, was sitting at ease on his knee, swinging her legs. "But you nice ones are always chicken-hearted. Treat her as she deserves, my duck, and make no bones about it. Just let her rip—and you stick to me!"

VI

ONE cold, windy afternoon, when dust was stirring and rain seemed imminent, Maurice Guest walked with bent head and his hat pulled over his eyes. He was returning from the *Zeitzerstrasse,* where, in a photographer's show-case, he had a few days earlier discovered a large photograph of Louise. This was a source of great pleasure to him. Here, no laws of breeding or delicacy hindered him from gazing at her as often as he chose.

On this particular day, whether he had looked too long, or whether the unrest of the weather, the sense of something impending, the dusty dryness that craved rain, had got into his blood and disquieted him: whatever it was, he felt restless and sick for news of her, and, at this very moment, was on his way to Madeleine, in the foolish hope of hearing her name.

But a little adventure befell him which made him forget his intention.

He was about to turn the corner of a street, when a sudden blast of wind swept round, bearing with it some half dozen single sheets of music. For a moment they whirled high, then sank fluttering to the ground, only to rise again and race one another along the road. Maurice instinctively gave chase, but it was not easy to catch them; no sooner had he secured one than the next was out of his reach.

Meanwhile their owner, a young and very pretty girl, looked on and laughed, without making any effort to help him; and the more he exerted himself, the more she laughed. In one hand she was carrying a violin-case, in the other a velvet muff, which now and again she raised to her lips, as if to conceal her mirth. It was a graceful movement, but an unnecessary one, for her laughter was of that charming kind, which never gives offence; and, besides that, although it was continuous, it was neither hearty enough nor frank enough to be unbecoming— the face was well under control. She stood there, with her head slightly on one side, and the parted lips showed both rows of small, even teeth; but the smile was unvarying, and, in spite of her merriment, her eyes did not for an instant quit the young man's face, as he darted to and fro.

Maurice could not help laughing himself, red and out of breath though he was.

"Now for the last one," he said in German.

At these words she seemed more amused than ever. "I don't speak German," she answered in English, with a strong American accent.

Having captured all the sheets, Maurice tried to arrange them for her.

"It's my Kayser," she explained with a quick, upward glance, adding the next minute with a fresh ripple of laughter: "He's all to pieces."

"You have too much to carry," said Maurice. "On such a windy day, too."

"That's what Joan said—Joan is my sister," she continued. "But I guess it's so cold this afternoon I had to bring a muff along. If my fingers are stiff I can't play, and then Herr Becker is angry." But she laughed again as she spoke, and it was plain that the master's wrath did not exactly incite fear. "Joan always comes along, but to-day she's sick."

"Will you let me help you?" asked Maurice, and a moment later he was walking at her side.

She handed over music and violin to him without a trace of hesitation; and, as they went along the *Promenade,* she talked to him with as little embarrassment as though they were old acquaintances. It was so kind of him to help her, she thought; she couldn't imagine how she would ever have got home without him, alone against the wind; and she was perfectly sure he must be American—no one but an American would be so nice. When Maurice denied this, she laughed very much indeed, and was not sure, this being the case, whether she could like him or not; as a rule, she didn't like English people; they were stiff and horrid, and were always wanting either to be introduced or to shake hands. Here she carried her muff up to her lips again, and her eyes shone mischievously at him over the dark velvet. Maurice had never known anyone so easily moved to laughter; whenever she spoke she laughed, and she laughed at everything he said.

Off the *Promenade,* where the trees were of a marvellous pale green, they turned into a street of high, spacious houses, the dark lines of which were here and there broken by an arched gateway, or the delicate tints of a spring garden. To a window in one of the largest houses, Maurice's little friend looked up, and smiled and nodded.

"There's my sister."

The young man looked, too, and saw a dark, thin-faced girl, who, when she found four eyes fixed on her, abruptly drew in her head, and as abruptly put it out again, leaning her two hands on the sill.

"She's wondering who it is," said Maurice's companion gleefully. Then, turning her face up, she made a speaking-trumpet of her hands, and cried: "It's all right, Joan.—Now I must run right up and tell her about it," she said to Maurice. "Perhaps she'll scold; Joan is very particular. Good-bye. Thank you ever so much for being so good to me—oh, won't you tell me your name?"

The very next morning brought him a small pink note, faintly scented. The pointed handwriting was still childish, but there was a coquettish flourish beneath the pretty signature: Ephie Cayhill. Besides a graceful word of thanks, she wrote: *We are at home every Sunday. Mamma would be very pleased.*

Maurice did not scruple to call the following week, and on doing so, found himself in the midst of one of those English-speaking coteries, which spring up in all large, continental towns. Foreigners were not excluded—Maurice discovered two or three of his German friends, awkwardly balancing their cups on their knees. In order, however, to gain access to the circle, it was necessary for them to have a smattering of English; they had also to be flint against any open or covert fun that might be made of them or their country; and above all, to be skilled in the art of looking amiable, while these visitors from other lands heatedly readjusted, to their own satisfaction, all that did not please them in the life and laws of this country that was temporarily their home.

Mrs. Cayhill was a handsome woman, who led a comfortable, vegetable existence, and found it a task to rise from the plump sofa-cushion. Her pleasant features were slack, and in those moments of life which called for a sudden decision, they wore the helpless bewilderment of a woman who has never been required to think for herself. Her grasp on practical matters was rendered the more lax, too, by her being an immoderate reader, who fed on novels from morning till night, and slept with a page turned down beside her bed. She was for ever lost in the joys or sorrows of some fictitious person, and, in consequence, remained for the most part completely ignorant of what was going on around her. When she did happen to become conscious of her surroundings, she was callous, or merely indifferent, to them; for, compared with romance, life was dull and diffuse; it lacked the wilful simplicity, the exaggerative omissions, and forcible perspectives, which make up art: in other words, life demanded that unceasing work of selection and rejection, which it is the story-teller's duty to perform for his readers. All novels were fish to Mrs. Cayhill's net; she lived in a world of intrigue and excitement, and, seated in her easy-chair by the sitting-room window, was generally as remote from her family as though she were in Timbuctoo.

There was a difference of ten years in age between her daughters, and it was the younger of the two whose education was being completed. Johanna, the elder, had been a disappointment to her mother. Left to her own devices at an impressionable age, the girl had developed bookish tastes at the cost of her appearance: influenced by a free-thinking tutor of her brothers', she had read Huxley and Haeckel, Goethe and Schopenhauer. Her wish had been for a university career, but she was not of a self-assertive nature, and when Mrs. Cayhill, who felt her world toppling about her ears at the mention of such a thing, said: " Not while I live! " she yielded, without a further word; and the fact that such an emphatic expression of opinion had been drawn from the mild-tempered mother, made it a matter of course that no other member of the family took Johanna's part. So she buried her ambitions, and kept her mother's house in an admirable, methodical way.

It was not the sacrifice it seemed, however, because Johanna adored her little sister, and would cheerfully have given up more than this for her sake. Ephie, who was at that time just emerging from childhood, was very pretty and precocious, and her mother had great hopes of her. She also tired early of her lesson-books, and, soon after she turned sixteen, declared her intention of leaving school. As at least a couple of years had still to elapse before she was old enough to be introduced in society, Mrs. Cayhill, taking the one decisive step of her life, determined that travel in Europe should put the final touches to Ephie's education: a little German and French; some finishing lessons on the violin; a run through Italy and Switzerland, and then to Paris, whence they would carry back with them a complete and costly outfit. So, valiantly, Mrs. Cayhill had her trunks packed, and, together with Johanna, who would as soon have thought of denying her age as of letting these two helpless beings go out into the world alone, they crossed the Atlantic.

For some three months now, they had been established in Leipzig. A circulating library, rich in English novels, had been discovered; Mrs. Cayhill was content; and it began to be plain to Johanna that the greater part of their two years' absence would be spent in this place. Ephie, too, had already had time to learn that, as far as music was concerned, her business was not so much with finishing as with beginning, and that the road to art, which she with all the rest must follow, was a steep one. She might have found it still more arduous, had Herr Becker, her master, not been a young man and very impressionable. And Ephie never looked more charming than when, with her rounded, dimpled arm raised in an exquisite curve, she leaned her cheek against the glossy brown wood of her violin.

She was pretty with that untouched, infantine prettiness, before which old and young go helplessly down. She was small and plump, with a full, white throat and neck, and soft, rounded hands and wrists, that were dimpled like a baby's. Her brown hair was drawn back from the low forehead, but, both here and at the back of her neck, it broke into innumerable little curls, which were much lighter in colour than the rest. Her skin, faintly tinged, was as smooth as the skin of a cherry; it had that exquisite freshness which is only to be found in a very young girl, and is lovelier than the bloom on ripe fruit. Her dark blue eyes were well opened, but the black lashes were so long and so peculiarly straight that the eyes themselves were usually hidden, and this made it all the more effective did she suddenly look up. Moulded like wax, the small, upturned nose seemed to draw the top lip after it; anyhow, the upper lip was too short to meet the lower, and consequently, they were always slightly apart, in a kind of questioning amaze. This mouth was the real beauty of the face: bright red, full, yet delicate, arched like a bow, with corners that went in and upwards, it belonged, by right of its absolute innocence, to the face of a little child; and the thought was monstrous that nature and the years would eventually combine to destroy so perfect a thing.

She also had a charming laugh, with a liquid note in it, that made one think of water bubbling on a dry summer day.

It was this laugh that held the room on Sunday after-

noon, and drew the handful of young men together, time after
time.

Mrs. Cayhill, who, on these occasions, was wont to lay aside
her book, was virtually a deeper echo of her little daughter,
and Johanna only counted in so far as she made and distributed
cups of tea at the end of the room. She did not look with
favour on the young men who gathered there, and her manner
to them was curt and unpleasing. Each of them in turn, as
he went up to her for his cup, cudgelled his brain for something to say; but it was no easy matter to converse with
Johanna. The ordinary small change and polite commonplace of conversation, she met with a silent contempt. In
musical chit-chat, she took no interest whatever, and pretended
to none, openly indeed "detested music," and was unable to distinguish Mendelssohn from Wagner, "except by the noise;"
while if a bolder man than the rest rashly ventured on the
literary ground that was her special demesne, she either smiled
at what he said, in a disagreeably sarcastic way, or flatly contradicted him. She was the thorn in the flesh of these young
men; and after having dutifully spent a few awkward moments at her side, they stole back, one by one, to the opposite
end of the room. Here Ephie, bewitchingly dressed in blue,
swung to and fro in a big American rocking-chair—going
backwards, it carried her feet right off the ground—and talked
charming nonsense, to the accompaniment of her own light
laugh, and her mother's deeper notes, which went on like an
organ-point, Mrs. Cayhill finding everything Ephie said,
matchlessly amusing.

As Dove and Maurice walked there together for the first
time—it now leaked out that Dove spent every Sunday afternoon in the *Lessingstrasse*—he spoke to Maurice of Johanna.
Not in a disparaging way; Dove had never been heard to
mention a woman's name otherwise than with respect. And,
in this case, he deliberately showed up Johanna's good quali-
ties, in the hope that Maurice might feel attracted by her,
and remain at her side; for Dove had fallen deeply in love with
Ephie, and had, as it was, more rivals than he cared for, in
the field.

"You should get on with her, I think, Guest," he said
slily. "You read these German writers she is so interested
in. But don't be discouraged by her manner. For though
she's one of the most unselfish women I ever met, her way of
speaking is sometimes abrupt. She reminds me, if it doesn't

sound unkind, of a faithful watch-dog, or something of the sort, which cannot express its devotion as it would like to."

When, after a lively greeting from Ephie, and a few pleasant words from Mrs. Cayhill, Maurice found himself standing beside Johanna, the truth of Dove's simile was obvious to him. This dark, unattractive girl had apparently no thought for anything but her tea-making; she moved the cups this way and that, filled the pot with water, blew out and lighted again the flame of the spirit-lamp, without paying the least heed to Maurice, making, indeed, such an ostentatious show of being occupied, that it would have needed a brave man to break in upon her duties with idle words. He remained standing, however, in a constrained silence, which lasted until she could not invent anything else to do, and was obliged to drink her own tea. Then he said abruptly, in a tone which he meant to be easy, but which was only jaunty: "And how do you like being in Germany, Miss Cayhill? Does it not seem very strange after America?"

Johanna lifted her shortsighted eyes to his face, and looked coolly and disconcertingly at him through her glasses, as if she had just become aware of his presence.

"Strange? Why should it?" she asked in an unfriendly tone.

"Why, what I mean is, everything must be so different here from what you are accustomed to—at least it is from what we are used to in England," he corrected himself. "The ways and manners, and the language, and all that sort of thing, you know."

"Excuse me, I do not know," she answered in the same tone as before. "If a person takes the trouble to prepare himself for residence in a foreign country, nothing need seem either strange or surprising. But English people, as is well known, expect to find a replica of England in every country they go to."

There was a pause, in which James, the pianist, who was a regular visitor, approached to have his cup refilled. All the circle knew, of course, that Johanna was "doing for a new man"; and it seemed to Maurice that James half closed one eye at him, and gave him a small, sympathetic nudge with his elbow.

So he held to his guns. When James had retired, he began anew, without preamble.

"My friend Dove tells me you are interested in German

literature?" he said with a slight upward inflection in his voice.

Johanna did not reply, but she shot a quick glance at him, and colouring perceptibly, began to fidget with the tea-things.

"I've done a little in that line myself," continued Maurice, as she made no move to answer him. "In a modest way, of course. Just lately I finished reading the *Jungfrau von Orleans.*"

"Is that so?" said Johanna with an emphasis which made him colour also.

"It is very fine, is it not?" he asked less surely, and as she again acted as though he had not spoken, he lost his presence of mind. "I suppose you know it? You're sure to."

This time Johanna turned scarlet, as if he had touched her on a sore spot, and answered at once, sharply and rudely. "And I suppose," she said, and her hands shook a little as they fussed about the tray, "that you have also read *Maria Stuart,* and *Tell,* and a page or two of Jean Paul. You have perhaps heard of Lessing and Goethe, and you consider Heine the one and only German poet."

Maurice did not understand what she meant, but she had spoken so loudly and forbiddingly that several eyes were turned on them, making it incumbent on him not to take offence. He emptied his cup, and put it down, and tried to give the matter an airy turn.

"And why not?" he asked pleasantly. "Is there anything wrong in thinking so? Schiller and Goethe *were* great poets, weren't they? And you will grant that Heine is the only German writer who has had anything approaching a style?"

Johanna's face grew stony. "I have no intention of granting anything," she said. "Like all English people—it flatters your national vanity, I presume—you think German literature began and ended with Heine.—A miserable Jew!"

"Yes, but I say, one can hardly make him responsible for being a Jew, can you? What has that got to do with it?" exclaimed Maurice, this being a point of view that had never presented itself to him. And as Johanna only murmured something that was inaudible, he added lamely: "Then you don't think much of Heine?"

But she declined to be drawn into a discussion, even into an expression of opinion, and the young man continued, with apology in his tone: "It may be bad taste on my part, of course. But one hears it said on every side. If you could tell me what I ought to read . . . or, perhaps, advise me a little?" he ended tentatively.

"I don't lend my books," said Johanna more rudely than she had yet spoken. And that was all Maurice could get from her. A minute or two later, she rose and went out of the room.

It became much less restrained as soon as the door had closed behind her. Ephie laughed more roguishly, and Mrs. Cayhill allowed herself to find what her little daughter said, droller than before. With an appearance of unconcern, Maurice strolled back to the group by the window. Dove was also talking of literature.

"That reminds me, how did you like the book I lent you on Wednesday, Mrs. Cayhill?" he asked, at the same instant springing forward to pick up Ephie's handkerchief, which had fallen to the ground.

"Oh, very much indeed, very interesting, very good of you," answered Mrs. Cayhill. "Ephie, darling, the sun is shining right on your face."

"What was it?" asked James, while Dove jumped up anew to lower the blind, and Ephie raised a bare, dimpled arm to shade her eyes.

Mrs. Cayhill could not recollect the title just at once—she had a "wretched memory for names"—and went over what she had been reading.

"Let me see, it was . . . no, that was yesterday: *Shadowed by Three,* a most delightful Book. On Friday, *Richard Elsmere,* and—oh, yes, I know, it was about a farm, an Australian farm."

"*The Story of an African Farm,*" put in Dove mildly, returning to his seat.

"Australian or African, it doesn't matter which," said Mrs. Cayhill. "Yes, a nice book, but a little coarse in parts, and very foolish at the end—the disguising, and the dying out of doors, and the looking-glass, and all that."

"I must say I think it a very powerful book," said Dove solemnly. "That part, you know, where the boy listens to the clock ticking in the night, and thinks to himself that with every tick, a soul goes home to God. A very striking idea!"

"Why, I think it must be a horrid book," cried Ephie. "All about dying. Fancy some one dying every minute. It couldn't possibly be true. For then the world would soon be empty."

"Always there are coming more into it," said Fürst, in his blunt, broken English.

A pause ensued. Dove flicked dust off his trouser-leg; and the American men present were suddenly fascinated by the bottoms of their cups. Ephie was the first to regain her composure.

"Now let us talk of something pleasant, something quite different—from dying." She turned and, over her shoulder, laughed mischievously at Maurice, who was sitting behind her. Then, leaning forward in her chair, with every eye upon her, she told how Maurice had saved her music from the wind, and, with an arch face, made him appear very ridiculous. By her prettily exaggerated description of a heated, perspiring young man, darting to and fro, and muttering to himself in German, her hearers, Maurice included, were highly diverted—and no one more than Mrs. Cayhill.

"You puss, you puss!" she cried, wiping her eyes and shaking a finger at the naughty girl.

The general amusement had hardly subsided when Fürst rose to his feet, and, drawing his heels together, made a flowery little speech, the gist of which was, that he would have esteemed himself a most fortunate man, had he been in Maurice's place. Ephie and her mother exchanged looks, and shook with ill-concealed mirth, so that Fürst, who had spoken seriously and in good faith, sat down red and uncomfortable; and Boehmer, who was dressed in what he believed to be American fashion, smiled in a superior manner, to show he was aware that Fürst was making himself ridiculous.

"Look here, Miss Ephie," said James; "the next time you have to go out alone, just send for me, and I'll take care of you."

"Or me," said Dove. "You have only to let me know."

"No, no, Mr. Dove!" cried Mrs. Cayhill. "You do far too much for her as it is. You'll spoil her altogether."

But at this, several of the young men exclaimed loudly: that would be impossible. And Ephie coloured becomingly, raised her lashes, and distributed winning smiles. When quiet had been restored, she assured them that they were all very kind, but she would never let anyone go with her but Joan— dear old Joan. They could not imagine how fond she was of Joan.

"She is worth more than all of you put together." And at the cries of: "Oh, oh!" she was thrown into a new fit of merriment, and went still further. "I would not give Joan's little finger for anyone in the world."

And meanwhile, as all her hearers—all, that is to say, except Dove, who sat moody, fingering his slight moustache, and gazing at Ephie with fondly reproachful eyes—as all of them, with Mrs. Cayhill at their head, made vehement protest against this sweeping assertion, Johanna sat alone in her bedroom, at the back of the house. It was a dull room, looking on a courtyard, but she was always glad to escape to it from the flippant chatter in the sitting-room. Drawing a little table to the window, she sat down and began to read. But, on this day, her thoughts wandered; and, ultimately, propping her chin on her hand, she fell into reverie, which began with something like "the fool and his Schiller!" and ended with her rising, and going to the well-stocked book-shelves that stood at the foot of the bed.

She took out a couple of volumes and looked through them, then returned them to their places on the shelf. No, she said to herself, why should she? What she had told the young man was true: she never lent her books; he would soil them, or, worse still, not appreciate them as he ought—she could not give anyone who visited there on Sunday, credit for a nice taste.

Unknown to herself, however, something worked in her, for, the very next time Maurice was there, she met him in the passage, as he was leaving, and impulsively thrust a paper parcel into his hand.

"There is a book, if you care to take it."

He did not express the surprise he felt, nor did he look at the title. But Ephie, who was accompanying him to the door, made a face of laughing stupefaction behind her sister's back, and went out on the landing with him, to whisper: "What *have* you been doing to Joan?"—at which remark, and at Maurice's blank face, she laughed so immoderately that she was forced to go down the stairs with him, for fear Joan should hear her; and, in the house-door, she stood, a white-clad little figure, and waved her hand to him until he turned the corner.

Having read the first volume of *Hammer und Amboss* deep into two nights, Maurice returned it and carried away the second. But it was only after he had finished *Problematische*

Naturen, and had expressed himself with due enthusiasm, that Johanna began to thaw a little. She did not discuss what he read with him; but, going on the assumption that a person who could relish her favourite author had some good in him, she gave the young man the following proof of her favour.

Between Ephie and him there had sprung up spontaneously a mutual liking, which it is hard to tell the cause of. For Ephie knew nothing of Maurice's tastes, interests and ambitions, and he did not dream of asking her to share them. Yet, with the safe instincts of a young girl, she chose him for a brother from among all her other acquaintances; called him " Morry "; scarcely ever coquetted with him; and let him freely into her secrets. It is easier to see why Maurice was attracted to her; for not only was Ephie pretty and charming; she was also adorably equable—she did not know what it was to be out of humour. And she was always glad to see him, always in the best possible spirits. When he was dull or tired, it acted like a tonic on him, to sit and let her merry chatter run over him. And soon, he found plenty of makeshifts to see her; amongst other things, he arranged to help her twice a week with harmony, which was, to her, an unexplorable abyss; and he ransacked the rooms and shelves of his acquaintances to find old Tauchnitz volumes to lend to Mrs. Cayhill.

The latter paid even less attention to the sudden friendship of her daughter with this young man than the ordinary American mother would have done; but Johanna's toleration of it was, for the most part, to be explained by the literary interests before mentioned. For Johanna was always in a tremble lest Ephie should become spoiled; and thoughtless Ephie could, at times, cause her a most subtle torture, by being prettily insincere, by assuming false coquettish airs, or by seeming to have private thoughts which she did not confide to her sister. This, and the knowledge that Ephie was now of an age when every day might be expected to widen the distance between them, sometimes made Johanna very gruff and short, even with Ephie herself. As her sister, she alone knew how much was good and true under the child's light exterior; she admired in Ephie all that she herself had not—her fair prettiness, her blithe manner, her easy, graceful words—and, had it been necessary, she would have gone down on her knees to remove the stones from Ephie's path.

Thus although on the casual observer, Johanna only made the impression of a dark, morose figure, which hovered round

6

two childlike beings, intercepting the sunshine of their lives, yet Maurice had soon come often enough into contact with her to appreciate her unselfishness; and, for the care she took of Ephie, he could almost have liked her, had Johanna shown the least readiness to be liked. Naturally, he did not understand how highly he was favoured by her; he knew neither the depth of her affection for Ephie, nor the exact degree of contempt in which she held the young men who dangled there on a Sunday—poor fools who were growing fat on emotion and silly ideas, when they should have been taking plain, hard fare at college. To Dove, Johanna had a particular aversion; chiefly, and in a contradictory spirit, because it was evident to all that his intentions were serious. But she could not hinder wayward Ephie from making a shameless use of him, and then laughing at him behind his back—a laugh in which Mrs. Cayhill was not always able to refrain from joining, though it must be said that she was usually loud in her praises of Dove, at the expense of all visitors who were not American.

"From these Dutch you can't expect much, one way or the other," she declared. "And young Guest sometimes sits there with a face as long as my arm. But Dove is really a most sensible young fellow—why, he thinks just as I do about America."

And as a special mark of favour, when Dove left the house on Sunday afternoon, his pockets bulged with *New York Heralds.*

VII

MEANWHILE, before the blinds in the *Brüderstrasse* were drawn up again, Maurice had found his way back to Madeleine. When they met, she smiled at him in a somewhat sarcastic manner, but no reference was made to the little falling-out they had had, and they began afresh to read and play together. On the first afternoon, Maurice was full of his new friends, and described them at length to her. But Madeleine damped his ardour.

"I know them, yes, of course," she said. "The usual Americans—even the blue-stocking, from whom heaven defend us. The little one is pretty enough as long as she keeps her mouth shut. But the moment she speaks, every illusion is shattered.—Why I don't go there on a Sunday? Good gracious, do you think they want me?—me, or any other petticoat? Are honours made to be divided?—No, Maurice, I don't like Americans. I was once offered a position in America, as 'professor of piano and voice-production' in a place called Schenectady; but I didn't hesitate. I said to myself, better one hundred a year in good old England, than five in a country where the population is so inflated with its importance that I should always be in danger of running amuck. And besides that, I should lose my accent, and forget how to say 'leg'; while the workings of the stomach would be discussed before me with an unpleasant freedom."

"You're too hard on them, Madeleine," said Maurice, smiling in spite of himself. But he was beginning to stand in awe of her sharp tongue and decided opinions; and, in the week that followed, he took himself resolutely together, and did not let a certain name cross his lips.

Consequently, he was more than surprised on returning to his room one day, to find a note from Madeleine, saying that she expected Louise that very afternoon at three.

It was not news to Maurice that Louise had come home. The evening before, as he turned out of the *Brüderstrasse,* a closed droschke turned into it. After the vehicle had lumbered past him and disappeared, the thought crossed his mind that she

might be inside it. He had not then had time to go back, but
early this very morning, he had passed the house and found the
windows open. So Madeleine had engaged her immediately!
As usual, Fürst had kept him waiting for his lesson; it was
nearly three o'clock already, and he was so hurried that he
could only change his collar; but, on the way there, in a sudden spurt of gratitude, he ran to a flower-shop, and bought a
large bunch of carnations.

He arrived at Madeleine's room in an elation he did not try
to hide; and over the carnations they had a mock reconciliation.
Madeleine wished to distribute the flowers in different vases
about the room, but he asked her to put them all together on the
centre table. She laughed and complied.

For several weeks now, musical circles had been in a stir
over the advent of a new piano-teacher named Schrievers—a
person who called himself a pupil of Liszt, held progressive
views, and, being a free lance, openly ridiculed the antiquated
methods of the Conservatorium. Madeleine was extremely
interested in the case, and, as they sat waiting, talked about
it to Maurice with great warmth, enlarging especially upon the
number of people who had the audacity to call themselves pupils
of Liszt. To Maurice, in his present frame of mind, the matter seemed of no possible consequence—for all he cared, the
whole population of the town might lay claim to having been
at Weimar—and he could not understand Madeleine finding
it important. For he was in one of those moods when the
entire consciousness is so intently directed towards some end,
that, outside this end, nothing has colour or vitality: all that
has previously impressed and interested one, has no more
solidity than papier mâché. Meanwhile she spoke on, and did
not appear to notice how time was flying. He was forced at
length to take out his watch, and exclaim, in feigned surprise,
at the hour.

"A quarter to four already!"

"Is it so late?" But on seeing his disturbance, she added:
"It will be all right. Louise was never punctual in her life."

He did his best to look unconcerned, and they spoke of that
evening's *Abendunterhaltung,* at which Fürst was to play. But
by the time the clock struck four, Maurice had relapsed, in
spite of himself, into silence. Madeleine rallied him.

"You must make shift with my company, Maurice. Not
but what I am sure Louise will come. But you see from this
what she is—the most unreliable creature in the world."

To pass the time, she suggested that he should help her to make tea, and they were both busy, when the electric bell in the passage whizzed harshly, and the next moment there came a knock at the door. But it was not Louise. Instead, two persons entered, one of whom was Heinrich Krafft, the other a short, thickset girl, in a man's felt hat and a closely buttoned ulster.

On recognising her visitors, Madeleine made a movement of annoyance, and drew her brows together. "You, Heinz!" she said.

Undaunted by this greeting, Krafft advanced to her and, taking her hands, kissed them, one after the other He was also about to kiss her on the lips, but she defended herself. "Stop! We are not alone."

"Just for that reason," said the girl in the ulster drily.

"What ill wind blows you here to-day?" Madeleine asked him.

As he was still wearing his hat, she took it off, and dropped it on the floor beside him; then she recollected Maurice, and made him known to the other two. Coming forward, Maurice recalled to Krafft's memory where they had already met, and what had passed between them. Before he had finished speaking, Krafft burst into an unmannerly peal of laughter. Madeleine laughed, too, and shook her finger at him. "You have been up to your tricks again!" Avery Hill, the girl in the ulster, did not laugh aloud, but a smile played round her mouth, which Maurice found even more disagreeable than the mirth of which he had been the innocent cause. He coloured, and withdrew to the window.

Krafft was so convulsed that he was obliged to sit down on the sofa, where Madeleine fanned him with a sheet of music. He had been seized by a kind of paroxysm, and laughed on and on, in a mirthless way, till Avery Hill said suddenly and angrily: "Stop laughing at once, Heinz! You will have hysterics."

In an instant he was sobered, and now he seemed to fall, without transition, into a mood of dejection. Taking out his penknife, he set to paring his nails, in a precise and preoccupied manner. Madeleine turned to Maurice.

"You'll wonder what all this is about," she said apologetically. "But Heinz is never happier than when he has succeeded in imposing on some one—as he evidently did on you."

"Indeed!" said Maurice. Their laughter had been offensive to him, and he found Krafft, and Madeleine with him, exceedingly foolish.

There was a brief silence. Krafft was absorbed in what he was doing, and Avery Hill, on sitting down, had lighted a cigarette, which she smoked steadily, in long-drawn whiffs. She was a pretty girl, in spite of her severe garb, in spite, too, of her expression, which was too composed and too self-sure to be altogether pleasing. Her face was fresh of skin, below smooth fair hair, and her lips were the red, ripe lips of Botticelli's angels and Madonnas. But the under one, being fuller than the other, gave the mouth a look of over-decision, and it would be difficult to imagine anything less girlish than were the cold grey eyes.

"We came for the book you promised to lend Heinz," she said, blowing off the spike of ash that had accumulated at the tip of the cigarette. "He could not rest till he had it."

Madeleine placed a saucer on the table with the request to use it as an ash-tray, and taking down a volume of De Quincey from the hanging shelf, held it out to Krafft.

"There you are. It will interest me to hear what you make of it."

Krafft ceased his paring to glance at the title-page. "I shall probably not open it," he said.

Madeleine laughed, and gave him a light blow on the hand with the book. "How like you that is! As soon as you know that you can get a thing, you don't want it any longer."

"Yes, that's Heinz all over," said Avery Hill. "Only what he hasn't got, seems worth having."

Krafft shut his knife with a click, and put it back in his pocket. "And that's what you women can't understand, isn't it?—that the best of things is the wishing for them. Once there, and they are nothing—only another delusion. The happiest man is the man whose wishes are never fulfilled. He always has a moon to cry for."

"Come, come now," said Madeleine. "We know your love for paradox. But not to-day. There's no time for philosophising to-day. Besides, you are in a pessimistic mood, and that's a bad sign."

"I and pessimism? Listen, heart of my heart, I have a new story for you." He moved closer to her, and put his arm round her neck. "There was once a man and his wife——"

But, at the first word, Madeleine put her hands to her ears.

"Mercy, have mercy, Heinz! No stories, I entreat you.
And behave yourself, too. Take your arm away." She tried
to remove it. "I have told you already, I can't have you here
to-day. I'm expecting a visitor."

He laid his head on her shoulder. "Let him come. Let
the whole world come. I don't budge. I am happy here."

"You must go and be happy elsewhere," said Madeleine
more decisively than she had yet spoken. "And before she
comes, too."

"She? What she?"

"Never mind."

"For that very reason, Mada."

She whispered a word in his ear. He looked at her, incredulously at first, then whimsically, with a sham dismay; and
then, as if Maurice had only just taken shape for him, he turned
and looked at him also, and from him to Madeleine, and back
to him, finally bursting afresh into a roar of laughter. Madeleine laid her hand over his mouth. "Take him away, do,"
she said to Avery Hill—" as a favour to me."

"Yes, when I have finished my cigarette," said the girl
without stirring.

Unsettled all the same, it would seem, by what he had heard,
Krafft rose and shuffled about the room, with his hands in his
pockets. Approaching Maurice, he even stood for a moment
and contemplated him, with a kind of mock gravity. Maurice
acted as if he did not see Krafft; long since, he had taken up a
magazine, and, half hidden in a chair between window and
writing-table, pretended to bury himself in its contents. But
he heard very plainly all that passed, and, at the effect produced on Krafft by the name of the expected visitor, his
hands trembled with anger. If the fellow had stood looking
at him for another second, he would have got up and knocked
him down. But Krafft turned nonchalantly to the piano,
where his attention was caught by a song that was standing on
the rack. He chuckled, and set about making merciless fun
of the music—the composer was an elderly singing-teacher, of
local fame. Madeleine grew angry, and tried to take it from
him.

"Hold your tongue, Heinz! If your own songs were more
like this, they would have a better chance of success. Now be
quiet! I won't hear another word. Herr Wendling is a very
good friend of mine."

"A friend! Heavens! She says friend as if it were an excuse

for him.—Mada, let your friend cease making music if he hopes for salvation. Let him buy a broom and sweep the streets—let him——"

"You are disgusting!"

She had got the music from him, but he was already at the piano, parodying, from memory, the conventional accompaniment and sentimental words of the song. "And this," he said, "from the learned ass who is not yet convinced that the *Feuerzauber* is music, and who groans like a dredge when the last act of *Siegfried* is mentioned. Wendling and Wagner! Listen to this!—for once, I am a full-blooded Wagnerite."

He felt after the chords that prelude Brünnhilde's awakening by Siegfried. Until now, Avery Hill had sat indifferent, as though what went on had nothing to do with her; but no sooner had Krafft commenced to play than she grew uneasy; her eyes lost their cold assurance, and, suddenly getting up and going round to the front of the piano, she pushed the young man's hands from the keys. Krafft yielded his place to her, and, taking up the chords where he had left them, she went on. She played very well—even Maurice in his disturbance could not but notice it—with a firm, masculine touch, and that inborn ease, that enviable appearance of perfect fitness, of being one with the instrument, which even the greatest players do not always attain. She had, besides, grip and rhythm, and her long, close-knit hands insinuated themselves artfully among the complicated harmonies.

When she began to play, Madeleine made "Tch, tch, tch!" and shook her head, in despair of now ever being rid of them. Krafft remained standing behind the piano at the window, leaning his forehead on the glass. Maurice, who watched them both surreptitiously, saw his face change, and grow thoughtful as he stood there; but when Avery Hill ceased abruptly, on a discord, he wheeled round at once and patted her on the back. While looking over to Maurice, he said: "No doubt you found that very pretty and affecting?"

"I think that's none of your business," said Maurice.

But Krafft did not take umbrage. "You don't say so?" he murmured with a show of surprise.

"Now, go, go, go!" cried Madeleine. "What have I done, to be subjected to such a visitation? No, Heinz, you don't sit down again. Here's your hat. Away with you!—or I'll have you put out by force."

And at last they really did go, to a cool bow from Maurice,

who still sat holding his magazine. But Madeleine had hardly closed the door behind them, when, like a whirlwind, Krafft burst into the room again.

"Mada, I forgot to ask you something," he said in a stage-whisper, drawing her aside. "Tell me—you *Kupplerin,* you!—does he know her?" He pointed over his shoulder with his thumb at Maurice.

Madeleine shook her head, in real vexation and distress, and laid a finger on her lip. But it was of no use. Stepping over to Maurice, Krafft bowed low, and held his hat against his breast.

"It is impossible for you to understand how deeply it has interested me to meet you," he said. "Allow me, from the bottom of my heart, to wish you success." Whereupon, before Maurice could say "damn!" he was gone again, leaving his elfin laugh behind him in the air, like smoke.

Madeleine shut the door energetically and gave a sigh of relief.

"Thank goodness! I thought they would never go. And now, the chances are, they'll run into Louise on the stairs. You'll wonder why I was so bent on getting rid of them. It's a long story. I'll tell it to you some other time. But if Louise had found them here when she came, she would not have stayed. She won't have anything to do with Heinz."

"I don't wonder at it," said Maurice. He stood up and threw the magazine on the table.

Madeleine displayed more astonishment than she felt. "Why what's the matter? You're surely not going to take what Heinz said, seriously? He was in a bad mood to-day, I know, and I noticed you were very short with him. But you mustn't be foolish enough to be offended by him. No one ever is. He is allowed to say and do just what he likes. He's our spoilt child."

Maurice laughed. "The fellow is either a cad, or an unutterable fool. You, Madeleine, may find his impertinence amusing. I tell you candidly, I don't!" and he went on to make it clear to her that the fault would not be his, were Krafft and he ever in the same room together again. "The kind of man one wants to kick downstairs. What the deuce did he mean by guffawing like that when you told him who was coming?"

"You mean about Louise?" Madeleine gave a slight shrug. "Yes, Maurice—unfortunately that was not to be avoided.

But sit down again, and let me explain things to you. When you hear——"

But he did not want explanations; he did not even want an answer to the question he had put; his chief concern now was to get away. To stay there, in that room, for another quarter of an hour, would be impossible, on such tenterhooks was he. To stay—for what? Only to listen to more slanderous hints, of the kind he had heard before. As it was, he did not believe he could face her frankly, should she still come. He felt as if, in some occult way, he had assisted at a tampering with her good name.

"You will surely not be so childish?" said Madeleine, on seeing him take up his hat.

"Childish?—you call it childish?" he exclaimed, growing angry with her, too. "Do you know what time it is? Three o'clock, you write me, and it's now a quarter past five. I have sat here doing nothing for over two mortal hours. It seems to me that's enough, without being made the butt of your friends' wit into the bargain. I'm sick of the whole thing. Good-bye."

"We seem bound to quarrel," said Madeleine calmly. "And always about Louise. But there's no use in being angry. I am not responsible for what Heinz says and does. And on the mere chance of his coming in to-day, to sit down and unroll another savoury story to you, about your idol—would you have thanked me for it? Remember the time I did try to open your eyes!—It's not fair either to blame me because Louise hasn't come. I did my best for you. I can't help it if she's as unstable as water."

"I think you dislike her too much to want to help it," said Maurice grimly. He stood staring at the carnations, and his resentment gave way to depression, as he recalled the mood in which he had bought them.

"Come back as soon as you feel better. I'm not offended, remember!" Madeleine called after him as he went down the stairs. When she was alone, she said "Silly boy!" and, still smiling, made excuses for him: he had come with such pleasurable anticipations, and everything had gone wrong. Heinz had behaved disagreeably, as only he could. While as for Louise, one was no more able to rely on her than on a wisp of straw; and she, Madeleine, was little better than a fool not to have known it.

She moved about the room, putting chairs and papers in

their places, for she could not endure disorder of any kind. Then she sat down to write a letter; and when, some half hour later, the girl for whom they had waited, actually came, she met her with exclamations of genuine surprise.

"Is it really you? I had given you up long ago. Pray, do you know what time it is?"

She took out her watch and dangled it before the other's eyes. But Louise Dufrayer hardly glanced at it. As, however, Madeleine persisted, she said: "I'm late, I know. But it was not my fault. I couldn't get away."

She unpinned her hat, and shook back her hair; and Madeleine helped her to take off her jacket, talking all the time. "I have been much annoyed with you. Does it never occur to you that you may put other people in awkward positions, by not keeping your word? But you are just the same as of old—incorrigible."

"Then why try to improve me?" said the other with a show of lightness. But almost simultaneously she turned away from Madeleine's matter-of-fact tone, passed her handkerchief over her lips, and after making a vain attempt to control herself, burst into tears.

Madeleine eyed her shrewdly. "What's the matter with you?"

But the girl who had sunk into a corner of the sofa merely shook her head, and sobbed; and Madeleine, to whom such emotional outbreaks were distasteful, went to the writing-table and busied herself there, with her back to the room. She did not ask for an explanation, nor did her companion offer any.

Louise abandoned herself to her tears with as little restraint as though she were alone, holding her handkerchief to her eyes with both hands, and giving deep, spasmodic sobs, which had apparently been held for some time in check.

Afterwards, she sat with her elbow on the end of the sofa, her face on her hand, and, still shaken at intervals by a convulsive breath, watched Madeleine make fresh tea. But when she took the cup that was handed to her, she was so far herself again as to inquire whom she was to have met, although her voice still did not obey her properly.

"Some one who is anxious to know you," replied Madeleine with an air of mystery. "But he couldn't, or rather would not, wait so long."

Louise showed no further curiosity. But when Madeleine said

with meaning emphasis that Krafft had also been there in the course of the afternoon, she shrank perceptibly and flushed.

" What! Does he still exist? " she asked with an effort at playfulness.

" As you very well know," answered Madeleine drily. " Tell me, Louise, how do you manage to keep out of his way? "

Louise made no rejoinder; she raised her cup to her lips, and the dark blood that had stained her face, in a manner distressing to see, slowly retreated. She continued to look down, and, the light of her big, dark eyes gone out, her face seemed wan and dead. Madeleine, studying her, asked herself, not for the first time, but, as always, with an unclear irritation, what the secret of the other's charm was. Beautiful she had never thought Louise; she was not even pretty, in an honest way—at best, a strange, foreign-looking creature, dark-skinned, black of eyes and hair, with flashing teeth, and a wonderfully mobile mouth—and some people, hopeless devotees of a pink and white fairness, had been known to call her plain. At this moment, she was looking her worst; the heavy, blue-black lines beneath her eyes were deepened by crying; her rough hair had been hastily coiled, unbrushed; and she was wearing a shabby red blouse that was pinned across in front, where a button was missing. There was nothing young or fresh about her; she looked her twenty-eight years, every day of them—and more.

And yet, Madeleine knew that those who admired Louise would find her as desirable at this moment as at any other. Hers was a nameless charm; it was present in each gesture of the slim hands, in each turn of the head, in every movement of the broad, slender body. Strangers felt it instantly; her very walk seemed provocative of notice; there was something in the way her skirts clung, and moved with her, that was different from the motion of other women's. And those whose type she embodied went crazy about her. Madeleine remembered as though it were yesterday, the afternoon on which Heinz had burst in to rave to her of his discovery; and how he would have dragged her out hatless to see this miracle. She remembered, too, after-days, when she had had him there, pacing the floor, and pouring out his feelings to her, infatuated, mad. And he was not the only one; they bowled over like ninepins; and it would be the same for years to come—was there any reason to wonder at Maurice Guest?

Meanwhile, as Madeleine sat thinking these and similar

things, Maurice was tramping through the *Rosental*. The May afternoon, of lucent sunshine and heaped, fleecy clouds, had tempted a host of people into the great park, but he soon left them all behind him, for he walked as though he were pursued. These people, placid, and content of face, and the brightness of the day, jarred on him; he was out of patience with himself, with Madeleine, with the world at large. Especially with Madeleine; he bore her a grudge for her hints and innuendoes, for being behind the scenes, as it were, and also for being so ready to enlighten him; but, most of all, for a certain malicious gratification, which was to be felt in every word she said about Louise.

He went steadily on, against the level bars of the afternoon sun; and, by the time he had tired himself bodily, he had worked off his inward vexation as well. As he walked back towards the town, he was almost ready to smile at his previous heat. What did all these others matter to him? They could not hinder him from carrying through what he had set his mind on. To-morrow was a day, and the next was another, and the next again; and life, considered thus in days and opportunities, was infinitely long.

He now felt not only an aversion to dwelling on his thoughts of an hour back, but also the need of forgetting them altogether. And, in nearing the *Lessingstrasse,* he followed an impulse to go to Ephie, and to let her merry laugh wipe out the last traces of his ill-humour.

Mrs. Cayhill and Johanna were both reading in the sitting-room, and though Johanna agreeably laid aside her book, conversation languished. Ephie was sent for, but did not come, and Maurice was beginning to wish he had thought twice before calling, when her voice was heard in the passage, and, a moment later, she burst into the room, with her arms full of lilac, branches of lilac, which she explained had been bought early that morning at the flower-market, by one of their fellow-boarders. She hardly greeted Maurice, but going over to him, held up her scented burden, and was not content till he had buried his face in it.

"Isn't it just sweet?" she cried, holding it high for all to see. "And the very first that is to be had. Again, Maurice, again, put your face right down into the middle of it—like that."

Mrs. Cayhill laughed, as Maurice obediently bowed his head, but Johanna reproved her sister.

"Don't be silly, Ephie. You behave as if you had never seen lilac before."

"Well, neither I have—not such lilac as this, and Maurice hasn't either," answered Ephie. "You shall smell it too, old Joan!"—and in spite of Johanna's protests, she forced her sister also to sink her face in the fragrant white and purple blossoms. But then she left them lying on the table, and it was Johanna who put them in water.

Mrs. Cayhill withdrew to her bedroom to be undisturbed, and Johanna went out on an errand. Maurice and Ephie sat side by side on the sofa, and he helped her to distinguish chords of the seventh, and watched her make, in her music-book, the big, tailless notes, at which she herself was always hugely tickled, they reminded her so of eggs. But on this particular evening, she was not in a studious mood, and book, pencil and india-rubber slid to the floor. Both windows were wide open; the air that entered was full of pleasant scents, while that of the room was heavy with lilac. Ephie had taken a spray from one of the vases, and was playing with it; and when Maurice chid her for thoughtlessly destroying it, she stuck the pieces in her hair. Not content with this, she also put bits behind Maurice's ears, and tried to twist one in the piece of hair that fell on his forehead. Having thus bedizened them, she leaned back, and, with her hands clasped behind her head, began to tease the young man. A little bird, it seemed, had whispered her any number of interesting things about Madeleine and Maurice, and she had stored them all up. Now, she repeated them, with a charming impertinence, and was so provoking that, in laughing exasperation, Maurice took her fluffy, flower-bedecked head between his hands, and stopped her lips with two sound kisses.

He acted impulsively, without reflecting, but, as soon as it was done, he felt a curious sense of satisfaction, which had nothing to do with Ephie, and was like a kind of unconscious revenge taken on some one else. He was not, however, prepared for the effect of his hasty deed. Ephie turned scarlet, and jumping up from the sofa, so that all the blossoms fell from her hair at once, stamped her foot.

"Maurice Guest! How dare you!" she cried angrily, and, to his surprise, the young man saw that she had tears in her eyes.

He had never known Ephie to be even annoyed, and was consequently dumbfounded; he could not believe, after the direct provocation she had given him, that his crime had been so great.

"But Ephie dear!" he protested. "I had no idea, upon my word I hadn't, that you would take it like this. What's the matter? It was nothing. Don't cry. I'm a brute."

"Yes, you are, a horrid brute! I shall never forgive you—never!" said Ephie, and then she began to cry in earnest.

He put his arm round her, and coaxing her to sit down, wiped away her tears with his own handkerchief. In vain did he beg her to tell him why she was so vexed. To all he said, she only shook her head, and answered: "You had no right to do it."

He vowed solemnly that it should never happen again, but at least a quarter of an hour elapsed before he succeeded in comforting her, and even then, she remained more subdued than usual. But when Maurice had gone, and she had dropped the scattered sprays of lilac out of the window on his head, she clasped her hands at the back of her neck, and dropped a curtsy to herself in the looking-glass.

"Him, too!" she said aloud.

She nodded at her reflected self, but her face was grave; for between these two, small, blue-robed figures was a deep and unsuspected secret.

And Maurice, as he walked away, wondered to himself for still a little why she should have been so disproportionately angry; but not for long; for, when he was not actually with Ephie, he was not given to thinking much about her. Besides, from there, he went straight to the latter half of an *Abendunterhaltung,* to hear Fürst play Brahms' *Variations on a Theme by Händel.*

VIII

THAT night he had a vivid dream. He dreamt that he was
in a garden, where nothing but lilac grew—grew with a
luxuriance he could not have believed possible, and on fantastic
bushes: there were bushes like steeples and bushes smaller than
himself, big and little, broad and slender, but all were of lilac,
and in flower—an extravagant profusion of white and purple
blossoms. He gazed round him in delight, and took an eager
step forward; but, before he could reach the nearest bush, he
saw that it had been an illusion: the bush was stripped and
bare, and the rest were bare as well. "You're too late. It
has all been gathered," he heard a voice say, and at this moment, he saw Ephie at the end of a long alley of bushes, coming towards him, her arms full of lilac. She smiled and nodded
to him over it, and he heard her laugh, but when she was
half-way down the path, he discovered his mistake: it was not
Ephie but Louise. She came slowly forward, her laden arms
outstretched, and he would have given his life to be able to
advance and to take what she offered him; but he could not
stir, could not lift hand or foot, and his tongue clove to
the roof of his mouth. Her steps grew more hesitating, she
seemed hardly to move; and then, just as she reached the spot
where he stood, he found that it was not she after all, but
Madeleine, who laughed at his disappointment and said: "I'm
not offended, remember!"—The revulsion of feeling was
too great; he turned away, without taking the flowers she
held out to him—and awoke.

This dream was present to him all the morning, like a
melody that haunts and recalls. But he worked more laboriously than usual; for he was aggrieved with himself for having
idled away the previous afternoon, and then, too, Fürst's playing
had made a profound impression on him. In vigorous imitation, he sat down to the piano again, after a hasty dinner
snatched in the neighbourhood; but as he was only playing
scales, he propped open before him a little volume of Goethe's
poems, which Johanna had lent him, and suiting his scales to
the metre of the lines, read through one after another of the
poems he liked best. At a particular favourite, he stopped playing and held the book in both hands.

He had hardly begun anew when the door of his room was

unceremoniously opened, and Dove entered, in the jocose way
he adopted when in a rosy mood. Maurice made a movement
to conceal his book, merely in order to avoid the explanation
he knew must follow; but it was too late; Dove had espied it.
He did not belie himself on this occasion; he was extremely
astonished to find Maurice " still at it," but much more so to
see a book open before him; and he vented his surprise loudly
and wordily.

" Liszt used to read the newspaper," said Maurice, for the
sake of saying something. He had swung round in the piano-
chair, and he yawned as he spoke, without attempting to dis-
guise it.

" Why, yes, of course, why not? " agreed Dove cordially,
afraid lest he had seemed discouraging. " Why not, indeed?
For those who can do it. I wish I could. But will you believe
me, Guest "—here he seated himself, and settled into an attitude for talking, one hand inserted between his crossed knees—
" will you believe me, when I say I find it a difficult business
to read at all?—at any time. I find it too stimulating, too
anregend, don't you know? I assure you, for weeks now, I
have been trying to read *Past and Present,* and have not yet
got beyond the first page. It gives one so much to think about,
opens up so many new ideas, that I stop myself and say: ' Old
fellow, that must be digested.' This, I see, is poetry "—he ran
quickly and disparagingly through Maurice's little volume, and
laid it down again. " I don't care much for poetry myself,
or for novels either. There's so much in life worth knowing
that is true, or of some use to one; and besides, as we all
know, fact is stranger than fiction."

They spoke also of Fürst's performance the evening before,
and Dove gave it its due, although he could not conceal his
opinion that Fürst's star would ultimately pale before that of
a new-comer to the town, a late addition to the list of Schwarz's
pupils, whom he, Dove, had been " putting up to things a
bit." This was a " Manchester man " and former pupil of
Hallé's, and it would certainly not be long before he set the
place in a stir. Dove had just come from his lodgings, where
he had been permitted to sit and hear him practise finger-
exercises.

" A touch like velvet," declared Dove. " And a stretch!—I
have never seen anything like it. He spans a tenth, nay, an
eleventh, more easily than we do an octave."

The object of Dove's visit was, it transpired, to propose that

7

Maurice should accompany him that evening to the theatre, where *Die Walküre* was to be performed; and as, on this day, Dove had reasons for seeing the world through rose-coloured glasses, he suggested, out of the fulness of his heart, that they should also invite Madeleine to join them. Maurice was nothing loath to have the meeting with her over, and so, though it was not quite three o'clock, they went together to the *Mozart-strasse.*

They found Madeleine before her writing-table, which was strewn with closely written sheets. This was mail-day for America, she explained, and begged the young men to excuse her finishing an important letter to an American journalist, with whom she had once "chummed up" on a trip to Italy.

"One never knows when these people may be of use to one," she was accustomed to say.

Having addressed and stamped the envelope, and tossed it to the others, she rose and gave a hand to each. At Maurice, she smiled in a significant way.

"You should have stayed, my son. Some one came, after all."

Maurice laid an imploring finger on his lips, but Dove had seized the opportunity of glancing at his cravat in the mirror, and did not seem to hear.

She agreed willingly to their plan of going to the theatre; she had thought of it herself; then, a girl she knew had asked her to come to hear her play in *Ensemblespiel.*

"However, I will let that slip. Schelper and Moran-Olden are to sing; it will be a fine performance. I suppose some one is to be there," she said laughingly to Dove, "or you would not be of the party."

But Dove only smiled and looked sly.

Without delay, Madeleine began to detail to Maurice, the leading motives on which the *Walküre* was built up; and Dove, having hummed, strummed and whistled all those he knew by heart, settled down to a discourse on the legitimacy and development of the motive, and especially in how far it was to be considered a purely intellectual implement. He spoke with the utmost good-nature, and was so unconscious of being a bore that it was impossible to take him amiss. Madeleine, however, could not resist, from time to time, throwing in a "Really!" "How extraordinary!" "You don't say so!" among his abstruse remarks. But her sarcasm was lost on Dove; and even if he had noticed it, he would only have smiled, unhit, being too sensible and good-humoured easily to take offence.

It was always a mystery to his friends where Dove got his information; he was never seen to read, and there was little theorising about art, little but the practical knowledge of it, in the circles to which he belonged. But just as he went about picking up small items of gossip, so he also gathered in stray scraps of thought and information, and being by nature endowed with an excellent memory, he let nothing that he had once heard escape him. He had, besides, the talker's gift of neatly stringing together these tags he had pulled off other people, of connecting them, and giving them a varnish of originality.

"By no means a fool," Madeleine was in the habit of saying of him. "He would be easier to deal with if he were."

Here, on the leading motive as handled by Wagner and Wagner's forerunners, he had an unwritten treatise ripe in his brain. But he had only just compared the individual motives to the lettered ribbons that issue from the mouths of the figures in medieval pictures, and began to hint at the *idée fixe* of Berlioz, when he was interrupted by a knock at the door.

"*Herein!*" cried Madeleine in her clear voice; and at the sight of the person who opened the door, Maurice involuntarily started up from his chair, and taking his stand behind it, held the back of it firmly with both hands, in self-defence.

It was Louise.

On seeing the two young men, she hesitated, and, with the door-handle still in her hand, smiled a faint questioning smile at Madeleine, raising her eyebrows and showing a thin line of white between her lips.

"May I come in?" she asked, with her head a little on one side.

"Why, of course you know you may," said Madeleine with some asperity.

And so Louise entered, and came forward to the table at which they had been sitting; but before anything further could be said, she raised her arms to catch up a piece of hair which had fallen loose on her neck. The young men were standing, waiting to greet her, Maurice still behind his chair; but she did not hurry on their account, or "just on their account did not hurry," as Madeleine mentally remarked.

Both watched Louise, and followed her movements. To their eyes, she appeared to be very simply dressed; it was only Madeleine who appreciated the cost and care of this seeming simplicity. She wore a plain, close-fitting black dress, of a smooth, shiny stuff, which obeyed and emphasised the lines and outlines of her body; and, as she stood, with her arms upraised, composedly aware of being observed, they could see the line of her side rising and falling with the rise and fall of each breath. Otherwise, she wore a large black hat, with feathers and an overhanging brim, which threw shadows on her face, and made her eyes seem darker than ever.

Letting her arms drop with a sigh of relief, she shook hands with Dove, and Dove—to Madeleine's diversion and Maurice's intense disgust—introduced Maurice to her as his friend. She looked full at the latter, and held out her hand; but before he could take it, she withdrew it again, and put both it and her left hand behind her back.

"No, no," she said. "I mustn't shake hands with you to-day. To-day is Friday. And to give one's hand for the first time on a Friday would bring bad luck—to you, if not to me."

She was serious, but both the others laughed, and Maurice, having let his outstretched hand fall, coloured, and smiled rather foolishly. She did not seem to notice his discomfiture; turning to Madeleine, she began to speak of a piece of music she wished to borrow; and then Maurice had a chance of observing her at his ease, and of listening to her voice, in which he heard all manner of impossible things. But while Madeleine, with Dove's assistance, was looking through a pile of music, Louise came suddenly up to him and said: "You are not offended with me, are you?" She had a low voice, with a childish cadence in it, which touched him like a caress.

"Offended? I with you?" He meant to laugh, but his voice shook.

She stared at him, openly astonished, not only at his words, but also at the tone in which they were said; and the strange, fervent gaze bent on her by this man whom she saw for the first time in her life, confused her and made her uneasy. Slowly and coldly she turned away, but Madeleine, who was charitably occupying Dove as long as she could, did not take any notice of her. And as the young man continued to stare at her, she looked out of the window at the lowering grey sky, and said, with a shudder: "What a day for June!"

All eyes followed hers, Maurice's with the rest; but almost instantly he brought them back again to her face.

"Louise is a true Southerner," said Madeleine; "and is wretched if there's a cloud in the sky."

Louise smiled, and he saw her strong white teeth. "It's not quite as bad as that," she said; and then, although herself not clear why she should have answered these searching eyes, she added, looking at Maurice: "I come from Australia."

If she had said she was a visitant from another world, Maurice would not, at the moment, have felt much surprise; but on hearing the name of this distant land, on which he would probably never set foot, a sense of desolation overcame him. He realised anew, with a pang, what an utter stranger he was to her; of her past life, her home, her country, he knew and could know nothing.

"That is very far away," he said, speaking out of this feeling, and then was vexed with himself for having done so. His words sounded· foolish as they lingered on in the stillness that followed them, and would, he believed, lay him open to Madeleine's ridicule. But he had not much time in which to repent of them; the music had been found, and she was going again. He heard her refuse an invitation to stay: she had an engagement at half-past four. And now Dove, who, throughout, had kept in the background, looked at his watch and took up his hat: he had previously offered, unopposed, to do the long wait outside the theatre, which was necessary when one had no tickets, and now it was time to go. But when Louise heard the word theatre, she laid a slim, ungloved hand on Dove's arm.

"The very thing for such a night!"

They all said *"Auf Wiedersehen!"* to one another; she did not offer to shake hands again, and Maurice nursed a faint hope that it was on his account. He opened the window, leant out, and watched them, until they went round the corner of the street.

Madeleine smiled shrewdly behind his back, but when he turned, she was grave. She did not make any reference to what had passed, nor did she, as he feared she would, put questions to him: instead, she showed him a song of Krafft's, and asked him to play the accompaniment for her. He gratefully consented, without knowing what he was undertaking. For the song, a setting of a poem by Lenau, was nominally in C sharp minor; but it was black with accidentals, and passed through many keys before it came to a close in D flat major. Besides this, the right hand had much hard passage-

work in quaint scales and broken octaves, to a syncopated bass
of chords that were adapted to the stretch of no ordinary hand.

"*Lieblos und ohne Gott auf einer Haide,*" sang Madeleine
on the high f sharp; but Maurice, having collected neither
his wits nor his fingers began blunderingly, could not right
himself, and after scrambling through a few bars, came to a
dead stop, and let his hands fall from the keys.

"Not to-day, Madeleine."

She laughed good-naturedly. "Very well—not to-day. One
shouldn't ask you to believe to-day that *die ganze Welt ist zum
Verzweifeln traurig.*"

While she made tea, he returned to the window, where he
stood with his hands in his pockets, lost in thought. He told
himself once more what he found it impossible to believe: that
he was going to see Louise again in a few hours; and not only
to see her, but to speak to her, to be at her side. And when
his jubilation at this had subsided, he went over in memory all
that had just taken place. His first impression, he could
afford now to admit it, had been almost one of disappointment:
that came from having dreamed so long of a shadowy being,
whom he had called by her name, that the real she was a
stranger to him. Everything about her had been different from
what he had expected—her voice, her smile, her gestures—
and in the first moments of their meeting, he had been chill
with fear, lest—lest . . . even yet he did not venture to
think out the thought. But this first sensation of strangeness
over, he had found her more charming, more desirable, than
even he had hoped; and what almost wrung a cry of pleasure
from him as he remembered it, was that not the smallest trifle
—no touch of coquetry, no insincerely spoken word—had
marred the perfect impression of the whole. To know her,
to stand before her, he recognised it now, gave the lie to false
slander and report. Hardest of all, however, was it to grasp
that the meeting had actually come to pass and was over: it
had been so ordinary, so everyday, the most natural thing in
the world; there had been no blast of trumpets, nor had any
occult sympathy warned her that she was in the presence of
one who had trembled for weeks at the idea of this moment—
and again he leaned forward and gazed at the spot in the street,
where she had disappeared from sight. He was filled with
envy of Dove—this was the latter's reward for his unfailing
readiness to oblige others—and in fancy he saw Dove walking
street after street at her side.

In reality, the two parted from each other shortly after turning the first corner.

On any other day, Dove would have been still more prompt to take leave of his companion; but, on this particular one, he was in the mood to be a little reckless. In the morning, he had received, with a delightful shock, his first letter from Ephie, a very frank, warmly written note, in which she relied on his great kindness to secure her, *without fail*—these words were deeply underscored—two places in the *parquet* of the theatre, for that evening's performance. Not the letter alone, but also its confiding tone, and the reliance it placed in him, had touched Dove to a deep pleasure; he had been one of the first to arrive at the box-office that morning, and, although he had not ventured, unasked, to take himself a seat beside the sisters, he was now living in the anticipation of promenading the *foyer* with them in the intervals between the acts, and of afterwards escorting them home.

On leaving Louise, he made for the theatre with a swinging stride—had he been in the country, stick in hand, he would have slashed off the heads of innumerable green and flowering things. As it was, he whistled—an unusual thing for him to do in the street—then assumed the air of a man hard pressed for time. Gradually the passers-by began to look at him with the right amount of attention; he jostled, as if by accident, one or two of those who were unobservant, then apologised for his hurry. It was not pleasurable anticipation alone that was responsible for Dove's state of mind, and for the heightening and radiation of his self-consciousness. In offering to go early to the theatre, and to stand at the doors for at least three-quarters of an hour, in order that the others, coming considerably later, might still have a chance of gaining their favourite seats: in doing this, Dove was not actuated by a wholly unselfish motive, but by the more complicated one, which, consciously or unconsciously, was present beneath all the friendly cares and attentions he bestowed on people. He was never more content with himself, and with the world at large, than when he felt that he was essential to the comfort and well-being of some of his fellow-mortals; than when he, so to speak, had a finger in the pie of their existence. It engendered a sense of importance, gave life fulness and variety; and this far outweighed the trifling inconveniences such well-doing implied. Indeed, he throve on them. For, in his mild way, Dove had a touch of Cæsarean mania—of a lust for power.

Left to herself, Louise Dufrayer walked slowly home to her
room in the *Brüderstrasse,* but only to throw a hasty look
round. It was just as she had expected: although it was long
past the appointed time, he was not there. At a flower-shop
in a big adjoining street, she bought a bunch of many-coloured
roses, and with these in her hands, went straight to where
Schilsky lived.

Mounting to the third floor of the house in the *Talstrasse,*
she opened, without ceremony, the door of his room, which
gave direct on the landing; but so stealthily that the young
man, who was sitting with his back to the door, did not
hear her enter. Before he could turn, she had sprung forward,
her arms were round his neck, and the roses under his nose.
He drew his face away from their damp fragrance, but did
not look up, and, without removing his cigarette, asked in a
tone of extreme bad temper: "What are you doing here,
Lulu? What nonsense is this? For God's sake, shut the
door!"

She ruffled his hair with her lips. "You didn't come.
And the day has seemed so long."

He tried to free himself, putting the roses aside with one
hand, while, with his cigarette, he pointed to the sheets of
music-paper that lay before him. "For a very good reason.
I've had no time."

She went back and closed the door; and then, sitting down
on his knee, unpinned her big hat, and threw it and the roses
on the bed. He put his arm round her to steady her, and as
soon as he held her to him, his ill-temper was vanquished.
He talked volubly of the instrumentation he was busy with.
But she, who could point out almost every fresh note he put
on paper, saw plainly that he had not been at work for more
than a quarter of an hour; and, in a miserable swell of doubt
and jealousy, such as she could never subdue, she asked:
"Were you practising as well?"

He took no notice of these words, and she did not trust herself to say more, until, with his free hand, he began jotting
again, making notes that were no bigger than pin-heads. Then
she laid her hand on his. "I haven't seen you all day."

But he was too engrossed to listen. "Look here," he said
pointing to a thick-sown bar. "That gave me the deuce of a
bother. While here"—and now he explained to her, in detail,
the properties of the tenor-tuba in B, and the bass-tuba in
F, and the use to which he intended to put these instru-

ments. She heard him with lowered eyes, lightly caressing
the back of his hand with her finger-tips. But when he ceased
speaking, she rubbed her cheek against his.

"It is enough for to-day. Lulu has been lonely."

Not one of his thoughts was with her, she saw that, as he
answered: "I must get this finished."

"To-night?"

"If I can. You know well enough, Lulu, when I'm in
the swing——"

"Yes, yes, I know. If only it wouldn't always come, just
when I want you most."

Her face lost its brightness; she rose from his knee and
roamed about the room, watched from the wall by her pictured
self.

"But is there ever a moment in the day when you don't
want me? You are never satisfied." He spoke abstractedly,
without interest in the answer she might make, and, relieved
of her weight, leant forward again, while his fingers played
some notes on the table. But when she began to let her hands
stray over the loose papers and other articles that encumbered
chairs, piano and washstand, he raised his head and watched
her with a sharp eye.

"For goodness' sake, let those things alone, can't you?"
he said after he had borne her fidgeting for some time.

"You have no secrets from me, I suppose?" She said it
with her tenderest smile, but he scowled so darkly in reply that
she went over to him again, to touch him with her hand.
Standing behind him, with her fingers in his hair, she said:
"Just to-day I wanted you so much. This morning I was
so depressed that I could have killed myself."

He turned his head, to give her a significant glance.

"Good reason for the blues, Lulu. I warned you. You
want too much of everything. And can't expect to escape
a *Kater*."

"Too much?" she echoed, quick to resent his words.
"Does it seem so to you? Would days and days of happiness be too much after we have been separated for a week?
—after Wednesday night?—after what you said to me yesterday?"

"Yesterday I was in the devil of a temper. Why rake up
old scores? Now go home. Or at least keep quiet, and let
me get something done."

He shook his head free of her caressing hand, and, worse

still, scratched the place where it had lain. She stood irresolute, not venturing to touch him again, looking hungrily at
him. Her eyes fell on the piece of neck, smooth, lightly
browned, that showed between his hair and the low collar;
and, in an uncontrollable rush of feeling, she stooped and kissed
it. As he accepted the caress, without demur, she said: " I
thought of going to the theatre to-night, dear."

He was pleased and showed it. " That's right—it's just
what you need to cheer you up."

" But I want you to come, too."

He struck the table with his fist. " Good God, can't you
get it into your head that I want to work? "

She laughed, with ready bitterness. " I should think I
could. That's nothing new. You are always busy when I
ask you to do anything. You have time for everything and
every one but me. If this were something you yourself wanted
to do to-night, neither your work nor anything else would
stand in the way of it; but my wishes can always be ignored.
Have you forgotten already that I only came home the day
before yesterday? "

He looked sullen. " Now don't make a scene, Lulu. It
doesn't do a whit of good."

" A scene! " she cried, seizing on his words. " Whenever
I open my lips now, you call it a scene. Tell me what I have
done, Eugen! Why do you treat me like this? Are you
beginning to care less for me? The first evening, the very
first, I get home, you won't stay with me—you haven't even
kept that evening free for me—and when I ask you about it,
and try to get at the truth—oh, do you remember all the cruel
things you said to me yesterday? I shall never forget them
as long as I live. And now, when I ask you to come out with
me—it is such a little thing—oh, I can't sit at home this evening, Eugen, I can't do it! If you really loved me, you would
understand."

She flung herself across the bed and sobbed despairingly.
Schilsky, who had again made believe during this outburst to
be absorbed in his work, cast a look of mingled anger and discomfort at the prostrate figure, and for some few moments,
succeeded in continuing his occupation with a show of indifference; but as, in place of abating, her sobs grew more
heart-rending, his own face began to twitch, and finally he
dropped pencil and cigarette, and with a loud expression of
annoyance went over to the bed.

"Lulu," he said persuasively. "Come, Lulu," and bending over her, he laid his hands on her shoulders and tried to force her to rise. She resisted him with all her might, but he was the stronger, and presently he had her on her feet, where, with her head on his shoulder, she wept out the rest of her tears. He held her to him, and although his face above her was still dark, did what he could to soothe her. He could never bear to see or to hear a woman cry, and this loud passionate weeping, so careless of anything but itself, racked his nerves, and filled him with an uneasy wrath against invisible powers.

"Don't cry, darling, don't cry!" he said again and again.

Gradually she grew calmer, and he, too, was still; but when her sobs were hushed, and she was clinging to him in silence, he put his hands on her shoulders and held her back from him, that he might look at her. His face wore a stubborn expression, which she knew, and which made him appear years older than he was.

"Now listen to me, Lulu," he said. "When you behave in this way again, you won't see me afterwards for a week—I promise you that, and you know I keep my word. Instead of being glad that I am in the right mood and can get something done, you come here—which you know I have repeatedly forbidden you to do—and make a fool of yourself like this. I have explained everything to you. I could not possibly stay on Wednesday night—why didn't you time your arrival better? But it's just like you. You would throw the whole of one's future into the balance for the sake of a whim. Yesterday I was in a beast of a temper—I've admitted it. But that was made all right last night; and no one but you would drag it up again."

He spoke with a kind of dogged restraint, which only sometimes gave way, when the injustice she was guilty of forced itself upon him. "Now, like a good girl, go home—go to the theatre and enjoy yourself. I don't mind you being happy without me. At least, go!—under any circumstances you ought not to be here. How often have I told you that!" His moderation swept over into the feverish irritation she knew so well how to kindle in him, and his lisp became so marked that he was almost unintelligible. "You won't have a rag of reputation left."

"If I don't care, why should you?" She felt for his hand. But he turned his back. "I won't have it, I tell you. You know what the student underneath said, the last time he met you on the stair."

She pressed her handkerchief to her lips to keep from bursting anew into sobs, and there was a brief silence—he stood at the window, gazing savagely at the opposite house-wall—before she said: "Don't speak to me like that. I'm going—now—this moment. I will never do it again—never again."

As he only mumbled disbelief at this, she put her arms round his neck, and raised her tear-stained face to his: her eyes were blurred and sunken with crying, and her lips were white. He knew every line of her face by heart; he had known it in so many moods, and under so many conditions, that he was not as sensitive to its influence as he had once been; and he stood unwilling, with his hands in his pockets, while she clung to him and let him feel her weight. But he was very fond of her, and, as she continued mutely to implore forgiveness—she, Lulu, his Lulu, whom every one envied him —his hasty anger once more subsided; he put his arms round her and kissed her. She nestled in against him, over-happy at his softening, and for some moments they stood like this, in the absolute physical agreement that always overcame their differences. In his arms, with her head on his shoulder, she smoothed back his hair; and while she gazed, with adoring eyes, at this face that constituted her world, she murmured words of endearment; and all the unsatisfactory day was annulled by these few moments of perfect harmony.

It was he who loosened his grasp. "Now, it's all right, isn't it? No more tears. But you really must be off, or you'll be late."

"Yes. And you?"

He had taken up his violin, and was tuning it, preparatory to playing himself back into the mood she had dissipated. He ran his fingers up and down, tried flageolets, and slashed chords across the strings.

But when she had sponged her face and pinned on her hat, he said, in response to her beseeching eyes, which, as so often before, made the granting of this one request, a touchstone of his love for her: "Look here, Lulu, if I possibly can, I'll drop in at the end of the first act. Look out for me then, in the *foyer*."

And with this, she was forced to be content.

IX

When, shortly after five o'clock, Madeleine and Maurice arrived at the New Theatre, they took their places at the end of a queue which extended to the corner of the main building; and before they had stood very long, so many fresh people had been added to the line, that it had lengthened out until it all but reached the arch of the theatre-café. Dove was well to the fore, and would be one of the first to gain the box-office. A quarter of an hour had still to elapse before the doors opened; and Maurice borrowed his companion's text-book, and read studiously, to acquaint himself with the plot of the opera. Madeleine took out Wolzogen's *Führer,* with the intention of brushing up her knowledge of the motives; but, before she had finished a page, she had grown so interested in what two people behind her were saying that she turned and took part in the conversation.

The broad expanse of the *Augustusplatz* facing the theatre was bare and sunny. A policeman arrived, and ordered the queue in a straighter line; then he strolled up and down, stroking and smoothing his white gloves. More people came hurrying over the square to the theatre, and ranged themselves at the end of the tail. As the hands of the big clock on the post-office neared the quarter past five, a kind of tremor ran through the waiting line; ·it gathered itself more compactly together. One clock after another boomed the single stroke; sounds came from within the building; the burly policeman placed himself at the head of the line. There was a noise of drawn bolts and grating locks, and after a moment's suspense, light shone out and the big door was flung open.

" Gent-ly! " shouted the policeman, but the leaders of the queue charged with a will, and about a dozen people had dashed forward, before he could throw down a stemming arm, on which those thus hindered leaned as on a bar of iron. Madeleine and Maurice were to the front of the second batch. And the arm down, in they flew also, Madeleine leading, through the swing-doors at the side of the corridor, up the steep, wooden stairs, one flight after another, higher and higher, round and round, past one, two, three, tiers—a mad

race, which ended almost in the arms of the gate-keeper at
the topmost gallery.

Dove was waiting with the tickets, and they easily secured
the desired places; not in the middle of the gallery, where, as
Madeleine explained while she tucked her hat and jacket under
the seat, the monstrous chandelier hid the greater part of the
stage, but at the right-hand side, next the lattice that separated the seats at seventy-five from those at fifty pfennigs.

" This is first-rate for seeing," said Maurice.

Madeleine laughed.   "You see too much—that's the
trouble.   Wait till you've watched the men running about the
bottom of the Rhine, working the cages the Rhine-daughters
swim in."

As yet, with the exception of the gallery, the great building
was empty.   Now the iron fire-curtain rose; but the sunken
well of the orchestra was in darkness, and the expanse of seats
on the ground floor far below, was still encased in white wrappings—here and there an attendant began to peel them off.
Maurice, poring over his book, had to strain his eyes to read,
and this, added to the difficulty of the German, and his own
sense of pleasurable excitement, made him soon give up the
attempt, and attend wholly to what Madeleine was saying.

It was hot already, and the air of the crowded gallery was
permeated with various, pungent odours: some people behind
them were eating a strong-smelling sausage, and the man on
the other side of the lattice reeked of cheap tobacco.   When
they had been in their seats for about a quarter of an hour,
the lights throughout the theatre went up, and, directly afterwards, the lower tiers and the ground floor were sprinkled
with figures.   One by one, the members of the orchestra
dropped in, turned up the lamps attached to their stands, and
taking their instruments, commenced to tune and flourish;
and soon stray motives and scraps of motives came mounting
up, like lost birds, from wind and strings; the man of the
drums beat a soft rattatoo, and applied his ear to the skins of
his instruments.   Now the players were in their seats, waiting
for the conductor; late-comers in the audience entered with an
air of guilty haste.   The chief curtain had risen, and the
stage was hidden only by stuff curtains, bordered with a runic
scroll.   A delightful sense of expectation pervaded the theatre.

Maurice had more than once looked furtively at his watch;
and, at every fresh noise behind him, he turned his head—
turned so often that the people in the back seats grew suspicious, and whispered to one another.   Madeleine had drawn

his attention to everything worth noticing; and now, with her opera-glass at her eyes, she pointed out to him people whom he ought to know. Dove, having eaten a ham-roll at the buffet on the stair, had ever since sat with his opera-glass glued to his face, and only at this moment did he remove it with a sigh of relief.

"There they are," said Madeleine, and showed Maurice the place in the *parquet,* where Ephie and Johanna Cayhill were sitting. But the young man only glanced cursorily in the direction she indicated; he was wondering why Louise did not come—the time had all but gone. He could not bring himself to ask, partly from fear of being disappointed, partly because, now that he knew her, it was harder than before to bring her name over his lips. But the conductor had entered by the orchestra-door; he stood speaking to the first violinist, and the next moment would climb into his seat. The players held their instruments in readiness—and a question trembled on Maurice's tongue. But at this very moment, a peremptory fanfare rang out behind the scene, and Madeleine said: "The sword motive, Maurice," to add in the same breath: "There's Louise."

He looked behind him. "Where?"

She nudged him. "Not here, you silly," she said in a loud whisper. "Surely you haven't been expecting her to come up here? *Parquet,* fourth row from the front, between two women in plaid dresses—oh, now the lights have gone."

"Ssh!" said at least half a dozen people about them: her voice was audible above the growling of the thunder.

Maurice took her opera-glass, and, notwithstanding the darkness into which the theatre had been plunged, travelled his eyes up and down the row she named—naturally without success. When the curtains parted and disclosed the stage, it was a little lighter, but not light enough for him; he could not find the plaids; or rather there were only plaids in the row; and there was also more than one head that resembled hers. To know that she was there was enough to distract him; and he was conscious of the music and action of the opera merely as something that was going on outside him, until he received another sharp nudge from Madeleine on his right-hand side.

"You're not attending. And this is the only act you'll be able to make anything of."

He gave a guilty start, and turned to the stage, where

Hunding had just entered to a pompous measure. In his
endeavours to understand what followed, he was aided by
his companions, who prompted him alternately. But Siegmund's narration seemed endless, and his thoughts wandered
in spite of himself.

"Listen to this," said Dove of a sudden. "It's one of the
few songs Wagner has written." He swayed his head from
side to side, to the opening bars of the love-song; and Maurice
found the rhythm so inviting that he began keeping time with
his foot, to the indignation of a music-loving policeman behind them, who gave an angry: "Pst!"

"One of the finest love-scenes that was ever written," whispered Madeleine in her decisive way. And Maurice believed
her. From this point on, the music took him up and carried
him with it; and when the great curtains fell, and shut off
the spring night, he applauded vigorously with the rest, keeping it up so long that Dove disappeared, and Madeleine grew
impatient.

"Let us go. The interval is none too long."

They went downstairs to the first floor of the building, and
entered a long, broad, brilliantly lighted corridor. Here the
majority of the audience was walking round and round, in a
procession of twos and threes; groups of people also stood at
both ends and looked on; others went in and out of the doors
that opened on the great loggia. Madeleine and Maurice
joined the perambulating throng, Madeleine bowing and smiling to her acquaintances, Maurice eagerly scanning the faces
that came towards him on the opposite side.

Suddenly, a stout gentleman, in gold spectacles, kid gloves
tight to bursting, and a brown frock coat, over the amplitude
of which was slung an opera-glass, started up from a corner,
and, seizing both Madeleine's hands, worked them up and
down. At the same time, he made a ceremonious little speech
about the length of time that had elapsed since their last meeting, and paid her a specious compliment on the taste she displayed in being present at so serious an opera. Madeleine
laughed, and said a few words in her hard, facile German:
the best was yet to come; "*die Moran*" was divine as Brünnhilde. Having bowed and said: "Lohse" to Maurice, the
stranger took no further notice of him, but, drawing Madeleine's hand through his arm, in a manner half gallant, half
paternal, invited her to take ices with him, at the adjoining
buffet.

Maurice remained standing in a corner, scrutinising those who passed him. He exchanged a few words with one of his companions of the dinner-table—a small-bodied, big-headed chemical student called Dickensey, who had a reputation for his cynicism. He had just asked Maurice whether Siegmund reminded him more of a pork-butcher or a prizefighter, and had offered to lay a bet that he would never attend a performance in this theatre when the doors of Hunding's house flew open, or the sword lit up, at exactly the right moment—when Maurice caught sight of Dove and the Cayhills. He excused himself, and went to join them.

Not one of the three looked happy. Johanna was unspeakably bored and did not conceal it; she gazed with contempt on the noisy, excited crowd. Dove was not only burning to devote himself to Ephie; he had also got himself into a dilemma, and was at this moment doing his best to explain the first act of the opera to Johanna, without touching on the relationship of the lovers. His face was red with the effort, and he hailed Maurice's appearance as a welcome diversion. But Ephie, too, greeted him with pleasure, and touching his arm, drew him back, so that they dropped behind the others. She was coquettishly dressed this evening, and looked so charming that people drew one another's attention to *die reizende kleine Engländerin.* But Maurice soon discovered that she was out of spirits, and disposed to be cross. For fear lest he was the offender, he asked if she had quite forgiven him, and if they were good friends again. "Oh, I had forgotten all about it!" But, a moment after, she was grave and quiet—altogether unlike herself.

"Are you not enjoying yourself, Ephie?"

"No, I'm not. I think it's stupid. And they're all so fat."

This referred to the singers, and was indisputable; Maurice could only agree with her, and try to rally her. Meanwhile, he continued surreptitiously to scour the hall, with an ever-growing sense of disappointment.

Then, suddenly, among those who were passing in the opposite direction, he saw Louise. In a flash he understood why he had not been able to find her in the row of seats: he had looked for her in a black dress, and she was all in white, with heavy white lace at her neck. Her companion was an Englishman called Eggis, of whom it was rumoured that he had found it advisable abruptly to leave his native land: here, he

8

made a precarious living by journalism, and by doing odd jobs for the consulate. In spite of his shabby clothes, this man, prematurely bald, with dissipated features, had polished manners and an air of refinement; and, thoroughly enjoying his position, he was talking to his companion with vivacity. It was plain that Louise was only half listening to him; with a faint, absent smile on her lips, she, too, restlessly scanned the crowd.

They all caught sight of Schilsky at the same moment, and Maurice, on whom nothing was lost, saw as well the quick look that passed between Louise and him, and its immediate effect: Louise flashed into a smile, and was full of gracious attentiveness to the little man at her side.

Schilsky leant against the wall, with his hands in his pockets, his conspicuous head well back. On entering the *foyer*, he had been pounced on by Miss Jensen. The latter, showily dressed in a large-striped stuff, had in tow a fellow-singer about half her own size, whom she was rarely to be seen without; but, on this occasion, the wan little American stood disconsolately apart, for Miss Jensen was paying no attention to him. In common with the rest of her sex, she had a weakness for Schilsky; and besides, on this evening, she needed specially receptive ears, for she had been studying the rôle of Sieglinde, and was full of criticisms and objections. As Ephie and Maurice passed them, she nodded to the latter and said: "Good evening, neighbour!" while Schilsky, seizing the chance, broke away, without troubling to excuse himself. Thus deserted, Miss Jensen detained Maurice, and so he lost the couple he wanted to keep in sight. But at the first pause in the conversation, Ephie plucked at his sleeve.

"Let us go out on the balcony."

They went outside on the loggia, where groups of people stood refreshing themselves in the mild evening air, which was pleasant with the scent of lilac. Ephie led the way, and Maurice followed her to the edge of the parapet, where they paused beside one of the pillars. Here, he found himself again in the neighbourhood of the other two. Louise, leaning both hands on the stone-work, was looking out over the square; but Schilsky, lounging as before, with his legs crossed, his hands in his pockets, had his back to it, and was letting his eyes range indifferently over the faces before him. As Maurice and Ephie came up, he yawned long and heartily, and, in so doing, showed all his defective teeth. Furtively watching them, Maurice saw him bend towards his companion and say something to her; at the same time, he touched with his finger-tips the lace she wore at the front of her dress. The familiarity of the action grated on Maurice, and he turned away his head. When he looked again, a moment or two later, he was disturbed anew. Louise was leaning forward, still in the same position, but Schilsky was plainly conversing by means of signs with some one else. He frowned, half closed his eyes, shook his head, and, as if by chance, laid a finger on his lips.

"Who's he doing that to?" Maurice asked himself, and followed the direction of the other's eyes, which were fixed on the corner where he and Ephie stood. He turned, and looked from side to side; and, as he did this, he caught a glimpse of Ephie's face, which made him observe her more nearly: it was flushed, and she was gazing hard at Schilsky. With a rush of enlightenment, Maurice looked back at the young man, but this time Schilsky saw that he was being watched; stooping, he said a nonchalant word to his companion, and thereupon they went indoors again. All this passed like a flash, but it left, none the less, a disagreeable impression, and before Maurice had recovered from it, Ephie said: "Let us go in."

They pressed towards the door.

"I'm poor company to-night, Ephie," he said, feeling already the need of apologising to her for his ridiculous suspicion. "But you are quiet, too." He glanced down at her as he spoke, and again was startled; her expression was set and defiant, but her baby lips trembled. "What's the matter? I believe you are angry with me for being so silent."

"I guess it doesn't make any difference to me whether you talk or not," she replied pettishly. "But I think it's just as dull and stupid as it can be. I wish I hadn't come."

"Would you like to go home?"

"Of course I wouldn't. I'll stop now I'm here—oh, can't we go quicker? How slow you are! Do make haste."

He thought he heard tears in her voice, and looked at her in perplexity. While he contemplated getting her into a quiet corner, and making her tell him truthfully what the matter was, they came upon Madeleine, who had been searching everywhere for Maurice. Madeleine had more colour in her cheeks than usual, and, in the pleasing consciousness that she was having a successful evening, she brought her good spirits to bear on Ephie, who stood fidgeting beside them.

"You look nice, child," she remarked in her patronising way. "Your dress is very pretty. But why is your face so red? One would think you had been crying."

Ephie, growing still redder, tossed her head. "It's no wonder, I'm sure. The theatre is as hot as an oven. But at least my nose isn't red as well."

Madeleine was on the point of retorting, but at this moment, the interval came to an end, and the electric bells rang shrilly. The people who were nearest the doors went out at once, upstairs and down. Among the first were Louise and Schilsky, the latter's head as usual visible above every one else's.

"I will go, too," said Ephie hurriedly. "No, don't bother to come with me. I'll find my way all right. I guess the others are in front."

"There's something wrong with that child to-night," said Madeleine as she and Maurice climbed to the gallery. "Pert little thing! But I suppose even such sparrow-brains have their troubles."

"I suppose they have," said Maurice. He had just realised that the longed-for interval was over, and with it more of the hopes he had nursed.

Dove was already in his seat, eating another roll. He moved along to make room for them, but not a word was to be got out of him, and as soon as he had finished eating, he raised the opera-glass to his eyes again. Behind his back, Madeleine whispered a mischievous remark to Maurice, but the latter smiled wintrily in return. He had searched swiftly and thoroughly up and down the fourth row of the *parquet,* only to find that Louise was not in it. This time there could be no doubt whatever; not a single white dress was in the row, and towards the middle a seat was vacant. They had gone home then; he would not see her again—and once more the provoking darkness enveloped the theatre.

This second act had no meaning for him, and he found the various scenes intolerably long. Dove volunteered no further aid, and Madeleine's explanations were insufficient; he was perplexed and bored, and when the curtains fell, joined in the applause merely to save appearances. The others rose, but he said he would not go downstairs; and when they had drawn back to let Dove push by and hurry away, Madeleine said she, too, would stay. However they would at least go into the corridor, where the air was better. After they had promenaded several times up and down, they descended to a lower floor, and there, through a little half-moon window that gave on the *foyer* below, they watched the living stream which, underneath, was going round as before. Madeleine talked without a pause.

"Look at Dove!" She pointed him out as he went by with the two sisters. "Did you ever see such a gloomy air? He might sit for Werther to-night. And oh, look, there's Boehmer with his widow—see, the pretty fattish little woman. She's over forty and has buried two husbands, but is crazy about Boehmer. They say she's going to marry him, though he's more than twenty years younger than she is."

At this juncture, to his astonishment, Maurice saw Schilsky and Louise. He uttered an involuntary exclamation, and Madeleine understood it. She stopped her gossip to say: "You thought she had gone, didn't you? Probably she has only changed her seat. They do that sometimes—he hates *parquet.*" And, after a pause: "How cross she looks! She's evidently in a temper about something. I never saw people hide their feelings as badly as they do. It's positively indecent."

Her strictures were justifiable; as long as the two below were in sight, and as often as they came round, they did not exchange word or look with each other. Schilsky frowned sulkily, and his loose-knitted body seemed to hang together more loosely than usual, while as for Louise—Maurice staring hard from his point of vantage could not have believed it possible for her face to change in this way. She looked suddenly older, and very tired; and her mobile mouth was hard.

When, an hour later, after a tedious colloquy between Brünnhilde and Wotan, this long and disappointing evening came to an end, to the more human strains of the *Feuerzauber,* and they, the last of the gallery-audience to leave, had tramped down the wooden stairs, Maurice's heart leapt to his throat to discover, as they turned the last bend, not only the two Cayhills waiting for them, but also, a little distance further off, Louise. She stood there, in her white dress, with a thin scarf over her head.

Madeleine was surprised too. "Louise! Is it you? And alone?"

The girl did not respond. "I want to borrow some money from you, Madeleine—about five or six marks," she said, without smiling, in one of those colourless voices that preclude further questioning.

Madeleine was not sure if she had more than a couple of marks in her purse, and confirmed this on looking through it under a lamp; but both young men put their hands in their pockets, and the required sum was made up. As they walked across the square, Louise explained. Dressed, and ready to start for the theatre, she had not been able to find her purse.

" I looked everywhere. And yet I had it only this morning. At the last moment, I came down here to Markwald's. He knows me; and he let me have the seats on trust. I said I would go in afterwards."

They waited outside the tobacconist's, while she settled her debt. Before she came out again, Madeleine cast her eyes over the group, and, having made a rapid surmise, said good-naturedly to Johanna: " Well, I suppose we shall walk together as far as we can. Shall you and I lead off? "

Maurice had a sudden vision of bliss; but no sooner had Louise appeared again, with the shopman bowing behind her, then Ephie came round to his side, with a naïve, matter-of-course air that admitted of no rebuff, and asked him to carry her opera-glass. Dove and Louise brought up the rear.

But Dove had only one thought: to be in Maurice's place. Ephie had behaved so strangely in the theatre; he had certainly done something to offend her, and, although he had more than once gone over his conduct of the past week, without finding any want of correctness on his part, whatever it was, he must make it good without delay.

" You know my friend Guest, I think," he said at last, having racked his brains to no better result—not for the world would he have had his companion suspect his anxiety to leave her. " He's a clever fellow, a very clever fellow. Schwarz thinks a great deal of him. I wonder what his impressions of the opera were. This was his first experience of Wagner; it would be interesting to hear what he has to say."

Louise was moody and preoccupied, but Dove's words made her smile.

"Let us ask him," she said.

They quickened their steps and overtook the others. And when Dove, without further ado, had marched round to Ephie's side, Louise, left slightly to herself, called Maurice back to her.

" Mr. Guest, we want your opinion of the *Walküre*."

Confused to find her suddenly beside him, Maurice was still more disconcerted at the marked way in which she slackened her pace to let the other two get in front. Believing, too, that he heard a note of mockery in her voice, he coloured and hesitated. Only a moment ago he had had several things worth saying on his tongue; now they would not out. He stammered a few words, and broke down in them half-way. She said nothing, and after one of the most embarrassing pauses he had ever experienced, he avowed in a burst of forlorn courage: "To tell the truth, I did not hear much of the music."

But Louise, who had merely exchanged one chance companion for another, did not ask the reason, or display any interest in his confession, and they went on in silence. Maurice looked stealthily at her: her white scarf had slipped back and her wavy head was bare. She had not heard what he said, he told himself; her thoughts had nothing to do with him. But as he stole glances at her thus, unreproved, he wakened to a sudden consciousness of what was happening to him: here and now, after long weeks of waiting, he was walking at her side; he knew her, was alone with her, in the summer darkness, and, though a cold hand gripped his throat at the thought, he took the resolve not to let this moment pass him by, empty-handed. He must say something that would rouse her to the fact of his existence; something that would linger in her mind, and make her remember him when he was not there. But they were half way down the *Grimmaischestrasse;* at the end, where the *Peterstrasse* crossed it, Dove and the Cayhills would branch off, and Madeleine return to them. He had no time to choose his phrases.

"When I was introduced to you this afternoon, Miss Dufrayer, you did not know who I was," he said bluntly. "But I knew you very well—by sight, I mean, of course. I have seen you often—very often."

He had done what he had hoped to do, had arrested her attention. She turned and considered him, struck by the tone in which he spoke.

"The first time I saw you," continued Maurice, with the same show of boldness—"you, of course, will not remember it. It was one evening in Schwarz's room—in April—months ago. And since then, I . . . well . . . I——"

She was gazing at him now, in surprise. She remembered at this minute, how once before, that day, his manner of saying some simple thing had affected her disagreeably. Then, she had eluded the matter with an indifferent word; now, she

was not in a mood to do this, or in a mood to show leniency.
She was dispirited, at war with herself, and she welcomed the
excuse to vent her own bitterness on another.

"And since then—well?"

"Since then . . . " He hesitated, and gave a nervous laugh
at his own daring. "Since then . . . well, I have thought
about you more than—than is good for my peace of mind."

For a moment amazement kept her silent; then she, too,
laughed, and the walls of the dark houses they were passing
seemed to the young man to re-echo the sound.

"Your peace of mind!"

She repeated the words after him, with such an ironical
emphasis that his unreflected courage curled and shrivelled.
He wished the ground had swallowed him up before he
said them. For, as they fell from her lips, the audacity he
had been guilty of, and the absurdity that was latent in the
words themselves, struck him in the face like pellets of hail.

"Your peace of mind! What has your peace of mind
to do with me?" she cried, growing extravagantly angry.
" I never saw you in my life till to-day; I may never see you
again, and it is all the same to me whether I do or not.—Oh,
my own peace of mind, as you call it, is quite hard enough to
take care of, without having a stranger's thrown at me! What
do you mean by making me responsible for it! I have never
done anything to you."

All the foolish castles Maurice had built came tumbling
about his ears. He grew pale and did not venture to look
at her.

"Make you responsible! Oh, how can you misunderstand
me so cruelly!"

His consternation was so palpable that it touched her in
spite of herself. Her face had been as naïvely miserable as a
child's; now it softened, and she spoke more kindly.

"Don't mind what I say. To-night I am tired . . . have a
headache . . . anything you like."

A wave of compassion drowned his petty feelings of injury,
and his sympathy found vent in a few inadequate words.

" Help me?—you? " She laughed, in an unhappy way.
" To help, one must understand, and you couldn't understand
though you tried. All you others lead such quiet lives; you
know nothing of what goes on in a life like mine. Every day I
ask myself why I have not thrown myself out of the win-

dow, or over one of the bridges into the river, and put an end to it."

Wrapped up though she was in herself, she could not help smiling at his frank gesture of dismay.

"Don't be afraid," she said, and the smile lingered on her lips. "I shall never do it. I'm too fond of life, and too afraid of death. But at least," she caught herself up again, "you will see how ridiculous it is for you to talk to me of your peace of mind. Peace of mind! I have never even been passably content. Something is always wanting. To-night, for instance, I feel so much energy in me, and I can make nothing of it—nothing! If I were a man, I should walk for hours, bareheaded, through the woods. But to be a woman . . . to be cooped up inside four walls . . . when the night itself is not large enough to hold it all!——"

She threw out her hands to emphasise her helplessness, then let them drop to her sides again. There was a silence, for Maurice could not think of anything to say; her fluency made him tongue-tied. He struggled with his embarrassment until they were all but within earshot of the rest, at the bottom of the street.

"If I . . . if you would let me . . . There is nothing in the world I wouldn't do to help you," he ended fervently.

She did not reply; they had reached the corner where the others waited. There was a general leave-taking. Through a kind of mist, Maurice saw that Ephie's face still wore a hostile look; and she hardly moved her lips when she bade him good-night.

Madeleine drew her own conclusions as she walked the rest of the way home between two pale and silent people. She had seen, on coming out of the theatre, that Louise was in one of her bad moods—a fact easily to be accounted for by Schilsky's absence. Maurice had evidently been made to suffer under it, too, for not a syllable was to be drawn from him, and after several unavailing attempts she let him alone.

As they crossed the *Rossplatz,* which lay wide and deserted in the starlight, Louise said abruptly: "Suppose, instead of going home, we walk to Connewitz?"

At this proposal, and at Maurice's seconding of it, Madeleine laughed with healthy derision.

"That is just like one of your crazy notions," she said. "What a creature you are! For my part, I decline with thanks. I have to get a Moscheles *étude* ready by to-morrow afternoon, and need all my wits. But don't let me hinder you. Walk to Grimma if you want to."

"What do you say? Shall you and I go on?" Louise turned to Maurice; and the young man did not know whether she spoke in jest or in earnest.

Madeleine knew her better. "Louise!" she said warningly. "Maurice has work to do to-morrow, too."

"You thought I meant it," said the girl, and laughed so ungovernably that Madeleine was again driven to remonstrance.

"For goodness' sake, be quiet! We shall have a policeman after us, if you laugh like that."

Nothing more was said until they stood before the house-door in the *Brüderstrasse*. There Louise, who had lapsed once more into her former indifference, asked Madeleine to come upstairs with her.

"I will look for the purse again; and then I can give you what I owe you. Or else I am sure to forget. Oh, it's still early; and the night is so long. No one can think of sleep yet."

Madeleine was not a night-bird, but she was also not averse to having a debt paid. Louise looked from her to Maurice. "Will you come, too, Mr. Guest? It will only take a few minutes," she said, and, seeing his unhappy face, and remembering what had passed between them, she spoke more gently than she had yet done.

Maurice felt that he ought to refuse; it was late. But Madeleine answered for him. "Of course. Come along, Maurice," and he crossed the threshold behind them.

After lighting a taper, they entered a paved vestibule, and mounted a flight of broad and very shallow stairs; half-way up, there was a deep recess for pot-plants, and a wooden seat was attached to the wall. The house had been a fine one in its day; it was solidly built, had massive doors with heavy brass fittings, and thick mahogany banisters. On the first floor were two doors, a large and a small one, side by side. Louise unlocked the larger, and they stepped into a commodious lobby, off which several rooms opened. She led the way to the furthest of these, and entered in front of her companions.

Maurice, hesitating just inside the door, found himself close to a grand piano, which stood free on all sides, was open, and disorderly with music. It was a large room, with three windows; and one end of it was shut off by a high screen, which stretched almost from wall to wall. A deep sofa stood in an oriel-window; a writing-table was covered with bric-à-brac, and three tall flower-vases were filled with purple lilac. But there was a general air of untidiness about the room; for strewn over the chairs and tables were numerous small articles of dress and the toilet—hairpins, a veil, a hat and a skirt—all traces of her intimate presence.

As she lifted the lamp from the writing-table to place it on the square table before the sofa, Madeleine called her attention to a folded paper that had lain beneath it.

"It seems to be a letter for you."

She caught at it with a kind of avidity, tore it open, and, heedless of their presence, devoured it, not only with her eyes, but with her parted lips and eager hands. When she looked up again, her cheeks had a tinge of colour in them; her eyes shone like faceted jewels; her smile was radiant and infectious. With no regard for appearances, she buttoned the note in the bosom of her dress.

"Now we will look for the purse," she said. "But come in, Mr. Guest—you are still standing at the door. I shall think you are offended with me. Oh, how hot the room is!—and the lilac is stifling. First the windows open! And then this scarf off, and some more light. You will help me to look, will you not?"

It was to Maurice she spoke, with a childlike upturning of her face to his—an irresistibly confiding gesture. She disappeared behind the screen, and came out bareheaded, nestling with both hands at the coil of hair on her neck. Then she lit two candles that stood on the piano in brass candlesticks, and Maurice lighted her round the room, while she searched in likely and unlikely places—inside the piano, in empty vases, in the folds of the curtains—laughing at herself as she did so, until Madeleine said that this was only nonsense, and came after them herself. When Maurice held the candle above the writing-table, he lighted three large photographs of Schilsky, one more dandified than the other; and he was obliged to raise his other hand to steady the candlestick.

At last, following a hint from Madeleine, they discovered the purse between the back of the sofa and the seat; and now Louise remembered that it had been in the pocket of her dressing-gown that afternoon.

"How stupid of me! I might have known," she said contritely. "So many things have gone down there in their day. Once a silver hair-brush that I was fond of; and I sometimes look there when bangles or hat-pins are missing," and letting her eyes dance at Maurice, she threw back her head and laughed.

Here, however, another difficulty arose; except for a few nickel coins, the purse was found to contain only gold, and the required change could not be made up.

"Never mind; take one of the twenty-mark pieces," she urged. "Yes, Madeleine, I would rather you did;" and when Madeleine hinted that Maurice might not find it too troublesome to come back with the change the following day, she turned to the young man, and saying: "Yes, if Mr. Guest would be so kind," smiled at him with such a gracious warmth that it was all he could do to reply with a decent unconcern.

But the hands of the clock on the writing-table were nearing half-past eleven, and now it was she who referred to the lateness of the hour.

"Thank you very much," she said to Maurice on parting. "And you must forget the nonsense I talked this evening. I didn't mean it—not a word of it." She laughed and held out her hand. "I wouldn't shake hands with you this afternoon, but now—if you will? For to-night I am not superstitious. Nothing bad will happen; I'm sure of that. And I am very much obliged to you—for everything. Good night."

Only a few minutes back, he had been steeped in pity for her; now it seemed as if no one had less need of pity or sympathy than she. He was bewildered, and went home to pass alternately from a mood of rapture to one of jealous despair. And the latter was torturous, for, as they walked, Madeleine had let fall such a vile suspicion that he had parted from her in anger, calling as he went that if he believed what she said to be true, he would never put faith in a human being again.

In the light of the morning, of course, he knew that it was incredible, a mere phantasm born of the dark; and towards four o'clock that afternoon, he called at the *Brüderstrasse* with the change. But Louise was not at home, and as he did not find her in on three successive days, he did not venture to return. He wrote his name on a card, and left this, together with the money, in an envelope.

X

AFTER parting from the rest, Dove and the two Cayhills continued their way in silence: they were in the shadow thrown by the steep vaulting of the *Thomaskirche,* before a word was exchanged between them. Johanna had several times glanced inquiringly at her sister, but Ephie had turned away her head, so that only the outline of her cheek was visible, and as Dove had done exactly the same, Johanna could only conclude that the two had fallen out. It was something novel for her to be obliged to talk when Ephie was present, but it was impossible for them to walk the whole way home as mum as this, especially as Dove had already heaved more than one deep sigh.

So, as they turned into the *Promenade,* Johanna said with a jerk, and with an aggressiveness that she could not subdue: "Well, that is the first and the last time anyone shall persuade me to go to a so-called opera by Wagner."

"Is not that just a little rash?" asked Dove. He smiled, unruffled, with a suggestion of patronage; but there was also a preoccupation in his manner, which showed that he was thinking of other things.

"You call that music," said Johanna, although he had done nothing of the kind. "I call it noise. I am not musical myself, thank goodness, but at least I know a tune when I hear one."

"If my opinion had been asked, I should certainly have suggested something lighter—*Lohengrin* or *Tannhäuser,* for instance," said Dove.

"You would have aone us a favour if you had," replied Johanna; and she meant what she said, in more ways than one. She had been at a loss to account for Ephie's sudden longing to hear *Die Walküre,* and had gone to the theatre against her will, simply because she never thwarted Ephie if she could avoid it. Now, after she had heard the opera, she felt aggrieved with Dove as well; as far as she had been able to gather from his vague explanations, from the bawling of the singers, and from subsequent events, the first act treated of relations so infamous that, by common consent, they are considered non-existent; and

Johanna was of the opinion that, instead of being so ready to take tickets for them, Dove might have let drop a hint of the nature of the piece Ephie wished to see.

After this last remark of Johanna's there was another lengthy pause. Then Dove, looking fondly at what he could see of Ephie's cheek, said: "I am afraid Miss Ephie has not enjoyed it either; she is so quiet—so unlike herself."

Ephie, who had been staring into the darkness, bit her lip: he was at it again. After the unfriendly way in which Maurice Guest had deserted her, and forced her into Dove's company, Dove had worried her right down the *Grimmaischestrasse,* to know what the matter was, and how he had offended her. She felt exasperated with every one, and if he began his worryings again, would have to vent her irritation somehow.

"Ephie has only herself to blame if she didn't enjoy it; she was bent on going," said Johanna, in the mildly didactic manner she invariably used towards her sister. "But I think she is only tired—or a little cross."

"Oh, that is not likely," Dove hastened to interpose.

"I am not cross, Joan," said Ephie angrily. "And if it was my fault you had to come—I've enjoyed myself very much, and I shall go again, as often as I like. But I won't be teased—I won't indeed!"

This was the sharpest answer Johanna had ever received from Ephie. She looked at her in dismay, but made no response, for of nothing was Johanna more afraid than of losing the goodwill Ephie bore her. Mentally she put her sister's pettishness down to the noise and heat of the theatre, and it was an additional reason for bearing Wagner and his music a grudge. Dove also made no further effort to converse connectedly, but his silence was of a conciliatory kind, and, as they advanced along the *Promenade,* he could not deny himself the pleasure of drawing the pretty, perverse child's attention to the crossings, the ruts in the road, the best bits of pavement, with a: "Walk you here, Miss Ephie," "Take care," "Allow me," himself meanwhile dancing from one side of the footpath to the other, until the young girl was almost distracted.

"I can see for myself, thank you. I have eyes in my head as well as anyone else," she exclaimed at length; and to Johanna's amazed: "Ephie!" she retorted: "Yes, Joan, you think no one has a right to be rude but yourself."

Johanna was more hurt by these words than she would have confessed. She had hitherto believed that Ephie—

affectionate, lazy little Ephie—accepted her individual pecu-
liarities as an integral part of her nature: it had not occurred
to her that Ephie might be standing aloof and considering her
objectively—let alone mentally using such an unkind word as
rudeness of her. But Ephie's fit of ill-temper, for such it undoubtedly was, made Johanna see things differently; it hinted
at unsuspected, cold scrutinies in the past, and implied a somewhat laming care of one's words in the days to come, which
would render it difficult ever again to be one's perfectly natural
self.

Had Johanna not been so occupied with her own feelings,
she would have heard the near tears in Ephie's voice; it was
with the utmost difficulty that the girl kept them back, and at
the house-door, she had vanished up the stairs long before Dove
had finished saying good-night. In the corridor, she hesitated
whether or no, according to custom, she should go to her
mother's room. Then she put a brave face on it, and opened the
door.

"Here we are, mummy. Good night. I hope the evening
wasn't too long."

Long?—on the contrary the hours had flown. Mrs. Cayhill,
left to herself, had all the comfortable sensations of a tippler
in the company of his bottle. She could forge ahead, undeterred
by any sense of duty; she had not to interrupt herself to laugh
at Ephie's wit, nor was she troubled by Johanna's cold eye—
that eye which told more plainly than words, how her elder
daughter regarded her self-indulgence. Propped up in bed on
two pillows, she now laid down her book, and put out her hand
to draw Ephie to her.

"Did you enjoy it, darling? Were you amused? But you
will tell me all about it in the morning."

"Yes, mother, in the morning. I am a little tired—but it
was very sweet," said Ephie bravely. "Good night."

Mrs. Cayhill kissed her, and nodded in perfect contentment
at the pretty little figure before her. Ephie was free to go.
And at last she was in her own room—at last!

She hastily locked both doors, one leading to the passage and
one to her sister's room. A moment later, Johanna was at the
latter, trying to open it.

"Ephie! What is the matter? Why have you locked the
door? Open it at once, I insist upon it," she cried anxiously,
and as loudly as she dared, for fear of disturbing the other in-
mates of the house.

But Ephie begged hard not to be bothered; she had a bad headache, and only wanted to be quiet.

"Let me give you a powder," urged her sister. "You are so excited—I am sure you are not well;" and when this, too, was refused: "You had nothing but some tea, child—you must be hungry. And they have left our supper on the table."

No, she was not hungry, didn't want any supper, and was very sleepy.

"Well, at least unlock your door, begged Johanna, with visions of the dark practices which Ephie, the soul of candour, might be contemplating on the other side. "I will not come in, I promise you," she added.

"Oh, all right," said Ephie crossly. But as soon as she heard that Johanna had gone, she returned to the middle of the room without touching the door; and after standing undecided for a moment, as if not quite sure what was coming next, she sat down on a chair at the foot of the bed, and suddenly began to cry. The tears had been in waiting for so long that they flowed without effort, abundantly, rolling one over another down her cheeks; but she was careful not to make a sound; for, even when sobbing bitterly, she did not forget that at any moment Johanna might enter the adjoining room and overhear her. And then, what a fuss there would be! For Ephie was one of those fortunate people who always get what they want, and but rarely have occasion to cry. All her desires had moved low, near earth, and been easily fulfilled. Did she break her prettiest doll, a still prettier was forthcoming; did anything happen to cross wish or scheme of hers, half a dozen brains were at work to think out a compensation.

But now she wept in earnest, behind closed doors, for she had received an injury which no one could make good. And the more she thought of it, the more copiously her tears flowed. The evening had been one long tragedy of disappointment: her fevered anticipation beforehand, her early throbs of excitement in the theatre, her growing consternation as the evening advanced, her mortification at being slighted—a sensation which she experienced for the first time. Again and again she asked herself what she had done to be treated in this way. What had happened to change him?

She was sitting upright on her chair, letting the tears stream unchecked; her two hands lay upturned on her knee; in one of them was a diminutive lace handkerchief, rolled to a ball, with which now and then she dabbed away the hottest tears. The windows of the room were still open, the blinds undrawn, and the street-lamps threw a flickering mesh of light on the wall. In the glass that hung over the washstand, she saw her dim reflection: following an impulse, she dried her eyes, and, with trembling fingers, lighted two candles, one on each side of the mirror. By this uncertain light, she leant forward with both hands on the stand, and peered at herself with a new curiosity.

She was still just as she had come out of the theatre: a many-coloured silk scarf was twisted round her head, and the brilliant, dangling fringes, and the stray tendrils of hair that escaped, made a frame for the rounded oval of her face. And then her skin was so fine, her eyes were so bright, the straight lashes so black and so long!—she put her head back, looked at herself through half-closed lids, turned her face this way and that, even smiling, wet though her cheeks were, in order that she might see the even line of teeth, with their slightly notched edges. The smile was still on her lips when the tears welled up again, ran over, trickled down and dropped with a splash, she watching them, until a big, unexpected sob rose in her throat, and almost choked her. Yes, she was pretty—oh, very, very pretty! But it made what had happened all the harder to understand. How had he had the heart to treat her so cruelly?

She knelt down by the open window, and laid her head on the sill. The moon, a mere sharp line of silver, hung fine and slender, like a polished scimitar, above the dark mass of houses opposite. Turning her hot face up to it, she saw that it was new, and instantly felt a throb of relief that she had not caught her first glimpse of it through glass. She bowed her head to it, quickly, nine times running, and sent up a prayer to the deity of fortune that had its home there. Good luck!—the fulfilment of one's wish! She wished in haste, with tight-closed eyes—and who knew but what, the very next day, her wish might come true! Tired with crying, above all, tired of the grief itself, she began more and more to let her thoughts stray to the morrow. And having once yielded to the allurements of hope, she even endeavoured to make the best of the past evening, telling herself that she had not been alone for a single instant; he had really had no chance of speaking to her. In the next breath, of course, she reminded herself that he might easily have made a chance, had he wished; and a healthier feeling of resentment stole over her. Rising from her cramped position, she shut the window. She resolved to show him that she was not a person who could be

9

treated in this off-hand fashion; he should see that she was not
to be trifled with.

But she played with her unhappiness a little longer, and even
had an idea of throwing herself on the bed without undressing.
She was very sleepy, though, and the desire to be between the
cool, soft sheets was too strong to be withstood. She slipped out
of her clothes, leaving them just where they fell on the floor,
like round pools; and before she had finished plaiting her hair,
she was stifling a hearty yawn. But in bed, when the light was
out, she lay and stared before her.

"I am very, very unhappy. I shall not sleep a wink," she
said to herself, and sighed at the prospect of the night-watch.

But before five minutes had passed her closed hand relaxed,
and lay open and innocent on the coverlet; her breath came
regularly—she was fast asleep. The moon was visible for a
time in the setting of the unshuttered window; and when she
wakened next day, toward nine o'clock, the full morning sun
was playing on the bed.

For several months prior to this, Ephie had worshipped
Schilsky at a distance. The very first time she saw him play,
he had made a profound impression on her: he looked so earnest
and melancholy, so supremely indifferent to every one about him,
as he stood with his head bent to his violin. Then, too, he had
beautiful hands; and she did not know which she admired more,
his auburn hair with the big hat set so jauntily on it, or the
thrillingly impertinent way he had of staring at you—through
half-closed eyes, with his head well back—in a manner at once
daring and irresistible.

Having come through a period of low spirits, caused by an
acute consciousness of her own littleness and inferiority, Ephie
so far recovered her self-confidence that she was able to look at
her divinity when she met him; and soon after this, she made
the intoxicating discovery that not only did he return her look,
but that he also took notice of her, and deliberately singled her
out with his gaze. And the belief was pardonable on Ephie's
part, for Schilsky made it a point of honour to stare any pretty
girl into confusion; besides which, he had a habit of falling
into sheep-like reveries, in which he saw no more of what or
whom he looked at, than do the glassy eyes of the blind. More
than once, Ephie had blushed and writhed in blissful torture
under these stonily staring eyes.

From this to persuading herself that her feelings were returned was only a step. Events and details, lighter than puff-balls, were to her links of iron, which formed a wonderful chain of evidence. She went about nursing the idea that Schilsky desired an introduction as much as she did; that he was suffering from a romantic and melancholy attachment, which forbade him attempting to approach her.

At this date, she became an adept at inventing excuses to go to the Conservatorium when she thought he was likely to be there; and, suddenly grown rebellious, she shook off Johanna's protectorship, which until now had weighed lightly on her. She grew fastidious about her dress, studied before the glass which colours suited her best, and the effect of a particular bow or ribbon; while on the days she had her violin-lessons, she developed a coquetry which made nothing seem good enough to wear, and was the despair of Johanna. When Schilsky played at an *Abendunterhaltung,* she sat in the front row of seats, and made her hands ache with applauding. Afterwards she lay wakeful, with hot cheeks, and dreamt extravagant dreams of sending him great baskets and bouquets of flowers, with coloured streamers to them, such as the singers in the opera received on a gala night. And though no name was given, he would know from whom they came. But on the only occasion she tried to carry out the scheme, and ventured inside a florist's shop, her scant command of German, and the excessive circumstantiality of the matter, made her feel so uncomfortable that she had fled precipitately, leaving the shopman staring after her in surprise.

Things were at this pass when, one day late in May, Ephie went as usual to take her lesson. It was two o'clock on a cloudless afternoon, and so warm that the budding lilac in squares and gardens began to give out fragrance. In the whitewashed, many-windowed corridors of the Conservatorium, the light was harsh and shadowless; it jarred on one, wounded the nerves. So at least thought Schilsky, who was hanging about the top storey of the building, in extreme ill-humour. He had been forced to make an appointment with a man to whom he owed money; the latter had not yet appeared, and Schilsky lounged and swore, with his two hands deep in his pockets, and his sulkiest expression. But gradually, he found himself listening to the discordant tones of a violin—at first unconsciously, as we listen when our thoughts are elsewhere engaged, then more and more intently. In one of the junior masters' rooms, some one had begun to play scales in the third position, uncertainly,

with shrill feebleness, seeking out each note, only to produce it
falsely.　As this scraping worked on him, Schilsky could not
refrain from rubbing his teeth together, and screwing up his
face as though he had toothache; now that the miserable little
tones had successfully penetrated his ear, they hit him like so
many blows.

"Damn him for a fool!" he said savagely to himself, and
found an outlet for his irritation in repeating these words
aloud.　Then, however, as an *étude* was commenced, with an
impotence that struck him as purely vicious, he could endure
the torment no longer.　He had seen in the *Bureau* the particular master, and knew that the latter had not yet come upstairs.
Going to the room from which the sounds issued, he stealthily
opened the door.

A girl was standing with her back to him, and was so engrossed in playing that she did not hear him enter.　On seeing
this, he proposed to himself the schoolboy pleasure of creeping
up behind her and giving her a well-deserved fright.　He did
so, with such effect that, had he not caught it, her violin would
have fallen to the floor.

He took both her wrists in his, held them firm, and, from his
superior height—he was head and shoulders taller than Ephie
—looked down on the miscreant.　He recognised her now as a
pretty little American whom he had noticed from time to time
about the building; but—but . . . well, that she was as
astoundingly pretty as this, he had had no notion.　His eyes
strayed over her face, picking out all its beauties, and he felt
himself growing as soft as butter.　Besides, she had crimsoned
down to her bare, dimpled neck; her head drooped; her long
lashes covered her eyes, and a tremulous smile touched the
corners of her mouth, which seemed uncertain whether to laugh
or to cry—the short upper-lip trembled.　He felt from her
wrists, and saw from the uneasy movement of her breast, how
wildly her heart was beating—it was as if one held a bird in
one's hand.　His ferocity died away; none of the hard words he
had had ready crossed his lips; all he said, and in his gentlest
voice, was: "Have I frightened you?"　He was desperately
curious to know the colour of her eyes, and, as she neither answered him nor looked up, but only grew more and more confused, he let one of her hands fall, and taking her by the chin,
turned her face up to his.　She was forced to look at him for a
moment.　Upon which, he stooped and kissed her on the mouth,
three times, with a pause between each kiss.　Then, at a noise in

the corridor, he swung hastily from the room, and was just in time to avoid the master, against whom he brushed up in going out of the door.

Herr Becker looked suspiciously at his favourite pupil's tell-tale face and air of extreme confusion; and, throughout the lesson, his manner to her was so cold and short that Ephie played worse than ever before. After sticking fast in the middle of a passage, she stopped altogether, and begged to be allowed to go home. When she had gone, and some one else was playing, Herr Becker stood at the window and shook his head: round this innocent baby face he had woven several pretty fancies.

Meanwhile Ephie flew rather than walked home, and having reached her room unseen, flung herself on the bed, and buried her burning cheeks in the white coolness of the pillows. Johanna, finding her thus, a short time after, was alarmed, put questions of various kinds, felt sure the sun had been too hot for her, and finally stood over the bed, holding her unfailing remedy, a soothing powder for the nerves.

"Oh, do for goodness' sake, leave me alone, Joan," said Ephie. "I don't want your powders. I am all right. Just let me be."

She drank the mixture, however, and catching sight of Johanna's anxious face, and aware that she had been cross, she threw her arms round her sister, hugged her, and called her a "dear old darling Joan." But there was something in the stormy tenderness of the embrace, in the flushed cheeks and glittering eyes that made Johanna even more uneasy. She insisted upon Ephie lying still and trying to sleep; and, after taking off her shoes for her, and noiselessly drawing down the blinds, she went on tiptoe out of the room.

Ephie burrowed more deeply in her pillow, and putting both hands to her ears, to shut out the world, went over the details of what had happened. It was like a fairy-story. She walked lazily down the sunny corridor, entered the class-room, and took off her hat, which Herr Becker hung up for her, after having playfully examined it. She had just taken her violin from its case, when he remembered something he had to do in the *Bureau,* and went out of the room, bidding her practise her scales during his absence; she heard again and smiled at the funny accent with which he said: "Shust a moment." She saw the bare walls of the room, the dust that lay white on the lid on the piano, was conscious of the difficulties of C sharp minor. She even knew

the very note at which *he* had been beside her—without a word
of warning, as suddenly as though he had sprung from the earth.
She heard the cry she had given, and felt his hands—the hands
she had so often admired—clasp her wrists. He was so close
to her that she felt his breath, and knew the exact shape of the
diamond ring he wore on his little finger. She felt, too, rather
than saw the audacious admiration of his eyes; and his voice was
not the less caressing because a little thick. And then—then—
she burrowed more firmly, held her ears more tightly to, laughed
a happy, gurgling laugh that almost choked her: never, as long
as she lived, would she forget the feel of his moustache as it
scratched her lips!

When she rose and looked at herself in the glass, it seemed extraordinary that there should be no outward difference in her;
and for several days she did not lose this sensation of being
mysteriously changed. She was quieter than usual, and her
movements were a little languid, but a kind of subdued radiance
peeped through and shone in her eyes. She waited confidently
for something to happen: she did not herself know what it
would be, but, after the miracle that had occurred, it was
beyond belief that things could jog on in their old familiar
course; and so she waited and expected—at every letter the
postman brought, each time the door-bell rang, whenever she
went into the street.

But after a week had dragged itself to an end, and she had not
even seen Schilsky again, she grew restless and unsure; and
sometimes at night, when Johanna thought she was asleep, she
would stand at her window, and, with a very different face
from that which she wore by day, put countless questions to herself, all of which began with why and how. And Johanna was
again beset by the fear that Ephie was sickening for an illness,
for the child would pass from bursts of rather forced gaiety to
fits of real fretfulness, or sink into brown studies, from which
she wakened with a start. But if, on some such occasion, Johanna said to her: "Where *are* your thoughts, Ephie?" she
would only laugh, and answer, with a hug: "Wool-gathering,
you dear old bumble-bee!"

From the lesson following the eventful one, Ephie played
truant, on the ground of headache, partly because her fancy
pictured him lying in wait like an ogre to eat her up, and partly
from a poor little foolish fear lest he should think her too easily
won. Now, however, she blamed herself for not having given
him an opportunity to speak to her, and began to frequent the

Conservatorium assiduously. When, after ten long days, she saw him again, an unfailing instinct guided her aright.

It was in the vestibule, as she was leaving the building, and they met face to face. Directly she espied him, though her heart thumped alarmingly, Ephie tossed her head, gazed fixedly at some distant object, and was altogether as haughty as her parted lips would allow of. And she played her part so well that Schilsky's attention was arrested; he remembered who she was, and stared hard at her as she passed. Not only this, but pleased, he could not have told why, he turned and followed her out, and standing on the steps, looked after her. She went down the street with her head in the air, holding her dress very high to display a lace-befrilled petticoat, and clattering gracefully on two high-heeled, pointed shoes. He screwed up his eyes against the sun, in order to see her better—he was shortsighted, too, but vanity forbade him to wear glasses— and when, at the corner of the street, Ephie rather spoilt the effect of her behaviour by throwing a hasty glance back, he laughed and clicked his tongue against the roof of his mouth.

"*Verdammt!*" he said with expression.

And both on that day and the next, when he admired a well-turned ankle or a pretty petticoat, he was reminded of the provoking little American, with the tossed head and baby mouth.

A few days later, in the street that ran alongside the Gewandhaus, he saw her again.

Ephie, who, in the interval, had upbraided herself incessantly, was none the less, now the moment had come, about to pass as before—even more frigidly. But this time Schilsky raised his hat, with a tentative smile, and, in order not to appear childish, she bowed ever so slightly. When he was safely past, she could not resist giving a furtive look behind her, and at precisely the same moment, he turned, too. In spite of her trouble, Ephie found the coincidence droll; she tittered, and he saw it, although she immediately laid the back of her hand on her lips. It was not in him to let this pass unnoticed. With a few quick steps, he was at her side.

He took off his hat again, and looked at her not quite sure how to begin.

"I am happy to see you have not forgotten me," he said in excellent English.

Ephie had impulsively stopped on hearing him come up with her, and now, colouring deeply, tried to dig a hole in the pavement with the toe of her shoe. She, too, could not think what to say; and this, together with the effect produced on her by his peculiar lisp, made her feel very uncomfortable. She was painfully conscious of his insistent eyes on her face, as he waited for her to speak; but there was a distressing pause before he added: "And sorry to see you are still angry with me."

At this, she found her tongue. Looking, not at him, but at a passer-by on the opposite side of the street, she said: "Why, I guess I have a right to be."

She tried to speak severely, but her voice quavered, and once more the young man was not sure whether the trembling of her lip signified tears or laughter.

"Are you always so cruel?" he asked, with an intentness that made her eyes seek the ground again. "Such a little crime! Is there no hope for me?"

She attempted to be dignified. "Little! I am really not accustomed——"

"Then I'm not to be forgiven?"

His tone was so humble that suddenly she had to laugh. Shooting a quick glance at him, she said:

"That depends on how you behave in future. If you promise never to——"

Before the words were well out of her mouth, she was aware of her stupidity; her laugh ended, and she grew redder than before. Schilsky had laughed, too, quite frankly, and he continued to smile at the confusion she had fallen into. It seemed a long time before he said with emphasis: "That is the last thing in the world you should ask of me."

Ephie drooped her head, and dug with her shoe again; she had never been so tongue-tied as to-day, just when she felt she ought to say something very cold and decisive. But not an idea presented itself, and meanwhile he went on: "The punishment would be too hard. The temptation was so great."

As she was still obstinately silent, he stooped and peeped under the overhanging brim of her hat. "Such pretty lips!" he said, and then, as on the former occasion, he took her by the chin and turned her face up to his.

But she drew back angrily. "Mr. Schilsky! . . . how dare you! Take your hand away at once."

"There!—I have sinned again," he said, and folded his hands in mock supplication. "Now I am afraid you will never forgive me.—But listen, you have the advantage of me; you know my name. Will you not tell me yours?"

Having retreated a full yard from him, Ephie regained some of her native self-composure. For the first time, she found herself able to look straight at him. "No," she said, with a touch of her usual lightness. "I shall leave you to find it out for yourself; it will give you something to do."

They both laughed. "At least give me your hand," he said; and when he held it in his, he would not let her go, until, after much seeming reluctance on her part, she had detailed to him the days and hours of her lessons at the Conservatorium, and where he would be likely to meet her. As before, he stood and watched her go down the street, hoping that she would turn at the corner. But, on this day, Ephie whisked along in a great hurry.

On after occasions, he waylaid her as she came and went, and either stood talking to her, or walked the length of the street beside her. At the early hour of the afternoon when Ephie had her lessons, he did not need to fear being seen by acquaintances; the sunshine was undisturbed in the quiet street. The second time they met, he told her that he had found out what her name was; and his efforts to pronounce it afforded Ephie much amusement. Their conversation was always of the same nature, half banter, half earnest. Ephie, who had rapidly recovered her assurance, invariably began in her archest manner, and it became his special pleasure to reduce her, little by little, to a crimson silence.

But one day, about a fortnight later, she came upon him at a different hour, when he was not expecting to see her. He was strolling up and down in front of the Conservatorium, waiting for Louise, who might appear at any moment. Ephie had been restless all the morning, and had finally made an excuse to go out: her steps naturally carried her to the Conservatorium, where she proposed to study the notice-board, on the chance of seeing Schilsky. When she caught sight of him, her eyes brightened; she greeted him with an inviting smile, and a saucy remark. But Schilsky did not take up her tone; he cut her words short.

"What are you doing here to-day?" he asked with a frown of displeasure, meanwhile keeping a watchful eye on the inner staircase—visible through the glass doors—down which Louise would come. "I haven't a moment to spare."

Mortally offended by his manner, Ephie drew back her extended hand, and giving him a look of surprise and resentment, was about to pass him by without a further word. But this was more than Schilsky could bear; he put out his hand to stop her, always, though, with one eye on the door.

"Now, don't be cross, little girl," he begged impatiently. "It's not my fault—upon my word it isn't. I wasn't expecting to see you to-day—you know that. Look here, tell me—this sort of thing is so unsatisfactory—is there no other place I could see you? What do you do with yourself all day? Come, answer me, don't be angry."

Ephie melted. "Come and visit us on Sunday afternoon," she said. "We are always at home then."

He laughed rudely, and took no notice of her words. "Come, think of something—quick!" he said.

He was on tenter-hooks to be gone, and showed it. Ephie grew flustered, and though she racked her brains, could make no further suggestion.

"Oh well, if you can't, you know," he said crossly, and loosened his hold of her arm.

Then, at the last moment, she had a flash of inspiration; she remembered how, on the previous Sunday, Dove had talked enthusiastically of an opera-performance, which, if she were not mistaken, was to take place the following night. Dove had declared that all musical Leipzig would probably be present in the theatre. Surely she might risk mentioning this, without fear of another snub.

"I am going to the opera to-morrow night," she said in a small, meek voice, and was on the verge of tears.

Schilsky hardly heard her; Louise had appeared at the head of the stairs. "The very thing," he said. "I shall look out for you there, little girl. Good-bye. *Auf Wiedersehen!*"

He went down the steps, without even raising his hat, and when Louise came out, he was sauntering towards the building again, as if he had come from the other end of the street.

Ephie went home in a state of anger and humiliation which was new to her. For the first few hours, she was resolved never to speak to Schilsky again. When this mood passed, she made up her mind that he should atone for his behaviour to the last iota: he should grovel before her; she would scarcely deign to look at him. But the nearer the time came for their meeting, the more were her resentful feelings swallowed up by the wish to see him. She counted off the hours till the opera commenced; she concocted a scheme to escape Johanna's surveillance; she had a story ready, if it should be necessary, of how she had once been introduced to Schilsky. Her fingers trembled with impatience as she fastened on a pretty new dress, which had just been sent home: a light, flowered stuff, with narrow bands of black velvet artfully applied so as to throw the fairness of her hair and skin into relief.

The consciousness of looking her best gave her manner a light sureness that was very charming. But from the moment they entered the *foyer,* Ephie's heart began to sink: the crowd was great; she could not see Schilsky; and in his place came Dove, who was not to be shaken off. Even Maurice was bad enough—what concern of his was it how she enjoyed herself? When, finally, she did discover the person she sought, he was with some one else, and did not see her; and when she had succeeded in making him look, he frowned, shook his head, and made angry signs that she was not to speak to him, afterwards going downstairs with the sallow girl in white. What did it mean? All through the tedious second act, Ephie wound her handkerchief round and round, and in and out of her fingers. Would it never end? How long would the fat, ugly Brünnhilde stand talking to Siegmund and the woman who lay so ungracefully between his knees? As if it mattered a straw what these sham people did or felt! Would he speak to her in the next interval, or would he not?

The side curtains had hardly swept down before she was up from her seat, hurrying Johanna away. This time she chose to stand against the wall, at the end of the *foyer.* After a short time, he came in sight, but he had no more attention to spare for her than before; he did not even look in her direction. Her one consolation was that obviously he was not enjoying himself; he wore a surly face, was not speaking, and, to a remark the girl in white made, he answered by an angry flap of the hand. When they had twice gone past in this way, and she had each time vainly put herself forward, Ephie began to take an interest in what Dove was saying, to smile at him and coquet with him, and the more openly, the nearer Schilsky drew. Other people grew attentive, and Dove went into a seventh heaven, which made it hard for him placidly to accept the fit of pettish silence, she subsequently fell into.

The crowning touch was put to this disastrous evening by the fact that Schilsky's companion of the *foyer* walked the greater part of the way home with them; and, what was worse, that she took not the slightest notice of Ephie.

XI

BEFORE leaving her bedroom the following morning, Ephie wrote on her scented pink paper a short letter, which began: "Dear Mr. Schilsky," and ended with: "Your sincere friend, Euphemia Stokes Cayhill." In this letter, she "failed to understand" his conduct of the previous evening, and asked him for an explanation. Not until she had closed the envelope, did she remember that she was ignorant of his address. She bit the end of her pen, thinking hard, and directly breakfast was over, put on her hat and slipped out of the house.

It was the first time Ephie had had occasion to enter the *Bureau* of the Conservatorium; and, when the heavy door had swung to behind her, and she was alone in the presence of the secretaries, each of whom was bent over a high desk, writing in a ledger, her courage almost failed her. The senior, an old, white-haired man, with a benevolent face, did not look up; but after she had stood hesitating for some minutes, an under-secretary solemnly laid down his pen, and coming to the counter, wished in English to know what he could do for her. Growing very red, Ephie asked him if he "would . . . could . . . would please tell her where Mr. Schilsky lived."

Herr Kleefeld leaned both hands on the counter, and disconcerted her by staring at her over his spectacles.

"Mr. Schilsky? Is it very important?" he said with a leer, as if he were making a joke.

"Why, yes, indeed," replied Ephie timidly.

He nodded his head, more to himself than to her, went back to his desk, opened another ledger, and ran his finger down a page, repeating aloud as he did so, to her extreme embarrassment: "Mr. Schilsky—let me see. Mr. Schilsky—let me see."

After a pause, he handed her a slip of paper, on which he had painstakingly copied the address: "*Talstrasse,* 12 III."

"Why, I thank you very much. I have to ask him about some music. Is there anything to pay?" stammered Ephie.

But Herr Kleefeld, leaning as before on the counter, shook his head from side to side, with a waggish air, which confused Ephie still more. She made her escape, and left him there, still wagging, like a china Mandarin.

Having addressed the letter in the nearest post office, she entered a confectioner's and bought a pound of chocolate creams; so that when Johanna met her in the passage, anxious and angry at her leaving the house without a word, she was able to assert that her candy-box had been empty, and she felt she could not begin to practise till it was refilled. But Johanna was very cantankerous, and obliged her to study an hour overtime to atone for her escapade.

Then followed for Ephie several unhappy days, when all the feeling she seemed capable of concentrated itself on the visits of the postman. She remained standing at the window until she had seen him come up the street, and she was regularly the first to look through the mails as they lay on the lobby table. Two days brought no reply to her letter. On the third fell a lesson, which she was resolved not to take. But when the hour came, she dressed herself with care and went as usual. Schilsky was nowhere to be seen. Half a week later, the same thing was repeated, except that on this day, she made herself prettier than ever: she was like some gay, garden flower, in a big white hat, round the brim of which lay scarlet poppies, and a dress of a light blue, which heightened the colour of her cheeks, and, reflected in her eyes, made them bluer than a fjord in the sun. But her spirits were low; if she did not see him this time, despair would crush her.

But she did—saw him while she was still some distance off, standing near the portico of the Conservatorium; and at the sight of him, after the uncertainty she had gone through during the past week, she could hardly keep back her tears. He did not come to meet her; he stood and watched her approach, and only when she reached him, indolently held out his hand. As she refused to notice it, and went to the extreme edge of the pavement to avoid it, he made a barrier of his arms, and forced her to stand still. Holding her thus, with his hand on her elbow, he looked keenly at her; and, in spite of the obdurate way in which she kept her eyes turned from him, he saw that she was going to cry. For a moment he hesitated, afraid of the threatening scene, then, with a decisive movement, he took her violin-case out of her hand. Ephie made an ineffectual effort to get possession of it again, but he held it above her reach, and saying: "Wait a minute," ran up the steps. He came back without it, and throwing a swift glance round him, took the young girl's arm, and walked her off at a brisk pace to the woods. She made a few, faint protests. But he replied: "You and I have something to say to each other, little girl."

A full hour had elapsed when Ephie appeared again. She was alone, and walked quickly, casting shy glances from side to side. On reaching the Conservatorium, she waited in a quiet corner of the vestibule for nearly a quarter of an hour, before Schilsky sauntered in, and released her violin from the keeping of the janitor, a good friend of his.

They had not gone far into the wood; Schilsky knew of a secluded seat, which was screened by a kind of boscage; and here they had remained. At first, Ephie had cried heartily, in happy relief, and he had not been able to console her. He had come to meet her with many good resolutions, determined not to let the little affair, so lightly begun, lead to serious issues; but Ephie's tears, and the tale they told, and the sobbed confessions that slipped out unawares, made it hard for him to be wise. He put his arm round her, dried her tears with his own handkerchief, kissed the hand he held. And when he had in this way petted her back to composure, she suddenly looked up in his face, and, with a pretty, confiding movement, said:

"Then you do care for me a little?"

It would have need a stronger than he to answer otherwise. "Of course I do," was easily said, and to avoid the necessity of more, he kissed the pink dimples at the base of her four fingers, as well as the baby crease that marked the wrist. The poppy-strewn hat lay on the seat beside them; the fluffy head and full white throat were bare; in the mellow light of the trees, the lashes looked jet-black on her cheeks; at each word, he saw her small, even teeth: and he was so unnerved by the nearness of all this fresh young beauty that, when Ephie with her accustomed frankness had told him everything he cared to know, he found himself saying, in place of what he had intended, that they must be very cautious. In the meantime, it would not do for them to be seen together: it might injure his prospects, be harmful to his future.

"Yes, but afterwards?" she asked him promptly.

He kissed her cheek. But she repeated the question, and he was obliged to reply: that would be a different matter. It was now her turn to be curious, and one of the first questions she put related to the dark girl he had been with at the theatre. Playing lightly with her fingers, Schilsky told her that this was one of his best friends, some one he had known for a long,

long time, to whom he owed much, and whom he could under no circumstances offend. Ephie looked grave for a moment; and, in the desire of provoking a pretty confession, he asked her if she had minded very much seeing him with some one else. But she made him wince by responding with perfect candour: "With her? Oh, no! She's quite old."

Before parting, they arranged the date of the next meeting, and, a beginning once made, they saw each other as often as was feasible. Ephie grew wonderfully apt at excuses for going out at odd times, and for prolonged absences. Sound fictions were needed to satisfy Johanna, and even Maurice Guest was made to act as dummy: he had taken her for a walk, or they had been together to see Madeleine Wade; and by these means, and also by occasionally shirking a lesson, she gained a good deal of freedom. Johanna would as soon have thought of herself being untruthful as of doubting Ephie, whom she had never known to tell a lie; and if she did sometimes feel jealous of all the new claims made on her little sister's attention, such a feeling was only temporary, and she was, for the most part, content to see Ephie content.

At night, in her own room, lying wakeful with hot cheeks and big eyes, Ephie went over in memory all that had taken place at their last meeting, or built high, top-heavy castles for the future. She was absurdly happy; and her mother and sister had never found her more charming and lovable, or richer in those trifling inspirations for brightening life, which happiness brings with it. She looked forward with secret triumph to the day when she would be able to announce her engagement to the celebrated young violinist, and the only shadow on her happiness was that she could not do this immediately. It did not once cross her mind to doubt the issue: she had always had her way, and, in her own mind, had long since arranged just how this matter was to fall out. She would return to America—where, of course, they would live—and get her clothes ready, and then he would come, and they would be married—a big wedding, with descriptions in the newspapers. They would have a big house, and he would play at concerts—as she had once heard Sarasate play in New York—and every one would stand on tiptoe to see him. She sat proud and conspicuous in the front row. "His wife. That is his wife!" people whispered, and they drew respectfully back to let her pass, as, in a very becoming dress, she swept into the little room behind the platform, which she alone was permitted to enter.

One day at this time there was a violent thunderstorm. Towards midday, the eastern sky grew black with clouds, which, for hours, had been ominously gathering; a sudden wind rose and swept the dust house-high through the streets; the thunder rumbled, and each roll came nearer. When, after a prolonged period of expectation, the storm finally burst, there was a universal sigh of relief.

The afternoon was damply refreshing. As soon as the rain ceased, Maurice shut his piano, and walked at a brisk pace to Connewitz, his head bared beneath the overhanging branches, which were still weighed down by their burden of drops. At the *Waldcafé* on the bank of the river, in a thickly grown arbour which he entered to drink a glass of beer, he found Philadelphia Jensen and the pale little American, Fauvre, taking coffee.

The lady welcomed him with a large, outstretched hand, in the effusively hearty manner with which she, as it were, took possession of people; and towards six o'clock, the three walked back through the woods together, Miss Jensen, resolute of bust as of voice, slightly ahead of her companions, carrying her hat in her hand, Fauvre dragging behind, hitting indolently at stones and shrubs, and singing scraps of melodies to himself in his deep baritone.

Miss Jensen, who had once been a journalist, was an earnest worker for woman's emancipation, and having now successfully mounted her hobby, spoke with a thought-deadening eloquence. Maurice had never been called on to think about the matter, and listened to her words absent-mindedly, comparing her, as she swept along, to a ship in full sail. She was just asserting that the ordinary German woman was little more than means to an end, the end being the man-child, when his attention was arrested, and, in an instant, jerked far away from Miss Jensen's theories. As they reached the bend of a path, a sound of voices came to them through the trees, and on turning a corner, Maurice caught a glimpse of two people who were going in the opposite direction, down a side-walk—a passing but vivid glimpse of a light, flowered dress, of a grey suit of clothes, and auburn hair. Ephie! He could have sworn to voice and dress; but to whom in all the world was she talking so confidentially? At the name that rose to his lips, he almost stopped short, but the next moment he was afraid lest his companions should also have seen who it was, and, quickening his steps, he incited Miss Jensen to talk on. First, however, that lady said in a surprised tone: " Say, that was Mr. Schilsky, wasn't it? Who was the lady? Did you perceive?" So there was no possible doubt of it.

After parting from his companions, he did an errand in the town, and from there went to the Cayhills' *Pension,* determined to ascertain whether it had really been Ephie he had seen, and if so, what the meaning of it was.

Mrs. Cayhill and Johanna were in the sitting-room; Johanna looked very surprised to see him. They had this moment risen from the supper-table, she told him; Ephie had only just got home in time. Before anything further could be said, Ephie herself came into the room; her face was flushed, and she did not seem well-pleased at his unexpected visit. She hardly greeted him, and instead, commenced talking about the weather.

" Then you had a pleasant walk?" asked Johanna in a preoccupied fashion, without looking up from the letter she was writing; and before Maurice could speak, Ephie, fondling her sister's neck, answered: " How could it be anything but sweet—after the rain?"

In the face of this frankness, it was on Maurice's tongue to say: " Then it was you, I saw?" but again she did not give him time. Still standing behind Johanna's chair, her eyes fixed on the young man's face with a curious intentness, she continued: " We walked right to Connewitz and back without a rest."

" I don't think you should take her so far," said Mrs. Cayhill, looking up from her book with her kindly smile. " She has never been used to walking and is easily tired—aren't you, my pet?"

" Yes, and then she can't get up the next morning," said Johanna, mildly dogmatic, considering the following sentence of her letter.

Gradually it broke upon Maurice that Ephie had been making use of his name. His consternation at the discovery was such that he changed colour. The others, however, were both too engrossed to notice it. Ephie grew scarlet, but continued to rattle on, covering his silence.

" Well, perhaps to-day it was a little too far," she admitted. " But mummy, I won't have you say I'm not strong. Why, Herr Becker is always telling me how full my tone is getting. Yes indeed. And look at my muscle."

She turned back the loose sleeve of her blouse, baring almost

10

the whole of her rounded arm; then, folding it sharply to her, she invited one after another to test its firmness.

"Quite a prize-fighter, I declare!" laughed Mrs. Cayhill, at the same time drawing her little daughter to her, to kiss her. But Johanna frowned, and told Ephie to put down her sleeve at once; there was something in the childish action that offended the elder sister, she did not know why. But Maurice had first to lay two of his fingers on the soft skin, and then to help her to button the cuff.

When, soon after this, he took his leave, Ephie went out of the room with him. In the dark passage, she caught at his hand.

"Morry, you mustn't tell tales on me," she whispered; and added pettishly: "Why ever did you just come to-night?"

He tried to see her face. "What is it all about, Ephie?" he asked. "Then it *was* you, I saw, in the *Nonne*—by the weir?"

"Me? In the *Nonne!*" She was genuinely surprised. "You saw me?"

He nodded. By the light that came from the stairs as she opened the hall-door, she noticed that he looked troubled, and an impulse rose in her to throw her arms round his neck and say: "Yes, yes, it was me. Oh, Morry, I am so happy!" But she remembered the reasons for secrecy that had been imposed on her, and, at the same time, felt somewhat defiantly inclined towards Maurice. After all, what business was it of his? Why should he take her to task for what she chose to do? And so she merely laughed, with assumed merriment, her own charming, assuaging laugh.

"In the wood?—you old goose! Listen, Morry, I told them I had been with you, because—why, because one of the girls in my class asked me to go to the *Café Français* with her, and we stayed too long, and ate too much ice-cream, and Joan doesn't like it, and I knew she would be cross—that's all! Don't look so glum, you silly! It's nothing," and she laughed again.

As long as this laugh rang in his ears—to the bottom of the street, that is—he believed her. Then, the evidence of his senses reasserted itself, and he knew that what she had told him was false. He had heard her voice in the wood too distinctly to allow of any mistake, and she was still wearing the same dress. Besides, she had lied so artlessly to the others, without a tremor of her candid eyes—why should she not lie to him, too? She was less likely to be considerate of him than of

Johanna. But his distress at her skill in deceit was so great that he said: "Ephie, little Ephie!" aloud to himself, just as he might have done had he heard that she was stricken down by a mortal illness.

On the top of this, however, came less selfish feelings. What was almost a sense of guilt took possession of him; he felt as if, in some way, he were to blame for what had happened; as if nature had intended him to stand in the place of a brother to this pretty, thoughtless child. And yet what could he have done? He did not now see Ephie as often as formerly, and hardly ever alone; on looking back, he began to suspect that she had purposely avoided him. The exercises in harmony, which had previously brought them together, had been discontinued. First, she had said that her teacher was satisfied with what she herself could do; then, that he had advised her to give up harmony altogether: she would never make anything of it. In the light of what had come to pass, Maurice saw that he had let himself be duped by her; she had lied then as now.

He puzzled his brains to imagine how she had learned to know Schilsky in the first instance, and when the affair had begun: what he had overheard that afternoon implied an advanced stage of intimacy; and he revolved measures by means of which a stop might be put to it. The only course he could think of was to lay the matter before Johanna; and yet what would the use of that be? Ephie would deny everything, make his story ludicrous, himself impossible, and never forgive him into the bargain. In the end, he might do more good by watching over her silently, at a distance. If it had only not been Schilsky who was concerned! Some of the ugly stories he had heard related of the young man rose up and took vivid shape before his eyes. If any harm came to Ephie, he alone would be to blame for it; not Johanna, only he knew the frivolous temptations the young girl was exposed to. Why, in Heaven's name, had he not taken both her hands, as they stood in the passage, and insisted on her confessing to him? No, credulous as usual, he had once more allowed himself to be hoodwinked and put off.

Thus he fretted, without arriving at any clearer conclusion than this: that he had unwittingly been made accessory to an unpleasant secret. But where his mind baulked, and refused to work, was when he tried to understand what all this might mean to the third person involved. Did Louise know or suspect anything? Had she, perhaps, for weeks past been suffering under the knowledge?

He stood irresolute, at the crossing where the *Mozartstrasse* joined the *Promenade.* A lamp-lighter was beginning his rounds; he came up with his long pole to the lamp at the corner, and, with a mild explosion, the little flame sprang into life. Maurice turned on his heel and went to see Madeleine.

The latter was making her supper off tea, bread, and cold sausage, and when she heard that he had not eaten, she set a cup and plate before him, and was glad that she happened to be late. Propped open on the table was a Danish Grammar, which she conned as she ate; for, in the coming holidays, she was engaged to go to Norway, as guide and travelling-companion to a party of Englishwomen.

"I had a letter from London to-day," she said, "with definite arrangements. So I at once bought this book. I intend to try and master at least the rudiments of the language— barbarous though it is—for I want to get some good from the journey. And if one has one's wits about one, much can be learnt from cab-drivers and railway-porters."

She traced on a map with her forefinger the route they proposed to follow, and laughed at the idea of the responsibility lying heavy on her. But when they had finished their supper, and she had talked informingly for a time of Norway, its people and customs, she looked at the young man, who sat irresponsive and preoccupied, and considered him attentively.

"Is anything the matter to-night? Or are you only tired?"

He was tired. But though she herself had suggested it, she was not satisfied with his answer.

"Something has bothered you. Has your work gone badly?"

No, it was nothing of that sort. But Madeleine persisted: could she be of any help to him?

"The merest trifle—not worth talking about."

The twilight had grown thick around them; the furniture of the room lost its form, and stood about in shapeless masses. Through the open window was heard the whistle of a distant train; a large fly that had been disturbed buzzed distractingly, undecided where to re-settle for the night. It was sultry again, after the rain.

"Look here, Maurice," Madeleine said, when she had observed him for some time in silence. "I don't want to be

officious, but there's something I should like to say to you.
It's this. You are far too soft-hearted. If you want to get on
in life, you must think more about yourself than you do. The
battle is to the strong, you know, and the strong, within limits,
are certainly the selfish. Let other people look after themselves; try not to mind how foolish they are—you can't improve them. It's harder, I daresay, than it is to be a person of
unlimited sympathies; it's harder to pass the maimed and crip-
pled by, than to stop and weep over them, and feel their sufferings through yourself. But *you* have really something in
you to occupy yourself with. You're not one of those people
—I won't mention names!—whose own emptiness forces them
to take an intense interest in the doings of others, and who, the
moment they are alone with their thoughts, are bored to desperation. Just as there are people who have no talent for making
a home home-like, and are only happy when they are out
of it."

Here she laughed at her own seriousness.

"But you are smiling inwardly, and thinking: the real old
school-marm!"

"You don't practise what you preach, Madeleine. Besides,
you're mistaken. At heart, I'm a veritable egoist."

She contradicted him. "I know you better than you know
yourself."

He did not reply, and a silence fell, in which the commonplace words she had last said, went on sounding and resounding, until they had no more likeness to themselves. Madeleine
rose, and pushed back her chair, with a grating noise.

"I must light the lamp. Sitting in the dark makes for
foolishness. Come, wake up, and tell me what plans you have
for the holidays."

"If I had a sister, I should like her to be like you," said
Maurice, watching her busy with the lamp. "Clear-headed,
and helpful to a fellow."

"I suppose men always will continue to consider that the
greatest compliment they can pay," said Madeleine, and turned
up the light so high that they both blinked.—And then she
scolded the young man soundly for his intention of remaining
in Leipzig during the holidays.

But when he rose to go, she said, with an impulsiveness that
was foreign to her: "I wish you had a friend."

It was his turn to smile. "Have you had enough of me?"

Madeleine, who was sitting with crossed arms, remained

grave. " I mean a man. Some one older than yourself, and
who has had experience. The best-meaning woman in the
world doesn't count."

Only a very few days later, an occasion offered when, with
profit to himself, he might have acted upon Madeleine's in-
troductory advice. He had been for a quick, solitary walk,
and was returning, in the evening between nine and ten o'clock,
along one of the paths of the wood, when suddenly, and close
at hand, he heard the sound of voices. He stopped in-
stantaneously, for by the jump his heart gave, he knew that
Louise was one of the speakers. What she said was inaudible
to him; but it was enough to be able to listen, unseen, to her
voice. Hearing it like this, as something existing for itself, he
was amazed at its depth and clearness; he felt that her personal presence had, until now, hindered him from appreciating
a beautiful but immaterial thing at its true worth. At first,
like a cadence that repeats itself, its tones rose and fell, but
with more subtle inflections than the ordinary voice has: there
was a note in it that might have belonged to a child's voice;
another, more primitive, that betrayed feeling with as little
reserve as the cry of an animal. Then it sank, and went on
in a monotone, like a Hebrew prayer, as if reiterating things
worn threadbare by repetition, and already said too often.
Gradually, it died away in the surrounding silence. There was
no response but a gentle rustling of the leaves overhead. It
began anew, and, in the interval, seemed to have gained in intensity; now there was a bitterness in it which, when it swelled,
made it give out a tone like the roughly touched strings of an
instrument; it seemed to be accusing, to be telling of unmerited
suffering. And, this time, it elicited a reply, but a casual, indifferent one, which might have related to the weather, or to
the time of night. Louise gave a shrill laugh, and then, as
plainly as if the words were being carved in stone before his
eyes, Maurice heard her say: " You have never given me a
moment's happiness."

As before, no answer was returned, and almost immediately
his ear caught a muffled sound of footsteps. At the same moment, a night-wind shook the tree-tops; there was a general
fluttering and swaying around him; and he came back to himself to find that he was standing rigid, holding on to a slender
tree that grew close by the path. His first conscious thought
was that this wind meant rain . . . there would be another
storm in the night . . . and the summer holidays—time of

partings—were at the door. She would go away . . . and he would perhaps never see her again.

Since the evening they had walked home from the theatre together, he had had no further chance of speaking to her. If they met in the street, she gave him, as Madeleine had foretold of her, a nod and a smile; and from this coolness, he had drawn the foolish inference that she wished to avoid him. Abnormally sensitive, he shrank out of her way. But now, the mad sympathy that had permeated him on the night she had made him her confidant grew up in him again; it swelled out into something monstrous—a gigantic pity that rebounded on himself. For he knew now why she suffered; and he was cast down both for her and for himself. It seemed unnatural that he was debarred from giving her just a fraction of the happiness she craved—he, who, had there been the least need for it, would have lain himself down for her to tread on. And in some of the subsequent nights when he could not sleep, he composed fantastic letters to her, in which he told her this and more, only to colour guiltily, with the return of daylight, at the impertinent folly of his thoughts.

But he could not forget the words he had heard her say; they haunted him like an importunate refrain. Even his busiest hours were set to them—" You have never given me a moment's happiness "—and they were alike a torture and a joy.

XII

THE second half of July scattered the little circle in all directions. Maurice spent a couple of days at the different railway-stations, seeing his friends off. One after another they passed into that anticipatory mood, which makes an egoist of the prospective traveller: his thoughts start, as it were, in advance; he has none left for the people who are remaining behind, and receives their care and attention as his due.

Dove was packed and strapped, ready to set out an hour after he had had his last lesson; and while he printed labels for his luggage, and took a circumstantial leave of his landlady and her family, with whom he was a prime favourite by reason of his decent and orderly habits, Maurice fetched for him from the lending library, the pieces of music set by Schwarz as a holiday-task. Dove was on tenter-hooks to be off. Of late, things had gone superlatively well with him: he had performed with applause in an *Abendunterhaltung,* and been highly commended by Schwarz; while, as for Ephie, she had been so sweet and winning, so modestly encouraging of his suit, that he had every reason to hope for success in this quarter also. Too dutiful a son, however, to take, unauthorised, such an important step as that of proposing marriage, he was now travelling home to sound two elderly people, resident in a side street in Peterborough, on the advisability of an American daughter-in-law.

The Cayhills had been among the first to leave, and would be absent till the middle of September. One afternoon, Maurice started them from the *Thüringer Bahnhof,* on their journey to Switzerland. Having seen Mrs. Cayhill comfortably settled with her bags, books and cushions, in the corner of a first-class carriage, and given Johanna assistance with the tickets, he stood till the train went, talking to Ephie; and he long retained a picture of her, standing with one foot on the step, in a becoming travelling-dress, a hat with a veil flying from it, and a small hand-bag slung across her shoulder, laughing and dimpling, and well aware of the admiring glances that were cast at her. It was a relief to Maurice that she was going away for a time; his feeling of responsibility with regard to her had not flagged, and he had made a point of seeing her more often, and of knowing more of her movements than before. As, however, he had not observed anything further to disturb him, his suspicions were on the verge of subsiding—as suspicions have a way of doing when we wish them to—and in the last day or two, he had begun to feel much less sure, and to wonder if, after all, he had not been mistaken.

" I shall miss you, Morry. I almost wish I were not going," said Ephie, and this was not untrue, in spite of the pretty new dresses her trunks contained. " Say, I don't believe I shall enjoy myself one bit. You will write, Morry, won't you, and tell me what goes on? All the news you hear and who you see and everything."——

" Be sure you write," said Madeleine, too, when he saw her off early in the morning to Berlin, where she was to meet her English charges. " Christiania, *poste restante,* till the first, and then Bergen. '*Fröken Wade,*' don't forget."

The train started; her handkerchief fluttered from the window until the carriage was out of sight.

Maurice was alone; every one he knew disappeared, even Fürst, who had obtained a holiday engagement in a villa near Dresden. An odd stillness reigned in the *Braustrasse* and its neighbourhood; from houses which had hitherto been clangorous with musical noises, not a sound issued. Familiar rooms and lodgings were either closely shuttered, or, in process of scouring, hung out their curtains to flutter on the sill.

The days passed, unmarked, eventless, like the uniform pages of a dull book. When the solitude grew unbearable, Maurice went to visit Frau Fürst, and had his supper with the family. He was a welcome guest, for he not only paid for all the beer that was drunk, but also brought such a generous portion of sausage for his own supper, that it supplied one or other of the little girls as well. Afterwards, they sat round the kitchen-table, listening, the children with the old-fashioned solemnity that characterised them, to Frau Fürst's reminiscences. Otherwise, he hardly exchanged a word with anyone, but sat at his piano the livelong day. Of late, Schwarz had been somewhat cool and off-hand in manner with him; the master had also not displayed the same detailed interest in his plans for the summer, as in those of the rest of the class. This was one reason why he had not gone away like every one else; the other, that he had been unwilling to write home for an increase of allowance. Sometimes, when the day was hot, he envied his friends refreshing themselves by wood, mountain or sea; but, in the main, he worked briskly at Czerny's *Fingerfertigkeit,* and with such perseverance that ultimately his fingers stumbled from fatigue.

With the beginning of August, the heat grew oppressive; all day long, the sun beat, fierce and unremittent, on this city of the plains, and the baked pavements were warm to the feet. Business slackened, and the midday rest in shops and offices was extended beyond its usual limit. Conservatorium and Gewandhaus, at first given over to relays of charwomen, their brooms and buckets, soon lay dead and deserted, too; and if, in the evening, Maurice passed the former building, he would see the janitor sitting at leisure in the middle of the pavement, smoking his long black cigar. The old trees in the *Promenade,* and the young striplings that followed the river in the *Lampestrasse,* drooped their brown leaves thick with dust; the familiar smell of roasting coffee, which haunted most house- and stair-ways, was intensified; and out of drains and rivers rose nauseous and penetrating odours, from which there was no escape. Every three or four days, when the atmosphere of the town had reached a pitch of unsavouriness which it seemed impossible to surpass, sudden storms swept up, tropical in their violence: blasts of thunder cracked like splitting beams; lightning darted along the narrow streets; rain fell in white, sizzling sheets. But the morning after, it was as hot as ever.

Maurice grew so accustomed to meet no one he knew, that one afternoon towards the middle of August, he was pulled up by a jerk of surprise in front of the *Pleissenburg,* on stumbling across Heinrich Krafft. He had stopped and impulsively greeted the young man, before he recalled his previous antipathy to him.

Krafft was sauntering along with his hands in his pockets, and, on being accosted, he looked vaguely and somewhat moodily at Maurice. The next moment, however, he laid a hand on the lappel of Maurice's coat, and, without preamble, burst into a witty and obscene anecdote, which had evidently been in his mind when they met. This story, and the fact that, by the North Sea, he had stood before breakers twenty feet high, were the only particulars Maurice bore away from their interview. His previous impatience with such eccentricity returned, but none the less, he looked grudgingly after the other's vanishing form.

A day or two later, towards evening, he saw Krafft again. As he was going through an outlying street, he came upon a group of children, who were amusing themselves by teasing a cat; the animal had been hit in the eye by a stone, and cowered, terrified and blinded, against the wall of a house. The children formed a half circle round it, and two of the biggest boys held a young and lively dog by the collar, inciting it and restraining it, and revelling in the cat's convulsive starts at each capering bark.

While Maurice was considering how to expostulate with them, Krafft came swiftly up behind, jerked two of the children apart, and, with a deft and perfectly noiseless movement, caught up the cat and hid its head under his coat. Then, cuffing the biggest boy, he kicked the dog, and ordered the rest to disperse. The children did so lingeringly; and once out of his reach, stood and mocked him.

He begged Maurice to accompany him to his lodgings, and there Maurice held the animal, a large, half-starved street-cat, while Krafft, on his knees before it, examined the wound. As he did this, he crooned in a wordless language, and the cat was quiet, in spite of the pain he caused it. But directly he took his hands off it, it jumped from the table, and fled under the furthest corner of the sofa.

Krafft next fetched milk and a saucer, from a cupboard in the wall, and went down on his knees again: while Maurice sat and watched and wondered at his tireless endeavours to induce the animal to advance. He explained his proceedings in a whisper.

"If I put the saucer down and leave it," he said, "it won't help at all. A cat's confidence must be won straight away."

He was still in this position, making persuasive little noises, when the door opened, and Avery Hill, his companion of a previous occasion, entered. At the sight of Krafft crouching on the floor, she paused with her hand on the door, and looked from him to Maurice.

"Heinz?" she said interrogatively. Then she saw the saucer of milk, and understood. "Heinz!" she said again; and this time the word was a reprimand.

"Ssh!—be quiet," said Krafft peevishly, without looking up.

The girl took no notice of Maurice's attempt to greet her. Letting fall on the grand piano, some volumes of music she was carrying, she continued sternly: "Another cat!—oh, it is abominable of you! This is the third he has picked up this

year," she said explanatorily, yet not more to Maurice than to
herself. " And the last was so dirty and destructive that Frau
Schulz threatened to turn him out, if he did not get rid of it.
He knows as well as I do that he cannot keep a cat here."

Her placidly tragic face had grown hard; and altogether, the
anger she displayed seemed out of proportion to the trival offence.

Krafft remained undisturbed. " It's not the least use scold-
ing. Go and make it right with the old crow.—Come, puss,
come."

The girl checked the words that rose to her lips, gave a
slight shrug, and went out of the room. They heard her, in
the passage, disputing with the landlady, who was justly indignant.

" If it weren't for you, Fräulein, I wouldn't keep him another day," she declared.

Meanwhile the cat, which, in the girl's presence, had shrunk
still further into its hiding-place, began to make advances. It
crept a step forward, retreated again, stretched out its nose to
sniff at the milk, and, all of a sudden, emerged and drank
greedily.

Krafft touched its head, and the animal paused in its hungry
gulping to rub its back against the caressing hand. When the
last drop of milk was finished, it withdrew to its corner, but
less suspiciously.

Krafft rose to his feet and stretched himself, and when
Avery returned, he smiled at her.

" Now then, is it all right? "

She did not reply, but went to the piano, to search for
something among the scattered music. Krafft clasped his hands
behind his head, and leaning against the table, watched her
with an ironical curl of the lip.

" *O Lene! Lene! O Magdalene!* " he sang under his
breath; and, for the second time, Maurice received the impression that a by-play was being carried on between these two.

" Look at this," said Krafft after a pause. " Here, ladies
and gentlemen, is one of those rare persons who have a jot of
talent in them, and off she goes—I don't mean at this moment,
but to-morrow, the day after, every day—to waste it in teaching children finger-exercises. If you ask her why she does it,
she will tell you it is necessary to live. Necessary to live!—
who has ever proved that it is? "

For an instant, it seemed as if the girl were going to flash out a bitter retort that might have betrayed her. Then she showed the same self-control as before, and went, without a word, into the next room. She was absent for a few minutes, and when she reappeared, carried what was unmistakably a bundle of soiled linen, going away with this on one arm, the volumes of music she had picked out on the other. She did not wish the young men good-night, but, in passing Maurice, she said in an unfriendly tone: "Do you know what time it is?" and to Krafft: "It is late, Heinz, you are not to play."

The door had barely closed behind her, when Krafft broke into the loud, repellent laugh that had so jarred on Maurice at their former meeting. He had risen at once, and now said he must go. But Krafft would not hear of it; he pressed him into his seat again, with an effusive warmth of manner.

"Don't mind her. Stay, like a good fellow. Of course, I am going to play to you."

He flicked the keys of the piano with his handkerchief, adjusted the distance of his seat, threw back his head, and half closing his eyes, began to play. Except for the unsteady flickerings cast on the wall by a street-lamp, the room was soon in darkness.

Maurice resumed his seat reluctantly. He had been dragged upstairs against his will; and throughout the foregoing scene, had sat an uncomfortable spectator. He had as little desire for the girl to return and find him there, as for Krafft to play to him. But no excuse for leaving offered itself, and each moment made it harder to interrupt the player, who had promptly forgotten the fact of his presence.

After he had listened for a time, however, Maurice ceased to think of escaping. Madeleine had once alluded to Krafft's skill as an interpreter of Chopin, but, all the same, he had not expected anything like what he now heard, and at first he could not make anything of it. He had hitherto only known Chopin's music as played in the sentimental fashion of the English drawing-room. Here, now, came some one who made it clear that, no matter how pessimistic it appeared on the surface, this music was, at its core, an essentially masculine music; it kicked desperately against the pricks of existence; what failed it was reticence, and philosophic calm. He could not, of course, know that various small things had combined to throw the player into one of his most prodigal moods: the rescue and taming of the cat, the passage-at-arms with Avery, her stimulating forbiddal, and, last and best, the one silent listener in the dark—this stranger, picked up at random in the streets, who had never yet heard him play, and to whom he might reveal himself with an indecency that friendship precluded.

When at length, Frau Schulz entered, in her bed-jacket, to say that it was long past ten o'clock, Krafft wakened as if out of a trance, and hid his eyes from the light. Frau Schulz, a robust person, disregarded his protests, and herself locked the piano and took the key.

"She makes me promise to," she whispered to Maurice, pointing over her shoulder at an imaginary person. "If I didn't, he'd go on all night. He's no more fit to look after himself than a baby—and he gets it again with his boots in the morning.—Yes, yes, call me names if it pleases you. Names don't kill. And if I am a hag, you're a rascal, that's what you are! The way you treat that poor, good creature makes one's blood boil."

Krafft waved her away, and opening the window, leaned out on the sill: a wave of warm air filled the room. Maurice rose with renewed decision, and sought his hat. But Krafft also took his down from a peg. "Yes, let us go out."

It was a breathless August night, laden with intensified scents and smells, and the moonlight lay thick and white on the ground: a night to provoke to extravagant follies. In the utter stillness of the woods, the young men passed from places of inky blackness into bluish white patches, dropped through the trees like monstrous silver thalers. The town lay behind them in a glorifying haze; the river stretched silver-scaled in the moonlight, like a gigantic fish-back.

Krafft walked in front of his companion, in preoccupied silence. His slender hands, dangling loosely, still twitched from their recent exertions, and from time to time, he turned the palms outward, with an impatient gesture. Maurice wished himself alone. He was not at ease under this new companionship that had thrust itself upon him; indeed, a strong mental antagonism was still uppermost in him, towards the moody creature at whose heels he followed; and if, at this moment, he had been asked to give voice to his feelings, the term "crazy idiot" would have been the first to rise to his lips.

Suddenly, without turning, or slackening his pace, Krafft commenced to speak: at first in a low voice, as if he were thinking aloud. But one word gave another, his thoughts came rapidly, he began to gesticulate, and finally, wrought on by the beauty of the night, by this choice moment for speech, still excited by his own playing, and in an infinite need of expression, he swept the silence before him with the force of a flood set free. If he thought Maurice were about to interrupt him, he made an imploring gesture, and left what he was saying unfinished, to spring over to the next theme ready in his brain. Names jostled one another on his tongue: he passed from Beethoven and Chopin to Berlioz and Wagner, to Liszt and Richard Strauss—and his words were to Maurice like the unrolling of a great scroll. In the same breath, he was with Nietzsche, and Apollonic and Dionysian; and from here he went on to Richard Dehmel, to *Anatol,* and the gentle " Loris " of the early verses; to Max Klinger, and the propriety of coloured sculpture; to *Papa Hamlet* and the future of the *Lied.* Maurice, listening intently, had fleeting glimpses into a land of which he knew nothing. He kept as still as a mouse, in order not to betray his ignorance; for Krafft was not didactic, and talked as if the subjects he touched on were as familiar to Maurice as to himself. On the other hand, Maurice believed it was a matter of indifference to him whether he was understood or not; he spoke for the pure joy of talking, out of the motley profusion of his knowledge.

Meanwhile, he had grown personal. And while he was still speaking with fervour of Vienna—which was his home—of gay, melancholy Wien, he flung round and put a question to his companion.

" Do you ever think of death? "

Maurice had been the listener for so long that he started.

" Death? " he echoed, and was as much embarrassed as though asked whether he believed in God. " I don't know. No, I don't think I do. Why should one think of death when one is alive and well? "

Krafft laughed at this, with a pitying irony. " Happy you! " he said. " Happy you! " His voice sank, and he continued almost fearfully: " I have the vision of it before me, always— wherever I go. Listen; I will tell you; it is like this." He laid his hand on Maurice's arm, and drew him nearer. " I know—no matter how strong and sound I may be at this moment; no matter how I laugh, or weep, or play the fool; no matter how little thought I give it, or whether I think about it all day long—I know the hour will come, at last, when I shall gasp, choke, grow black in the face, in the vain struggle for another single mouthful of that air which has always been mine at will. And no one will be able to help me; there is no escape from that hour; no power on earth can keep it from me. And it is all a matter of chance when it happens—a great lottery: one draws to-day, one to-morrow; but my turn will surely come, and each day that passes brings me twenty-four hours nearer the end." He drew still closer to Maurice. " Tell me, have you never stood before a doorway—the doorway of some strange house that you have perhaps never consciously gone past before—and waited, with the atrocious curiosity that death and its hideous paraphernalia waken in one, for a coffin to be carried out?—the coffin of an utter stranger, who is of interest to you now, for the first and the last time. And have you not thought to yourself, with a shudder, that some day, in this selfsame way, under the same indifferent sky, among a group of loiterers as idly curious as these, you yourself will be carried out, feet foremost, like a bale of goods, like useless lumber, all will and dignity gone from you, never to enter there again?—there, where all the little human things you have loved, and used, and lived amongst, are lying just as you left them—the book you laid down, the coat you wore—now all of a greater worth than you. You are mere dead flesh, and behind the horrid lid lie stark and cold, with rigid fingers and half-closed eyes, and the chief desire of every one, even of those you have loved most, is to be rid of you, to be out of reach of sight and smell of you. And so, after being carted, and jolted, and unloaded, you will be thrown into a hole, and your body, ice-cold, and as yielding as meat to the touch—oh, that awful icy softness!—your flesh will begin to rot, to be such that not your nearest friend would touch you. God, it is unbearable! "

He wiped his forehead, and Maurice was silent, not knowing what to say; he felt that such rational arguments as he might be able to offer, would have little value in the face of this intensely personal view, which was stammered forth with the bitterness of an accusation. But as they crossed the suspension-bridge, Krafft stopped, and stood looking at the water, which glistened in the moonlight like a living thing.

"No, it is impossible for me to put death out of my mind," he went on. " And yet, a spring into this silver fire down here would end all that, and satisfy one's curiosity as well. Why is one not readier to make the spring?—and what would one's sensations be? The mad rush through the air—the crash—the sinking in the awful blackness . . ."

" Those of fear and cold. You would wish yourself out

again," answered Maurice; and as Krafft nodded, without seeming to resent his tone, he ventured to put forward a few points for the other side of the question. He suggested that always to be brooding over death unfitted you for life. Every one had to die when his time came; it was foolish to look upon your own death as an exception to the rule. Besides, when sensation had left you—the soul, the spirit, whatever you liked to call it—did it matter what afterwards became of your body? It was, then, in reality, nothing but lumber, fresh nourishment for the soil; and it was morbid to care so much how it was treated, just because it had once been your tenement, when it was now as worthless as the crab's empty shell.

He stuttered this out piece-wise, in his halting German; then paused, not sure how his companion would take the didactic tone he had fallen into. But Krafft had turned, and was gazing at him, considering him attentively for the first time. When Maurice ceased to speak, he nodded a hasty assent: "Yes, yes, it is quite true. Go on." And as the former, having nothing more to say, was mute, he added: "You are like some one I once knew. He was a great musician. I saw him die; he died by inches; it lasted for months; he could neither die nor live."

"Why do you brood over these things, if you find them so awful? Are you not afraid your nerves will go through with you, and make you do something foolish?" asked Maurice, and was himself astonished at his boldness.

"Of course I am. My life is a perpetual struggle against suicide," answered Krafft.

In the distance, a church-clock struck a quarter to twelve, and it was on Maurice's tongue to suggest that they should move homewards, when, with one of his unexpected transitions, Krafft turned to him and said in a low voice: "What do you say? Shall you and I be friends?"

Maurice hesitated, in some embarrassment. "Why yes; I should be very glad."

"And you will let me say ' *du* ' to you?"

"Certainly. If you are sure you won't regret it in the morning."

Krafft stretched out his hand. As Maurice held in his the fine, slim fingers, which seemed mere skin and muscle, a hitherto unknown feeling of kindliness came over him for the young man at his side. At this moment, he had the lively sensation that he was the stronger and wiser of the two, and

that it was even a little beneath him to take the other too
seriously.

"You think so poorly of me then? You think no good thing
can come out of me?" asked Krafft, and there was an appeal-
ing note in his voice, which, but a short time back, had been
so overbearing.

Had Maurice known him better, he would have promptly
retorted: "Don't be a fool." As it was, he laughed. "Who
am I to sit in judgment? The only thing I do know is, that
if I had your talent—no, a quarter of it—I should pull myself
together and astonish the world."

"It sounds so easy; but I have too many doubts of myself,"
said Krafft, and laid his hand on Maurice's shoulder. "And
I have never had anyone to keep me up to the mark—till now.
I have always needed some one like you. You are strong and
sympathetic; and one has the feeling that you understand."

Maurice was far from certain that he did. However, he
answered in a frank way, doing his best to keep down the sentimental tone that had invaded the conversation. At heart,
he was little moved by this new friendship, which had begun
with the word itself; he told himself that it was only a whim of
Krafft's, which would be forgotten in the morning. But, as
they stood thus on the bridge, shoulder to shoulder, he did not
understood how he could ever have taken anything this frail
creature did, amiss. At the moment, there was a clinging helplessness about Krafft, which instinctively roused his manlier
feelings. He said to himself that he had done wrong in lightly
condemning his companion; and, impelled by this sudden burst
of protectiveness, he seized the moment, and spoke earnestly to
Krafft of earnest things, of duty, not only to one's fellows, but
to oneself and one's abilities, of the inspiring gain of unre-
mitted endeavour.

Afterwards, they sauntered home—first to Maurice's lodging,
then to Krafft's, and once again to Maurice's. At this stage,
Krafft was frankness itself; Maurice learnt to his surprise that
the slim, boyish lad at his side was over twenty-seven years of
age; that, for several semesters, Krafft had studied medicine in
Vienna, then had thrown up this "disgusting occupation," to
become a clerk in a wealthy uncle's counting-house. From this,
he had drifted into journalism, and finally, at the instigation of
Hans von Bülow, to music; he had been for two and a half
years with Bülow, on travel, and in Hamburg, and was at
present in Leipzig solely to have his "fingers put in order."

His plans for the future were many, and widely divergent. At one time, a musical career tempted him irresistibly; every one but Schwarz—this finger-machine, this generator of living metronomes—believed that he could make a name for himself as a player of Chopin. At other times, and more often, he contemplated retiring from the world and entering a monastery. He spoke with a morbid horror—yet as if the idea of it fascinated him—of the publicity of the concert-platform, and painted in glowing colours a monastery he knew of, standing on a wooded hill, not far from Vienna. He had once spent several weeks there, recovering from an illness, and the gardens, the trimly bedded flowers, the glancing sunlight in the utter silence of the corridors, were things he could not forget. He had lain day for day on a garden-bench, reading Novalis, and it still seemed to him that the wishless happiness of those days was the greatest he had known.

Beside this, Maurice's account of himself sounded tame and unimportant; he felt, too, that the circumstances of English life were too far removed from his companion's sphere, for the latter to be able to understand them.

On waking next morning, Maurice recalled the incidents of the evening with a smile; felt a touch of warmth at the remembrance of the moment when he had held Krafft's hand in his; then classed the whole episode as strained, and dismissed it from his mind. He had just shut the piano, after a busy forenoon, when Krafft burst in, his cheeks pink with haste and excitement. He had discovered a room to let, in the house he lived in, and nothing would satisfy him but that Maurice should come instantly to see it. Laughing at his eagerness, Maurice put forward his reasons for preferring to remain where he was. But Krafft would take no denial, and not wishing to hurt his feelings, Maurice gave way, and agreed at least to look at the room.

It was larger and more cheerful than his own, and had also a convenient alcove for the bedstead; and after inspecting it, Maurice felt willing to expend the extra marks it cost. They withdrew to Krafft's room to come to a decision. There, however, they found Avery Hill, who, as soon as she heard what they contemplated, put a veto on it. Growing pale, as she always did where others would have flushed, she said: "It is an absurd idea—sheer nonsense! I won't have it, understand that! Pray, excuse me," she continued to Maurice, speaking in a more friendly tone than she had yet used to him, "but

you must not listen to him. It is just one of his whims—
nothing more. In less than a week, you would wish yourself
away again. You have no idea how changeable he is—how
impossible to live with."

Maurice hastened to reassure her. Krafft did not speak; he
stood at the window, with his back to them, his forehead pressed
against the glass.

So Maurice continued to live in the *Braustrasse,* under the
despotic rule of Frau Krause, who took every advantage of his
good-nature. But after this, not a day passed without his
seeing Krafft; the latter sought him out on trivial pretexts.
Maurice hardly recognised him: he was gentle, amiable, and
amenable to reason; he subordinated himself entirely to Maurice,
and laid an ever-increasing weight on his opinion. Maurice became able to wind him round his finger; and the
hint of a reproof from him served to throw Krafft into a state
of nervous depression. Without difficulty, Maurice found himself to rights in his rôle of mentor, and began to flatter himself that he would ultimately make of Krafft a decent member
of society. As it was, he soon induced his friend to study in
a more methodical way; they practised for the same number of
hours in the forenoon, and met in the afternoon; and Krafft
only sometimes broke through this arrangement, by appearing
in the *Braustrasse* early in the morning, and, despite remonstrance, throwing himself on the sofa, and remaining there, while
Maurice practised. The latter ended by growing accustomed
to this whim as to several other things that had jarred on him—
such as Krafft's love for a dirty jest—and overlooked or for-
gave them. At first embarrassed by the mushroom growth of
a friendship he had not invited, he soon grew genuinely attached to Krafft, and missed him when he was absent from
him.

Avery Hill could hardly be termed third in the alliance;
Maurice's advent had thrust her into the background, where
she kept watch over their doings with her cold, disdainful eye.
Maurice was not clear how she regarded his intrusion. Sometimes, particularly when she saw the improvement in Heinrich's
way of life, she seemed to tolerate his presence gladly; at others
again, her jealous aversion to him was too open to be overlooked.
The jealousy was natural; he was an interloper, and Heinz
neglected her shamefully for him; but there was something
else behind it, another feeling, which Maurice could not make
out. He by no means understood the relationship that existed

between his friend and this girl of the stone-grey eyes and stern, red lips. The two lived almost door by door, went in and out of each other's rooms at all hours, and yet, he had never heard them exchange an affectionate word, or seen a mark of endearment pass between them. Avery's attachment—if such it could be called—was noticeable only in the many small ways in which she cared for Krafft's comfort; her manner with him was invariably severe and distant, with the exception of those occasions when a seeming trifle raised in her a burst of the dull, passionate anger, beneath which Krafft shrank. Maurice believed that his friend would be happier away from her; in spite of her fresh colouring, he, Maurice, found her wanting in attraction, nothing that a woman ought to be. But her name was rarely mentioned between them; Krafft was, as a rule, reticent concerning her, and when he did speak of her, it was in a tone of such contempt that Maurice was glad to shirk the subject.

"It's all she wants," Krafft had replied, when his companion ventured to take her part. "She wouldn't thank you to be treated differently. Believe me, women are all alike; they are made to be trodden on. Ill-usage brings out their good points—just as kneading makes dough light. Let them alone, or pamper them, and they spread like a weed, and choke you"—and he quoted a saying about going to women and not forgetting the whip, at which Maurice stood aghast.

"But why, if you despise a person like that—why have her always about you?" he cried, at the end of a flaming plea for woman's dignity and worth.

Krafft shrugged his shoulders. "I suppose the truth is we are dependent on them—yes, dependent, from the moment we are laid in the cradle. It's a woman who puts on our first clothes and a woman who puts on our last. But why talk about these things?"—he slipped his arm through Maurice's. "Tell me about yourself; and when you are tired of talking, I will play."

It usually ended in his playing. They ranged through the highways and byways of music.

One afternoon—it was a warm, wet, grey day towards the end of August—Maurice found Krafft in a strangely apathetic mood. The weather, this moist warmth, had got on his nerves, he said; he had been unable to settle to anything; was weighed down by a lassitude heavier than iron. When Maurice entered, he was stretched on the sofa, with closed eyes; on his chest slept Wotan, the one-eyed cat, now growing sleek and fat. While Maurice was trying to rally him, Krafft sprang up. With a precipitance that was the extreme opposite of his previous sloth, he lowered both window-blinds, and, lighting two candles, set them on the piano, where they dispersed the immediate darkness, but no more.

"I am going to play *Tristan* to you."

Maurice had learnt by this time that it was useless to try to thwart Krafft. He laughed and nodded, and having nothing in particular to do, lay down in the latter's place on the sofa.

Krafft shook his hair back, and began the prelude to the opera in a rapt, ecstatic way, finding in the music an outlet for all his nervousness. At first, he played from memory; when this gave out, he set the piano-score up before him, then forgot it again, and went on playing by heart. Sometimes he sang the different parts, in a light, sweet tenor; sometimes recited them, with dramatic fervour. Only he never ceased to play, never gave his hearer a moment in which to recover himself.

Frau Schulz's entry with the lamp, and her grumblings at the *"unverschämte Spektakel"* passed unheeded. A strength that was more than human seemed to take possession of the frail youth at the piano. Evening crept on afternoon, night on evening, and still he continued, drunk with the most emotional music conceived by a human brain.

Even when hands and fingers could do no more, the frenzy that was in him would not let him rest: he paced the room, and talked—talked for hours, his eyes ablaze. A church-clock struck ten, then half-past, then eleven, and not for a moment was he still; his speech seemed, indeed, to gather impetus as it advanced, like a mountain torrent.

Then, all of a sudden, in the middle of a vehement defence of anti-Semitism, to which he had been led by the misdeeds of those "arch-charlatans," Mendelssohn and Meyerbeer, he stopped short, like a run-down clock, and, falling into a chair before the table, buried his face in his arms. There was silence, the more intense for all that had preceded it. Wotan wakened from sleep, and was heard to stretch his limbs, with a yawn and a sigh. The spell was broken; Maurice, his head in a whirl, rose stiff and cramped from his uncomfortable position on the sofa.

"You rascal, you make one lose all sense of time. And I am starving. I must snatch something at Canitz's as I go by."

Krafft started, and raised a haggard face with twitching lips. "You are not going to leave me?—like this?."

Maurice was both hungry and tired—worn out, in fact.

"We will go somewhere in the town," said Krafft. "And then for a walk. The rain has stopped—look!"

He drew up one of the blinds, and they saw that the stars were shining.

"Yes, but what about to-morrow?—and to-morrow's work?"

"To-morrow may never come. And to-night is."

"Those are only words. Do you know the time?"

Krafft turned quickly from the window. "And if I make it a test of the friendship you have professed for me, that you stay here with me to-night?—You can sleep on the sofa."

"Why on earth get personal?" said Maurice; he could not find his hat, which had fallen in a dark corner. "Heinz, dear boy, be reasonable. Come, give me the house-key—like a good fellow."

"It's the first—the only thing, I have asked of you."

"Nonsense. You have asked dozens."

Krafft took a few steps towards him, and threw the key on the floor at his feet. Wotan, who was at the door, mewing to be let out, sprang back in affright.

"Go, go, go!" Krafft cried. "I never want to see you again."

Earlier than usual the next morning, Maurice returned to set things right, and to laugh with Heinz at their extravagance of the night before. But Krafft was not to be seen. From Frau Schulz, who flounced past him in the passage, first with hot water, then with black coffee, Maurice learned that Krafft had been brought home early that morning, in a disgraceful state of intoxication. Frau Schulz still boiled at the remembrance.

"*So 'n Schwein, so 'n Schwein!*" she cried. "But this time he goes. I have said it before and, fool that I am, have always let them persuade me. But this is the end. Not a day after the fifteenth will I have him in the house."

Maurice slipped away.

Two days passed before he saw his friend again. He found him pale and dejected, with reddish, heavy eyes and a sneering smile. He was wholly changed; his words were tainted with the perverse irony, which, at the beginning of their acquaintance, had made his manner so repellent. But now, Maurice was not, at once, frightened away by it; he could not believe Heinrich's pique was serious, and gave himself trouble to win his friend back. He chid, laughed, rallied, was earnest and apologetic, and all this without being conscious of having done wrong.

"I think you had better leave him alone," said Avery, after watching his fruitless efforts. "He doesn't want you."

It was true; now Krafft had no thought for anyone but Avery. It was Avery here, and Avery there. He called her by a pet name, was anxious for her comfort, and hung affectionately on her arm.—The worst of it was, that he did not seem in the least ashamed of his fickleness.

Maurice made one further attempt to move him, then, hurt and angry, intruded no more. At first, he was chiefly angry. But, gradually, the hurt deepened, and became a sense of injury, which made him avoid the street Krafft lived in, and shun him when they met. He missed him, after the close companionship of the past weeks, and felt as if he had been suddenly deprived of a part of himself. And he would no doubt have missed him more keenly still, if, just at this juncture, his attention had not been engrossed by another and more important matter.

XIII

THE commencement of the new term had just assembled the incoming students to sign their names in the venerable roll-book, when the report spread that Schilsky was willing to play his symphonic poem, *Zarathustra,* to those of his friends who cared to hear it. Curiosity swelled the number, and Fürst lent his house for the occasion.

"You'll come, of course," said the latter to Maurice, as they left Schwarz's room after their lesson; and Madeleine said the same thing while driving home from the railway-station, where Maurice had met her. She was no more a friend of Schilsky's than he was, but she certainly intended to be present, to hear what kind of stuff he had turned out.

On the evening of the performance, Maurice and she walked together to the *Brandvorwerkstrasse.* Madeleine had still much to say. She had returned from her holiday in the best of health and spirits, liberally rewarded for her trouble, and possessed of four new friends, who, no doubt, would all be of use to her when she settled in England again. This was to be her last winter in Leipzig, and she was drawing up detailed plans of work. From now on, she intended to take private lessons from Schwarz, in addition to those she received in the class.

"Even though they do cost ten marks each, it makes him ever so much better disposed towards you."

She also told him that she had found a letter from Louise waiting for her, in which the latter announced her return for the following week. Louise wrote from England, and all her cry was to be back in Leipzig.

"Of course—now he is here," commented Madeleine. "You know, I suppose, that he has been travelling with Zollinger? He has the luck of I don't know what."

The Cayhills would be absent till the middle of the month: Maurice had received from Ephie one widely written note, loud in praise of a family of "perfectly sweet Americans," whom they had learnt to know in Interlaken, but also expressing eagerness to be at home again in "dear old Leipzig."

Dove had arrived a couple of days ago—and here Madeleine laughed.

"He is absolutely shiny with resolution," she declared. "Mind, Maurice, if he takes you into confidence—as he probably will—you are not on any account to dissuade him from proposing. A snub will do him worlds of good."

They were not the first to climb the ill-lighted stair that wound up to the Fürsts' dwelling. The entry-door on the fourth storey stood open, and a hum of voices came from the sitting-room. The circular hat-stand in the passage was crowded with motley headgear.

As they passed the kitchen, the door of which was ajar, Frau Fürst peeped through the slit, and seeing Maurice, called him in. The coffee-pot was still on the stove; he must sit down and drink a cup of coffee.

"There is plenty of time. Schilsky has not come yet, and I have only this moment sent Adolfchen for the beer."

Maurice asked her if she were not coming in to hear the music. She laughed good-naturedly at the idea.

"Bless your heart, what should I do in there, among all you young people? No, no, I can hear just as well where I am. When my good husband had his evenings, it was always from the kitchen that I listened."

Pausing, with a saucepan in one hand, a cloth in the other, she said: "You will hear something good to-night, Herr Guest. Oh, he has talent, great talent, has young Schilsky! This is not the usual work of a pupil. It has form, and it has ideas, and it is new and daring. I know one of the motives from hearing Franz play it," and she hummed a theme as she replaced on the shelf, the scrupulously cleaned pot. "For such a young man, it is wonderful; but he will do better still, depend upon it, he will."

Here she threw a hasty glance round the tiny kitchen, at three of the children sitting as still as mice in the corner, laid a finger on her lips, and, bursting with mystery, leaned over the table and asked Maurice if he could keep a secret.

"He is going away," she whispered.

Maurice stared at her. "Going away? Who is? What do you mean?" he asked, and was so struck by her peculiar manner that he set his cup down untouched.

"Why Schilsky, of course." She thought his astonishment was disbelief, and nodded confirmingly. "Yes, yes, he is going away. And soon, too."

"How do you know?" cried Maurice. Sitting back in his chair, he stemmed his hands against the edge of the table, and looked challengingly at Frau Fürst.

"Ssh!—not so loud," said the latter. "It's a secret, a dead secret—though I'm sure I don't know why. Franz——"

At this very moment, Franz himself came into the kitchen. He looked distrustfully at his whispering mother.

"Now then, mother, haven't you got that beer yet?" he demanded. His genial bonhomie disappeared, as if by magic, when he entered his home circle, and he was particularly gruff with this adoring woman.

"*Gleich, Fränzchen, gleich,*" she answered soothingly, and whisked about her work again, with the air of one caught napping.

Maurice followed Fürst's invitation to join the rest of the party.

The folding-doors between the "best room" and the adjoining bedroom had been opened wide, and the guests were distributed over the two rooms. The former was brilliantly lighted by three lamps and two candles, and all the sitting-accommodation the house contained was ranged in a semicircle round the grand piano. Here, not a place was vacant; those who had come late were in the bedroom, making shift with whatever offered. Two girls and a young man, having pushed back the feather-bed, sat on the edge of the low wooden bedstead, with their arms interlaced to give them a better balance. Maurice found Madeleine on a rickety little sofa that stood at the foot of the bed. Dove sat on a chest of drawers next the sofa, his long legs dangling in the air. Beside Madeleine, with his head on her shoulder, was Krafft.

"Oh, there you are," cried Madeleine. "Well, I did my best to keep the place for you; but it was of no use, as you see. Just sit down, however. Between us, we'll squeeze him properly."

Maurice was glad that the room, which was lighted only by one small lamp, was in semi-darkness; for, at the sound of his own voice, it suddenly became clear to him that the piece of gossip Frau Fürst had volunteered, had been of the nature of a blow. Schilsky's departure threatened, in a way he postponed for the present thinking out, to disturb his life; and, in an abrupt need of sympathy, he laid his hand on Krafft's knee.

"Is it you, old man? What have you been doing with yourself?"

Krafft gave him one of those looks which, in the early days of their acquaintance, had proved so disconcerting—a look of struggling recollection.

"Oh, nothing in particular," he replied, without hostility, but also without warmth. His mind was not with his words, and Maurice withdrew his hand.

Madeleine leaned forward, dislodging Krafft's head from its resting-place.

"How long have you two been ' *du* ' to each other?" she asked, and at Maurice's curt reply, she pushed Krafft from her. "Sit up and behave yourself. One would think you had an evil spirit in you to-night."

Krafft was nervously excited: bright red spots burnt on his cheeks, his hands twitched, and he jerked forward in his seat, and threw himself back again, incessantly.

"No, you are worse than a mosquito," cried Madeleine, losing patience. "Anyone would think you were going to play yourself. And he will be as cool as an iceberg. The sofa won't stand it, Heinz. If you can't stop fidgeting, get up."

He had gone, before she finished speaking; for a slight stir in the next room made them suppose for a moment that Schilsky was arriving. Afterwards, Krafft was to be seen straying about, with his hands in his pockets; and, on observing his rose-pink cheeks and tumbled curly hair, Madeleine could not refrain from remarking: "He ought to have been a girl."

The air was already hot, by reason of the lamps, and the many breaths, and the firmly shut double-windows. The clamour for beer had become universal by the time Adolfchen arrived with his arms full of bottles. As there were not enough glasses to go round, every two or three persons shared one between them —a proceeding that was carried out with much noisy mirth. Above all other voices was to be heard that of Miss Jensen, who, in a speckled yellow dress, with a large feather fan in her hand, sat in the middle of the front row of seats. It was she who directed how the beer should be apportioned; she advised a few late-comers where they would still find room, and engaged Fürst to place the lights on the piano to better advantage. Next her, a Mrs. Lautenschläger, a plump little American lady, with straight yellow hair which hung down on her shoulders, was relating to her neighbour on the other side, in a tone that could be clearly heard in both rooms, how she had " discovered " her voice.

"I come to Schwarz, last fall," she said shaking back her

hair, and making effective use of her babyish mouth; "and he thinks no end of me. But the other week I was sick, and as I lay in bed, I sung some—just for fun. And my landlady— she's a regular singer herself—who was fixing up the room, she claps her hands together and says: 'My goodness me! Why *you* have a voice!' That's what put it in my head, and I went to Sperling to hear what he'd got to say. He was just tickled to death, I guess he was, and he's going to make something dandy of it, so I stop long enough. I don't know what my husband'll say though. When I wrote him I was sick, he says: 'Come home and be sick at home'—that's what he says."

Miss Jensen could not let pass the opportunity of breaking a lance for her own master, the Swede, and of cutting up Sperling's method, which she denounced as antiquated. She made quite a little speech, in the course of which she now and then interrupted herself to remind Fürst—who was as soft as a pudding before her—of something he had forgotten to do, such as snuffing the candles or closing the door.

"Just let me hear your scale, will you?" she said patronisingly to Mrs. Lautenschläger. The latter, nothing loath, stuck out her chin, opened her mouth, and, for a short time, all other noises were drowned in a fine, full volume of voice.

On their sofa, Madeleine and Maurice sat in silence, pretending to listen to Dove, who was narrating his journey. Madeleine was out of humour; she tapped the floor, and had a crease in her forehead. As for Maurice, he was in such poor spirits that she could not but observe it.

"Why are you so quiet? Is anything the matter?"

He shook his head, without speaking. His vague sense of impending misfortune had crystallised into a definite thought; he knew now what it signified. If Schilsky went away from Leipzig, Louise would probably go, too, and that would be the end of everything.

"I represented to him," he heard Dove saying, "that I had seen the luggage with my own eyes at Flushing. What do you think he answered? He looked me up and down, and said: '*Ich werde telegraphieren und Erkundigungen einziehen.*' Now, do you think if you said to an English station-master: 'Sir, I saw the luggage with my own eyes,' he would not believe you? No, in my opinion, the whole German railway-system needs revision. Would you believe it, we did not make fifty kilometers in the hour, and yet our engine broke down before Magdeburg?"

So this would be the end; the end of foolish dreams and weak hopes, which he had never put into words even to himself, which had never properly existed, and yet had been there, nevertheless, a mass of gloriously vague perhapses. The end was at hand—an end before there had been any beginning.

" . . . the annoyance of the perpetual interruptions," went on the voice on the other side. "A lady who was travelling in the same compartment—a very pleasant person, who was coming over to be a teacher in a school in Dresden—I have promised to show her our lions when she visits Leipzig: well, as I was saying, she was quite alarmed the first time he entered in that way, and it took me some time, I assure you, to make her believe that this was the German method of revising tickets."

The break occasioned by the arrival of the beer had been of short duration, and the audience was growing impatient; at the back of the room, some one began to stamp his feet; others took it up. Fürst perspired with anxiety, and made repeated journeys to the stair-head, to see if Schilsky were not coming. The latter was almost an hour late by now, and jests, bald and witty, were made at his expense. Some one offered to take a bet that he had fallen asleep and forgotten the appointment, and at this, one of the girls on the bed, a handsome creature with bold, prominent eyes, related an anecdote to her neighbours, concerning Schilsky's powers of sleep. All three exploded with laughter. In a growing desire to be asked to play, Boehmer had for some time hung about the piano, and was now just about to drop, as if by accident, upon the stool, when the cry of: " No Bach! " was raised—Bach was Boehmer's specialty—and re-echoed, and he retired red and discomfited to his place in a corner of the room, where his companion, a statuesque little English widow, made biting observations on the company's behaviour. The general rowdyism was at its height, when some one had the happy idea that Krafft should sing them his newest song. At this, there was a unanimous shriek of approval, and several hands dragged Krafft to the piano. But himself the wildest of them all, he needed no forcing. Flinging himself down on the seat, he preluded wildly in imitation of Rubinstein. His hearers sat with their mouths open, a fixed smile on their faces, laughter ready in their throats, and only Madeleine was coolly contemptuous.

" Tom-fool! " she said in a low voice.

Krafft was confidently expected to burst into one of those

songs for which he was renowned. Few of his friends were able to sing them, and no one but himself could both sing and play them simultaneously: they were a monstrous, standing joke. Instead of this, however, he turned, winked at his audience, and began a slow, melancholy ditty, with a recurring refrain. He was not allowed to finish the first verse; a howl of disapproval went up; his hearers hooted, jeered and stamped.

" Sick cats! "

" Damn your *' wenig Sonne!' "*—this was the refrain.

" Put your head in a bag! "

" Pity he drinks! "

" Give us one of the rousers—the rou . . . sers! "

Krafft himself laughed unbridledly. *"Das ich spricht!"* he announced. " In C sharp major."

There was a hush of anticipation, in which Dove, stopping his *Bretzel* half-way to his mouth, was heard to say in his tone of measured surprise: " C sharp major! Why, that is——"

The rest was drowned in the wild chromatic passages that Krafft sent up and down the piano with his right hand, while his left followed with full-bodied chords, each of which exceeded the octave. Before, however, there was time to laugh, this riot ceased, and became a mournful cadence, to the slowly passing harmonies of which, Krafft sang:

I am weary of everything that is, under the sun.
I sicken at the long lines of rain, which are black against the sky;
They drip, for a restless heart, with the drip of despair:
For me, winds must rage, trees bend, and clouds sail stormily.

The whirlwind of the prelude commenced anew; the chords became still vaster; the player swayed from side to side, like a stripling-tree in a storm. Madeleine said, " Tch! " in disgust, but the rest of the company, who had only waited for this, burst into peals of laughter; some bent double in their seats, some leant back with their chins in the air. Even Dove smiled. Just, however, as those whose sense of humour was most highly developed, mopped their faces with gestures of exhaustion, and assured their neighbours that they " could not, really could not laugh any more," Fürst entered and flapped his hands.

" Here he comes! "

A sudden silence fell, broken only by a few hysterical giggles from the ladies, and by a frivolous American, who cried: " Now for *Also schrie Zenophobia!*" Krafft stopped playing, but remained sitting at the piano, wiping down the keys with his handkerchief.

Schilsky came in, somewhat embarrassed by the lull which had succeeded the hubbub heard in the passage, but wholly unconcerned at the lateness of the hour: except in matters of practical advancement, time did not exist for him. As soon as he appeared, the two ladies in the front row began to clap their hands; the rest of the company followed their example, then, in spite of Fürst's efforts to prevent it, rose and crowded round him. Miss Jensen and her friend made themselves particularly conspicuous. Mrs. Lautenschläger had an infatuation for the young man, of which she made no secret; she laid her hand caressingly on his coat-sleeve, and put her face as near his as propriety admitted.

"Disgusting, the way those women go on with him!" said Madeleine. "And what is worse, he likes it."

Schilsky listened to the babble of compliments with that mixture of boyish deference and unequivocal superiority, which made him so attractive to women. He was too good-natured to interrupt them and free himself, and would have stood as long as they liked, if Fürst had not come to the rescue and led him to the piano. Schilsky laid his hand affectionately on Krafft's shoulder, and Krafft sprang up in exaggerated surprise. The audience took its seats again; the thick manuscript-score was set up on the music-rack, and the three young men at the piano had a brief disagreement with one another about turning the leaves: Krafft was bent on doing it, and Schilsky objected, for Krafft had a way of forgetting what he was at in the middle of a page. Krafft flushed, cast an angry look at his friend, and withdrew, in high dudgeon, to a corner.

Standing beside the piano, so turned to those about him that the two on the sofa in the next room only saw him sideways, and ill at that, Schilsky gave a short description of his work. He was nervous, which aggravated his lisp, and he spoke so rapidly and in such a low voice that no one but those immediately in front of him, could understand what he said. But it did not matter in the least; all present had come only to hear the music; they knew and cared nothing about Zarathustra and his spiritual development; and one and all waited impatiently for Schilsky to stop speaking. The listeners in the bedroom merely caught disjointed words—*Werdegang, Notschrei, Taranteln*—but not one was curious enough even to lean forward in his seat. Madeleine made sarcastic inward comments on the behaviour of the party.

"It's perfectly clear to you, I suppose," she could not refrain from observing as, at the finish, Dove sagely wagged his head in agreement.

It transpired that there was an ode to be sung before the last section of the composition, and a debate ensued who should sing it. The two ladies in the front had quite a little quarrel—without knowing anything about the song—as to which of their voices would best suit it. Schilsky was silent for a moment, tapping his fingers, then said suddenly: "Come on, Heinz," and looked at Krafft. But the latter, who was standing morose, with folded arms, did not move. He had a dozen reasons why he should not sing; he had a cold, was hoarse, was out of practice, could not read the music from sight.

"Good Heavens, what a fool Heinz is making of himself tonight!" said Madeleine.

But Schilsky thumped his fist on the lid, and said, if Krafft did not sing it, no one should; and that was the end of the matter. Krafft was pulled to the piano.

Schilsky took his seat, and, losing his nervousness as soon as he touched the keys, preluded firmly and easily, with his large, white hands. Now, every one leaned forward to see him better; especially the ladies threw themselves into positions from which they could watch hair and hands, and the slender, swaying figure.

"Isn't he divine?" said the bold-eyed girl on the bed, in a loud whisper, and hung upon her companion's neck in an ecstatic attitude.

After the diversity of noises which had hitherto interfered with his thinking connectedly, Maurice welcomed the continuous sound of the music, which went on without a break. He sat in a listening attitude, shading his eyes with his hand. Through his fingers, he surreptitiously watched the player. He had never before had an opportunity of observing Schilsky so closely, and, with a kind of blatant generosity, he now pointed out to himself each physical detail that he found prepossessing in the other, every feature that was likely to attract—in the next breath, only to struggle with his honest opinion that the composer was a slippery, loose-jointed, caddish fellow, who could never be proved to be worthy of Louise. But he was too down-hearted at what he had learnt in the course of the evening, to rise to any active feeling of dislike.

12

Intermittently he heard, in spite of himself, something of
Schilsky's music; but he was not in a frame of mind to understand, or to retain any impression of it.   He was more effec-
tively jerked out of his preoccupation by single spoken words,
which, from time to time, struck his ear: this was Fürst, who,
in the absence of a programme, announced from his seat beside Schilsky, the headings of the different sections of the work:
Werdegang; Seiltänzer—here Maurice saw Dove conducting
with head and hand—*Notschrei; Schwermut; Taranteln*—and
here again, but vaguely, as if at a distance, he heard suppressed
laughter.   But he was thoroughly roused when Krafft, picking
up a sheet of music and coming round to the front of the piano,
began to sing *Das trunkene Lied.*   By way of introduction,
the low F in the bass of F minor sounded persistently, at syncopated intervals; Schilsky inclined his head, and Krafft sang,
in his sweet, flute-like voice:

> Oh, Mensch!   Gieb Acht!
> Was spricht die tiefe Mitternacht?
> "Ich schlief, ich schlief,
> Aus tiefem Schlaf bin ich erwacht:
> Die Welt ist tief,
> Und tiefer als der Tag gedacht.

—the last phrase of which was repeated by the accompaniment, a semitone higher.

> Tief ist ihr Weh,
> Lust—tiefer noch als Herzeleid:

As far as this, the voice had been supported by simple, full-
sounding harmonies.   Now, from out the depths, still of f
minor, rose a hesitating theme, which seemed to grope its way:
in imagination, one heard it given out by the bass strings; then
the violas reiterated it, and dyed it purple; voice and violins
sang it together; the high little flutes carried it up and beyond,
out of reach, to a half close.

> Weh spricht: vergeh!

Suddenly and unexpectedly, there entered a light yet mournful phrase in F major, which was almost a dance-rhythm, and
seemed to be a small, frail pleading for something not rightly
understood.

Doch alle Lust will Ewigkeit,
Will tiefe, tiefe Ewigkeit."

The innocent little theme passed away, and the words were sung again to a stern and fateful close in D flat major.

The concluding section of the work returned to these motives, developed them, gathered them together, grouped them and interchanged them, in complicated thematic counterpoint. Schilsky was barely able to cope with the difficulties of the score; he exerted himself desperately, laboured with his head and his whole body, and surmounted sheerly unplayable parts with the genial slitheriness that is the privilege of composers.

When, at last, he crashed to a close and wiped his face in exhaustion, there was a deafening uproar of applause. Loud cries were uttered and exclamations of enthusiasm; people rose from their seats and crowded round the piano to congratulate the player. Mrs. Lautenschläger could not desist from kissing his hand. A tall, thin Russian girl in spectacles, who had assiduously taken notes throughout, asked in a loud voice, and her peculiar, hoppy German, for information about the orchestration. What use had he made of the cymbals? She trusted a purely Wagnerian one. Schilsky hastened to reopen the score, and sat himself to answer the question earnestly and at length.

"Come, Maurice, let us go," said Madeleine, rising and shaking the creases from her skirt. "There will be congratulations enough. He won't miss ours."

Maurice had had an idea of lingering till everybody else had gone, on the chance of picking up fresh facts. But he was never good at excuses. So they slipped out into the passage, followed by Dove; but while the latter was looking for his hat, Madeleine pulled Maurice down the stairs.

"Quick, let us go!" she whispered; and, as they heard him coming after them, she drew her companion down still further, to the cellar flight, where they remained hidden until Dove had passed them, and his steps had died away in the street.

"We should have had nothing but his impressions and opinions all the way home," she said, as they emerged. "He was bottled up from having to keep quiet so long—I saw it in his face. And I couldn't stand it to-night. I'm in a bad temper, as you may have observed—or perhaps you haven't."

No, he had not noticed it.

" Well, you would have, if you hadn't been so taken up with yourself. What on earth is the matter with you? "

He feigned surprise: and they walked in silence down one street and into the next. Then she spoke again. " Do you know—but you're sure not to know that either—you gave me a nasty turn to-night? "

" I? " His surprise was genuine this time.

"Yes, you—when I heard you say ' *du* ' to Heinz."

He looked at her in astonishment; but she was not in a hurry to continue. They walked another street-length, and all she said was: " How refreshing the air is after those stuffy rooms! "

As they turned a corner, however, she made a fresh start.

" I think it's rather hard on me," she said, and laughed as she spoke. " Here am I again, having to lecture you! The fact is, I suppose, one's *métier* clings to one, in spite of oneself. But there must be something about you, too, Maurice Guest, that makes one want to do it—want to look after you, so to speak—as if you couldn't be trusted to take care of yourself. Well, it disturbed me to-night. to see how intimate you and Heinz have got."

" Is that all? Why on earth should that trouble you? And anyhow," he added, " the whole affair came about without any wish of mine."

" How? " she demanded; ana when he had told her: " And since then? "

He went into detail, coolly, without the resentment he had previously felt towards Krafft.

" And that's all? "

" Isn't it enough—for a fellow to go on in that way? "

" And you feel aggrieved? "

" No, not now. At first I was rather sore, though, for Heinz is an interesting fellow, and we were very thick for a time."

" Yes, of course—until Schilsky comes back. As soon as he appears on the scene, Master Heinz gives you the cold shoulder. Or perhaps you didn't know that Heinz is the attendant spirit of that heaven-born genius? "

Maurice did not reply, and when she spoke again, it was with renewed seriousness. " Believe me, Maurice, he is no friend for you. It's not only that you ought to be above letting yourself be treated in this way, but Heinz's friendship won't do you any good. He belongs to a bad set here—and Schilsky, too. If you were long with Heinz, you would be bound to get drawn into it, and then it would be good-bye to anything you might have done—to work and success. No, take my advice—it's sincerely meant—and steer clear of Heinz."

Maurice smiled to himself at her womanly idea of Krafft leading him to perdition. "But you're fond of him yourself, Madeleine," he said. "You can't help liking him either."

"I daresay I can't. But that is quite a different matter—quite;" and as if more than enough had now been said, she abruptly left the subject.

Before going home that night, Maurice made the old round by way of the *Brüderstrasse,* and stood and looked up at the closed windows behind which Louise lived. The house was dark, and as still as was the deserted street. Only the Venetian blinds seemed to be faintly alive; the outer windows, removed for the summer, had not yet been replaced, and a mild wind flapped the blinds, just as it swayed the tops of the trees in the opposite garden. There was a breath of autumn in the air. He told himself aloud, in the nightly silence, that she was going away—as if by repeating the words, he might ultimately grow used to their meaning. The best that could be hoped for was that she would not go immediately, but would remain in Leipzig for a few weeks longer. Then a new fear beset him. What if she never came back again?—if she had left the place quietly, of set purpose?—if these windows were closed for good and all? A dryness invaded his throat at the possibility, and on the top of this evening of almost apathetic resignation to the inevitable, the knowledge surged up in him that all he asked was to be allowed to see her just once more. Afterwards, let come what might. Once again, he must stand face to face with her—must stamp a picture of her on his brain, to carry with him for ever.

For ever!—— And through his feverish sleep ran, like a thread, the words he had heard Krafft sing, of an eternity that was deep and dreamless, a joy without beginning or end.

Madeleine had waved her umbrella at him. He crossed the road to where she was standing in rain-cloak and galoshes. She wished to tell him that the date of her playing in the *Abendunterhaltung* had been definitely fixed. About to go, she said:

"Louise is back—did you know?"

Of course he knew, though he did not tell her so—knew almost the exact hour at which the blinds had been drawn up, the windows opened, and a flower-pot, in a gaudy pink paper, put out on the sill.

Not many days after this, he came upon Louise herself. She was standing talking, at a street-corner, to the shabby little Englishman, Eggis, with whom she had walked the *foyer* of the theatre. Maurice was about to bow and pass by, but she smiled and held out her hand.

"You are back, too, then? To-day I am meeting all my friends."

She had fur about her neck, although the weather was not really cold, and her face rose out of this setting like a flower from its cup.

This meeting, and the few cordial words she had spoken, helped him over the days that followed. Sometimes, while he waited for the blow to fall, his daily life grew very unimportant; things that had hitherto interested him, now went past like shadows; he himself was a mere automaton. But sometimes, too, and especially after he had seen Louise, and touched her living hand, he wondered whether he were not perhaps tormenting himself unnecessarily. Nothing more had come to light; no one had hinted by a word at Schilsky's departure; it might yet prove to be all a mistake.

Then, however, he received a postcard from Madeleine, saying that she had something interesting to tell him. He went too early, and spent a quarter of an hour pacing her room. When she entered, she threw him a look, and, before she had finished taking off her wraps, said:

"Maurice, I have a piece of news for you. Schilsky is going away."

He nodded; his throat was dry.

"Why, you don't mean to say you knew?" she cried, and paused half-way out of her jacket.

Maurice went to the window, and stood with his back to her. In one of the houses opposite, at a window on the same level, a girl was practising the violin; his eyes followed the mechanical movements of the bow.

He cleared his throat. "Do you— Is it likely— I mean, do you think?——"

Madeleine understood him. "Yes, I do. Louise won't stay here a day longer than he does; I'm sure of that."

But otherwise she knew no more than Maurice; and she did

not offer to detain him, when, a few minutes later, he alleged a pressing appointment. Madeleine was annoyed, and showed it; she had come in with the intention of being kind to him, of encouraging him, and discussing the matter sympathetically, and it now turned out that not only had he known it all the time, but had also kept it a secret from her. She did not like under-hand ways, especially in people whom she believed she knew inside out.

Now that the pledge of secrecy had been removed from him, Maurice felt that he wanted facts; and, without thinking more about it than if he had been there the day before, he climbed the stairs that led to Krafft's lodging.

He found him at supper; Avery was present, too, and on the table sat Wotan, who was being regaled with strips of skin off the sausage. Krafft greeted Maurice with a touch of his former effusiveness; for he was in a talkative mood, and needed an audience. At his order, Avery put an extra plate on the table, and Maurice had to share their meal. It was not hard for him to lead Krafft round to the desired subject. It seemed that one of the masters in the Conservatorium had expressed a very unequivocal opinion of Schilsky's talents as a composer, and Krafft was now sarcastic, now merry, at this critic's expense. Maurice laid down his knife, and, in the first break, asked abruptly: "When does he go?"

"Go?—who?" said Krafft indifferently, tickling Wotan's nose with a piece of skin which he held out of reach.

"Who?—why, Schilsky, of course."

It sounded as if another than he had said the words: they were so short and harsh. The plate Avery was holding fell to the floor. Krafft sat back in his chair, and stared at Maurice, with a face that was all eyes.

"You knew he was going away?—or didn't you?" asked Maurice in a rough voice. "Every one knows. The whole place knows."

Krafft laughed. "The whole place knows: every one knows," he repeated. "Every one, yes—every one but me. Every one but me, who had most right to know. Yes, I alone had the right; for no one has loved him as I have."

He rose from the table, knocking over his chair.

"Or else it is not true?"

"Yes, it is true. Then you didn't know?" said Maurice, bewildered by the outburst he had evoked.

"No, we didn't know." It was Avery who spoke. She

was on her knees, picking up the pieces of the plate with slow, methodical fingers.

Krafft stood hesitating. Then he went to the piano, opened it, adjusted the seat, and made all preparations for playing. But with his fingers ready on the keys, he changed his mind, and, instead, laid his arms on the folded rack and his head on his arms. He did not stir again, and a long silence followed. The only sound that was to be heard came from Wotan, who, sitting on his haunches on a corner of the table, washed the white fur of his belly with an audible swish.

XIV

Whistling to him to stop, Fürst ran the length of a street-block after Maurice, as the latter left the Conservatorium.

"I say, Guest," he said breathlessly, on catching up with him. "Look here, I just wanted to tell you, you must be sure and join us to-night. We are going to give Schilsky a jolly send-off."

They stood at the corner of the *Wächterstrasse;* it was a blowy day. Maurice replied evasively, with his eyes on the unbound volume of Beethoven that Fürst was carrying; its tattered edges moved in the wind.

"When does he go?" he asked, without any show of concern.

Fürst looked warily round him, and dropped his voice. "Well, look here, Guest, I don't mind telling you," he said; he was perspiring from his run, and dried his neck and face. "I don't mind telling you; you won't pass it on; for he has his reasons—family or domestic reasons, if one may say so, tra-la-la!"—he winked, and nudged Maurice with his elbow— "for not wanting it to get about. It's deuced hard on him that it should have leaked out at all. I don't know how it happened; for I was mum, 'pon my honour, I was."

"Yes. And when does he go?" repeated his hearer with the same want of interest.

"To-morrow morning early, by the first train."

Now to be rid of him! But it was never easy to get away from Fürst, and since Maurice had declared his intention of continuing to take lessons from him, as good as impossible. Fürst was overpowering in his friendliness, and on this particular occasion, there was no escape for Maurice before he had promised to make one of the party that was to meet that night, at a café in the town. Then he bluffly alleged an errand in the *Plagwitzerstrasse,* and went off in an opposite direction to that which his companion had to take.

As soon as Fürst was out of sight, he turned into the path that led to the woods. Overhead, the sky was a monotonous grey expanse, and a soft, moist wind drove in gusts, before

which, on the open meadow-land, he bent his head. It was a
wind that seemed heavy with unfallen rain; a melancholy
wind, as the day itself was melancholy, in its faded colours,
and cloying mildness. With his music under his arm, Maurice
walked to the shelter of the trees. Now that he had learnt the
worst, a kind of numbness came over him; he had felt so intensely in the course of the past week that, now the crisis was
there, he seemed destitute of feeling.

His feet bore him mechanically to his favourite seat, and
here he remained, with his head in his hands, his eyes fixed on
the trodden gravel of the path. He had to learn, once and for
all, that, by to-morrow, everything would be over; for, notwithstanding the wretchedness of the past days, he was as
far off as ever from understanding. But he was loath to begin;
he sat in a kind of torpor, conscious only of the objects his
eyes rested on: some children had built a make-believe house
of pebbles, with a path leading up to the doorway, and at this
he gazed, estimating the crude architectural ideas that had
occurred to the childish builders. He felt the wind in his hair,
and listened to the soothing noise it made, high above his head.
But gradually overcoming this physical dullness, his mind began to work again. With a sudden vividness, he saw himself
as he had walked these very woods, seven months before; he
remembered the brilliant colouring of the April day, and the
abundance of energy that had possessed him. Then, on looking into the future, all his thoughts had been of strenuous endeavour and success. Now, success was a word like any other,
and left him cold.

For a long time, in place of passing on to his real preoccupation, he considered this, brooding over the change that had
come about in him. Was it, he asked himself, because he had
so little whole-hearted endurance, that when once a thing was
within his grasp, that grasp slackened? Was it that he was
able to make the effort required for a leap, then, the leap over,
could not right himself again? He believed that the slackening interest, the inability to fix his attention, which he had
had to fight against of late, must have some such deeper significance; for his whole nature—the inherited common sense
of generations—rebelled against tracing it back to the day on
which he had seen a certain face for the first time. It was
too absurd to be credible that because a slender, dark-eyed girl
had suddenly come within his range of vision, his life should
thus lose form and purpose—incredible and unnatural as well—

and, in his present mood, he would have laughed at the suggestion that this was love. To his mind, love was something frank and beautiful, made for daylight and the sun; whereas his condition was a source of mortification to him. To love, without any possible hope of return; to love, knowing that the person you loved regarded you with less than indifference, and, what was worse, that this person was passionately attached to another man—no, there was something indelicate about it, at which his blood revolted. It was the kind of thing that it suited poets to make tragedies of, but it did not—should not—happen in sober, daily life. And if, as it seemed in this case, it was beyond mortal's power to prevent it, then the only fitting thing to do was promptly to make an end. And because, over the approach of this end, he suffered, he now called himself hard names. What had he expected? Had he really believed that matters could always dally on, in this pleasant, torturous way? Would he always have been content to be third party, and miserable outsider? No; the best that could happen to him was now happening: let the coming day once be past, let a very few weeks have run their course, and the parting would have lost its sting; he would be able to look back, regretfully no doubt, but as on something done with, irrecoverable. Then he would apply himself to his work with all his heart; and it would be possible to think of her, and remember her, calmly. If once an end were put to these daily chances of seeing her, which perpetually fanned his unrest, all would go well.

And yet . . . did he close his eyes and let her face rise up before him—her sweet, white face, with the unfathomable eyes, and pale, sensuous mouth—he was shaken by an emotion that knocked his resolutions as flat as a breath knocks a house of cards. It was not love, nor anything to do with love, this he could have sworn to: it was merely the strange physical effect her presence, or the remembrance of her presence, had had upon him, from the first day on: a tightening of all centres, a heightening of all faculties, an intense hope, and as intense a despair. And in this moment, he confessed to himself that he would have been over-happy to live on just as he had been doing, if only sometimes he might see her. He needed her, as he had never felt the need of anyone before; his nature clamoured for her, imperiously, as it clamoured for light and air. He had no concern with anyone but her—her only—and he could not let her go. It was not love; it was a bodily weakness, a pitiable infirmity: he even felt it degrading that another person should be able to exercise such an influence over him, that there should be a part of himself over which he had no control. Not to see her, not to be able to gather fresh strength from each chance meeting, meant that the grip life had of him would relax—he grew sick even at the thought of how, in some unknown place, in the midst of strangers, she would go on living, and giving her hand and her smile to other people, while he would never see her again. And he said her name aloud to himself, as if he were in bodily pain, or as if the sound of it might somehow bring him aid: he inwardly implored whatever fate was above him to give him the one small chance he asked—the chance of fair play.

The morning passed, without his knowing it. When, considerably after his usual dinner-hour, he was back in his room, he looked at familiar objects with unseeing eyes. He was not conscious of hunger, but going into the kitchen begged for a cup of the coffee that could be smelt brewing on Frau Krause's stove. When he had drunk this, a veil seemed to lift from his brain; he opened and read a letter from home, and was pricked by compunction at the thought that, except for a few scales run hastily that morning, he had done no work. But while he still stood, with his arm on the lid of the piano, an exclamation rose to his lips; and taking up his hat, he went down the stairs again, and out into the street. What was he thinking of? If he wished to see Louise once more, his place was under her windows, or in those streets she would be likely to pass through.

He walked up and down before the house in the *Brüderstrasse,* sometimes including a side street, in order to avoid making himself conspicuous; putting on a hurried air, if anyone looked curiously at him; lingering for a quarter of an hour on end, in the shadow of a neighbouring doorway. Gradually, yet too quickly, the grey afternoon wore to a close. He had paced to and fro for an hour now, but not a trace of her had he seen; nor did even a light burn in her room when darkness fell. A fear lest she should have already gone away, beset him again, and got the upper hand of him; and wild schemes flitted through his mind. He would mount the stairs, and ring the door-bell, on some pretext or other, to learn whether she was still there; and his foot was on the lowest stair, when his courage failed him, and he turned back. But the idea had taken root; he could not bear much longer the uncertainty he was in; and so, towards seven o'clock, when he had hung about for three hours, and there was still no sign of life in her room, he went boldly up the broad, winding stair and rang the bell. When the door was opened, he would find something to say.

The bell, which he had pulled hard, pealed through the house, jangled on, and, in a series of after-tinkles, died away. There was no immediate answering sound; the silence persisted, and having waited for some time, he rang again. Then, in the distance, he heard a door creak; soft, cautious footsteps crept along the passage; a light moved; the glass window in the upper half of the door was opened, and a little old woman peered out, holding a candle above her head. On seeing the pale face close before her, she drew back, and made as if to shut the window; for, as a result of poring over newspapers, she lived in continual expectation of robbery and murder.

" She is not at home," she said with tremulous bravado, in answer to the young man's question, and again was about to close the window. But Maurice thrust in his hand, and she could not shut without crushing it.

" Then she is still here? Has she gone out? When will she be back? " he queried.

" How should I know? And look here, young man, if you don't take away your hand and leave the house at once, I shall call from the window for a policeman."

He went slowly down the stairs and across the street, and took up anew his position in the dark doorway—a proceeding which did not reassure Fräulein Grünhut, who, regarding his inquiries as a feint, was watching his movements from between the slats of a window-blind. But Maurice had not stood again for more than a quarter of an hour, when a feeling of nausea seized him, and this reminded him that he had practically eaten nothing since the morning. If he meant to hold out, he must snatch a bite of food somewhere; afterwards, he would return and wait, if he had to wait all night.

In front of the *Panorama* on the *Rossplatz,* he ran into the arms of Fürst, and the latter, when he heard where Maurice was going, had nothing better to do than to accompany him, and drink a *Schnitt.* Fürst, who was in capital spirits at the prospect of the evening, laughed heartily, told witty anecdotes, and slapped his fat thigh, the type of rubicund good-humour; and as he was not of an observant turn of mind, he did not notice his companion's abstraction. Hardly troubling to dissemble, Maurice paid scant attention to Fürst's talk; he ate avidly, and as soon as he had finished, pushed back his chair and called to the waiter for his bill.

"I must go," he said, and rose. "I have something important to do this evening, and can't join you."

Fürst, cut short in the middle of a sentence, let his double chin fall on his collar, and gazed open-mouthed at his companion.

"But I say, Guest, look here! . . ." Maurice heard him expostulate as the outer door slammed behind him.

He made haste to retrace his steps. The wind had dropped; a fine rain was beginning to fall; it promised to be a wet night, of empty streets and glistening pavements. There was no visible change in the windows of the *Brüderstrasse;* they were as blankly dark as before. Turning up his coat-collar, Maurice resumed his patrollings, but more languidly; he was drowsy from having eaten, and the air was chill. A weakness overcame him at the thought of the night-watch he had set himself; it seemed impossible to endure the crawling past of still more hours. He was tired to exhaustion, and a sudden, strong desire arose in him, somehow, anyhow, to be taken out of himself, to have his thoughts diverted into other channels. And this feeling grew upon him with such force, the idea of remaining where he was, for another hour, became so intolerable, that he forgot everything else, and turned and ran back towards the *Panorama,* only afraid lest Fürst should have gone without him.

The latter was, in fact, just coming out of the door. He stared in astonishment at Maurice.

"I've changed my mind," said Maurice, without apology. "Shall we go? Where's the place?"

Fürst mumbled something inaudible; he was grumpy at the other's behaviour. Scanning him furtively, and noting his odd, excited manner, he concluded that Maurice had been drinking.

They walked without speaking; Fürst hummed to himself. In the thick-sown, business thoroughfare, the *Brühl,* they entered a dingy café; and while Fürst chattered with the landlord and *Büffetdame,* with both of whom he was on very friendly terms, Maurice went into the side-room, where the *Kneipe* was to be held, and sat down before a long, narrow table, spread with a soiled red and blue-checked tablecloth. He felt cold and sick again, and when the wan *piccolo* set a beer-mat before him, he sent the lad to the devil for a cognac. The

waiter came with the liqueur-bottle; Maurice drank the contents of one and then another of the tiny glasses. A genial
warmth ran through him and his nausea ceased. He leaned
his head on his hands, closed his eyes, and, soothed by the heat
of the room, had a few moments' pleasant lapse of consciousness.

He was roused by the entrance of a noisy party of three.
These were strangers to him, and when they had mentioned
their names and learned his, they sat down at the other end of
the table and talked among themselves. They were followed
by a couple of men known to Maurice by sight. One, an
Italian, a stout, animated man, with prominent, jet-black eyes
and huge white teeth, was a fellow-pupil of Schilsky's, and a
violinist of repute, notwithstanding the size and fleshiness of
his hands, which were out of all proportion to the delicate build
of his instrument. The other was a slender youth of fantastic
appearance. He wore a long, old-fashioned overcoat, which
reached to his heels, and was moulded to a shapely waist; on
his fingers were numerous rings; his bushy hair was scented
and thickly curled, his face painted and pencilled like a woman's. He did not sit down, but, returning to the public
room, leaned over the counter and talked to the *Büffetdame,*
in a tone which had nothing in common with Fürst's hearty
familiarity.

Next came a couple of Americans, loud, self-assertive, careless of dress and convention; close behind them still another
group, and at its heels, Dove. The latter entered the room
with an apologetic air, and on sitting down at the head of the
table, next Maurice, mentioned at once that, at heart, he was
not partial to this kind of thing, and was only there because
he believed the present to be an exceptional occasion: who knew
but what, in after years, he might not be proud to claim
having made one of the party on this particular evening?—
the plain truth being that Schilsky was little popular with his
own sex, and, in consequence of the difficulty of beating up a
round dozen of men, Fürst had been forced to be very pressing
in his invitations, to have recourse to bribes and promises, or,
as in the case of Dove, to stimulating the imagination. The
majority of the guests present were not particular who paid for
their drink, provided they got it.

At Krafft's entry, a stifled laugh went round. To judge
from his appearance, he had not been in bed the previous night:
sleep seemed to hang on his red and sunken eyelids; his hands

and face were dirty, and when he took off his coat, which he had worn turned up at the neck, it was seen that he had either lost or forgotten his collar. Shirt and waistcoat were insufficiently buttoned. His walk was steady, but his eyes had a glassy stare, and did not seem to see what they rested on. A strong odour of brandy went out from him; but he had not been many minutes in the room before a stronger and more penetrating smell made itself felt. The rest of the company began to sniff and ejaculate, and Fürst, having tracked it to the corner where the overcoats hung, drew out of one of Krafft's pockets a greasy newspaper parcel, evidently some days old, containing bones, scraps of decaying meat, and rancid fish. The *piccolo,* summoned by a general shout, was bade to dispose of the garbage instantly, and to hang the coat in a draughty place to air. Various epithets were hurled at Krafft, who, however, sat picking his teeth with unconcern, as if what went on around him had nothing to do with him.

They were now all collected but Schilsky, and much beer had been drunk. Fürst was in his usual state of agitation lest his friend should forget to keep the appointment; and the spirits of those—there were several such present—who suffered almost physical pain from seeing another than themselves the centre of interest, went up by leaps and bounds. But at this juncture, Schilsky's voice was heard in the next room. It was raised and angry; it snarled at a waiter. Significant glances flew round the table: for the young man's outbursts of temper were well known to all. He entered, making no response to the greetings that were offered him, displaying his anger with genial indifference to what others thought of him. To the *piccolo* he tossed coat and hat, and swore at the boy for not catching them. Then he let his loose-limbed body down on the vacant chair, and drank off the glass of *Pilsener* that was set before him.

There was a pause of embarrassment. The next moment, however, several men spoke at once: Fürst continued a story he was telling, some one else capped it, and the mirth these anecdotes provoked was more than ordinarily uproarious. Schilsky sat silent, letting his sullen mouth hang, and tapping the table with his fingers. Meanwhile, he emptied one glass of beer after another. The *piccolo* could hardly cope with the demands that were made on him, and staggered about, top-heavy, with his load of glasses.

But it was impossible to let the evening pass as flatly as

this; besides, as the general hilarity increased, it made those present less sensitive to the mood of the guest of honour. Fürst was a born speaker, and his heart was full. So, presently, he rose to his feet, struck his glass, and, in spite of Schilsky's deepening scowl, held a flowery speech about his departing friend. The only answer Schilsky gave was a muttered request to cease making an idiot of himself.

This was going rather too far; but no one protested, except Ford, the pianist, who said in English: " Speesch? Call that a speesch? "

Fürst, inclined in the first moment of rebuff to be touchy, allowed his natural goodness of heart to prevail. He leaned forward, and said, not without pathos: " Old man, we are all your friends here. Something's the matter. Tell us what it is."

Before Schilsky could reply, Krafft awakened from his apparent stupor to say with extreme distinctness: " I'll tell you. There's been the devil to pay."

" Now, chuck it, Krafft! " cried one or two, not without alarm at the turn things might take.

But Schilsky, whose anger had begun to subside under the influence of the two litres he had drunk, said slowly and thickly: " Let him be. What he says is the truth—gospel truth."

" Oh, say, that's to' bad! " cried one of the Americans—a lean man, with the mouth and chin of a Methodist.

All kept silence now, in the hope that Schilsky would continue. As he did not, but sat brooding, Fürst, in his rôle of peacemaker, clapped him on the back. " Well, forget it for to-night, old man! What does it matter? To-morrow you'll be miles away."

This struck a reminiscence in Ford, who forthwith tried to sing:

> I'm off by the morning train,
> Across the raging main——

" That's easily said! " Schilsky threw a dark look round the table. " By those who haven't been through it. I have. And I'd rather have lost a hand."

Krafft laughed—that is to say, a cackle of laughter issued from his mouth, while his glazed eyes stared idiotically. " He shall tell us about it. Waiter, a round of *Schnaps!*"

" Shut up, Krafft! " said Fürst uneasily.

" Damn you, Heinz! " cried Schilsky, striking the table.

He swallowed his brandy at a gulp, and held out the glass to be refilled. His anger fell still more; he began to commiserate himself. "By Hell, I wish a plague would sweep every woman off the earth!"

"The deuce, why don't you keep clear of them?"

Schilsky laughed, without raising his heavy eyes. "If they'd only give one the chance. Damn them all!—old and young—I say. If it weren't for them, a man could lead a quiet life."

"It'll all come out in the wash," consoled the American.

Maurice heard everything that passed, distinctly; but the words seemed to be bandied at an immeasurable distance from him. He remained quite undisturbed, and would have felt like a god looking on at the doings of an infinitesimal world, had it not been for a wheel which revolved in his head, and hindered him from thinking connectedly. So far, drinking had brought him no pleasure; and he had sense enough to find the proximity of Ford disagreeable; for the latter spilt half the liquor he tried to swallow over himself, and half over his neighbour.

A fresh imprecation of Schilsky's called forth more laughter. On its subsidence, Krafft awoke to his surroundings again. "What has the old woman given you?" he asked, with his strange precision of speech and his drunken eyes.

Schilsky struck the table with his fist. "Look at him!— shamming drunk, the bitch!" he cried.

"Never mind him; he don't count. How much did she give you?"

"Oh, gee, go on!"

But Schilsky, turned sullen again, refused to answer.

"Out with it then, Krafft!—you know, you scoundrel, you!"

Krafft put his hand to the side of his mouth. "She gave him three thousand marks."

On all sides the exclamations flew.

"Oh, gee-henna!"

"Golly for her!"

"*Drei tausend Mark!—Alle Ehre!*"

Again Krafft leaned forward with a maudlin laugh. "*Jawohl*—but on what condition?"

"Heinz, you ferret out things like a pig's snout," said Fürst. with an exaggerated, tipsy disgust.

"What, the old louse made conditions, did she?"

"Is she jealous?"

There was another roar at this. Schilsky looked as black as thunder.

Again Fürst strove to intercede. " Jealous?—in seven devils' name, why jealous? The old scarecrow! She hasn't an ounce of flesh to her bones."

Schilsky laughed. "Much you know about it, you fool! Flesh or no flesh, she's as troublesome as the plumpest. I wouldn't go through the last month again for all you could offer me. Month?—no, nor the last six months either! It's been a hell of a life. Three of 'em, whole damned three, at my heels, and each ready to tear the others' eyes out."

" Three! Hullo! "

" Three? Bah!—what's three?" sneered the painted youth.

Schilsky turned on him. "What's three? Go and try it, if you want to know, you pap-sodden suckling! Three, I said, and they've ended by making the place too hot to hold me. But I'm done now. No more for me!—if my name's what it is."

Having once broken through his reserve, he talked on, with heated fluency; and the longer he spoke, the more he was carried away by his grievances. For, all he had asked for, he assured his hearers, had been peace and quiet—the peace necessary to important work. "Jesus and Mary! Are a fellow's chief obligations not his obligations to himself?" At the same time, it was not his intention to put any of the blame on Lulu's shoulders: she couldn't help herself. "Lulu is Lulu. I'm damned fond of Lulu, boys, and I've always done my best by her—is there anyone here who wants to say I haven't?"

There was none; a chorus of sympathetic ayes went up from the party that was drinking at his expense.

Mollified, he proceeded, asserting vehemently that he would have gone miles out of his way to avoid causing Lulu pain. "I'm a soft-hearted fool—I admit it!—where a woman is concerned." But he had yielded to her often enough—too often—as it was; the time had come for him to make a stand. Let those present remember what he had sacrificed only that summer for Lulu's sake. Would anyone else have done as much for his girl? He made bold to doubt it. For a man like Zeppelin to come to him, and to declare, with tears in his eyes, that he could teach him no more—could he afford to treat a matter like that with indifference? Had he really been free to make a choice?

Again he looked round the table with emphasis, and those

who had their muscles sufficiently under control, hastened to
lay their faces in seemly folds.

Then, however, Schilsky's mood changed; he struck the
table so that the glasses danced. " And shall I tell you what
my reward has been for not going? Do you want to know
how Lulu has treated me for staying on here? 'You are a
quarter of an hour late: where have you been? You've only
written two bars since I saw you this morning: what have
you been doing? A letter has come in a strange writing:
who is it from? You've put on another tie: who have
you been to see?' Himmelsakrament!" He drained his
glass. " I've had the life of a dog, I tell you—of a dog!
There's not been a moment in the day when she hasn't spied
on me, and followed me, and made me ridiculous. Over every
trifle she has got up a fresh scene. She's even gone so far as
to come to my room and search my pockets, when she knew I
wasn't at home."

" Yes, yes," sneered Krafft. " Exactly! And so, gentlemen,
he was now for slinking off without a word to her."

" Oh, pfui!" spat the American.

" Call him a liar!" said a voice.

" Liar?" repeated Schilsky dramatically. " Why liar? I
don't deny it. I would have done it gladly if I could—isn't
that just what I've been saying? Lulu would have got over
it all the quicker alone. And then, why shouldn't I confess
it? You're all my friends here." He dropped his voice.
" I'm afraid of Lulu, boys. I was afraid she'd get round me,
and then my chance was gone. She might have shot me, but
she wouldn't have let me go. You never know how a woman
of that type'll break out—never!"

" But she didn't!" said Krafft. " You live."

Schilsky understood him.

" Some brute," he cried savagely, " some dirty brute had
nothing better to do than to tell her."

" Ha, ha, ha!" laughed the painted boy.

Fürst blew his nose. " It wasn't me. I was mum. 'Pon
my honour, I was."

" My God!" said Schilsky, and fell to remembering it.
" What a time I've been through with her this afternoon!"
He threatened to be overcome by the recollection, and supported his head on his hands. " A woman has no gratitude,"
he murmured, and drew his handkerchief from his pocket. " It
is a weak, childish sex—with no inkling of higher things."

Here, however, he suddenly drew himself up. "Life is very hard!" he cried, in a loud voice. "The perpetual struggle between duty and inclination for a man of genius . . . .!"

He grew franker, and gave gratuitous details of the scene that had taken place in his room that afternoon. Most of those present were in ecstasies at this divulging of his private life, which went forward to the accompaniment of snores from Ford, and the voice of Dove, who, with portentous gravity, sang over and over again, the first strophe of *The Last Rose of Summer.*

"A fury!" said Schilsky. "A . . . a what do you call it?—a . . . Meg . . . a Meg——" He gave it up and went on: "By God, but Lulu knows how! Keep clear of her nails, boys—I'd advise you!" At this point, he pulled back his collar, and exhibited a long, dark scratch on the side of his neck. "A little remembrance she gave me to take away with me!" While he displayed it, he seemed to be rather proud of it; but immediately afterwards, his mood veered round again to one of bitter resentment. To illustrate the injustice she had been guilty of, and his own long-suffering, he related, at length, the story of his flirtation with Ephie, and the infinite pains he had been at to keep Louise in ignorance of what was happening. He grew very tender with himself as he told it. For, according to him, the whole affair had come about without any assistance of his. "What the deuce was I to do? Chucked herself full at my head, did the little one. No invitation necessary—a ripe plum, boys! Touch the plum—and off it tumbles! As pretty a little thing, too, as ever was made! Had everything arranged by the second meeting. Papa to set us up; house in New York; money *in Hülle und Fülle!*"

At the mention of New York, the lean American looked grave. "Look here, you, don't think you're the whole shoot because you've got a wave in your hair!" he murmured in English.

But Schilsky did not hear him; his voice droned on, giving the full particulars of this particular case. He grew momentarily opener.

"One no sooner out of the door than the other was in," he asserted, and laughed long to himself.

For some time past, Maurice had been possessed by the idea that what was happening concerned him very nearly, and that he ought to interfere and put his foot down. His hands

had grown cold, and he sat vainly trying to speak: nothing,
however, came, but little drunken gulps and hiccups. But the
first mention of Ephie's name seemed to put new strength into
him; he made a violent effort, and rose to his feet, holding on
to the table with both hands. He could not, however, manage
to attract attention; no one took any notice of him; and besides this, he had himself no notion what it was that he really
wanted to say.

"And drowns his sorrows in the convivial glass!" he suddenly shouted in English, at the top of his voice, which he had
found. He had a vague belief that he was quoting a well-
known line of poetry, and, though he did not in the least understand how it applied to the situation, he continued to repeat it, with varying shades of fervour, till some one called
out: "Oh, stop your blasted rot!"

He laughed hoarsely at this, could not check himself, and was
so exhausted when he had finished that it took him some time
to remember why he was on his feet. Schilsky was still relating: his face was darkly red, his voice husky, and he flapped
his arms with meaningless gestures. A passionate rebellion,
a kind of primitive hatred, gripped Maurice, and when Schilsky paused for breath, he could contain himself no longer.
He felt the burning need of contradicting the speaker, even
though he could not catch the drift of what was said.

"It's a lie!" he cried fiercely, with such emphasis that
every face was turned to him. "A damned lie!"

"A lie? What the devil do you mean?" responded not
one but many voices—the whole table seemed to be asking
him, with the exception of Dove, who sang on in an ever
decreasing tempo.

"Get out!—Let him alone; he's drunk. He doesn't know
what he's saying—He's got rats in his head!" he heard voices
asserting. Forthwith he began a lengthy defence of himself,
broken only by gaps in which his brain refused to work. Conscious that no one was listening to him, he bawled more and
more loudly.

"Oh, quit it, you double-barrelled ass!" said the American.

Schilsky, persuaded by those next him to let the incident pass
unnoticed, contented himself with a: "*Verfluchte Schweinerei!*"
spat, after Fürst's gurgled account of Maurice's previous in-
sobriety, across the floor behind him, to express his contempt,
and proceeded as dominatingly as before with the narration of
his love-affairs.

The blood rushed to Maurice's head at the sound of this voice which he could neither curb nor understand. Rage mastered him—a vehement desire to be quits. He kicked back his chair, and rocked to and fro.

"It's a lie—a dirty lie!" he cried. "You make her unhappy—God, how unhappy you make her! You illtreat her. You've never given her a day's happiness. S . . . said so . . . herself. I heard her . . . I swear . . . I——"

His voice turned to a whine; his words came thick and incoherent.

Schilsky sprang to his feet and aimed the contents of a half-emptied glass at Maurice's face. "Take that, you blasted spy!—you Englishman!" he spluttered. "I'll teach you to mix your dirty self in my affairs!"

Every one jumped up; there was noise and confusion; simultaneously two waiters entered the room, as if they had not been unprepared for something of this kind. Fürst and another man restrained Schilsky by the arms, reasoning with him with more force than coherence. Maurice, the beer dripping from chin, collar and shirt-front, struggled furiously with some one who held him back.

"Let me get at him—let me get at him!" he cried. "I'll teach him to treat a woman as he does. The sneak—the cur —the filthy cad! He's not fit to touch her hand—her beautiful hand—her beau . . . ti . . . ful——" Here, overpowered by his feelings, as much as by superior strength, he sank on a chair and wept.

"I'll break his bones!" raved Schilsky. "What the hell does he mean by it?—the *infame Schuft,* the *Aas,* the dirty *Engländer!* Thinks he'll sneak after her himself, does he?— What in Jesus' name is it to him how I treat her? I'll take a stick to her if I like—it's none of his blasted business! Look here, do you see that?" He freed one hand, fumbled in his pocket, and, almost inarticulate with rage and liquor, brandished a key across the table. "Do you see that? That's a key, isn't it, you drunken hog? Well, with that key, I can let myself into Lulu's room at any hour I want to; I can go there now, this very minute, if I like—do you think she'll turn me out, you infernal spy? Turn me out?—she'd go down on her knees here before you all to get me back to her!"

Unwilling to be involved in the brawl, the more sober of the party had begun to seek out their hats and to slink away. A little group round Schilsky blarneyed and expostulated.

Why should the whole sport of the evening be spoilt in this
fashion? What did it matter what the damned cranky Englishman said? Let him be left to his swilling. They would clear
out, and wind up the night at the *Bauer;* and at four, when that
shut, they would go on to the *Bayrische Bahnhof,* where they
could not only get coffee, but could also see Schilsky off by a
train soon after five. These persuasions prevailed, and, still
swearing, and threatening, and promising, by all that was holy,
to bring Lulu there, by the hair of her head if necessary, to show
whether or no he had the power over her he boasted of, Schilsky
finally allowed himself to be dragged off, and those who were
left lurched out in his wake.

With their exit an abrupt silence fell, and Maurice sank
into a heavy sleep, in which he saw flowery meadows and heard
a gently trickling brook. . . .

"Now then, up with you!—get along!" some one was
shouting in his ear, and, bit by bit, a pasty-faced waiter entered
his field of view. "It's past time, anyhow," and yawning
loudly, the waiter turned out all the gas-jets but one. " Don't
yer hear? Up with you! You'll have to look after the other—
now, damn me, if there isn't another of you as well! " and,
from under the table, he drew out a recumbent body.

Maurice then saw that he was still in the company of Dove,
who sat staring into space—like a dead man. Krafft, propped
on a chair, hung his head far back, and the collarless shirt exposed the whole of his white throat.

The waiter hustled them about. Maurice was comparatively
steady on his legs; and it was found that Dove could walk.
But over Krafft, the man scratched his head and called a com-
rade. At the mention of a droschke, however, Maurice all
but wept anew with ire and emotion: this was his dearest
friend, the friend of his bosom; he was ready at any time to
stake his life for him, and now he was not to be allowed even
to see him home.

A difficulty arose about Maurice's hat: he was convinced
that the one the waiter jammed so rudely on his head did not
belong to him; and it seemed as if nothing in the world had
ever mattered so much to him as now getting back his own
hat. But he had not sufficient fluency to explain all he meant;
before he had finished, the man lost patience; and suddenly,
without any transition, the three of them were in the street.
The raw night air gave them a shock; they gasped and choked
a little. Then the wall of a house rose appositely and met

them. They leaned against it, and Maurice threw the hat from him and trampled on it, chuckling at the idea that he was revenging himself on the waiter.

It was a journey of difficulties; not only was he unclear what locality they were in, but innumerable lifeless things confronted them and formed obstacles to their progress; they had to charge an advertisement-column two or three times before they could get round it. Maurice grew excessively angry, especially with Dove. For while Heinz let himself be lugged this way and that, Dove, grown loud and wilful, had ideas of his own, and, in addition to this, sang the whole time with drunken gravity:

> Sez the ragman, to the bagman,
> I'll do yees no harm.

"Stop it, you oaf!" cried Maurice, goaded to desperation. "You beastly, blathering, drunken idiot!"

Then, for a street-length, he himself lapsed into semi-consciousness, and when he wakened, Dove was gone. He chuckled anew at the thought that somehow or other they had managed to outwit him.

His intention had been to make for home, but the door before which they ultimately found themselves was Krafft's. Maurice propped his companion against the wall, and searched his own pockets for a key. When he had found one, he could not find the door, and when this was secured, the key would not fit. The perspiration stood out on his forehead; he tried again and again, thought the keyhole was dodging him, and asserted the fact so violently that a window in the first storey was opened and a head thrust out.

"What in the name of Heaven are you doing down there?" it cried. "You drunken *Schwein,* can't you see the door's open?"

In the sitting-room, both fell heavily over a chair; after that, with infinite labour, he got Heinz on the sofa. He did not attempt to make a light; enough came in from a street-lamp for him to see what he was doing.

Lying on his face, Krafft groaned a little, and Maurice suddenly grasped that he was taken ill. Heinz was ill, Heinz, his best friend, and he was doing nothing to help him! Shedding tears, he poured out a glass of water. He believed he was putting the carafe safely back on the table, but it dropped with a crash to the floor. He was afraid Frau Schulz would come in, and said in a loud voice: " It's that fellow there, he's dead drunk, beastly drunk!" Krafft would not drink the water, and in the attempt to force him, it was spilled over him. He stirred uneasily, put up his arms and dragged Maurice down, so that the latter fell on his knees beside the sofa. He made a few ineffectual efforts to free himself; but one arm held him like a vice; and in this uncomfortable position, he went to sleep.

PART II

O viva morte, e dilettoso male!

PETRARCH.

I

THE following morning, towards twelve o'clock, a note from Madeleine was handed to Maurice. In it, she begged him to account to Schwarz for her absence from the rehearsal of a trio, which was to have taken place at two.

Go and explain that it is quite impossible for me to come, she wrote. *Louise is very ill; the doctor is afraid of brain fever. I am rushing off this moment to see about a nurse—and shall stay till one comes.*

He read the words mechanically, without taking in their meaning. From the paper, his eyes roved round the room; he saw the tumbled, unopened bed, from which he had just risen, the traces of his boots on the coverings. He could not remember how he had come there; his last recollection was of being turned out of Krafft's room, in what seemed to be still the middle of the night. Since getting home, he must have slept a dead sleep.

"Ill? Brain fever?" he repeated to himself, and his mind strove to pierce the significance of the words. What had happened? Why should she be ill? A racking uneasiness seized him and would not let him rest. His inclination was to lay his aching head on the pillow again; but this was out of the question; and so, though he seldom braved Frau Krause, he now boldly went to her with a request to warm up his coffee.

When he had drunk it, and bathed his head, he felt considerably better. But he still could not call to mind what had occurred. The previous evening was blurred in its details; he only had a sense of oppression when he thought of it, as of something that had threatened, and still did. He was glad to have a definite task before him, and went out at once, in order to catch Schwarz before he left the Conservatorium; but it was too late; the master's door was locked. It was a bright, cold day with strong sunlight; Maurice's eyes ached, and he shrank from the wind at every corner. Instead of going home, he went to Madeleine's room and sat down to wait for her.

She had evidently been away since early morning; the piano was dusty and unopened; the blind at the head of it had not been drawn up. It was a pleasant dusk; he put his arms on the table, his head on his arms, and, in spite of his anxiety, fell into a sound sleep.

He was wakened by Madeleine's entrance. It was three o'clock. She came bustling in, took off her hat, laid it on the piano, and at once drew up the blind. She was not surprised to find him there, but exclaimed at his appearance.

"Good gracious, Maurice, how dreadful you look! Are you ill?"

He hastened to reassure her, and she was a little put out at her wasted sympathy.

"Well, no wonder, I'm sure, after the doings there were last night. A pretty way to behave! And that you should have mixed yourself up in it as you did!—I wouldn't have believed it of you. How I know? My dear boy, it's the talk of the place."

Her words called up to him a more lucid remembrance of the past evening than he had yet been capable of. In his eagerness to recollect everything, he changed colour and looked away. Madeleine put his confusion down to another cause.

"Never mind, it's over now, and we won't say any more about it. Sit still, and I'll make you some tea. That will do your head good—for you have a splitting headache, haven't you? I shall be glad of some myself, too, after all the running about I've had this morning. I'm quite worn out."

When she heard that he had had no dinner, she sent for bread and sausage, and was so busy and unsettled that only when she sat down, with her cup before her, did he get a chance to say: "What is it, Madeleine? Is she very ill?"

Madeleine shrugged her shoulders. "Yes, she is ill enough. It's not easy to say what the matter is, though. The doctor is to see her again this evening. And I found a nurse."

"Then she is not going away?" He did not mean to say the words aloud; they escaped him against his will.

His companion raised her eyebrows, filling her forehead with wrinkles. "Going away?" she echoed. "I should say not. My dear Maurice, what is more, it turns out she hadn't an idea he was going either. What do you say to that?" She flushed with sincere indignation. "Not an idea—until yesterday. My lord had the intention of sneaking off without a word, and of leaving her to find it out for herself. Oh, it's an abominable affair altogether!—and has been from beginning to end. There's much about Louise, as you know, that I don't approve of, and I think she has behaved weakly—not to call it by a harder name—all through. But now, she has my entire sympathy. The poor girl is in a pitiable state."

"Is she . . . dangerously ill?"

"Well, I don't think she'll die of it, exactly—though it might be better for her if she did. Na! . . . let me fill up your cup. And eat something more. Oh, he is . . . no words are bad enough for him; though honestly speaking, I think we might have been prepared for something of this kind, all along. It seems he made his arrangements for going on the quiet. Frau Schaefele advanced him the money; for of course he has nothing of his own. But what condition do you think the old wretch made? That he should break with Louise. Fürst has told me all about it. I went to him at once this morning. She was always jealous of Louise—though to him she only talked of the holiness of art and the artist's calling, and the danger of letting domestic ties entangle you, and rubbish of that kind. I believe she was at the bottom of it that he didn't marry Louise long ago. Well, however that may be, he now let himself be persuaded easily enough. He was hearing on all sides that he had been here too long; and candidly, I think he was beginning to feel Louise a drag on him. I know of late they were not getting on well together. But to be such a coward and a weakling! To slink off in this fashion! Of course, when it came to the last, he was simply afraid of her, and of the scene she would make him. Bravery has as little room in his soul as honesty or manliness. He would always prefer a back-door exit. Such things excite a man, don't you know?—and ruffle the necessary artistic composure." She laughed scornfully. "However, I'm glad to say, he didn't escape scot-free after all. Everything went well till yesterday afternoon, when Louise, who was as unsuspecting as a child, heard of it from some one—they say it was Krafft. Without thinking twice—you know her . . . or rather you don't— she went straight to Schilsky and confronted him. I can't tell you what took place between them, but I can imagine something of it, for when Louise lets herself go, she knows no bounds, and this was a matter of life and death to her."

Madeleine rose, blew out the flame of the spirit-lamp, and refilled the teapot.

"Fräulein Grünhut, her landlady, heard her go out yesterday afternoon, but didn't hear her come in, so it must have been late in the evening. Louise hates to be pried on, and the old woman is lazy, so she didn't go to her room till about half-past eight this morning, when she took in the hot water. Then she found Louise stretched on the floor, just as she had come in last night, her hat lying beside her. She was conscious, and her eyes were open, but she was stiff and cold, and wouldn't speak or move. Grünhut couldn't do anything with her, and was mortally afraid. She sent for me; and between us we got her to bed, and I went for a doctor. That was at nine, and I have been on my feet ever since."

"It's awfully good of you."

"No, she won't die," continued Madeleine meditatively, stirring her tea. "She's too robust a nature for that. But I shouldn't wonder if it affected her mind. As I say, she knows no bounds, and has never learnt self-restraint. It has always been all or nothing with her. And this I must say: however foolish and wrong the whole thing was, she was devoted to Schilsky, and sacrificed everything—work, money and friends —to her infatuation. She lived only for him, and this is a moral judgment on her. Excess of any kind brings its own punishment with it."

She rose and smoothed her hair before the mirror.

"And now I really must get to work, and make up for the lost morning. I haven't touched a note to-day. As for you, Maurice, if you take my advice, you'll go home and go to bed. A good sleep is what you're needing. Come to-morrow, if you like, for further news. I shall go back after supper, and hear what the doctor says. Good-bye."

"Good-bye, Madeleine. You're a brick."

Having returned to his room, he lay face downwards on the sofa. He was sick at heart. Viewed in the light of the story he had heard from Madeleine, life seemed too unjust to be endured. It propounded riddles no one could answer; the vast output of energy that composed it, was misdirected; on every side was cruelty and suffering. Only the heartless and selfish —those who deserved to suffer—went free.

He pressed the back of his hand to his tired eyes; and, despite her good deeds, he felt a sudden antipathy to Madeleine, who, on a day like this, could take up her ordinary occupation.

In the morning, on awakening from a heavy sleep, he was seized by a fear lest Louise should have died in the night.

Through brooding on it, the fear became a certainty, and he went early to Madeleine, making a detour through the *Brüderstrasse,* where his suspicions were confirmed by the lowered blinds. He had almost two hours to wait; it was eleven o'clock before Madeleine returned. Her face was so grave that his heart seemed to stop beating. But there was no change in the sick girl's condition; the doctor was perplexed, and spoke of a consultation. Madeleine was returning at two o'clock to relieve the nurse.

"You are foolishly letting it upset you altogether," she reproved Maurice. "And it won't mend matters in the least. Go home and settle down to work, like a sensible fellow."

He tried to follow Madeleine's advice. But it was of no use; when he had struggled on for half an hour, he sprang up, realising how monstrous it was that he should be sitting there, drilling his fingers, getting the right notes of a turn, the specific shade of a crescendo, when, not very far away, Louise perhaps lay dying. Again he felt keenly the contrariness of life; and all the labour which those around him were expending on the cult of hand and voice and ear, seemed of a ludicrous vanity compared with the grim little tragedy that touched him so nearly; and in this mood he remained, throughout the days of suspense that now ensued.

He went regularly every afternoon to Madeleine, and, if she were not at home, waited till she returned, an hour, two hours, as the case might be. This was the vital moment of the day—when he read her tidings from her face.

At first they were always the same: there was no change. Fever did not set in, but, day and night, Louise lay with wide, strained eyes; she refused nourishment, and the strongest sleeping-draught had no effect. Then, early one morning, for some trifling cause which, afterwards, no one could recall, she broke into a convulsive fit of weeping, went on till she was exhausted, and subsequently fell asleep.

On the day Maurice learnt that she was out of danger, he walked deep into the woods. The news had lifted such a load from his mind that he felt almost happy. But before he reached home again, his brain had begun to work at matters which, during the period of anxiety, it had left untouched. At first, in desperation, he had been selfless enough to hope that Schilsky would return, on learning what had happened. Now, however, that he had not done so, and Louise had passed safely through the ordeal, Maurice was ready to tremble lest anything

14

should occur to soil the robe of saintly suffering, in which he draped her.

He began to take up the steady routine of his life again. Fürst received him with open arms, and no allusion was made to the night in the *Brühl*. With the cessation of his anxiety, a feeling of benevolence towards other people awakened in him, and when, one afternoon, Schwarz asked the assembled class if no one knew what had become of Krafft, whether he was ill, or anything of the kind, it was Maurice who volunteered to find out. He remembered now that he had not seen Krafft at the Conservatorium for a week or more.

Frau Schulz looked astonished to see him, and, holding the door in her hand, made no mien to let him enter. Herr Krafft was away, she said gruffly, had been gone for about a week, she did not know where or why. He had left suddenly one morning, without her knowledge, and the following day a postcard had come from him, stating that all his things were to lie untouched till his return.

"He was so queer lately that I'd be just as pleased if he stayed away altogether," she said. "That's all I can tell you. Maybe you'd get something more out of her. She knows more than she says, anyhow," and she pointed with her thumb at the door of the adjoining *Pension*.

Maurice rang there, and a dirty maid-servant showed him Avery's room. At his knock, she opened the door herself, and first looked surprised, then alarmed at seeing him.

"What's the matter? Has anything happened?" she stammered, like one on the look-out for bad news.

"Then what do you want?" she asked in her short, unpleasant way, when he had reassured her.

"I came up to see Heinz. And they tell me he is not here; and Frau Schulz sent me to you. Schwarz was asking for him. Is it true that he has gone away?"

"Yes, it's true."

"Where to? Will he be away long?"

"How should I know?" she cried rudely. "Am I his keeper? Find out for yourself, if you must know," and the door slammed to in his face.

He mentioned the incident to Madeleine that evening. She looked strangely at him, he thought, and abruptly changed the subject. A day or two later, on the strength of a rumour that reached his ears, he tackled Fürst, and the latter, who, up to this time, had been of a praiseworthy reticence, let fall a hint which made Maurice look blank with amazement. Nevertheless, he could not now avoid seeing certain incidents in his friendship with Krafft, under a different aspect.

About a fortnight had elapsed since the beginning of Louise's illness; she was still obliged to keep her bed. More than once, of late, Madeleine had returned from her daily visit, decidedly out of temper.

"Louise rubs me up the wrong way," she complained to Maurice. "And she isn't in the least grateful for all I've done for her. I really think she prefers having the nurse about her to me."

"Sick people often have such fancies," he consoled her.

"Louise shows hers a little too plainly. Besides, we have never got on well for long together."

But one afternoon, on coming in, she unpinned her hat and threw it on the piano, with a decisive haste that was characteristic of her in anger.

"That's the end; I don't go back again. I'm not paid for my services, and am under no obligation to listen to such things as Louise said to me to-day. Enough is enough. She is well on the mend, and must get on now as best she can. I wash my hands of the whole affair."

"But you're surely not going to take what a sick person says seriously?" Maurice exclaimed in dismay. "How can she possibly get on with only those strangers about her?"

"She's not so ill now. She'll be all right," answered Madeleine; she had opened a letter that was on the table, and did not look up as she spoke. "There's a limit to everything—even to my patience with her rudeness."

And on returning the following day, he found, sure enough, that, true to her word, Madeleine had not gone back. She maintained an obstinate silence about what had happened, and requested that he would now let the matter drop.

The truth was that Madeleine's conscience was by no means easy.

She had gone to see Louise on that particular afternoon, with even more inconvenience to herself than usual. On admitting her, Fräulein Grünhut had endeavoured to detain her in the passage, mumbling and gesticulating in the mystery-mongering way with which Madeleine had no patience. It incited her to answer the old woman in a loud, clear voice; then, brusquely putting her aside, she opened the door of the sick girl's room.

As she did so, she utttered an exclamation of surprise. Louise, in a flannel dressing-gown, was standing at the high tiled stove behind the door. Both her arms were upraised and held to it, and she leant her forehead against the tiles.

"Good Heavens, what are you doing out of bed?" cried Madeleine; and, as she looked round the room: "And where is Sister Martha?"

Louise moved her head, so that another spot of forehead came in contact with the tiles, and looked up at Madeleine from under her heavy lids, without replying.

Madeleine laid one by one on the table some small purchases she had made on the way there.

"Well, are you not going to speak to me to-day?" she said in a pleasant voice, as she unbuttoned her jacket. "Or tell me what I ask about the Sister?" There was not a shade of umbrage in her tone.

Louise moved her head again, and looked away from Madeleine to the wall of the room. "I have got up," she answered, in such a low voice that Madeleine had to pause in what she was doing, to hear her; "because I could not bear to lie in bed any longer. And I've sent the Sister away—because . . . oh, because I couldn't endure having her about me."

"You have sent Sister Martha away?" echoed Madeleine. "On your own responsibility? Louise!—how absurd! Well, I suppose I must put on my hat again and fetch her back. How can you get on alone, I should like to know? Really, I have no time to come oftener than I do."

"I'm quite well now. I don't need anyone."

"Come, get back into bed, like a good girl, and I will make you some tea," said Madeleine, in the gently superior tone that one uses to a sick person, to a young child, to anyone with whom it is not fitting to dispute.

Instead, Louise left the stove, and sat down in a low American rocking-chair, where she crouched despondently.

"I wish I had died," she said in a toneless voice.

Madeleine smiled with exaggerated cheerfulness, and rattled the tea-cups. "Nonsense! You mustn't talk about dying—now that you are nearly well again. Besides, you know, such things are easily said. One doesn't mean them."

"I wish I had died. Why didn't you let me die?" repeated Louise in the same apathetic way.

Madeleine did not reply; she was cogitating whether it would be more convenient to go after the nurse at once, and what she ought to do if she could not get her to come back. For Louise would certainly have despatched her in tragedy-fashion.

Meanwhile the latter had laid her arms along the low arms of the chair, and now sat gazing from one to the other of her hands. In their way, these hands of hers had acquired a kind of fame, which she had once been vain of. They had been photographed; a sculptor had modelled them for a statue of Antigone—long, slim and strong, with closely knit fingers, and pale, deep-set nails: hands like those of an adoring Virgin; hands which had an eloquent language all their own, but little or no agility, and which were out of place on the keys of a piano. Louise sat looking at them, and her face was so changed—the hollow setting of the eyes reminded perpetually of the bones beneath; the lines were hammered black below the eyes; nostrils and lips were pinched and thinned—that Madeleine, secretly observing her, remarked to herself that Louise looked at least ten years older than before. Her youth, and, with it, such freshness as she had once had, were gone from her.

" Here is your tea."

The girl drank it slowly, as if swallowing were an effort, while Madeleine went round the room, touching and ordering, and opening a window. This done, she looked at her watch.

" I will go now," she said, " and see if I can persuade Sister Martha to come back. If you haven't mortally offended her, that is."

Louise started up from her chair, and put her cup, only half emptied, on the table.

" Madeleine!—please—please, don't! I can't have her back again. I am quite well now. There was nothing more she could do for me. I shall sleep a thousand times better at night if she is not here. Oh, don't bring her back again! Her voice cut like a knife, and her hands were so hard."

She trembled with excitement, and was on the brink of tears.

" Hush!—don't excite yourself like that," said Madeleine, and tried to soothe her. " There's no need for it. If you are really determined not to have her, then she shall not come—and that's the end of it. Not but what I think it foolish of you all the same," she could not refrain from adding. " You are still weak. However, if you prefer it, I'll do my best to run up this evening to see that you have everything for the night."

" I don't want you either."

Madeleine shrugged her shoulders, and her pity became tinged with impatience.

"The doctor says you must go away somewhere, for a change," she said as she beat up the pillows and smoothed out the crumpled sheets, preparatory to coaxing her patient back to bed.

Louise shook her head, but did not speak.

"A few weeks' change of air is what you need to set you up again."

"I cannot go away."

"Nonsense! Of course you can. You don't want to be ill all the winter?"

"I don't want to be well."

Madeleine sniffed audibly. "There's no reasoning with you. When you hear on all sides that it's for your own good——"

"Oh, stop tormenting me!" cried Louise, raising a drawn face with disordered hair. "I won't go away! Nothing will make me. I shall stay here—though I never get well again."

"But why? Give me one sensible reason for not going.— You can't!"

"Yes . . . if . . . if Eugen should come back."

The words could only just be caught. Madeleine stood, holding a sheet with both hands, as though she could not believe her ears.

"Louise!" she said at last, in a tone which meant many things.

Louise began to cry, and was shaken by hard, dry sobs. Madeleine did not look at her again, but went severely on with her bedmaking. When she had finished, she crossed to the washstand, and poured out a glass of water.

Louise took it, humbled and submissive, and gradually her sobs abated. But now Madeleine, in place of getting ready to leave, as she had intended, sat down at the centre table, and revolved what she felt it to be her duty to say. When all sound of crying had ceased, she began to speak, persuasively, in a quiet voice.

"You have brought the matter up yourself, Louise," she said, "and, now the ice is broken, there are one or two things I should like to say to you. First then, you have been very ill, far worse than you know—the immediate danger is over now, so I can speak of it. But who can tell what may happen if you persist in remaining on here by yourself, in the state you are in?"

Louise did not stir; her face was hidden.

"The reason you give for staying is not a serious one, I hope," Madeleine proceeded cautiously choosing her words. "After all the . . . the precautions that were taken to ensure the . . . break, it is not all likely . . . he would think of returning. And Louise," she added with warmth, "even though he did—suppose he did—after the way he has behaved, and his disgraceful treatment of you——"

Louise looked up for an instant. "That is not true," she said.

"Not true?" echoed Madeleine. "Well, if you are able to admire his behaviour—if you don't consider it disgraceful—no, more than that—infamous——" She stopped, not being able to find a stronger epithet.

"It is not true," said Louise in the same expressionless voice. But now she lifted her head, and pressed the palms of her hands together.

Madeleine pushed back her chair, as if she were about to rise. "Then I have nothing more to say," she said; and went on: "If you are ready to defend a man who has acted towards you as he has—in a way that makes a respectable person's blood boil—there is indeed nothing more to be said." She reddened with indignation. "As if it were not bad enough for him to go, after all you have done for him, but that he must do it in such a mean, underhand way—it's enough to make one sick. The only thing to compare with it is his conduct on the night before he left. Do you know, pray, that on the last evening, at a *Kneipe* in the *Goldene Hirsch,* he boasted of what you had done for him—boasted about everything that had happened between you—to a rowdy, tipsy crew? More than that, he gave shameless details, about you going to his room that afternoon——"

"It's not true, it's not true," repeated Louise, as if she had got these few words by heart. She rose from her chair, and leaned on it, half turning her back to Madeleine, and holding her handkerchief to her lips.

Madeleine shrugged her shoulders. "Do you think I should say it, if it weren't?" she asked. "I don't invent scandal. And you are bound to hear it when you go out again. He did this, and worse than I choose to tell you, and if you felt as you ought to about it, you would never give him another thought. He's not worth it. He's not worth any respectable person's——"

"Respectable!" burst in Louise, and raised two blazing eyes to her companion's face. "That's the second time. Why

do you come here, Madeleine, and talk like that to me? He
did what he was obliged to—that's all: for I should never have
let him go. Can't you see how preposterous it is to think that
by talking of respectability, and unworthiness, you can make
me leave off caring for him?—when for months I have lived
for nothing else? Do you think one can change one's feelings
so easily? Don't you understand that to love a person once is
to love him always and altogether?—his faults as well—everything he does, good or bad, no matter what other people think
of it? Oh, you have never really cared for anyone yourself,
or you would know it."

"It's not preposterous at all," retorted Madeleine. "Yes—
if he had deserved all the affection you wasted on him, or if
unhappy circumstances had separated you. But that's not the
case. He has behaved scandalously, without the least attempt at shielding you. He has made you the talk of the place.
And you may consider me narrow and prejudiced, but this I
must say—I am boundlessly astonished at you. When he has
shown you as plainly as he can that he's tired of you, that you
should still be ready to defend him, and have so little proper
pride that you even say you would take him back!——"

Louise turned on her. "You would never do that, Madeleine, would you?—never so far forget yourself as to crawl
to a man's feet and ask—ask?—no, implore forgiveness, for
faults you were not conscious of having committed. You
would never beg him to go on loving you, after he had ceased
to care, or think nothing on earth worth having if he
would not—or could not. As I would; as I have done." But
chancing to look at Madeleine, she grew quieter. "You would
never do that, would you?" she repeated. "And do you know
why?" Her words came quickly again; her voice shook with
excitement. "Because you will never care for anyone more than
yourself—it isn't in you to do it. You will go through life,
right on to the end, without knowing what it is to care for some
one—oh, but I mean absolutely, unthinkingly——"

She broke down, and hid her face again. Madeleine had carried the cups and saucers to a side-table, and now put on
her hat.

"And I hope I never shall," she said, forcing herself to speak
calmly. "If I thought it likely, I should never look at a man
again."

But Louise had not finished. Coming round to the front of
the rocking-chair, and leaning on the table, she gazed at Made-

leine with wild eyes, while her pale lips poured forth a kind
of revenge for the suffering, real and imaginary, that she had
undergone at the hands of this cooler nature.

"And I'll tell you why. You are doubly safe; for you will
never be able to make a man care so much that—that you are
forced to love him like this in return. It isn't in you to do it.
I don't mean because you're plain. There are plenty of plainer
women than you, who can make men follow them. No, it's
your nature—your cold, narrow, egotistic nature—which only
lets you care for things outside yourself in a cold, narrow way.
You will never know what it is to be taken out of yourself,
taken and shaken, till everything you are familiar with falls
away."

She laughed; but tears were near at hand. Madeleine had
turned her back on her, and stood buttoning her jacket, with a
red, exasperated face.

"I shall not answer you," she said. "You have worked
yourself into such a state that you don't know what you're
saying. All the same, I think you might try to curb your
tongue. I have done nothing to you—but be kind to you."

"Kind to me? Do you call it kind to come here and try to
set me against the man I love best in the world? And who
loves me best, too. Yes; he does. He would never have gone,
if he hadn't been forced to—if I hadn't been a hindrance to
him—a drag on him."

"It makes me ashamed of my sex to hear you say such things.
That a woman can so far lose her pride as to——"

"Oh, other women do it in other ways. Do you think I
haven't seen how you have been trying to make some one here
like you?—doing your utmost, without any thoughts of pride or
self-respect.—And how you have failed? Yes, failed. And if
you don't believe me, ask him yourself—ask him who it is that
could bring him to her, just by raising her finger. It's to me
he would come, not to you—to me who have never given him
look or thought."

Madeleine paled, then went scarlet. "That's a direct untruth. You!—and not to egg a man on, if you see he admires
you! You know every time a passer-by looks at you in the
street. You feed on such looks—yes, and return them, too. I
have seen you, my lady, looking and being looked at, by a
stranger, in a way no decent woman allows.—For the rest, I'll
trouble you to mind your own business. Whatever I do or
don't do, trust me, I shall at least take care not to make myself

the laughing-stock of the place. Yes, you have only succeeded in making yourself ridiculous. For while you were cringing before him, and aspiring to die for his sake, he was making love behind your back to another girl. For the last six months. Every one knew it, it seems, but you."

She had spoken with unconcealed anger, and now turned to leave the room. But Louise was at the door before her, and spread herself across it.

"That's a lie, Madeleine! Of your own making. You shall prove it to me before you go out of this room. How dare you say such a thing!—how dare you!"

Madeleine looked at her with cold aversion, and drew back to avoid touching her.

"Prove it?" she echoed. "Are his own words not proof enough! He told the whole story that night, just as he had first told all about you. It had been going on for months. Sometimes, you were hardly out of his room, before the other was in. And if you don't believe me, ask the person you're so proud of having attracted, without raising your finger."

Louise moved away from the door, and went back to the table, on which she leaned heavily. All the blood had left her face and the dark rings below her eyes stood out with alarming distinctness. Madeleine felt a sudden compunction at what she had done.

"It's entirely your own fault that I told you anything whatever about it," she said, heartily annoyed with herself. "You had no right to provoke me by saying what you did. I declare, Louise, to be with you makes one just like you. If it's any consolation to you to know it, he was drunk at the time, and there's a possibility it may not be true."

"Go away—go out of my room!" cried Louise. And Madeleine went, without delay, having almost a physical sensation about her throat of the slender hands stretched so threateningly towards her.—And this unpleasant feeling remained with her until she turned the corner of the street.

II

On the afternoon when Maurice found that Madeleine had kept her word he went home and paced his room in perplexity. He pictured Louise lying helpless, too weak to raise her hand. His brain went stupidly over the few people to whom he might turn for aid. Avery Hill?—Johanna Cayhill? But Avery was occupied with her own troubles; and Johanna's relationship to Ephie put her out of the question. He was thinking fantastic thoughts of somehow offering his own services, or of even throwing himself on the goodness of a person like Miss Jensen, whose motherly form must surely imply a corresponding motherliness of heart, when Frau Krause entered the room, bearing a letter which she said had been left for him an hour or two previously. She carried a lamp in her hand, and eyed her restless lodger with suspicion.

"Why, in the name of goodness, didn't you bring this in when it came?" he demanded. He held the unopened letter at arm's length, as if he were afraid of it.

Frau Krause bridled instantly. Did he think she had nothing else to do than to carry things in and out of his room? The letter had lain on the chest of drawers in the passage; he could have seen it for himself, had he troubled to look.

Maurice waved her away. He was staring at the envelope; he believed he knew the handwriting. His heart beat with precise hammerings. He laid the letter on the table, and took a few turns in the room before he picked it up again. On examining it anew, it seemed to him that the lightly gummed envelope had been tampered with, and he made a threatening movement towards the door, then checked himself, remembering that if the letter were what he believed, it would be written in English. He tore it open, destroying the envelope in his nervousness. There was no heading, and it was only a few lines long.

I must speak to you. Will you come to me this evening?
Louise Dufrayer.

His heart was thumping now. He was to go to her, she said

so herself; to go this moment, for it was evening already. As
it was, she was perhaps waiting for him, wondering why he
did not come. He had not shaved that day, and his first impulse was to call for hot water. In the same breath he gave up
the idea: it was out of the question by the poor light of the
lamp, and the extraordinary position of the looking-glass. He
made, however, a hasty toilet in his best, only to colour at himself when finished. Was there ever such a fool as he? His
act contained the germ of an insult: and he rapidly changed
back to his workaday wear.

All this took time, and it was eight o'clock before he rang
the door-bell in the *Brüderstrasse*. Now, the landlady did not
mistake him for a possible thief. But she looked at him in an
unfriendly way, and said grumblingly that Fräulein had been
expecting him for an hour or more. Then she pointed to the
door of the room, and left him to make his way in alone.

He knocked gently, but no one answered. The old woman,
who stood watching his movements, signed to him to enter, and
he turned the handle. The large room was dark, except for the
light shed by a small lamp, which stood on the table before
the sofa. From somewhere out of the dusk that lay beyond, a
white figure rose and came towards him.

Louise was in a crumpled dressing-gown, and her hair was
loosened from its coil on her neck. Maurice saw so much, before she was close beside him, her eyes searching his face.

" Oh, you have come," she said with a sigh, as if a load had
been lifted from her mind. " I thought you were not coming."

" I only got your note a few minutes ago. I . . . I came at
once," he said, and stammered, as he saw how greatly illness
had changed her.

" I knew you would."

She did not give him her hand, but stood gazing at him; and
her look was so helpless and forlorn that he grew uncomfortable.

" You have been ill? " he said, to render the pause that followed less embarrassing.

" Yes; but I'm better now." She supported herself on the
table; her indecision seemed to increase, and several seconds
passed before she said: " Won't you sit down? "

He took one of the stuffed arm-chairs she indicated; and she
went back to the sofa. Again there was silence. With her
elbows on her knees, her chin on her two hands, Louise stared
hard at the pattern of the tablecloth. Maurice sat stiff and
erect, waiting for her to tell him why she had summoned him.

"You will think it strange that I should send for you like this . . . when I know you so slightly," she began at length. "But . . . since I saw you last . . . I have been in trouble," —her voice broke, but her eyes remained fixed on the cloth. "And I am quite alone. I have no one to help me. Then I thought of you; you were kind to me once; you offered to help me." She paused, and wound her handkerchief to a ball.

"Anything!—anything that lies in my power," said Maurice fervently. He fidgeted his hands round the brim of his hat, which he was holding to him.

"Won't you tell me what it is?" he asked, after another long break. "I should be so glad, and grateful—yes, indeed, grateful—if there were anything I could do for you."

She met his eyes, and tried to say something, but no sound came over her lips. She was trying to fasten her thoughts on what she had to say, but, in spite of her efforts, they eluded her. For more than twenty-four hours she had brooded over one idea; the strain had been too great; and, now that the moment had come, her strength deserted her. She would have liked to lay her head on her arms and sleep; it almost seemed to her now, in the indifference of sheer fatigue, that it did not matter whether she spoke or not. But as she looked at the young man, she became conscious of an expression in his face, which made her own grow hard.

"I won't be pitied."

Maurice turned very red. His heart had gone out to her in her distress; and his feelings were painted on his face. His discomfiture at her discovery was so palpable that it gave her courage to go on.

"You were one of those, were you not, who were present at a certain café in the *Brühl,* one evening, three weeks ago." It was more of a statement than a question. Her eyes held him fast. His retreating colour rose again; he had a presentiment of what was coming.

"Then you must have heard——" she began quickly, but left the sentence unended.

His suspicions took shape, and he made a large, vague gesture of dissent.

"You heard all that was said," she continued, without paying any heed to him. "You heard how . . . how some one —no, how the man I loved and trusted . . . how he boasted about my caring for him; and not only that, but how, before

that drunken crowd, he told how I had been to him . . .
to his room . . . that afternoon——" She could not finish,
and pressed her knotted handkerchief to her lips.

Maurice looked round him for assistance. "You are mistaken," he declared. "I heard nothing of the kind. Remember, I, too, was among those . . . in the state you mention,"
he added as an afterthought, lowering his voice.

"That is not it." Leaning forward, she opened her eyes so
wide that he saw a rim of white round the brown of the pupils.
"You must also have heard . . . how, all this time, behind
my back, there was some one else . . . someone he cared
for . . . when I thought it was only me."

The young man coloured, with her and for her. "It is not
true; you have been misled," he said with vehemence. And,
again, a flash of intuition suggested an afterthought to him.
"Can you really believe it? Don't you think better of him than
that?"

For the first time since she had known him, Louise gave him
a personal look, a look that belonged to him alone, and held a
warm ray of gratitude. Then, however, she went on unsparingly: "I want you to tell me who it was."

He laid his hat on a chair, and used his hands. "But if I
assure you it is not true? If I give you my word that you have
been misinformed?"

"Who was it? What is her name?"

He rose, and went away from the table.

"I knew him better than you," she said slowly, as he did not
speak: "you or anyone else—a hundred thousand times better
—and I *know* it is true."

Still he did not answer.

"Then you won't tell me?"

"Tell you? How can I? There's nothing to tell."

"I was wrong then. You have no pity for me?"

"Pity!—I no pity?" he cried, forgetting how, a minute ago,
she had resented his feeling it. "But all the same I can't tell
you what you ask me. You don't realise what it means: putting
a slur on a young girl's name . . . which has never been
touched."

Directly he had said this, he was aware of his foolishness;
but she let the admission contained in the words pass unnoticed.

"Then she is not with him?" she cried, springing to her
feet, and there was a jubilation in her voice, which she did not

attempt to suppress. Maurice made no answer, but in his face was such a mixture of surprise and disconcertion that it was answer enough.

She remained standing, with her head bowed; and Maurice, who, in his nervousness, had gripped the back of his chair, held it so tightly that it left a furrow in his hand. He was looking into the lamp, and did not at first see that Louise had raised her head again and was contemplating him. When she had succeeded in making him look at her, she sat down on the sofa and drew the folds of her dressing-gown to her.

"Come and sit here. I want to speak to you."

But Maurice only shot a quick glance at her, and did not move.

She leaned forward, in her old position. She had pushed the heavy wings of hair up from her forehead, and this, together with her extreme pallor, gave her face a look of febrile intensity.

"Maurice Guest," she said slowly, "do you remember a night last summer, when, by chance, you happened to walk with me, coming home from the theatre?—Or have you perhaps forgotten?"

He shook his head.

"Then do you remember, too, what you said to me? How, since the first time you had seen me—you even knew where that was, I believe—you had thought about me . . . thought too much, or words to that effect. Do you remember?"

"Do you think when a man says a thing like that he forgets it?" asked Maurice in a gruff voice. He turned, as he spoke, and looked down on her with a kind of pitying wisdom. "If you knew how often I have reproached myself for it!" he added.

"There was no need for that," she answered, and even smiled a little. "We women never resent having such things said to us—never—though it is supposed we do, and though we must pretend to. But I remember, too, I was in a bad mood that night, and was angry with you, after all. Everything seemed to have gone against me. In the theatre—in . . . Oh, no, no!" she cried, as she remembrance of that past night, with its alternations of pain and pleasure, broke over her. "My God!"

Maurice hardly breathed, for fear he should remind her of his presence. When the paroxysm had passed, she crossed to the window; the blinds had not been drawn, and leaning her forehead on the glass, she looked out into the darkness. In spite of his trouble of mind, the young man could not but comment on the ironic fashion in which fate was treating him: not once, in all the hours he had spent on the pavement below, had Louise come, like this, to the window; now that she did so, he was in the room beside her, wishing himself away.

Then, with a swift movement, she came back to him, and stood at his side.

"Then it was not true?—what you said that night."

"True?" echoed Maurice. He instinctively moved a step away from her, and threw a quick glance at the pale face so near his own. "If I were to tell you how much more than that is true, you wouldn't have anything more to do with me."

For the second time, she seemed to see him and consider him. But he kept his head turned stubbornly away.

"You feel like that," she began in slow surprise, to continue hurriedly: "You care for me like that, and yet, when I ask the first and only thing I shall ever ask of you, you won't do it? It is a lesson to me, I suppose, not to come to you for help again.—Oh, I can't understand you men! You are all—all alike."

"I would do anything in the world for you. Anything but this."

She repeated his last words after him. "But I want nothing else."

"This I can't tell you."

"Then you don't really care. You only think you do. If you can't do this one small thing for me! Oh, there is no one else I can turn to, or I would. Oh, please tell me!—you who make-believe to care for me. You won't? When it comes to the point, a man will do nothing—nothing at all."

"I would cut off my hands for you. But you are asking me to do something I think wrong."

"Wrong! What is wrong?—and what is right? They are only words. Is it right that I should be left like this?—thrown away like a broken plate? Oh, I shall not rest till I know who it was that took him from me. And you are the only person who can help me. Are you not a little sorry for me? Is there nothing I can do to make you sorry?"

"You won't realise what you are asking me to do."

He spoke in a constrained voice, for he felt the impossiblity of standing out much longer against her. Louise caught the note of yielding, and taking his hand in hers, laid it against her forehead.

"Feel that! Feel how it throbs and burns! And so it has gone on for hours now, for days. I can't think or feel—with that fever in me. I must know who it was, or I shall go mad. Don't torture me then—you, too! You are good, Be kind to me now. Be my friend, Maurice Guest."

Maurice was vanquished; in a low voice he told her what she wished to hear. She read the syllables from his lips, repeated the name slowly after him, then shook her head; she did not know it. Letting his hand drop, she went back to the sofa.

"Tell me everything you know about her," she said imperiously. "What is she like?—what is she like? What is the colour of her hair?"

Maurice was a poor hand at description. Questioned thus, he was not even sure whether to call Ephie pretty or not; he knew that she was small, and very young, but of her hair he could say little, except that it was not black.

Louise caught at the detail. "Not black, no, not black!" she cried. "He had black enough here," and she ran her hands through her own unruly hair.

There was nothing she did not want to know, did not try to force from his lips; and a relentless impatience seized her at his powerlessness.

"I must see her for myself," she said at length, when he had stammered into silence. "You must bring her to me."

"No, that you really can't ask me to do."

She came over to him again, and took his hands. "You will bring her here to-morrow—to-morrow afternoon. Do you think I shall hurt her? Is she any better than I am? Oh, don't be afraid! We are not so easily soiled."

Maurice demurred no more.

"For until I see her, I shall not know—I shall not know," she said to herself, when he had pledged his word.

The tense expression of her face relaxed; her mouth drooped; she lay back in the sofa-corner and shut her eyes. For what seemed a long time, there was no sound in the room. Maurice thought she had fallen asleep. But at his first light movement she opened her eyes.

"Now go," she said. "Please, go!" And he obeyed.

The night was cold, but, as he stood irresolute in the street, he wiped the perspiration from his forehead. He felt very perplexed. Only one thing was clear to him: he had promised to bring Ephie to see her the next day, and, however wrong it might be, the promise was given and must be kept. But what

15

he now asked himself was: did not the bringing of the child,
under these circumstances, imply a tacit acknowledgment that
she was seriously involved?—a fact which, all along, he had
striven against admitting. For, after his one encounter with
Ephie and Schilsky, in the woods that summer, and the first
firing of his suspicions, he had seen nothing else to render him
uneasy; a few weeks later, Ephie had gone to Switzerland, and,
on her return in September, or almost directly afterwards—
three or four days at most—Schilsky had taken his departure.
There had been, of course, his drunken boasts to take into account, but firstly, Maurice had only retained a hazy idea of their
nature, and, in the next place, the events which had followed that
evening had been of so much greater importance to him that
he had had no thoughts to spare for Ephie—more especially as
he then knew that Schilsky was out of the way. But now the
whole affair rose vividly before his mind again, and in his heart
he knew that he had always believed—just as Louise believed—
in Ephie's guilt. No: guilt was too strong a word. Yet however harmless the flirtation might have been in itself, it had been
carried on in secret, in an underhand way: there had been nothing straightforward or above-board about it; and this alone was
enough to compromise a young girl.

The Cayhills had been in Leipzig again for three weeks, but
so occupied had Maurice been during this time, that he had
only paid them one hasty call. Now he felt that he must see
Ephie at once, not only to secure her word that she would come
out with him, the following day, but also to read from her frank
eyes and childish lips the assurance of her innocence, or, at least,
the impossibility of her guilt.

But as he walked to the *Lessingstrasse,* he remembered, without being able to help it, all the trifles which, at one time or another, had disturbed his relations with Ephie. He recalled each
of the thin, superficial untruths, by means of which she had defended herself, the day he had met her with Schilsky: it seemed
incredible to him now that he had not seen through them instantly. He called up her pretty, insincere behaviour with the
circle of young men that gathered round her; the language of
signs by which she had conversed with Schilsky in the theatre.
He remembered the astounding ease with which he had made
her acquaintance in the first case, or rather, with which she had
made his. Even the innocent kiss she had once openly incited
him to, and on the score of which she had been so exaggeratedly
angry—this, too, was summoned to bear witness against her.

Each of these incidents now seemed to point to a fatal frivolity, to a levity of character which, put to a real test, would offer no resistance.

Supper was over in the *Pension,* but only Mrs. Cayhill sat in her accustomed corner. Ephie was with the rest of the boarders in the general sitting-room, where Johanna conducted Maurice. Boehmer was paying an evening visit, as well as a very young American, who laughed: " Heh, heh! " at everything that was said, thereby displaying two prominently gold teeth. Mrs. Tully sat on a small sofa, with her arm round Ephie's waist: they were the centre of the group, and it did not appear likely that Maurice would get an opportunity of speaking to Ephie in private. She was in high spirits, and had only a saucy greeting for him. He sat down beside Johanna, and waited, ill at ease. Soon his patience was exhausted; rising, he went over to the sofa, and asked Ephie if he might come to take her for a walk, the next afternoon. But she would not give him an express promise; she pouted: after all these weeks, it suddenly occurred to him to come and see them, and then, the first thing he did, was to ask a favour of her. Did he really expect her to grant it?

" Don't, Ephie, love, don't! " cried Mrs. Tully in her sprightly way. " Men are really shocking creatures, and it is our duty, love, to keep them in their place. If we don't, they grow presumptuous," and she shot an arch look at Boehmer, who returned it, fingered his beard, and murmured: " Cruel—cruel! "

" And even if I wanted to go when the time came, how do you expect me to know so long beforehand? Ever so many things may happen before to-morrow," said Ephie brilliantly; at which Mrs. Tully laughed very much indeed, and still more at Boehmer's remark that it was an ancient privilege of the ladies, never to be obliged to know their own minds.

" It's a libel—take that, you naughty boy! " she cried, and slapped him playfully on the hand. " Ephie, love, how shall we punish him? "

" He is not to come again for a week," answered Ephie slily; and at Boehmer's protestations of penitence and despair, both she and Mrs. Tully laughed till the tears stood in their eyes, Ephie all the more extravagantly because Maurice stood unsmiling before her.

" I ask this as a direct favour, Ephie. There's something I want to say to you—something important," he added in a low voice, so that only she could hear it.

Ephie changed colour at once, and tried to read his face.

" Then I may come at five? You will be ready? Good night."

Johanna followed him into the passage, and stood by while he put on his coat. They had used up all their small talk in the sitting-room, and had nothing more to say to each other. When however they shook hands, she observed impulsively: " Sometimes I wish we were safe back home again." But Maurice only said: " Indeed? " and displayed no curiosity to know the reason why.

After he had gone, Ephie was livelier than before, as long as she was being teased about her pale, importunate admirer. Then, suddenly, she pleaded a headache, and went to her own room.

Johanna, listening outside the door, concluded from the stillness that her sister was asleep. But Ephie heard Johanna come and go. She could not sleep, nor could she get Maurice's words out of her mind. He had something important to say to her. What could it be? There was only one important subject in the world for her now; and she longed for the hour of his visit—longed, hoped, and was more than half afraid.

III

SINCE her return to Leipzig, Ephie's spirits had gone up and down like a barometer in spring. In this short time, she passed through more changes of mood than in all her previous life. She learned what uncertainty meant, and suspense, and helplessness; she caught at any straw of hope, and, for a day on end, would be almost comforted; she invented numberless excuses for Schilsky, and rejected them, one and all. For she was quite in the dark about his movements; she had not seen him since her return, and could hear nothing of him. Only the first of the letters she had written to him from Switzerland had elicited a reply, and he had left all the notes she had sent him, since getting back, unanswered.

Her fellow-boarder, Mrs. Tully, was her only confidant; and that, only in so far as this lady, knowing that what she called "a little romance" was going on, had undertaken to enclose any letters that might arrive during Ephie's absence. Johanna had no suspicions, or rather she had hitherto had none. In the course of the past week, however, it had become plain even to her blind, sisterly eyes that something was the matter with Ephie. She could still be lively when she liked, almost unnaturally lively, and especially in the company of Mrs. Tully and her circle; but with these high spirits alternated fits of depression, and once Johanna had come upon her in tears. Driven into a corner, Ephie declared that Herr Becker had scolded her at her lesson; but Johanna was not satisfied with this explanation; for formerly, the master's blame or praise had left no impression on her little sister's mind. Even worse than this, Ephie could now, on slight provocation, be thoroughly peevish— a thing so new in her that it worried Johanna most of all. The long walks of the summer had been given up; but Ephie had adopted a way of going in and out of the house, just as it pleased her, without a word to her sister. Johanna scrutinised her keenly, and the result was so disturbing that she resolved to broach the subject to her mother.

On the morning after Maurice's visit, therefore, she appeared in the sitting-room, with a heap of undarned stockings in one

hand, her work-basket in the other, and with a very determined
expression on her face. But the moment was not a happy one:
Mrs. Cayhill was deep in *Why Paul Ferrol Killed his Wife;*
and would be lost to her surroundings until the end of the
book was reached. Had Johanna been of an observant turn
of mind, she would have waited a little; for, finding the
intermediate portion of the novel dry reading, Mrs. Cayhill
was getting over the pages at the rate of three or four a minute,
and would soon have been finished.

But Johanna sat down at the table and opened fire.

" I wish to speak to you, mother," she said firmly.

Mrs. Cayhill did not even blink. Johanna drew several
threads across a hole she was darning, before she repeated, in
the same decided tone: " Do you hear me, mother? There is
something I wish to speak to you about."

" Hm," said Mrs. Cayhill, without raising her eyes from the
page. She heard Johanna, and was even vaguely distracted by
her from the web of circumstance that was enveloping her hero;
but she believed, from experience, that if she took no notice of
her, Johanna would not persist. What the latter had to say
would only be a reminder that it was mail-day, and no letters
were ready; or that if she did not put on her bonnet and go out
for a walk, she would be obliged to take another of her nerve-
powders that night: and Mrs. Cayhill hated moral persuasion
with all her heart.

" Put down your book, mother, please, and listen to me,"
continued Johanna, without any outward sign of impatience,
and as she spoke, she drew another stocking over her hand.

" What *is* the matter, Joan? I wish you would let me be,"
answered Mrs. Cayhill querulously, still without looking up.

" It's about Ephie, mother. But you can't hear me if you
go on reading."

" I can hear well enough," said Mrs. Cayhill, and turning
a page, she lost herself, to all appearance, in the next one.
Johanna did not reply, and for some minutes there was silence,
broken only by the turning of the leaves. Then, compelled by
something that was stronger than herself, Mrs. Cayhill laid her
book on her knee, gave a loud sigh, and glanced at Johanna's
grave face.

" You are a nuisance, Joan. Well, make haste now—what
is it? "

" It's Ephie, mother. I am not easy about her lately. I don't
think she can be well. She is so unlike herself."

"Really, Joan," said Mrs. Cayhill, laughing with an exaggerated carelessness. "I think I should be the first to notice if she were sick. But you like to make yourself important, that's what it is, and to have a finger in every pie. There is nothing whatever the matter with the child."

"She's not well, I'm sure," persisted Johanna, without haste. "I have noticed it for some time now. I think the air here is not agreeing with her. I constantly hear it said that this is an enervating place. I believe it would be better for her if we went somewhere else for the winter—even if we returned home. Nothing binds us, and health is the first and chief——"

"Go home?" cried Mrs. Cayhill, and turned her book over on its face. "Really, Joan, you are absurd! Because Ephie finds it hard to settle down again, after such a long vacation —and that's all it is—you want to rush off to a fresh place, when . . . when we are just so comfortably fixed here for the winter, and where we have at last gotten us a few friends. As for going home, why, every one would suppose we'd gone crazy. We haven't been away six months yet—and when Mr. Cayhill is coming over to fetch us back—and . . . and everything."

She spoke with heat; for she knew from experience that what her elder daughter resolved on, was likely to be carried through.

"That is all very well, mother," continued Johanna unmoved. "But I don't think your arguments are sound if we find that Ephie is really sick, and needs a change."

"Arguments not sound! What big words you love to use, Joan! You let Ephie be. She grows prettier every day, and she's a favourite wherever she goes."

"That's another thing. Her head is being turned, and she will soon be quite spoilt. She begins to like the fuss and attention so well that——"

"You had your chances too, Joan. You needn't be jealous."

Johanna had heard this remark too often to be sensitive to it.

"When it comes to serious 'chances,' as you call them, no one will be more pleased for Ephie or more interested than I. But this is something different. You see that yourself, mother, I am sure. These young men who come about the house are so foolish, and immature, and they have such different ideas of things from ourselves. They think so . . . so "—Johanna hesitated for a word—" so laxly on earnest subjects. And it is telling on Ephie.—Look, for instance, at Mr. Dove! I don't want to say anything against him, in particular. He is really more serious than the rest. But for some time now, he has been making himself ridiculous,"—Johanna had blushed for Dove on the occasion of his last visit. "No one could be more in earnest than he is; but Ephie only makes fun of him, in a heartless way. She won't see what a grave matter it is to him."

Mrs. Cayhill laughed, not at all displeased. "Young people will be young people. You can't put old heads on young shoulders, Joan, or shut them up in separate houses. Ephie is an extremely pretty girl, and it will be the same wherever we go.—As for young Dove, he knows well enough that nothing can come of it, and if he chooses to continue his attentions, why, he must take the consequences—that's all. Absurd!—a boy and girl flirtation, and to make so much of it! A mountain of a molehill, as usual. And half the time, you only imagine things, and don't see what is going on under your very nose. Anyone but you, I'm sure, would find more to object to in the way young Guest behaves than Dove."

"Maurice Guest?" said Johanna, and laid her hands with stocking and needle on the table.

"Yes, Maurice Guest," repeated Mrs. Cayhill, with complacent mockery. "Do you think no one has eyes but yourself?— No, Joan, you're not sharp enough. Just look at the way he went on last night! Every one but you could see what was the matter with him. Mrs. Tully told me about it afterwards. Why, he never took his eyes off her."

"Oh, I'm sure you are mistaken," said Johanna earnestly, and was silent from sheer surprise. "He has been here so seldom of late," she added after a pause, thinking aloud.

"Just for that very reason," replied Mrs. Cayhill, with the same air of wisdom. "A nice-minded young man stays away, if he sees that his feelings are not returned, or if he has no position to offer.—And another thing I'll tell you, Joan, though you do think yourself so clever. You don't need to worry if Ephie *is* odd and fidgety sometimes just now. At her age, it's only to be expected. You know very well what I mean. All girls go through the same thing. You did yourself."

After this, she took up her book again, having, she knew, successfully silenced her daughter, who, on matters of this nature, was extremely sensitive.

Johanna went methodically on with her darning; but the new idea which her mother had dropped into her mind, took root and grew. Strange that it had not occurred to her before! Dove's state of mind had been patent from the first; but she had had no suspicions of Maurice Guest. His manner with Ephie had hitherto been that of a brother: he had never behaved like the rest. Yet, when she looked back on his visit of the previous evening, she could not but be struck by the strangeness of his demeanour: his distracted silence, his efforts to speak to Ephie alone, and the expression with which he had watched her. And Ephie?—what of her? Now that Johanna thought of it, a change had also come over Ephie's mode of treating Maurice; the gay insouciance of the early days had given place to the pert flippancy which, only the night before, had so pained her sister. What had brought about this change? Was it pique? Was Ephie chafing, in secret, at his prolonged absences, and was she, girl-like, anxious to conceal it from him?

Johanna gathered up her work to go to her own room and think the matter out in private. In the passage, she ran into the arms of Mrs. Tully, whom she disliked; for, ever since coming to the *Pension,* this lady had carried on a kind of cult with Ephie, which was distasteful in the extreme to Johanna.

"Oh, Miss Cayhill!" she now exclaimed. "I was just groping my way—it is indeed groping, is it not?—to your sitting-room. *Where* is your sister? I want *so* much to ask her if she will have tea with me this afternoon. I am expecting a few friends, and should be *so* glad if she would join us."

"Ephie is practising, Mrs. Tully," said Johanna in her coolest tone. "And I cannot have her disturbed."

"She is so very, very diligent," said Mrs. Tully with enthusiasm. "I always remark to myself on hearing her, how very idle a life like mine is in comparison. I am able to do *so* little; just a mere trifle here and there, a little atom of good, one might say. I have no talents.—And you, too, dear Miss Cayhill. So studious, so clever! I hear of you on every side," and, letting her eyes rest on Johanna's head, she wondered why the girl wore her hair so unbecomingly.

Johanna did not respond.

"If only you would let your hair grow, it would make such a difference to your appearance," said Mrs. Tully suddenly, with disconcerting outspokenness.

Johanna drew herself up.

"Thanks," she said. "I have always worn my hair like this, and at my age, have no intention of altering it," and leaving Mrs. Tully protesting vehemently at such false modesty, she went past her, into her own room, and shut the door.

She sat down by the window to sew. But her hands soon fell to her lap, and with her eyes on the backs of the neighbouring houses, she continued her interrupted reflections. First, though, she threw a quick, sarcastic side-glance on her mother and herself. As so often before, when she had wanted to pin her mother's attention to a subject, the centre of interest had shifted in spite of her efforts, and they had ended far from where they had begun: further, she, Johanna, had a way, when it came to the point, not of asking advice or of faithfully discussing a question, but of emphatically giving her opinion, or of stating what she considered to be the facts of the case.

From an odd mixture of experience and self-distrust, Johanna had, however, acquired a certain faith in her mother's opinions— these blind, instinctive hits and guesses, which often proved right where Johanna's carefully drawn conclusions failed. Here, once more, her mother's idea had broken in upon her like a flash of light, even though she could not immediately bring herself to accept it. Maurice and Ephie! She could not reconcile the one with the other. Yet what if the child were fretting? What if he did not care? A pang shot through her at the thought that any outsider should have the power to make Ephie suffer. Oh, she would make him care!—she would talk to him as he had never been talked to in his life before.

The sisters' rooms were connected by a door; and, gradually, in spite of her preoccupation, Johanna could not but become aware how brokenly Ephie was practising. Coaxing, encouragement, and sometimes even severity, were all, it is true, necessary to pilot Ephie through the two hours that were her daily task; but as idle as to-day, she had never been. What could she be doing? Johanna listened intently, but not a sound came from the room; and impelled by a curiosity to observe her sister in a new light, she rose and opened the door.

Ephie was standing with her back to it, staring out of the window, and supporting herself on the table by her violin, which she held by the neck. At Johanna's entrance, she started, grew very red, and hastily raised the instrument to her shoulder.

"What are you doing, Ephie? You are wasting a great deal of time," said Johanna in the tone of mild reproof that came natural to her, in speaking to her little sister. "Is anything the matter to-day? If you don't practice better than this, you won't have the *étude* ready by Friday, and Herr Becker will make you take it again—for the third time."

"He can if he likes. I guess I don't care," said Ephie non-

chalantly, and, seizing the opportunity offered for a break, she
sat down, and laid bow and fiddle on the table.

"Have you remembered everything he pointed out to you at
your last lesson?" asked Johanna, going over to the music-stand,
and peering at the pages with her shortsighted eyes. "Let me
see—what was it now? Something about this double-stopping
here, and the fingering in this position."

Ephie laughed. "Old Joan, what do you know about it?"

"Not much, dear, I admit," said Johanna pleasantly. "But
try and master it, like a good girl. So you can get rid of it,
and go on to something else."

Ephie sat back, clasped her hands behind her head, and gave
a long sigh. "Yes, to the next one," she said. "Oh, if you
only knew how sick I am of them, Joan! The next won't be
a bit better than this. They are all alike—a whole book of
them."

Johanna looked down at the little figure with the plump,
white arms, and discontented expression; and she tried to find
in the childish face something she had previously not seen there.

"Are you tired of studying, Ephie?" she asked. "Would
you like to leave off, and go away?"

"Go away from Leipzig? Where to?" Ephie did not un-
clasp her hands, but her eyes grew vigilant.

"Oh, there are plenty of other places, child. Dresden—or
Weimar—or Stuttgart—where you could take lessons just as
well. Or if you are tired of studying altogether, there is no
need for you to go on with it. We can return home, any day.
Sometimes, I think it would be better if we did. You have not
been yourself lately, dear. I don't think you are very well."

"I not myself?—not well? What rubbish you talk, Joan! I
am quite well, and wish you wouldn't tease me. I guess you
want to go away yourself. You are tired of being here. But
nothing shall induce me to go. I love old Leipzig. And
I still have heaps to learn before I leave off studying. I don't
even know whether I shall be ready by spring. It all depends.—
And now, Joan, go away." She took up her violin and put it on
her shoulder. "Now it's you who are wasting time. How can
I practise when you stand there talking?"

Johanna was silent. But after this, she did not venture to
mention Maurice's name; and she had turned to leave the room
when she remembered her meeting with Mrs. Tully.

"I would rather you did not go to tea, Ephie," she ended,
and then regretted having said it.

"That's another of your silly prejudices, Joan. I want to know why you feel so about Mrs. Tully. I think she's lovely. Not that I'd have gone anyway. I promised Maurice to go for a walk with him at five. I know what her 'few friends' means, too—just Boehmer, and she asks me along so people will think he comes to see me, and not her. He sits there, and twirls his moustache, and makes eyes at her, and she makes them back. I'm only for show. No, I shouldn't have gone. I can't bear Boehmer. He's such a goat."

"You didn't think that as long as he came to see us," expostulated Johanna.

"No, of course not. But so he only comes to see her, I do. —And sometimes, Joan, why it's just embarrassing. The last afternoon, why, he had a headache or something, and she made him lie on the sofa, with a rug over him, so she could bathe his head with eau-de-cologne. I guess she's going to marry him. And I'm not the only one. The other day I heard Frau Walter and Frau von Baerle talking in the dining-room after dinner, and they said the little English widow was very *heiratslustig.*"

"Ephie, I don't like to hear you repeat such foolish gossip," said Johanna in real distress. "And if you can understand and remember a word like that, you might really take more pains with your German. It is not impossible for you to learn, you see."

"Joan the preacher, and Joan the teacher, and Joan the wise old bird," sang Ephie, and laughed. "I think Mrs. Tully is real kind. She's going to show me a new way to do my hair. This style is quite out in London, she says."

"Don't let her touch your hair. It couldn't be better than it is," said Johanna quickly. But Ephie turned her head this way and that, and considered herself in the looking-glass.

Now that she knew Maurice was expected that afternoon, Johanna awaited his arrival with impatience. Meanwhile, she believed she was not wrong in thinking Ephie unusually excited. At dinner, where, as always, the elderly boarders made a great fuss over her, her laughter was so loud as to grate on Johanna's ear; but afterwards, in their own sitting-room, a trifle sufficed to put her out of temper. A new hat had been sent home, a hat which Johanna had not yet seen. Now that it had come, Ephie was not sure whether she liked it or not; and all the cries of admiration her mother and Mrs. Tully uttered, when she put it on, were necessary to reassure her. Johanna was silent, and this unspoken disapproval irritated Ephie.

"Why don't you say something, Joan?" she cried crossly. "I suppose you think it's homely?"

"Frankly, I don't care for it much, dear. To my mind, it's overtrimmed."

This was so precisely Ephie's own feeling that she was more annoyed than ever; she taunted Johanna with old-fashioned, countrified tastes; and, in spite of her mother's comforting assurances, retired in a pet to her own room.

That afternoon, as they sat together at tea, Mrs. Cayhill, who for some time had considered Ephie fondly, said: "I can't understand you thinking she isn't well, Joan. I never saw her look better."

Ephie went crimson. "Now what has Joan been saying about me?" she asked angrily.

Johanna had left the table, and was reading on the sofa.

"I only said what I repeated to yourself, Ephie. That I didn't think you were looking well."

"Just fancy," said Mrs. Cayhill, laughing good-humouredly, "she was saying we ought to leave Leipzig and go to some strange place. Even back home to America. You don't want to go away, darling, do you?"

"No, really, Joan is too bad," cried Ephie, with a voice in which tears and exasperation struggled for the mastery. "She always has some new fad in her head. She can't leave us alone —never! Let her go away, so she wants to. I won't. I'm happy here. I love being here. Even if you both go away, I shall stop."

She got up from the table, and went to a window, where she stood biting her lips, and paying small attention to her mother's elaborate protests that she, too, had no intention of being moved.

Johanna did not raise her eyes from her book. She could have wept: not only at the spirit of rebellious dislike, which was beginning to show more and more clearly in everything Ephie said. But was no one but herself awake to the change that was taking place in the child, day by day? She would write to her father, without delay, and make him insist on their returning to America.

From the moment Maurice entered the room, she did not take her eyes off him; and, under her scrutiny, the young man soon grew nervous. He sat and fidgeted, and found nothing to say.

Ephie was wayward: she did not think she wanted to go

out; it looked like rain. Johanna refrained from interfering;
but Maurice was most persistent: he begged Ephie not to dis-
appoint him, and, when this failed, said angrily that she had
no business to bring him there for such capricious whims. This
treatment cowed Ephie; and she went at once to put on her hat
and jacket.

" He wants to speak to her; and she knows it; and is trying
to avoid it," said Johanna to herself; and her heart beat fast
for both of them. But she was alone with Maurice; she must
not lose the chance of sounding him a little.

" Where do you think of going for a walk? " she asked,
and her voice had an odd tone to her ears.

" Where? Oh, to the *Rosental*—or the *Scheibenholz*—or
along the river. Anywhere. I don't know."

She coughed. " Have you noticed anything strange about
Ephie lately? She is not herself. I'm afraid she is not well."

He had noticed nothing. But he did not face Johanna; and
he held the photograph he was looking at upside down.

She leaned out of the window to watch them walk along
the street. At this moment, she was fully convinced of the
correctness of her mother's assumption; and by the thought
of what might take place within the next hour, she was much
disturbed. During the rest of the afternoon, she found it
impossible to settle to anything; and she wandered from one
room to another, unable even to read. But it struck six,
seven, eight o'clock; it was supper-time; and still Ephie had not
come home. Mrs. Cayhill grew anxious, too, and Johanna
strained her eyes, watching the dark street. At nine and
at ten, she was pacing the room, and at eleven, after a messenger had been sent to Maurice's lodging and had found no
one there, she buttoned on her rain-cloak, to accompany one
of the servants to the police-station.

" Why did I let her go?—Oh, why did I let her go! "

IV

MAURICE and Ephie walked along the *Lessingstrasse* without speaking—it was a dull, mild day, threatening to rain, as it had rained the whole of the preceding night. But Ephie was not accustomed to be silent; she found the stillness disconcerting, and before they had gone far, she shot a furtive look at her companion. She did not intend him to see it ; but he did, and turned to her. He cleared his throat, and seemed about to speak, then altered his mind. Something in his face, as she observed it more nearly, made Ephie change colour and give an awkward laugh.

"I asked you before how you liked my hat," she said, with another attempt at the airiness which, to-day, she could not command. "And you didn't say. I guess you haven't looked at it. You're in such a hurry."

Maurice turned his head; but he did not see the hat. Instead, he mentally answered a question Louise had put to him the day before, and which he had then not known how to meet. Yes, Ephie was pretty, radiantly pretty, with the fresh, unsullied charm of a flower just blown.

"Joan was so stupid about it," she went on at random; her face still wore its uncertain smile. "She said it was overtrimmed, and top-heavy, and didn't become me. As if she ever wore anything that suited her! But Joan is an old maid. She hasn't a scrap of taste. And as for you, Maurice, why I just don't believe you know one hat from another. Men are so stupid."

Again they went forward in silence.

"You are tiresome to-day," she said at length, and looked at him with a touch of defiance, as a schoolgirl looks at the master with whom she ventures to remonstrate.

"Yes, I'm a dull companion."

"Knowing it doesn't make it any better."

But she was not really cross; all other feelings were swallowed up by the uneasiness she felt at his manner of treating her.

"Where are we going?" she suddenly demanded of him,

with a little quick upward note in her voice. "This is not the way to the *Scheibenholz*."

"No." He had been waiting for the question. "Ephie," —he cleared his throat anew. "I am taking you to see a friend —of mine."

"Is that what you brought me out for? Then you didn't want to speak to me, as you said? Then we're not going for a walk?"

"Afterwards, perhaps. It's like this. Some one I know has been very ill. Now that she is getting better, she needs rousing and cheering up, and that kind of thing; and I said I would bring you to call on her. She knows you by sight— and would like to know you personally," he added, with a lame effort at explanation.

"Is that so?" said Ephie with sudden indifference; and her heart, which had begun to thump at the mention of a friend, quieted down at once. In fancy, she saw an elderly lady with shawls and a footstool, who had been attracted by her fresh young face; the same thing had happened to her before.

Now, however, that she knew the object of their walk, she was greatly relieved, as if a near danger had been averted; but she had not taken many steps forward before she was telling herself that another hope was gone. The only thing to do was to take the matter into her own hands; it was now or never; and simply a question of courage.

"Maurice, say, do many people go away from here in the fall?—leave the Con., I would say?" she asked abruptly. "I mean is this a time more people leave than in spring?"

Maurice started; he had been lost in his own thoughts, which all centred round this meeting he had weakly agreed to arrange. Again and again he had tried to imagine how it would fall out. But he did not know Louise well enough to foresee how she would act; and the nearer the time came, the stronger grew his presentiment of trouble. His chief remaining hope was that there would be no open speaking, that Schilsky's name would not be mentioned; and plump into the midst of this hope fell Ephie's question. He turned on her; she coloured furiously, and walked into a pool of water; and, at this moment, everything was as clear to Maurice as though she had said: "Where is he? Why has he gone?"

"Why do you ask?" he queried with unconscious sharpness. "No, Easter is the general time for leaving. But people who

play in the *Prüfungen* then, sometimes stay for the summer
term. Why do you ask?"

"Gracious, Maurice, how tiresome you are! Must one
always say why? I only wanted to know. I missed people
I used to see about, that's all."

"Yes, a number have not come back."

He was so occupied with what they were saying that he,
in his turn, stepped into a puddle, splashing the water up over
her shoe. Ephie was extremely annoyed.

"Look!—look what you've done!" she cried, showing him
her spikey little shoe. "Why don't you look where you're.
going? How clumsy you are!" and, in a sudden burst of ill-
humour: "I don't know why you're bringing me here. It's
a horrid part of the city anyway. I didn't have any desire to
come. I guess I'll turn back and go home."

"We're almost there now."

"I don't care. I don't want to go."

"But you shall, all the same. What's the matter with you
to-day that you don't know your own mind for two minutes
together?"

"You didn't inquire if I wanted to come. You're just
horrid, Maurice."

"And you're a capricious child."

He quickened his pace, afraid she might still escape him;
and Ephie had hard work to keep up with him. As she trotted
along, a few steps behind, there arose in her a strong feeling
of resentment against Maurice, which was all the stronger
because she suspected that she was on the brink of hearing
her worst suspicions confirmed. But she could not afford to
yield to the feeling, when the last chance she had of getting
definite information was passing from her. Knitting both
hands firmly inside her muff, she asked, with an earnestness
which, to one who knew, was fatally tale-telling: "Did anyone you were acquainted with leave, Maurice?"

"Yes," said the young man at her side, with brusque determination. He remained untouched by the tone of appeal
in which Ephie put the question; for he himself suffered under
her continued hedging. "Yes," he said, "some one did, and
that was a man called Schilsky—a tall, red-haired fellow, a
violinist. But he has only just gone. He came back after
the vacation to settle his affairs, and say good-bye to his
friends. Is there anything else you want to know?"

He regretted the words as soon as they were out of his

mouth. After all, Ephie was such a child. He could not see her face, which was hidden by the brim of the big hat, but there was something pathetic in the line of her chin, and the droop of her arms and shoulders. She seemed to shrink under his words—to grow smaller. As he stood aside to let her pass before him, through the house-door in the *Brüderstrasse,* he had a quick revulsion of feeling. Instead of being rough and cruel to her, he should have tried to win her confidence with brotherly kindness. But he had had room in his mind for nothing but the meeting with Louise, and now there was no more time; they were going up the stairs. All he could do was to say gently: "I ought to tell you, Ephie, that the person we are going to see has been very, very ill—and needs treating with the utmost consideration. I rely on your tact and good-feeling."

But Ephie did not reply; the colour had left her face, and for once, the short upper-lip closed firmly on the lower one. For some minutes amazed anger with Maurice was all she felt. Then, however, came the knowledge of what his words meant: he knew—Maurice knew; he had seen through her fictions; he would tell on her; there would be dreadful scenes with Joan; there would be reproaches and recriminations; she would be locked up, or taken away. As for what lay beyond, his assertion that Schilsky had been there—had been and gone, without a word to her—that was a sickening possibility, which, at present, her mind could not grasp. She grew dizzy under these blows that rained down on her, one after the other. And meanwhile, she had to keep up appearances, to go on as though nothing had happened, when it seemed impossible even to drag herself to the top of the winding flight of stairs. She held her head down; there was a peculiar clicking in her throat, which she could not master; she felt at every step as if she would have to burst out crying.

At the glass of the door, and at the wizened old face that appeared behind it, she looked with unseeing eyes; and she followed Maurice mechanically along the passage to a door at the end.

In his agitation the young man forgot to knock; and as they entered, a figure sprang up from the sofa-corner, and made a few impulsive steps towards them.

Maurice went over to Louise and took her hand.

"I've brought her," he said in a low tone, and with a kind of appeal in voice and eyes, which he was not himself

aware of. Louise answered the look, and went on looking at
him, as if she were fearful of letting her eyes stray. Both
turned at an exclamation from Ephie. She was still standing
where Maurice had left her, close beside the door; but her
face was flaming, and her right hand fumbled with the door-
handle.

"Ephie!" said Maurice warningly. He was afraid she
would turn the handle, and, going over to her, took her by
the arm.

"Say, Maurice, I'm going home," she said under her breath.
"I can't stop here. Oh, why did you bring me?"

"Ssh!—be a good girl, Ephie," he replied as though speaking to a child. "Come with me."

An inborn politeness struggled with Ephie's dread. "I can't.
I don't know her name," she whispered. But she let him draw
her forward to where Louise was standing; and she held out
her hand.

"Miss ——?" she said in a small voice, and waited for
the name to be filled in.

Louise had watched them whispering, with a stony face,
but, at Ephie's gesture, life came into it. Her eyes opened
wide; and drawing back from the girl's outstretched hand,
yet without seeming to see it, she turned with a hasty movement, and went over to the window, where she stood with
her back to them.

This was the last straw; Ephie dropped on a chair, and
hiding her face in her hands, burst into the tears she had
hitherto restrained. Her previous trouble was increased a
hundredfold. For she had recognised Louise at once; she felt
that she was in a trap; and the person who had entrapped her
was Maurice. Holding a tiny lace handkerchief to her eyes,
she sobbed as though her heart would break.

"Don't cry, dear, don't cry," said the young man. "It's
all right." But his thoughts were with Louise. He was apprehensive of what she might do next.

As if in answer to his fear, she crossed the room.

"Ask her to take her hands down. I want to see her face."

Maurice bent over Ephie, and touched her shoulder.

"Ephie, dear, do you hear? Look up, like a good girl, and
speak to Miss Dufrayer."

But Ephie shook off his hand.

Over her bowed head, their eyes met; and the look Louise
gave the young man was cold and questioning. He shrugged

his shoulders: he could do nothing; and retreating behind the writing-table, he left the two girls to themselves.

"Stand up, please," said Louise in an unfriendly voice; and as Ephie did not obey, she made a movement to take her by the wrists.

"No, no!—don't touch me," cried Ephie, and rose in spite of herself. "What right have you to speak to me like this?"

She could say no more, for, with a quick, unforeseen movement, Louise took the young girl's face in both hands, and turned it up. And after her first instinctive effort to draw back, Ephie kept still, like a fascinated rabbit, her eyes fixed on the dark face that looked down at her.

Seconds passed into minutes; and the minutes seemed hours. Maurice watched, on the alert to intervene, if necessary.

At the entrance of her visitors, Louise had been unable to see distinctly, so stupefied was she by the thought that the person on whom her thoughts had run, with a kind of madness, for more than forty-eight hours, was actually in the room beside her—it was just as though a nightmare phantom had taken bodily form. And then, too, though she had spent each of these hours in picturing to herself what this girl would be like, the reality was so opposed to her imagining that, at first, she could not reconcile the differences.

Now she forced herself to see every line of the face. Nothing escaped her. She saw how loosened tendrils of hair on neck and forehead became little curls; saw the finely marked brows, and the dark blue veins at the temples; the pink and white colouring of the cheeks; the small nose, modelled as if in wax; the fascinating baby mouth, with its short upper-lip. Like most dark, sallow women, whose own brief freshness is past, the elder girl passionately admired such may-blossom beauty, as something belonging to a different race from herself. And this was not all: as she continued to look into Ephie's face, she ceased to be herself; she became the man whose tastes she knew better than her own; she saw with his eyes, felt with his senses. She pictured Ephie's face, arch and smiling, lifted to his; and she understood and excused his weakness. He had not been able to help what had happened: this was the prettiness that drew him in, the kind he had invariably turned to look back at, in the street—something fair and round, adorably small and young, something to be petted and protected, that clung, and was childishly subordinate. For her dark sallowness, for her wilful mastery, he had only had a passing fancy. She was not his type, and she knew it. But to have known it vaguely, when it did not matter, and to know it at a moment like the present, were two different things.

In a burst of despair she let her arms fall to her sides; but her insatiable eyes gazed on; and Ephie, though she was now free, did not stir, but remained standing, with her face raised, in a silly fascination. And the eyes, having taken in the curves of cheeks and chin, and the soft white throat, passed to the rounded, drooping shoulders, to the plumpness of the girlish figure, embracing the whole body in their devouring gaze. Ephie went hot and cold beneath them; she felt as if her clothes were being stripped from her, and she left standing naked. Louise saw the changing colour, and interpreted it in her own way. His—all his! He was not the mortal—she knew it only too well—to have this flower within his reach, and not clutch at it, instinctively, as a child clutches at sunbeams. It would not have been in nature for him to do otherwise than take, greedily, without reflection. At the thought of it, a spasm of jealousy caught her by the throat; her hanging hands trembled to hurt this infantile prettiness, to spoil these lips that had been kissed by his.

Maurice was at her side. "Don't hurt her," he said, and did not know how the words came to his lips.

The spell was broken. The unnatural expression died out of her face; she was tired and apathetic.

"Hurt her?" she repeated faintly. "No, don't be afraid. I shall not hurt her. But if I beat her with ropes till all my strength was gone, I couldn't hurt her as she has hurt me."

"Hush! Don't say such things."

"I? I hurt you?" said Ephie, and began to cry afresh. "How could I? I don't even know you."

"No, you don't know me; and yet you have done me the cruellest wrong."

"Oh, no, no," sobbed Ephie. "No, indeed!"

"He was all I had—all I cared for. And you plotted, and planned, and stole him from me—with your silly baby face."

"It's not true," wept Ephie. "How could I? I didn't know anything about you. He . . . he never spoke of you."

Louise laughed. "Oh, I can believe that! And you thought, didn't you, you poor little fool, that he only cared for you? That was why my name was never mentioned. He didn't need to scheme, and contrive, and lie, lie abominably, for fear I should come to hear what he was doing!"

"No, indeed," sobbed Ephie. "Never! And you've no right to say such things of him."

"I no right?" Louise drew herself up. "No right to say what I like of him? Are you going to tell me what I shall say and what I shan't of the man I loved?—yes, and who loved me, too, but in a way you couldn't understand—you who think all you have to do is to smile your silly smile, and spoil another person's life. You didn't know, no, of course not!—didn't know this was his room as well as mine. Look, his music is still lying on the piano; that's the chair he sat in, not many days ago; here," she took Ephie by the shoulder and drew her behind the screen, where a small door, papered like the wall, gave, direct from the stair-head, a second entrance to the room—"here's the door he came in at.—For he came as he liked, whenever he chose."

"It's not true; it can't be true," said Ephie, and raised her tear-stained face defiantly. "We are engaged—since the summer. He's coming back to marry me soon."

"He's coming back to marry you!" echoed Louise in a blank voice. "He's coming back to marry you!"

She moved a few steps away, and stood by the writing-table, looking dazed, as if she did not understand. Then she laughed.

Ephie cried with renewed bitterness. "I want to go home."

But Maurice did not pay any attention to her. He was watching Louise, with a growing dismay. For she continued to laugh, in a breathless way, with a catch in the throat, which made the laughter sound like sobbing. On his approaching her, she tried to check herself, but without success. She wiped her lips, and pressed her handkerchief to them, then took the handkerchief between her teeth and bit it. She crossed to the window, and stood with her back to the others; but she could not stop laughing. She went behind the low, broad screen that divided the room, and sat down on the edge of the bed; but still she had to laugh on. She came out again into the other part of the room, and saw Maurice pale and concerned, and Ephie's tears dried through pure fear; but the sight of these two made her laugh more violently than before. She held her face in her hands, and pressed her jaws together as though she would break them; for they shook with a nervous convulsion. Her whole body began to shake, with the efforts she made at repression.

Ephie cowered in her seat. "Oh, Maurice, let us go. I'm so afraid," she implored him.

"Don't be frightened! It's all right." But he was following Louise about the room, entreating her to regain the mastery of herself. When he did happen to notice Ephie more closely, he said: "Go downstairs, and wait for me there. I'll come soon."

Ephie did not need twice telling: she turned and fled. He heard the hall-door bang behind her.

"Do try to control yourself. Miss Dufrayer—Louise! Every one in the house will hear you."

But she only laughed the more. And now the merest trifles helped to increase the paroxysm—the way Maurice worked his hands, Ephie's muff lying forgotten on a chair, the landlady's inquisitive face peering in at the door. The laugh continued, though it had become a kind of cackle—a sound without tone. Maurice could bear it no longer. He went up to her and tried to take her hands. She repulsed him, but he was too strong for her. He took both her hands in his, and pressed her down on a chair. He was not clear himself what to do next; but, the moment he touched her, the laughter ceased. She gasped for breath; he thought she would choke, and let her hands go again. She pressed them to her throat; her breath came more and more quickly; her eyes closed; and falling forward on her knees, she hid her face in the cushioned seat of the sofa.

Then the tears came, and what tears! In all his life, Maurice had never heard crying like this. He moved as far away from her as he could, stood at the window, staring out and biting his lips, while she sobbed, regardless of his presence, with the utter abandon of a child. Like a child, too, she wept rebelliously, unchastenedly, as he could not have believed it possible for a grown person to cry. Such grief as this, so absolute a despair, had nothing to do with reason or the reasoning faculties; and the words were not invented that would be able to soothe it.

But, little by little, a change came over her crying. The rebellion died out of it; it grew duller, and more blunted, hopeless, without life. Her strength was almost gone. Now, however, there was another note of childishness in it, that of complete exhaustion, which it is so hard to hear. The tears rose to his own eyes; he would have liked to go to her, to lay his hand on her head, and treat her tenderly, to make her cease and be happy once more; but he did not dare. Had he done so, she might not have repelled him; for, in all intensely passionate grief, there comes a moment of subsidence, when the grief and its origin are forgotten, and the one over-ruling desire is the desire to be comforted, no matter who the comforter and what his means, so long as they are masterful and strong.

She grew calmer; and soon she was only shaken at widening intervals by a sob. Then these, too, ceased, and Maurice held his breath. But as, after a considerable time had elapsed, she still lay without making sound or movement, he crossed the room to look at her. She was fast asleep, half sitting, half lying, with her head on the cushions, and the tears wet on her cheeks. He hesitated between a wish to see her in a more comfortable position, and an unwillingness to disturb her. Finally, he took an eider-down quilt from the bed, and wrapped it round her; then slipped noiselessly from the room.

It was past eight o'clock.

*   *   *   *   *

Ephie ran down the stairs as if a spectre were at her heels, and even when in the street, did not venture to slacken her speed. Although the dusk was rapidly passing into dark, a good deal of notice was attracted by the sight of a well-dressed young girl running along, holding a handkerchief to her face, and every now and then emitting a loud sob. People stood and stared after her, and some little boys ran with her. Instead of dropping her pace when she saw this, Ephie grew confused, and ran more quickly than before. She had turned at random, on coming out of the house; and she was in a part of the town she did not know. In her eagerness to get away from people, she took any turn that offered; and after a time she found that she had crossed the river, and was on what was almost a country road. A little further off, she knew, lay the woods; if once she were in their shelter, she would be safe; and, without stopping to consider that night was falling, she ran towards them at full speed. On the first seat she came to she sank breathless and exhausted.

Her first sensation was one of relief at being alone. She unpinned and took off the big, heavy hat, and laid it on the seat beside her, in order to be more at her ease; and then she cried, heartily, and without precautions, enjoying to the full the luxury of being unwatched and unheard. Since tea-time, she seemed to have been fighting her tears, exercising

a self-restraint that was new to her and very hard; and not
to-day alone—oh, no, for weeks past, she had been obliged to
act a part. Not even in her bed at night had she been free
to indulge her grief; for, if she cried then, it made her pale
and heavy-eyed next day, and exposed her to Joan's comments.
And there were so many things to cry about: all the
emotional excitement of the summer, with its ups and downs
of hope and fear; the never-ceasing need of dissimulation; the
gnawing uncertainty caused by Schilsky's silence; the growing
sense of blankness and disappointment; Joan's suspicions;
Maurice's discovery; the knowledge that Schilsky had gone
away without a word to her; and, worst of all, and most
inexplicable, the terrible visit of the afternoon—at the remembrance of the madwoman she had escaped from, Ephie's
tears flowed with renewed vigour. Her handkerchief was
soaked and useless; she held her fur tippet across her eyes to
receive the tears as they fell; and when this grew too wet, she
raised the skirt of her dress to her face. Not a sound was to
be heard but her sobbing; she was absolutely alone; and she
wept on till those who cared for her, whose chief wish was
to keep grief from her, would hardly have recognized in her
the child they loved.

How long she had been there she did not know, when she
was startled to her feet by a loud rustling in the bushes
behind her. Then, of a sudden, she became aware that it
was pitch-dark, and that she was all by herself in the woods.
She took to her heels, in a panic of fear, and did not stop
running till the street-lamps came into sight. When she was
under their friendly shine, and could see people walking on
the other side of the river, she remembered that she had left
her hat lying on the seat. At this fresh misfortune, she began
to cry anew. But not for anything in the world would she
have ventured back to fetch it.

She crossed the Pleisse and came to a dark, quiet street, where
few people were; and here she wandered up and down. It
was late; at home they would be sitting at supper now, exhaust-
ing themselves in conjectures where she could be. Ephie was
very hungry, and at the thought of the warmth and light of
the supper-table, a lump rose in her throat. If it had
been only her mother, she might have faced her—but Joan!
Home in this plight, at this hour, hatless, and with swollen
face, to meet Joan's eyes and questions!—she shivered at the
idea. Moreover, the whole *Pension* would get to know what

had happened to her; she would need to bear inquisitive looks
and words; she would have to explain, or, still worse, to invent
and tell stories again; and of what use were they now, when
all was over? A feeling of lassitude overcame her—an inability to begin fresh. All over: he would never put his arm
round her again, never come towards her, careless and smiling,
and call her his " little, little girl."

She sobbed to herself as she walked. Everything was
bleak, and black, and cheerless. She would perhaps die of
the cold, and then all of them, Joan in particular, would
be filled with remorse. She stood and looked at the inky water
of the river between its stone walls. She had read of people
drowning themselves; what if she went down the steps and
threw herself in?—and she feebly fingered at the gate. But
it was locked and chained; and at the idea of her warm, soft
body touching the icy water; at the picture of herself lying
drowned, with dank hair, or, like the Christian Martyr, floating away on the surface; at the thought of their grief, of *him*
wringing his hands over her corpse, she was so moved that
she wept aloud again, and amost ran to be out of temptation's
way.

It had begun to drizzle. Oh, how tired she was! And
she was obliged constantly to dodge impertinently staring men.
In a long, wide street, she entered a door-way that was not
quite so dark as the others, and sat down on the bottom step
of the stairs. Here she must have dozed, for she was roused
by angry voices on the floor above. It sounded like some one
who was drunk; and she fled trembling back to the street.

A neighbouring clock struck ten. At this time of night, she
could not go home, even though she wished to. She was wandering the streets like any outcast, late at night, without a hat
—and her condition of hatlessness she felt to be the chief stigma.
But she was starving with hunger, and so tired that she could
scarcely drag one foot after the other. Oh, what would they
say if they knew what their poor little Ephie was enduring!
Her mother—Joan—Maurice!

Maurice! The thought of him came to her like a ray of
light. It was to Maurice she would turn. He would be
good to her, and help her; he had always been kind to her, till
this afternoon. And he knew what had happened; it would
not be necessary to explain.—Oh, Maurice, Maurice!

She knew his address, if she could but find the street. A
droschke passed, and she tried to hail it; but she did not like to

advance too far out of the shadow, on account of her bare head. Finally, plucking up courage, she inquired the way of a feather-hatted woman, who had eyed her with an inquisitive stare.

It turned out that the *Braustrasse* was just round the corner; she had perhaps been in the street already, without knowing it; and now she found it, and the house, without difficulty. The street-door was still open; or she would never have been bold enough to ring.

The stair was poorly lighted, and full of unsavoury smells. In her agitation, Ephie rang on a wrong floor, and a strange man answered her timid inquiry. She climbed a flight higher, and rang again. There was a long and ominous pause, in which her heart beat fast; if Maurice did not live here either, she would drop where she stood. She was about to ring a second time, when felt slippers and an oil lamp moved along the passage, the glass window was opened, and a woman's face peered out at her. Yes, Herr Guest lived there, certainly, said Frau Krause, divided between curiosity and indignation at having to rise from bed; and she held the lamp above her head, in order to see Ephie better. But he was not at home, and, even if he were, at this hour of night . . . The heavy words shuffled along, giving the voracious eyes time to devour.

At the thought that her request might be denied her, Ephie's courage took its last leap.

" Why, I must see him. I have something important to tell him. Could I not wait? " she urged in her broken German, feeling unspeakably small and forlorn. And yielding to a desire to examine more nearly the bare, damp head and costly furs, Frau Krause allowed the girl to pass before her into Maurice's room.

She loitered as long as she could over lighting the lamp that stood on the table; and meanwhile threw repeated glances at Ephie, who, having given one look round the shabby room, sank into a corner of the sofa and hid her face: the coarse-browed woman, in petticoat and night-jacket, seemed to her capable of robbery or murder. And so Frau Krause unwillingly withdrew, to await further developments outside: the holy, smooth-faced Herr Guest was a deep one, after all.

When Maurice entered, shortly before eleven, Ephie started up from a broken sleep. He came in pale and disturbed, for Frau Krause had met him in the passage with angry mutterings about a *Frauenzimmer* in his room; and his thoughts had

at once leaped fearfully to Louise. When he saw Ephie, he
uttered a loud exclamation of surprise.

"Good Lord, Ephie! What on earth are you doing here?"

She sprang at his hands, and caught her breath hysterically.
"Oh, Morry, you've come at last. Oh, I thought you would
never come. Where have you been? Oh, Morry, help me—
help me, or I shall die!"

"Whatever is the matter? What are you doing here?"

At his perturbed amazement, she burst into tears, still clinging fast to his hands. He led her back to the sofa, from which
she had sprung.

"Hush, hush! Don't cry like that. What's the matter,
child? Tell me what it is—at once—and let me help you."

"Oh, yes, Morry, help me, help me! There's no one else.
I didn't know where to go. Oh, what shall I do!"

Her own words sounded so pathetic that she sobbed piteously.
Maurice stroked her hand, and waited for her to grow quieter.
But now that she had laid the responsibility of herself on other
shoulders, Ephie was quite unnerved: after the dark and fearful wanderings of the evening, to be beside some one who knew,
who would take care of her, who would tell her what to do!

She sobbed and sobbed. Only with perseverance did Maurice
draw from her, word by word, an account of where she had
been that evening, broken by such cries as: "Oh, what shall
I do! I can't ever go home again—ever! . . . and I lost
my hat. Oh, Morry, Morry! And I didn't know he had
gone away—and it wasn't true what I said, that he was coming back to marry me soon. I only said it to spite her, because
she said such dreadful things to me. But we were engaged, all
the same; he said he would come to New York to marry me.
And now . . . oh, dear, oh, Morry! . . ."

"Then he really promised to marry you, did he?"

"Yes, oh, yes. Everything was fixed. The last day I was
there," she wept. "But I didn't know he was going away;
he never said a word about it. Oh, what shall I do! Go after
him, and bring him back, Morry. He must come back. He
can't leave me like this, he can't—oh, no, indeed!"

"You don't mean to say you went to see him, Ephie?—alone?
—at his room?" queried Maurice slowly, and he did not
know how sternly. "When? How often? Tell me everything. This is no time for fibbing."

But he could make little of Ephie's sobbed and hazy version
of the story; she herself could not remember clearly now; the

impressions of the last few hours had been so intense as to obliterate much of what had gone before. " I thought I would drown myself . . . but the water was so black. Oh, why did you take me to that dreadful woman? Did you hear what she said? It wasn't true, was it? Oh, it can't be!"

" It was quite true, Ephie. What he told *you* wasn't true. He never really cared for anyone but her. They were—were engaged for years."

At this, she wept so heart-rendingly that he was afraid Frau Krause would come in and interfere.

"You *must* control yourself. Crying won't alter things now. If you had been frank and candid with us, it would never have happened." This was the only reproach he could make her; what came after was Johanna's business, not his. "And now I'm going to take you home. It's nearly twelve o'clock. Think of the state your mother and sister will be in about you."

But at the mention of Johanna, Ephie flung herself on the sofa again and beat the cushions with her hands.

" Not Joan, not Joan! " she wailed. " No, I won't go home. What will she say to me? Oh, I am so frightened! She'll kill me, I know she will." And at Maurice's confident assurance that Johanna would have nothing but love and sympathy for her, she shook her head. " I know Joan. She'll never forgive me. Morry, let me stay with you. You've always been kind to me. Oh, don't send me away!"

" Don't be a silly child, Ephie. You know yourself you can't stay here."

But he gave up urging her, coaxed her to lie down, and sat beside her, stroking her hair. As he said no more, she gradually ceased to sob, and in what seemed to the young man an incredibly short time, he heard from her breathing that she was asleep. He covered her up, and stood a sheet of music before the lamp, to shade her eyes. In the passage he ran up against Frau Krause, whom he charged to prevent Ephie in the event of her attempting to leave the house.

Buttoning up his coat-collar, he hastened through the mist-like rain to fetch Johanna.

There was a light in every window of the *Pension* in the *Lessingstrasse;* the street-door and both doors of the flat stood open. As he mounted the stairs a confused sound of voices struck his ear; and when he entered the passage, he heard Mrs. Cayhill crying noisily. Johanna came out to him at once;

she was in hat and cloak. She listened stonily to his statement that Ephie was safe at his lodgings, and put no questions; but, on her returning to the sitting-room, Mrs. Cayhill's sobs stopped abruptly, and several women spoke at once.

Johanna preserved her uncompromising attitude as they walked the midnight streets. But as Maurice made no mien to explain matters further, she so far conquered her aversion as to ask: "What have you done to her?"

The young man's consternation at this view of the case was so evident that even she felt the need of wording her question differently.

"Answer me. What is Ephie doing at your rooms?"

Maurice cleared his throat. "It's a long and unpleasant story, Miss Cayhill. And I'm afraid I must tell it from the beginning.—You didn't suspect, I fear, that . . . well, that Ephie had a fancy for some one here?"

At these words, which were very different from those she had expected, Johanna eyed him in astonishment.

"A fancy!" she repeated incredulously. "What do you mean?"

"Even more—an infatuation," said Maurice with deliberation. "And for some one I daresay you have never even heard of—a . . . a man here, a violinist, called Schilsky."

The elaborate fabric she had that day reared, fell together about Johanna's ears. She stared at Maurice as if she doubted his sanity; and she continued to listen, with the same icy air of disbelief, to his stammered and ineffectual narrative, until he said that he believed "it" had been "going on since summer."

At this Johanna laughed aloud. "That is quite impossible," she said. "I knew everything Ephie did, and everywhere she went."

"She met him nearly every day. They exchanged letters, and ——"

"It is impossible," repeated Johanna with vehemence, but less surely.

"—— and a sort of engagement seems to have existed between them."

"And you knew this and never said a word to me?"

"I didn't know—not till to-night. I only suspected something—once . . . long ago. And I couldn't—I mean—one can't say a thing like that without being quite sure——"

But here he broke down, conscious, as never before, of the negligence he had been guilty of towards Ephie. And Johanna was not likely to spare him: there was, indeed, a bitter antagonism to his half-hearted conduct in the tone in which she said: "I stood to Ephie in a mother's place. You might have warned me—oh, you might, indeed!"

They walked on in silence—a hard, resentful silence. Then Johanna put the question he was expecting to hear.

"And what has all this to do with to-night?"

Maurice took up the thread of his narrative again, telling how Ephie had waited vainly for news since returning from Switzerland, and how she had only learnt that afternoon that Schilsky had been in Leipzig, and had gone away again, without seeing her, or letting her know that he did not intend to return.

"And how did she hear it?"

"At a friend's house."

"What friend?"

"A friend of mine, a —— No; I had better be frank with you: the girl this fellow was engaged to for a year or more."

"And Ephie did not know that?"

He shook his head.

"But you knew, and yet took her there?"

It was a hopeless job to try to exonerate himself. "Yes, there were reasons—I couldn't help it, in fact. But I'm afraid I should not be able to make you understand."

"No, never!" retorted Johanna, and squared her shoulders.

But there was more to be said—she had worse to learn—before Ephie was handed over to her care.

"And Ephie has been very foolish," he began anew, without looking at her. "It seems—from what she has told me to-night—that she has been to see this man . . . been at his rooms . . . more than once."

At first, he was certain, Johanna did not grasp the meaning of what he said; she turned a blank face curiously to him. But, a moment later, she gave a low cry, and hardly able to form the words for excitement, asked: "Who . . . what . . . what kind of a man was he—this . . . Schilsky?"

"Rotten," said Maurice; and she did not press him further. He heard her breath coming quickly, and saw the kind of stiffening that went through her body; but she kept silence, and did not speak again till they were almost at his house-door. Then she said, in a voice that was hoarse with feeling: "It has been all my fault. I did not take proper care of her. I was blind and foolish. And I shall never be able to forgive myself for it—never. But that Ephie—my little

Ephie—the child I—that Ephie could . . . could do a thing like this . . . " Her voice tailed off in a sob.

Maurice struck matches, to light her up the dark staircase; and the condition of the stairs, the disagreeable smells, the poverty of wall and door revealed, made Johanna's heart sink still further: to surroundings such as these had Ephie accustomed herself. They entered without noise; everything was just as Maurice had left it, except that the lamp had burned too high and filled the room with its fumes. As Johanna paused, undecided what to do, Ephie started up, and, at the sight of her sister, burst into loud cries of fear. Hiding her face, she sobbed so alarmingly that Johanna did not venture to approach her. She remained standing beside the table, one thin, ungloved hand resting on it, while Maurice bent over Ephie and tried to soothe her.

" Please fetch a droschke," Johanna said grimly, as Ephie's sobs showed no signs of abating; and when, after a lengthy search in the night, Maurice returned, she was standing in the same position, staring with drawn, unblinking eyes at the smoky lamp, which no one had thought of lowering. Ephie was still crying, and only Maurice might go near her. He coaxed her to rise, wrapped his rug round her, and carried her, more than he led her, down the stairs.

" Be good enough to drive home with us," said Johanna. And so he sat with his arm round Ephie, who pressed her face against his shoulder, while the droschke jolted over the cobbled streets, and Johanna held herself pale and erect on the opposite seat. She mounted the stairs in front of them. Ephie was limp and heavy going up; but no sooner did she catch sight of Mrs. Cayhill than, with a cry, she rushed from the young man's side, and threw herself into her mother's arms.

" Oh, mummy, mummy!"

Downstairs, in the rain-soaked street, Maurice found the droschke-driver waiting for his fare. It only amounted to a couple of marks, and it was no doubt a just retribution for what had happened that he should be obliged to lay it out; but, none the less, it seemed like the last straw—the last dismal touch—in a day of forlorn discomfort.

V

A few weeks later, a great variety of cabin-trunks and saratogas blocked the corridor of the *Pension*. The addresses they bore were in Johanna's small, pointed handwriting.

On this, the last afternoon of the Cayhills' stay in Leipzig, Maurice saw Johanna again for the first time. She had had her hands full. In the woods, on that damp October night, and on her subsequent wanderings, Ephie had caught a severe cold; and the doctor had feared an inflammation of the lungs. This had been staved off; but there was also, it seemed, a latent weakness of the chest, hitherto unsuspected, which kept them anxious. Ephie still had a dry, grating cough, which was troublesome at night, and left her tired and fretful by day. They were travelling direct to the South of France, where they intended to remain until she had quite recovered her strength.

Maurice sat beside Johanna on the deep sofa where he and Ephie had worked at harmony together. But the windows of the room were shut now, and the room itself looked unfamiliar; for it had been stripped of all the trifles and fancy things that had given it such a comfortable, home-like air, and was only the bare, lodging-house room once more. Johanna was as self-possessed as of old, a trifle paler, a trifle thinner of lip.

She told him that they intended leaving quietly the next morning, without partings or farewells. Ephie was still weak, and the less excitement she had to undergo, the better it would be for her.

"Then I shall not see Ephie again?" queried Maurice in surprise.

Johanna thought not: it would only recall the unhappy night to her memory; besides, she had not asked to see him, as she no doubt would have done, had she wished it.—At this, the eleventh hour, Johanna did not think it worth while to tell Maurice that Ephie bore him an unalterable grudge.

"I never want to see him again."

That was all she said to Johanna; but, during her illness, she had brooded long over his treachery. And even if things had come all right in the end, she would never have been able

to forgive his speaking to her of Schilsky in the way he had
done.   No, she was finished with Maurice Guest; he was
too double-faced, too deceitful for her.—And she cried bitterly,
with her face turned to the wall.

The young man could not but somewhat lamely agree with
Johanna that it was better to let the matter end thus: for
he felt that towards the Cayhills he had been guilty of a breach
of trust such as it is difficult to forgive.   At the same time,
he was humanly hurt that Ephie would not even say good-bye
to him.

He asked their further plans, and learnt that as soon as Ephie
was well again, they would sail for New York.

" My father has cabled twice for us."

Johanna's manner was uncompromisingly dry and short.
After her last words, there was a long pause, and Maurice
made a movement to rise.   But she put out her hand and detained him.

" There is something I should like to say to you."   And
thereupon, with the abruptness of a nervous person :   " When
I have seen my sister and mother safe back, I intend leaving
home myself.   I am going to Harvard."

Maurice realised that the girl was telling him a fact of considerable importance to herself, and did his best to look interested.

" Really?   That's always been a wish of yours, hasn't it? "

" Yes."   Johanna coloured, hesitated as he had never known
her to do, then burst out :   "And now there is nothing in the
way of it."   She drew her thumb across the leaf-corners of a
book that was lying on the table.   " Oh, I know what you will
say : how, now that Ephie has turned out to be weak and untrust-
worthy, there is all the more reason for me to remain with her, to
look after her.   But that is not possible."   She faced him sharply,
as though he had contradicted her.   " I am incapable of pretending to be the same when my feelings have changed; and,
as I told you—as I knew that night—I shall never be able to
feel for Ephie as I did before.   I am ready, as I said, to take
all the blame for what has happened ; I was blind and thoughtless.
But if the care and affection of years count for nothing; if I
have been so little able to win her confidence; if, indeed, I have
only succeeded in making her dislike me, by my care of her,
so that when she is in trouble, she turns from me, instead of
to me—why, then I have failed lamentably in what I had
made the chief duty of my life.

"Besides," she continued more quietly, "there is another reason: Ephie is going to fall a victim to her nerves. I see that; and my poor, foolish mother is doing her best to foster it.—You smile? Only because you do not understand what it means. It is no laughing matter. If an American woman once becomes conscious of her nerves, then Heaven help her!—Now I am not of a disinterested enough nature to devote myself to sick-nursing where there is no real sickness. And then, too, my mother intends taking a French maid back with her, and a person of that class will perform such duties much more competently than I."

She spoke with bitterness. Maurice mumbled some words of sympathy, wondering why she should choose to say these things to him.

"Even at home my place is filled," continued Johanna. "The housekeeper who was appointed during our absence has been found so satisfactory that she will continue in the post after our return. Everywhere, you see, I have proved superfluous. There, as here."

"I'm sure you're mistaken," said Maurice with more warmth. "And, Miss Joan, there's something I should like to say, if I may. Don't you think you take what has happened here a little too seriously? No doubt Ephie behaved foolishly. But was it after all any more than a girlish escapade?"

"Too seriously?"

Johanna turned her shortsighted eyes on the young man, and gazed at him almost pityingly. How little, oh, how little, she said to herself, one mortal knew and could know of another, in spite of the medium of speech, in spite of common experiences! Some of the nights at the beginning of Ephie's illness returned vividly to her mind, nights, when she, Johanna, had paced her room by the hour, filled with a terrible dread, a numbing uncertainty, which she would sooner have died than have let cross her lips. She had borne it quite alone, this horrible fear; her mother had been told of the whole affair only what it was absolutely necessary for her to know. And, naturally enough, the young man who now sat at her side, being a man, could not be expected to understand. But the consciousness of her isolation made Johanna speak with renewed harshness.

"Too seriously?" she repeated. "Oh, I think not. The girlish escapade, as you call it, was the least of it. If that had been all, if it had only been her infatuation for some one

who was unworthy of her, I could have forgiven Ephie till
seventy times seven. But, after all these years, after the way I
have loved her—no, idolised her!—for her to treat me as she did
—do you think it possible to take that too seriously? There
was no reason she should not have had her little secrets. If she
had let me see that something was going on, which she did not
want to tell me about, do you think I should have forced
her?"—and Johanna spoke in all good faith, forgetful of how
she had been used to clip and doctor Ephie's sentiments. "But
that she could deceive me wilfully, and lie so lightly, with a
smile, when, all the time, she was living a double life, one to
my face and one behind my back—that I cannot forgive.
Something has died in me that I used to feel for her. I could
never trust her again, and where there is no trust there can be
no real love."

"She didn't understand what she was doing. She is so
young."

"Just for that reason. So young, and so skilled in deceit.
That is hardest of all, even to think of: that she could wear
her dear innocent face, while behind it, in her brain, were cold,
calculating thoughts how she could best deceive me! If there
had been but a single sign to waken my suspicions, then, yes,
then I could have forgiven her," said Johanna, and again forgot
how often of late she had been puzzled by the subtle change in
Ephie. "If I could just know that, in spite of her efforts,
she had been too candid to succeed!"

She had unburdened herself and it had been a relief to her,
but nothing could be helped or mended. Both knew this, and
after a few polite questions about her future plans and studies,
Maurice rose to take his leave.

"Say good-bye to them both for me, and give Ephie my
love."

"I will. I think she will be sorry afterwards that she
did not see you. She has always liked you."

"Good-bye then. Or perhaps it is only *auf Wiedersehen?*"

"I hardly think so." Johanna had returned to her usual
sedate manner. "If I do visit Europe again, it will not be for
five or six years at least."

"And that's a long time. Who knows where I may be, by
then!"

He held Johanna's hand in his, and saw her gauntly slim
figure outlined against the bare sitting-room. It was not likely
that they would ever meet again. But he could not summon up

any very lively feelings of regret. Johanna had not touched him deeply; she had left him as cool as he had no doubt left her; neither had found the key to the other. Her chief attraction for him had been her devotion to Ephie; and now, having been put to the test, this was found wanting. She had been wounded in her own pride and self-love, and could not forgive. At heart she was no more generous and unselfish than the rest.

He repeated farewell messages as he stood in the passage. Johanna held the front door open for him, and, as he went down the stairs, he heard it close behind him, with the extreme noiselessness that was characteristic of Johanna's treatment of it.

The following morning, shortly after ten o'clock, a train steamed out of the *Thüringer Bahnhof,* carrying the Cayhills with it. The day was misty and cheerless, and none of the three travellers turned her head to give the town a parting glance. They left unattended, without flowers or other souvenirs, without any of the demonstratively pathetic farewells, the waving of hats, and crowding about the carriage-door, which one of the family, at least, had connected inseverably with their departure. And thus Ephie's musical studies came to an abrupt and untimely end.

*   *   *   *   *

"My faith in women is shattered. I shall never believe in a woman again."

Dove paced the floor of Maurice's room with long and steady strides, beneath which a particular board creaked at intervals. His voice was husky, and the ruddiness of his cheeks had paled.

At the outset of Ephie's illness, Dove had called every morning at the *Pension,* to make inquiries and to leave his regards. But when the story leaked out, as it soon did, in an exaggerated and distorted form, he straightway ceased his visits. Thus he was wholly unprepared for the family's hurried departure, the news of which was broken to him by Maurice. Dove was dumbfounded. Not a single sententious phrase crossed his lips; and he remained unashamed of the moisture that dimmed his eyes. But he maintained his bearing commendably; and it was impossible not to admire the upright, manly air with which he walked down the street.

The next day, however, he returned, and was silent no longer. He made no secret of having been hard hit; just as

previously he had let his friends into his hopes and intentions,
so now every one heard of his reverses. He felt a tremendous
need of unbosoming himself; he had been so sure of success,
or, at least, so unthinking of failure, and the blow to his self-
esteem was a rude one.

Maurice sat with his hands in his pockets, and tried to urge
reason. But Dove would not admit even the possibility of his
having been mistaken. He had received innumerable proofs
of Ephie's regard for him.

"Remember how young she was! Girls of that age never
know their own minds," said Maurice. But Dove was inclined to take Johanna's sterner view, and to cry: "So young
and so untender!" for which he, too, substituted "untrue";
and, just on this score, to deduce unfavourable inferences for
Ephie's whole moral character. As Maurice listened to him,
he could not help thinking that Johanna's affection had been
of the same nature as Dove's, in other words, had had a touch
of the masculine about it: it had existed only as long as it
could guide and subordinate; it denied to its object any midget
attempt at individual life; it set up lofty moral standards, and
was implacable when a smaller, frailer being found it impossible
to live up to them.

At the same time, he was sorry for Dove, who, in his blindness, had laid himself open to receive this snubbing; and he
listened patiently, even a thought flattered by his confidence,
until he learnt from Madeleine that Dove was making the
round of his acquaintances, and behaving in the same way to
anyone who would let him. Then he found that the openness
with which Dove related his past hopes, and the marks of affection Ephie had given him, bordered on indecency. He said
so, with a wrathful frankness; but Dove could not see it in
that light, and was not offended.

As the personal smart weakened, the more serious question
that Dove had to face was, what he was going to tell his relatives at home. For it now came out that he had represented
the affair to them as settled; in his perfectly sincere optimism,
he had regarded himself as an all but engaged man. And the
point that disturbed him was, how to back out with dignity,
yet without violating the truth, on which he set great store.

"I'm sure he needn't let that trouble him," said Madeleine,
on hearing of his dilemma. "He has only to say that *he* has
changed his mind, which is true enough."

This was the conclusion Dove eventually came to himself—

though not with such unseemly haste as Madeleine. Having approached the matter from all sides, he argued that it would be more considerate to Ephie to put it in this light than to tell the story in detail. And consequently, two elderly people in Peterborough nodded to each other one morning over the breakfast-table, and agreed that Edward had done well. They had not been much in favour of the American match, but they had trusted implicitly in their son's good sense, and now, as ever, he had acted in the most becoming way. He had never given them an hour's uneasiness since his birth.

Dove wrote:

Circumstances have arisen, my dear parents, which make it incontrovertibly clear to me that the young lady to whom I was paying my addresses when I consulted you in summer and myself would not have known true happiness in our union. On more intimate acquaintance it transpired that our characters were totally unsuited. I have therefore found it advisable to banish the affair from my mind and to devote myself wholly to my studies.

As time passed, and Dove was able to view what had happened more objectively, he began to feel and even to hint that, all things considered, he had had a rather lucky escape; and from this, it was not very far to believing that if he had not just seen through the whole affair from the beginning, he had at any rate had some inkling of it; and now, instead of giving proofs of Ephie's affection, he narrated the gradual growth of his suspicions, and how these had ultimately been verified. In conclusion, he congratulated himself on having drawn back, with open eyes, while there was still time.

" Like his cheek! " said Madeleine. " But he could imagine himself into being the Shah of Persia, if he sat down and gave his mind to it. I don't believe the snub is going to do him a bit of good. He bobs up again like a cork, irrepressible. *Have you heard him quote:* ' Frailty thy name is woman! ' or: ' If women could be fair and yet not fond '?—It's as good as a play."

But altogether, Madeleine was very sharp of tongue since she learnt the part Maurice had played in what, for a day, was the scandal of the English-speaking colony. She had taken him to task at once, for his " lamentable interference."

" Haven't I warned you, Maurice, not to mix yourself up

in Louise's affairs? No good can come of it. She breeds mischief. And if that absurd child had really drowned herself"—in the version of the story that had reachéd Madeleine's ears, Maurice was represented fishing Ephie bodily from the river—"you would have had to bear the whole brunt of the blame. It ought to teach you a lesson. For you're just the kind of boy women will always take advantage of, a mean advantage, you know. Consider how you were treated in this case—by both of them! They were not a scrap grateful to you for what you did—women never are. They only look down on you for letting them have their own way. Kindness and complaisance don't move them. A well-developed biceps and a cruel mouth —that's what they want, and that's all!" she wound up with a flourish, in an extreme bad temper.

She sat, one dull November afternoon, at her piano, and continued to run her fingers over the keys. Maurice leant on the lid, and listened to her. But they had barely exchanged a word, when there was a light tap at the door, and Krafft entered. Both started at his unexpected appearance, and Madeleine cried: "You come in like a ghost, to frighten people out of their wits."

Krafft was buttoned to the chin in a travelling-ulster, and looked pale and thin.

"What news from St. Petersburg?" queried Madeleine with a certain asperity.

But Maurice recalled an errand he had to do in town; and, on hearing this, Krafft, who was lolling aimlessly, declared that he would accompany him.

"But you've only just come!" expostulated Madeleine. "What in the name of goodness did you climb the stairs for?"

He patted her cheek, without replying.

The young men went away together, Maurice puffing somewhat ostentatiously at a cigarette. The wind was cold, and Krafft seemed to shrink into his ulster before it, keeping his hands deep in his pockets. But from time to time, he threw a side-glance at his friend, and at length asked, in the tone of appeal which Maurice found it hard to withstand: "What's the matter, *Liebster?* Why are you so different?—so changed?"

"The matter? Nothing—that I'm aware of," said Maurice, and considered the tip of his cigarette.

"Oh, yes, there is," and Krafft laid a caressing hand on his companion's arm. "You are changed. You're not frank with me. I feel such things at once."

"Well, how on earth am I to know when to be frank with you, and when not? Before you . . . not very long ago, you behaved as if you didn't want to have anything more to do with me."

"You are changed, and, if I'm not mistaken, I know why," said Krafft, ignoring his answer. "You have been listening to gossip—to what my enemies say of me."

"I don't listen to gossip. And I didn't know you had enemies, as you call them."

"I?—and not have enemies?" He flared up as though Maurice had affronted him. "My good fellow, did you ever hear of a man worth his salt, who didn't have enemies? It's the penalty one pays: only the dolts and the 'all-too-many' are friends with the whole world. No one who has work to do that's worth doing, can avoid making enemies. And who knows what a friend is, who hasn't an enemy to match him? It's a question of light and shade, theme and counter-theme, of artistic proportion." He laughed, in his superior way. But directly afterwards, he dropped back into his former humble tone. "But that you, my friend, are so ready to let yourself be influenced—I should not have believed it of you."

"What I heard, I heard from Fürst; and I have no reason to suspect him of falsehood.—Of course, if you assure me it was not true, that's a different thing." He turned so sharply that he sent a beautiful flush over Krafft's face. "Come, give me your word, Heinz, and things will be straight again."

But Krafft merely shrugged his shoulders, and his colour subsided as rapidly as it had risen.

"Are you still such an outsider," he asked, "after all this time—in my society—as to attach importance to a word? What is 'giving a word'? Do you really think it is of any value? May I not give it to-night, and take it back to-mor-row, according to the mood I am in, according to whether I believe it myself or not, at the moment?—You think a thing must either be true or not true? You are wrong. Do you be-lieve, when you answer a question in the affirmative or the negative, that you are actually telling the truth? No, my friend, to be perfectly truthful one would need to lose one-self in a maze of explanation, such as no questioner would have the patience to listen to. One would need to take into account the innumerable threads that have gone to making the state-ment what it is. Do you think, for instance, if I answered yes or no, in the present case, it would be true? If I deny what you heard—does that tell you that I have longed with all my heart for it to come to pass? Or say I admit it—I should need to unroll my life before you to make you understand. No, there's no such thing as absolute truth. If there were, the finest subtleties of existence would be lost. There is neither positive truth nor positive untruth; life is not so coarse-fibred as that. And only the grossest natures can be satisfied with a blunt yes or no. Truth?—it is one of the many miserable conventions the human brain has tortured itself with, and its first principle is an utter lack of the imaginative faculties.—*Adieu!*"

VI

In the days that followed, Maurice threw himself heart and soul into his work. He had lost ground of late, he saw it plainly now: after his vigorous start, he had quickly grown slack. He was not, to-day, at the stage he ought to be, and there was not a doubt but that Schwarz saw it, too. Now that he came to think of it, he had more than once been aware of a studied coolness in the master's manner, of a rather ostentatious indifference to the quality of the work he brought to the class: and this he knew by hearsay to be Schwarz's attitude towards those of his pupils in whom his interest was waning. If he, Maurice, wished to regain his place in the little Pasha's favour, he must work like a coal-heaver. But the fact was, the strenuous industry to which he now condemned himself, was something of a relaxation after the mental anxiety he had recently undergone; this striking of a black and white keyboard was a pleasant, thought-deadening employment, and could be got through, no matter what one's mood.—And so he rose early again, and did not leave the house till he had five hours' practice behind him.

Wer sich der Einsamkeit ergiebt, ach, der ist bald allein: at the end of a fortnight, Maurice smiled to find the words of Goethe's song proved on himself. If he did not go to see his friends, none of them came to him. Dove, who was at the stage of: " I told you so," in the affair of the Cayhills, had found fresh listeners, who were more sympathetic than Maurice could be expected to be: and Madeleine was up to her ears in work, as she phrased it, with the " C minor Beethoven."

" Agility of finger equals softening of the brain " was a frequent gibe of Krafft's; and now and then, at the close of a hard day's work, Maurice believed that the saying contained a grain of truth. Opening both halves of his window, he would lean out on the sill, too tired for connected thought. But when dusk fell, he lay on the sofa, with his arms clasped under his head, his knees crossed in the air.

At first, in his new buoyancy of spirit, he was able to keep foolish ideas behind him, as well as to put away all recollection of the disagreeable events he had been mixed up in of late: after having, for weeks, borne a load that was too heavy for him, he breathed freely once more. The responsibility of taking care of Ephie had been removed from him—and this by far outweighed the little that he missed her. The matter had wound up, too, in a fairly peaceable way; all being considered, things might have been worse. So, at first, he throve under his light-heartedness; and only now became aware how great the strain of the past few weeks had been. His chief sensation was relief, and also of relief at being able to feel relieved—indeed, the moment even came when he thought it would be possible calmly to accept the fact of Louise having left the town, and of his never being likely to see her again.

Gradually, however, he began to be astonished at himself, and in the background of his mind, there arose a somewhat morbid curiosity, even a slight alarm, at his own indifference. He found it hard to understand himself. Could his feelings, those feelings which, a week or two ago, he had believed unalterable, have changed in so short a time? Was his nature one of so little stability? He began to consider himself with something approaching dismay, and though, all this time, he had been going about on a kind of mental tiptoe, for fear of rousing something that might be dormant in him, he now could not help probing himself, in order to see if the change he observed were genuine or not. And this with a steadily increasing frequency. Instead of continuing thankful for the respite, he ultimately grew uneasy under it. Am I a person of this weak, straw-like consistency, to be tossed about by every wind that blows? Is there something beneath it all that I cannot fathom?

He had not seen Louise since the night he had left her asleep beside the sofa; and he was resolved not to see her—not, at least, until she wished to see him. It was much better for him that the uncertainties of the bygone months did not begin anew; then, too, she had called him to her when she was in trouble, and not for anything in the world would he presume on her appeal. Besides, his presence would recall to her the unpleasant details connected with Ephie's visit, which he hoped she had by this time begun to forget. Thus he argued with himself, giving several reasons where one would have served; and the upshot of it was, that his own state of mind occupied him considerably.

His friends noticed the improvement in him; the careworn expression that had settled down on him of late gave way to

his old air of animation; and on all the small topics of the day,
he brought a sympathetic interest to bear, such as people had
ceased to expect from him. Madeleine, in particular, was satisfied with her "boy," as she took to calling him. She noted
and checked off, in wise silence, each inch of his progress along
the road of healthy endeavour; and the relations between them
bcame almost as hearty as at the commencement of their friendship. Privately, she believed that the events of the past month
had taught him a lesson, which he would not soon forget. It was
sufficient, however, if they had inspired him with a distrust of
Louise, which would keep him from her for the present; for
Madeleine had grounds for believing that before many weeks
had passed, Louise would have left Leipzig.

So she kept Maurice as close to her as work permitted; and
as the winter's flood of concerts set in, in full force, he accompanied her, almost nightly, to the Old Gewandhaus or the
Alberthalle; for Madeleine was an indefatigable concert-goer,
and never missed a performer of note, rarely even a first appearance at the *Hôtel de Prusse* or a *Blüthner Matinée.* On
the night she herself played in an *Abendunterhaltung,* with
the easily gained success that attended all she did, Maurice
went with her to the green-room, and was the first afterwards
to tell her how her performance had "gone." That same
evening she took him with her to the house of friends of hers,
the Hensels. There he met some of the best musical society
of the place, made a pleasant impression, and was invited to
return.

Meanwhile, winter had set in, with extreme severity. Piercing north winds drove down the narrow streets, and raged
round the corners of the Gewandhaus square: on emerging
from the *Probe* on a Wednesday morning, one's breath was
cut clean off, and the tears raced down one's cheeks. When
the wind dropped, there were hard black frosts—a deadly,
stagnant kind of cold, which seemed to penetrate every pore of
the skin and every cranny of the house. Then came the snow,
which fell for three days and nights on end, and for several
nights after, so that the town was lost under a white pall:
house-entrances were with difficulty kept free, and the swept
streets were banked with walls of snow, four and five feet high.
The night-frosts redoubled their keenness; the snow underfoot
crackled like electric sparks; the sleighs crunched the roads.
But except for this, and for the tinkling of the sleigh-bells,
the streets were as noiseless as though laid with straw, and espe-

cially while fresh snow still formed a soft coating on the crisp
layer below.   All dripping water hung as icicles; water froze
in ewers and pitchers; milk froze in cans and jugs; and this
though the great stoves in the dwelling-rooms were heated to
bursting-point.   Red-nosed, red-eared men, on whose beards
and moustaches the breath had turned to ice-drops, cried to
one another at street-corners that such a winter had not been
known for thirty years; and, as they spoke, they stamped their
feet, and clapped their hands, to keep the chilly blood agoing.
Women muffled and veiled themselves like Orientals, hardly
showing the tips of their noses; and all manner of strange,
antiquated fur-garments saw the day.   At night, if one opened
a window, and peered out at the houses crouching beneath their
thick white load, and at the deserted, snow-bound streets, over
which the street-lamps threw a pale, uncertain light—at night,
familiar things took on an unfamiliar aspect, and the well-
known streets might have been the untrodden ways that led to
a new world.

Early in November, all ponds and pools were bearing, and
forthwith many hundreds of people forgot the severity of the
weather, and thronged out with their skates.

Maurice was among the first.   He was a passionate skater;
and it was the one form of sport in which he excelled.   As
four o'clock came round, he could contain himself no longer;
he would rather have gone without his dinner, than have missed,
on the *Johannateich,* the two hours that elapsed before the
sweepers, crying: *"Feierabend!"* drove the skaters before
them, with their brooms.   In a tightly buttoned square jacket,
the collar of which was turned up as far as it would go, with
the flaps of his astrachan cap drawn over his ears, his hands in
coarse woollen gloves, Maurice defied the cold, flying round the
two ponds that formed the *Johannateich,* or practising intricate
figures with a Canadian acquaintance in a corner.

Madeleine watched him approvingly from one of the wooden
bridges that spanned the neck connecting the ponds.   She re-
joiced at his glowing face and vigorous, boyish pleasure, also
at the skill that marked him out as one of the best skaters
present.   For some time, Maurice tried in vain to persuade her
to join him.   Madeleine, usually so confident, was here diffident
and timid.   She had never in her life attempted to skate, and
was sure she would fall.   And what should she do if she broke
a thumb or strained a finger?—with her *Prüfung* just before
the door.   She would never have the courage to confess to

Schwarz how it had happened; for he was against "sport" in any form. But Maurice laughed at her fears.

"There is not the least chance of your falling," he cried up to her. "Do come down, Madeleine. Before you've gone round twice, you'll be able to throw off all those mufflings."

Finally, she let herself be persuaded, and according to his promise, Maurice remained at her side from the moment of her first, hesitating steps, each of which was accompanied by a faint scream, to the time when, with the aid of only one of his hands, she made uncertain efforts at striking out. She did not learn quickly; but she was soon as enthusiastic a skater as Maurice himself; and he fell into the habit of calling for her, every afternoon, on his way to the ponds.

Dove was also of assistance in the beginning, and, as usual, was well up in the theory of the thing, though he did not shine in practice.

"Oh, bother, never mind how you go at first. That'll come afterwards," said Maurice impatiently. But Dove thought the rules should be observed from the beginning, and gave Madeleine minute instructions how to place her feet.

Towards five o'clock, the ice grew more crowded, and especially was this the case on Wednesdays and Saturdays, when the schools had half-holidays. On one of these latter days, Maurice did not find Madeleine at home; and he had been on the ponds for nearly an hour, before he espied her on a bench beside the *garderobe,* having her skates put on by a blue-smocked attendant. He waved his cap to her, and skated over.

"Why are you so late?"

"Oh, thank goodness, there you are. I should never have dared to stand up alone in this crowd. Aren't these children awful? Get away, you little brutes! If you touch me, I'll fall.—Here, give me change," she said to the ice-man, holding out a twenty-pfennig piece.

Maurice saw that she was unusually excited, and as soon as he had drawn her out of reach of the children, asked her the reason.

"I've something interesting to tell you, Maurice."

But here Dove, coming up behind, took possession of her left hand, with no other greeting than the military salute, which, on the ice, he adopted for all his friends, male and female, alike; and Madeleine hastily swallowed the rest of her sentence.

They skated round the larger of the ponds several times without stopping. The cold evening air stung their faces; the sun had gone down in a lurid haze; Madeleine's skirts swayed behind her and lent her a fictitious grace.

But presently she cried a halt, and while she rested in a quiet corner, they watched Maurice doing a complicated figure, which he and his Canadian friend had invented the day before. Dove was explaining how it was done—"It is really not so hard as it looks"—when, with a cry of "*Achtung!*" some one whizzed in among them, scattered the group, and, revolving on himself, ended with a jump in the air. It was James. He took out his handkerchief and blew his nose, in the most unconcerned manner possible.

"I don't think such acrobatic tricks should be allowed," said Madeleine disapprovingly; she had been forced to grab Dove's arm to keep her balance.

"Say, do you boys know the river has six inches and will be open to-morrow, if it isn't to-day?" asked James, stooping to tighten a strap.

"Is that so? Oh gee, that's fine!" cried Miss Martin, who had skated leisurely up in his rear. "Say, you people, why don't we fix up a party an' go up it nights? A lady in my boarding-house done that with some folks she was acquainted with last year. Seems to me we oughtn't to be behind."

Miss Martin was a skilled and graceful skater, and looked her best in a dark fur hat and jacket, which set off her abundance of pale flaxen hair. Others had followed her, and it was resolved to form a party for the next evening, provided Dove had previously ascertained if the river actually was "free," in order that they ran no risk of being ignominiously turned off.

"The ice may be a bit rough, but it's a fine run to Connewitz."

"An' by moonlight, too—but say, is there a moon? Why, I presume there ought to be," said Miss Martin.

"'Doth the moon shine that night we play our play?'" quoted Dove, examining a tiny pocket-calendar.

"Oh gee, that's fine!" repeated Miss Martin, on hearing his answer. "Say, we must dance a *Française*. Mr. Guest, you an' I'll be partners, I surmise," and ceasing to waltz and pirouette with James, she took a long sweep, then stood steady, and let her skates bear her out to the middle of the pond. Her skirts clung close in front, and swept out behind her lithe figure, until it was lost in the crowd.

"Don't you wish *you* could skate like that?" asked the sharp-tongued little student, called Dickensey, who was standing beside Madeleine. Madeleine, who held him in contempt because his trousers were baggy at the knees, and because he had once appeared at a ball in white cotton gloves, answered with asperity that there were other things in life besides skating. She had no further chance of speaking to Maurice in private, so postponed telling her news till the following evening.

Shortly after eight o'clock, the next night, a noisy party whistled and hallooed in the street below Maurice's window. He was the last to join, and then some ten or eleven of them picked their steps along the hard-frozen ruts of the *Schleussiger Weg,* a road that followed the river to the outskirts of the town. Just above the *Germaniabad,* a rough seat had been erected on the ice, for the convenience of skaters. They were the first to make use of it; the snow before it was untrodden; and the Pleisse wound white and solitary between its banks of snow.

They set off in a higgledy-piggledy fashion, each striking out for himself. When, however, they had passed the narrower windings, gone under the iron bridge which was low enough to catch the unwary by the forehead, and when the full breadth of the river was before them, they took hands, and, forming a long line, skated in time to the songs some one struck up, and in which all joined: *The Rose of Sharon, Jingle Bells, There is a Tavern in our Town.* As they advanced to the corners where the big trees trailed their naked branches on the ice, just as in summer they sank their leaves in the water, Miss Jensen, who, despite her proportions, was a surprisingly good skater, sent her big voice over the snow-bound stillness, in an aria from the *Prophet;* and after this, Miss Martin, not to be done, struck up the popular *Allerseelen.* This was the song of the hour; they all knew it, and up and down and across the ice rang out their voices in unison: *Wie einst im Mai, wie einst im Mai.*

Inside Wagner's *Waldcafé* at Connewitz, they sat closely packed round one of the wooden tables, and drank beer and coffee, and ate *Berliner Pfannkuchen.* The great iron stove was almost red-hot; the ladies threw off their wrappings; cold faces glowed and burnt, and frozen hands tingled. One and

18

all were in high spirits, and the jollity reached a climax when, having exchanged hats, James and Miss Jensen cleared a space in the middle of the floor and danced a nigger-dance, the lady with her skirts tucked up above her ankles. In the adjoining room, some one began to play a concertina, and then two or three couples stood up and danced, with much laughter and many outcries at the narrowness of the space. Even Dove joined in, his partner being a very pretty American, whom Miss Martin had brought with her, and whose side Dove had not left for a moment. Only Madeleine and Dickensey sat aloof, and for once were agreed: Americans were really "very bad form." There was no livelier pair than Maurice and Miss Martin; the latter's voice could be heard above all others, as she taught Maurice new steps in a corner of the room. Her flaxen hair had partly come loose, and she did not stop to put it up. They were the first to run through the dark garden, past the snow-laden benches and arbours, which, in summer, were buried in greenery; and, from the low wooden landing-place, they jumped hand in hand on to the ice, and had shot a long way down the river before any of the rest could follow them.

But this did not please Madeleine. As it was, she was vexed at not having had the opportunity of a quiet word with Maurice; and when she had laboriously skated up, with Dickensey, to the spot where, in a bright splash of moonlight, Maurice and Miss Martin were cutting ingenious capers, she cried to the former in a peremptory tone: "There's something wrong with my skate, Maurice. Will you look at it, please?" and as sharply declined Dickensey's proffered aid.

Maurice came to her side at once, and in this way she detained him. But Dickensey hovered not far off, and Miss Martin was still in sight. Madeleine caught her skate in a crack, fell on her knee, and said she had now loosened the strap altogether. She sat down on a heap of snow, and Dickensey's shade vanished good-naturedly round a corner.

"Well, *you* seem to be enjoying yourself," she said as Maurice drew off his gloves and knelt down.

"Why, yes, aren't you?" he replied so frankly that she did not continue the subject.

"I've been trying all the evening to get a word with you. I told you yesterday, you remember, that I wanted to speak to you. Sit down here, for a moment, so that we can talk in peace," and she spread part of her skirt over the snow-heap.

Maurice complied, and she could not discover any trace of reluctance in his manner.

"I want your advice," she continued. "I was taken quite by surprise myself. Schwarz sent for me, you know, after counterpoint. It was about my *Prüfung* at Easter. If I play then, it's a case of the C minor Beethoven. Well, now he says it's a thousand pities for me to break off just at the stage I'm at, and he wants me to stay for another year. If I do, he'll give me the G major—that's a temptation, isn't it? On the other hand, I shall have been here my full time—three years—at Easter. That's a year longer than I originally intended, and I feel I'm getting too old to be a pupil. But this talk with Schwarz has upset my plans. I'm naturally flattered at his interesting himself in me. He wouldn't do it for every one. And I do feel I could gain an immense deal in another year.— Now, what do you think?"

"Why, stay, of course, Madeleine. If you can afford it, that is. I can't imagine anyone wanting to leave."

"Oh, my capital will last so long, and it's a good enough investment."

"But wasn't a place being kept open for you in a school?"

"Yes; but I don't think a year more or less will make much difference to them. I must sound them, of course, though," said Madeleine, and did not mention that she had written and posted the letter the night before. "Then you advise me to stay?"

"Why, of course," he repeated, and was mildly astonished at her. "If everything is as smooth as you say."

"You would miss me, if I left?"

"Why, of course I should," he said again, and wondered what in the world she was driving at.

"Well, all the better," replied Madeleine. "For when one has really got to like a person, one would rather it made a difference than not."

She was silent after this, and sat looking down the stretch of ice they had travelled: the moon was behind a cloud, and the woods on either side were masses of dense black shadow. Not a soul was in sight; the river was like a deserted highway. Madeleine stared down it, and did not feel exactly satisfied with the result of her investigation. She had not expected anything extraordinary—Heaven forbid!—but she had been uncomfortably conscious of Maurice's surprise. To her last remark, he

had made no answer: he was occupied with the screw of one of
his skates.

She drew his attention to the fact that, if she remained in
Leipzig for another twelvemonth, they would finish at the same
time; and thereupon she sketched out a plan of them going
somewhere together, and starting a music-school of their own.
Maurice, who thought she was jesting, laughingly assented.
But Madeleine was in earnest: " Other people have done it—
why shouldn't we? We could take a 'cellist with us, and go
to America, or Australia, or Canada—there are hundreds of
places. And there's a great deal of money in it, I'm sure. A
little capital would be needed to begin with, but not much, and
I could supply that. You've always said you dreaded going
back to the English provinces to decay—here's your chance! "

She saw the whole scheme cut and dried before her. As
they skated after the rest, she continued to enlarge upon it, in
a detailed way that astonished Maurice. He confessed that,
with a head like hers to conduct it, such a plan stood a fair
chance of success; and thus encouraged, Madeleine undertook
to make a kind of beginning at once, by sounding some of the
numerous friends she had, scattered through America. Her
idea was that they should go over together, and travel to various places, giving concerts, and acquainting themselves, as
they did so, with the musical conditions of the towns they
visited.

" And the 'cellist shall be an American—that will draw."

According to the pace at which they were skating, the others
should have remained well out of reach. But on turning a
corner, they came upon the whole party dancing a *Française*—
which two members whistled—on a patch of ice that was
smoother than the rest.

" Here, Guest, come along, we want you," was the cry as
soon as Maurice appeared; and, to Madeleine's deep displeasure, she was thrown on Dove, whose skill had not sufficed. When the dancing was over, Maurice once more found
himself with Miss Martin, whom, for some distance, he pushed
before him, she standing steady on her skates, and talking to
him over her shoulder.

" That wasn't a bit pretty of you, Mr. Guest," she asserted,
with her long, slow, twanged speech. " It was fixed up yesterday, I recollect, that you were to dance the *Française* with
me. Yes, indeed. An' then I had to take up with Mr. Dove.
Now Mr. Dove is just a lovely gentleman, but he don't skate

elegantly, an' he nearly tumbled me twice. Yes, indeed. But I presume when Miss Wade says come, then you're most obliged to go.

"How is it one don't ever see you now?" she queried a moment later. "It isn't anyhow so pleasurable at dinner as it used to be. But I hear you're working most hard—it's to' bad."

"It's what one comes to here."

"I guess it is. But I do like to see my friends once in a while. Say, now, Mr. Guest, won't you drink coffee with me one afternoon? I'll make you some real American coffee if you do, sir. What they call coffee here don't count."

She turned, offered him her hand, and they began to skate in long, outward curving lines.

"I think one has just a fine time here, don't you?" she continued. "Momma, she came right with me, an' stopped a bit, till I was fixed up in a boarding-house. But she didn't find it agreeable, no sir. She missed America, an' presumed I would, too. When she was leaving, she said to me: 'El'nor Martin, if you find you can't endure it among these Dutch, just you cable, and poppa he'll come along an' fetch you right home.' But I'm sure I haven't desired to quit, no, not once. I think it's just fine. But then I've gotten me so many friends I don't ever need to feel lonesome. Why, my friend Susie Fay, she says: 'Why, El'nor, I guess you're acquainted with most every one in the place.' An' I reckon she's not far out. Anyways there ain't more than two Americans in the city I don't know. An' I see most all strangers that come. Say, are you acquainted with Miss Moses? She's from Chicago, an' resides in a boarding-house way down by the *Colonnaden*. I got acquainted with her yesterday. She's a lovely lady, an', why, she's just as smart as she can be. Say, if you like, I'll invite her along, so you can get acquainted with her too."

Maurice expressed pleasure at the prospect; and Miss Martin continued to rattle on, with easy frankness, of herself, her family, and her friends. He listened vaguely, with half an ear, since it was only required of him to throw in an occasional word of assent. But suddenly his attention was arrested, and brought headlong back to what she was saying: in the string of names that fell from her tongue, he believed he had caught one he knew.

"Miss Dufrayer?" he queried.

"That's it," replied his companion. "Louise Dufrayer.

Well, sir, as I was going on to remark, when first I was acquainted with her, she was just as sweet as she could be; yes,
indeed; why, she was just dandy.   But she hasn't behaved a
bit pretty—I presume you heard tell of what took place here
this fall? "

"Then you know Miss Dufrayer? "

" Yes, indeed.   But I don't see her any more, an' I guess
I don't want to.   Not but what I've heard she feels pretty
mean about it now—beg pardon?—how I know?   Why, indeed, the other day, Schwarz come in an' told us how she's
moping what she can—moping herself to death—if I recollect, those were his very words.   Yes, indeed.   She don't take
lessons no more, I presume.   I think she should go right away
from this city.   It ain't possible to be acquainted with her any
more, for all she's so lonesome, an' one feels sort of bad about
it, yes, indeed.   But momma, the last thing she said to me
was: 'Now El'nor Martin, just keep your eyes open, an'
don't get acquainted with people you might feel bad about
afterwards.'   An' I presume momma was right.   I don't—
Oh, say, do look at her, isn't she a peach? "—this, as her
pretty friend, with Dove in tow, came gliding up to them.
" Say, Susie Fay, are you acquainted with Mr. Guest? "

" Mr. Guest.   Pleased to know you," said Susie cordially;
and Miss Martin was good-natured enough to skate off with
Dove, leaving Maurice to her friend.

But afterwards, at the bench, as he was undoing Madeleine's skates, he overheard pretty Susie remark, without much
care to moderate her voice: " Say, El'nor Martin, that's the
quietest sort of young man I've ever shown round a district.
Why, seems to me, he couldn't say ' shoh.'   Guess you
shouldn't have left us, El'nor."

And Miss Martin guessed so, too.

VII

WHEN he had seen Madeleine home, Maurice returned to his room, and not feeling inclined to sleep, sat down to read. But his thoughts strayed; he forgot to turn the page; and sat staring over the book at the pattern of the tablecloth. Incidents of the evening flashed before him: Miss Jensen, in James's hat, with her skirts pinned up; Madeleine earnest and decisive on the bank of snow; the maze and laughter of the *Française;* Miss Martin's slim, straight figure as he pushed her before him. He did not try to control these details, nor was he conscious of a mental effort; they stood out for an instant, as vivid sensations, then glided by, to make room for others. But, as he let them pass, he became aware that below them, in depths of his mind he had believed undisturbed, there was present a feeling of strange unhappiness, which he did not know the cause of: these sharp pictures resembled an attempt on the part of his mind, to deceive him as to what was really going on in him. But he did not want to know, and he allowed his thoughts to take wider flights: recalling the scheme Madeleine had proposed, he considered it with a clearness of view, which, at the time, had been impossible. From this, he turned to America itself, and reflected on the opportunities the country offered. He saw the two of them sweeping through vast tracts of uncultivated land, in a train that outdid all real trains in swiftness; saw unknown tropical places, where the yellow fruit hung low and heavy, and people walked shadeless, sandy roads, in white hats, under white umbrellas. He saw Madeleine and himself on the awning-spanned deck of an ocean steamer, anchoring in a harbour where the sea was the colour of turquoise, touched to sapphire where the mountains came down to the shore.

"Moping herself to death ": the phrase crystallised in his brain with such suddenness that he said it aloud. Now he knew what it was that was troubling him. He had not consciously recalled the words, nor had they even made a very incisive impression on him at the time; but they had evidently lain dormant, now to return and to strike him, as if no others had been said. He explained to himself what they

meant. It was this: outside, in the crisp, stinging air, people
lived and moved, busy with many matters, or sported, as he
and his companions had done that evening: inside, she sat
alone, mournful, forsaken. He saw her in the dark sofa-
corner, with her head on her hands. Day passed and night
passed, but she was always in the same place; and her head
was bowed so low that her white fingers were lost in the
waves of her hair. He saw her thus with the distinctness of a
vision, and except in this way could not see her at all.

He felt it little short of shameful that he should have carelessly amused himself; and, as always where she was concerned, a deep, unreasoning sense of his own unworthiness
filled him. He demanded of himself, with a new energy, what
he could do to help her. Fantastic plans rose as usual in
his mind, and as usual were dismissed. For the one thing he
was determined not to do, was to thrust himself on her un-
called. Her solitude was of her own choosing, and no one had
the right to break in upon it. It was perhaps her way of
doing penance; and, at this thought, he felt a thrill of satisfaction.

At night, he consoled himself that things would seem different in the morning; but when he wakened from a restless
sleep, crowded with dreams one more grotesque than another,
he was still prone to be gloomy. He could think more clearly
by daylight—that was all: his pitying sympathy for her had
only increased. It interfered with everything he did, just as
it had formerly done—just in the old way. And he had been
on the brink of believing himself grown indifferent, and
stronger in common sense. Fool that he was! Only a word
was needed to bring his card-house down. The placidity of
the past weeks had been a mere coating of thin ice, which had
given way beneath the first test. A distrust of himself took
him, a distrust so deep that it amounted to aversion; for in his
present state of mind he discerned only a despicable weakness.
But though he was thus bewildered at his own inconsistency,
he was still assured that he would not approach Louise—not,
that is, unless she sent for him. So much control he still had
over his actions: and he went so far as to make his staying away
a touchstone of his stability. This, too, although reason told
him the end of it all would be, that Louise would actually leave
Leipzig, without sending for him, or even remembering his
existence.

He worked steadily enough. A skilled observer might have

remarked a slight contraction of the corners of his mouth; none of his friends, however, noticed anything, with the exception of Madeleine, and all she said was: "You look so cross sometimes. Is anything the matter?"

Late one afternoon, they were on the ice as usual. While Madeleine talked to Dickensey, Maurice practised beside them. In making a particularly complicated, gyration, he all but overbalanced himself, and his cap fell on the ice. As he was brushing the snow off it, he chanced to raise his eyes. A number of people were standing on the wooden bridge, watching the skaters; to the front, some children climbed and pushed on the wooden railing. His eye was ranging carelessly over them, when he started so violently that he again let his cap drop. He picked it up, threw another hasty look at the bridge, then turned and skated some distance away, where he could see without being seen. Yes, he had not been mistaken; it was Louise; he recognised her although a fur hat almost covered her hair. She was gazing down, with an intentness he knew in her; one hand rested on the parapet. And then, as he looked, his blood seemed to congeal: she was not alone; he saw her turn and speak to some one behind her. For a moment things swam before him. Then, a blind curiosity drove him forward to find out whom she spoke to. People moved on the bridge, obstructing his view, then several went away, and there was no further hindrance to his seeing: her companion was the shabby little Englishman, of doubtful reputation, with whom he had met her once or twice that summer. He felt himself grow cold. But now that he had certainty, his chief idea was to prevent the others from knowing, too; he grew sick at the thought of Madeleine's sharp comments, and Dickensey's cynicism. Rejoining them, he insisted—so imperiously that Madeleine showed surprise—on their skating with him on the further pond; and he kept them going round and round without a pause.

When the bridge was empty, and he had made sure that Louise was not standing anywhere about the edge of the ice, he left his companions, and, without explanation, crossed to the benches and took off his skates. He did not, however, go home; he went into the *Scheibenholz,* and from there along outlying roads till he reached the river; and then, screwing on his skates again, he struck out with his face to the wind. Dusk was falling; at first he met some skaters making for home; but these were few, and he soon left them behind.

When the state of the ice did not allow of his skating further, he plunged into the woods again, beyond Connewitz, tumbling in his haste, tripping over snow-bound roots, sinking knee-deep in the soft snow. His endeavour was to exhaust himself. If he sat at home now, before this fever was out of him, he might be tempted to knock his head against the wall of his room. Movement, space, air—plenty of air!—that was what he needed.

Hitherto, he had been surprised at his own conduct; now he was aghast: the hot rush of jealousy that had swept through him at the sight of the couple on the bridge, was a revelation even to himself. His previous feelings had been those of a child compared with this—a mere weak revolt against the inevitable. But what had now happened was not inevitable; that was the sting of it: it was a violent chance-effect. And his distress was so keen that, for the first time, she, too, had to bear her share of blame. He said jeeringly to himself, that, quixotic as ever, he had held aloof from her, leaving her in solitude to an atonement of his own imagining; and meanwhile, some one who was not troubled by foolish ideals stepped in and took his place. For it *was* his place; he could not rid himself of that belief. If anyone had a right to be at her side it was he, unless, indeed, all that he had undergone on her behalf during the past months counted for nothing.

Of course this Eggis was an unscrupulous fellow; but it was just such men as this—he might note that for future use —who won where others lost. At the same time, he shrank from the idea of imitating him; and even had he been bold enough, not a single errand could he devise to serve him as an excuse. He could not go to her and say: I come because I have seen you with some one else. And yet that would be the truth; and it would lurk beneath all he said.

The days of anxiety that followed were hard to bear. He dreaded every street-corner, for fear Louise and the other should turn it; dreaded raising his eyes to the bridges over the ice; and was so irritable in temper that Madeleine suggested he should go to Dresden in the Christmas holidays, for change of air.

For, over all this, Christmas had come down—the season of gift-making, and glittering Christmas trees, of *Bowle, Stollen,* and *Honigkuchen.* For a fortnight beforehand, the open squares and places were set out with fir-trees of all sizes —their pungent fragrance met one at every turn: the shops were ablaze till late evening, crowded with eagerly seeking purchasers; the streets were impassible for the masses of country people that thronged them. Every one carried brown paper parcels, and was in a hurry. As the time drew near, subordinates and officials grew noticeably polite; the very house-porter touched his cap at your approach. Bakers' shops were piled high with *Weihnachtsstollen,* which were a special mark of the festival: cakes shaped like torpedoes, whose sugared, almonded coats brisked brown and tempting. But the spicy scent of the firs was the motive that recurred most persistently: it clung even to the stairways of the houses.

Maurice had assisted Madeleine with her circumstantial shopping; and at dusk on Christmas Eve, he helped her to carry her parcels to the house of some German friends. He himself was invited to Miss Jensen's, where a party of English and Americans would celebrate the evening in their own fashion; but not till eight o'clock. When he had picked out at a confectioner's, a *Torte* for the Fürsts, he did not know how to kill time. He was in an unsettled mood, and the atmosphere of excitement, which had penetrated the familiar details of life, jarred on him. It seemed absurdly childish, the way in which even the grown-up part of the population surrendered itself to the sentimental pleasures of the season. But foreigners were only big children; or, at least, they could lay aside age and dignity at will. He felt misanthropic, and went for a long walk; and when he had passed the last tree-market, where poor buyers were bargaining for the poor trees that were left, he met only isolated stragglers. In some houses, the trees were already lighted.

On his return, he went to a flower-shop in the *Königsplatz,* and chose an azalea to take to Miss Jensen. While he was waiting for the pot to be swathed in crimped paper, his eye was caught by a large bunch of red and yellow roses, which stood in a vase at the back of the counter. He regarded them for a moment, without conscious thought; then, suddenly colouring, he stretched out his hand.

"I'll take those roses, too. What do they cost?"

The girl who served him—a very pretty girl, with plaits of straw-coloured hair, wound Madonna-like round her head —named a sum that seemed exorbitant to his inexperience, and told a wordy story of how they had been ordered, and then countermanded at the last moment.

"A pity. Such fine flowers!"

Her interest was awakened in the rather shabby young man, who paid the price without flinching; and she threw inquisitive looks at him as she wrapped the roses in tissue-paper.

A moment later, Maurice was in the street with the flowers in his hand. He had acted so spontaneously that he now believed his mind to have been made up before he entered the shop; no, more, as if all that had happened during the past week had led straight up to his impulsive action. Or was it only that, at the sight of the flowers, a kind of refrain had begun to run through his head: she loves roses, loves roses?

But he did not give himself time for reflection; he hurried through the cold night air, sheltering the flowers under his coat. Soon he was once more in the *Brüderstrasse,* on the stair, every step of which, though he had only climbed it some three or four times, he seemed to know by heart. As, however, he waited for the door to be opened, his heart misgave him; he was not sure how she would regard his gift, and, in a burst of cowardice, he resolved just to hand in the roses, without even leaving his name. But his first ring remained unanswered, and before he rang again, he had time to be afraid she would not be at home—a simple, but disappointing solution.

There was another pause. Then he heard sounds, steps came along the passage, and the door was opened by Louise herself.

He was so unprepared for this that he could not collect his wits; he thrust the flowers into her hand, with a few stammered words, and his foot was on the stair before she could make a movement to stop him.

Louise had peered out from the darkness of the passage to the dusk of the landing, with the air of one roused from sleep. She looked from him to the roses in her hand, and back at him. He tried to say something else, raised his hat, and was about to go. But, when she saw this, she impulsively stepped towards him.

"Are they for me?" she asked. And added: "Will you not come in? Please, come in."

At the sound of her voice, Maurice came back from the stair-head. But it was not possible for him to stay: friends—engaged—a promise of long standing.

"Ah then . . . of course." She retreated into the shadow of the doorway. "But I am quite alone. There is no one in but me."

" Why, however does that happen? " Maurice asked
quickly, and was ready at once to be wrath with all the world.
He paused irresolute, with his hand on the banisters.

" I said I didn't mind. But it is lonely."

" I should think it was.—On this night of all others, too."

He followed her down the passage. In the room there was
no light except what played on the walls from the street-
lamps, the blinds being still undrawn. She had been sitting
in the dark. Now, she took the globe off the lamp, and would
have lighted it, but she could not find matches.

" Let me do it," said Maurice, taking out his own; and,
over the head of this trifling service, he had a feeling of intense satisfaction. By the light that was cast on the table, he
watched her free the roses from their paper, and raise them to
her face. She did not mention them again, but it was ample
thanks to see her touch several of them singly, as she put them
in a jug of water.

But this done, they sat on opposite sides of the table, and
had nothing to say to each other. After each banal observation he made came a heart-rending pause; she let a subject
drop as soon as it was broached. It was over two months now
since Maurice had seen her, and he was startled by the change
that had taken place in her. Her face seemed to have grown
longer; and there were hollows in the fine oval of the cheeks,
in consequence of which the nose looked larger, and more
pinched. The chin-lines were sharpened, the eyes more sunken,
while the shadows beneath them were as dark as though they
were plastered on with bistre. But it was chiefly the expression of the face that had altered: the lifelessness of the eyes
was new to it, and the firm compression of the mouth: now,
when she smiled, no thin line of white appeared, such as he
had been used to watch for.

Even more marked than this, though, was the change that
had taken place in her manner. He had known her as passionately self-assertive; and he could not now accustom himself to
the condition of apathy in which he found her. " Moping to
death " had been no exaggeration; help was needed here, and at
once, if she were not to be irretrievably injured.

As he thought these things, he talked at random. There
were not many topics, however, that could be touched on with
impunity, and he returned more than once to the ice and the
skating, as offering a kind of neutral ground, on which he
was safe. And Louise listened, and sometimes assented; but

her look was that of one who listens to the affairs of another world. Could she not be persuaded to join them on the *Johannateich*, he was asking her. What matter though she did not skate! It was easily learned. Madeleine had been a beginner that winter, and now seldom missed an afternoon.

"Oh, if Madeleine is there, I should not go," she said with a touch of the old arrogance.

Then he told her of the frozen river, with its long, lonely, grey-white reaches. Her eyes kindled at this, he fancied, and in her answer was more of herself. "I have never trodden on ice in my life. Oh, I should be afraid—horribly afraid!"

For those who did not skate there were chairs, he urged— big, green-painted, sledge-like chairs, which ran smoothly. The ice was many inches thick; there was not the least need to be afraid.

But she only smiled, and did not answer.

"Then I can't persuade you?" he asked, and was annoyed at his own powerlessness. She can go with Eggis, he told himself, and simultaneously spoke out the thought. "I saw you on the bridge the other day."

But if he had imagined this would rouse her, he was wrong.

"Yes?" she said indifferently, and with that laming want of curiosity which prevents a subject from being followed up.

They sat in silence for some seconds. With her fingers, she pulled at the fringe of the tablecloth. Then, all of a sudden rising from her chair, she went over to the jug of roses, which she had placed on the writing-table, bent over the flowers with a kind of perceptible hesitation, and as suddenly came back to her seat.

"Suppose we went to-night," she said, and for the first time looked hard at Maurice.

"To-night?" he had echoed, before he could check himself.

"Ah yes—I forgot. You are going out."

"That's the least of it," he answered, and stood up, fearful lest she should sink back into her former listlessness. "But it's Christmas Eve. There wouldn't be a soul on the river but ourselves. Are you sure you would like it?"

"Just for that reason," she replied, and wound her hand-kerchief in and out of her hands, so afraid was she now that he would refuse. "I could be ready in five minutes."

With his brain in a whirl, Maurice went back to the flower-shop, and, having written a few words of apology on a card, ordered this to be sent with his purchase to Miss Jensen.

When he returned, Louise was ready. But he was not satisfied: she did not know how cold it would be: and he made her
put on a heavy jacket under her fur cape, and take a silk shawl,
in which, if necessary, she could muffle up her head. He himself carried a travelling-rug for her knees.

"As if we were going on a journey!" she said, as she
obeyed him. Her eyes shone with a spark of their old light,
in approval of the adventurous nature of their undertaking.

The hard-frozen streets, over which a cutting wind drove,
were deserted. In many windows, the golden glory of the
Christbaum was visible; the steep blackness of the houses was
splashed with patches of light. At intervals, a belated holiday-
maker was still to be met with hurrying townwards: only they
two were leaving the town, and its innocent revels, behind
them. Maurice had a somewhat guilty feeling about the whole
affair: they also belonged by rights to the town to-night.
He was aware, too, of a vague anxiety, which he could not
repress; and these feelings successfully prevented him taking
an undue pleasure in what was happening to him. He had
swung his skates, fetched in passing, over his shoulder; and
they walked as quickly as the slippery snow permitted. Louise
had not spoken since leaving the house; she also stood mutely
by, while the astonished boatman, knocked out in the middle
of his festivities, unlocked the boat-shed where the ice-chairs
were kept. The Christmas punch had made him merry; he
multiplied words, and was even a little facetious at their expense. According to him, a snow-storm was imminent, and
he warned them not to be late in returning.

Maurice helped Louise into the chair, and wrapped the rug
round her. If she were really afraid, as she had asserted, she
did not show it. Even after they had started, she remained as silent as before; indeed, on looking back, Maurice
thought they had not exchanged a word all the way to Connewitz. He pushed in a kind of dream; the wind was with
them, and it was comparatively easy work; but the ice was
rough, and too hard, and there were seamy cracks to be avoided.
The snow had drifted into huge piles at the sides; and, as they
advanced, it lay unswept on their track. It was a hazily bright
night, but rapid clouds were passing. Not a creature was to
be seen: had a rift opened in the ice, and had they two gone
through it, the mystery of their disappearance would never have
been solved.

Slight, upright, unfathomable as the night, Louise sat before him. What her thoughts were on this fantastic journey, he never knew, nor just what secret nerve in her was satisfied by it. By leaning sideways, he could see that her eyes were fixed on the grey-white stretch to be travelled: her warm breath came back to him; and the coil of her hair, with its piquant odour, was so close that, by bending, he could have touched it with his lips. But he was still in too detached a mood to be happy; he felt, throughout, as if all this were happening to some one else, not to him.

At their journey's end, he helped her, cold and stiff, along the snowy path to the *Waldcafé*. In a corner of the big room, which was empty, they sat beside the stove, before cups of steaming coffee. The landlady served them herself, and looked with the same curious interest as the boatman at the forlorn pair.

Louise had laid her fur cap aside with her other wraps, and had drawn off her gloves; and now she sat with her hand propping her chin. She was still disinclined to speak; from the expression of her eyes, Maurice judged that her thought were very far away. Sitting opposite her, he shaded his own eyes with his hand, and scrutinised her closely. In the stronger light of this room, he could see more plainly than before the havoc trouble had made of her face. And yet, in spite of the shadows that had descended on it, it was still to him the most adorable face in the world. He could not analyse his feelings any better now than in the beginning; but this face had exactly the same effect upon him now as then. It seemed to be a matter of the nerves. Nor was it the face alone: it was also the lines of throat and chin, when she turned her head; it was the gesture with which she fingered the knot of hair on her neck; above all, her hands, whose every movement was full of meaning: yes, these things sent answering ripples through him, as sound does through air.

He had stared too openly: she felt his eyes, and raised her own. For a few seconds, they looked at each other. Then she held out her hand.

"You are my friend."

He pressed it, without replying; he could not think of anything suitable to say; what rose to his lips was too emotional, too tell-tale. But he made a vow that, from this day on, she should never doubt the truth of what she said.

"You are my friend."

He would take care of her as no one had ever yet tried to

do. She might safely give herself into his charge. The unobtrusive aid that was mingled tenderness and respect, should always be hers.

"Are you warmer now?"

He could not altogether suppress the new note that had got into his voice. All strangeness seemed to have been swept away between them; he was wide-awake to the fact that he was sitting alone with her, apart from the rest of the world.

He looked at his watch: it was time to go; but she begged for a little longer, and so they sat on for another half-hour, in the warm and drowsy stillness.

Outside, they found a leaden sky; and they had not gone far before snow began to fall: great flakes came flying to them, smiting their faces, stinging their eyes, melting on their lips. The wind was against them; they were exposed to the full force of the blizzard. Maurice pushed till he panted; but their progress was slow. At intervals, he stopped, to shake the snow off the rug, and to enwrap Louise afresh; and each violent gust that met him when he turned a corner, smote him doubly; for he pictured to himself the fury with which it must hurl itself against her, sitting motionless before it.

It took them twice as long to return; and when Louise tried to get out of the chair, she found herself so paralysed with cold that she could hardly stand. Blinded by the snow, she clung to Maurice's arm; he heard her teeth chatter, as they toiled their way along the *Arndtstrasse,* through the thick, new snow-layer. Not a droschke was to be seen; and they were half-way home before they met one. The driver was drunk or asleep, and had first to be roused. Louise sank limply into a corner.

The cab slithered and slipped over the dangerous roads, jolting them from side to side. Maurice had laid the rug across her knees, and she had ceased to shiver. But, by the light of a street-lamp which they passed, he was dismayed to see that tears were running down her cheeks.

"What is it? Are you so cold?—Just a little patience. We shall soon be there."

He took her hand, and chafed it. At this, she began to cry. He did not know how to comfort her, and looked out of the window, scanning each house they passed, to see if it were not the last. She was still crying when the cab drew up. The house-key had been forgotten; there was nothing for it but to ring for the landlady, and to stand in the wind till she came down. The old woman was not so astonished as Maurice had expected; but she was very wroth at the folly of the proceeding, and did not scruple to say so.

"*So 'ne Dummheit, so 'ne Dummheit!*" she mumbled, as, between them, they got Louise up the stairs; and she treated Maurice's advice concerning cordials and hot drinks with scant courtesy.

"*Ja, ja—jawohl!*" she sniffed. And, on the landing, the door was shut in his face.

VIII

WHAT she needed, what she had always needed, was a friend, he said to himself. She had never had anyone to stand by her and advise her to wisdom, in the matter of impulsive acts and wishes. He would be that friend. He had not, it was true, made a very happy beginning, with the expedition that had ended so unfortunately; but he promised himself not to be led into an indiscretion of the kind again. It was a friend's part to warn in due time, and to point out the possible consequences of a rash act. He only excused his behaviour because he had not seen her for over two months, and had felt too sorry for her to refuse the first thing she asked of him. But from now on, he would be firm. He would win her back to life—reawaken her interest in what was going on around her. He would devote himself to serving her: not selfishly, as others had done, with their own ends in view; the gentle, steady aid should be hers, which he had always longed to give her. He felt strong enough to face any contingency: it seemed, indeed, as if his love for her had all along been aiming at this issue; as if each of the unhappy hours he had spent, since first meeting her, was made up for by the words: "You are my friend."

A deep sense of responsibility filled him. In obedience, however, to a puritanic streak in his nature, he hedged himself round with restrictions, lest he should believe he was setting out on all too primrose a path. He erected limiting boundaries, which were not to be overstepped. For example, on the two days that followed the memorable Christmas Eve, he only made inquiries at the door after Louise, and when he learned that the cold she had caught was better, did not return. For, on one point, his mind was made up: idle tongues should have no fresh cause for gossip.

At the expiry of a fortnight, however, he began to fear that if he remained away any longer, she would think him indifferent to her offer of friendship. So, late one afternoon, he called to see her. But when he was face to face with her, he doubted whether she had given him a thought in the interval: she seemed mildly surprised at his coming. It was even possible that she had forgotten, by now, what she had said to him; and

he sought anew for a means of impressing himself on her consciousness.

She was crouched in the rocking-chair, close beside the stove,
and was wrapped in a thick woollen shawl; but the hand she
gave him was as cold as stone. She was trying to keep warm,
she said; she had not been properly warm since the night on
the ice.

"But there's an easy remedy for that," said Maurice, who
came in ruddy from the sharp air. "You must go out and
walk. Then you will soon get warm."

But she shuddered at the suggestion, and also made an expressive gesture to indicate the general laxity of her dress—
the soiled dressing-gown, her untidy hair. Then she leaned
forward again, holding both hands, palms out, to the mica
pane in the door of the stove, through which the red coals
glowed.

"If only winter were over!"

He gazed at the expressive lines of hand and wrist, and was
reminded of an adoring Madonna he had somewhere seen en-
graved: her hands were held back in the same way; the thumbs
slightly thrown out, the three long fingers together, the little
one apart: here as there, was the same supple, passionate indolence. But he could find no more to say than on the occasion of his former visit; she did not help him; and more and
more did it seem to the young man as if the words he had
gone about hugging to him, had never been spoken. After a
desperate quarter of an hour, he rose to take leave. But simultaneously, she, too, got up from the rocking-chair, and, standing pale and uncertain before him, asked him if she might
trouble him to do something for her. A box had been sent to
her from England, she told him, while she tumbled over the
dusty letters and papers accumulated on the writing-table, and
had been lying unclaimed at the custom-house for several weeks
now—how many she did not know, and she spread out her
fingers, with a funny little movement, to show her ignorance.
She had only remembered it a day or two ago; the dues would
no doubt be considerable. If it were not too much trouble . . .
she would be so grateful; she would rather ask him than Mr.
Eggis.

"I should be delighted," said Maurice.

He went the next morning, at nine o'clock, spent a trying
hour with uncivil officials, and, in the afternoon, called to
report to Louise. As he was saying good-bye to her, he in-

quired if there were nothing else of a similar nature he could do for her; he was glad to be of use. Smiling, Louise admitted that there were other things, many of them, more than he would have patience for. She should try him and see, said Maurice, and laid his hat down again, to hear what they were.

As a consequence of this, the following days saw him on various commissions in different quarters of the town, scanning the names of shops, searching for streets he did not know. But matters did not always run smoothly; complications arose, for instance, over a paid bill that had been sent in a second time, and over an earlier one that had not been paid at all; and Maurice was forced to confess his ignorance of the circumstances. When this had happened more than once, he sat down, with her consent, at the writing-table, to work through the mass of papers, and the contents of a couple of drawers.

In doing this, he became acquainted with some of the more intimate details of her life—minute and troublesome details, for which she had no aptitude. From her seat at the stove, Louise watched him sorting and reckoning, and she was as grateful to him as it was possible for her to be, in her present mood. No one had ever done a thing of the kind for her before; and she was callous to the fact of its being a stranger, who had his hands thus in her private life. When, horrified beyond measure at the confusion that reigned in all belonging to her, Maurice asked her how she had ever succeeded in keeping order, she told him that, before her illness, there had, now and again, come a day of strength and purpose, on which she had had the "courage" to face these distasteful trifles and to end them. But she did not believe such a day would ever come again.

Bills, bills, bills: dozens of bills, of varying dates, sent in once, twice, three times, and invariably tossed aside and forgotten—a mode of proceeding incomprehensible to Maurice, who had never bought anything on credit in his life. And not because she was in want of money: there were plenty of gold pieces jingling loose in a drawer; but from an aversion, which was almost an inability, to take in what the figures meant. And the amounts added up to alarming totals; Maurice had no idea what a woman's dress cost, and could only stand amazed; but the sum spent on fruit and flowers alone, in two months, represented to his eyes a small fortune. Then there was the Blüthner, the unused piano; the hire of it had not been paid since the previous summer. Three terms were owed at Klemm's musical library, from which no music was now borrowed; fees were still being charged against her at the Conservatorium, where she had given no formal notice of leaving. It really did not matter, she said, with that carelessness concerning money, which was characteristic of her; but it went against the grain in Maurice to let several pounds be lost for want of an effort; and he spent a diplomatic half-hour with the secretaries in the *Bureau,* getting her released from paying the whole of the term that had now begun. As, however, she would not appear personally, she was under the necessity of writing a letter, stating that she had left the Conservatorium; and when she had promised twice to do it, and it was still unwritten, Maurice stood over her, and dictated the words into her pen. A day or two afterwards, he prevailed upon her to do the same for Schwarz, to inform him of her illness, and to say that, at Easter, if she were better, she would come to him for a course of private lessons. This was an idea of Maurice's own, and Louise looked up at him before putting down the words.

"It's not true. But if you think I should say so—it doesn't matter."

This was the burden of all she said: nothing mattered, nothing would ever matter again. There was not the least need for the half-jesting tone in which Maurice clothed his air of authority. She obeyed him blindly, doing what he bade her without question, glad to be subordinate to his will. As long as he did not ask her to think or to feel, or to stir from her chair beside the stove.

But it was only with regard to small practical things; in matters of more importance she was not to be moved. And the day came, only too soon, when the positive help Maurice could give her was at an end; she did not owe a pfennig to anyone; her letters and accounts were filed and in order. Then she seemed to elude him again. He did what lay in his power: brought her books that she did not read, brought news and scraps of chit-chat, which he thought might interest her and which did not, and an endless store of sympathy. But to all he said and did, she made the same response: it did not matter.

Since the night on the river, she had not set foot across the threshold of her room; nervous fears beset her. Maurice was bent on her going out into the open air; he also wished her to mix with people again, and thus rid herself of the morbid fancies that were creeping on her. But she shrank as he spoke of it, and pressed both hands to her face: it was too cold, she murmured, and too cheerless; and then the streets! . . . the publicity of the streets, the noise, the people! This was what she said to him; to herself she added: and all the old familiar places, to each of which a memory was attached! He spent hours in urging her to take up some regular occupation; it would be her salvation, he believed, and, not allowing himself to be discouraged, he returned to the attack, day after day. But she only smiled the thin smile with which she defeated most of his proposals for her good. Work?—what had she to do with work? It had never been anything to her but a narcotic, enabling her to get through those hours of the day in which she was alone.

She let Maurice talk on, and hardly heard what he said. He meant well, but he did not understand. No one understood. No one but herself knew the weight of the burden she had borne since the day when her happiness was mercilessly destroyed. Now she could not raise a finger to help herself. On waking, in the morning, she turned with loathing from the new day. In the semi-darkness of the room, she lay motionless, half sleeping, or dreaming with open eyes. The clock ticked benumbingly the long hours away; the wind howled, or the wind was still; snow fell, or it was frostily clear; but nothing happened—nothing at all. The day was well advanced before she left her bed for the seat by the stove; there she brooded until she dragged herself back to bed. One day was the exact counterpart of another.

The only break in the deathlike monotony was Maurice's visit. He came in, fresh, and eager to see her; he held her hand and said kind things to her; he talked persuasively, and she listened or not, as she felt disposed. But little though he was able to touch her, she unconsciously began to look to his visits; and one day, when he was detained and could not come, she was aware of a feeling of injury at his absence.

As time went by, however, Maurice felt more and more clearly that he was making no headway. His uneasiness increased; for her want of spirit had something about it that he could not understand. It began to look to him like a somewhat morbid indulgence in grief.

"This can't go on," he said sternly.

She was in one of her most pitiable moods; for there were gradations in her unhappiness, as he had learned to know.

"This can't go on. You are killing yourself by inches—
and I'm a party to it."

For the first time, there was a hint of impatience in his
manner. To his surprise, Louise raised her head, raised it
quickly, as he had not seen her make a movement for weeks.

"By inches? Inches only? Oh, I am so strong . . . Nothing hurts me. Nothing is of any use."

"If you look in the glass, you will see that you're hurting
yourself considerably."

"You mean that I'm getting old?—and ugly?" she caught
him up. "Do you think I care?—Oh, if I had only had the
courage, that day! A few grains of something, and it would
have been all over, long ago. But I wasn't brave enough.
And now I have no more courage in, me than strength in my
little finger."

Maurice looked meditatively at her, without replying: this
was the single occasion on which she had been roused to a
retort of any kind; and, bitter though her words were, he could
not prevent the spark of hope which, by their means, was lit
in him.

And from this day on, things went forward of themselves.
Again and again, some harmless observation on his part drew
forth a caustic reply from her; it was as if, having once experienced it, she found an outcry of this kind a relief to her
surcharged nerves. At first, what she said was directed chiefly
against herself—this self for which she now nursed a fanatic
hatred, since it had failed her in her need. But, little by
little, he, too, was drawn within the circle of her bitterness;
indeed, it sometimes seemed as if his very kindness incited her,
by laying her under an obligation to him, which it was in her
nature to resent: at others, again, as if she merely wished to
try him, to see how far she might go.

"Do I really deserve that thrust?" he once could not
help asking. He smiled, as he spoke, to take the edge off his
words.

Louise threw a penitent glance at him, and, for all answer,
held out her hand.

But, the very next day, after a similar incident, she crossed
the room to him, with the swiftness of movement that was
always disturbing in her, contrasting as it did with her customary indolence. "Forgive me. I ought not to. And you
are the only friend I have. But there's so much I must say
to some one. If I don't say it, I shall go mad."

"Why, of course. That's what I'm here for," said Maurice.

And so it went on—a strange state of things, in which he never called her by her name, and seldom touched her hand. He had himself well under control—except for the moment immediately before he saw her, and the moment after. He could not yet meet her, after the briefest absence, unmoved.

For a week on end that penetrating rawness had been abroad, which precedes and accompanies a thaw; and one day, early in February, when, after the unequalled severity of the winter, the air seemed of an incredible mildness, the thaw was there in earnest; on the ice of more than three months' standing, pools of water had formed overnight. By the *Johannateich,* Maurice and Madeleine stood looking dubiously across the bank of snow, which, here and there, had already collapsed, leaving miniature crater-rings, flecked with moisture. Several people who could not tear themselves away, were still flying about the ice, dexterously avoiding the watery places; and Dove and pretty Susie Fay called out to them that it was better than it looked. But Maurice was fastidious and Madeleine indifferent; she was really rather tired of skating, she admitted, as they walked home, and was ashamed to think of the time she had wasted on it. As, however, this particular afternoon was already broken into, she would have been glad to go for a walk; but Maurice did not take up her suggestion, and parted from her at her house-door.

"Spring is in the air," he sought to tempt Louise, when, a few minutes later, he entered her room.

She, too, had been aware of the change; for it had aggravated her dejection. She raised her eyes to his like a tired child, and had not strength enough to make her usual stand against him. Oh, if he really wished it so much, she would go out, she said at last. And so he left her to dress, and ran to the Conservatorium, arriving just in time for a class.

Later on, a curious uneasiness drew him back to see how she had fared. It was almost dark, but she had not returned; and he waited for half an hour before he heard her step in the hall. Directly she came .in, he knew that something was the matter.

In each of her movements was a concentrated, but noiseless energy: she shut the door after her as if it were never to open again; tore off rather than unpinned the thick black veil in

which she had shrouded herself; threw her hat on the sofa,
furs and jacket to the hat; then stood motionless, pressing her
handkerchief to her lips.   Her face had emerged from its
wrappings with renewed pallor; her eyes shone as if with bella-
donna.   She took no notice of the silent figure in the corner,
did not even look in his direction.

"You've got back," said Maurice, for the sake of saying
something. "It's late."

At his words, she dropped on a chair, put her arms on the
table, and hid her face in them.

"What's the matter? Has anything happened?" he asked,
in quick alarm, as she burst into violent sobs. He should have
been accustomed to her way of crying by this time—it sounded
worse than it was, as he knew—but it invariably racked him
afresh. He stood over her; but the only comfort he ventured
on was to lay his hand on her hair—this wild black hair, which
met his fingers springily, with a will of its own.

"What is the matter?" he besought her. "Tell me, Louise
—tell me what it is."

He had to ask several times before he received an answer.
Finally, she sobbed in a muffled voice, without raising her head:
"How could you make me go out! Oh, how *could* you!"

"What do you mean? I don't understand. What is it?"
He had visions of her being annoyed or insulted.

But she only repeated: "How could you! Oh, it was cruel
of you!" and wept afresh.

Word by word, Maurice drew her story from her. There was
not very much to tell.

She had gone out, and had walked hurriedly along quiet
by-streets to the *Rosental*.   But before she had advanced a
hundred yards, her courage began to fail, and the further
she went, the more her spirits sank.   Her surroundings were
indescribably depressing: the smirched, steadily retreating snow
was leaving bare all the drab brownness it had concealed
—all the dismal little gardens, and dirty corners.   Houses,
streets and people wore their most bedraggled air. Particularly
the people: they were as ugly as the areas of roof and stone, off
which the soft white coating had slid; their contours were as
painful to see. And the mud—oh, God, the mud! It spread
itself over every inch of the way; the roads were rivers of
filth, which spattered and splashed; at the sides of the streets,
the slush was being swept into beds. Before she had gone any
distance, her boots and skirts were heavy with it; and she

hated mud, she sobbed—hated it, loathed it, it affected her
with a physical disgust—and this he might have known when
he sent her out. In the *Rosental,* it was no better; the paths
were so soaked that they squashed under her feet; on both sides
lay layers of rotten leaves from the autumn; the trees were only
a net-work of blackened twigs, their trunks surrounded by an
undergrowth that was as ragged as unkempt hair. And everything was mouldering: the smell of moist, earthy decay reminded her of open graves. Not a soul was visible but herself. She sat on a seat, the only living creature in the scene,
and the past rose before her with resistless force: the intensity
of her happiness; the base cruelty of his conduct; her misery,
her unspeakable misery; her forlorn desolation, which was of
a piece with the desolation around her, and which would never
again be otherwise, though she lived to be an old woman.—How
long she sat thinking things of this kind, she did not know. But
all of a sudden she started up, frightened both by her wretched
thoughts and by the loneliness of the wood; and she fled,
not looking behind her, or pausing to take breath, till she reached
the streets. Into the first empty droschke she met, she had
sunk exhausted, and been driven home.

It was of no use trying to reason with her, or to console
her.

"I can't bear my life," she sobbed. "It's too hard . . .
and there is no one to help me. If I had done anything to
deserve it . . . then it would be different . . . then I shouldn't
complain. But I didn't—didn't do anything—unless it was
that I cared too much. At least it was a mistake—a dreadful
mistake. I should never have shown him how I cared: I
should have made him believe he loved me best. But I was a
fool. I flung it all at his feet. And it was only natural he
should get tired of me. The wonder was that I held him so
long. But, oh, how can one care as I did, and yet be able to
plot and plan? I couldn't. It isn't in me to do it."

She wept despairingly, with her head on her outstretched
arms. When she raised it again, her tear-stained face looked
out, Medusa-like, from its setting of ruffled hair. More to herself than to the young man, as if, on this day, secret springs
had been touched in her, she continued with terse disconnected-
ness: "I couldn't believe it; I wouldn't—even when I heard
it from his own lips. You thought, all of you, that I was ill;
but I wasn't; I was only trying to get used to the terrible
thought—just as a suddenly blinded man has to get used to

being always in the dark. And while I was still struggling came Madeleine, with her cruel tongue, and told me—you know what she told me. Oh, if his leaving me had been hard to bear, this stung like scorpions. I wonder I didn't go mad. I should have, if you hadn't come to help me. For a day and night, I did not move from the corner of that sofa there. I turned her words over till there was no sense left in them. My nails cut my palms."

Her clasped hands were slightly stretched from her: her whole attitude betrayed the tension at which she was speaking. "Oh, my God, how I hated him . . . hated him . . . how I hate him still! If I live to be an old, old woman, I shall never forgive him. For, in time, I might have learnt to bear his leaving me, if it had only been his work that took him from me. It was always between us, as it was; but it was at least only a pale brain thing, not living flesh and blood. But that all the time he should have been deceiving me, taking pains to do it—that I cannot forgive. At first, I implored, I prayed there might be some mistake: you, too, told me there was. And I hoped against hope—till I saw her. Then, I knew it was true—as plainly as if it had been written on that wall." She paused for breath, in this bitter pleasure of laying her heart bare. "For I wasn't the person he could always have been satisfied with—I see it now. He liked a woman to be fair, and soft, and gentle—not dark, and hot-tempered. It was only a phase, a fancy, that brought him to me, and it couldn't have lasted for ever. But all I asked of him was common honesty— to be open with me: it wasn't much to ask, was it? Not more than we expect of a stranger in the street. But it was too much for him, all the same. And so . . . now . . . I have nothing left to remind me that I ever knew him. That night, when I had seen her, I burned everything—every photograph, every scrap of writing I had ever had from him . . . if only one could burn memories too! I had to tear my heart over it; I used to think I felt it bleeding, drop by drop. For all the suffering fell on me, who had done nothing. He went free."

"Are you sure of that? It may have been hard for him, too —harder than you think." Maurice was looking out of the window, and did not turn.

She shook her head. "The person who cares, can't scheme and contrive. He didn't care. He never really cared for me— only for himself; at heart, he was cold and selfish. No, I paid for it all—I who hate and shrink from pain, who would do anything to avoid it. I want to go through life knowing only what is bright and happy; and time and again, I am crushed and flung down. But, in all my life, I haven't suffered like this. And now perhaps you understand, why I never want to hear his name again, and why I shall never—not if I live to be a hundred years old—never forgive him. It isn't in me to do it. As a child, I ground my heel into a rose if it pricked me."

There was a silence. Then she sighed, and pushed her hair back from her forehead. "I don't know why I should say all this to you," she said contritely. "But often, just with you, I seem to forget what I am saying. It must be, I think, because you're so quiet yourself."

At this, Maurice turned and came over to her. "No, it's for another reason. You need to say these things to some one. You have brooded over them to yourself till they are magnified out of all proportion. It's the best thing in the world for you to say them aloud." He drew up a chair, and sat down beside her. "Listen to me. You told me once, not very long ago, that I was your friend. Well, I want to speak to you to-night as that friend, and to play the doctor a little as well. Will you not go away from here, for a time?—go away and be with people who know nothing of . . . all this—people you don't need to be afraid of? Let yourself be persuaded. You have such a healthy nature. Give it a chance."

She looked at him with a listless forbearance. "Don't go on. I know everything you are going to say.—That's always the way with you calm, quiet people, who are not easily moved yourselves. You still put faith in these trite remedies; for you've never known the ills they're supposed to cure."

"Never mind me. It's you we have to think of. And I want you to give my old-fashioned remedy a trial."

But she did not answer, and again a few minutes went by, before she stretched out her hand to him. "Forget what I've said to-night. I shall never speak of it again.—But then you, too, must promise not to make me go out alone—to think and remember—in all the dirt and ugliness of the streets."

And Maurice promised.

IX

THE unnatural position circumstances had forced him into, was to him summed up in the fact that he had spoken in defence of the man he despised above all others. Only at isolated moments was he content with the part he played; it was wholly unlike what he had intended. He had wished to be friend and mentor to her, and he was now both; but nevertheless, there was something wrong about his position. It seemed as if he had at first been satisfied with too low a place in her esteem, ever to allow of him taking a higher one. He was conscious that in her liking for him, there was a drop of contempt. And he tormented himself with such a question as: should a new crisis in her life arise, would she, now that she knows you, turn to you? And in moments of despondency he answered no. He felt the tolerance that lurked in her regard for him. Kindness and care on his part were not enough.

None of his friends had an idea of what was going on. No one he knew lived in the neighbourhood of the *Brüderstrasse;* and, the skating at an end, he was free to spend his time as he chose. When another brief nip of frost occurred, he alleged pressure of work, and did not take advantage of it.

Then, early one morning, Dove paid him a visit, with a list in his hand. Since the night of the skating party, his acquaintances had not seen much of Dove; for he had been in close attendance on the pretty little American, who made no scruple of exacting his services. Now, after some preamble, it came out that he wished to include Maurice in a list of mutual friends, who were clubbing to give a ball—a "Bachelors' Ball," Dove called it, since the gentlemen were to pay for the tickets, and to invite the ladies. But Maurice, vexed at the interruption, made it clear that he had neither time nor inclination for an affair of this kind: he did not care a rap for dancing. And after doing his best to persuade him, and talking round the matter for half an hour, Dove said he did not of course wish to press anyone against his will, and departed to disturb other people.

Maurice had also to stand fire from Madeleine; for she had counted on his inviting her. She was first incredulous, then offended, at his refusal: and she pooh-poohed his strongest argument—that he did not own a dress-suit. If that was all, she knew a shop in the *Brühl,* where such things could be hired for a song.

Maurice now thought the matter closed. Not many days later, however, Dove appeared again, with a crestfallen air. He had still over a dozen tickets on his hands, and, at the low price fixed, unless all were sold, the expenses of the evening would not be covered. In order to get rid of him, Maurice bought a ticket, on the condition that he was not expected to use it, and also suggested some fresh people Dove might try; so that the latter went off with renewed courage on his disagreeable errand.

Maurice mentioned the incident to Louise that evening, as he mentioned any trifle he thought might interest her. He sat on the edge of his chair, and did not mean to stay; for he had found her on the sofa with a headache.

So far, she had listened to him with scant attention; but at this, she raised her eyebrows.

" Then you don't care for dancing? "—she could hardly believe it.

He repeated the words he had used to Dove.

She smiled faintly, looking beyond him, at a sombre patch of sky.

" I should think not. If it were me!——" She raised her hand, and considered her fingers.

" If it were you? —yes? "

But she did not continue.

It had been almost a spring day: that, no doubt, accounted for her headache. Maurice made a movement to rise. But Louise turned quickly on her side, and, in her own intense way, said: " Listen. You have the ticket, you say? Use it, and take me with you. Will you? "

He smiled as at the whim of a child. But she was in earnest.

" Will you? "

" No, of course not."

He tempered his answer with the same smile. But she was not pleased—he saw that. Her nostrils tightened, and then dilated, as they had a way of doing when she was annoyed. For some time after, she did not speak.

But the very next day, when he was remonstrating with her over some small duty which she had no inclination to perform, she turned on him with an unreasonable irritation. " You only want me to do disagreeable things. Anything that is pleasant, you set yourself against."

It took him a minute to grasp that she was referring to what he had said the evening before.

"Yes, but then . . . I didn't think you were in earnest."

"Am I in the habit of saying things I don't mean? And haven't you said yourself that I am killing myself, shut up in here?—that I must go out and mix with people? Very well, here is my chance."

He kept silence: he did not know whether she was not mainly inspired by a spirit of contradiction, and he was afraid of inciting her, by resistance, to say something she would be unable to retract. "I don't think you've given the matter sufficient thought," he said at last. "It can't be decided offhand."

She was angry, even more with herself than with him. "Oh, I know what you mean. You think I shall be looked askance at. As if it mattered what people say! All my life I haven't cared, and I shall not begin now, when I have less reason than ever before."

He did not press the subject; he hoped she would change her mind, and thus render further discussion unnecessary. But this was not the case; she clung to the idea, and was deaf to reason. To a certain extent, he could feel for her; but he was too troubled by the thought of unpleasant possibilities, not to endeavour to persuade her against it: he knew, as she did not, how unkindly she had been spoken of; and he was not sure whether her declared bravado was strong enough to sustain her. But the more he reasoned, the more determined she was to have her own way; and she took his efforts in very bad part.

"You pretend to be solicitous about me," she said one afternoon, from her seat by the fire. "Yet when a chance of diversion comes you begrudge it to me. You would rather I mouldered on here."

"That's not generous of you. It is only you I am thinking of—in all this ridiculous affair."

The word stung her. "Ridiculous? How dare you say that! I'm still young, am I not? And I have blood in my veins, not water. Well, I want to feel it. For months now, I have been walled up in this tomb. Now I want to live. Not—do you understand?—to go out alone, on a filthy day, with no companion but my own thoughts. I want to dance—to forget myself—with light and music. It's the most natural thing in the world. Anyone but you would think so."

"It is not life you mean; it's excitement."

"What it means is that you don't want to take me.—Yes, that's what it is. But I can get some one else. I will send for Eggis; he will have no objection."

"Why drag in that cad's name? You know very well if you do go, it will be with me, and no one else."

A slight estrangement grew up between them. Maurice was hurt: she had shown too openly the small value she set on his opinion. In addition to this, he was disagreeably affected by her craving for excitement at any cost. To his mind, there was more than a touch of impropriety in the proceeding; it was just as if a mourner of a few months' standing should suddenly discard his mourning, and with it all the other decencies of grief.

She had not been entirely wrong in accusing him of unreadiness to accompany her. When he pictured to himself the astonished faces of his friends, he found it impossible to look forward to the event with composure. He saw now that it would have been better to make no secret of his friendship with Louise; so harmless was it that every one he knew might have assisted at it; but now, the very abruptness of its disclosure would put it in a bad light. Through Dove, he noised it abroad that he would probably be present at the ball after all; but he shunned Madeleine with due precaution, and could not bring himself even to hint who his companion might be. In his heart, he still thought it possible that Louise might change her mind at the last moment—take fright in the end, at what she might have to face.

But the night came, and this had not happened. While he dressed himself in the hired suit, which was too large here, too small there, he laid a plan of action for the evening. Since it had to be gone through with, it must be carried off in a high-handed way. He would do what he could to make her presence in the hall seem natural; he would be attentive, without devoting himself wholly to her; and he would induce her to leave early.

He called for her at eight o'clock. The landlady said that Fräulein was not quite ready, and told him to wait in the passage. But the door of the room was ajar, and Louise herself called to him to come in.

It was comparatively dark; for she had the lamp behind the

screen, where he heard her moving about. Her skirts rustled; drawers and cupboards were pulled noisily open. Then she came out, with the lamp in her hand.

Maurice was leaning against the piano. He raised his eyes, and made a step forward, to take the lamp from her. But after one swift, startled glance, he drew back, colouring furiously. For a moment he could not collect himself: his heart seemed to have leapt into his throat, and there to be hammering so hard that he had no voice with which to answer her greeting.

Owing to what he now termed his idiotic preoccupation with himself, he had overlooked the fact that she, too, would be in evening dress. Another thing was, he had never seen Louise in any but street-dress, or the loose dressing-gown. Now he called himself a fool and absurd; this was how she was obliged to be. Convention decreed it, hence it was perfectly decorous; it was his own feelings that were unnatural, overstrained. But, in the same breath, a small voice whispered to him that all dresses were not like this one; also that every girl was not of a beauty, which, thus emphasised, made the common things of life seem poor and stale.

Louise wore a black dress, which glistened over all its surface, as if it were sown with sparks; it wound close about her, and out behind her on the floor. But this was only the sheath, from which rose the whiteness of her arms and shoulders, and the full column of her throat, on which the black head looked small. Until now, he had seen her bared wrist—no more. Now the only break on the long arm was a band of black velvet, which as it were insisted on the petal-white purity of the skin, and served in place of a sleeve.

Strange thoughts coursed through the young man's mind. His first impulse had been to avert his eyes; in this familiar room it did not seem fitting to see her dressed so differently from the way he had always known her. Before, however, he had followed this sensation to an end, he made himself the spontaneous avowal that, until now, he had never really seen her. He had known and treasured her face—her face alone. Now he became aware that to the beautiful head belonged also a beautiful body, that, in short, every bit of her was beautiful and desirable. And this feeling in its turn was overcome by a painful reflection: others besides himself would make a similar observation; she was about to show herself to a hundred other eyes: and this struck him as such an unbearable profanation, that he could have fallen on his knees to her, to implore her to stay at home.

Unconscious of his embarrassment, Louise had gone to the console-glass; and there, with the lamp held first above her head, then placed on the console-table, she critically examined her appearance. As if dissatisfied, she held a velvet bow to the side of her hair, and considered the effect; she took a powder-puff, and patted cheeks and neck with powder. Next she picked up a narrow band of velvet, on which a small star was set, and put it round her throat. But the clasp would not meet behind, and, having tried several times in vain to fasten it, she gave an impatient exclamation.

"I can't get it in."

As Maurice did not offer to help her, she went out of the room with the thing in her hand. During the few seconds she was absent, the young man racked his brain to invent telling reasons which would induce her not to go; but when she returned, slightly flushed at the landlady's ready flattery, she was still so engrossed in herself, and so unmindful of him, that he recognised once more his utter powerlessness. He only half existed for her this evening: her manner was as different as her dress.

She gathered her skirts high under her cloak, displaying her feet in fur-lined snow-boots. In the turmoil of his mind, Maurice found nothing to say as they went. But she did not notice his silence; there was a suppressed excitement in her very walk; and she breathed in the cold, crisp air with open lips and nostrils, like a wild animal.

"Oh, how glad I am I came! I might still have been sitting in that dull room—when I haven't danced for years—and when I love it so!"

"I can't understand you caring about it," he said, and the few words contained all his bitterness.

"That is only because you don't know me," she retorted, and laughed. "Dancing is a passion with me. I have dance-rhythms in my blood, I think.—My mother was a dancer."

He echoed her words in a helpless way, and a set of new images ran riot in his brain. But Louise only smiled, and said no more.

They were late in arriving; dancing had already begun; the cloak-rooms were black with coats and mantles. In the narrow passage that divided the rooms, two Englishmen were putting on their gloves. As Maurice changed his shoes, close to the door, he overheard one of these men say excitedly: " By Jove, there's a pair of shoulders! Who the deuce is it? "

Maurice knew the speaker by sight: he was a medical student, named Herries, who, on the ice, had been conspicuous for his skill as a skater. He had a small dark moustache, and wore a bunch of violets in his buttonhole.

" You haven't been here long enough, old man, or you wouldn't need to ask," answered his companion. Then he dropped his voice, and made a very disparaging remark—not so low, however, but what the listener was forced to hear it, too.

Both laughed a little. But though Maurice rose and clattered his chair, Herries persisted, with an Englishman's supreme indifference to the bystander: " Do you think she can dance? "

" Can't tell. Looks a trifle heavy."

" Well, I'll risk it. Come on. Let's get some one to introduce us."

The blood had rushed to Maurice's head and buzzed there: another second, and he would have stepped out and confronted the speaker. But the incident had passed like a flash. And it was better so: it would have been a poor service to her, to begin the evening with an unpleasantness. Besides, was this not what he had been bracing himself to expect? He looked stealthily over at Louise; considering the proximity of the rooms, it was probable that she, too, had overheard the derogatory words. But when she had put on her gloves, she took his arm without a trace of discomfiture.

They entered the hall at the close of a polka, and slipped unnoticed into the train of those who promenaded. But they had not gone once round, when they were the observed of all eyes; although he looked straight in front of him, Maurice could see the astonished eyebrows and open mouths that greeted their advance. At one end of the hall was an immense mirror: he saw that Louise, who was flushed, held her head high, and talked to him without a pause. In a kind of bravado, she made him take her round a second time; and after the third, which was a solitary progress, they remained standing with their backs to the mirror. Eggis at once came up, with Herries in his train, and, on learning that she had no programme, the latter ran off to fetch one. Before he returned, a third man had joined them, and soon she was the centre of a little circle. Herries, having returned with the programme, would not give it up until he had put his initials opposite several dances. Louise only smiled—a rather artificial smile that had been on her lips since she entered the hall.

Maurice had fallen back, and now stood unnoticed behind the group. Once Louise turned her head, and raised her eyebrows interrogatively; but a feeling that was mingled pride and dismay restrained him; and as, even when the choosing of dances was over, he did not come forward, she walked down the hall on Herries's arm. The musicians began to tune; Dove, as master of ceremonies, was flying about, with his hands in gloves that were too large for him; people ranged themselves for the lancers in lines and squares. Maurice lost sight for a moment of the couple he was watching. As soon as the dance began, however, he saw them again; they were waltzing to the *Francaise,* at the lower end of the hall.

He was driven from the corner in which he had taken refuge, by hearing some one behind him say, in an angry whisper: " I call it positively horrid of her to come." It was Susie Fay who spoke; through some oversight, she had not been asked to dance. Moving slowly along, behind the couples that began a schottische, he felt a tap on his arm, and, looking round, saw Miss Jensen. She swept aside her ample skirts, and invited him to a seat beside her. But he remained standing.

"You don't care for dancing?" she queried. And, when he had replied: " Well, say, now, Mr. Guest,—we are all dying to know—however have you gotten Louise Dufrayer along here this evening? It's the queerest thing out."

" Indeed? " said the young man drily.

"Well, maybe queer is not just the word. But, why, we all presumed she was perfectly inconsolable—thinking only of another world. That's so. And then you work a miracle, and out she pops, fit as can be."

" I persuaded her . . . for the sake of variety," mumbled Maurice.

Little Fauvre, the baritone, had come up; but Miss Jensen did not heed his meek reminder that this was their dance.

" That was excessively kind of you," said the big woman, and looked at Maurice with shrewd, good-natured eyes. " And no doubt, Louise is most grateful. She seems to be enjoying herself.—Keep quiet, Fauvre, do, till I am ready.—But I don't like her dress. It's a lovely goods, and no mistake. But it ain't suitable for a little hop like this. It's too much."

" How Miss Dufrayer dresses is none of my business."

"Well, maybe not.—Now, Fauvre, come along "—she called it " Fover." " I reckon you think you've waited long enough."

Maurice, left to himself again, was astonished to hear Madeleine's voice in his ear. She had made her way to him alone.

" For goodness' sake, pull yourself together," she said cuttingly. " Every one in the hall can see what's the matter with you."

Before he could answer, she was claimed by her partner— one of the few Germans scattered through this Anglo-American gathering. " Is zat your brozzer? " Maurice heard him ask as they moved away. He watched them dancing together, and found it a ridiculous sight: round Madeleine, tall and angular, the short, stout man rotated fiercely. From time to time they stopped, to allow him to wipe his face.

Maurice contemplated escaping from the hall to some quiet room beyond. But as he was edging forward, he ran into Dove's arms, and that was the end of it. Dove, it seemed, had had his eye on him. The originator of the ball confessed that he was not having a particularly good time; he had everything to superintend—the dances, the musicians, the arrangements for supper. Besides this, there were at least a dozen too many ladies present; he believed some of the men had simply given their tickets away to girl-friends, and had let them come alone. So far, Dove had been forced to sacrifice himself entirely, and he was hot and impatient.

" Besides, I've routed half a dozen men out of the billiard-room, more than once," he complained irrelevantly, wiping the moisture from his brow. " But it's of no——Now just look at that! " he interrupted himself. " The 'cellist has had too much to drink already, and they're handing him more beer. Another glass, and he won't be able to play at all.—I say, you're not dancing. My dear fellow, it really won't do. You must help me with some of these women."

Taking Maurice by the arm, he steered him to a corner of the hall where sat two little provincial English sisters, looking hopeless and forlorn. Who had invited them, it was impossible to say; but no one wished to dance with them. They were dressed exactly alike, were alike in face, too—as like as two nuts, thought Maurice, as he bowed to them. Their hair was of a nutty brown, their eyes were brown, and they wore brown dresses. He led them out to dance, one after the other, and they were overwhelmingly grateful to him. He could hardly tell them apart; but that did not matter; for, when he took one back to her seat, the other sat waiting for her turn.

In dancing, he was thrown together with more of his friends, and he was not slow to catch the looks—cynical, contemptuous, amused—that were directed at him. Some were disposed to wink, and to call him a sly dog; others found food for malicious gossip in the way Louise had deserted him; and, when he met Miss Martin in a quadrille, she snubbed his advances with a definiteness that left no room for doubt.

Round dances succeeded to square dances; the musicians' playing grew more mechanical; flowers drooped, and dresses were crushed. An Englishman or two ran about complaining of the ventilation. As often as Maurice saw Louise, she was with Herries. At first, she had at least made a feint of dancing with other people; now she openly showed her preference. Always this dapper little man, with the violets and the simpering smile.

They were the two best dancers in the hall. Louise, in particular, gave herself up to the rhythm of the music with an abandon not often to be seen in a ball-room. Something of the professional about it, said Maurice to himself as he watched her; and, in his own estimation, this was the hardest thought he had yet had of her.

At supper, he sat between the two little sisters, whose bird-like chatter acted upon him as a reiterated noise acts on the nerves of one who is trying to sleep. He could hardly bring himself to answer civilly. At the further end of the table, on the same side as he, sat Louise. She was with those who had been her partners during the evening. They were drinking champagne, and were very lively. Maurice could not see her face; but her loud, excited laugh jarred on his ears.

Afterwards, the same round was to begin afresh, except that the sisters had generously introduced him to a friend. But when the first dance was over, Maurice abruptly excused himself to his surprised partner, and made his way out of the hall.

At the disordered supper-table, a few people still lingered; and deserters were again knocking balls about the green cloth of the billiard-table. Maurice went past them, and up a flight of stairs that led to a gallery overlooking the hall. This gallery was in semi-darkness. At the back of it, chairs were piled one on top of the other; but the two front rows had been left standing, from the last concert held in the building, and here, two or three couples were sitting out the dance. He went into the extreme corner, where it was darkest.

At last he was alone. He no longer needed to dance with girls he did not care a jot for, or to keep up appearances. He was free to be as wretched as he chose, and he availed himself unreservedly of the chance. It was not only the personal slight Louise had put upon him throughout the evening, making use of him, as it were, to the very door, and then throwing him off: but that she could be attracted by a mere waxen prettiness, and well-fitting clothes—for the first time, distrust of her was added to his hurt amazement.

He had not been in his hiding-place for more than a very few minutes, when the door he had entered by reopened, and a couple came down the steps to the corner where he was sitting.

"Oh, there's some one there!" cried Louise at the sight of the dark figure. "Maurice! Is it you? What are you doing here?"

"Sssh!" said Herries warningly, afraid lest her clear voice should carry too far.

"Yes. It's me," said Maurice stiffly, and rose. "But I'm going. I shan't disturb you."

"Disturb?" she said, and laughed a little. "Nonsense! Of course not." From her position on Herries's arm, she looked down at him, uncertain how to proceed. Then she laughed again. "But how fortunate that I found you! The next is our dance, isn't it?"—she pretended to examine her programme. "It will begin in a minute. I think I'll wait here."

"The next may be, but not the next again, remember," said Herries, before he allowed her to withdraw her arm. Louise nodded and laughed. *"Auf Wiedersehen!"*

But after the door had closed behind Herries, she remained standing, a step higher than Maurice, tipping her face with her handkerchief.

When she descended the step, and was on a level with him, he could see how her eyes glittered.

"Was that lie necessary?—for me?"

"What's the matter, Maurice? Why are you like this? Why have you not asked me to dance?"

He was unpleasantly worked on by her free use of his name.

"I, you? Have I had a chance?"

"Wasn't it for you to make the chance? Or did you expect me to come to you: Mr. Guest, will you do me the honour of dancing with me?—Oh, please, don't be cross. Don't spoil my pleasure—for this one night at least."

But she laughed again as she spoke, as though she did not fear his power to do so, and laid her hand on his arm: and, at her touch, he seemed to feel through sleeve and glove, the superabundance of vitality that was throbbing in her this evening. She was unable to be still for a moment; in the delicate pallor of her face, her eyes burned, black as jet.

"Are you really enjoying yourself so much? What *can* you find in it all?"

"Come—come down and dance. Listen!—can you resist that music? Quick, let us go down."

"I dance badly. I'm not Herries."

"But I can suit my step to anyone's. Won't you dance with me?—when I ask you?"

She had been leaning forward, looking over the balustrade at the couples arranging themselves below. Now she turned, and put her arm through his.

They went down the stairs, into the hall. Close beside the door at which they entered, they began to dance.

In all these months, Maurice had scarcely touched her hand. Now convention required that he should take her in his arms: he had complete control over her, could draw her closer, or put her further away, as he chose. For the first round or two, this was enough to occupy him entirely: the proximity of the lithe body, the nearness of the dark head, the firm, warm resistance that her back offered to his hand.

They were dancing to the music of the *Wiener Blut,* most melancholy gay of waltzes, in which the long, legato, upward sweep of the violins says as plainly as in words that all is vanity. But with the passing of the players to the second theme, the melody made a more direct appeal: there was a passionate unrest in it, which disquieted all who heard it. The dancers, with flushed cheeks and fixed eyes, responded instinctively to its challenge: the lapidary swing with which they followed the rhythm became less circumspect; and a desire to dance till they could dance no more, took possession of those who were fanatic. No one yielded to the impulse more readily than Louise; she was quite carried away. Maurice felt the change in her; an uneasiness seized him, and increased with every turn. She had all but closed her eyes; her hair brushed his shoulder; she answered to the lightest pressure of his arm. Even her face looked strange to him: its expression, its individuality, all that made it hers, was as if wiped out. Involuntarily he straightened himself, and his own movements grew stiffer, in his effort to impart to her some of his own restraint. But it was useless. And, as they turned and turned, to the maddening music, cold spots broke out on his forehead: in this manner she had danced with all her previous partners, and would dance with those to come. Such a pang of jealousy shot through him at the thought that, without knowing what he was doing, he pulled her sharply to him. And she yielded to the tightened embrace as a matter of course.

With a jerk he stopped dancing and loosened his hold of her.

She stood and blinked at lights and people: she had been far away, in a world of melody and motion, and could not come back to herself all at once. Wonderingly she looked at Maurice; for the music was going on, and no one else had left off dancing; and, with the same of comprehension, but still too dazed to resist, she followed him up the stairs.

" It's easy to see you don't care for dancing," she said, when they were back in the corner of the gallery. Her breath came unsteadily, and again she touched her face with the small, scented handkerchief.

"No. Not dancing like that," he answered rudely. But now again, as so often before, directly it was put into words, his feeling seemed strained and puritanic.

Louise leaned forward in her seat to look into his face.

" Like what?—what do you mean? Oh, you foolish boy, what is the matter with you to-night? You will tell me next I can't dance."

" You dance only too well."

" But you would rather I was a wooden doll—is that it? How is one to please you? First you are vexed with me because *you* did not ask *me* to dance; and when I send my partner away, on your account, you won't finish one dance with me, but exact that I shall sit here, in a dark corner, and let that glorious music go by. I don't know what to make of you." But her attention had already wandered to the dancers below. " Look at them!— Oh, it makes me envious! No one else has dreamt of stopping yet. For no matter how tired you are beforehand, when you dance you don't feel it, and as long as the music goes on, you must go on, too, though it lasted all night.—Oh, how often I have longed for a night like this! And then I've never met a better dancer than Mr. Herries."

" And for the sake of his dancing, you can forget what a puppy he is?"

" Puppy?" At the warmth of his interruption, she laughed, the low, indolent laugh, by means of which she seemed determined, on this night, to keep anything from touching her too nearly. "How crude you men are! Because he is handsome and dances well, you reason that he must necessarily be a simpleton."

"Handsome? Yes—if a tailor's dummy is handsome."

But Louise only laughed again, like one over whom words had no power. "If he were the veriest scarecrow, I would forgive him—for the sake of his dancing."

She leant forward, letting her gloved arms lie along her knees; and above the jet-trimmed line of her bodice, he saw her white chest rise and fall. At a slight sound behind, she turned and looked expectantly at the door.

"No, not yet," said the young man at her side. "Besides, even if it were, this is my dance, remember. You said so yourself."

"You are rude to-night, Maurice—and *langweilig*." She averted her face, and tapped her foot. But the content that lapped her made it impossible for her to take anything earnestly amiss, and even that others should show displeasure jarred on her like a false note.

"Don't be angry. To-morrow it will all be different again. Let me have just this one night of pleasure—let me enjoy myself in my own way."

"To hear you talk, one would think I had no wish but to spoil your pleasure."

"Oh, I didn't mean that. You misunderstand everything."

"What I say or think has surely no weight with you?"

She gave up the attempt to pacify him, and leaning back in her chair, stifled a yawn. Then with an exclamation of: "How hot it is up here!" she peeled off her gloves. With her freed hands, she tidied her hair, drawing out and thrusting in again the silver dagger that held the coil together. Then she let her bare arms fall on her lap, where they lay in strong outline against the black of her dress. One was almost directly under Maurice's eyes; even by the poor light, he could see the mark left on the inside of the wrist, by the buttons of the glove. It was a generously formed arm, but so long that it looked slender, and its firm white roundness was flawless from wrist to shoulder. He shut his eyes, but he could see it through his eyelids. Sitting beside her like this, in the semi-darkness, morbidly aware of the perfume of her hair and dress, he suddenly forgot that he had been rude, and she indifferent. He was conscious only of the wish to drive it home to her, how unhappy she was making him.

"Louise," he said so abruptly that she started. "I'm going

to ask you to do something for me. I haven't made many demands, have I?—since you first called me your friend." He paused and fumbled for words. "Don't—don't dance any more to-night. Don't dance again."

She stooped forward to look at him. "Not dance again?—I? What do you mean?"

"What I say. Let us go home."

"Home? Now? When it's only half over?—You don't know what you are saying." But her surprise was already on the wane.

"Oh, yes, I do. I'm not going to let you dance again."

She laughed, in spite of herself, at the new light in which he was showing himself. But, the moment after, she ceased to laugh; for, with an audacity he had not believed himself capable of, Maurice took the arm that was lying next him, and, midway between wrist and elbow, put his lips to it, kissing it several times, in different places.

Taken unawares, Louise was helpless. Then she freed herself, ungently. "No, no, I won't have it. Oh, how can you be so foolish! My gloves—where is my glove? Pick it up, and give it to me—at once!"

He groped on the dusty floor; the veins in his forehead hammered. She had moved to a distance, and now stood busy with the gloves; she would not look at him.

In the uneasy silence that ensued, Herries opened the door: a moment later, they went out together. Maurice remained standing until he saw them appear below. Then he dropped back into his seat, and covered his face with his hands.

He did not regret what he had done; he did not care in the least, whether he had made her angry with him or not. On the contrary, the feeling he experienced was akin to relief: disapproval and mortification, jealousy and powerlessness—all the varying emotions of the evening—had found vent and alleviation in the few hastily snatched kisses. He no longer felt injured by her treatment of him: that hardly seemed to concern him now. His sensations, at this minute, resolved themselves into the words: "She is mine, she is mine!" which went round and round in his brain. And then, in a sudden burst of clearness, he understood what it meant for him to say this. It meant that the farce of friendship, at which he had played, was at an end; it meant that he loved her—not as hitherto, with a touch of elegiac resignation—but with a violence that made him afraid. It seemed incredible to him now that he had spent two months in close fellowship with her: it was ludicrous, inhuman. For he now saw, that his ultimate desire had been neither to help her nor to restore her to life—that was a comedy he had acted for the benefit of the traditions in his blood. Brutally, at this moment, he acknowledged that he had only wished to hear her voice and to touch her hand: to make for himself so indispensable a place among the necessities of her life that no one could oust him from it.—Mine—mine! Instinct alone spoke in him to-night—that same blunt instinct which had reared its head the first time he saw her, but which, until now, he had kept under, like a medieval ascetic. No reason came to his aid; he neither looked into the future nor did he consider the past: he only swore to himself in a kind of stubborn wrath that she was his, and that no earthly power should take her from him.

One by one the slow-dragging hours wore away. The dancers' ranks were thinned; but those who remained, gyrated as insensately as ever. There was an air of greater freedom over the ball-room. The chaperons who, earlier in the evening, had sat patiently on the red velvet sofas, had vanished with their charges, and, in their train, the more sedate of the company: it was past three o'clock, and now, every few minutes, a cloaked couple crossed a corner of the hall to the street-door.

When Maurice went downstairs, he could not find Louise, and some time elapsed before she and Herries emerged from the supper-room. Although the lines beneath her eyes were like rings of hammered iron, she danced anew, went on to the very end, with a few other infatuated people. Finally, the tired musicians rose stiffly to pack their instruments; and, with a sigh of exhaustion, she received on her shoulders the cloak Maurice stood holding.

They were among the last to leave the hall; the lights went out behind them. Herries walked a part of the way home with them, and talked much and idly—ineffable in his self-conceit, thought Maurice. But Louise urged him on, saying wild, disconnected things, as if, as long as words were spoken, it did not matter what they were. Again and again her laugh resounded: it was hoarse, and did not ring true.

"She has had too much champagne," Maurice said to himself, as he walked silent at her side.

In the *Rossplatz*, Herries, who was in a becoming fur cap, and a coat with a fur-lined collar, took a circumstantial leave of her. He raised both her hands to his lips.

"To the memory of those divine waltzes—our waltzes!" he

said sentimentally. "And to all the others the future has in
store for us!"

She left her hands in his, and smiled at him.

"Till to-morrow then," said Herries. "Or shall you forget
your promise?"

"It is you who will forget—not I."

After this, Maurice and she walked on alone together. It
was that dreariest of all the hours between sunset and dawn,
when it is scarcely night any longer, and yet not nearly day. The
crisp frost of the previous evening had given place to a bleak
rawness; the day that was coming would crawl in, lugubriously,
unable to get the better of the darkness. The houses about them
were wrapped in sleep; they two were the only people abroad,
and their footsteps echoed in the damp streets. But, for once,
Louise was not affected by the gloom of her surroundings. She
walked swiftly, and her chief aim seemed to be to render any
but the most trival words impossible. Now, however, her
strained gaiety had the aspect of a fever; Maurice believed that,
for the most part, she did not know what she was saying.

Until they stood in front of the house-door, she kept up the
tension. But when the young man had fitted the key in the
lock and turned it, she looked at him, and, for the first time
this night, gave him her full attention.

"Good night—my friend!"

She was leaning against the woodwork; beneath the lace
scarf, her eyes were bent on him with a strange expression.
Maurice looked down into them, and, for a second or two, held
them with his own, in one of those looks which are not for ordinary use between a man and a woman. Louise shivered under
it, and gave a nervous laugh; the next moment, she made a slight
movement towards him, an involuntary movement, which was
so imperceptible as to be hardly more than an easing of her
position against the doorway, and yet was unmistakable—as
unmistakable as was the little upward motion with which she
resigned herself at the outset of a dance. For an instant, his
heart stopped beating; in a flash he knew that this was the
solution: there was only one ending to this night of longing
and excitement, and that was to take her in his arms, as she
stood, to hold her to him in an infinite embrace, till his own
nerves were stilled, and the madness had gone from her. But
the returning beat of his blood brought the knowledge that a
morrow must surely come—a morrow for both of them—a
cold, grey day to be faced and borne. She was not herself,

in the bonds of her unnatural excitement; it was for him to be wise.

He took her limply hanging hand, and looked at her gravely and kindly.

" You are very tired."

At his voice, the wild light died out of her eyes; she seemed to shrink into herself. " Yes, very tired. And oh, so cold! "

" Can't you get a cup of tea?—something to warm you? "

But she did not hear him; she was already on the stair. He waited till her steps had died away, then went headlong down the street. But, when he came to think things over, he did not pride himself on the self-control he had displayed. On the contrary, he was tormented by the wish to know what she would have said or done had he yielded to his impulse; and, for the remainder of the night, his brain lost itself in a maze of hazardous conjecture. Only when day broke, a cheerless February day, was he satisfied that he could not have acted differently.

Upstairs, in her room, Louise lay face downwards on her bed, and there, her arms thrown wildly out over the pillows, all the froth and intoxication of the evening gone from her—there lay, and wished she were dead.

* * * * *

Three days later, towards four o'clock in the afternoon, Maurice watched the train that carried her from him steam out of the *Dresdener Bahnhof.*

The clearness he had gained as to his own motives, and the ruthless probing of himself it induced, both led to the same conclusion: Louise must go away. The day after the ball, too, he had found her in a state of collapse, which was unparalleled even in the ups and downs of the past weeks.

" Anything!—do anything you like with me. I wish I had never been born; " and, though no muscle of her face moved, large slow tears ran down her sallow cheeks.

Unconsciously twisting and bending Herries's card, which was lying on the table, Maurice laid his plan before her. And having won the above consent, he did not let the grass grow under his feet. He applied to Miss Jensen for practical aid, and that lady was tactful enough to give it without curiosity. She knew Dresden well, recommended it as a lively place, and wrote forthwith to a *Pension* there, engaging rooms for a lady who had just recovered from a severe illness. By tacit agree-

ment, this was understood to cover any extravagance or im-
prudence, of which Louise might make herself guilty.

Now she had gone, and with her, the central interest of his
life. But the tired gesture with which he took off his hat and
wiped his forehead, as he walked home, was expressive of the
relief he felt that he was not going to see her again for some
time.

He let a fortnight elapse—a fortnight of colourless days, unbroken by word or sign from her. Then, one night, he spent
several hours writing to her—writing a carefully worded letter,
in which he put forward the best reasons he could devise, for her
remaining away altogether.

To this he received no answer.

X

FROM one of the high, wooden benches, at the back of the amphitheatre in the *Alberthalle,* where he had lain at full length, listening to the performance of a Berlin pianist, Krafft rose, full to the brim of impressions, and eager to state them.

"That man," he began, as he left the hall between Maurice and Avery Hill, "is a successful teacher. And therewith his fate as an artist is sealed. No teacher can get on to the higher rungs of the ladder, and no inspired musician be a satisfactory teacher. If the artist is obliged to share his art, his pupils, should they be intelligent, may pick up something of his skill, learn the trick of certain things; but the moment he begins to set up dogmas, it is the end of him.—As if it were possible for one person to prescribe to another, of a totally different temperament, how he ought to feel in certain passages, or be affected by certain harmonies! If I, for example, choose to play the later Beethoven sonatas as I would the Brahms Concerto in B flat, with a thoroughly modern irony, what is it that hinders me from doing it, and from satisfying myself, and kindred souls, who are honest enough to admit their feelings? Tradition, nothing in the world but tradition; tradition in the shape of the teacher steps in and says anathema: to this we are not accustomed, *ergo,* it cannot be good.—And it is just the same with those composers who are also pedagogues. They know, none better, that there are no hard and fast rules in their art; that it is only convention, or the morbid ear of some medieval monk, which has banished, say, consecutive fifths from what is called 'pure writing'; that further, you need only to have the regulation number of years behind you, to fling squeamishness to the winds. In other words, you learn rules to unlearn them with infinite pains. But the pupil, in his innocence, demands a rigid basis to go on—it is a human weakness, this, the craving for rules—and his teachers pamper him. Instead of saying: develop your own ear, rely on yourself, only what you teach yourself is worth knowing—instead of this, they build up walls and barriers to hedge him in, behind which, for their benefit, he must go through the antics of a performing dog. But nemesis overtakes them; they fall a victim to their own wiles, just as the liar finally believes his own lies. Ultimately, they find their chief delight in the adroitness with which they themselves overcome imaginary obstacles."

His companions were silent. Avery Hill had a nine hours' working-day behind her, and was tired; besides, she made a point of never replying to Krafft's tirades. Once only, of late, had she said to him in Maurice's presence: "You would reason the skin off one's bones, Heinz. You are the most self-conscious person alive." Krafft had been much annoyed at this remark, and had asked her to call him a Jew and be done with it; but afterwards, he admitted to Maurice that she was right.

"And it's only the naïve natures that count."

Maurice had found his way back to Krafft; for, in the days of uncertainty that followed the posting of his letter, he needed human companionship. Until the question whether Louise would return or not was decided, he could settle to nothing; and Krafft's ramblings took him out of himself. Since the ball, his other friends had given him the cold shoulder; hence it did not matter whether or no they approved of his renewed intimacy with Krafft—he said "they," but it was Madeleine who was present to his mind. And Krafft was an easy person to take up with again; he never bore a grudge, and met Maurice readily, half-way.

It had not taken the latter long to shape his actions for what he believed to be the best. But his thoughts were beyond control. He was as helpless against sudden spells of depression as against dreams of an iridescent brightness. He could no more avoid dwelling on the future than reliving the past. If Louise did not return, these memories were all that were left him. If she did, what form were their relations to each other going to assume?—and this was the question that cost him most anxious thought.

A thing that affected him oddly, at this time, was his growing inability to call up her face. It was incredible. This face, which he had supposed he knew so well that he could have drawn it blindfold, had taken to eluding him; and the more impatient he became, the poorer was his success. The disquieting thing, however, was, that though he could not materialise her face, what invariably rose before his eyes was her long, bare arm, as it had lain on the black stuff of her dress. At first, it only came when he was battling to secure the face; then it took to appearing at unexpected moments; and eventually, it became a kind of nightmare, which haunted him. He would start up from dreaming of it, his hair moist with perspiration, for, strangely enough, he was always on the point of doing it harm: either his teeth were meeting in it, or he had drawn the blade of a knife down the middle of the blue-veined whiteness, and the blood spurted out along the line, which reddened instantly in the wake of the knife.

April had come, bringing April weather; it was fitfully sunny, and a mild and generous dampness spurred on growth: shrubs and bushes were so thickly sprinkled with small buds that, at a distance, it seemed as though a transparent green veil had been flung over them. In the Gewandhaus, according to custom, the Ninth Symphony had brought the concert season to a close; once more, the chorus had struggled victoriously with the *Ode to Joy*. And early one morning, Maurice held a note in his hand, in which Louise announced that she had " come home," the night before.

She had been away for almost two months, and, to a certain extent, he had grown inured to her absence. At the sight of her handwriting, he had the sensation of being violently roused from sleep. Now he shrank from the moment when he should see her again; for it seemed that not only the present, but all his future depended on it.

Late in the evening, he returned from the visit, puzzled and depressed.

Seven had boomed from church-clocks far and near, before he reached the *Brüderstrasse,* but, nevertheless, he had been kept waiting in the passage for a quarter of an hour: and he was in such an apprehensive frame of mind that he took the delay as a bad omen.

When he crossed the threshold, Louise came towards him with one of those swift movements which meant that she was in good spirits, and confident of herself. She held out her hands, and smiled at him with all her dark, mobile face, saying words that were as impulsive as her gesture. Maurice was always vaguely chilled by her outbursts of light-heartedness: they seemed to him strained and unreal, so accustomed had he grown to the darker, less adaptable side of her nature.

"You have come back? " he said, with her hand in his.

"Yes, I'm here—for the present, at least."

The last words caught in his ear, and buzzed there, making his foreboding a certainty. On the spot, his courage failed him; and though Louise continued to ring all the changes her voice was capable of, he did not recover his spirits. It was not merely the sense of strangeness, which inevitably attacked him after he had not seen her for some time; on this occasion, it was more. Partly, it might be due to the fact that she was dressed in a different way; her hair was done high on her head, and she wore a light grey dress of modish cut and design. Her face, too, had grown fuller; the hollows in her cheeks had vanished; and her skin had that peculiar clear pallor that was characteristic of it in health.

He was stupidly silent; he could not join in her careless vivacity. Besides, throughout the visit, nothing was said that it was worth his while coming to hear.

But when she wished him good-bye, she said, with a strange smile: " Altogether, I am very grateful to you, Maurice, for having made me go away."

He himself no longer felt any satisfaction at what he had done. As soon as he left her, he tried to comprehend what had happened: the change in her was too marked for him to be able to console himself that he had imagined it. Not only had she seemingly recovered, as if by magic, from the lassitude of the winter—he could even have forgiven her the alteration in her style of dress, although this, too, helped to alienate her from him. But what he ended by recognising, with a jealous throb, was that she had mentally recovered as well; she was once more the self-contained girl he had first known, with a gift for keeping an outsider beyond the circle of her thoughts and feelings. An outsider! The weeks of intimate companionship were forgotten, seemed never to have been. She had no further need of him, that was the clue to the mystery, and the end of the matter.

And so it continued, the next day, and the next again; Louise deliberately avoided touching on anything that lay below the surface. She vouchsafed no explanation of the words that had disquieted him, nor was the letter Maurice had written her once mentioned between them.

But, though she seemed resolved not to confide in him, she could not dispense with the small, practical services, he was able to render her. They were even more necessary to her than before; for, if one thing was clear, it was that she no longer intended to cloister herself up inside her four walls: the day after her return, she had been out till late in the afternoon, and had come home with her hands full of parcels. She took it now as a matter of course that Maurice should accompany her; and did not, or would not, notice his abstraction.

After the lapse of a very short time, however, the young man began to feel that there was something feverish in the continual high level of her mood. She broke down, once or twice, in trying to sustain it, and was more of her eloquently silent self again: one evening, he came upon her, in the dusk, when she was sitting with her chin on her hand, looking out before her with the old questioning gaze.

Occasionally he thought that she was waiting for something: in the middle of a sentence, she would break off, and grow absent-minded; and more than once, the unexpected advent of the postman threw her into a state of excitement, which she could not conceal. She was waiting for a letter. But Maurice was proud, and asked no questions; he took pains to use the cool, friendly tone, she herself adopted.

Not a week had dragged out, however, since her return, before he was suffering in a new way, in the oldest, cruellest way of all.

The *Pension* at which she had stayed in Dresden, had been frequented by leisured foreigners: over twenty people, of various nationalities, had sat down daily at the dinner-table. Among so large a number, it would have been easy for Louise to hold herself aloof. But, as far as Maurice could gather, she had felt no inclination to do this. From the first, she seemed to have been the nucleus of an admiring circle, chief among the members of which was a family of Americans—a brother and two sisters, rich Southerners, possessed of a vague leaning towards art and music. The names of these people recurred persistently in her talk; and, as the days went by, Maurice found himself listening for one name in particular, with an irritation he could not master. Raymond van Houst— a ridiculous name!—fit only for a backstairs romance. But as often as she spoke of Dresden, it was on her lips. Whether in the Galleries, or at the Opera, on driving excursions, or on foot, this man had been at her side; and soon the mere mention of him was enough to set Maurice's teeth on edge.

One afternoon, he found her standing before an extravagant mass of flowers, which were heaped up on the table; there were white and purple violets, a great bunch of lilies of the valley, and roses of different colours. They had been sent to her from Dresden, she said; but, beyond this, she offered no explanation. All the vases in the room were collected before her; but she had not begun to fill them: she stood with her hands in the flowers, tumbling them about, enjoying the contact of their moist freshness.

To Maurice's remark that she seemed to take a pleasure in destroying them, she returned a casual: "What does it matter?" and taking up as many violets as she could hold, looked defiantly at him over their purple leaves. Through all she said and did ran a strong undercurrent of excitement.

But before Maurice left, her manner changed. She came over to him, and said, without looking up: "Maurice . . . I want to tell you something."

"Yes; what is it?" He spoke with the involuntary coolness this mood of hers called out in him; and she was quick to feel it. She returned to the table.

"You ask so prosaically: you are altogether prosaic to-day. And it is not a thing I can tell you off-hand. You would need to sit down again. It's a long story; and you were going; and it's late. We will leave it till to-morrow: that will be time enough. And if it is fine, we can go out somewhere, and I'll tell you as we go."

It was a brilliant May afternoon: great white clouds were piled one on the top of another, like bales of wool; and their fantastic bulging roundnesses made the intervening patches of blue seem doubly distant. The wind was hardly more than a breath, which curled the tips of thin branches, and fluttered the loose ends of veils and laces. In the *Rosental*, where the meadow-slopes were emerald-green, and each branch bore its complement of delicately curled leaves, the paths were so crowded that there could be no question of a connected conversation. But again, Louise was not in a hurry to begin.

She continued meditative, even when they had reached the *Kaiserpark,* and were sitting with their cups before them, in the long, wooden, shed-like building, open at one side. She had taken off her hat—a somewhat showy white hat, trimmed with large white feathers—and laid it on the table; one dark wing of hair fell lower than the other, and shaded her forehead.

Maurice, who was on tenter-hooks, subdued his impatience as long as he could. Finally, he emptied his cup at a draught, and pushed it away.

"You wanted to speak to me, you said."—His manner was curt, from sheer nervousness.

His voice startled her. "Yes, I have something to tell you," she said, with a hesitation he did not know in her. "But I must go back a little.—If you remember, Maurice, you wrote to me while I was away, didn't you?" she said, and looked not at him, but at her hands clasped before her. "You gave me a number of excellent reasons why it would be better for me not to come back here. I didn't answer your letter at the time because . . . What should you say, Maurice, if I told you now, that I intended to take your advice?"

"You are going away?" The words jerked out gratingly, of themselves.

"Perhaps.—That is what I want to speak to you about. I have a chance of doing so."

"Chance? How chance?" he asked sharply.

"That's what I am going to tell you, if you will give me time."

Drawing a letter from her pocket, she smoothed the creases out of the envelope, and handed it to him.

While he read it, she looked away, looked over the enclosure. Some people were crossing it, and she followed them with her eyes, though she had often seen their counterparts before. A man in a heavy ulster—notwithstanding the mildness of the day—stalked on ahead, unconcerned about the fate of his family, which dragged, a woman and two children, in the rear: like savages, thought Louise, where the male goes first, to scent danger. But the crackling of paper recalled her attention; Maurice was folding the sheet, and replacing it in the envelope, with a ludicrous precision. His face had taken on a pinched expression, and he handed the letter back to her without a word.

She looked at him, expecting him to say something; but he was obdurate. "This was what I was waiting all these days to tell you," she said.

"You knew it was coming then?" He scarcely recognised his own voice; he spoke as he supposed a judge might speak to a proven criminal.

Louise shrugged her shoulders. "No. Yes.—That is, as far as it's possible to know such a thing."

Through the crude glass window, the sun cast a medley of lines and lights on her hands, and on the checkered table-cloth. There were two rough benches, and a square table; the coffee-cups stood on a metal tray; the lid of the pot was odd, did not match the set: all these inanimate things, which, a moment ago, Maurice had seen without seeing them, now stood out before his eyes, as if each of them had acquired an independent life, and no longer fitted into its background.

"Let us go home," he said, and rose.

"Go home? But we have only just come!" cried Louise, with what seemed to him pretended surprise. "Why do you want to go home? It is so quiet here: I can talk to you. For I need your advice, Maurice. You must help me once again."

"I help you?—in this? No, thank you. All I can do, it seems, is to wish you joy." He remained standing, with his hand on the back of the bench.

But at the cold amazement of her eyes, he took his seat again. "It is a matter for yourself—only you can decide. It's none of my business." He moved the empty cups about on the cloth.

"But why are you angry?"

"Haven't I good reason to be? To see you—you!—accepting an impertinence of this kind so quietly. For it *is* an impertinence, Louise, that a man you hardly know should write to you in this cocksure way and ask you to marry him. Impertinent and absurd!"

"You have a way of finding most things I want to do absurd," she answered. "In this case, though, you're mistaken. The tone of the letter is all it should be. And, besides, I know Mr. Van Houst very well."

Maurice looked at her with a sardonic smile.

"Seven weeks is a long time," she added.

"Seven weeks!—and for a lifetime!"

"Oh, one can get to know a man inside out, in seven weeks," she said, with wilful flippancy. "Especially if, from the first, he shows so plainly . . . Maurice, don't be angry. You have always been kind to me; you're not going to fail me now that I really need help? I have no one else, as you very well know." She smiled at him, and held out her hand. He could not refuse to take it; but he let it drop again immediately.

"Let me tell you all about it, and how it happened, and then you will understand," Louise went on, in a persuasive voice—he had once believed that the sound of this voice would reconcile him to any fate. "You think the time was short, but we were together every day, and sometimes all day long. I knew from the first that he cared for me; he made no secret of it. If anything, it is a proof of tactfulness on his part that he should have written rather than have spoken to me himself.

I like him for doing it, for giving me time. And then, listen, Maurice, what I should gain by marrying him. He is rich, really rich, and good-looking—in an American way—and thirty-two years old. His sisters would welcome me—one of them told me as much, and told me, too, that her brother had never cared for anyone before. He would make an ideal husband," she added with a sudden recklessness, at the sight of Maurice's unmoved face. "Americanly chivalrous to the finger-tips, and with just enough of the primitive animal in him to ward off monotony."

Maurice raised his hand, as if in self-defence. "So you, too, then, like any other woman, would marry just for the sake of marrying?" he asked, with bitter disbelief.

"Yes.—And just especially and particularly I."

"For Heaven's sake, let us get out of here!"

Without listening to her protest, he went to find the waiter. Louise followed him out of the enclosure, carrying hat and gloves in her hand.

They struck into narrow by-paths going back, to avoid the people. But it was impossible to escape all, and those they met, eyed them with curiosity. The clear English voices rang out unconcerned; the pale girl with the Italian eyes was visibly striving to appease her companion, who marched ahead, angry and impassive.

For a few hundred yards neither of them spoke. Then Louise began anew.

"And that is not all. You judge harshly and unfairly because you don't know the facts. I am almost quite alone in the world. I have no relatives that I care for, except one brother. I lived with him, on his station in Queensland, until I came here. But now he's married, and there would be no room for me in the house—figuratively speaking. If I go back now, I must share his home with his wife, whom I knew and disliked. While here is some one who is fond of me, and is rich, and who offers me not only a home of my own, but, what is far more to me, an entirely new life in a new world."

"Excellent reasons! But in reckoning them up, you have forgotten what seems to me the most important one of all; whether or no you care for him, for this . . . this . . ." in his trouble, he could not find a suitable epithet.

But Louise refused to be touched. "I like him," she answered, and looked across the slope of meadow they were passing. "I liked him, yes, as any woman would like a man who

treated her as he did me. He was very good to me. And not
in the least repugnant.—But care?" she interrupted herself.
"If by care, you mean . . . Then no, a hundred thousand
times, no! I shall never care for anyone in that way again,
and you know it. I had enough of that to last me all my
life."

"Very well, then, and I say, if you married a man you
care for as little as that, I should never believe in a woman
again.—Not, of course, that it matters to you what I believe in
and what I don't! But to hear you—you, Louise!—counting
up the profits to be gained from it, like . . . like—oh, I don't
know what! I couldn't have believed it of you."

"You are a very uncomfortable person, Maurice."

"I mean to be. And more than uncomfortable. Listen to
me! You talk of it lightly and coolly; but if you married this
man, without caring for him more than you say you do, just
for the sake of a home, or his money, or his good manners, or
the primitive animal, or whatever it is that attracts you in him:"
—he grew bitter again in spite of himself—" if you did this,
you would be stifling all that is good and generous in your
nature. For you may say what you like; the man is little more
than a stranger to you. What can you know of his real character? And what can he know of you?"

"He knows as much of me as I ever intend him to know."

"Indeed! Then you wouldn't tell him, for instance, that
only a few months ago, you were eating your heart out for some
one else?"

Louise winced as though the words had struck her in the
face. Before she answered, she stood still, in the middle of
the path, and pinned on, with deliberate movements, the big
white hat, beneath the drooping brim and nodding feathers
of which, her eyes were as black as coals.

"No, I should not," she said. "Why should I? Do you
think it would make him care more for me to know that I had
nearly died of love for another man?"

"Certainly not. And it might also make him less ready
to marry you."

"That's exactly what I think."

One was as bitter as the other; but Maurice was the more
violent of the two.

"And so you would begin the new life you talk of, with lies
and deceit?—A most excellent beginning!"

"If you like to call it that. *I* only know, that no one with any sense thinks of dragging up certain things when once they are dead and buried. Or are you, perhaps, simple enough to believe any man living would get over what I have to tell him, and care for me afterwards in the same way?"

He turned, with tell-tale words on his tongue. But the expression of her face intimidated him. He had only to look at her to know that, if he spoke of himself at this moment, she would laugh him to scorn.

But the beloved face acted on him in its own way; his sense of injury weakened. "Louise," he said in an altered tone; "whatever you say to the contrary, in a matter like this, I can't advise you. For I don't understand—and never should. —But of one thing I'm as sure as I am that the sun will rise to-morrow, and that is, that you won't do it. Do you honestly think you could go on living, day after day, with a man you don't sincerely care for?—of whom the most you can say is that he's not repugnant to you? You little know what it would mean!—And you may reason as you will; I answer for you; and I say no, and again no. It isn't in you to do it. You are not mean and petty enough. You can't hide your feelings, try as you will.—No, you couldn't deceive some one, by pretending to care for him, for months on end. You would be miserably unhappy; and then—then I know what would happen. You would be candid—candid about everything—when it was too late."

There was no mistaking the sincerity of his words. But Louise was boundlessly irritated, and made no further effort to check her resentment.

"You have an utterly false and ridiculous idea of me, and of everything belonging to me."

"I haven't spent all this time with you for nothing. I know you better than you know yourself. I believe in you, Louise. And I know I am right. And some day you'll know it, too."

These words only incensed her the more.

"What you know—or think you know—is nothing to me. If you had listened to me patiently, as I asked you to, instead of losing your temper, and taking what I said as a personal affront, then, yes, then I should have told you something else besides. How, when I came back, a fortnight ago, I was quite resolved to marry this man, if he asked me—marry him and cut myself off for ever from my old life and its hateful memories.—And why not? I'm still young. I still have a right to pleasure—

and change—and excitement.—And in all these days, I didn't
once hesitate—not till the letter came yesterday—and then not
till night. It wasn't like me; for when once I have made up
my mind, I never go back. So I determined to ask you—ask
you to help me to decide. For you had always been kind to me.
—But this is what I get for doing it." Her anger flared up
anew. "You have treated me abominably, to-day, Maurice;
and I shan't forget it. All your ridiculous notions about right
and wrong don't matter a straw. What does matter is, that
when I ask for help, you should behave as if—as if I were going
to commit a crime. Your opinion is nothing to me. If I decide
to marry the man, I shall do it, no matter what you say."

"I'm sure you will."

"And if I don't, let me tell you this: it won't be because
of anything you've said to-day. Not from any high-flown notions of honesty, or generosity, as you would like to make yourself believe; but merely because I haven't the energy in me.
I couldn't keep it up. I want to be quiet, to have an easy
life. The fact that some one else had to suffer, too, wouldn't
matter to me, in the least. It's myself I think of, first and
foremost, and as long as I live it will always be myself."

Her voice belied her words; he expected each moment that
she would burst out crying. However, she continued to walk
on, with her head erect; and she did not take back one of the
unkind things she had said.

They parted without being reconciled. Maurice stood and
watched her mount the staircase, in the vain hope that she
would turn, before reaching the top.

He did not see how the fine May afternoon declined, and
passed into evening; how the high stacks of cloud were broken
up at sunset, and shredded into small flakes and strips of cloud,
which, saturated with gold, vanished in their turn: how the
shadows in the corners turned from blue to black; nor did he
note the mists that rose like steam from the ground, intensifying
the acrid smell of garlic, with which the woods abounded.
Screened by the thicket, he sat on his accustomed seat, and gave
himself up to being miserable.

For some time he was conscious only of how deeply he had
been wounded—just as one suffers from the bruise after the
blow. At the moment, he had been stunned into a kind of
quiescence; now his nerves throbbed and tingled. But, little by
little, a vivid recollection of what had actually occurred returned to sting him: and certain details stood out fixed and un-

forgettable. Yet, in reliving the hours just past, he felt
no regret at the fact that they had quarrelled. What first
smote him was an unspeakable amazement at Louise. The
knowledge that, for weeks on end, she had been contemplating marriage, was beyond his belief. Hardly recovered
from the throes of a suffering believed incurable, and while he
was still going about her with gloved hands, as it were, she
was ready to throw herself into the arms of the first likely man
she met. He could not help himself: in this connection, every
little trait in her that was uncongenial to him, started up with
appalling distinctness. Hitherto, he had put it down to his
own sensitiveness; he was over-nice. But for the most part,
he had forgiven her on account of all she had come through;
for he believed that this grief had swept destructively through
her nature, leaving a jagged wound, which only time could
heal. Now, as if to prove to him what a fool he was, she
showed him that he had been mistaken in this also; she could
recover her equilibrium, while he still hedged her round with
solicitude—recover herself, and transfer her affection to another person. Good God! Was it so easy, a matter of so little
moment, to grow fond of one who was almost a stranger to
her?—for, in spite of what she said to the contrary, he was
persuaded that she had a stronger feeling for this man than
she had been willing to admit: this riper man, with his experienced way of treating women. Was, then, his own idea
of her wholly false? Was there, after all, something in her
nature that he could not, would not, understand? He denied it
fiercely, almost before he had formulated the question: no
matter what her actions were, or what words she said, deep down
in her was an intense will for good, a spring of noble impulse.
It was only that she had never had a proper chance. But he
denied it to a vision of her face: the haunting eyes which,
at first sight, had destroyed his peace of mind; the dead black
hair against the ivory-coloured skin. It was in these things
that the truth lay, not in the blind promptings of her inclination.

For the first time, the idea of marriage took definite shape in
his mind. For all he knew, it might have been lying dormant
there, all along; but he would doubtless have remained unconscious of it, for weeks to come, had it not been for the
events of the afternoon. Now, however, Louise had made it
plain that his feelings for her were of an exaggerated delicacy;
plain that she herself had no such scruples. He need hesitate no
longer. But marry! . . . marriage! . . . he marry Louise!—

at the thought of it, he laughed. That he, Maurice Guest, should, for an instant, put himself on a par with her American suitor! The latter, rich, leisured, able to satisfy her caprices, surround her with luxury: himself, younger than she by several years, without prospects, with nothing to offer her but a limitless devotion. He tried to imagine himself saying: "Louise, will you marry me?" and the words stuck in his throat; for he saw the amused astonishment of her eyes. And not merely at the presumption he would be guilty of; what was as clear to him as day was that she did not really care for him; not as he cared for her; not with the faintest hint of a warmer feeling. If he had never grasped this before, he did so now, to the full. Sitting there, he affirmed to himself that she did not even like him. She was grateful to him, of course, for his help and friendship; but that was all. Beyond this, he would not have been surprised to learn from her own lips that she actually disliked him: for there was something irreconcilable about their two natures. And never, for a moment, had she considered him in the light of an eligible lover—oh, how that stung! Here was she, with an attraction for him which nothing could weaken; and in him was not the smallest lineament, of body or of mind, to wake a response in her. He was powerless to increase her happiness by a hair's breadth. Her nerves would never answer to the inflection of his voice, or the touch of his hand. How could such things be? What anomaly was here?

To-day, her face rose before him unsought—the sweet, dark face with the expression of slight melancholy that it wore in repose, as he loved it best. It was with him when, stiff and tired, he emerged from his seclusion, and walked home through the trails of mist that hung, breast-high, on the meadow-land. It was with him under the street-lamps, and, to its accompanying presence, the strong conviction grew in him that evasion on his part was no longer possible. Sooner or later, come what might, the words he had faltered over, even to himself, would have to be spoken.

XI

ONE day, some few weeks later, Madeleine sat at her writing-table, biting the end of her pen. A sheet of note-paper lay before her; but she had not yet written a word. She frowned to herself, as she sat.

Hard at work that morning, she had heard a ring at the door-bell, and, a minute after, her landlady ushered in a visitor, in the shape of Miss Martin. Madeleine rose from the piano with ill-concealed annoyance, and having seated Miss Martin on the sofa, waited impatiently for the gist of her visit; for she was sure that the lively American would not come to see her without an object. And she was right: she knew to a nicety when the important moment arrived. Most of the visit was preamble; Miss Martin talked at length of her own affairs, assuming, with disarming candour, that they interested other people as much as herself. She went into particulars about her increasing dissatisfaction with Schwarz, and retailed the glowing accounts she heard on all sides of a teacher called Schrievers. He was not on the staff of the Conservatorium; but he had been a favourite of Liszt's, and was attracting many pupils. From this, Miss Martin passed to more general topics, such as the blow Dove had recently received over the head of his attachment to pretty Susie Fay. " Why, Sue, she feels perfectly *dreadful* about it. She can't understand Mr. Dove thinking they were anything but real good friends. Most every one here knew right away that Sue had her own boy down home in Illinois. Yes, indeed."

Madeleine displayed her want of interest in Dove's concerns so plainly, that Miss Martin could not do otherwise than cease discussing them. She rose to end her call. As, however, she stood for the momentary exchange of courtesies that preceded the hand-shake, she said, in an off-hand way: " Miss Wade, I presume I needn't inquire if you're acquainted with the latest about Louise Dufrayer? I say, I guess I needn't inquire, see-ing you're so well acquainted with Mr. Guest. I presume, though, you don't see so much of him now. No, indeed. I hear he's thrown over all his friends. I feel real disappointed about him. I thought he was a most agreeable young man.

But, as momma says, you never can tell. An' I reckon Louise is most to blame. Seems like she simply *can't* exist without a beau. But I wonder she don't feel ashamed to show herself, the way she's talked of. Why, the stories I hear about her! ... an' they're always together. She's gotten her a heap of new things, too—a millionaire asked her to marry him, when she was in Dresden, but he wasn't good enough for her, no ma'am, an' all on account of Mr. Guest.—Yes, indeed. But I must say I feel kind of sorry for him, anyway. He was a real pleasant young man."

" Maurice Guest is quite able to look after himself," said Madeleine drily.

" Is that so? Well, I presume you ought to know, you were once so well acquainted with him—if I may say, Miss Wade, we all thought it was you was his fancy. Yes, indeed."

" Oh, I always knew he liked Louise."

But this was the chief grudge she, too, bore him: that he had been so little open with her. His seeming frankness had been merely a feint; he had gone his own way, and had never really let her know what he was thinking and planning. She now recalled the fact that Louise had only once been mentioned between them, since the time of her illness, over six months ago; and she, Madeleine, had foolishly believed his reticence to be the result of a growing indifference.

Since the night of the ball, they had shunned each other, by tacit consent. But, though she could avoid him in person, Madeleine could not close her ears to the gossipy tales that circulated. In the last few weeks, too, the rumours had become more clamatory: these two misguided creatures had obviously no regard for public opinion; and several times, Madeleine had been obliged to go out of her own way, to escape meeting them face to face. On these occasions, she told herself that she had done with Maurice Guest; and this decision was the more easy as, since the beginning of the year, she had moved almost entirely in German circles. But now the distasteful tattle was thrust under her very nose. It seemed to put things in a different light to hear Maurice pitied and discussed in this very room. In listening to her visitor, she had felt once more how strong her right of possession was in him; she was his oldest friend in Leipzig. Now she was ready to blame herself for having let her umbrage stand in the way of them continuing friends: had he been dropping in as he had formerly done, she might have prevented things from going so far, and certainly have been of use in hindering them from growing worse; for, with Louise, one was never sure. And so she determined to write to him, without delay. In this, though, she was piqued as well by a violent curiosity. Louise said to have given up a good match for his sake!— she could not believe it. It was incredible that she could care for him as he cared for her. Madeleine knew them both too well; Maurice was not the type of man by whom Louise was attracted.

She wrote in a guarded way.

It seems absurd that old friends should behave as we are doing. If anything that happened was my fault, forgive it, and show me you don't bear me a grudge, by coming to see me to-morrow afternoon.

They had not met for close on four months, and, for the first few minutes after his arrival, Madeleine was confused by the change that had taken place in Maurice. It was not only that he was paler and thinner than of old: his boyish manner had deserted him; and, when he forgot himself, his eyes had a strange, brooding expression.

"Other-worldly . . . almost," thought Madeleine; and, in order to surmount an awkwardness she had been resolved not to feel, she talked glibly. Maurice said he could not stay long, and wished to keep his hat in his hand; but before he knew it, he was sitting in his accustomed place on the sofa.

As they stirred their tea, she told him how annoyed she had felt at having recently had a performance postponed in favour of Avery Hill: and how the latter was said to be going crazy, with belief in her own genius. Maurice seemed to be in the dark about what was happening, and made no attempt to hide his ignorance. She could see, too, that he was not interested in these things; he played with a tassel of the sofa, and did not notice when she stopped speaking.

It is his turn now, she said to herself, and left the silence that followed unbroken. Before it had lasted long, however, he looked up from his employment of twisting the tassel as far round as it would go, and then letting it fly back. " I say, Madeleine, now I'm here, there's something I should like to ask you. I hope, though, you won't think it impertinence on my part." He cleared his throat. " Once or twice lately I've heard a report about you—several times, indeed. I didn't pay

any attention to it—not till a few days back, that is—when I
saw it—or thought I saw it—confirmed with my own eyes.   I
was at Bonorand's on Monday evening; I was behind you."

In an instant Madeleine had grasped what he was driving
at.   "Well, and what of that, pray?" she asked.   "Do
you think I should have been there, if I had been ashamed
of it?"

"I saw whom you were with," he went on, and treated the
tassel so roughly that it came away in his hand.   "I say,
Madeleine, it can't be true, what they say—that you are thinking of . . . of marrying that old German?"

Madeleine coloured, but continued to meet his eyes.   "And
why not?" she asked again.—"Don't destroy my furniture,
please."

"Why not?" he echoed, and laid the tassel on the table.
"Well, if you can ask that, I should say you don't know the
facts of the case.   If I had a sister, Madeleine, I shouldn't care
to see her going about with that man.   He's an old—don't you
know he has had two wives, and is divorced from both?"

"Fiddle-dee-dee!   You and your sister!   Do you think a
man is going to come to nearly fifty without knowing something
of life?   That he hasn't been happy in his matrimonial relations is his misfortune, not his fault."

"Then it's true?"

"Why not?" she asked for the third time.

"Then, of course, I've nothing more to say.   I've no right
to interfere in your private affairs.   I hoped I should still be
in time—that's all."

"No, you can't go yet, sit still," she said peremptorily.   "I
too, have something to say.—But will you first tell me, please,
what it can possibly matter to you, whether you are in time, as
you call it, or not?"

"Why, of course, it matters.—We haven't seen much of each
other lately; but you were my first friend here, and I don't
forget it.   Particularly in a case like this, where everything is
against the idea of you marrying this man: your age—your
character—all common sense."

"Those are only words, Maurice.   With regard to my age,
I am over twenty-seven, as you know.   I need no boy of eighteen for a husband.   Then I am plain: I shall never attract
anyone by my personal appearance, nor will a man ever be led
to do foolish things for my sake.   I have worked hard all my
life, and have never known what it is to let to-morrow take

care of itself.—Now here, at last, comes a man of an age not wholly unsuitable to mine, whatever you may say. What though he has enjoyed life? He offers me, not only a certain social standing, but material comfort for the rest of my days. Whereas, otherwise, I may slave on to the end, and die eventually in a governesses' home."

"*You* would never do that. You are not one of that kind. But do you think, for a moment, you'd be happy in such a position of dependence?"

"That's my own affair. There would certainly be nothing extraordinary in it, if I were."

"As you put it, perhaps not. But —— If it were even some one of your own race! But these foreigners think so queerly. And then, too, Madeleine, you'll laugh, I daresay, but I've always thought of you as different from other women —strong and independent, and quite sure of yourself. The kind of girl that makes others seem little and stupid. No one here was good enough for you."

Madeleine's amazement was so great that she did not reply immediately. Then she laughed. "You have far too high an opinion of me. Do you really think I like standing alone? That I do it by preference?—You were never more mistaken, if you do. It has always been a case of necessity with me, no one ever having asked me to try the other way. I suppose like you, they thought I enjoyed it. However, set your mind at rest. Your kind intervention has not come too late. There is still nothing definite."

"I'm glad to hear it."

"I don't say there mayn't be," she added. "Herr Lohse and I are excellent friends, and it won't occur to me not to accept the theatre-tickets and other amusements he is able to give me. —But it is also possible that for the sake of your ideals, I may die a solitary old maid."

Here she was overcome by the comical side of the matter, and burst out laughing.

"What a ridiculous boy you are! If you only knew how you have turned the tables on me. I sent for you, this afternoon, to give you a sound talking-to, and instead of that, here you sit and lecture me."

"Well, if I have achieved something ——"

"It's too absurd," she repeated more tartly. "For you to come here in this way to care for my character, when you yourself are the talk of the place."

His face changed, as she had meant it to do. He choked back a sharp rejoinder. " I'd be obliged, if you'd leave my affairs out of the question."

" I daresay you would. But that's just what I don't intend to do. For if there are rumours going the round about me, what on earth is one to say of you? I needn't go into details. You know quite well what I mean. Let me tell you that your name is in everybody's mouth, and that you are being made to appear not only contemptible, but ridiculous."

" The place is a hot-bed of scandal. I've told you that before," he cried, angry enough now. " These dirty-minded *Musiker* think it outside the bounds of possibility for two people to be friends." But his tone was unsure, and he was conscious of it.

" Yes—when one of the two is Louise."

" Kindly leave Miss Dufrayer out of the question."

" Oh, Maurice, don't Miss Dufrayer me!—I knew Louise before you even knew that she existed.—But answer me one question, and I'm done. Are you engaged to Louise? "

" Most certainly not."

" Well, then, you ought to be.—For though you don't care what people say about yourself, your conscience will surely prick you when you hear that you're destroying the last shred of reputation Louise had left.—I should be sorry to repeat to you what is being said of her."

But after he had gone, she reproached herself for having put such a question to him. At the pass things had reached, it was surely best for him to go through with his infatuation, and get over it. Whereas she, in a spasm of conventionality, had pointed him out the sure road to perdition; for the worst thing that could happen would be for him to bind himself to Louise, in any fashion. As if her reputation mattered! The more rapidly she got rid of what remained to her, the better it would be for every one, and particularly for Maurice Guest.

Had Maurice been in doubt as to Madeleine's meaning, it would have been removed within a few minutes of his leaving the house. As he turned a corner of the Gewandhaus, he came face to face with Krafft. Though they had not met for weeks, Heinrich passed with no greeting but a disagreeable smile. Maurice was not half-way across the road, however, when Krafft came running back, and, taking the lappel of his friend's coat, allowed his wit to play round the talent Maurice displayed for wearing dead men's shoes.

*   *   *   *   *

Carmen was given that night in the theatre; Maurice had fetched tickets from the box-office in the morning. An ardent liking for the theatre had sprung up in Louise of late; and they were there sometimes two or three evenings in succession. Besides this, *Carmen* was her favourite opera, which she never missed. They heard it from the second-top gallery. Leaning back in his corner, Maurice could see little of the stage; but the bossy waves of his companion's head were sharply outlined for him against the opposite tier.

Louise was engrossed in what was happening on the stage; her eyes were wide open, immovable. He had never known anyone surrender himself so utterly to the mimic life of the theatre. Under the influence of music or acting that gripped her, Louise lost all remembrance of her surroundings: she lived blindly into this unreal world, without the least attempt at criticism. Afterwards, she returned to herself tired and dispirited, and with a marked distaste for the dullness of real life. Here, since the first lively clash of the orchestra, since the curtain rose on gay Seville, she had been as far away from him as if she were on another planet. Not, he was obliged to confess to himself, that it made very much difference. Though he was now her constant companion, though his love for her was stronger than it had ever been, he knew less of her to-day than he had known six months ago, when one all-pervading emotion had made her life an open book.

Since that unhappy afternoon on which he learnt the contents of the letter from Dresden, they had spent a part of nearly every day in each other's company. Louise had borne him no malice for what he had said to her; indeed, with the generous forgetfulness of offence, which was one of the most astonishing traits in her character, she met him, the day after, as though nothing had passed between them. By common consent, they never referred to the matter again; Maurice did not know to this day, whether or how she had answered the letter. For, although she had forgiven him, she was not quite the same with him as before; a faint change had come over their relation to each other. It was something so elusive that he could not have defined it; yet nevertheless it existed, and he was often acutely conscious of it. It was not that she kept her thoughts to herself; but she did not say *all* she thought—that was it. And this shade of reserve, in her who had been so frank, ate into him sorely. He accepted it, though, as a chastisement, for he had been in a very contrite frame of mind on awakening to the knowledge that he had all but lost her. And so the days had slipped away. An outsider had first to open his eyes to the fact that it was impossible for things to go on any longer as they were doing; that, for her sake, he must make an end, and quickly.

And yet it had been so easy to drift, so hard to do otherwise, when Louise accepted all he did for her as a matter of course, in that high-handed way of hers which took no account of details. He felt sorry for her, too, for she was not happy. There was a gnawing discontent in her just now, and for this, in great measure, he held himself responsible: for a few weeks she had been buoyed up by the hope of a new life, and he had been the main agent in destroying this hope. In return, he had had nothing to offer her—nothing but a rigid living up to certain uncomfortable ideals, which brought neither change nor pleasure with them: and, despite his belief in the innate nobility of her nature, he could not but recognise that ideals were for her something colder and sterner than for other people.

She made countless demands on his indulgence, and he learnt to see, only too clearly, what a dependent creature she was. It was more than a boon, it was a necessity to her, to have some one at her side who would care for her comfort and well-being. He could not picture her alone; for no one had less talent than she for the trifles that compose life. Her thoughts seemed always to be set on something larger, vaguer, beyond.

He devoted as much time to her as he could spare from his work, and strove to meet her half-way in all she asked. But it was no slight matter; for her changes of mood had never been so abrupt as they were now. He did not know how to treat her. Sometimes, she was cold and unapproachable, so wrapped up in herself that he could not get near her; and perhaps only an hour later, her lips would curve upwards in the smile which made her look absurdly young, and her eyes, too, have all the questioning wonder of a child's. Or she would be silent with him, not unkindly, but silent as a sphinx; and, on the same day, a fit of loquacity would seize her, when she was unable to speak quickly enough for the words that bubbled to her lips. He managed to please her seldomer than ever. But however she behaved, he never faltered. The right to be beside her was now his; and the times she was the hardest on him were the times he loved her best.

As spring, having reached and passed perfection, slipped over into summer, she was invaded by a restlessness that nothing could quell. It got into her hands and her voice, into all her movements, and worked upon her like a fever—like a crying need. So intense did it become that it communicated itself to him also. He, too, began to feel that rest and stillness were impossible for them both, and to be avoided at any cost.

" I have never really seen spring," Louise said to him, one day, in excuse of some irrational impulse that had driven her out of the house. And the quick picture she drew, of how, in her native land, the brief winter passed almost without transition into the scathing summer; her suggestion of unchanging leaves, brown barrenness, and arid dryness; of grass burnt to cinders, of dust, drought, and hot, sandy winds: all this helped him to understand something of what she was feeling. A remembrance of this parched heat was in her veins, making her eager not to miss any of the young, teeming beauty around her, or one of the new strange scents; eager to let the magic of this awakening permeate her and amaze her, like a primeval happening. But, though he thus grasped something of what was going on in her, he was none the less uneasy under it: just as her feverish unburdening of herself after hours of silence, so now her attitude towards this mere change of nature disquieted him; she over-enjoyed it, let herself go in its exuberance. And, as usual, when she lost hold of her nerves, he found himself retreating into his shell, practising self-control for two.

Often, how often he could not count, the words that had to be said had risen to his lips. But they had never crossed them —in spite of the wanton greenness of the woods, which should have been the very frame in which to tell a woman you loved her. But not one drop of her nervous exaltation was meant for him: she had never shown, by the least sign, that she cared a jot for him; and daily he became more convinced that he was chasing a shadow, that he was nothing to her but the *staffage* in the picture of her life. He was torn by doubts, and mortally afraid of the one little word that would put an end to them.

He recollected one occasion when he had nearly succeeded in telling her, and when, but for a trick of fate, he would have done so. They were on their way home from the *Nonne,* where the delicate undergrowth of the high old trees was most prodigal, and where Louise had closed her eyes, and drunk in the rich, earthy odours. They had paused on the suspension-bridge, and stood, she with one ungloved hand on the railing, to watch the moving water. Looking at her, it had seemed to him that just on this afternoon, she might listen to what he had to say with a merciful attentiveness; she was quiet, and her face was gentle. He gripped the rail with both hands. But, before he could open his lips, a third person turned from the wood-path on to the bridge, making it tremble with his steps—a jaunty cavalry officer, with a trim moustache and bright dancing eyes. He walked past them, but threw a searching look at Louise, and, a little further along the bridge, stood still, as if to watch something that was floating in the water, in reality to look covertly back at her. She had taken no notice of him as he passed, but when he paused, she raised her head; and then she looked at him—with a preoccupied air, it was true, but none the less steadily, and for several seconds on end. The words died on Maurice's lips: and going home, he was as irresponsive as she herself . . .

"I love you, Louise—love you." He said it now, sitting back in his dark corner in the theatre; but amid the buzz and hum of the music, and the shouting of the toreadors, he might have called the words aloud, and still she would not have heard them.

Strangely enough, however, at this moment, for the first time during the evening, she turned her head. His eyes were fixed on her, in a dark, exorbitant gaze. Her own face hardened.

"The opera-glass!"

Maurice opened the leather case, and gave her the glass. Their fingers met, and hers groped for a moment round his hand. He withdrew it as though her touch had burnt him. Louise flashed a glance at him, and laid the opera-glass on the ledge in front of her, without making use of it.

Slowly the traitorous blood subsided. To the reverberating music, which held all ears, and left him sitting alone with his fate, Maurice had a moment of preternatural clearness. He realised that only one course was open to him, and that was to go away. *Bei Nacht und Nebel,* if it could not be managed otherwise, but, however it happened, he must go. More wholly for her sake than Madeleine had dreamed of: unless he wanted to be led into some preposterous folly that would embitter the rest of his life. Who could say how long the wall he had built up round her—of the knowledge he shared with her, of pity for what she had undergone—would stand against the onset of this morbid, overmastering desire?

To the gay, feelingless music, he thought out his departure in detail, sparing himself nothing.

But in the long interval after the second act, when they were downstairs on the *loggia,* where it was still half daylight; where the lights of cafés and street-lamps were only beginning here and there to dart into existence; where every man they met seemed to notice Louise with a start of attention: here Maurice was irrevocably convinced that it would be madness to resign his hard-won post without a struggle. For that it would long remain empty, he did not for a moment delude himself.

They hardly exchanged a word during the remainder of the evening. His mouth was dry. Carmen, and her gaudy fate, drove past him like the phantasmagoria of a sleepless night.

When the opera was over, and they stood waiting for the crowd to thin, he scanned his companion's face with anxiety, to discover her mood. With her hand on the wire ledge, Louise watched the slow fall of the iron curtain. Her eyes were heavy; she still lived in what she had seen.

Her preoccupation continued as they crossed the square; her movements were listless. Maurice's thoughts went back to a similar night, a year ago, when, for the first time, he had walked at her side: it had been just such a warm, lilac-scented night as this, and then, as now, he had braced himself up to speak. At that time he had known her but slightly; perhaps, for that very reason, he had been bolder in taking the plunge.

He turned and looked at her. Her face was averted: he could only see the side of her cheek, and the clear-cut line of her chin.

"Are you tired, Louise?" he asked, and, in the protective tenderness of his tone, her name sounded like a term of endearment.

She made a vague gesture, which might signify either yes or no.

"It was too hot for you up there, to-night," he went on. "Next time, I shall take you a seat downstairs—as I've always wanted to." As she still did not respond, he added, in a changed voice: "Altogether, though, it will be better for you to get accustomed to going alone to the theatre."

She turned at this, with an indolent curiosity. "Why?"

" Because—why, because it will soon be necessary. I'm going away."

He had made a beginning now, clumsily, and not as he had intended, but it was made, and he would stand fast.

" You are going away? "

She said each word distinctly, as if she doubted her ears.

" Yes."

" Why, Maurice? "

" For several reasons. It's not a new decision. I've been thinking about it for some time."

" Indeed? Then why choose just to-night to tell me?— you've had plenty of other chances. And to-night I had en- joyed the theatre, and the music, and coming out into the air . . . "

" I'm sorry. But I've put it off too long as it is. I ought to have told you before.—Louise . . . you must see that things can't go on like this any longer? "

His voice begged her for once to look at the matter as he did. But she heard only the imperative.

" Must? " she repeated. " I don't see—not at all."

" Yes.—For your sake, I must go."

" Ah!—that makes it clearer. People have been talking, have they? Well, let them talk."

" I can't hear you spoken of in that way."

" Oh, you're very good. But if we, ourselves, know that what's being said is not true, what can it matter? "

" I refuse to be the cause of it."

" Do you, indeed? " She laughed. " You refuse? After do- ing all you can to make yourself indispensable, you now say: get on as best you can alone; I've had enough; I must go.—Don't say it's on my account—that the thought of yourself is not at the bottom of it—for I wouldn't believe you though you did."

" I give you my word, I have only thought of you. I meant it . . . I mean it, for the best."

She quickened her steps, and he saw that she was nervously worked up.

" No man can want to injure the woman he respects—as I respect you."

Her shoulders rose, in her own emotional way.

" But tell me one thing," he begged, as she walked in- exorable before him. " Say it will matter a little to you if I go—that you will miss me—if ever so little . . . Louise! "

" Miss you? What does it matter whether I miss you or

not? It seems to me that counts least of all. You, at any rate, will have acted properly. You will have nothing to reproach yourself with.—Oh, I wouldn't be a man for anything on earth! You are all—all alike. I hate you and despise you—every one of you!"

They were within a few steps of the house. She pressed on, and, without looking back at him, or wishing him good-night, disappeared in the doorway.

XII

It was a hot evening in June: the perfume of the lilac, now in fullest bloom, lay over squares and gardens like a suspended wave. The sun had gone down in a cloudless sky; an hour afterwards, the pavements were still warm to the touch, and the walls of the buildings radiated the heat they had absorbed. The high old houses in the inner town had all windows set open, and the occupants leaned out on their window-cushions, with continental nonchalance. The big garden-cafés were filled to the last seat. In the woods, the midges buzzed round people's heads in accompanying clouds; and streaks of treacherous white mist trailed, like fixed smoke, over the low-lying meadow-land.

Maurice and Louise had rowed to Connewitz; but so late in the evening that most of the variously shaped boats, with coloured lanterns at their bows, were returning when they started.

Louise herself had proposed it. When he went to her that afternoon, he found her stretched on the sofa. A theatre-ticket lay on the table—for she had taken him at his word, and shown him that she could do without him. But to-night she had no fancy for the theatre: it was too hot. She looked very slight and young in her white dress; but was moody and out of spirits.

On the way to Connewitz, they spoke no more than was necessary. Coming back, however, they had the river to themselves; and she no longer needed to steer. He placed cushions for her at the bottom of the boat; and there she lay, with her hands clasped under her neck, watching the starry strip of sky, which followed them, between the tops of the trees above, like a complement of the river below.

The solitude was unbroken; they might have gone down in the murky water, and no one would ever know how it had happened: a snag caught unawares; a clumsy movement in the light boat; half a minute, and all would be over.—Or, for the first and the last time in his life, he would take her in his arms, hold her to him, feel her cheek on his; he would kiss her, with kisses that were at once an initiation and a farewell; then, covering her eyes with his hands, he would gently, very gently, tilt the boat. A moment's hesitation; it sought to right itself; rocked violently, and overturned: and beneath it, locked in each other's arms, they found a common grave. . . .

In fancy, he saw it all. Meanwhile, he rowed on, with long, leisurely strokes; and the lapping of the water round the oars was the only sound to be heard.

At home, on the lid of his piano, lay the prospectuses of music-schools in other towns. They were still arriving, in answer to the impulsive letters he had written off, the night after the theatre. But the last to come had remained unopened. —He was well aware of it: his lingering on had all the appearance of a weak reluctance to face the inevitable. For he could never make mortal understand what he had come through, in the course of the past week. He could no more put into words the isolated spasms of ecstasy he had experienced—when nothing under the sun seemed impossible—than he could describe the slough of misery and uncertainty, which, on occasion, he had been forced to wade through. For the most part, he believed that the words of contempt Louise had spoken, came straight from her heart; but he had also known the faint stirring of a new hope, and particularly was this the case when he had not seen Louise for some time. Then, at night, as he lay staring before him, this feeling became a sudden refulgence, which lighted him through all the dark hours, only to be remorselessly extinguished by daylight. Most frequently, however, it was so slender a hope as to be a mere distracting flutter at his heart. Whence it sprang, he could not tell—he knew Louise too well to believe, for a moment, that she would make use of pique to hide her feelings. But there was a something in her manner, which was strained; in the fact that she, who had never cared, should at length be moved by words of his; in a certain way she had looked at him, once or twice in these days; or in a certain way she had avoided looking at him. No, he did not know what it was. But nevertheless it was there—a faint, inarticulate existence—and, compared with it, the tangible facts of life were the shadows of a shadow.

Surely she had fallen asleep. He said her name aloud, to try her. "Louise!" She did not stir, and the word floated out into the night—became an expression of the night itself.

They had passed the weir and its foaming, and now glided under the bridges that spanned the narrower windings of the river. The wooden bathing-house looked awesome enough to harbour mysteries. Another sharp turn, among sedge and rushes, and the outlying streets of the town were on their right. The boat-sheds were in darkness, when they drew up alongside the narrow landing-place. Maurice got out with the chain in his hand, and secured the boat. Louise did not follow immediately: her hair had come down, and she was stiff from the cramped position in which she had been lying. When she did rise to her feet, she could hardly stand. He put out his hand, and steadied her by the arm.

"A heavy dew must be falling. Your sleeve is wet."

She made a movement to draw her arm away; at the same moment, she tangled her foot in her skirt, tripped, and, if he had not caught her, would have fallen forward.

"Take care what you're doing! Do you want to drown yourself?"

"I don't know. I shouldn't mind, I think," she answered tonelessly.

His own balance had been endangered. Directly he had righted himself, he set her from him. But it could not be undone: he had had her in his arms, felt all her weight on him. The sensation seemed to take his strength away: after the long, black, silent evening, her body was doubly warm, doubly real. He walked her back, along the deserted streets, at a pace she could not keep up with. She lagged behind. She was very pale, and her face wore an expression of almost physical suffering. She looked resolutely away from Maurice; but when her eyes did chance to rest on him, she was swept by such a sense of nervous irritation that she hated the sight of him, as he walked before her.

Upstairs, in her room, when he had laid the cushions on the sofa; when the lamp was lighted and set on the table; when he still stood there, pale, and wretched, and undecided, Louise came to an abrupt decision. Advancing to the table, she leaned her hands on it, and bending forward, raised her white face to his.

"You told me you were going away; why do you not go? Why have you not already gone?" she asked, and her mouth was hard. "I am waiting . . . expecting to hear."

His answer was so hasty that it was all but simultaneous.

"Louise!—can't you forgive me?—for what I said the other night?"

"I have nothing to forgive," she replied, coldly in spite of herself. "You said you must go. I can't keep you here against your will."

"It has made you angry with me. I have made you un-happy."

"You are making us both unhappy," she said in a low voice. "Now, it is I who say, things can't go on like this."

"I know it." He drew a deep breath. "Louise! . . . if only you could care a little! "

There was silence after these words, but not a silence of conclusion; both knew now that more must follow. He raised his head, and looked into her eyes.

"Can you not see how I love you—and how I suffer? "

It was a statement rather than a question, but he was not aware of this: he was only amazed that, after all, he should be able to speak so quietly, in such an even tone of voice.

There was another pause of suspense; his words seemed like balls of down that he had tossed into the still air: they sank, lingeringly, without haste; and she stood, and let them descend on her. His haggard eyes hung on her face; and, as he watched, he saw a change come over it: the enmity that had been in it, a few seconds back, died out; the lips softened and relaxed; and when the eyes were raised to his again, they were kind, full of pity.

"I'm sorry. Poor boy . . . poor Maurice."

She seemed to hesitate; then, with one of her frankest ges-tures, held out her hand. At its touch, soft and living, he forgot everything: plans and resolutions, hopes and despairs, happiness and unhappiness no longer existed for him; he knew only that she was sorry for him, that some swift change in her had made her sympathise and understand. He looked down, with dim eyes, at the sweet, pale face, now alight with compassion; then, with disarming abruptness, he took her head between his hands, and kissed her, repeatedly, where-ever his lips chanced to fall—on the warm mouth, the closed eyes, temples, and hair.

He was gone before she recovered from her surprise. She had instinctively stemmed her hands against his shoulders; but, when she was alone, she stood just as he left her, her eyes still shut, letting the sensation subside, of rough, unexpected kisses. She had been taken unawares; her heart was beating. For a moment or two, she remained in the same attitude; then she passed her hand over her face. "That was foolish of him . . . very," she said. She looked down at herself and saw her hands. She stretched them out before her, with a sudden sense of emptiness.

"If I could care! Yes—if I could only care!"

At two o'clock that morning, Maurice wrote:

Forgive me—I didn't know what I was doing. For I love you, Louise—no woman has ever been loved as you are. I know it is folly on my part. I have nothing to offer you. But be my wife, and I will work my fingers to the bone for you.

He went out into the summer night, and posted the letter. Returning to his room, he threw himself on the sofa, and fell into a heavy sleep, from which he did not wake till the morning was well advanced.

Work was out of the question that day, when he waited as if for a sentence of death. He paced his narrow room, incessantly, afraid to go out, for fear of missing her reply. The hours dragged themselves by, as it is their special province to do in crises of life; and with each one that passed, he grew more convinced what her answer to his letter would be.

It was late in the afternoon when the little boy she employed as a messenger, put a note into his hands.

Come to me this evening.

It was all but evening now; he went, just as he was, on the heels of the child.

The windows of her room were open. She sprang up to meet him, then paused. He looked desperately yet stealthily at her. The commiseration of the previous night was still in her face; but she was now quite sure of herself: she drew him to the sofa and made him sit down beside her. Then, however, for a few seconds, in which he waited with hammering pulses, she did not speak. The dull fear at his heart became a certainty; and, unable to bear the suspense any longer, he took one of her hands and laid it on his forehead.

Then she said: "Maurice—poor, foolish Maurice!—it is not possible. You see that yourself, I'm sure."

"Yes. I know quite well: it is presumption."

"Oh, I don't mean that. But there are so many reasons. And you, too, Maurice . . . Look at me, and tell me if what you wrote was not just an attempt to make up for what happened last night." And as he did not reply, she added: "You mustn't make yourself reproaches. I, too, was to blame."

"It was nothing of the sort. I've been trying for weeks

now to tell you. I love you—have loved you since the first time I saw you."

He let go of her hand, and she sat forward, with her arms along her knees. Her eyes were troubled; but she did not lose her calm manner of speaking. "I'm sorry, Maurice, very sorry—you believe me, don't you, when I say so? But believe me, too, it's not so serious as you think. You are young. You will get over it, and forget—if not soon, at least in time. You must forget me, and some day you will meet the nice, good woman, who is to be your wife. And when that happens, you will look back on your fancy for me as something foolish, and unreal. You won't be able to understand it then, and you will be grateful to me, for not having taken you at your word."

Maurice laughed. All the same, he tried to bear his dismissal well: he rose, wrung her hand, and left her.

In the seclusion of his own room, he went through the blackest hour of his life.

He began to make final preparations for his departure. His choice had fallen on Stuttgart: it was far distant from Leipzig; he would be well out of temptation's way—the temptation suddenly to return. He wrote a letter home, apprising his relatives of his intention: by the time they received the letter, it would be too late for them to interfere. Otherwise, he took no one into his confidence. He would greatly have liked to wait until the present term was over; another month, and the summer vacation would have begun, and he would have been able to leave without making himself conspicuous. But every day it grew more impossible to be there and not to see her— for four days now he had kept away, fighting down his unreasoning desire to know what she was doing. He intended only to see her once more, to bid her good-bye.

The afternoon before his interview with Schwarz—he had arranged this with himself for the morning, at the master's private house—he sat at his writing-table, destroying papers and old letters. There was a heap of ashes in the cold stove by the time he took out, tied up in a separate packet, the few odd scraps of writing he had received from Louise. He balanced the bundle in his hand, hesitating what to do with it. Finally, he untied the string, to glance through the letters once again.

At the sight of the bold, black, familiar writing, in which each word—two or three to a line—seemed to have a life of its own; at the well-conned pages, each of which he knew by

23

heart; at the characteristic, almost masculine signature, and the faint perfume that still clung to the paper: at the sight of these things all that he had been thinking and planning since seeing her last, was effaced from his mind. As often before, where she was concerned, a wild impulse, surging up in him, took entire possession of him; and hours of patient and laborious reasoning were by one swift stroke blotted out.

He rose, locked the letters up again, rested his arm on the lid of the piano, his head on his arm. The more he toyed with his inclination to go to her, the more absorbent it became, and straightway it was an ungovernable longing: it came over him with a dizzy force, which made him close his eyes; and he was as helpless before it as the drunkard before his craving to drink. Standing thus, he saw with a flash of insight that, though he went away as far as steam could carry him, he would never, as long as he lived, be safe from overthrows of this kind. It was something elemental, which he could no more control than the flow of his blood. And he did not even stay to excuse himself to himself: he went headlong to her, with burning words on his lips.

"My poor boy," she said, when he ceased to speak. "Yes, I know what it is—that sudden rage that comes over one, to rush back, at all costs, no matter what happens afterwards.— I'm so sorry for you, Maurice. It is making me unhappy."

"You are not to be unhappy. It shall not happen again, I promise you.—Besides, I shall soon be gone now." But at his own words, the thought of his coming desolation pierced him anew. "Give me just one straw to cling to! Tell me you won't forget me all at once; that you will miss me and think of me—if ever so little."

"You asked me that the other night. Was what I said then, not answer enough?—And besides, in these last four days, since I have been alone, I've learnt just how much I shall miss you, Maurice. It's my punishment, I suppose, for growing so dependent on anyone."

"You must go away, too. You can't stay here by yourself. We must both go, in opposite directions, and begin afresh."

She did not reply at once. "I shouldn't know where to go," she said, after a time. "Will nothing else do, Maurice? Is there no other way?—Oh, why can't we go on being friends, as we were!"

He shook his head. "I've struggled against it so long—you don't know. I've never really been your friend—only I couldn't hurt you before, by telling you. And it has worn me out; I'm good for nothing. Louise!—think, just once more —ask yourself, once more, if it's quite impossible, before you send me into the outer darkness."

She was silent.

"I don't ask you to love me," he went on, in a low voice. "I've come down from that, in these wretched days. I would be content with less, much less. I only ask you to let yourself be loved—as I could love you. If only you could say you liked me a little, all the rest would come, I'm confident of it. In time, I should make you love me. For I would take, oh, such care of you! I want to make you happy, only to make you happy. I've no other wish than to show you what happiness is."

"It sounds so good . . . you are good, Maurice. But the future—tell me, have thought of the future?"

"I should think I have.—Do you suppose it means nothing to me to be so despicably poor as I am? To have absolutely nothing to offer you?"

She took his hand. "That's not what I mean. And you know it. Come, let us talk sensibly this afternoon, and look things straight in the face.—You want to marry me, you say, and let the rest come? That is very, very good of you, and I shall never forget it.—But what does it mean, Maurice? You have been here a little over a year now, haven't you?— and still have about a year to stay. When that's over, you will go back to England. You will settle in some small place, and spend your life, or the best part of your life, there—oh, Maurice, you are my kind friend, but I tell you frankly, I couldn't face life in an English provincial town. I'm not brave enough for that."

He gleaned a ray of hope from her words. "We could live here—anywhere you liked. I would make it possible. I swear I would."

She shook her head, and went on, with the same reasonable sweetness. "And then, there's another thing. If I married you, sooner or later you would have to take me home to your people. Have you really thought of that, and how you would feel about it, when it came to the point?—No, no, it's impossible for me to marry you."

"But that—that American!—you would have married him?"

"That was different," she said, and her voice grew thinner.

" It's the knowing that tells, Maurice. You would have that still to learn. You don't realise it yet, but afterwards, it would come home to you.—Listen! You have always been kind to me, I owe you such a debt of gratitude, that I'm going to be frank, brutally frank with you. I've told you often that I shall never really care for anyone again. You know that, don't you? Well, I want to tell you, too—I want you to understand quite, quite clearly that . . . that I belonged to him altogether—entirely—that I . . . Oh, you know what I mean ! "

Maurice covered his face with his hands. " The past is the past. It should never be mentioned between us. It doesn't matter—nothing matters now."

" You say that—every one says that—beforehand," she an- swered; and not only her words, but also her way of saying them, seemed to set her down miles away from him, on a lonely pinnacle of experience. " Afterwards, you would think dif- ferently."

" Louise, if you really cared, it would be different. You wouldn't say such things, then—you would be only too glad not to say them."

In her heart she knew that he was right, and did not con- tradict him. The busy little clock on the writing-table ticked away a few seconds. With a jerk, Maurice rose to his feet. Louise remained sitting, and he looked down on her black head. His gaze was so insistent that she felt it, and raised her eyes. His forlorn face moved her.

" Why is it—what is the matter with me?—that I must upset your life like this? I can't bear to see you so unhappy.— And yet I haven't done anything, have I? I have always been honest .with you; I've never made myself out to be better than I am. There must be something wrong with me, I think, that no one can ever be satisfied to be just my friend.—Yet with you I thought it was different. I thought things could go on as they were. Maurice, isn't it possible? Say it is! Show me just one little spark of good in myself! "

" I'm not different from other men, Louise. I deluded my- self long enough, God knows! "

She made a despondent gesture, and turned away. " Well, then, if either of us should go, I'm the one. You have your work. I do nothing; I have no ties, no friends—I never even seem to have been able to make acquaintances. And if I went, you could stay quietly on. In time, you would forget me.—

If I only knew where to go! I am so alone, and it is all so hard. I shall never know what it is to be happy myself, or to make anyone else happy—never!" and she burst into tears.

It was his turn now to play the comforter. Drawing a chair up before her, he took her hand, and said all he could think of to console her. He could bear anything, he told her, but to see her unhappy. All would yet turn out to be for the best. And, on one point, she was to set her mind at rest: her going away would not benefit him in the least. He would never consent to stay on alone, where they had been so much together.

"I've nothing to look forward to, nothing," she sobbed. "There's nothing I care to live for."

As soon as she was quieter, he left her.

For an hour or more Louise lay huddled up on the sofa, with her face pressed to her arm.

When she sat up again, she pushed back her heavy hair, and, clasping her hands loosely round her knees, stared before her with vacant eyes. But not for long; tired though she was, and though her head ached from crying, there was still a deep residue of excitement in her. The level beams of the sun were pouring blindly into the room; the air was dense and oppressive. She rose to her feet and moved about. She did not know what to do with herself: she would have liked to go out and walk; but the dusty, jarring light of the summer streets frightened her. She thought of music, of the theatre, as a remedy for the long evening that yawned before her: then dismissed the idea from her mind. She was in such a condition of restlessness, this night, that the fact of being forced to sit still between two other human beings, would make her want to scream.

The sun was getting low; the foliage of the trees in the opposite gardens was black, with copper edges, against the refulgence of the sky. She leaned her hands on the sill, and gazed fixedly at the stretch of red and gold, which, like the afterglow of a fire, flamed behind the trees. Her eyes were filled with it. She did not think or feel: she became one, by looking, with the sight before her. As she stood there, nothing of her existed but her two widely opened eyes; she was a miracle wrought by the sunset; she *was* the sunset—in one of those vacancies of mind, which all intense gazers know.

How long she had remained thus she could not have told, when a strange thing happened to her. From some sub-conscious layer of her brain, which started into activity because the rest of it was so passive, a small, still thought glided in, and took possession of her mind. At first, it was so faint that she hardly grasped it; but, once established there, it became so vivid that, with one sweep, it blotted out trees and sunset; so real that it seemed always to have been present to her. Without conscious effort on her part, the solution to her difficulties had been found; a decision had been arrived at, but not by her; it was the work of some force outside herself.

She turned from the window, and pressed her hands to her blinded eyes. Good God! it was so simple. To think that this had not occurred to her before!—that, throughout the troubled afternoon, the idea had never once suggested itself! There was no need of loneliness and suffering for either of them. He might stay; they both might stay; she could make him happy, and ward off the change she so dreaded.—Who was she to stick at it?

But she remained dazed, doubtful as it were of this peaceful ending; her hand still covered her eyes. Then, with one of the swift movements by which it was her custom to turn thought into action, she went to the writing-table, and scrawled a few, big words.

Maurice, I have found a way. Come back to-morrow evening.

She hesitated only over the last two words, and, before writing them, sat with her chin in her hand, and deliberately considered. Then she addressed the envelope, and stamped it: it would be soon enough if he got it through the post, the following morning.

But, with her, to resolve was to act; she was ill at ease under enforced procrastination; and had often to fight against a burning impatience, when circumstances delayed the immediate carrying out of her will. In this case, however, she had voluntarily postponed Maurice's return for twenty-four hours, when he might have been with her in less than one: for, in her mind, there lurked the seductive thought of a long, summer day, with an emotion at its close to which she could look forward.

In the meantime, she was puzzled how to fill up the evening. After all, she decided to go to the theatre, where she arrived in time to hear the last two acts of *Aïda*. From a seat in the *parquet,* close to the orchestra, she let the showy music play round her. Afterwards, she walked home through the lilac-haunted night, went to bed, and at once fell asleep.

Next morning, she wakened early—that was the sole token of disturbance, she could detect in herself. It was very still; there was a faint twittering of birds, but the noises of the street had not yet begun. She lay in the subdued yellow light of her room, with one arm across her eyes.

Fresh from sleep, she understood certain things as never before. She saw all that had happened of late—her slow recovery, her striving and seeking, her growing friendship with Maurice—in a different light. On this morning, too, she was able to answer one of the questions that had puzzled her the night before. She saw that the relations in which they had stood to each other, during the bygone months, would have been impossible, had she really cared for him. She liked him, yes, had always liked him; and, in addition, his patience and kindness had made her deeply grateful to him. But that was all. Neither his hands, nor his voice, nor his eyes, nor anything he did, had had the power to touch her—*so* to touch her, that her own hands and eyes would have met his half-way; that the old familiar craving, which was partly fear and partly attraction, would have made her callous to his welfare. Had there been a breath of this, things would have come to a climax long ago. Hot and eager as she was, she could not have lived on coolly at his side—and, at this moment, she found it difficult to make up her mind whether she admired Maurice or the reverse, for having been able to carry his part through.

And yet, though no particle of personal feeling drew her to him, she, too, had suffered, in her own way, during these weeks of morbid tension, when he had been incapable either of advancing or retreating. How great the strain had been, she recognised only in the instant when he had spanned the breach, in clear, unmistakable words. If he had not done it, she would have been forced to; for she could never find herself to rights, for long, in half circumstances: if she were not to grow bewildered, she had to see her road simple and straight before her. His words to her after they had been on the river together—more, perhaps, his bold yet timid kisses—had given her back strength and assurance. She was no longer the miserable instrument on which he tried his changes of mood; she was again the giver and the bestower, since she held a heart and a heart's happiness in the hollow of her hand.

What people would think and say was a matter of indif-

ference to her: besides, they practically believed the worst of her
already. No; she had nothing to lose and, it might be, much to
gain. And after all, it meant so little! The first time, perhaps; or if one cared too much. But in this case, where she
had herself well in hand, and where there was no chance of the
blind desire to kill self arising, which had been her previous
undoing; where the chief end aimed at was the retention of a
friend—here, it meant nothing at all.

The thought that she might possibly have scruples on his
part to combat, crossed her mind. She stretched her arm
straight above her head, then laid it across her eyes again. She
would like him none the less for these scruples, did they exist:
now, she believed that, at heart, she had really appreciated his
reserve, his holding back, where others would have been so
ready to pounce in. For the first time, she considered him
in the light of a lover, and she saw him differently. As if the
mere contemplation of such a change brought her nearer to him,
she was stirred by a new sensation, which had him as its object.
And under the influence of this feeling, she told herself that
perhaps just in this gentler, kindlier love, which only sought
her welfare, true happiness lay. She strained to read the
future. There would be storms neither of joy nor of pain;
but watchful sympathy, and the fine, manly tenderness that
shields and protects. Oh, what if after all her passionate craving for happiness, it was here at her feet, having come to her
as good things often do, unexpected and unsought!

She could lie still no longer; she sprang up, with an alacrity
that had been wanting in her movements of late. And throughout the long day, this impression, which was half a hope and
half a belief, was present to her mind, making everything she
did seem strangely festive. She almost feared the moment when
she would see him again, lest anything he said should dissipate
her hope.

When he came, her eyes followed him searchingly. With an
instinct that was now morbidly sharpened, Maurice was aware
of the change in her, even before he saw her eyes. His own
were one devouring question.

She made him sit down beside her.

" What is it, Louise? Tell me—quickly. Remember, I've
been all day in suspense," he said, as seconds passed and she did
not speak.

" You got my note then? "

" What is it?—what did you mean? "

"Just a little patience, Maurice. You take one's breath away. You want to know everything at once. I sent for you because—oh, because . . . I want you to let us go on being friends."

"Is that all?" he cried, and his face fell. "When I have told you again and again that's just what I can't do?"

She smiled. "I wish I had known you as a boy, Maurice—oh, but as quite a young boy!" she said in such a changed voice that he glanced up in surprise. Whether it was the look she bent on him, or her voice, or her words, he did not know; but something emboldened him to do what he had often done in fancy: he slid to his knees before her, and laid his head on her lap. She began to smooth back his hair, and each time her hand came forward, she let it rest for a moment.—She wondered how he would look when he knew.

"You can't care for me, I know. But I would give my life to make you happy."

"Why do you love me?" She experienced a new pleasure in postponing his knowing, postponing it indefinitely.

"How can I say? All I know is how I love you—and how I have suffered."

"My poor Maurice," she said, in the same caressing way. "Yes, I shall always call you poor.—For the love I could give you would be worthless compared with yours."

"To me it would be everything.—If you only knew how I have longed for you, and how I have struggled!"

He took enough of her dress to bury his face in. She sat back, and looked over him into the growing dusk of the room: and, in the alabaster of her face, nothing seemed to live except her black eyes, with the half-rings of shadow.

Suddenly, with the unexpectedness that marked her movements when she was very intent, she leant forward again, and, with her elbow on her knee, her chin on her hand, said in a low voice: "Is it for ever?"

"For ever and ever."

"Say it's for ever." She still looked past him, but her lips had parted, and her face wore the expression of a child's listening to fairy-tales. At her own words, a vista seemed to open up before her, and, at the other end, in blue haze, shone the great good that had hitherto eluded her.

"I shall always love you," said the young man. "Nothing can make any difference."

"For ever," she repeated. "They are pretty words."

Then her expression changed; she took his head between her hands.

"Maurice . . . I'm older than you, and I know better than you, what all this means. Believe me, I'm not worth your love. I'm only the shadow of my old self. And you are still so young and so . . . so untried. There's still time to turn back, and be wise."

He raised his head.

"What do you mean? Why are you saying these things? I shall always love you. Life itself is nothing to me, without you. I want you . . . only you."

He put his arms round her, and tried to draw her to him. But she held back. At the expression of her face, he had a moment of acute uncertainty, and would have loosened his hold. But now it was she who knotted her hands round his neck, and gave him a long, penetrating look. He was bewildered; he did not understand what it meant; but it was something so strange that, again, he had the impulse to let her go. She bent her head, and laid her face against his; cheek rested on cheek. He took her face between his hands, and stared into her eyes, as if to tear from them what was passing in her brain. Over both, in the same breath, swept the warm, irresistible wave of self-surrender. He caught her to him, roughly and awkwardly, in a desperate embrace, which the kindly dusk veiled and redeemed.

XIII

" Now you will not leave me, Maurice? "

" Never . . . while I live."

" And you . . ."

" No. Don't ask me yet. I can't tell you."

" Maurice! "

" Forgive me! Not yet. That after all you should care a little! After all . . . that you should care so much! "

" And it is for ever? "

" For ever and ever . . . what do you take me for? But not here! Let us go away—to some new place. We will make it our very own."

Their words came in haste, yet haltingly; were all but inaudible whispers; went flying back and forwards, like brief cries for aid, implying a peculiar sense of aloofness, of being cut adrift and thrown on each other's mercy.

Louise raised her head.

" Yes, we will go away. But now, Maurice—at once! "

" Yes. To-night . . . to-morrow . . . when you like."

The next morning, he set out to find a place. Three weeks of the term had still to run, and he was to have played in an *Abendunterhaltung,* before the vacation. But, compared with the emotional upheaval he had undergone, this long-anticipated event was of small consequence. To Schwarz, he alleged a succession of nervous headaches, which interfered with his work. His looks lent colour to the statement; and though, as a rule, highly irritated by opposition to his plans, Schwarz only grumbled in moderation. He would have let no one else off so easily, and, at another time, the knowledge of this would have rankled in Maurice, as affording a fresh proof of the master's indifference towards him. As it was, he was thankful for the freedom it secured him.

On the strength of a chance remark of Madeleine's, which he had remembered, he found what he looked for, without difficulty. It could not have been better: a rambling inn, with restaurant, set in a clearing on the top of a wooded hill, with an open view over the undulating plains.

That night, he wrote to Louise from the Rochlitzer Berg, painting the nest he had found for them in glowing colours,

and begging her to come without delay.   But the whole of the
next day passed without a word from her, and the next again,
and not till the morning of the third, did he receive a note,
announcing her arrival for shortly after midday.   He took it
with him to the woods, and lay at full length on the moss.

Although he had been alone now for more than forty-eight
hours—a July quiet reigned over the place—he had not managed
to think connectedly.   He was still dazed, disbelieving of what
had happened.   Again and again he told himself that his dreams
and hopes—which he had always pushed forward into a vague
and far-off future—had actually come to pass.   She was his,
all his; she had given herself ungrudgingly: as soon as he could
make it possible, she would be his wife.   But, in the meantime, this was all he knew: his nearer vision was obstructed
by the stupefying thought of the weeks to come.   She was to
be there, beside him, day after day, in a golden paradise of love.
He could only think of it with moist eyes; and he swore to himself that he would repay her by being more infinitely careful
of her than ever man before of the woman he loved.   But
though he repeated this to himself, and believed it, his feelings had unwittingly changed their pole.   On his knees before
her, he had vowed that her happiness was the end of all his
pleading; now it was frankly happiness he sought, the happiness of them both, but, first and foremost, happiness.   And it
could hardly have been otherwise: the one unpremeditated
mingling of their lives had killed thought; he could only feel
now, and, throughout these days, he was conscious of each movement he made, as of a song sung aloud.   He wandered up and
down the wooded paths, blind to everything but the image of
her face, which was always with him, and oftenest as it had
bent over him that last evening, with the strange new fire in
its eyes.   Closing his own, he felt again her arms on his shoulders, her lips meeting his, and, at such moments, it could happen
that he threw his arms round a tree, in an ungovernable rush
of longing.   Beyond the moment when he should clasp her to
him again, he could not see: the future was as indistinct as were
the Saxon plains, in the haze of morning or evening.

He set out to meet her far too early in the day, and when
he had covered the couple of miles that lay between the inn on
the hill and the railway-station at the foot, he was obliged to
loiter about the sleepy little town for over an hour.   But
gradually the time ticked away; the hands of his watch pointed
to a quarter to two, and presently he found himself on the

shadeless, sandy station which lay at the end of a long, sandy street, edged with two rows of young and shadeless trees; found himself looking along the line of rail that was to bring her to him. Would the signal never go up? He began to feel, in spite of the strong July sunlight, that there was something illusive about the whole thing. Or perhaps it was just this harsh, crude light, without relieving shadows, which made his surroundings seem unreal to him. However it was, the nearer the moment came when he would see her again, the more improbable it seemed that the train, which was even now overdue, should actually be carrying her towards him—her to him! He would yet waken, with a shock. But then, coming round a corner in the distance, at the side of a hill, he saw the train. At first it appeared to remain stationary, then it increased in size, approached, made a slight curve, and was a snaky line; it vanished, and reappeared, leaving first a white trail of cloud, then thick rounded puffs of cloud, until it was actually there, a great black object, with a creak and a rattle.

He had planted himself at the extreme end of the platform, and the carriages went past him. He hastened, almost running, along the train. At the opposite end, a door was opened, the porter took out some bags, and Louise stepped down, and turned to look for him. He was the only person on the station, besides the two officials, and in passing she had caught a glimpse of his face. If he looks like that, every one will know, she thought to herself, and her first words, as he came breathlessly up, were: " Maurice, you mustn't look so glad! "

He had never really seen her till now, when, in a white dress, with eyes and lips alight, she stood alone with him on the wayside platform. To curb his first, impetuous gesture, Louise had stretched out both her hands. He stood holding them, unable to take his eyes from her face. At her movement to withdraw them, he stooped and kissed them.

" Not look glad? Then you shouldn't have come."

They left her luggage to be sent up later in the day, and set out on their walk. Going down the shadeless street, and through the town, she was silent. At first, as they went, Maurice pointed out things that he thought would interest her, and spoke as if he attached importance to them. While, in reality, nothing mattered, now that she was beside him. And gradually, he, too, lapsed into silence, walking by her side across the square, and through the narrow streets, with the solemnly festive feelings of a child on Sunday. They crossed the moat, passed through the gates and courtyard of the old castle, and began to ascend the steep path that was a short-cut to the woods. It was exposed to the full glare of the sun, and, on reaching the sheltering trees, Louise gave a sigh of relief, and stood still to take off her hat.

"It's so hot. And I like best to be bareheaded."

"Yes, and now I can see you better. Is it really you, at last? I still can't believe it.—That you should have come to me!"

"Yes, I'm real," she smiled, and thrust the pins through the crown of the hat. "But very tired, Maurice. It was so hot, and the train was so slow."

"Tired?—of course, you must be. Come, there's a seat just round this corner. You shall rest there."

They sat, and he laid his arm along the back of the bench. With his left hand he turned her face towards him. "I must see you. I expect every minute to wake and find it's not true."

"And yet you haven't even told me you're glad to see me."

"Glad? No. Glad is only a word."

She leaned lightly against the protective pressure of his arm. On one of her hands lying in her lap, a large spot of sunlight settled. He stooped and put his lips to it. She touched his head.

"Were the days long without me?"

"Why didn't you come sooner?"

Not that he cared, or even cared to know, now that she was there. But he wanted to hear her speak, to remember that he could now have her voice in his ears, whenever he chose. But Louise was not disposed to talk; the few words she said, fell unwillingly from her lips. The stillness of the forest laid its spell upon them: each faint rustling among the leaves was audible; not a living thing stirred except themselves. The tall firs and beeches stretched infinitely upwards, and the patches of light that lay here and there on the moss, made the cool darkness seem darker.

When they walked on again, Maurice put his arm through hers, and, in this intimacy of touch, was conscious of every step she took. It made him happy to suit his pace to hers, to draw her aside from a spreading root or loose stone, and to feel her respond to his pressure. She walked for the most part languidly, looking to the ground. But at a thickly wooded turn of the path, where it was very dark, where the sunlight seemed far away, and the pine-scent was more pungent than elsewhere, she stopped, to drink in the spicy air with open lips and nostrils.

" It's like wine. Maurice, I'm glad we came here—that you found this place. Think of it, we might still be sitting indoors, with the blinds drawn, knowing that the pavements were baking in the sun. While here! . . . Oh, I shall be happy here! "

She was roused for a moment to a rapturous content with her surroundings. She looked childishly happy and very young. Maurice pressed her arm, without speaking: he was so foolishly happy that her praise of the place affected him like praise of himself. Again, he had a chastened feeling of exhilaration: as though an acme of satisfaction had been reached, beyond which it was impossible to go.

On catching sight of the rambling wooden building, in the midst of the clearing that had been made among the encroaching trees, Louise gave another cry of pleasure, and before entering the house, went to the edge of the terrace, and looked down on the plains. But upstairs, in her room on the first storey, he made her rest in an arm-chair by the window. He himself prepared the tea, proud to perform the first of the trivial services which, from now on, were to be his. There was nothing he would not do for her, and, as a beginning, he persuaded her to lie down on the sofa and try to sleep.

Once outside again, he did not know how to kill time ; and the remainder of the afternoon seemed interminable. He endeavoured to read, but could not take in the meaning of two consecutive sentences. He was afraid to go far away, in case she should wake and miss him. So he loitered about in the vicinity of the house, and returned every few minutes, to see if her blind were not drawn up. Finally, he sat down at one of the tables on the terrace, where he had her window in sight. Towards six o'clock, his patience was exhausted; going upstairs, he listened outside the door of her room. Not a sound. With infinite precaution, he turned the handle, and looked in.

She was lying just as he had left her, fast asleep. Her head was a little on one side; her left hand was under her cheek, her right lay palm upwards on the rug that covered her. Maurice sat down in the arm-chair.

At first, he looked furtively, afraid of disturbing her; then more openly, in the hope that she would waken. Sitting thus, and thinking over the miracle that had happened to him, he now sought to find something in her face for him alone, which had previously not been there. But his thoughts wandered as he gazed. How he loved it!—this face of hers. He was invariably worked on afresh by the blackness of the lustreless hair; by the pale, imperious mouth; by the dead white pallor of the skin, which shaded to a dusky cream in the curves of neck and throat, and in the lines beneath the eyes was of a bluish brown. Now the lashes lay in these encircling rings. Without doubt, it was the eyes that supplied life to the face: only when they were open, and the lips parted over the strong teeth, was it possible to realise how intense a vitality was latent in her. But his love would wipe out the last trace of this wan tiredness. He would be infinitely careful of her: he would shield her from the impulsiveness of her own nature; she should never have cause to regret what she had done. And the affection that bound them would day by day grow stronger. All his work, all his thoughts, should belong to her alone; she would be his beloved wife; and through him she would learn what love really was.

He rose and stood over her, longing to share his feelings with her. But she remained sunk in her placid sleep, and as he stood, he became conscious of a different sensation. He had never seen her face—except convulsed by weeping—when it was not under full control. Was it because he had stared so long at it, or was it really changed in sleep? There was something about it, at this moment, which he could not explain: it almost looked less fine. The mouth was not so proudly reticent as he had believed it to be; there was even a want of restraint about it; and the chin had fallen. He did not care to see it like this: it made him uneasy. He stooped and touched her hand. She started up, and could not remember where she was. She put both hands to her forehead. " Maurice!—what is it? Have I been asleep long? "

He held his watch before her eyes. With a cry she sprang to her feet. Then she sent him downstairs.

They were the only guests. They had supper alone in a longish room, at a little table spread with a coloured cloth. The window was open behind them, and the branches of the trees outside hung into the room. In honour of the occasion, Maurice ordered wine, and they remained sitting, after they had finished supper, listening to the rustling and swishing of the trees. The only drawback to the young man's happiness was the pertinacious curiosity of the girl who waited on them. She lingered after she had served them, and stared so hard that Maurice turned at length and asked her what the matter was.

The girl coloured to the roots of her hair.

"Ach, Fräulein is so pretty," she answered naïvely, in her broad Saxon dialect.

Both laughed, and Louise asked her name, and if she always lived there. Thus encouraged, Amalie, a buxom, thick-set person, with a number of flaxen plaits, came forward and began to talk. Her eyes were fixed on Louise, and she only occasionally glanced from her to the young man.

" It's nice to have a sweetheart," she said suddenly.

Louise laughed again and coloured. " Haven't you got one, Amalie? "

Amalie shook her head, and launched out into a tale of faith-lessness and desertion. " Yes, if I were as pretty as you, Fräu-lein, it would be a different thing," she ended, with a hearty sigh.

Maurice clattered up from the table. " All right, Amalie, that'll do."

They went out of doors, and strolled about in the twilight. He had intended to show her some of the pretty nooks in the neighbourhood of the house. But she was not as affable with him as she had been with Amalie; she walked at his side with an air of preoccupied indifference.

When they sat down on a seat, on the side of the hill, the moon had risen. It was almost at the full, and a few gently sailing scraps of cloud, which crossed it, made it seem to be coming towards them. The plains beneath were veiled in haze; detached sounds mounted from them: the prolonged barking of a dog, the drone of an approaching train. Round about them, the air was heavy with the scent of the sun-warmed pines. Maurice had taken her hand and sat holding it: it was the one thing that existed for him. All else was vague and un-real: only their two hearts beat in all the universe. But there was no interchange between them of binding words or endear-ments, such as pass between most lovers.

How long they sat, neither could have told. But suddenly, far below, a human voice was raised in a long cry, which echoed against the side of the hill. Louise shivered: and he had a moment of apprehension.

" You're cold. We have sat too long. Let us go."

They rose, and walked slowly back to the house.

Although the doors were still open, the building was in dark-ness, and they had to grope their way up the stairs. Outside her room, he paused to light the candle that was standing on the table, but Louise opened the door and went in. As she did so,

24

she gave a cry. The blind had not been lowered, and a patch of greenish-white moonlight lay on the floor before the window, throwing the rest of the room into massy shadow. She went forward and stood in it.

"Don't make a light," she said to him over her shoulder.

Maurice put down the matches, with which he had been fumbling, went quickly in after her, and shut the door.

Before anyone else was astir, he had flung out into the freshness of the morning. It was cool in the shade of the woods; grass and moss were a little moist with dew. He did not linger under the trees; he needed movement; and striding along the driving-road, which ran down the hill where the incline was easiest, he went out on the plains, among the little villages that dotted the level land like huge clumps of mushrooms. He carried his cap in his hand, and let the early sun play on his head.

When he returned, it was nine o'clock, and he was ravenously hungry. Amalie carried the coffee and the crisp brown rolls to one of the small tables on the terrace, and herself stood, after she had served him, and looked over the edge of the hill. When he had finished eating, he opened a volume of *Dichtung und Wahrheit,* which he carried in his pocket, and began to read. But after a few lines, his thoughts wandered; the book had a chilling effect on him in his present mood; the writing seemed stiff and strained—the work of a very old man.

At first, that morning, he had not ventured to review even in thought the past hours. Now, however, that he was again within a stone's throw of Louise, memories crowded upon him; he gazed, with a passion of gratefulness, at her window. One detail stood out more vividly than all the rest. It was that of waking suddenly at dawn, from a dreamless sleep, and of finding on his pillow, a thick tress of black ruffled hair. For a moment, he had hardly been able to believe his eyes; and even yet, the mere remembrance of this dusky hair on the pillow's whiteness, seemed to bring what had happened home to him, as nothing else could have done.

She had slept on, undisturbed, and she was still asleep, to judge from the lowered blind. But though hours seemed to pass while he sat there, he was not dissatisfied; it was enough to know how near she was to him.

When she came, she was upon him before he was aware of it. At the light step behind, he sprang from his seat.

"At last!"

"Are you tired of waiting for me?"

She was in the same white dress, and a soft-brimmed hat fell over her forehead. He did not answer her words; for Amalie followed on her heels with fresh coffee, and made a great business of re-setting the table.

"*Wünsche guten Appetit!*"

The girl retired to a distance, but still lingered, keeping them in sight. Maurice leaned across the table. "Tell me how you are. Have you forgotten me?" He tried to take her hand.

"Take care, Maurice. We can be seen here."

"How that girl stares! Why doesn't she go away?"

"She is envying me my sweetheart again . . . who won't let me eat my breakfast."

"I've been alone for hours, Louise. Tell me what I want to know."

"Yes—afterwards. The coffee is getting cold."

He sat back and watched her movements, with fanatic eyes. She was not confused by the insistence of his gaze; but she did not return it. She was paler than usual; and the lines beneath her eyes were blacker. Maurice believed that he could detect a new note in her voice this morning; and he tried to make her speak, in order that he might hear it; but she was as chary of her words as of her looks. Attracted by the two strangers, a little child of the landlord's came running up to stare shyly. She spread a piece of bread with honey, and gave it to the child. He was absurdly jealous, and she knew it.

For the rest of the morning, she would have been content to bask in the sun, but when she saw how impatient he was, she gave way, and they went out of the sight of other people, into the friendly, screening woods.

"I thought you would never come."

"Why didn't you wake me? Oh, gently, Maurice! You forget that I've just done my hair."

"To-day I shall forget everything. Let me look at you again . . . right into your eyes."

"To-day you believe I'm real, don't you? Are you satisfied?"

"And you, Louise, you?—Say you're happy, too!"

They came upon the *Friedrich August Turm,* a stone tower, standing on the highest point of the hill, beside a large quarry; and, too idly happy to refuse, climbed the stone steps, led by a persuasive old pensioner, who, on the platform at the top, adjusted the telescope, and pointed out the distant landmarks, with something of an owner's pride. On this morning, Maurice would not have been greatly surprised to hear that the streaky headline of the Dover coast was visible: he had eyes for her alone, as, with assumed interest, she followed the old man's hand, learned where Leipzig lay, and how, on a clear day, its many spires could be distinguished.

"Over there, Maurice . . . a little more to the right. How far away we seem!"

Leaning against the parapet, he continued to look at her. The few ordinary words meant in reality something quite different. It was as if she had said to him: "Yes, yes, be at rest—I am still yours;" and he told himself, with a feverish pleasure, that, from now on, everything she said in the presence of others would be a cloak for what she really meant to say. He had been right, there *was* a new tone in her voice this morning, an imperceptible vibration, a sensuous undertone, which seemed to have been left over from those moments when it had quivered like a roughly touched string beneath a bow. Going down the steps behind her, he heard her dress swish from step to step, and saw the fine grace of her strong, supple body. At a bend in the stair, he held her back and kissed her neck, just where the hair stopped growing. On the ground-floor, she paused to pick out a trifle from a table set with mementoes. The old man praised his wares with zeal, taking up this and that in his old, reddened hands, on which the skin was drawn and glazed, like a coating of gelatine. Louise chose a carved wooden pen; a tiny round of glass was set in the handle, through which might be seen a view of the tower, with an encircling motto.

After this, he had her to himself, for the rest of the day. They sat on a seat that was screened by trees, and thickly grown about. His arm lay along the back of the bench, and every now and then his hand sought and pressed the warm, soft round of her shoulder. In this attitude, he poured out his heart to her. Hitherto, the very essence of his love had been taciturn endurance; now, he felt how infinitely much he had to say to her: all that he had undergone since knowing her first, all the hopes and feelings that had so long been pent up in him, struggled to escape. Now, there was no hindrance to his telling her everything; it was not only permissible, but right that he should: henceforth there must be no strangeness between them, no knowledge, pleasant or unpleasant, that she did not share. And he went back, and dwelt on details and events long past, which, unknown to himself, his memory had stored up; but it was chiefly the restless misery of the past half year that was his theme

—he took the same pleasure in reciting it, now that it was over, as the convalescent in relating his sufferings. Besides that, it was easier, there being nothing to conceal; whereas, in referring to an earlier time, a certain name had to be shirked and gone round about, like a plague-spot. His impassioned words knew no halt; he was amazed at his own eloquence. And the burden of months fell away from him as he talked.

The receptiveness of her silence spurred him on. She sat motionless, with loosely clasped hands; and spots of light settled on her bare head, and on the white stuff of her dress. Occasionally, at something he said, a smile would raise the corners of her mouth; sometimes, but less often, she turned her head with incredulous eyes. But, though she was emotionally so irresponsive, Maurice had the feeling that she was content, even happy, to sit inactive at his side, and listen to his story.

Each of these first wonderful days was of the same pattern. They themselves lost count of time, so like was one day to another; and yet each that passed was a little eternity in itself. The weather was superb, and to them, in their egotism, it came to seem in the order of things that they should rise in the morning to cloudless skies and golden sunshine; that the cool green seclusion of the woods should be theirs, where they were more securely shut off from the world than inside the house. Louise lay on the moss, with her arms under her head, or sat with her back against a tree-trunk. Maurice was always in front of her, so that he could see her face as he talked—this face of which he could never see enough.

He was happy, in a dazed way; he could not appraise the extent of his happiness all at once. Its chief outward sign was the nervous flood of talk that poured from his lips—as though they had been sealed and stopped for years. But Louise urged him on; what he had first felt dimly, he soon knew for certain: that she was never tired of learning how much he loved her, how he had hoped, and ventured, and despaired, and how he had been prepared to lose her, up to the very last day. She also made him describe to her more than once how he had first seen her: his indelible impression of her as she played; her appearance at his side in the concert-hall; how he had followed her out and looked for her, and had vainly tried to learn who she was.

"I stood quite close to you, you say, Maurice? Perhaps I even looked at you. How strange things are!"

Still, the interest she displayed was of a wholly passive kind; she took no part herself in this building up of the past. She

left it to him, just as she left all that called for firmness or
decision, in this new phase of her life. The chief step taken, it
seemed as if no further initiative were left in her; she let herself be loved, waited for everything to come from him, was
without will or wish. He had to ask no self-assertion of her
now, no impulsive resolutions. Over all she did, lay a subtle
languor; and her abandon was absolute—he heard it in the
very way she said his name.

In the first riotous joy of possession, Maurice had been conscious of the change in her as of something inexpressibly sweet
and tender, implying a boundless faith in him. But, before long,
it made him uneasy. He had imagined several things as likely
to happen; had imagined her the cooler and wiser of the two,
checking him and chiding him for his over-devotion; had
imagined even moments of self-reproach, on her part, when she
came to think over what she had done. What he had not
imagined was the wordless, unthinking fashion in which she
gave herself into his hands. The very expression of her face
altered in these days: the somewhat defiant, bitter lines he had
so loved in it, and behind which she had screened herself, were
smoothed out; the lips seemed to meet differently, were sweeter,
even tremulous; the eyes were more veiled, far less sure of themselves. He did not admit to himself how difficult she made
things for him. Strengthened, from the first, by his good resolutions, he was determined not to let himself be carried off his feet.
But it would have been easier for him to stand firm, had she met
him in almost any other way than this—even with a frank return of feeling, for then they might have spoken openly, and
have helped each other. As it was, he had no thoughts but of
her; his watchful tenderness knew no bounds; but the whole
responsibility was his. It was he who had to maintain the happy
mean in their relations; he to draw the line beyond which it was
better for all their after-lives that they should not go. He
affirmed to himself more than once that he loved her the more
for her complete subjection: it was in keeping with her open-
handed nature which could do nothing by halves. Yet, as time
passed, he began to suffer under it, to feel her absence of will as
a disquieting factor—to find anything to which he could compare it, he had to hark back to the state she had been in when
he first offered her aid and comfort. That was the lassitude
of grief, this of . . . he could not find a word. But it began
to tell on him, and more than once made him a little sharp with
her; for, at moments, he would be seized by an overpowering

temptation to shake her out of her lassitude, to rouse her as he very well knew she could be roused. And then, strange desires awoke in him; he did not himself know of what he was capable.

One afternoon, they were in the woods as usual. It was very sultry; not a leaf stirred. Louise lay with her elbow on the moss-grown roots of a tree; her eyes were heavy. Maurice, before her, smoked a cigarette, and watched for the least recognition of his presence, thinking, meanwhile, that she looked better already for these days spent out-of-doors—the tiny lines round her eyes were fast disappearing. By degrees, however, he grew restless under her protracted silence; there was something ominous about it. He threw his cigarette away, and, taking her hand, began to pull apart the long fingers with the small, pink nails, or to gather them together, and let them drop, one by one, like warm, but lifeless things.

"What *are* you thinking of?" he asked at last, and shut her hand firmly within his.

She started. "I? . . . thinking? I don't know. I wasn't thinking at all."

"But you were. I saw it in your face. Your thoughts were miles away."

"I don't know, Maurice. I couldn't tell you now." And a moment later, she added: "You think one must always be thinking, when one is silent."

"Yes, I'm jealous of your thoughts. You tell me nothing of them. But now you have come back to me, and it's all right."

He drew her nearer to him by the hand he held, and, putting his arm under her neck, bent her head back on the moss. Her stretched throat was marked by two encircling lines; he traced them with his finger. She lay and smiled at him. But her eyes remained shaded: they were meditative, and seemed to be considering him, a little deliberately.

"Tell me, Louise," he said suddenly; "why do you look at me like that? It's not the first time—I've seen it before. And then, I can't help thinking there's some mistake—that after all you don't really care for me. It is so—so critical."

"You are curious to-day, Maurice."

"Yes. There's so much I want to know, and you tell me nothing. It is I who talk and talk—till you must be tired of hearing me."

"No, I like to listen best. And I have nothing to say."

"Nothing? Really nothing?"

"Only that I'm glad to be here—that I am happy."

He kissed her on the throat, the eyes and the lips; kissed her, until, under his touch, that vague, elusive influence began to emanate from her, which, he was aware, might some day overpower him, and drag him down. They were quite alone, shut in by high trees; no one would find them, or disturb them. And it was just this mysterious power in her that his nerves had dreamed of waking: yet now, some inexplicable instinct made him hesitate, and forbear. He drew his arm from under her head, and rose to his feet, where he stood looking down at her. She lay just as he had left her, and he felt unaccountably impatient.

"There it is again!" he cried. "You are looking at me just as you did before."

Louise passed her hand over her eyes, and sat up. "Why, Maurice, what do you mean? It was nothing—only something I was trying to understand."

But what it was that she did not understand, he could not get her to tell him.

A fortnight passed. One morning, when a soft south breeze was in motion, Maurice reminded her with an air of playful severity, that, so far, they had not learned to know even their nearer surroundings; while of all the romantic explorings in the pretty Muldental, which he had had in view for them, not one had been undertaken. Louise was not fond of walking in the country; she tired easily, and was always content to bask in the sun and be still. But she did not attempt to oppose his wish; she put on her hat, and was ready to start.

His love of movement reasserted itself. They went down the driving-road, and out upon the long, ribbon-like roads that zigzagged the plains, connecting the dotted villages. These roads were edged with fruit-trees—apple and cherry. The apples were still hard, green, polished balls, but the berries were at their prime. And everywhere men were aloft on ladders, gathering the fruit for market. For the sum of ten pfennigs, Maurice could get his hat filled, and, by the roadside, they would sit down to make a second breakfast off black, luscious cherries, which stained the lips a bluish purple. When it grew too hot for the open roads, they descended the steep, wooded back of the hill, to the romantic little town of Wechselburg at its base. Here, a massive bridge of reddish-yellow stone spanned the winding, slate-grey Mulde; a sombre, many-windowed castle of the same stone as the bridge looked out over a wall of magnificent chestnuts.

On returning from these, and various other excursions, they were pleasantly tired and hungry. After supper, they sat upstairs by the window in her room, Louise in the big chair, Maurice at her feet, and there watched the darkness come down, over the tops of the trees.

Somewhat later in the month, the fancy took her to go to a place called Amerika. Maurice consulted the landlord about the distance. Their original plan of taking the train a part of the way was, however, abandoned when the morning came; for it was an uncommonly lovely day, and a fresh breeze was blowing. So, having scrambled down to Wechselburg again, they struck out on the flat, and began their walk. The whole day lay before them; they were bound to no fixed hours; and, throughout the morning, they made frequent halts, to gather the wild raspberries that grew by the roadside. Having passed under a great railway viaduct, which dominated the landscape, they stopped at a village inn, to rest and drink coffee. About two o'clock, they came to Rochsburg, and finally arrived, towards the middle of the afternoon, at the picturesque restaurant that bore the name of Amerika. Here they dined. Afterwards, they returned to Rochsburg, but much less buoyantly—for Louise was growing footsore—paid a bridge-toll, were shown through the castle, and, at sunset, found themselves on the little railway-station, waiting for an overdue train. The restaurant in which they sat, was a kind of shed, roofed by a covering of Virginia creeper; the station stood on an eminence; the plains stretched before them, as far as they could see; the evening sky was an unbroken sheet of red and gold.

The half-hour's journey over—it was made in a narrow wooden compartment, crowded with peasants returning from a market—they left the train, and began to climb the hill. But, by now, Louise was at the end of her strength, and Maurice began to fear that he would never get her home; she could with difficulty drag one foot after the other, and had to rest every few minutes, so that it was nearly ten o'clock before they entered the house. In her room, he knelt before her and took off her boots; Amalie carried her supper up on a tray. She hardly touched it: her eyes were closing with fatigue, and she was asleep as soon as her head touched the pillow.

Next day she did not waken till nearly noon, and she remained in bed till after dinner. For the rest of the day, she sat in the arm-chair. Maurice wished to read to her, but she preferred quiet—did not even want to be talked to. The weather was on her nerves, she said—for it had grown very sultry, and the sky was overcast. The landlord prophesied a thunderstorm. In the evening, however, as it was still dry, and he had been in the house all day, Maurice went out for a solitary walk.

He swung down the road at a pace he could only make when he was alone. It had looked threatening when he left the house, but, as he went, the clouds piled themselves up with inconceivable rapidity, and before he was three miles out on the plain, the storm broke, with a sudden fury from which there was no escape. He took to his heels, and ran to the next village, some quarter of a mile in front of him. There, in the smoky room of a tiny inn, together with a handful of country-people, he was held a prisoner for over two hours; the rain pelted, and the thunder cracked immediately overhead. When, drenched to the skin, he reached the top of the hill again, it was going on for midnight. He had been absent for close on four hours.

The candle in her room was guttering in its socket. By its failing light, he saw that she was lying across the bed, still dressed. Over her bent Amalie.

He had visions of sudden illness, and brushed the girl aside.

"What is it? What's the matter?"

At his voice, Louise lifted a wild face, stared at him as though she did not recognise him, then rose with a cry, and flung herself upon him.

"Take care! I'm wet through."

For all answer, she burst into tears, and trembled from head to foot.

"What is it, darling? Were you afraid?"

But she only clung to him and trembled.

Amalie was weeping with equal vehemence; he ordered her out of the room. Notwithstanding his dripping clothes, he was forced to support Louise. In vain he implored her to speak; it was long before she was in a state to reply to his questionings. Outside the storm still raged; it was a wild night.

"What was it? Were you afraid? Did you think I was lost?"

"I don't know—Oh, Maurice! You will never leave me, will you?"

She wounded her lips against his shoulder.

"Leave you! What has put such foolish thoughts into your head?"

"I don't know.—But on a night like this, I feel that anything might happen."

"And did it really matter so much whether I came back or not?"

He felt her arms tighten round him.

"Did you care as much as that?—Louise!"

"I said: my God!—what if he should never come back! And then, then . . ."

"Then——?"

"And then the noise of the storm . . . and I was so alone . . . and all the long, long hours . . . and at every sound I said, there he is . . . and it never was you . . . till I knew you were lying somewhere . . . dead . . . under a tree."

"You poor little soul!" he began impulsively, then stopped, for he felt the sudden thrill that ran through her.

"Say that again, Maurice!—say it again!"

"You poor, little fancy-ridden soul!"

"Oh, if you knew how good it sounds!—if I could make you understand! You're the only person who has ever said a thing like that to me—the only one who has ever been in the least sorry for me. Promise me now—promise again—that you will never leave me.—For you are all I have."

"Promise?—again? When you are more to me than my own life?"

"And you will never get tired of me?—never?"

"My own dear wife!"

She strained him to her with a strength for which he would not have given her credit. He tried to see her face.

"Do you know what that means?"

"Yes, I know. It means, if you leave me now, I shall die."

By the next morning, all traces of the storm had vanished; the sun shone; the slanting roads were hard and dry again. Other storms followed—for it was an exceptionally hot summer—and many an evening the two were prisoners in her room, listening to the angry roar of the trees, which lashed each other with a sound like that of the open sea.

Every Sunday in August, too, brought a motley crowd of guests to the inn, and then the whole terrace was set out with little tables. Two waiters came to assist Amalie; a band played in an arbour; carts and wagonettes were hitched to the front of the house; and the noise and merry-making lasted till late in the night. Together they leaned from the window of Louise's room, to watch the people; they hardly ventured out of doors, for it was unpleasant to see their favourite nooks invaded by strangers. Except on Sundays, however, their seclusion remained undisturbed; half a dozen visitors were staying in the other wing of the building, and of these they sometimes caught a glimpse at meals; but that was all: the solitude they desired was still theirs.

And so the happy days slid past; August was well advanced, by this time, and the tropical heat was at its height. In the beginning, it had been Maurice who regretted the rapid flight of the days: now it was Louise. Occasionally, a certain shadow settled on her face, and, at such moments, he well knew what she was thinking of: for, once, out of the very fulness of his content, he had said to her with a lazy sigh: "To-day is the first of August," and then, for the first time, he had seen this look of intense regret cross her face. She had entreated him not to say any more; and, after that, the speed with which the month decreased, was not mentioned between them.

But his carelessly dropped words had sown their seed. A couple of weeks later, the remembrance of the work he had still to do for Schwarz, before the beginning of the new term, broke over him like a douche of cold water. It was a resplendent morning; he had been leaning out of the window, idly tapping his fingers on the sill. Suddenly they seemed to him to have grown stiff, to have lost their agility; and by the thoughts that now came, he was so disquieted that he shut himself up in his own room.

At his first words to her, Louise, who was still in bed, turned pale. "Yes, yes, be quiet!—I know," she said, and buried her face in the down pillow.

In this position she remained for some seconds; Maurice stood staring out of the window. Then, without raising her face, she held out her hand to him.

He took it; but he did not do what she expected he would: sit down on the side of the bed, and put his arm round her. He stood holding it, absent-mindedly. She stole a glance at him, and turned still paler. Then, with a jerk, she released her hand, sat up in bed, and pushed her hair from her face.

"Maurice! . . . then if it has to be . . . then to-day . . . please, please, to-day! Don't ask me to stay here, and think, and remember, that it's all over—that this is the end—that we shall never, never be here in this little room again. Oh, I couldn't bear it!—I can't bear it, Maurice. Let us go away—please, let us go!"

In vain he urged reason; there was no gainsaying her: she

brushed aside, without listening to it, his objection that their rooms in Leipzig would not be ready for them. Throwing back the bedclothes, she got up at once and dressed herself, with cold fingers, then flung herself upon the packing, helped and hindered by Amalie, who wept beside her. The hour that followed was like a bad dream. Finally, however, the luggage was carried downstairs, the bill paid, and the circumstantial good-byes were said: they set off, at full speed, down the wood-path to the station, to catch the midday train. Louise was white with exhaustion: her breath came sobbingly. In a first-class carriage, he made her lie down on the seat. With her hand in his, he said what he could to comfort her; for her face was tragic.

"We will come again, darling. It is only *auf Wiedersehen,* remember!"

But she shook her head.

"We shall never be here again."

Leipzig, at three o'clock on an August afternoon, lay baking in the sun. He put her in a covered droschke, himself carrying the bags, for he could not find a porter.

"At seven, then! Try to sleep. You are so pale."

"Good-bye—good-bye!"

His hand rested on the door of the droschke. She laid hers on it, and clung to it as though she would never let it go.

PART III

. . . dove il Sol tace.

—DANTE.

I

FRAU KRAUSE was ill pleased at his unlooked-for reappearance, and did not scruple to say so. From the condition of disorder in which he found his room, Maurice judged that it had been occupied, during his absence, by the entire family. Having been caught napping, Frau Krause carried the matter off with a high hand: she gave him to understand that his behaviour in descending upon her thus, was not that of a decent lodger. Maurice never parleyed with her; ascertaining by a glance that his books and music had been left untouched, he made his escape from the pails of water that were straightway brought into evidence, as well as from her irate assurances that the room would be ready for him in a quarter of an hour.

He went into the town, and did various small errands necessary to the taking up anew of the old life. After he had had dinner, and had looked through the newspapers, the temptation was strong to go to Louise, and to spend the hot afternoon hours at her side. But he resisted ; for that would have been a poor beginning to the sensible way of life they would have to follow, from now on. Besides, with the certainty of seeing her again in a very short time, it was not impossible to be patient. No more uncertainty, no more doubts and fears!—the day for these was over.—And so, having satisfied himself that his room was still uninhabitable, he strolled to the Conservatorium, to see what notices had remained affixed to the notice-board. As he was leaving again, he met the janitor, and from him learned that his name was down for the first *Abendunterhaltung* of the coming month.

In the shadeless street, he paused irresolute. The heat of the slumbrous afternoon was oppressive; all animation seemed suspended. The trees in streets and gardens drooped, brownish-yellow, and heavy with dust. The sun met the eyes blindingly, and was reflected from every house-wall. Maurice went for a walk in the woods. In his pocket he had a letter, still unread, which he had found waiting for him that day. It was

385

from his mother, and his eyes slid carelessly over the pages.
There were the usual reproaches for his prolonged silences, the
never-failing reminders that his time in Leipzig would come to
an end the following spring, as well as several details of domestic interest.   Then, however, followed a piece of news
which rallied his attention.

You will doubtless be interested to hear, she wrote, *that
your friend the old music teacher in Norwich died suddenly
last week. His pupils had fallen off greatly of late and when
everything had been sold there was scarcely enough to cover
the funeral expenses. Your father thinks that though a young
person from London of the name of Smith or Smythe has lately
set up there and attracted many of the best paying families.
yet the old connection might be worked up again and it would
be worth your while trying to do it. At first you could live
at home and go over once or twice a week. Your father has
been making inquiries about a suitable room.*

This news called up a feeling of repugnance in Maurice:
it came like a message from another world; the very baldness
of its expression seemed to throw him back, at one stroke, into
the hated atmosphere of his home.   He folded the letter and
replaced it in the envelope, with such a conscious hostility to
all that his blood-relations did or said, as he had not felt since
the day when, in their midst, he had struggled to assert his
independence.   How little they understood him!   It was like
them, in their unimaginative dulness, to suppose that they could
arrange his life for him—draw up the lines on which it was to
be spent.   He saw himself bound down hand and foot again,
to the occupation he so hated; saw himself striving to oust
the young person from London, just as no doubt his old friend
had striven; saw himself becoming proficient in all the mean,
petty tricks of rival teachers, and either vanquishing or being
vanquished, in the effort to earn a living.

However he viewed them, his prospects had nothing hopeful
in them.   They were vague, too, to the last degree.   On one
question alone was his mind made up: he meant to marry
Louise at the earliest possible date.   Whatever else happened,
this should come to pass.   For the first time, he thought with
something akin to remorse, over the turn affairs had taken.
He had been blind and dizzy with his infatuation, sick for
her to his very marrow—he could only look back on those

feverish weeks in June as on the horrors of a nightmare—and he would not have missed a single hour of the happy days at Rochlitz. But, none the less, he had always felt a peculiar aversion to people who allowed their feelings to get the better of them. Now, he himself was one of them. If only she were his wife! Had she consented, he would have married her there and then, without reflection. They might have lived on, just as they were going to do, and have kept their marriage a secret, reserving to themselves the pleasure of knowing that their intimacy was legal. At it was, he must console himself with the thought that, married or not, they were indissolubly bound: he knew now better than before, that no other woman would ever exist for him; and surely, in the case of an all-absorbing passion such as this, the over-stepping of conventional boundaries would not be counted too heavily against them: laws and conventions existed only for the weak and vacillating loves of the rest of the world.

Then, however, and almost against his will, the other side of the question forced itself upon his notice. As the marriage had not already taken place, as, indeed, Louise chose to evade the subject when he brought it up, he could not but admit to himself, rather wrily, that it would be pleasanter for him if it were now postponed until he was independent of home-support. His family would, he knew, bitterly resent his taking the step; and in regard to them, he was proud. Where Louise was concerned, of course, it was a different matter: there, no misplaced pride should stand in the way. She had ample means for her own needs; it was merely a question of earning enough to keep himself. The sole advantage of the present state of affairs was, that it might still be concealed; whereas even a secret marriage implied a possible publicity: it might somehow leak out, and, in the event of this, he knew that his parents would immediately cut off supplies. If once he were independent of them, he could do as he liked. He set his teeth at the thought of it. To no small extent, his way was mapped out for him. Marrying Louise meant giving up all idea of returning home. He understood now, more clearly than before, how unfitted she was for the narrow life that would there be expected of her. And even if he had longed for approval and consent, he would never have had courage to ask her to face the petty, ignoble details of conventional propriety, which such a sanction implied. No, if he wished to ensure her happiness, he must secure to her the freer atmosphere in which she

was accustomed to live. He must burn his ships behind him,
and the most satisfactory thing was, that he was able to do it
without a pang.

He racked his brains as to the means of making a livelihood.
There was nothing he would not do. He was more ready to
work than ever a labourer with a starving family at his back.
But, having let every possibility pass before his mind's eye,
he was forced to the conclusion that the only occupation open
to him was the one he had come to Leipzig to escape. He
was fit for nothing but to be a teacher. All he could do at
the piano, hundreds of others could do better; his talents as
a conductor were, he had learned, of the meagrest; the pleasing
little songs he might compose, of small value. Yet, if this
were the price he had to pay for making her his wife, he was
content to pay it: no sacrifice was too great for him. And
then, to be a teacher here meant something different from what
it meant in England. Here, it was possible to retain your self-
respect—the caste of the class was another to begin with—and
also to remain in touch with all that was best worth knowing.
As a foreigner, he might add to his earnings by teaching English;
but piano-lessons would of necessity be his chief source of income. They were plentiful enough: Avery Hill supported
herself entirely by them, and Fürst kept his family. Of course,
though, this was due to Schwarz: his influence was a key to
all doors. Both of these were favourite pupils; while a melancholy fact, which had to be faced, was, that he did not stand
well with Schwarz. Somehow, they had never taken to each
other: he, perhaps, had had too open an eye for the master's
foibles, and Schwarz had no doubt been aware, from the first,
of his pupil's fatally divided interests. The crown had probably
been set by his ill-considered flight in July. If he wished ultimately to achieve something, the interest he had forfeited must
be regained, cost what it might? He would work, in these coming months, as never before. Could he make a brilliant, even a
wholly respectable job of the trio he was to play, it would go far
towards reinstating him in Schwarz's good graces: and he might
then venture to approach the master with a request for assistance.
This was the first piece of work that lay to his hand, and he
would do it with all his might. After that, the rest.

There was no time to lose. A mild despair overcame him
at the thought of the intricate sonata, the long, mazy concerto by Hummel, which had formed his holiday task. In
exactly a fortnight from this date, the vacation came to an

end, and, as yet, he did not know a note of them. Through the motionless heat of the paved streets, he went home, and turning Frau Krause out of his room, sat down at the piano to scales and exercises. Not until he felt suppleness and strength coming back to his fingers, did he allow his thoughts to wander. Then, however, they leapt to Louise; after this break in his consciousness, he seemed to have been absent from her for days.

The sun was full on her windows; curtains and blinds were drawn against it. While he hesitated, still dazzled by the glare of the streets, she sprang to meet him, laying both hands on his shoulders.

"At last!"

He blinked, and laughed, and held her at arm's length. "At last?—Why, what does that mean?"

"That I have been waiting for you, and hoping you would come—for hours."

"But, dearest, I'm too early as it is. It's not six o'clock."

"Yes, I know. But I was so sure you would come sooner, —that you wouldn't be able to stay away! Oh, the afternoon has been endless; and the heat was suffocating. I couldn't dress, and I haven't unpacked a thing."

Now he saw that she was in her dressing-gown, and that the bags and valises stood in a corner, just as they had been carried up from the droschke.

With her hands still on his shoulders, she put back her head. A thin line of white appeared between her lips, and, under their drooped lids, her eyes shone with a moist brilliance. She looked at him eagerly for some seconds, and it seemed to him wistfully, too. Then, in an inexplicable change of mood, she let her arms fall, and turned away. She had grown pale and despondent. There was only one thing for him to do: to put his arms round her and draw her to his knee. Holding her thus, he whispered in her ear words such as she loved to hear. He had grown skilled in repeating them. Under the even murmur of his voice, her face grew tranquil; she sank little by little into a state of well-being; her one fear was that he would cease speaking.

On the writing-table, a gold-faced clock ticked solemnly: its minutes went by unheeded. Maurice was the first to feel the disillusioning shudder of reality; simultaneously, the remembrance returned to him of what he had come intending to tell her.—He loosened her arms.

"Louise!" he said in an altered voice. "Look up, dear— and let me see your eyes. You won't believe me, I think, but I came this evening meaning to talk very sensibly—nothing but common sense, in fact. There's a great deal I want to say to you. Come, let us be two rational people—yes? As a beginning, I'll draw up the blinds. The sun's behind the houses now, and the room is so close."

Louise shrank from the violent, dusty light; and her face, a moment back rapturously content, took on at once a look of apprehension.

"Not to-night, Maurice—not to-night! It's too . . . too hot for common sense to-night."

He laughed and took her hand. "Be my own brave girl, and help me. You have only to look at me, as you know, to make me forget everything. And that mustn't be. We have got to be serious for a little—have you ever thought, Louise, how seldom you and I have talked seriously together? There was never time, was there? . . . in all these weeks. There was only time to tell you how much you are to me.—But now— well, so many things were running in my head this afternoon. This letter from home was the beginning of them. Read it— this page here, at least—and then I'll tell you what I've been thinking."

He put the letter into her hand, and she ran her eyes over the page. But she laid it down without comment.

A fear crossed his mind. "Don't misunderstand it," he said hastily. "You know that point was settled months ago. There's no question of going back for me now—and I'm glad of it. I never want to see England again. But it gave me a lot to think about—how the staying here was to be managed, and things like that."

He was conscious of becoming somewhat wordy; and as she did not respond, his uneasiness grew. In his anxiety to make her think as he did, he clasped his hand over hers.

"I needn't say again, need I, darling, what the past weeks have meant to me? I'm so grateful to you for them that I could only prove it with years of my life. But—and don't misunderstand this either, or think I don't love you more now than ever before—you know I do. But, look at it as we will, those weeks were play—glorious play, worth half one's existence, but still only play. They couldn't last for ever. Now we've come back, and we have to face work and the workaday world—you see what I mean, I'm sure?"

There was a note of entreaty in his voice. As she still kept silence, he gave his whole strength to demolishing the mute opposition he felt in her.

"From now on, dear, we must make up our minds to be two very sensible people. I've an enormous amount of work to get through, in the coming months. And at Easter, I shall probably be thrown on my own resources. But I'll fight my way somehow—here, beside you. We'll live our own life. Just you and I.—Let me tell you what I propose to do,"— and here, he laid before her, in their entirety, his plans for winning over Schwarz, for gaining a foothold, and for making a modest income. "A good *Prüfung,*" he concluded, "and I'll be able to get anything I want out of him. In the meantime, I've got to make a decent job next month of the trio—I'm pretty well in his black books, I can guess, for going off as I did in July. I must work as I've never done before. Each single day must be mapped out, and nothing allowed to interfere. It's an undertaking; but you'll help me, won't you, darling?—as only you can. I've let things go, far too much—I see it now. But it was impossible—frankly, I didn't care. I only wanted you. Now, it will . . . it must be different. The unrest is gone; you belong to me, and I to you. We are sure of each other."

"Oh, it's stifling! There's no air in the room."

She rose from his side, and went to the open window, where she stood with her back to him. As a result of his words, her life seemed suddenly to stretch before her, just as dry, and dusty, and commonplace, as the street she looked down on.

"I want to show you, too," he continued behind her, "that you haven't utterly thrown yourself away. I know how little I can do; but honest endeavour must count for something. I ask nothing better than to work for you, Louise—and you know it."

A wave of warm air came in at the window; the dying afternoon turned to twilight.

"Yes . . . and I? What am I to do? What room is there for me in your plans of work?"

He glanced sharply at her; but she had not moved.

"Louise, dearest! I know that what I say must sound selfish and inconsiderate. And yet I can't help it. I'm forced to ask you to wait . . . merely to wait. And for what? Good Heavens, no one realises it as I do! I have nothing to offer you, in return—but my love for you. But if you knew

how strong that is—if you knew how happy I am resolved to
make you! Have a little patience, darling! It will all come
right in the end—if only you love me. And you do, don't you?
Say once more you do."

She turned so swiftly that the tail of her dressing-gown
twisted, and fell over on itself.

"Can you still ask that? Have you not had proof enough?
Is there an inch of you that doesn't believe in my love for
you? Oh, Maurice! . . . It's only that I'm tired to-night—
and restless. I was so wretched at having to come back.
And the heat has got on my nerves. I wish a great storm
would come, and shake the house, and make the branches of
the trees beat against the panes—do you remember? And we
were so safe. The worse the storm was, the closer you held
me." She sat down beside him, on the arm of the sofa. "Such
a night seemed doubly wild after the long, still days that had
gone before it—do you remember?—Oh, why had it all to end?
Weren't we happy enough? Or did we ask too much? Why
must time go just the same over happiness and unhappiness
alike?" She got up again, and strayed back to the window.
"Days like those will never—can never—come again. Even
as it is, coming back has made a difference. Could you even
yesterday have spoken as you do to-day? Was there any room
then for common sense between us? No, we were too happy.
It was enough to know we were alive."

"Be reasonable, darling. I am as sorry as you that these
weeks are over; but, glorious as they were, they couldn't last for
ever. And trust me; we shall know other days just as happy.
—But if, because I talk like this, you imagine I don't love you
a hundred times better even than yesterday—but you don't
mean that. You know me better, my Rachel!"

"Yes. Perhaps you're right—you are right. But I am
right, too."

She came back, and sat down on the sofa again, and propped
her chin on her hand.

"You're tired to-night, dear—that's all. To-morrow things
will look different, and you'll see the truth of what I say. At
night, things get distorted——"

"No, no, one only really sees in the dark," she interrupted
him.

—"but in the morning, one can smile at one's fears. Trust
me, Louise, and believe in me. All our future happiness
depends on how we act just now."

"Our future happiness . . . yes," she said slowly. "But what of the present?"

"Isn't it worth while sacrificing a brief present to a long future?"

She threw him a quick glance. "You talk like an orthodox Christian, Maurice," she said, and added: "The present is here: it belongs to us. The future is so unclear—who knows what it will bring us!"

"And isn't it just for that very reason that I speak as I do? If everything lay clear and straight before us, do you think I should bother about anything but you? It's the uncertainty of the whole thing that troubles me. But however vague it is, I can tell you one thing that will happen. And you know, dearest, what that is—the only ambition I have left: to make you my wife at the earliest possible moment."

She gazed at him meditatively.

"Why wouldn't you let me have my way at first?" he cried. "Why were you against it? We could have kept it a secret: no one need have known a thing about it. And I should never have asked you to go to England, or to see my people. Call it narrow, if you must, I can't help it; it's the only thing for us to do. Why won't you agree? Tell me what you have against it. Listen!" He knelt down and put his arms round her. "We have still a fortnight—that's time enough. Let us go to England to-morrow, and be married—without a word to anyone—in the first registrar's office we find. Only marry me!"

"Would it make you love me more?"

She looked at him intently, turning the whole weight of her dark glance upon him.

"You!" he said. "You to ask such a thing! You with these eyes . . . and this hair! And these hands!—I love every line of them . . . You can't understand, can you, you bundle of emotions, that I should care for you as I do, and yet be able to talk soberly? It seems to you a man's way of loving—and poor at that. But if you imagine I don't love you all the more for what you have sacrificed for me—no, you didn't say that, I know, but it comes to the same thing in the end."

She made no answer; and a feeling of discouragement began to creep over him. He rose to his feet.

"A man who loves a woman as I love you," he said almost violently, "has only one wish—can have only one. I shall never rest or be thoroughly happy till you consent to marry me. That you can refuse as you do, seems to prove that you don't care for me enough."

She put her arms round his neck: her wide sleeves fell back, leaving her arms bare. "Maurice," she said gently, "why must you worry yourself?—You know if you are set on our marrying, I'll give way. But I don't want to be married— not yet. There's plenty of time. It's only a small matter now; it doesn't seem as if it could make any difference; and yet it might. The sense of being bound; of some one—no, of the law permitting us to love each other . . . no, Maurice, not yet.—Listen! I'm older and wiser than you, and I *know*. Happiness like this doesn't come every day. Instead of brooding and hesitating, one must seize it while it's there: it's such a slippery thing; it's gone before you know it. You can't bind it fast, and say it shall last so and so long. We have it now; don't let us talk and reason about it.—Oh, to-day, I'm nervous! Let me make a confession. As a child I had presentiments—things I foresaw came true, and on the morning of a misfortune, I've felt such a load on my chest that I could hardly breathe. Well, to-day, when I came into this room again, it seemed as if two black wings shut out the sunlight; and I was afraid. The past weeks have been so unreasonably happy—such happiness mustn't be let go. Help me to hold it; I can't do it alone. Don't try to make it fast to the future; while you do that, it's going—do you think one can draw out happiness like a thread? Oh, help me!—don't let anything take it from us. And I will give up everything to it. Only you must always be beside me, Maurice, and love me. Don't let anything come between us! For my sake, for my sake!"

In the face of this outpouring, his own opinions seemed of little matter; his one concern was to ward off the tears that he saw were imminent. He held her to him, stroked her hair, and murmured words of comfort. But when she raised her head again, her eyelids were reddened, as though she had actually wept.

"Now I know you. Now you are my own again," she whispered. "How could I know you as you were then? I'd never seen you like that—seen you cold and sensible."

He looked down at her without speaking, in a preoccupied way.

She touched his face with her finger. "Here are lines I don't know—I see them now for the first time—lines of reason, of common sense, of all that is strange to me in you."

He caught her hand, continuing to gaze at her with the same expression of aloofness. "I need them for us both. You have none."

Her lips parted in a smile. Then this faded, and she looked at him with eyes that reminded him of an untamed animal, or of a startled child.

"Mine . . . still mine!" she said passionately.—And in the hours it took to reassure her, his primly reasoned conclusions were blown like chaff before the wind.

II

THE next fortnight flew by; and familiar faces began to appear again. The steps and inner vestibule of the Conservatorium became a lounge for seeing acquaintances. In the café at the corner, the click of billiard balls was to be heard from early morning on.

Maurice looked forward to meeting his friends, with some embarrassment. It was unlikely that the events of the summer had remained a secret; for that, there was a clique in the place over-much on the alert for scandal, to which unfortunately the name of Louise Dufrayer lent itself only too readily. He could not decide what position to take up, with regard to their present intimacy; to flaunt it openly, to be pointed at as her lover, would for her sake be repugnant to him. It made him reject an idea he had revolved, of begging her to let him announce their engagement: for, in the present state of things, the word "*Bräutigam*" had an evil sound. Eventually, he came to the conclusion that they must be more cautious than they had ever been, and give absolutely no food for talk.

One day, in the *Grassistrasse,* he came upon a little knot of men he knew. And it was just as he supposed; the secret was a secret no longer. He saw it at once in their treatment of him. There was a spice of deference in their manner: and their looks expressed curiosity, envious surprise, even a kind of brotherly welcome. After this, Maurice changed his mind: the only course open to him was to brazen things out. He would not wait for his friends to show him what they thought; he would be beforehand with them.

A chance soon offered of putting his intentions into practice. On entering Seyffert's one afternoon, he espied Dove, who had just returned. Dove sat alone at a small table, reading the *Tageblatt;* before him stood a cup of cocoa. When he saw Maurice, he raised the newspaper a trifle higher, so that it covered the level of his eyes. But Maurice went across the room, and touched him on the shoulder. Dove dropped his shield, and sprang up, exclaiming with surprise. Maurice sat down beside him, and, by dint of a little wheedling, put Dove at his ease. The latter was bubbling over with new experiences and future prospects. It seemed that in Peterborough, Dove's native town, the art of music was taking strides that were nothing short of marvellous. To hear Dove talk, the palm for progress must be awarded to Peterborough, over and above all the other towns of Great Britain; and he was agog with plans and expectations. During the holidays, he had held conversations with several local magnates, all of whom expressed themselves in favour of his scheme for founding a school of music, and promised him their support. Dove had returned to Leipzig in a bran-new outfit, and a hard hat; his studies were coming to an end in spring, and he began to think already of casting the skin of Bohemianism.

Maurice listened to him leniently—even drew Dove out a little. But he kept his eye on the clock. In less than half an hour, he would be with Louise; from some corner of the semi-darkened room, she would spring towards him, and throw herself into his arms.

The majority of the classes were not yet assembled, when one day, a rumour rose, and spreading, ran from mouth to mouth. Those who heard it were at first incredulous; as, however, it continued to make headway, they whistled to themselves, or vented their surprise in a breathless *"Ach!"* Later in the day, they stood about in groups, and excitedly discussed the subject. Ten of Schwarz's most advanced pupils had left the master for the outsider named Schrievers. At the head of the list stood Fürst.

The Conservatorium, royally endowed and municipally controlled, held to its time-honoured customs with tenacity. The older masters laboured to uphold tradition, and such younger ones as were progressively inclined, had not the influence to effect a change. Unattached teachers were regarded with suspicion—unless they happened to be former pupils of the institution, in which case it was assumed that they carried out its precepts. There had naturally always been plenty of others as well; but these were comparatively powerless: they could give their pupils neither imposing certificates, nor gala public performances, such as the *Prüfungen,* and, for the most part, they flourished unknown. This was previous to the arrival of Schrievers. It was now about a year and a half ago that his settling in Leipzig had caused a flutter in musical circles. Then, however, he had been forgotten, or at least remembered only at intervals, when it was heard that he had caught another fish, in the shape of a renegade pupil.

Schrievers was a burly, red-bearded man, still well under middle age, and possessed of plenty of push and self-confidence. It soon transpired that he was an out-and-out champion of modern ideas in music; for, from the first, he was connected with a leading paper, in which he made his views known. He had a trenchant pen, and, with unfailing consistency, criticised the musical conditions of Leipzig adversely. The progressive *Lisztverein,* of which he was soon the leading spirit, alone escaped; the opera, bereft of Nikisch, and the Gewandhaus, under its gentle and aged conductor, were treated by him with biting sarcasm. But his chief butt was the Conservatorium, and its ancient methods. He asserted that not a jot of the curriculum had been altered for fifty years; and its speedy downfall was the sole result to be expected and hoped for. The fact that, at this time, some seven hundred odd students were enrolled on its books went far to discredit this pious hope; but, nevertheless, Schrievers harped always on the same string; and just as perpetual dropping wears a stone, so his continued diatribes ate into emotional and sensitive natures. He began to attract a following, and, simultaneously, to make himself known as a pupil of Liszt. This brought him a fresh batch of enemies. Even a small German town is seldom without its Liszt-pupil, and in Leipzig several were settled, none of whom had ever heard of Martin Schrievers. They refused to admit him to their jealous clique. In their opinion, he belonged to that goodly class of persons, who, having by hook or by crook, contrived to spend an hour in the Abbé of Weimar's presence, afterwards abused the sacred name of pupil. He was hated by these chosen few with more vigour than by the conservative pedagogues, who, naturally enough, saw the ruin of art in all he did.

Various reasons were given for his success, no one being willing to believe that it was due to his merits as a teacher. Some said that he recognised in a twinkling the weak points of the individual with whom he had to deal. He humoured foibles, was tender of self-conceit. He also flattered his pupils by giving them music that was beyond their powers of execution: those, for instance, who had worked long and with feeble interest at Czerny, Dussek and Hummel, were dazzled at the prospect of Liszt and Chopin, which was suddenly thrust beneath their eyes. Other ill-wishers believed that his chief bait was the musical *soirées* he gave when a famous pianist came to the town. By virtue of his journalistic position, he was personally acquainted with all the great; they visited at his house, and his pupils had thus not merely the opportunity of getting to know artists like Rubinstein and d'Albert, and of hearing them play in private, but, what was more to the point, of themselves taking part in the performance, and perhaps receiving a golden word from the great man's lips. And though no huge parchment scroll was forthcoming on the termination of one's studies, yet Schrievers held the weapon of criticism in his hand, and, at the first tentative public appearance of the young performer, could make or mar as he chose. He lived on good terms, too, with his fellow-critics, so that wire-pulling was easy—incomparably more so than were the embarrassing visits, open to any snub, which were common if one was only a pupil of the Conservatorium, and which, in the case of the lady-pupils, included costly bouquets of flowers.

Among those who had deserted Schwarz were some, like Miss Martin, malcontents, who had flitted from place to place, and from master to master, in the perpetual hope of discovering that ideal teacher who would estimate them at their true worth. These were radiantly satisfied with the change. Miss Martin bore, wherever she went, an octave-study by Liszt, and flaunted it in the faces of her friends: and Miss Moses, who had been under Bendel, could not say two sentences without throwing in: "That Chopin *étude* I studied last," or: "The Polonaise in E flat I'm working at;" for, beforehand, she too had been a humble performer of Haydn and Bertini. James had the prospect of playing a Concerto by Liszt—forbidden fruit to the pupils of the Conservatorium—in one of the concerts of the *Lisztverein,* and was sure, in advance, of being favourably criticised. Boehmer wished to specialise in Bach, and if Schwarz set himself against one thing more than another, it was a one-sided musical taste: within the bounds of classicism, the master demanded catholic sympathies; those students who had romantic leanings towards Chopin and Schumann, were castigated with severely classical compositions; and, vice versa, he had insisted on Boehmer widening his horizon on Schubert and Mendelssohn. And there were also several others, who, having been dragged forward by Schwarz, from inefficient beginnings, now left him, to write their acquired skill to Schrievers' credit. Fürst was the greatest riddle of all. It was he who, on subsequent concert-tours, was to have extended the fame of the Conservatorium; he was the show pupil of the institution, and, in the coming *Prüfungen,* was to

have distinguished himself, and his master with him, by playing
Beethoven's Concerto in E flat.

Other teachers besides Schwarz had been forsaken for the
new-comer, but in no case by so large a body of students.
They bore their losses philosophically. Bendel, one of the few
masters who spoke English—it was against the principles of
Schwarz to know a word of it: foreign pupils had to learn
his language, not he theirs—Bendel, frequented chiefly by the
American colony, was of a phlegmatic temperament and not
easily roused. He alluded to the backsliders with an ironical
jest, preferring to believe that they were the losers. But
Schwarz was of a diametrically opposite nature. In the short,
thickset man, with the all-seeing eyes, and the head of carefully waved hair, just streaked with grey—a head at once too
massive and too fine for the clumsy body—in Schwarz, dwelt
a fierce and indomitable pride. His was one of those moody,
sensitive natures, quick to resent, always on the look-out for
offence. He was ever ready to translate things into the personal; for though he had an overweening sense of his own
importance, there was yet room in him for a secret doubt; and
with this doubt, he, as it were, put other people to the test. The
loss of the flower of his flock made him doubly unsure; he felt
himself a marked man, for Bendel and other enemies to jeer
at. Aloud, he spoke long and vehemently, as if mere noisy
words would heal the wound. And the pupils who had remained faithful to him, gathered all the more closely round
him, and burned as he did. If wishes could have injured or
killed, Fürst's career would then and there have come to an
end: his ingratitude, his treachery, and his lack of moral fibre,
were denounced on every hand.

One day, at this time, Maurice entered Schwarz's room.
The class was assembled; but, although the hour was well
advanced, no one had begun to play. The master stood at the
window, with his back to the grass-grown courtyard. He was
haranguing, in a strident voice, the three pupils who sat along
the wall. From what followed, Maurice gathered that that
very afternoon Schwarz had been informed of the loss of four
more pupils; and though, as every one knew, he had hitherto
not set much store by any of them, he now discovered latent
talent in all four, and was, at the same time, exasperated that
such nonentities should presume to judge him.

To infer from the appearance of those present, the storm
had raged for a considerable period. And still it went on. After

the expiry of a further interval, Krafft who, throughout, had sat shading his eyes with his hand, awoke as though from sleep, yawned heartily, stretched himself and, taking out his watch, studied it with profound attention. For the first time, Schwarz was checked in his flow of words; he coughed, fumbled for an epithet, then stopped, and, to the general surprise, motioned Krafft to the piano.

But Heinrich was in a bad mood. He stifled another yawn before beginning, and played in a mechanical way.

Schwarz had often enough made allowance for this pupil's varying moods; he was not now in the humour to do so.

"*Halt!*" he cried before the first page was turned. "What in God's name is the meaning of this? Do you come here to read from sight?"

Krafft continued to play as if nothing had been said.

"Do you hear me?" thundered Schwarz.

"It's impossible," said Krafft, and proceeded.

"*Barmherziger Gott!*——" The master's short neck reddened, and twisted in its collar.

"Give me music I care to play, and I'll show you how it should be done. I can make nothing of this," answered Krafft.

Schwarz strode up to the piano, and swept the volume from the rack; it fell with a crash on the keys and on Krafft's hands, and effectually hindered him from continuing.

What had gone before was as a summer shower to a deluge. With his arms stiffly knotted behind his back, Schwarz paced the floor with a tread that shook it. His steely blue eyes flashed with passion; the veins stood out on his forehead; his large, prominent mouth gaped above his tuft of beard; he struck ludicrous attitudes, pouring out, meanwhile, without stint—for he had soon passed from Krafft's particular case of insubordination to the general one—pouring out the savage anger and deep-felt injury that had accumulated in him. Finally, he invited the class to rise and leave him, there and then. For what, in God's name, were they waiting? Let them up and away, without more ado!

On receiving the volume of Beethoven on his fingers, Krafft straightened out the pages, and taking down his hat from its peg, left the room, with movements of a calculated coolness. But only a pupil of Bülow's might take such a liberty; the rest had to assist quietly at the painful scene. Maurice studied his finger nails, and Dove did not once remove his eyes from the leg of the piano. They, at least, knew from experience that,

in time, the storm would pass; also that it sounded worse than
it actually was. But a new-comer, a stout Bavarian lad, with
hair cut like Rubinstein's, who was present at the lesson for
the first time, was pale and frightened, and sat drinking in
every word.

Towards the end of the hour, when quiet was re-established,
one's inclination was rather to escape from the room and be
free, than to sit down to play something that demanded coolness and concentration. Dove, who was not sensitive to externals, came safely through the ordeal; but Maurice made a
poor job of the trio in which he had hoped to excel. Schwarz
did not even offer to turn the pages. This, Beyerlein, the
new-comer, did, in a nervous desire to ingratiate himself; but
he was still so flustered that, at a critical moment, he brought
the music down on the keys. Schwarz said nothing; wrapped
in the moody silence that invariably followed his outbursts, he
hardly seemed aware that anyone was playing. After two
movements of the trio, he signed to Beyerlein to take his turn,
and proffered no comment on Maurice's work. Maurice would
have hurried away, without a further word, had he not already
learned the early date of his performance. He knew, too, that
if the practical side of the affair—rehearsals with string players, and so on—was not satisfactorily arranged, he would be
blamed for it. So he reminded Schwarz of the matter. From
what ensued, it was plain that the master still bore him a
grudge for absconding in summer. Schwarz glared coldly at
him, as if unsure to what Maurice alluded; and when the
latter had recalled the details of the case to his mind, he said
rudely: "You went your way, Herr Guest. Now I go
mine." He commenced to turn the leaves of his ponderous
note-book, and after Maurice had stood for some few minutes,
listening to Beyerlein trip and stumble through Mozart, he
felt that, for this day at least, he could put up with no more,
and left the class.

III

SHAKING all disagreeable impressions from him, he sped through the fading light of the September afternoon.

This was the time—it was six o'clock—at which he could rejoin Louise with a free mind. It was the exception for him to go earlier, or at other hours; but, did he chance to go, no matter when, she met him in the same way—sprang towards him from the window, where she had been sitting or standing, with her eyes on the street.

"I believe you watch for me all day long," he said to her once.

On this particular afternoon, when he had used much the same words to her, she put back her head and looked up at him, with a pale, unsmiling face.

"Not quite," she answered slowly. "But I have a fancy, Maurice—a foolish fancy—that once you will come early—in the morning—and we shall have the whole day together again. Perhaps even go away somewhere . . . before summer is quite over."

"And I promise you, dearest, we will. Just let me get through the next fortnight, and then I shall be freer. We'll take the train, and go back to Rochlitz, or anywhere you like. In the meantime, take more care of yourself. You are far too pale. You will go out to-morrow, yes?—to please me?"

But this was a request he had often made, and generally in vain.

Since the afternoon of their return, Louise had made no further attempt to stem or alter circumstance. She accepted Maurice's absences without demur. But one result was, that her feelings were hoarded up for the few hours he passed with her: these were then a working-off of emotion; and it seemed impossible to cram enough into them, to make good the starved remainder of the day.

Maurice was vaguely troubled. He was himself so busy at this time, and so full of revived energy, that he could not imagine her happy, living as she did, entirely without occupation. At first he had tried to persuade her to take up her music again; but she would not even consider it. To all his arguments, she made the same reply.

"I have no real talent. With me, it was only an excuse—
to get away from home."

Nor could he induce her to renew her acquaintance with
people she had known.

"Do you know, I once thought you didn't care a jot what
people said of you?" It was not a very kind thing to say;
it slipped out unawares.

But she did not take it amiss. "I used not to," she answered with her invincible frankness. "But now—it seems—
I do."

"Why, dearest? Aren't you happy enough not to care?"

For answer, she took his face between her hands, and looked
at him with such an ill-suppressed fire in her eyes that all he
could do was to draw her into his arms.

His pains for her good came to nothing. He took her his
favourite books, but—with the exception of an occasional novel
—Louise was no reader. In those he brought her, she seldom
advanced further than the first few pages; and she could sit
for an hour without turning a leaf. He had never seen her
with a piece of sewing or any such feminine employment in
her hands. Nor did she spend time on her person; as a rule,
he found her in her dressing-gown. He had to give up trying
to influence her, and to become reconciled to the fact that she
chose to live only for him. But on this September day, after
the unpleasant episode with Schwarz, he had a fancy to go for
a walk; Louise was unwilling; and he felt anew how preposterous it was for her to spend these fine autumn days, in this
half-dark room.

"You are burying yourself alive—just as you did last
winter."

She laid her hand on his lips. "No, no!—don't say that.
Now I am happy."

"But are you really? Sometimes I'm not sure." He was
tired himself this evening, and found it difficult to be convinced. "It troubles me when I think how dull it must be
for you. Dearest, are you—can you really be happy like this?"

"I have you, Maurice."

"But only for an hour or two in the twenty-four. Tell
me, what do you think of?"

"Of you."

"All that time? Of poor, plain, ordinary me?"

"You are mine," she said with vehemence, and looked at
him with what he called her "hungry-beast" eyes.

"You would like to eat me, I think."

"Yes. And I should begin here; this is the bit of you I love best"—and before he knew what she was going to do, she had stooped, and he felt her teeth in the skin of his neck.

"That's a strange way of showing your love," he said, and involuntarily put his hand to the spot, where two bluish-red marks had appeared.

"It's my way. I want you—I *want* you. I want to feel that you're mine—to make you more mine than you've ever been. I wish I had a hundred arms. I would hold you with them all, and never let you go."

"But, dearest, one would think I wanted to go. Do you really believe if I had my own way, I should be anywhere but here with you?"

"No.—I don't know.—How should I know?"

"Doubts?—beloved!"

"No, no, not doubts. It's only—oh, I don't know what it is. If you could always be with me, Maurice, they wouldn't come. For what I never meant to happen *has* happened. I have grown to care too much—far too much. I want you, I need you, at every moment of the day. I want you never to be out of my sight."

Maurice held her at arm's length, and looked at her. "You can say that—at last!" And drawing her to him: "Patience, darling. Just a little patience. Some day you will never be alone again."

"I do have patience, Maurice. But let me be patient in my own way. For I'm not like you. I have no room in me now for other things. I can't think of anything else. If I had my way, we should shut ourselves up alone, and live only for each other. Not share it, not make it just a part of what we do."

"But man can't live on nectar and honey alone. It wouldn't be life."

"It wouldn't be life, no. It would be more than life."

Some of the evening shadows seemed to invade her face. Her expression was childishly pathetic. He drew her to his knee.

"I should like to see you happier, Louise—yes, yes, I know! —but I mean perfectly happy, as you were sometimes at Rochlitz. Since we came back, it has never been just the right thing—say what you like."

"If only we had never come back!"

"If you still think so, darling, when I've finished here, we'll go away at once. In the meantime, patience."

"Oh, I don't mean to be unreasonable!" But her head was on his shoulder, his arms were round her; and in this position, nothing mattered greatly to her.

Patience?—yes, there was need for him to exhort her to patience. It ate already into her soul as iron bands eat into flesh. The greater part of her life was now spent in practising it. And for sheer loathing of it, she turned over, on waking, and kept her eyes closed, in an attempt to prolong the night. For the day stretched empty before her; the hours passed, one by one, like grey-veiled ghosts. Yet not for a moment had she harboured his idea of regular occupation; she knew herself too well for that. In the fever into which her blood had worked itself, she could settle to nothing: her attention was centred wholly in herself; and all her senses were preternaturally acute. But she suffered, too, under the stress of her feeling; it blunted her, and made her, on the one hand, regardless of everything outside it, on the other, morbidly sensitive to trifles. She waited for him, hour after hour, crouched in a corner of the sofa, or stretched at full length, with closed eyes.

Long before it was time for him to come, she was stationed at the window. She learned to know the people who appeared in the street between the hours of four and six so accurately that she could have described them blindfold. There was the old-faced little girl who delivered milk; there was the postman who emptied into his canvas receptacle, the blue letter-box affixed to the opposite wall; the student with the gashed face and red cap, who lived a couple of doors further down, and always whistled the same tune; the big Newfoundland dog that stalked majestically at his side, and answered to the name of Tasso—she knew them all. These two last hours were weighted with lead. He came, sometimes a poor half-hour too soon, but usually not till past six o'clock. Never, in her life, had she waited for anyone like this, and, towards the end of the time, a sense of injury, of more than mortal endurance, would steal through her and dull her heart towards him, in a way that frightened her.

When, at length, she saw him turn the corner, when she had caught and answered his swift upward glance, she drew back into the shadow of the room, and hid her face in her hands.

Then she listened.

He had the key of the little papered door in the wall. Between the sound of his step on the stair, and the turning of the key in the lock, there was time for her to undergo a moment of suspense that drove her hand to her throat. What if, after the tension of the afternoon, her heart, her nerves—parts of her over which she had no control—should not take their customary bound towards him? What if her pulses should not answer his? But before she could think her thought to the end, he was there; and when she saw his kind eyes alight, his eager hands outstretched, her nervous fears were vanquished. Maurice hardly gave himself time to shut the door, before catching her to him in a long embrace. And yet, though she did not suspect it, he, too, had a twinge of uncertainty on entering. Her bodily presence still affected him with a sense of strangeness—it took him a moment to get used to her again, as it were—and he was forced to reassure himself that nothing had changed during his absence, that she was still all his own.

When the agitation of these first, few, speechless minutes had subsided, a great tenderness seized Louise; freeing one hand, she smoothed back his hair from his forehead, with movements each of which was a caress. As for him, his first impetuous rush of feeling was invariably followed by an almost morbid pity for her, which, in this form, was a new note in their relation to each other, or a harking back to the oldest note of all. When he considered how dependent she was on him, how her one desire was to have him with her, he felt that he could never repay her or do enough for her: and, whatever his own state of mind previous to coming, when once he was there, he exerted himself to the utmost, to cheer her. It was always she who needed consolation; and, by means of his endearments, she was petted back to happiness like a tired child.

In his efforts to take her out of herself, Maurice told her how he had spent the day: where he had been, and whom he had met—every detail that he thought might interest her. She listened, in grateful silence, but she never put a question. This at an end, he returned once more, in a kind of eternal circle, to the one subject of which she never wearied. He might repeat, for the thousandth time, how dear she was to him, without the least fear that the story would grow stale in the telling.

And once here, amidst the deep tenderness of his words, he felt her slowly come to life again, and unfold like a flower. After the long, dead day, Louise was consumed by a desire to drain such moments as these to the dregs. She did not let a word of his pass unchallenged, and all that she herself said, was an attempt to discover some spasm of mental ecstasy, which they had not yet experienced. Sometimes, the feeling grew so strong that it forced her to give an outward sign. Slipping to her knees, she gazed at him with the eyes of a faithful animal.

"What have I done to make you look at me like that?" asked Maurice, amazed.

"What can I do to show you how I love you? Tell me what I can do."

"Do?—what do you want to do? Be your own dear self—that's all, and more than enough."

But she continued to look beseechingly at him, waiting for the word that might be the word of her salvation.

"Haven't you done enough already, in giving yourself to me?" he asked, seeing how she hung on his lips.

But she repeated: "What can I do? Let me do something. Oh, I wish you would hurt me, or be unkind to me!"

He tried to make her understand that he wished for no such humble adoration, that, indeed, he could not be happy under it. If either was to serve the other, it was he; he asked nothing better than to put his hands under her feet. But he could neither coax her nor laugh her out of her absorption: she had the will to self-abasement; and she remained unsatisfied, waiting for the word he would not speak.

Once or twice, during these weeks, they went out in the evening, and, in the corner of some quiet restaurant, took a festive little meal. But, for the most part, she preferred to stay at home. She was not dressed, she said, or she was tired, or it was too hot, or it had rained. And Maurice did not urge her; for, on the last occasion, the evening had been spoiled for him by the conduct of some people at a neighbouring table; they had stared at Louise, and whispered remarks about her. At home, she herself prepared the supper, moving indolently about the room, her dressing-gown dragging after her, from table to cupboard, and back again, often with a pause at his side, in which she forgot what she had set out for. Maurice disputed each trifling service with her; he could only think of Louise as made to be waited on, slow to serve herself.

"Let me do it, dearest."

She had risen anew to fetch something. Now she stood beside him, and put her arms round his neck.

"What can I do for you? Tell me what I can do," she said, and crushed his head against her breast.

He loosened her fingers, and drew her to his knee. "What

do you want me to say, dear discontent? Do?—you were never meant to do anything in this world. Your hands were made to lie one on top of the other . . . so! Look at them. Most white and most useless! "

" There are things not made with hands," she answered obscurely. She let him do what he liked; but she kept her face turned away; and over her eyes passed a faint shadow of resignation.

But this mood also was a transient one; hours followed, when she no longer sought and questioned, but when she gave, recklessly, in a wild endeavour to lose the sense of twofold being. And before these outbreaks, the young man was helpless. His past life, and such experience as he had gathered in it, grew fantastic and unreal, might all have belonged to some one else: the sole reality in a world of shadows was this soft human body that he held in his arms.

Point by point, however, each of which wounded, consciousness fought itself free again. Such violent extremes of emotion were, in truth, contrary to his nature. They made him unsure. And, as the pendulum swung back, something vital in him made protest.

" Sometimes, it seems as if there were something else . . . something that's not love at all . . . more like hate—yes, as if you hated me . . . would like to kill me."

Her whole body was moved by the sigh she drew.

" If I only could! Then I should know that you were mine indeed."

" Is it possible for me to be more yours than I am? "

" Part of you would never be mine, though we spent all our lives together."

He roused himself from his lethargy. " How can you say that?—And yet I think I know what you mean. It's like a kind of rage that comes over one— Yes, I've felt it, too. Listen, darling—there are things one can't say in daylight. I, too, have felt . . . sometimes . . . that in spite of all my love for you—I mean our love for each other—yet there was still something, a part of you, I had no power over. The real you is something—some one I don't really know . . . in spite of all the kisses. Yes"—and the more he tried to find words for what he meant, the more convinced he grew of its truth. " Nothing keeps us apart; you love me, are here in my arms, and yet . . . yet there's a bit of you I can't influence— that is still strange to me. How often I have to ask you why

you look at me in a certain way, or what you are thinking of!
I never know your thoughts; I've never once been able to read
them; you always keep something back.—Why is it, dear? Is
it my fault? If I could just once get at your real self—if I
knew that once, only once, in all these weeks, you had been mine
—every bit of you—then . . . yes, then, I believe I would
be satisfied to . . . to—I don't know what!"

He had spoken in an even, monotonous voice, almost more to
himself than to her. Now, however, he was forced to the
opposite extreme of anxious solicitude. " No, no, I didn't really
mean it. Darling! . . . hush!—don't cry like that. I didn't
know what I was saying; it isn't true, not a word of it."

She had flung herself across him; her own elemental weeping
shook her from head to foot. He realised, for the first time,
the depth and strength of it, now that it, as it were, went
through him, too. Gathering her to him, he made wild and foolish promises. But nothing soothed her: she wept on, until the
dawn crept in, thinly grey, round the windows. But when it
grew so light that the objects in the room were recovering their
form, she fell asleep, and he hardly dared to breathe, for fear of
disturbing her.

By day, the sensations he had tried to express to her seemed
the figments of the night. He needed only to be absent from her
to feel the old restlessness tug at his heart-strings. At such moments, it seemed to him ridiculous to torment himself about an
infinitesimal flaw in their love, and one which perhaps existed
only in his imagination. To be with her again was his sole
desire; and to feel her cheek on his, to be free to run his hands
through her exciting hair, belonged, when he was separated
from her, to that small category of things for which he would
have bartered his soul.

One evening, towards the end of September, Louise watched
for him at the window. It had been a warm autumn day, rich
in varying lights and shades. Now it was late, nearly half-past
six, and still he had not come: her eyes were tired with staring
down the street.

When at last he appeared, she saw that he was carrying
flowers. Her heart, which at the sight of him, had set up a
glad and violent beating, settled down again at once, to its normal course. She knew what the flowers meant : in a spirit of
candour, which had something disarming in it, he invariably
brought them when he could not stay long with her ; and she
had learned to dread seeing them in his hand.

In very truth, he was barely inside the room before he told her that he could only stay for an hour. He was to play his trio the following evening, and now, at the last moment, the 'cellist had been taken ill. He had spent the greater part of the afternoon looking for a substitute, and having found one, had still to interview him again, to let him know the time at which Schwarz had appointed an extra rehearsal for the next day.

Maurice had mentioned more than once the date of his playing; but it had never seemed more to Louise than a disturbing outside fact, to be put out of mind or kissed away. She had forgotten all about it, and the knowledge of this overcame her disappointment; she tried to atone, by being reasonable. Maurice had steeled himself against pleadings and despondency, and was grateful to her for making things easy. He wished to outdo himself in tender encouragement; but she remained evasive: and since, in spite of himself, he could not hinder his thoughts from slipping forward to the coming evening, he, too, had moments of preoccupied silence.

When the clock struck eight, he rose to go. In saying goodnight, he turned her face up, and asked her had she decided if she were coming to hear him play.

It was on her direct lips to reply that she had not thought anything about it. A glance at his face checked her. He was waiting anxiously for her answer: it was a matter of importance to him. Her previous sense of remissness was still with her, hampering her, making her unfree; and for a minute she did not know what to say.

"Would you mind much if I asked you not to come?" he said as she hesitated.

"No, of course not," she hastened to respond, glad to be relieved of the decision. "If you would rather I didn't."

"It's a fancy of mine, dearest—foolish, I know—that I shall get on better if you're not there."

"It's all right. I understand."

When he had gone, she returned to her place at the window. It was a fine night: there was no moon; but the stars glittered furiously in the inky-blue sky, a stretch of which was visible above the gardens. The vastness of the night, the distance of sky and stars, made her shiver. Leaning her wrists on the cold, moist sill, she looked down into the street; it was not very far; but a jump from where she was, to the pavement, would suffice to put an end to every feeling. She was very lonely; no one wanted her. Here she might stand, at this forlorn post, for hours, for the whole night; no one would either know or care.—And her feeling of error, of unfreedom and desolation grew so hard to bear that, for fear she should actually throw herself down, she banged the window to, with a crash that resounded through the street.

But there was something else at work in her to-night, which she could not understand. She struggled with it, as one struggles with a forgotten melody, which hovers behind the consciousness, and will not emerge.

Except for the light thrown by a small lamp, the room was in shadow. She went slowly back to the sofa. On the way she trod on the roses; they had been knocked down and forgotten. She picked them up, and laid them on the cushioned seat beside her. They were dark crimson, and gave out a strong scent: Maurice had seldom brought her such beautiful roses. She sat with her elbows on her knees, her hands closed and pressed to her cheeks, as though she could only think with her muscles at a strain. In memory, she went over what he had said, reflected on what his words meant, and strove, honestly, to project herself into that part of his life, of which she knew nothing. But it was not easy; for one thing, the smell of the roses was too strong; it seemed to hinder her imagination. They had the scent that only deep red roses have—one which seems to come from a distance, from the very heart of cool, pure things—and more and more, she felt as if something within her were trying to find vent in it, something that swelled up, subsided, and mounted again, with what was almost a physical effort. It had been the truth when she told him that she understood; but it had touched her strangely all the same: for it had let her see into an unsuspected corner of his nature. He, too, then, had a cranny in his brain, where such fancies lodged—such an eccentric, artist fancy, or whim, or superstition—as that, out of several hundred people, a single individual could distract and disturb. He . . . too!

The little word had done it. Now she knew—knew what the roses had been trying to tell her. And as if invisible hands had touched a spring in her brain, thereby opening some secret place, the memory of a certain hour returned to her, returned with such force that she fell on her knees, and pressed her face to the seat of the sofa. On the floor beside her lay the roses. Why, oh why, had he needed to bring them to her, on this night of all others?

On the day she remembered, they had been lavished over the

room—one June evening, two years ago. And ever afterwards, the scent of blood-red roses had been associated for her with one of the sweet, leading themes in Beethoven's violin concerto. There was a special concert that night at the Conservatorium; the hall was filled to the last place. She waited with him in the green-room, until his turn came to play. Then she went into the hall, and stood at the back, under the gallery. Once more, she was aware of the stir that ran through the audience, as Schilsky walked down the platform. Hardly, however, had he drawn his bow across the strings, when she felt a touch on her arm, and a Russian, who was an intimate friend of his, beckoned her outside. There, he told her that he had been sent to ask her to leave the hall; and they smiled at each other, in understanding of the whim. Afterwards, she learned how, just about to step on to the platform, Schilsky had had a presentiment that things would go wrong if she remained inside. In his gratitude, and in the boyish exultation with which success filled him, he had collected all the roses, and wantonly pulled them to pieces. Red petals fell like flakes of red snow; and, crushed and bruised, the fragile leaves had yielded a scent, tenfold increased.

While it lasted, the vision was painfully intense: on returning to herself, she was obliged to look round and think where she was. The lamp burned steadily; the dull room was just as she had left it. With a cry, she buried her face in the cushions again, and held her hands to her ears.

More, more, and more again! She was as hungry for these memories as a child for dainties. She was starved for them. And now, dead to the present, she relived the past happy hours of triumph and excitement, not one of which had hung heavy, in each of which her craving for sensation had been stilled. She saw herself as she had then been, proud, secure, unspeakably content. Forgotten words rang in her ears, words of love and of anger, words that were like ointment and like knives. Then, not a day had been empty or tedious; life was always highly coloured, and there was neither pleasure nor pain that she had not tasted to the full. Even the suffering she had gone through, for his sake, was no longer hateful to her. Anything—anything rather than this dead level of monotony on which she had fallen.

When, finally, she raised her head, she might, for all she knew, have been absent for days. Things had lost their familiar aspect; she had once more lived right through the great experience of her life. Putting her hands to her forehead, she tried to force her thoughts back to reality. Then, stiffly, she rose from her knees. In doing so, she touched the roses. With a gesture that was her real awakening, she caught them up and pressed them to her face. It was a satisfaction to her that fingers and cheeks were pricked by their thorns. She was conscious of wishing to hurt herself. With her lips on the cool buds, she stammered broken words: " Maurice—my poor Maurice! " and kissed the flowers, feeling as if, in some occult way, he would be aware of her kisses, of the love she was thus expending on him.

For, in a sudden revulsion of feeling, she was sensible of a great compassion for him; and with each pressure of her lips to the roses, she implored his forgiveness for her unpremeditated desertion. She called to mind his tenderness, his unceasing care of her, and, closing her eyes, stretched out her arms to him, in the empty room. Already she began to live for the following evening, when he would come again. Now, only to sleep through as many as she could of the hours that separated them! She would be to him the next night, what she had never yet been: his own rival in fondness. And as a beginning, she crossed the room, and put the fading roses in a pitcher of water.

IV

Towards seven o'clock the following evening, Maurice loitered about the vestibule of the Conservatorium. In spite of his attempt to time himself, he had arrived too early, and his predecessor on the programme had still to play two movements of a sonata by Beethoven.

As he stood there, Madeleine entered by the street-door.

"Is that you?" she asked, in the ironical tone she now habitually used to him. "You look just as if you were posing for the John in a Rubens Crucifixion.—Feel shaky? No? You ought to, you know. One plays all the better for it.—Well, good luck to you! I'll hold my thumbs."

He went along the passage to the little green-room, at the heels of his string-players. On seeing them go by, it had occurred to him that he might draw their attention to a passage in the *Variations,* with which he had not been satisfied at rehearsal that day. But when he caught them up, they were so deep in talk that he hesitated to interrupt. The 'cellist, a greasy little fellow with a mop of touzled hair, was relating an adventure he had had the night before. His droll way of telling it was more amusing than the long-winded story, and he himself was more tickled by it than was the violinist, a lanky German-American boy, with oily black hair and a pimpled face. Throughout, both tuned their instruments assiduously, with that air of inattention common to string-players.

Meanwhile, the sonata by Beethoven ran its course. While the story-teller still smacked his lips, it came to an end, and the performer, a tall, Polish girl, with a long, sallow, bird-like neck, round which was wound a piece of black velvet, descended the steps. Behind her was heard the applause of many hands. As this showed no sign of ceasing, Schwarz, who had come out of the hall by a lower door, bade her return and bow her thanks. At his words, the girl burst into tears.

"*Na, na, na!*" he said soothingly. "What's all this about? You did excellently."

She seized his hand and clung to it. The 'cellist ran to fetch water; the other two young men were embarrassed, and looked away.

Here, however, several friends burst into the room, and bore

415

Fräulein Prybowski off. Schwarz gave the signal, the string-players picked up their instruments, and the little procession, with Maurice at its head, mounted the steps to the platform.

Although before an audience for the first time in his life, Maurice had never felt more composed. Passing by the organ, and the empty seats of the orchestra, he descended to the front of the platform, where two grand pianos stood side by side; and, as he went, he noted that the hall was exceptionally well filled. He let down the lid of the piano to the peg for chamber-music; he lowered the piano-chair, and flicked the keys with his handkerchief. And Schwarz, sitting by him, to turn the pages of the music, felt so sure of this pupil's coolness that he yawned, and stroked the insides of his trouser-legs.

Maurice was just ready for the start, when the 'cellist, who was restless, discovered that the stand which had been placed for him was insecure; rising from his seat, he went to fetch another from the back of the platform. In the delay that ensued, Maurice looked round at the audience. He saw innumerable heads and faces, all turned expectantly towards him, like lines of globular fruits. His eye ranged indifferently over the oc-cupants of the front seats—strange faces, which told him noth-ing—until his attention was arrested by a face almost directly beneath him, in the second row. For the flash of a second, he thought he knew the person to whom it belonged, and struggled to recall a name. Then, almost as swiftly, he dismissed the idea. It was, however, a face of that kind which, once seen, is never forgotten—a frog-like face, with protruding eyes, and the frog's expressive leer. Somewhere, not very long ago, this face had been before him, and had stared at him in the same discon-certing manner—but where? when? In the few seconds that remained, his brain worked furiously, sped back in desperate haste over all the likely places where he might have seen it. And a restaurant evolved itself; a table in a secluded corner; chrysan-themums and their acrid scent; a screen, round which this re-pulsive face had peered. It had fixed them both, with such malevolence that it had destroyed his pleasure, and he had per-suaded Louise to go home. His memory was now so alert that he could recall the man's two companions as well.

The scene built itself up with inconceivable rapidity. And while he was still absorbed by it, Schwarz raised a decisive hand. It was the signal to begin; he obeyed unthink-ingly; and was at the bottom of the first page before he knew it.

Throughout the whole of the opening movement, he was not rightly awake to what he was doing. His fingers, like well-drilled soldiers, went automatically through their work, neither blundering nor forgetting; but the mind which should have controlled them was unable to concentrate itself: he heard himself play as though he were listening to some one else. He was only roused by the burst of applause that succeeded the final chords. As he struck the first notes of the *Andante with Variations,* he nerved himself for an effort; but now, as if it were the result of his previous inattention, an odd uneasiness beset him ; and on his beginning to weigh each note as he played it, his fingers hesitated and grew less sure. Having failed, through over-care, in the rounding of a turn, he resolved to let things go as they would, and his thoughts wander at will. The movements of the trio succeeded one another; the *Variations* ceased, and were followed by the crisp gaiety of the *Minuet.* The lights above his head were reflected in the shining ebony of the piano; regularly, every moment or two, he was struck by the appearance of Schwarz's broad, fat hand, which crossed his range of vision to turn a leaf; he meditated absently on a sharp uplifting of this hand that occurred, as though the master were dissatisfied with the rhythm—the 'cellist's fault, no doubt: he had been inexact at rehearsal, and, this evening, was too much taken up with his own witticisms beforehand, to think about what he had to do. And thus the four divisions of the trio slipped past, separated by a disturbing noise of hands, which continued to seem as unreal to Maurice as everything else. Only as the last notes of the *Prestissimo* died away, in the disappointing, ineffectual scales in C major, with which the trio closed—not till then did he grasp that the event to which he had looked forward for many weeks was behind him, and also that no one present knew less of how it had passed off than he himself.

With his music in his hand, he turned to Schwarz, to learn what success he had had, from the master's face. According to custom, Schwarz shook hands with him; he also nodded; but he did not smile. He was, however, in a hurry; the old, white-haired director had left his seat, and stood waiting to speak to him. Both 'cellist and violinist had vanished on the instant; the audience, eager as ever at the end of a concert to shake off an imposed restraint, had risen while Maurice still played the final notes; and, by this time, the hall was all but empty.

27

He slowly ascended the platform. Now that it was over, he felt how tired he was; his very legs were tired, as though he had walked for miles. The green-room was deserted; the gas-jet had been screwed down to a peep. None of his friends had come to say a word to him. He had really hardly expected it; but, all the same, a hope had lurked in him that Krafft would perhaps afterwards make some sign—even Madeleine. As, however, neither of them appeared, he seemed to read a confirmation of his failure in their absence, and he loitered for some time in the semi-darkness, unwilling to face the dispersing crowd. When at length he went down the passage, only a few stragglers remained. One or two acquaintances congratulated him in due form, but he knew neither well enough to try to get at the truth. As he was nearing the street-door, however, Dove came out of the *Bureau*. He made for Maurice at once; his manner was eager, his face bore the imprint of interesting news.

"I say, Guest!" he cried, while still some way off. "An odd coincidence. Young Leumann is to play this very same trio next week. A little chap in knickerbockers, you know— a pupil of Bendel's. He is said to have a glorious *legato*—just the very thing for the *Variations*."

"Indeed?" said Maurice with a well-emphasised dryness. His tone nudged Dove's memory.

"By the way, all congratulations, of course," he hastened to add. "Never heard you play better. Especially the *Menuetto*. Some people sitting behind me were reminded of Rubinstein."

"Well, good-night, I'm off," said Maurice, and, even as he spoke, he shot away, leaving his companion in some surprise.

Once out of Dove's sight, he took off his hat and passed his hand over his forehead. Any slender hope he might have had was now crushed; his playing had been so little remarkable that even Dove had been on the point of overlooking it altogether.

Louise threw herself into his arms. At last! she exulted to herself. But his greeting had not its usual fervour; instead of kissing her, he laid his face against her hair. Instantly, she became uncertain. She did not quite know what she had been expecting; perhaps it had been something of the old, pleasurable excitement that she had learnt to associate with an occasion like the present. She put back her head and looked at him, and her look was a question.

"Yes. At least it's over, thank goodness!" he said in reply.

Not knowing what answer to make to this, she led him to the sofa. They sat down, and, for a few minutes, neither spoke. Then, he did what on the way there, he had imagined himself doing: laid his head on her lap, and himself placed her hands on his hair. She passed them backwards and forwards; her sense of having been repulsed, yielded, and she tried to change the current of his thoughts.

"Did you notice, Maurice, as you came along, how full the air was of different scents to-night?" she asked as her cool hands went to and fro. "It was like an evening in July. I was at the window trying to make them out. But the roses were too strong for them; for you see—or rather you have not seen—all the roses I have got for you—yes, just dark red roses. This afternoon I went to the little shop at the corner, and bought all they had. The pretty girl served me—do you remember the pretty girl with the yellow hair, who tried to make friends with you last summer? You like roses, too, don't you?—though not as much as I do. They were always my favourite flowers. As a child, I used to imagine what it would be like to gather them for a whole day, without stopping. But, like all my wishes then, this had to be postponed, too, till that wonderful future, which was to bring me *all* I wanted. There were only a few bushes where I lived; it was too dry for them. But the smell of them takes me back—always. I have only to shut my eyes, and I am full of the old extravagant longings —the childish impatience with time, which seemed to crawl so slowly . . . even to stand still."

"Tell me all about it," he murmured, without raising his head.

She smiled and humoured him.

"I like flowers best for their scents," she went on. "No matter what beautiful colours they have. A camelia is a foolish flower; like a blind man's face—the chief thing is wanting. But then, of course, the smell must remind one of pleasant things. It's strange, isn't it, how much association has to do with pleasure?—or pain. Some things affect me so strongly that they make me wretched. There's music I can't listen to; I have to put my hands to my ears, and run away from it; and all because it takes me back to an unhappy hour, or to a time of my life that I hated. There are streets I never walk through, even words I dread to hear anyone say, because they are connected with some one I disliked, or a day I would rather not have lived. And it is just the same with smells. Wood smouldering outside!—and all the country round is smoky with bush fires. Mimosa in the room—and I can feel the sun beating down on deserted shafts and the stillness of the bush. Rotting leaves and the smell of moist earth, and I am a little girl again, in short dresses, standing by a grave—my father's—to which I was driven in a high buggy, between two men in black coats. I can't remember crying at all, or even feeling sorry; I only smelt the earth—it was in the rainy season and there was water in the grave.—But flowers give me my pleasantest memories. Passion-flowers and periwinkles—you will say they have no smell, but it's not true. Flat, open passion-flowers—red or white—with purplish-fringed centres, have a honey-smell, and make me think of long, hot, cloudless days, which seemed to have neither beginning nor end. And little periwinkles have a cool green smell; for they grew along an old paling fence, which was shady and sometimes even damp. And violets? I never really cared for violets; not till . . . I mean . . . I never . . . "

She had entangled herself, and broke off so abruptly that he moved. He was afraid this soothing flow of words was going to cease.

"Yes, yes, go on, tell me some more—about violets."

She hastened to recover herself. " They are silly little flowers. Made to wither in one's dress . . . or to be crushed. Unless one could have them in such masses that they filled the room. But lilac, Maurice, great sprays and bunches of lilac—white and purple—you know, don't you, who will always be associated with lilac for me? Do you remember some of those evenings at the theatre, on the balcony between the acts? The gallery was so hot, and out there it seemed as if the whole town were steeped in lilac. Or walking home—those glorious nights —when some one was so silent . . . so moody—do you remember? "

At the peculiar veiled tone that had come into her voice; at this reminder of a past day of alternate rapture and despair, so different from the secured happiness of the present; at the thought of this common memory that had built itself up for them round a flower's scent, a rush of grateful content overcame Maurice, and, for the first time since entering the room, he looked up at her with a lover's eyes.

Safe, with her arms round him, he was strong enough to face

the worst. " How good you are to me, dearest! And I don't deserve it. To-night, you might just have sent me away again, when I came. For I was in a disagreeable mood—and still am. But you won't give me up just yet for all that, will you? However despondent I get about myself? For you are all I have, Louise—in the whole world. Yes, I may as well confess it to you, to-night was a failure—not a noisy, open one . . . but all the same, it's no use calling it anything else."

He had laid his head on her lap again, so did not see her face. While he spoke, Louise looked at him, in a kind of unwilling surprise. Instinctively, she ceased to pass her hands over his hair.

" Oh, no, Maurice," she then protested, but weakly, without conviction.

" Yes—failure," he repeated, and put more emphasis than before on the word. " It's no good beating about the bush.—And do you realise what it—what failure means for us, Louise? "

" Oh, no," she said again, vaguely trying to ward off what she foresaw was coming. " And why talk about it to-night? You are tired. Things will seem different in the morning. Shut your eyes again, and lie quite still."

But, the ice once broken, he felt the need of speaking—of speaking out relentlessly all that was in him. And, as he talked, he found it impossible to keep still; he paced the room. He was very pale and very voluble, and made a clean breast of everything that troubled him; not so much, however, with the idea of confessing it to her, as of easing his own mind. And now, again, he let her see into his real self, and, unlike the previous occasion, it was here more than a glimpse that she caught. He was distressingly frank with her. She heard now, for the first time, of the foolish ambitions with which he had begun his studies in Leipzig; heard of their gradual subsidence, and his humble acceptance of his inferiority, as well as of his present fear that, when his time came to an end, he would have nothing to show for it—and under the influence of what had just happened, this fear grew more vivid. It was one thing, he made clear to her, and unpleasant enough at best, to have to find yourself to rights as a mediocrity, when you had hoped with all your heart that you were something more. But what if, having staked everything on it, you should discover that you had mistaken your calling altogether?

" To-night, you see, I think I should have been a better chimney-sweep. The real something that makes the musician

—even the genuinely musical outsider—is wanting in me. I've learnt to see that, by degrees, though I don't know in the least what it is.—But even suppose I were mistaken—who could tell me that I was? One's friends are only too glad to avoid giving a downright opinion, and then, too, which of them would one care to trust? I believe in the end I shall go straight to Schwarz, and get him to tell me what he thinks of me—whether I'm making a fool of myself or not."

"Oh, I wouldn't do that," Louise said quickly.

It was the first time she had interrupted him. She had sat and followed his restless movements with a look of apprehension. A certain board in the floor creaked when he trod on it, and she found herself listening, each time, for the creaking of this board. She was sorry for him, but she could not attach the importance he did to his assumed want of success, nor was she able to subdue the feeling of distaste with which his doubtings inspired her. It was so unnecessary, too, this outpouring; she had never felt curious about the side of his nature which was not the lover's side. To-night, it became clear to her that she would have preferred to remain in ignorance of it. And besides, what he said was so palpable, so undeniable, that she could not understand his dragging the matter to the surface: she had never thought of him but as one of the many honest workers, who swell the majority, and are not destined to rise above the crowd. She had not dreamed of his considering himself in another light, and it was painful to her now, to find that he had done so. To put an end to such embarrassing confidences, she went over to him, and, with her hands on his shoulders, her face upturned, said all the consoling words she could think of, to make him forget. They had never yet failed in their effect. But to-night too much was at work in Maurice, for him to be influenced by them. He kissed her, and touched her cheek with his hand, then began anew; and she moved away, with a slight impatience, which she did not try to conceal.

"You brood too much, Maurice . . . and you exaggerate things, too. What if every one took himself so seriously? —and talked of failure because on a single occasion he didn't do himself justice?"

"It's more than that with me, dear.—But it's a bad habit, I know—not that I really mean to take myself too seriously; but all my life I have been forced to worry about things, and to turn them over."

"It's unhealthy always to be looking into yourself. Let things go more, and they'll carry you with them."

He took her hands. "What wise-sounding words! And I'm in the wrong, I know, as usual. But, in this case, it's impossible not to worry. What happened this evening seems a trifle to you, and no doubt would to every one else, too. But I had made a kind of touchstone of it; it was to help to decide the future—that hideously uncertain future of ours! I believe now, as far as I'm concerned, I don't care whether I ever come to anything or not. Of course, I should rather have been a success—we all would!—but caring for you has swallowed up the ridiculous notions I once had. For your sake—it's you I torment myself about. *What* is to become of us?"

"If that's all, Maurice! Something will turn up, I'm sure it will. Have a little patience, and faith in luck . . . or fate . . . or whatever you like to call it."

"That's a woman's way of looking at things."

He was conscious of speaking somewhat unkindly; but he was hurt by her lack of sympathy. Instead, however, of smoothing things over, he was impelled, by an unconquerable impulse, to disclose himself still further. "Besides, that's not all," he said, and avoided her eyes. "There's something else, and I may just as well make a clean breast of it. It's not only that the future is every bit as shadowy to-night as it has always been: I haven't advanced it by an inch. But I feel to-night that if I could have been what I once hoped to be—no, how shall I put it? You know, dear, from the very beginning there has been something wrong, a kind of barrier between us— hasn't there? How often I've tried to find out what it is! Well, to-night I seem to know. If *I* were not such an out-and-out mediocrity, if I had really been able to achieve something, you would care for me—yes, that's it!—as you can't possibly care now. You would have to; you wouldn't be able to help yourself."

Her first impulsive denial died on her lips; as he continued to speak, she seemed to feel in his words an intention to wound her, or, at least, to accuse her of want of love. When she spoke, it was in a cool voice, as though she were on her guard against being touched too deeply.

"That has nothing whatever to do with it," she said. "It's you yourself, Maurice, I care for—not what you can or can't do."

But these words added fuel to his despondency. "Yes, that's just it," he answered. "For you, I'm in two parts, and one of them means nothing to you. I've felt it, often enough, though I've never spoken of it till to-night. Only one side of me really matters to you. But if I'd been able to accomplish what I once intended—to make a name for myself, or something of that sort—then it would all have been different. I could have forced you to be interested in every single thing I did—not only in the me that loves you, but in every jot of my outside life as well."

Louise did not reply: she had a moment of genuine despondency. The staunch tenderness she had been resolved to feel for him this evening, collapsed and shrivelled up; for the morbid self-probing in which he was indulging made her see him with other eyes. What he said belonged to that category of things which are too true to be put into words: why could not he, like every one else, let them rest, and act as if they did not exist? It was as clear as day: if he were different, the whole story of their relations would be different, too. But as he could not change his nature, what was the use of talking about it, and of turning out to her gaze, traits of mind with which she could not possibly sympathise? Standing, a long white figure, beside the piano, she let her arms hang weakly at her sides. She did not try to reason with him again, or even to comfort him; she let him go on and on, always in the same strain, till her nerves suddenly rebelled at the needless irritation.

"Oh, *why* must you be like this to-night?" she broke in on him. "Why try to destroy such happiness as we have? Can you never be content?"

From the way in which he seized upon these words, it seemed as if he had only been waiting for her to say them. "Such happiness as we have!" he repeated. "There!—listen!—you yourself admit it. Admit all I've been saying.—And do you think I can realise that, and be happy? No, I've suffered under it from the first day. Oh, why, loving you as I do, could I not have been different?—more worthy of you. Why couldn't I, too, be one of those favoured mortals . . .? Listen to me," he said lowering his voice, and speaking rapidly. "Let me make another confession. Do you know why to-night is doubly hard to bear? It's because—yes, because I know you must be forced—and not to-night only, but often—to compare me—what I am and what I can do—with . . . with . . . you know who I mean. It's inevitable—the comparison must be

thrust on you every day of your life. But does that, do you
think, make it any the easier for me?"

As the gist of what he was trying to say was borne in upon
her, Louise winced. Her face lost its tired expression, and
grew hard. "You are breaking your word," she said, in a
tone she had never before used to him. "You promised me
once, the past should never be mentioned between us."

"I'm not blind, Louise," he went on, as though she had not
spoken. "Nor am I in a mood to-night to make myself any
illusions. The remembrance of what he was—he was never
doubtful of himself, was he?—must always—*has* always—
stood between us, while I have racked my brains to discover
what it was. To-night it came over me like a flash that it was
he—that he . . . he spoiled you utterly for anyone else;
made it impossible for you to care for anyone who wasn't made
of the same stuff as he was. It would never have occurred to
him, would it, to torment you and make you suffer for his own
failure? For the very good reason that he never was a failure.
Oh, I haven't the least doubt what a sorry figure I must cut
beside him!"

The unhappy words came out slowly, and seemed to linger
in the air. Louise did not break the pause that followed, and
by her silence, assented to what he said. She still stood motionless beside the piano.

"Or tell me," Maurice cried abruptly, with a ray of hope;
"tell me the truth about it all, for once. Was it mere exaggeration, or was he really worth so much more than all the rest
of us? Of course he could play—I know that—but so can
many a fool. But all the other part of it—his incredible talent,
or luck in everything he touched—was it just report, or was it
really something else?—Tell me."

"He was a genius," she answered, very coldly and distinctly; and her voice warned him once more that he was
trespassing on ground to which he had no right. But he was
too excited to take the warning.

"A genius!" he echoed. "He was a genius! Yes, what
did I tell you? Your very words imply a comparison as you
say them. For I?—what am I? A miserable bungler, a
wretched dilettant—or have you another word for it? Oh,
never mind—don't be afraid to say it!—I'm not sensitive to-
night. I can bear to hear your real opinion of me; for it could
not possibly be lower than my own. Let us get at the truth
for once, by all means!—But what I want to know," he cried

a moment later, " is, why one should be given so much and the other so little. To one all the talents and all your love; and the other unhappy wretch remains an outsider his whole life long. When you speak in that tone about him, I could wish with all my heart that he had been no better than I am. It would give me pleasure to know that he, too, had only been a dabbling amateur—the victim of a pitiable wish to be what he hadn't the talent for."

He could not face her amazement; he stared at the yellow globe of the lamp till his eyes smarted.

" It no doubt seems despicable to you," he went on, " but I can't help it. I hate him for the way he was able to absorb you. He's my worst enemy, for he has made it impossible for you—the woman I love—to love me wholly in return.—Of course, you can't—you *won't* understand. You're only aghast at what you think my littleness. Of all I've gone through, you know nothing, and don't want to know. But with him, it was different; you had no difficulty in understanding him. He had the power over you. Look!—at this very moment, you are siding, not with me, but with him. All my struggling and striving counts for nothing.—Oh, if I could only understand you! " He moved to and fro in his agitation. " Why is a woman so impossible? Does nothing matter to her but tangible success? Do care and consideration carry no weight?— even matched against the blackguardly egoism of what you call genius?—Or will you tell me that he considered you? Didn't he treat you from beginning to end like the scoundrel he was? "

She raised hostile eyes. " You have no right to say that," she said in a small, icy voice, which seemed to put him at an infinite distance from her. " You are not able to judge him. You didn't know him as . . . as I did."

With the last words a deeper note came into her voice, and this was all Maurice heard. A frenzied fear seized him.

" Louise! " he cried violently. " You care for him still! "

She started, and raised her arms, as if to ward off a blow. " I don't . . . I don't . . . God knows I don't! I hate him—you know I do! " She had clapped both hands to her face, and held them there. When she looked up again, she was able to speak as quietly as before. " But do you want to make me hate you, too? Do you think it gives me a higher opinion of you, to hear you talk like that about some one I once cared for? How can I find it anything but ungenerous? —Yes, you are right, he *was* different—in every way. He didn't know what it meant to be envious of anyone. He was as different from you as day from night."

Maurice was hurt to the quick. "Now I know your real opinion of me! Till now you have been considerate enough to hide it. But to-night I have heard it from your own lips. You despise me!"

"Well, you drove me to say it," she burst out, wounded in her turn. "I should never have said it of my own accord— never! Oh, how ungenerous you are! It's not the first time you've goaded me into saying something, and then turned round on me for it. You seem to enjoy finding out things you can feel hurt by.—But have I ever complained? Did I not take you just as you were, and love you—yes, love you! I knew you couldn't be different—that it wasn't your fault if you were faint-hearted and . . . and— But you?—what do you do? You talk as if you worship the ground I walk on: but you can't let me alone. You are always trying to change me— to make me what you think I ought to be."

Her words came in haste, stumbling one over the other, as it became plain to her how deeply this grievance, expressed now for the first time, had eaten into her soul. "You've never said to yourself, she's what she is because it's her nature to be. You want to remake my nature and correct it. You are always believing something is wrong. You knew very well, long ago, that the best part of me had belonged to some one else. You swore it didn't matter. But to-night, because there's absolutely nothing else you can cavil at, you drag it up again—in spite of your promises. I have always been frank with you. Do you thank me for it? No, it's been my old fault of giving everything, when it would have been wiser to keep something back, or at least to pretend to. I might have taken a lesson from you, in parsimonious reserve. For there's a part of you, you couldn't give away—not if you lived with a person for a hundred years."

Of all she said, the last words stung him most.

"Yes, and why?" he cried. "Ask yourself why! You are unjust, as only a woman can be. You say there's a part of me you don't know. If that's true, what does it mean? It means you don't want to know it. You don't want it even to exist. You want everything to belong to you. You don't care for me well enough to be interested in that side of my life which has nothing to do with you. Your love isn't strong enough for that."

"Love!—need we talk about love?" Her face was so unhappy that it seemed to have grown years older. "Love is something quite different. It takes everything just as it is. You have never really loved me."

"I have never really loved you?"

He repeated the words after her, as if he did not understand them, and with his right hand grasped the table; the ground seemed to be slipping from under his feet. But Louise did not offer to retract what she had said, and Maurice had a moment of bewilderment: there, not three yards from him, sat the woman who was the centre of his life; Louise sat there, and, with all appearance of believing it, cast doubts on his love for her. At the thought of it, he was exasperated.

"I not love you!"

His voice was rough, had escaped control. "You have only to lift your finger, and I'll throw myself from that window on to the pavement."

Louise sat as if turned to stone.

"Don't you hear?" he cried more loudly. "Look up! . . . tell me to do it!"

Still she did not move.

"Louise, Louise!" he implored, throwing himself down before her. "Speak to me! Don't you hear me?—Louise!"

"Oh, yes, I hear," she said at last. "I hear how ready you are with promises you know you will not be asked to keep. But the small, everyday things—those are what you won't do for me."

"Tell me . . . tell me what I shall do!"

"All I ask of you is to be happy. And to let me be happy, too."

He stammered promises and entreaties. Never, never again! —if only this once she would forgive him; if only she would smile at him, and let the light come back to her eyes. He had not been responsible for his actions this evening.

"It was more of a strain than I knew. And after it was over, I had to vent my disappointment somehow; and it was you, poor darling, who suffered. Forgive me, Louise!—But try, dear, a little to understand why it was. Can't you see that I was only like that through fear—yes, fear!—that somehow you might slip from me. I can't help feeling, one day you will have had enough of me, and will see me for what I really am."

He tried to put his arms round her, but she held back: she

had no desire to be reconciled. The sole response she made to his beseeching words was: " I want to be happy."

" But you shall.—Do you think I live for anything else? Only forgive me! Remember the happiest hours we have spent together. Come back to me; be mine again! Tell me I am forgiven."

He was in despair; he could not get at her, under her coating of insensibility. And since his words had no power to move her, he took to kissing her hands. She left them limply in his; she did not resist him. From this, he drew courage: he began to treat her more inconsiderately, compelling her to bend down to him, making her feel his strength; and he did not cease his efforts till her head had sunk forward, heavy and submissive, on his shoulder.

They were at peace again: and the joys of reconciliation seemed almost worth the price they had paid for them.

V

THE following morning, having drunk his coffee, Maurice pushed back the metal tray on which the delf-ware stood, and remained sitting idle with his hands before him. It was nine o'clock, and the houses across the road were beginning to catch stray sunbeams. By this time, his daily work was as a rule in full swing; but to-day he was in no hurry to commence. He was even more certain now than he had been on the night before, of his lack of success; and the idea of starting anew on the dull round filled him with distaste. He had been so confident that his playing would, in some way or other, mark a turning-point in his musical career; and lo! it had gone off with as little fizz and effect as a damp rocket. Lighting a cigarette, he indulged in ironical reflections. But, none the less, he heard the minutes ticking past, and as he was not only a creature of habit, but had also a troublesome northern conscience, he rose before the cigarette had formed its second spike of ash, and went to the piano: no matter how rebellious he felt, this was the only occupation open to him; and so he set staunchly out on the unlovely mechanical exercising, which no pianist can escape. Meanwhile, he recapitulated the scene in the concert hall, from the few anticipatory moments, when the 'cellist related amatory adventures, to the abrupt leave he had taken of Dove at the door of the building. And in the course of doing this, he was invaded by a mild and agreeable doubt. On such shadowy impressions as these had he built up his assumption of failure! Was it possible to be so positive? The unreal state of mind in which he had played, hindered him from acting as his own judge. The fact that Schwarz had not been effusive, and that none of his friends had sought him out, admitted of more than one interpretation. The only real proof he had was Dove's manner to him; and was not Dove always too full of his own affairs, or, at least, the affairs of those who were not present at the moment, to have any attention to spare for the person he was actually with? At the idea that he was perhaps mistaken, Maurice grew so unsettled that he rose from the piano. But, by the time he took his seat again, he had wavered; say what he would, he could not get rid of the belief that if he had achieved anything out of the common, Madeleine would not have made it her business to avoid him. After this, however, his fluctuating hopes rallied, then sank once more, until it ended in his leaving the piano. For it was of no use trying to concentrate his thoughts until he knew.

Even as he said this to himself, his resolution was taken. There was only one person to whom he could apply, and that was Schwarz. The proceeding might be unusual, but then the circumstances in which he was placed were unusual, too. Besides, he asked neither praise nor flattery, merely a candid opinion.

If, however, he faced Schwarz on this point, there were others on which he might as well get certainty at the same time. The matter of the *Prüfung,* for instance, had still to be decided. So much depended on the choice of piece. His fingers itched towards Chopin or Mendelssohn, for the sole reason that the *technique* of these composers was in his blood. Whereas Beethoven!—he knew from experience how difficult it was to get a satisfactory effect out of the stern barenesses of Beethoven. They demanded a skill he could never hope to possess.

Between five and six that afternoon, he made his way to the *Sebastian Bach-Strasse,* where Schwarz lived. It was hot in the new, shadeless streets through which he passed, and also in crossing the *Johannapark;* hardly a hint of September was in the air. He walked at a slow pace, in order not to arrive too early, and, for some reason unclear to himself, avoided stepping on the joins of the paving-stones.

On hearing that he had not come for a lesson, the dirty maid-servant, who opened the third-floor door to him, showed him as a visitor into the best sitting-room. Maurice remained standing, in prescribed fashion. But he had no sooner crossed the threshold than he was aware of loud voices in the adjoining room, separated from the one he was in by large folding-doors.

" If you think," said a woman's voice, and broke on " think " —" if you think I'm going to endure a repetition of what happened two years ago, you're mistaken. Never again shall she enter this house! Oh, you pig, you wretch! Klara has told me; she saw you through the keyhole—with your arm round her waist. And I know myself, scarcely a note was struck in the hour. You have her here on any pretext; you keep her in the class after all the others have gone. But this time I'm not going to sit still till the scandal comes out, and she has to leave

the place. A man of your age!—the father of four children!—
and this ugly little hussy of seventeen! Was there ever such
a miserable woman as I am! No, she shall never enter this
house again."

"And I say she shall!" came from Schwarz so fiercely that
the listener started. "Aren't you ashamed, woman, at your
age, to set a servant spying at keyholes?—or, what is more
likely, spying yourself? Keep to your kitchen and your pots,
and don't dictate to me. I am the master of the house."

"Not in a case like this. It concerns me. It concerns the
children. I say she shall never enter the door again."

"And I say she shall. Go out of the room!"

A chair grated roughly on a bare floor; a door banged with
such violence that every other door in the house vibrated.

In the silence that ensued, Maurice endeavoured to make his
presence known by walking about. But no one came. His
eyes ranged round the room. It was, with a few slight
differences, the ordinary best room of the ordinary German
house. The windows were heavily curtained, and, in front
of them, to the further exclusion of light and air, stood re-
spectively a flower-table, laden with unlovely green plants,
and a room-aquarium. The plush furniture was stiffly grouped
round an oblong table and dotted with crochet-covers; under a
glass shade was a massy bunch of wax flowers; a vertikow, dec-
orated with shells and grasses, stood cornerwise beside the sofa;
and, at the door, rose white and gaunt a monumental Berlin
stove. But, in addition to this, which was *de rigueur,* there
were personal touches: on the walls, besides the usual group of
family photographs, in oval frames, hung the copy of a Madonna by Gabriel Max, two etchings after Defregger, several
large group-photographs of Schwarz's classes in different years,
a framed concert programme, yellow with age, and a silhouette
of Schumann. Over one of the doors hung a withered laurel-
wreath of imposing dimensions, and with faded silken ends,
on which the inscription was still legible: *Dem grossen
Künstler, Johannes Schwarz!*—Open on a chair, with an em-
broidered book-marker between its pages, lay *Atta Troll;* and
by the stove, a battered wooden doll sat against the wall, in
a relaxed attitude, with a set leer on its painted face.

Maurice waited, in growing embarrassment. He had unconsciously fixed his eyes on the doll; and, in the dead silence
of the house, the senseless face of the creature ruffled his nerves:
crossing the room, he knocked it over with his foot, so that its

head fell with a bump on the parquet floor, where it lay in a still more tipsy position. There was no doubt that he had arrived at a most inopportune moment; it seemed, too, as if the girl had forgotten even to announce him.

On cautiously opening the door, with the idea of slipping away, he heard a child screaming in a distant room, and the mother's voice sharp in rebuke. The servant was clattering pots and pans in the kitchen, but she heard Maurice, and put her head out of the door. Her face was red and swollen with crying.

" What!—you still here? " she said rudely. " I'd forgotten all about you."

" It doesn't matter—another time," murmured Maurice.

But the girl had spoken in a loud voice to make herself heard above the screaming, which was increasing in volume, and, at her words, a door at the end of the passage, and facing down it, was opened by about an inch, and Frau Schwarz peered through the slit.

" Who is it? "

The servant tossed her head, and made no reply. She went back into her kitchen, and, after a brief absence, during which Frau Schwarz continued surreptitiously to scrutinise Maurice, came out carrying a large plateful of *Berliner Pfannkuchen.* With these she crossed to an opposite room, and, as she there planked the plate down on the table, she announced the visitor. A surly voice muttered something in reply. As, however, the girl insisted in her sulky way, on the length of time the young man had waited, Schwarz called out stridently: " Well, then, in God's name, let him come in! And Klara, you tell my wife, if that noise isn't stopped, I'll throw either her or you downstairs."

Klara appeared again, scarlet with anger, jerked her arm at Maurice, to signify that he might do the rest for himself, and, retreating into her kitchen, slammed the door. Left thus, with no alternative, Maurice drew his heels together, gave the customary rap, and went into the room.

Schwarz was sitting at the table with his head on his hand, tracing the pattern of the cloth with the blade of his knife. A coffee-service stood on a tray before him; he had just refilled his cup, and helped himself from the dish of *Pfannkuchen,* which, freshly baked, sent an inviting odour through the room. He hardly looked up on Maurice's entrance, and cut short the young man's apologetic beginnings.

28

"Well, what is it? What brings you here?"

As Maurice hesitated before the difficulty of plunging off-hand into the object of his visit, Schwarz pointed with his knife at a chair: he could not speak, for he had just put the best part of a *Pfannkuchen* in his mouth, and was chewing hard. Maurice sat down, and holding his hat by the brim, proceeded to explain that he had called on a small personal matter, which would not occupy more than a minute of the master's time.

"It's in connection with last night that I wished to speak to you, Herr Professor," he said: the title, which was not Schwarz's by right, he knew to be a sop. "I should be much obliged to you if you would give me your candid opinion of my playing. It's not easy to judge oneself—although I must say, both at the time, and afterwards, I was not too well pleased with what I had done—that is to say . . ."

"*Wie? Was?*" cried Schwarz, and threw a hasty glance at his pupil, while he helped himself anew from the dish.

Maurice uncrossed his legs, and crossed them again, the same one up.

"My time here comes to an end at Easter, Herr Professor. And it's important for me to learn what you think of the progress I have made since being with you. I don't know why," he added less surely, "but of late I haven't felt satisfied with myself. I seem to have got a certain length and to have stuck there. I should like to know if you have noticed it, too. If so, does the fault lie with my want of talent, or——"

"Or with *me,* perhaps?" broke in Schwarz, who had with difficulty thus far restrained himself. He laughed offensively. "With *me*—eh?" He struck himself on the chest, several times in succession, with the butt-end of his knife, that there might be no doubt to whom he referred. "Upon my soul, what next I wonder!—what next!" He ceased to laugh, and grew ungovernably angry. "What the devil do you mean by it? Do you think I've nothing better to do, at the end of a hard day's work, than to sit here and give candid opinions, and discuss the progress made by each strummer who comes to me twice a week for a lesson? Oho, if you are of that opinion, you may disabuse your mind of it! I'm at your service on Tuesday and Friday afternoon, when I am paid to be; otherwise, my time is my own."

He laid two of the cakes one on top of the other, sliced them through, and put the piece thus obtained in his mouth.

Maurice had risen, and stood waiting for the breathing-space into which he could thrust words of apology.

"I beg your pardon, Herr Professor," he now began. "You misunderstand me. Nothing was further from my mind than——"

But Schwarz had not finished speaking; he rapped the table with his knife-handle, and, working himself up to a white heat, continued: "But plain and plump, I'll tell you this, Herr Guest"—he pronounced it "Gvest." "If you are not satisfied with me, and my teaching, you're at liberty to try some one else. If this is a preliminary to inscribing yourself under that miserable humbug, that wretched charlatan, who pretends to teach the piano, do it, and have done with it! No one will hinder you—certainly not I. You're under no necessity to come here beforehand, and apologise, and give your reasons—none of the others did. Slink off like them, without a word!—it's the more decent way in the long run. They at least knew they were behaving like blackguards."

"You have completely misunderstood me, Herr Schwarz. If you will give me a moment to explain——"

But Schwarz was in no mood for explanations; he went on again, paying no heed to Maurice's interruption.

"Who wouldn't rather break stones by the roadside than be a teacher?" he asked, and sliced and ate, sliced and ate. "Look at the years of labour I have behind me—twenty and more!—in which I've toiled to the best of my ability, eight and nine hours, day after day, and eternally for ends that weren't my own!—And what return do I get for it? A new-comer only needs to wave a red flag before them, and all alike rush blindly to him. A pupil of Liszt?—bah! Who was Liszt? A barrel-organ of execution; a perverter of taste; a worthy ally of that upstart who ruined melody, harmony, and form. Don't talk to me of Liszt!"

He spoke in spurts, blusteringly, but indistinctly, owing to the fullness of his mouth.

"But I'm not to be imposed on. I know their tricks. Haven't I myself had pupils turn to me from Bülow and Rubinstein? Is that not proof enough? Would they have come if they hadn't known what my method was worth? And I took them, and spared no pains to make something of them. Haven't I a right to expect a little gratitude from them in return?—Gratitude? Such a thing doesn't exist; it's a word without meaning, a puffing of the air. Look at him for whom I did more than for all the rest. Did I take a pfennig from him in payment?—when I saw that he had talent? Not I! And I did it all. When he came to me, he couldn't play a scale. I gave him extra lessons without charge, I put pupils in his way, I got him scholarships, I enabled him to support his family—they would have been beggars in the street, but for me. And now soon will be! Yes, I have had his mother here, weeping at my feet, imploring me to reason with him and bring him back to his senses. *She* sees where his infamy will land them. But I? I snap my fingers in his face. He has sown, and he shall reap his sowing.—But the day will come, I know it, when he will return to me, and all the rest will follow him, like the sheep they are. Let them come! They'll see then whether I have need of them or not. They'll see then what they were worth to me. For I can produce others—others, I say!—who will put him and his fellows out of the running. Do they think I'm done for, because of this? I'll show them the contrary. I'll show them! Why, I set no more store by the lot of you than I do by this plate of cakes!"

Again he ate voraciously, and for a few moments, the noise his jaws made in working was the only sound in the room. Maurice stood in the same attitude, with his hat in his hand.

"I regret more than I can express, having been the cause of annoying you, Herr Professor," he said at length with stiff formality. "But I should like to repeat, once more, that my only object in coming here was to speak to you about last night. I felt dissatisfied with myself and . . ."

"Dissatisfied?" echoed Schwarz, bringing his jaws together with a snap. "And what business of yours is it to feel dissatisfied, I'd like to know? Leave that to me! You'll hear soon enough, I warrant you, when *I* have reason to be dissatisfied. Until then, do me the pleasure of minding your own business."

"Excuse me," said Maurice with warmth, "if this isn't my own business! . . . As I see it, it's nobody's but mine. And it seemed to me natural to appeal to you, as the only person who could decide for me whether I should have anything further to do with art, or whether I should throw it up altogether."

Schwarz, who was sometimes not averse to a spirited opposition, caught at the one unlucky word on which he could hang his scorn.

"*Art!*" he repeated with jocose emphasis—he had finished the plate of cakes, risen from the table, and was picking his teeth at the window. " Art!—pooh, pooh!—what's art got to do with it? In your place, I should avoid taking such high-flown words on my tongue. Call it something else. Do you think it makes a jot of difference whether you call it art or . . . pludderdump? Not so much "—and he snapped his fingers—" will be changed, though you never call it any-thing! Vanity!—it's nothing but vanity! A set of raw youths inflate themselves like frogs, and have opinions on art, as on what they have eaten for their dinner.—Do your work and hold your tongue! A scale well played is worth all the words that were ever said—and that, the majority of you can't do."

He closed his toothpick with a snap, spat dexterously at a spittoon which stood in a corner of the room, and the inter-view was over.

As Maurice descended the spiral stair, he said to himself that, no matter how long he remained in Leipzig, he would never trouble Schwarz with his presence again. The man was a loose-mouthed bully. But in future he might seek out others to be the butt of his clumsy wit. He, Maurice, was too good for that.—And squaring his shoulders, he walked erectly down the street, and across the *Johannapark*.

But none the less, he did not go straight home. For, below the comedy of intolerance at which he was playing, lurked, as he well knew, the consciousness that his true impres-sion of the past hour had still to be faced. He might post-pone doing this; he could not shirk it. It was all very well: he might repeat to himself that he had happened on Schwarz at an inopportune moment. That did not count. For him, Maurice, the opportune moment simply did not exist; he was one of those people who are always inopportune, come and go as they will. He might have waited for days; he would never have caught Schwarz in the right mood, or in the nick of time. How he envied those fortunate mortals who always arrived at the right moment, and instinctively said the right thing! That talent had never been his. With him it was a perpetual blunder.

One thing, though, that still perplexed him, was that not once, since he had been in Leipzig, had he caught a glimpse of that native goodness of heart, for which he had heard Schwarz lauded. The master had done his duty by him—nothing more. Neither had had any personal feeling for the other; and the words Schwarz had used this afternoon had only been the outcome of a long period of reserve, even of distrust. At this

moment, when he was inclined to take the onus of the mis-
understanding on his own shoulders, Maurice admitted, besides his constant preoccupation—or possibly just because of
it—an innate lack of sympathy in himself, an inability, either
of heart or of imagination, to project himself into the lives and
feelings of people he did not greatly care for. Otherwise, he
would not have gone to Schwarz on such an errand as to-
day's; he would have remembered that the master was likely
to be sore and suspicious. And, from now on, things would be
worse instead of better. Schwarz had no doubt been left under
the impression that Maurice had wished to complain of his
teaching; and impressions of this nature were difficult to erase.

There was nothing to be done, however, but to plod along
in the familiar rut. He must stomach aspersions and injuries,
behave as if nothing had happened. His first hot intention of
turning his back on Schwarz soon yielded to more worldly-wise
thoughts. Every practical consideration was against it. He
might avenge himself, if he liked, by running to the rival teacher
like a crossed child; Schrievers would undoubtedly receive him
with open arms, and promise him all he asked. But what could
he hope to accomplish, under a complete change of method, in
the few months that were left? He would also have to forfeit
his fees for the coming term, which were already paid. Schrievers' lessons were expensive, and out of the small sum that remained to him to live on, it would be impossible to take more
than half a dozen. Another than he might have appealed to
Schrievers' satisfaction in securing a fresh convert; but Maurice had learnt too thoroughly by now, that he was not one of
those happy exceptions—exceptions by reason of their talent or
their temperament—to whom a master was willing to devote
his time free of charge.

Over these reflections night had fallen; and he walked
speedily back by the dark wood-paths. But before he reached
the meadows, from which he could see lights blinking in the
scattered villas, his steps had lagged again. His discouragement had nothing chimerical in it at this moment; it was part
and parcel of himself.—The night was both chilly and misty,
and it was late. But a painful impression of the previous
evening lingered in his mind. Louise would be annoyed with
him for keeping her waiting; and he shrank, in advance, from
the thought of another disagreeable scene. He was not in the
mood to-night, to soothe and console.

As he entered the *Mozartstrasse,* he saw that there was a light

in Madeleine's window. She was at home, then. He imagined
her sitting quiet and busy in her pleasant room, which, except
for the ring of lamplight, was sunk in peaceful shadow. This
was what he needed: an hour's rest, dim light, and Madeleine's
sympathetic tact.

Without giving himself time for thought, he mounted the
stair and pressed the bell-knob on the third floor.

On seeing who her visitor was, Madeleine rose with alacrity
from the writing-table.

"Maurice! Is it really you?"

"I was passing. I thought I would run up . . . you're surprised to see me?"

"Oh, well—you're a stranger now, you know."

She was vexed with herself for showing astonishment. Moving some books, she made room for him to sit down on the sofa,
and, as he was moody, and seemed in no hurry to state why he
had come, she asked if she might finish the letter she was
writing.

"Make yourself comfortable. Here's a cushion for your
head."

Through half-closed eyes, he watched her hand travelling
across the sheet of note-paper, and returning at regular intervals, with a sure swoop, to begin a fresh line. There was
no sound except the gentle scratching of her pen.

Madeleine did not look up till she had finished her letter
and addressed the envelope. Maurice had shut his eyes.

"Are you asleep?" she roused him. "Or only tired?"

"I've a headache."

"I'll make you some tea."

He watched her preparing it, and, by the time she handed
him his cup, he was in the right mood for making her his
confidant.

"Look here, Madeleine," he said; "I came up to-night—
The fact is, I've done a foolish thing. And I want to talk to
some one about it."

Her eyes grew more alert.

"Let me see if I can help you."

He shook his head. "I'm afraid you can't. But first of all,
tell me frankly, how you thought I got on last night."

"How you got on?" echoed Madeleine, unclear what this
was to lead to. "Why, all right, of course.—Oh, well, if you
insist on the truth!—The fact is, Maurice, you did no better
and no worse than the majority of those who fill the *Abend*

programmes. What you didn't do, was to reach the standard
your friends had set up for you."

"Thanks. Now listen," and he related to her in detail his
misadventure of the afternoon.

Madeleine followed with close attention. But more distinctly than what he said, she heard what he did not say. His
account of the two last days, with the unintentional sidelight it
threw on just those parts he wished to keep in darkness, made
her aware how complicated and involved his life had become.
But before he finished speaking, she brought all her practical
intelligence to bear on what he said.

"Maurice!" she exclaimed, with a consternation that was
three parts genuine. "I should like to shake you. How *could*
you!—what induced you to do such a foolish thing?" And,
as he did not speak: "If only you had come to me before, instead of after! I should have said: hold what ridiculous opinions you like yourself, but for goodness' sake keep clear of
Schwarz with them. Yes, ridiculous, and offensive, too. Anyone would have taken your talk about being dissatisfied just
as he did. And after the way he has been treated of late, he's
of course doubly touchy."

"I knew that, when it was too late. But I meant merely to
speak straight out to him, Madeleine—one man to another.
You surely don't want to say he's incapable of allowing one to
have an independent opinion? If that's the case, then he's
nothing but the wretched little tyrant Heinz declares him
to be."

"Wait till you have taught as long as he has," said Madeleine, and, at his muttered: "God forbid!" she continued with
more warmth: "You'll know then, too, that it doesn't matter
whether your pupils have opinions or not. He has seen this
kind of thing scores of times before, and knows it must be
kept down."

She paused, and looked at him. "To get on in life, one must
have a certain amount of tact. You are too naïve, Maurice, too
unsuspecting—one of those people who would like to carry on
social intercourse on a basis of absolute truth, and then be
surprised that it came to an end. You are altogether a
very difficult person to deal with. You are either too candid,
or too reserved. There's no middle way in you. I haven't the
least doubt that Schwarz finds you both perplexing and irritat-
ing; he takes the candour for impertinence, and the reserve for
distrust."

Maurice smiled faintly. "Go on—don't spare me. No one ever troubled before to tell me my failings."

"Oh, I'm quite in earnest. As I look at it, it's entirely your own fault that you don't stand better with Schwarz. You have never condescended to humour him, as you ought to have done. You thought it was enough to be truthful and honest, and to leave the rest to him. Well, it wasn't. I won't hear a word against Schwarz; he's goodness itself to those who deserve it. A little bluff and rude at times; but he's too busy to go about in kid gloves for fear of hurting sensitive people's feelings."

"Why did you never take private lessons from him?" was her next question. "I told you months ago, you remember, that you ought to.—Oh, yes, you said they were too expensive, I know, but you could have scraped a few marks together somehow. You managed to buy books, and books were quite unnecessary. One lesson a fortnight would have brought you more into touch with Schwarz than all you have had in the class. As it is, you don't know him any better than he knows you." And as she refilled his tea-cup, she added: "You quoted Heinz to me just now. But you and I can't afford to measure people by the same standards as Heinz. We are everyday mortals, remember.—Besides, in all that counts, he is not worth Schwarz's little finger."

"You're a warm advocate, Madeleine."

"Yes, and I've reason to be. No one here has been as kind to me as Schwarz. I came, a complete stranger, and with not more than ordinary talent. But I went to him, and told him frankly what I wanted to do, how long I could stay, and how much money I had to spend. He helped me and advised me. He has let me study what will be of most use to me afterwards, and he takes as much interest in my future as I do myself. How can I speak anything but well of him?—What I certainly didn't do, was to go to him and talk ambiguously about feeling dissatisfied with him . . ."

"With myself, Madeleine. Haven't I made that clear?"

But Madeleine only sniffed.

"Well, it's over and done with now," she said after a pause. "And talking about it won't mend it.—Tell me, rather, what you intend to do. What are your plans?"

"Plans? I don't know. I haven't any. Sufficient unto the day, etc."

But of this she disapproved with open scorn. "Rubbish!

When your time here is all but up! And no plans!—One thing, I can tell you anyhow, is, after to-day you needn't rely on Schwarz for assistance. You've spoilt your chances with him. The only way of repairing the mischief would be the lesson I spoke of—one a week as long as you're here."

"I couldn't afford it."

"No, I suppose not," she said sarcastically, and tore a piece of paper that came under her fingers into narrow strips. "Tell me," she added a moment later, in a changed tone: "where do you intend to settle when you return to England? And have you begun to think of advertising yourself yet?"

He waved his hand before his face as if he were chasing away a fly. "For God's sake, Madeleine! . . . these alluring prospects!"

"Pray, what else do you expect to do?"

"Well, the truth is, I . . . I'm not going back to England at all. I mean to settle here."

Madeleine repressed the exclamation that rose to her lips, and stooped to brush something off the skirt of her dress. Her face was red when she raised it. She needed no further telling; she understood what his words implied as clearly as though it were printed black on white before her. But she spoke in a casual tone. "However are you going to make that possible?"

He endeavoured to explain.

"I don't envy you," she said drily, when he had finished. "You hardly realise what lies before you, I think. There are people here who are glad to get fifty pfennigs an hour, for piano lessons. Think of plodding up and down stairs, all day long, for fifty pfennigs an hour!"

He was silent.

"While in England, with a little tact and patience, you would soon have more pupils than you could take at five shillings."

"Tact and patience mean push and a thick skin. But don't worry! I shall get on all right. And if I don't—life's short, you know."

"But you are just at the beginning of it—and ridiculously young at that! Good Heavens, Maurice!" she burst out, unable to contain herself. "Can't you see that after you've been at home again for a little while, things that have seemed so important here will have shrunk into their right places? You'll be glad to have done with them then, when you are in orderly circumstances again."

"I'm afraid not," answered the young man. "I'm not a good forgetter."

"A good forgetter!" repeated Madeleine, and laughed sarcastically. She was going on to say more, but, just at this moment, a clock outside struck ten, and Maurice sprang to his feet.

"So late already? I'd no idea. I must be off."

She stood by, and watched him look for his hat.

"Here it is." She picked it up, and handed it to him, with an emphasised want of haste.

"Good night, Madeleine. Thanks for the truth. I knew I could depend on you."

"It was well meant. And the truth is always beneficial, you know. Good night.—Come again, soon."

He heard her last words half-way down the stairs, which he took two at a time.

The hour he had now to face was a painful ending to an unpleasant day. It was not merely the fact that he had kept Louise waiting, in aching suspense, for several hours. It now came out that, after their disagreement of the previous night, she had confidently expected him to return to her early in the day, had expected contrition and atonement. That he had not even suspected this made her doubly bitter against him. In vain he tried to excuse himself, to offer explanations. She would not listen to him, nor would she let him touch her. She tore her dress from between his fingers, brushed his hand off her arm; and, retreating into a corner of the room, where she stood like an animal at bay, she poured out over him her accumulated resentment. All she had ever suffered at his hands, all the infinitesimal differences there had been between them, from the beginning, the fine points in which he had failed—things of which he had no knowledge—all these were raked up and cast at him till, numb with pain, he lost even the wish to comfort her. Sitting down at the table, he laid his head on his folded arms.

At his feet were the fragments of the little clock, which, in her anger at his desertion of her, she had trodden to pieces.

VI

THEIR first business the next morning was to buy another clock. By daylight, Louise was full of remorse at what she had done, and in passing the writing-table, averted her eyes. They went out early to a shop in the *Grimmaischestrasse;* and Maurice stood by and watched her make her choice.

She loved to buy, and entered into the purchase with leisurely enjoyment. The shopman and his assistant spared themselves no trouble in fetching and setting out their wares. Louise handled each clock as it was put before her, discussed the merits of different styles, and a faint colour mounted to her cheeks over the difficulty of deciding between two which she liked equally well. She had pushed up her veil; it swathed her forehead like an Eastern woman's. Her eagerness, which was expressed in a slight unsteadiness of nostril and lip, would have had something childish in it, had it not been for her eyes. They remained heavy and unsmiling; and the disquieting half-rings below them were more bluely brown than ever. Leaning sideways against the counter, Maurice looked away from them to her hands; her fingers were entirely without ornament, and he would have liked to load them with rings. As it was, he could not even pay for the clock she chose; it cost more than he had to spend in a month.

In the street again, she said she was hungry, and, glad to be able .to add his mite to her pleasure, he took her by the arm and steered her to the *Café Français,* where they had coffee and ices. The church-steeples were booming eleven when they emerged; it did not seem worth while going home and settling down to work. Instead, they went to the *Rosental.*

It was a brilliant autumn day, rich in light and shade, and there was only a breath abroad of the racy freshness that meant subsequent decay. The leaves were turning red and orange, but had not begun to fall; the sky was deeply blue; outlines were sharp and precise. They were both in a mood this morning to be susceptible to their surroundings; they were even eager to be affected by them, and made happy. The disagreements of the two preceding nights were like bad dreams, which they

444

were anxious to forget, or at least to avoid thinking of. Her painful, unreasonable treatment of him, the evening before, had not been touched on between them; after his incoherent attempts to justify himself, after his bitter self-reproaches, when she lay sobbing in his arms, they had both, with one accord, been silent. Neither of them felt any desire for open-hearted explanations; they were careful not to stir up the depths anew. Louise was very quiet; had it not been for her eyes, he might have believed her happy. But here, just as an hour before in the watchmaker's shop, they brooded, unable to forget. And yet there was a pliancy about her this morning, a readiness to meet his wishes, which, as he walked at her side, made him almost content. The old, foolish dreams awoke in him again, and vistas opened, of a gentle comradeship, which might still come true, when the strenuous side of her love for him had worn itself out. If only an hour like the present could have lasted indefinitely!

It was a happy morning. They ended it with an improvised lunch at the *Kaiserpark;* and it remained imprinted on their minds as an unexpected patch of colour, in an unending row of grey days, given up to duty.

The next one, and the next again, Louise continued in the same yielding mood, which was wholly different from the emotional expansiveness of the past weeks. Maurice took a glad advantage of her willingness to please him, and they had several pleasant walks together: to Napoleon's battlefields; along the *Grüne Gasse* and the *Poetenweg* to Schiller's house at Gohlis; and into the heart of the *Rosental—das wilde Rosental—*where it was very solitary, and where the great trees seemed to stagger under their load of stained leaves.

A burst of almost July radiance occurred at this time; and one day, Louise expressed a wish to go to the country, in order that, by once more being together for a whole day on end, they might relive in fancy the happy weeks they had spent on the Rochlitzer Berg. It was never her way to urge over-much, which made it hard to refuse her; so it was arranged that they should set off betimes the following Saturday.

Maurice had his reward in the cry of pleasure she gave when he wakened her to tell her that it was a fine day.

" Get up, dear! It's less than an hour till the train goes."

For the first time for weeks, Louise was her impetuous self again. She threw things topsy-turvy in the room. It was he who drew her attention to an unfastened hook, and an unbound ribbon. She only pressed forward.

"Make haste!—oh, make haste! We shall be late."

An overpowering smell of newly-baked rolls issued from the bakers' shops, and the errand-boys were starting out with their baskets. Women and house-porters were coming out to wash pavements and entrances: the collective life of the town was waking up to another uneventful day; but they two were hastening off to long hours of sunlight and fresh air, unhampered by the passing of time, or by fallacious ideas of duty; were setting out for a new bit of world, to strange meals taken in strange places, reached by white roads, or sequestered wood-paths. In the train, they were crushed between the baskets of the market-women, who were journeying from one village to another. These sat with their wizened hands clasped on their high stomachs, or on the handles of their baskets, and stared, like stupid, placid animals, at the strange young foreign couple before them. Partly for the frolic of astonishing them, and also because he was happy at seeing Louise so happy, Maurice kissed her hand; but it was she who astonished them most. When she gave a cry, or used her hands with a sudden, vivid effect, or flashed her white teeth in a smile, every head in the carriage was turned towards her; and when, in addition, she was overtaken by a fit of loquacity, she was well-nigh devoured by eyes.

They did not travel as far as they had intended. From the carriage window, she saw a wayside place that took her fancy.

"Here, Maurice; let us get out here."

Having breakfasted, and left their bags at an inn, they strayed at random along an inviting road lined with apple-trees. When Louise grew tired, they rested in the arbour of a primitive *Gasthaus,* and ate their midday meal. Afterwards, in a wood, he spread a rug for her, and she lay in a nest of sun-spots. Only their own voices broke the silence. Then she fell asleep, and, until she opened her eyes again, and called to him in surprise, no sound was to be heard but the sudden, crisp rustling of some bird or insect. When evening fell, they returned to their lodging, ate their supper in the smoky public room—for, outside, mists had risen—and then before them stretched, undisturbed, the long evening and the longer night, to be spent in a strange room, of which they had hitherto not suspected the existence, but which, from now on, would be indissolubly bound up with their other memories.

The first day passed in such a manner was as flawless as any they had known in the height of summer—with all the added attractions of closer intimacy. In its course, the shadows lifted

from her eyes; and Maurice ceased to remember that he had
made a mess of his affairs. But the very next one failed—as
far as Louise was concerned—to reach the same level: it was
like a flower ever so slightly overblown. The lyric charms that
had so pleased her—the dewy freshness of the morning, the
solitude, the unbroken sunshine—were frail things, and,
snatched with too eager a hand, crumbled beneath the touch.
They were not made to stand the wear and tear of repetition.
It was also impossible, she found, to live through again days
such as they had spent at Rochlitz; time past was past irrevocably, with all that belonged to it. And it was further, a mistake
to believe that a more intimate acquaintance meant a keener
pleasure; it was just the stimulus of strangeness, the piquancy
of feeling one's way, that had made up half the fascination of
the summer.

With sure instinct, Louise recognised this, even while she
exclaimed with delight. And her heart sank: not until this
moment had she known how high her hopes had been, how
firmly she had pinned her faith upon the revival of passion
which these days were to bring to pass. The knowledge that
this had been a delusion, was hard to bear. In thought, she was
merciless to herself, when, on waking, the second morning, she
looked with unexpectant eyes over the day that lay before her.
Could nothing satisfy her, she asked herself? Could she not
be content for twenty-four hours on end? Was it eternally
her lot to come to the end of things, before they had properly
begun? It seemed, always, as if she alone must be pressing
forward, without rest. Here, on the second of these days of
love and sunshine, she saw, with absolute clearness, that neither
this nor any other day had anything extraordinary to give her;
and sitting silent at dinner, under an arbour of highly-coloured
creeper, she was overcome by such a laming discouragement, that
she laid her knife and fork down, and could eat no more.

Maurice, watching her across the table, believed that she was
over-tired, and filled up her glass with wine.

But she did not yield without a struggle. And it was not
merely rebellion against the defects of her own nature, which
prompted her. The prospect of the coming months filled her
with dismay. When this last brief spell of pleasure was
over, there was nothing left, to which she could look forward. The approaching winter stretched before her like a star-
less night; she was afraid to let her mind dwell on it. What
was she to do?—what was to become of her, when the short

dark days came down again, and hemmed her in ? The thought of it almost drove her mad.   Desperate with fear, she shut her eyes and went blindly forward, determined to extract every particle of pleasure, or, at least, of oblivion, that the present offered.

Under these circumstances, the poor human element in their relations became once again, and more than ever before, the pivot on which their lives turned.   Louise aimed deliberately at bringing this about.   Further, she did what she had never yet done: she brought to bear on their intercourse all her own hard-won knowledge, and all her arts.   She drew from her store of experience those trifling, yet weighty details, which, once she has learned them, a woman never forgets.   And, in addition to this, she took advantage of the circumstances in which they found themselves, utilising to the full the stimulus of strange times and places: she fired the excitement that lurked in sur-reptitious embrace and surrender, under all the dangers of a possible surprise.   She was perverse and capricious; she would turn away from him till she reduced him to despair; then to yield suddenly, with a completeness that threatened to undo them both.   Her devices were never-ending.   Not that they were necessary: for he was helpless in her hands when she assumed the mastery.   But she could not afford to omit one of the means to her end, for she had herself to lash as well as him.   And so, once more, as at the very beginning, hand grew to be a weight in hand, something alive, electric; and any chance contact might rouse a blast in them.   She neither asked nor showed mercy.   Drop by drop, they drained each other of vitality, two sufferers, yet each thirsty for the other's life-blood; for, with this new attitude on her part, an element of cruelty had entered into their love.   When, with her hands on his shoulders, her insatiable lips apart, Louise put back her head and looked at him, Maurice was acutely aware of the hostile feeling in her.   But he, too, knew what it was; for, when he tried to urge prudence on her, she only laughed at him; and this low, reckless laugh, her savage eyes, and morbid pallor, in-variably took from him every jot of concern.

They returned to Leipzig towards the middle of the first week, in order not to make their absence too conspicuous.   But they had arranged to go away again, on the following Saturday, and, in the present state of things, the few intervening days seemed endless.   Louise shut herself up, and would see little of him.

The next week, and the next again, were spent in the same fashion. A fine and mild October ran its course. For the fourth journey, towards the end of the month, they had planned to return to Rochlitz. At the last moment, however, Maurice opposed the scheme, and they left the train at Grimma. It was Friday, and a superb autumn day. They put up, not in the town itself, but at an inn about a mile and a half distant from it. This stood on the edge of a wood, was a favourite summer resort, and had lately been enlarged by an additional wing. Now, it was empty of guests save themselves. They occupied a large room in the new part of the building, at the end of a long corridor, which was shut off by a door from the rest of the house. They were utteily alone; there was no need for them even to moderate their voices. In the early morning hours, and on the journey there, Maurice had thought he noticed something unusual about Louise, and, more than once, he had asked her if her head ached. But soon he forgot his solicitude.

Next morning, he felt an irresistible inclination to go out: opening the window, he leaned on the sill. A fresh, pleasant breeze was blowing; it bent the tops of the pines, and drove the white clouds smoothly over the sky. He suggested that they should walk to the ruined cloister of Nimbschen; but Louise responded very languidly, and he had to coax and persuade. By the time she was ready to leave the untidy room, the morning was more than half over, and the shifting clouds had balled themselves into masses. Before the two emerged from the wood, an even network of cloud had been drawn over the whole sky; it looked like rain.

They walked as usual in silence, little or nothing being left to say, that seemed worth the exertion of speech. Each step cost Louise a visible effort; her arms hung slack at her sides; her very hands felt heavy. The pallor of her face had a greyish tinge in it. Maurice began to regret having hurried her out against her will.

They were on a narrow path skirting a wood, when she suddenly expressed a wish for some tall bulrushes that grew beside a stream, some distance below. Maurice went down to the edge of the water and began to cut the rushes. But the ground was marshy, and the finest were beyond his reach.

On the path at the top of the bank, Louise stood and followed his movements. She watched his ineffectual efforts to seize the further reeds, saw how they slipped back from be-

29

tween his hands; she watched him take out his knife and open
it, endeavour once more to reach those he wanted, and, still
unsuccessful, choose a dry spot to sit down on; saw him take
off his boots and stockings, then rise and go cautiously out on
the soft ground.   Ages seemed to pass while she watched him
do these trivial things; she felt as if she were gradually turning
to stone as she stood.   How long he was about it!   How
deliberately he moved!   And she had the odd sensation, too,
that she knew beforehand everything he would and would not
do, just as if she had experienced it already.   His movements
were of an impossible circumstantiality, out of all proportion
to the trifling service she had asked of him; for, at heart, she
cared as little about the rushes as about anything else.   But it
was an unfortunate habit of his, and one she noticed more and
more as time went on, to make much of paltry details, which,
properly, should have been dismissed without a second thought.
It implied a certain tactlessness, to underline the obvious in
this fashion.   The very way, for instance, he stretched out his
arm, unclasped his knife, leant forward, and then stooped back
to lay the cut reeds on the bank.   Oh, she was tired!—tired to
exasperation!—of his ways and actions—as tired as she was
of his words, and of the thousand and one occurrences, daily
repeated, that made up their lives.   She would have liked to
creep away, to hide herself in an utter seclusion; while, instead,
it was her lot to assist, hour after hour, at making much of what,
in the depths of her soul, did not concern her at all.   Nothing,
she felt, would ever really concern her again.   She gazed fixedly
before her, at him, too, but without seeing him, till her sight
was blurred; trees and sky, stream and rushes, swam together
in a formless maze.   And all of a sudden, while she was still
blind, there ran through her such an intense feeling of aversion,
such a complete satedness with all she had of late felt and
known, that she involuntarily took a step backwards, and pressed
her palms together, in order to hinder herself from screaming
aloud.   She could bear it no longer.   In a flash, she grasped
that she was unable, utterly unable, to face the day that was
before her.   She knew in advance every word, every look and
embrace that it held for her: rather than undergo them afresh,
she would throw herself into the water at her feet.   Anywhere, anywhere!—only to get away, to be alone, to cover her
face and see no more!   Her hand went to her throat; her
breath refused to come; she shivered so violently that she was
afraid she would fall to the ground.

Maurice, all unsuspecting, sat with his back to her, and laced his boots.

But he was startled into an exclamation, when he climbed the bank and saw the state she was in.

"Louise! Good Heavens, what's the matter? Are you ill?"

He took her by the arm, and shook her a little, to arrest her attention.

"Maurice! . . . no!" Her voice was hoarse. "Oh, let me go home!"

He repeated the words in amazed alarm. "But what is it, darling? Are you ill? Are you cold?—that you're trembling like this?"

"No . . . yes. Oh, I want to go home!—back to Leipzig."

"Why, of course, if you want to. At once."

The rushes lay forgotten on the ground. Without further words, they hastened to the inn. There, Maurice helped her to throw her things into the bag she had not wholly unpacked, and, having paid the bill, led her, with the same feverish haste, through woods and town to the railway-station. He was full of distressed concern for her, but hardly dared to show it; for, to all his questions, she only shook her head. Walking at his side, she dug her nails into her palms till she felt the blood come, in her effort to conceal and stifle the waves of almost physical repugnance that passed through her, making it impossible for her to bear even the touch of his hand. In the train, she leaned back in the corner, and, shutting her eyes, pretended to be asleep.

They took a droschke home; the driver whipped up his horse; the landlady was called in to make the first fire of the season. Louise went to bed at once. She wanted nothing, she said, but to lie still in the darkened room. He should go away; she preferred to be alone. No, she was not ill, only tired, but so tired that she could not keep her eyes open. She needed rest: tomorrow she would be all right again. He should please, please, leave her, and go away. And, turning her face to the wall, she drew the bedclothes over her head.

At his wits' end to know what it all meant, Maurice complied. But at home in his room, he could settle to nothing; he trembled at every footstep on the stair. No message came, however, and when he had seen her again that evening, he felt more reassured.

"It's nothing—really nothing. I'm only tired . . . yes,

it was too much. Just let me be, Maurice—till to-morrow."
And she shut her eyes again, and kept them shut, till she heard
the door close behind him.

He was reassured, but still, for the greater part of the night,
he lay sleepless. He was always agitated anew by the abrupt
way in which Louise passed from mood to mood; but this was
something different; he could not understand it. In the morning, however, he saw things in a less tragic light; and, on
sitting down to the piano, he experienced almost a sense of satisfaction at the prospect of an undisturbed day's work.

Meanwhile Louise shrank, even in memory, from the feverish weeks just past, as she had shrunk that day from his touch.
And she struggled to keep her thoughts from dwelling on them.
But it was the first time in her life that she felt a like shame
and regret; and she could not rid her mind of the haunting
images. She knew the reason, too; darkness brought the
knowledge. She had believed, had wished to believe, that the
failure was her fault, a result of her unstable nature; whereas
the whole undertaking had been merely a futile attempt to
bolster up the impossible, to stave off the inevitable, to post-
pone the end. And it had all been in vain. The end! It
would come, as surely as day followed night—had perhaps
indeed already come; for how else could the nervous aversion
be explained, which had seized her that day? What, during
the foregoing weeks, she had tried not to hear; what had sounded
in her ears like the tone of a sunken bell, was there at last,
horrible and deafening. She had ceased to care for him, and
ceased, surfeited with abundance, with the same vehement
abruptness as she had once begun. The swiftness with which
things had swept to a conclusion, had, confessedly, been ac-
celerated by her unhappy temperament; but, however gentle the
gradient, the point for which they made would have remained
the same. What she was now forced to recognise was, that the
whole affair had been no more than an episode; and the fact of
its having begun less brutally than others, had not made it a
whit better able than these to withstand decay.

A bitter sense of humiliation came over her. What was
she? Not a week ago—she could count the days on her fingers—
the mere touch of his hand on her hair had made her thrill; and
now the sole feeling she was conscious of was one of dislike.
She looked back over the course of her relations with him, and
many things, unclear before, became plain to her. She had gone
into the intimacy deliberately, with open eyes, knowing that she

cared for him only in a friendly way. She had believed, then, that the gift of herself would mean little to her, while it would secure her a friend and companion. And then, too—she might as well be quite honest with herself—she had nourished a romantic hope that a love which commenced as did this shy, adoring tenderness, would give her something finer and more enduring than she had hitherto known. Wrong, all wrong, from beginning to end! It had been no better than those loves which made no secret of their aim and did not strut about draped in false sentiment. The end of all was one and the same. But besides this, it had come to mean more to her than she had ever dreamt of allowing. You could not play with fire, it seemed, and not be burned. Or, at least, she could not. She was branded with wounds. The fierce demands in her, over which she had no control, had once more reared their heads and got the mastery of her, and of him, too. There had been no chance, beneath their scorching breath, for a pallid delicacy of feeling.

It did not cross her mind that she would conceal what she felt from him. Secrecy implied a mental ingenuity, a tiresome care of word and deed. His eyes must be opened; he, too, must learn to say the horrid word "end." How infinitely thankful she had now reason to be that she had not yielded to his persuasions, and married him! No, she had never seriously considered the idea, even at the height of her folly. But then, she was never quite sure of herself; there was always a chance that some blind impulse would spring up in her and overthrow her resolutions. Now, he must suffer, too—and rightly. For, after all, he had also been to blame. If only he had not importuned her so persistently, if only he had let her alone, nothing of this would have happened, and there would be no reason for her to lie and taunt herself. But, in his silent, obstinate way, he had given her no peace; and you could not—she could not!— go on living unmoved, at the side of a person who was crazy with love for you.

For two nights, she slept little. On the third, worn out, she fell soon after midnight into a deep sleep, from which, the following morning, she wakened refreshed.

When Maurice came, about half-past twelve, her eyes followed him with a new curiosity, as he drew up a chair and sat down at her bedside. She wondered what he would say when he knew, and what change would come over his face. But she made no beginning to enlightening him. In his presence, she was seized by an ungovernable desire to be distracted, to be taken out of herself. Also, it was not, she began to grasp, a case of stating a simple fact, in simple words; it meant all the circumstantiality of complicated explanation; it meant a still more murderous tearing up of emotion. And besides this, there was another factor to be reckoned with, and that was the peculiar mood he was in. For, as soon as he entered the room, she felt that he was different from what he had been the day before.

She heard the irritation in his voice, as he tried to persuade her to come out to dinner with him. In fancy she saw it all: saw them walking together to the restaurant, at a brisk pace, in order to waste none of his valuable time; saw dinner taken quickly, for the same reason; saw them parting again at the house-door; then herself in the room alone, straying from sofa to window and back again, through the long hours of the long afternoon. A kind of mental nausea seized her at the thought that the old round was to begin afresh. She brought no answer over her lips. And after waiting some time in vain for her to speak, Maurice rose, and, still under the influence of his ill-humour, drew up the three blinds, and opened a window. A cold, dusty sunlight poured into the room.

Louise gave a cry, and put her hands to her eyes.

"The room is so close, and you're so pale," he said in self-excuse. "Do you know you've been shut up in here for three days now?"

"My head aches."

"It will never be any better as long as you lie there. Dearest, what is it? *What's* the matter with you?"

"You're unhappy about something," he went on, a moment later. "What is it? Won't you tell me?"

"Nothing," she murmured. She lay and pressed her palms to her eyeballs, so firmly that when she removed them, the room was a blur. Maurice, standing at the window, beat a tattoo on the pane. Then, with his back to her, he began to speak. He blamed himself for what he called the folly of the past weeks. "I gave way when I should have been firm. And this is the result. You have got into a nervous, morbid state. But it's nonsense to think it can go on."

For the first time, she was conscious of a somewhat critical attitude on his part; he said "folly" and "nonsense." But she made no comment; she lay and let his words go over her. They had so little import now. All the words that had ever been said could not alter a jot of what she felt—of her intense inward experience.

Her protracted silence, her heavy indifference infected him; and for some time the only sound to be heard was that of his fingers drumming on the glass. When he spoke again, he seemed to be concluding an argument with himself; and indeed, on this particular day, Maurice found it hard to detach his thoughts from himself, for any length of time.

" It's no use, dear. Things can't go on like this any longer. I've got to buckle down to work again. I've . . . I . . . I haven't told you yet: Schwarz is letting me play the Mendelssohn."

She thought she would have to cry aloud; here it was again: the chilling atmosphere of commonplace, which her nerves were expected to live and be well in; the well-worn phrases, the " must this," and " must that," the confident expectation of interest in doings that did not interest her at all. She could not—it would kill her to begin it anew! And, in spite of her efforts at repression, an exclamation forced its way through her lips.

At this, Maurice went quickly back to her.

" Forgive me . . . talking about myself, when you are not well."

He knelt down beside the bed, and removed her hands from her face. She did not open her eyes, kept quite still. At this moment, she felt mainly curious: would the strange aversion to his touch return? He was kissing her palms, pressing them to his face. She drew a long, deep sigh: it did not come back. On the contrary, the touch of his hand was pleasant to her. He stroked her cheek, pushed back a loose piece of hair from her forehead; and, as he did this, she was aware of the old sense of well-being. Beneath his hand, irksome thoughts fell away. Backwards and forwards it travelled, as gently as though she were a sick person. And, little by little, so gradually that, at first, she herself was not conscious of them, other wishes came to life in her again. She began to desire more than mere peace. The craving came over her to forget her self-torturings, and to forget them in a dizzy whirl. Reaching up, she put her arms round his neck, and drew him down. He kissed her eyelids. At this she opened her eyes, enveloping him in a look he had learnt to know well. For a second he sustained it: his life was concentrated in the liquid fire of these eyes, in these eager parted lips. She pressed them to his, and he felt a smart, like a bee's sting.

With a jerk, he thrust her arms away, and rose to his feet; to keep his balance he was obliged to grasp the back of a chair. Taking out his handkerchief, he pressed it to his lip.

"Maurice!"

"It's late . . . I must go . . . I must work, I tell you." He stood staring at the drop of blood on his handkerchief.

"Maurice!"

He looked round him in a confused way; he was strangely angry, and hasty to no purpose. "Won't you . . . then you won't come out with me?"

"Maurice!" The word was a cry.

"Oh, it's foolish! You don't know what you're doing." He had found his coat, and was putting it on, with unsure hands. "Then, if . . . this evening, then! As usual. I'll come as usual."

The door shut behind him; a minute later, the street-door banged. At the sound Louise seemed to waken. Starting up in bed, she threw a wild look round the empty room; then, turned on her face, and bit a hole in the linen of the pillow.

Maurice worked that afternoon as though his future was conditioned by the number of hours he could practise before evening. Throughout these three days, indeed, his zeal had been unabating. He would never have yielded so calmly to the morbid fashion in which she had cooped herself up, had not the knowledge that his time was his own again, been something of a relief to him. Yes, at first, relief was the word for what he felt. For, after making one good resolution on top of another, he had, when the time came, again been a willing defaulter. He had allowed the chance to slip of making good, by redoubled diligence, his foolish mistake with regard to Schwarz. Now it was too late; though the master had let him have his way in the choice of piece for the coming *Prüfung,* it had mainly been owing to indifference. If only he did not prove unequal to the choice now it was made! For that he was out of the rut of steady work, was clear to him as soon as he put his hands to the piano.

But he had never been so forlornly energetic as on this particular afternoon. Yet there was something mechanical, too, about his playing; neither heart nor brain was in it. Mendelssohn's effective roulades ran thoughtlessly from his fingers: in the course of a single day, he had come to feel a deep contempt for the emptiness of these runs and flourishes. He pressed forward, however, hour after hour without a break, as though he were a machine wound up for the purpose. But with the entrance of dusk, his fictitious energy collapsed. He did not even trouble to light the lamp, but, throwing himself on the sofa, covered his eyes with his arm.

The twilight induced sensations like itself—vague, formless, intolerable. A sudden recognition of the uselessness of human striving grew up in him, with the rapidity of a fungus. Effort and work, ambition and success, alike led nowhere, were so many blind alleys: ambition ended in smoke; success was a fleeing phantom, which one sought in vain to grasp. To the great mass of mankind, it was more than immaterial whether one of its units toiled or no; not a single soul was benefited by it. Most certainly not the toiler himself. It was only given to a few to achieve anything; the rest might stand aside early in the day. Nothing of their labours would remain, except the scars they themselves bore.

He was unhappy; to-night he knew it with a painful clearness. The shock had been too rude. For him, change had to be prepared, to come gradually. Sooner or later, no doubt, he would right himself again; but in the meantime his plight was a sorry one. It was his duty to protect himself against another onslaught of the kind—to protect them both. For there was no blinking the fact: a few more weeks like the foregoing, and they would have been two of the wretchedest creatures on earth. They were miserable enough as it was, he in his, she in her own way. It must never happen again. She, too, had doubtless become sensible of this, in the course of the past three days. But had she? Could he say that? What had she thought?—what had she felt? And he told himself that was just what he would never know.

He saw her as she had lain that morning, her arms long and white on the coverlet. He recalled all he had said, and tried to piece things together; an inner meaning seemed to be eluding him. Again, in memory, he heard the half-stifled cry that had drawn him to her side, felt her hands in his, the springy resistance of her hair, the delicate skin of her eyelids. Then, he had not understood the sudden impulse that had made him spring to his feet. But now, as he lay in the dusk, and summed up these things, a new thought, or hardly a thought so much as an intuition, flashed through his mind, instantly to take entire possession of him—just as if it had all along been present, in waiting. Simultaneously, the colour mounted to his face: he refused to harbour such a thought, and put it from him, angry with himself. But it was not to be kept down; it rose again, in an inexplicable way—this suggestion, which was like a slur cast on her. Why, he demanded of himself, should it not have occurred to him before?—once, twenty, a hundred times? For the same thing had often happened: times without number, she had striven to keep him at her side. Was its presence to-day a result of his aimless irritation? Or was it because, after holding him at arm's length for three whole days, she had asked, on returning to him, neither affection nor comradeship, only the blind gratification of sense?

He did not know. But forgotten hints and trifles—words, acts, looks—which he had never before considered consciously, now recurred to him as damning evidence. With his arm still across his eyes, he lay and let it work in him; let doubts and frightful uncertainties grow up in his brain; suffered the most horrible suffering of all—doubt of the one beloved. He seemed to be looking at things from a new point, seeing them in different proportions—all his own poor hopes and beliefs as well— and, while the spasm of distrust lasted, he felt inclined to doubt whether she had ever really cared for him. He even questioned his own feeling for her, seeking to discover whether it, too, had not been based on a mere sensual fancy. He saw them satisfying an instinct, without reason and without nobility. And, by this light, he read a reason for the past months, which made him groan aloud.

He rose and paced the room. If what he was thinking of her were true, then it would be better for both their sakes if he never saw her again. But, even while he said this, he knew that he would have to see her, and without loss of time. What he needed was to stand face to face with her, to look into her eyes, which, whatever they might do, had never learned to hide the truth, and there gain the certainty that his imaginings were monstrous—the phantoms of a melancholy October twilight.

It was nearly nine o'clock, but there was no light in her room. He pictured her lying in the dark, and was filled with remorse. But he said her name in vain; the room was empty. Lighting the lamp, he saw that the bedclothes had been thrown back over the foot-end of the unmade bed, as though she had only just left it. The landlady said that she had gone out, two hours previously, without leaving any message. All he could do

was to sit down and wait; and in the long half-hour that now
went by, the black thoughts that had driven him there were forgotten. His only wish was to have her safe beside him again.

Towards ten o'clock he heard approaching sounds. A moment later Louise came in. She blinked at the light, and began
to unfasten her veil before she was over the threshold.

He gave a sigh of relief. "At last! Thank goodness! Where
have you been?"

"Did you think I was lost? Have you been here long?"

"For hours. Where else should I be? But you—where
have you been?"

Standing before the table, she fumbled with the veil, which
she had pulled into a knot. He did not offer to help her; he
stood looking at her, and both voice and look were a little stern.

"Why did you go out?"

She did not look at him. "Oh, just for a breath of air.
I felt I . . . I *had* to do something.

From the moment of her entrance, even before she had spoken,
Maurice was aware of that peculiar aloofness in her, which
invariably made itself felt when she was engrossed by something
in which he had no part.

"That's hardly a reason," he said nervously.

With the veil stretched between her two hands, she turned
her head. "Do you want another? Well, after you left me
to-day, I lay and thought and thought . . . till I felt I should
go mad, if I lay there any longer."

"Yes, but all of a sudden, like this! After being in bed for
three days . . . to go out and . . ."

"But I have not been ill!"

"Go out and wander about the streets, at night."

"I didn't mean to be so late," she said, and folded the veil
with an exaggerated care. "But I was hindered; I had a little
adventure."

"What do you mean?"

"Oh, nothing much. A man followed me—and I couldn't
get rid of him."

"Go on, please!" He was astonished at the severity of his
own voice.

"Oh, don't be so serious, Maurice!" She had folded the
veil to a neat square, stuck three hatpins in it, and thrown it
with her hat and jacket on the sofa. "No one has tried to
murder me," she said, and raised both her hands to her hair. "I
was standing before Haase's window—the big jeweller's in the

Peterstrasse, you know. I've always loved jewellers' windows
—especially at night, when they're lighted up. As a child, I
thought heaven must be like the glitter of diamonds on blue
velvet—the Jasper Sea, you know, and the pearly floor."

" Never mind that now! "

" Well, I was standing there, looking in, longer perhaps than
I knew. I felt that some one was beside me, but I didn't see
who it was, till I heard a man's voice say: *' Schöne Sachen,
Fräulein, was?'* Of course, I took no notice; but I didn't run
away, as if I were afraid of him. I went on looking into the
window, till he said: *' Darf ich Ihnen etwas kaufen?'* and
more nonsense of the same kind. Then I thought it was time
to go. He followed me down the *Peterstrasse,* and when I came
to the *Rossplatz,* he was still behind me. So I determined to
lead him a dance. I've been walking about, with him at my
heels, for over an hour. In a quiet street where there was no
one in sight, he spoke to me again, and refused to go away until
I told him where I lived. I pretended to agree, and, on the
condition that he didn't follow me any further, I gave him a
number in the *Querstrasse;* and in case he broke his word, I
came home that way. I hope he'll spend a pleasant evening
looking for me."

She laughed—her fitful, somewhat unreal laugh, which was
always displeasing to him. To-night, taken in conjunction with
her story, and her unconcerned way of telling it, it jarred on
him as never before.

" Let me catch him here, and I'll make it impossible for him
to insult a woman again! " he cried. " For it *is* an insult—
though you don't see it in that light. You laugh as you
tell it, as if something amusing had happened to you. You
are so strange sometimes.—Tell me, dearest, *why* did you go
out? When I asked you, you wouldn't come."

" No. Then I wasn't in the mood." Her smile faded.

" No. But after dark—and quite alone—then the mood takes
you."

" But I've done it hundreds of times before. I can take care
of myself."

" You are never to do it again—do you hear?—Why didn't
you give the fellow in charge? " he asked a moment later, in a
burst of distrust.

Again Louise laughed. " Oh, a German policeman would
find that rather funny than otherwise. It's the rule, you know,
not the exception. And the same thing has happened to me be-

fore. So often that it's literally not worth mentioning. I shouldn't have spoken of it to-night if you hadn't been so persistent. Besides," she added as an afterthought—and, in the face of his grave displeasure, she found herself wilfully exaggerating the levity of her tone—"besides, this wasn't the kind of man one gives in charge. Not the usual commercial-traveller type. A Graf, or Baron, at least."

He was as nettled as she had intended him to be. "You talk just as if you had had experience in the class of man.—Do you really think it makes things any better? To my mind, it's a great deal worse.—But the thing is—you don't know how . . . You're not to go out alone again at night. I forbid it. This is the first time for weeks; and see what happens! And it's not—you may well say it has happened to you before. I don't know what it is, but— The very cab-drivers look at you as they've no business to—as they don't look at other women!"

"Well, can I help that?—how men look at me?" she asked indignantly. "Do you wish to say it's my fault? That I do anything to make them?"

"No. Though it might be better if you did," he answered gloomily. "The unpleasant thing is, though you do nothing . . . that it's there all the same . . . something . . . I don't know what."

"No, I don't think you do, and neither do I. But I do know that you are being very rude to me." As he made no reply, she went on: "You will, however, at least give me credit for knowing how to keep men at a distance, though I can't hinder them from looking at me.—And, for your own comfort, remember in future that I'm not an inexperienced child. There's nothing I don't know."

"You needn't throw that up at me."

"*I* at *you?*" she laughed hotly. "That's surely reversing the order of things, isn't it? It ought to be the other way about."

"Unfortunately it isn't." The look he gave her was made up of mingled anger and entreaty; but as she took no notice of it, he turned away, and going to the window, leaned his forehead against the glass. What affected him so disagreeably was not the incident of the man following her, but her light way of regarding it. And as the knowledge of this came home to him, he was impelled to go on speaking. "It's a trifle to make a fuss about, I know," he said. "And I shouldn't give it a second thought, if I could *only* feel, Louise, that you looked at it as I do . . . and felt about it as I do. You seem so indifferent to what it really means—it's almost as if you enjoyed it. Other women are different. They resent such a thing instinctively. While you don't even take offence. And men feel that in you, somehow. That's what makes them look at you and follow you about. That's what attracts them— and always has done—far too easily."

"You among the rest!"

"For God's sake, hold your tongue! You don't know what you're saying."

"Oh, I know well enough." She put her hair back from her forehead, and passed her handkerchief over her lips. "Instead of lecturing me in this way, you might be grateful, I think, that I didn't accept the man's offer and go somewhere to supper with him. It's dull enough here. You don't make things very gay for me. To-day, altogether, you are treating me as if I were a criminal."

He did not answer; the words "You among the rest!" went on sounding in his ears. Yes, there was truth in them, a horrible truth. Who was he to sit in judgment?—either on her, or on those others who yielded to the attraction that went out from her. Had not he himself been in love with her before he even knew her name? Had he then accused her?— laid the blame at her door?

She caught a moth that was fluttering round the lamp, and carried it to the window. When, a moment later, he turned and gave her another unhappy look, she felt a kind of pity for him, forced as he was, by his nature, to work himself into unhappiness over such a trivial matter.

"Don't let us say unkind things to each other," she said slowly. "I'm sorry. If I had known it would worry you so much, I shouldn't have said a word about it. That would have been easy."

He felt her touch on his arm. As it grew warm and close, he, too, was filled with the wish to be at one with her again— to be lulled into security. He pressed her hand.

"Forgive me! To-day I've been bothered—pestered with black thoughts. Or else I shouldn't go on like this."

Now she was silent; both stared out into the night. And then a strange thing happened. He began to speak again, and words rose to his lips, of which, a moment before, he had had no idea, but which he now knew for absolute truth. He said: "I don't want to excuse myself; I'm jealous, I admit it. And yet there *is* an excuse for me, Louise. For saying such things to you, I mean. To-night I— Have you ever thought, dear, what a difference it would make to us, if you had . . . I mean if I knew . . . that you had never cared for anyone . . . if you had never belonged to anyone but me? That's what I wish now more than anything else in the world. If I could just say to myself: no one but me has ever held her in his arms; and no one ever will. Do you think then, darling, I could speak as I have done to-night?"

A moment back, he had had no thought of such a thing; now, here it was, expressed, over his lips—another of those strange, inlying truths, which were existent in him, and only waited for a certain moment to come to light. Strangest of all, perhaps, was the manner in which it impressed itself on him. In it seemed to be summed up his trouble of the afternoon, his suspense and irritation of the later hours. It was as if he had suddenly found a formula for them, and, as he stated it, he was dumbfounded by its far-reaching significance.

A church-clock pealed a single stroke.

" Oh, yes, perhaps," said Louise, in a low voice. She could not rouse herself to a very keen interest in his feelings.

" No, not perhaps. Yes—a thousand times yes! Everything would be changed by it. Then I couldn't torment you. And our love would have a certainty such as it can now never have."

" But you knew, Maurice! I told you—everything! You said it didn't matter."

" And it doesn't, and never shall. But to make it undone, I would cheerfully give years of my life. You're a woman— you can't understand these things—or know what we miss. You mine only—life wouldn't be the same."

For a moment she did not answer. Then the same toneless voice came out of the darkness at his side. " But I *am* yours only—now. And it's a foolish thing to wish for the impossible."

VII

IT was, indeed, a preposterous thought to have at this date: no one knew that better than himself. And as long as he was with Louise, he kept it at bay; it was a fatuous thing even to allow himself to think, considering the past, and considering all he knew.

But next morning, as he sat with busy fingers, and a vacant mind, it returned. He thrust it angrily away, endeavouring to concentrate his attention on the music open before him. For a time, he believed he had succeeded. Then, the idea was unexpectedly present to him again, and this time more forcibly than before; it came like a sharp, swift stab of remembrance, and forced an exclamation over his lips. Discouraged, he let his hands drop from the keys of the piano; for now he knew that he would probably never be rid of it again. This was always the way with unpleasant thoughts and impressions: if they returned, after he had resolved to have done with them, they were henceforth part and parcel of himself, fixed ideas, against which his will was powerless.

In the hope of growing used to the haunting reflection, and to the unhappiness it implied, he thought it through to the end—this strange, unsought knowledge, which had lain unsuspected in him, and now became articulate. Once considered, however, it made many things clear. He could even account to himself now, for the blasphemous suggestions that had plagued him not twenty-four hours ago. If he had then not, all unconsciously, had the feeling that Louise had known too long and too well what love was, to be willing to live without it, such thoughts as those would never have risen in him.

In vain he asked himself, why he should only now understand these things. He could find no answer. Throughout the time he had known Louise, he had been better acquainted with her mode of life than anyone else: her past had lain open to him; she had concealed nothing, had been what she called "brutally frank" with him. And he had protested, and honestly believed, that what had preceded their intimacy did not matter to him. Who could foresee that, on a certain day, an idea of this kind would break out in him—

like a canker? But this query took him a step further. Was
it not deluding himself to say break out? Had not this shadow
lurked in their love from the very beginning? Had it not
formed an invisible barrier between them? It was possible—
no, it was true; though he only recognised its truth at the
present time. It had existed from the first: something which
each of them, in turn, had felt, and vaguely tried to express.
It had little or nothing to do with the fact that they had defied
convention. That, regrettable though it might be, was beside
the mark. The confounding truth was, that, in an emotional
crisis of an intensity of the one they had come through, it was
imperative to be able to say: our love is unparalleled, unique;
or, at least: I am the only possible one; I am yours, you are
mine, only. That had not been the case. What he had been
forced to tell himself was, that he was not the first. And
now he knew that, for some time past, he had been aware
that he would always occupy the second place; she was
forced to compare him with another, to his disadvantage. And
he knew more. For the first time, he allowed his thoughts to
rove, unchecked, over her previous life, and he was no longer
astonished at the imperfections of the present. To him, the
gradual unfolding of their love had been a wonderful revelation; to her, a repetition, and a paler and fainter one, of a tale
she already knew by heart. And the knowledge of this awakened a fresh distrust in him. If she had loved that first time,
as she had asserted, as he had seen with his own eyes that she
did, desperately, abandonedly, how had it been possible for her
to change front so quickly, to turn to him and love anew?
Was such a thing credible? Was a woman's nature capable
of it? And had it not been this constant fear, lest he should
never be able to efface the image of his predecessor, which,
yesterday, had boldly stalked out as a dread that what had
drawn her to him, had not been love at all?

But this mood passed. He himself cared too well to doubt,
for long, that in her own way she really loved him. What,
however, he was obliged to admit was, that what she felt could
in no way be counted the equal of his love for her: that had
possessed a kind of primeval freshness, which no repetition,
however passionately fond, could achieve. And yet, in his
mind, there was still room for doubt—eager, willing doubt.
It was due to his ignorance. He became aware of this, and,
while brooding over these things, he was overmanned by the desire to learn, from her own lips, more about her past, to hear

30

exactly what it had meant to her, in order that he might compare it with her present life, and with her feelings for him. Who could say if, by doing this, he might not drive away what was perhaps a phantom of his own uneasy brain?

He resolved to make the endeavour. But he was careful not to let her suspect his intention. First of all, he was full of compunction for his bad temper of the night before; he was also slightly ashamed of what he was going to do; and then, too, he knew that she would resent his prying. What he did must be done with tact. He had no wish to make her unhappy over it. And so, when he saw her again, he tries his best to make her forget how disagreeable he had been.

But the desire to know remained, became a morbid curiosity. If this were satisfied, he believed it would make things easier for both of them. But he was infinitely cautious. Sometimes, without a word, he took her face between his hands and looked into her eyes, as if to read in them an answer to the questions he was afraid to put—looked right into the depth of her eyes, where the pupils swam in an oval of bluish white, overhung by lids which were finely creased in their folds, and netted with tiny veins. But he said not a word, and the eyes remained unfathomable, as they had always been.

Meanwhile, he did what he could to set his life on a solid basis again. But he was unable to arouse in himself a very vital interest in his work; some prompter-nerve in him seemed to have been injured. And often, he was overcome by the feeling that this perpetual preoccupation with music was only a trifling with existence, an excuse for not facing the facts of life. He would sometimes rather have been a labourer, worn out with physical toil. He was much alone, too; when he was not with Louise, he was given over to his own thoughts, and, day by day, fostered by the long, empty hours of practice, these moved more and more steadily in the one direction. The craving for a knowledge of the facts, for certainty in any form —this became a reason for, a plea in extenuation of, what he felt escaping him.

Louise did not help him; she assented to what he did without comment, half sorry for him in what seemed to her his wilful blindness, half disdainful. But she, too, made a discovery in these tame, flat days, and this was, that it was one thing to say to herself: it is over and done with, and another to make the assertion a fact. Energy for the effort was lacking in her; for the short, sharp stroke, which with her meant action, was invariably born of intense happiness or unhappiness. Now, as the days went by, she asked herself why she should do it. It was so much easier to let things slide, until something happened of itself, either to make the break, or to fill up the still greater emptiness in her life which a break would cause. And if he were content with what she could give him, well and good; she made no attempt to deceive him. And it seemed to her that he *was* content, though in a somewhat preoccupied way. But a little later, she acknowledged to herself that this was not the whole truth. There was habit to fight against—habit which could still give her hours of self-forgetfulness—and one could not forgo, all at once, and under no pressing necessity to do so, this means of escape from the cheerlessness of life.

But not for long did matters remain at this negative stage. Whereas, until now, the touch of her lips had been sufficient to chase away the shadows, the moment came, when, as he held her in his arms, Maurice was paralysed by the abrupt remembrance: she has known all this before. How was it then? To what degree is she mine, was she his? What fine, ultimate shade of feeling is she keeping back from me?—His ardour was damped; and as Louise also became aware of his sudden coolness, their hands sank apart, and had no strength to join anew.

Thus far, he had gone about his probings with skill, questioning her in a roundabout way, trying to learn by means of inference. But after this, he let himself go, and put a barefaced question. The subject once broached, there was no further need of concealment, and he flung tact and prudence to the winds. He could not forget—he was goaded on by—the look she had given him, as the ominous words crossed his lips: it made him conscious once more of the unapproachable nature of that first love of hers. He grew reckless; and while he had hitherto only sought to surprise her and entrap her, he now began to try to worm things out of her, all the time spying on her looks and words, ready to take advantage of the least slip on her part.

At first, before she understood what he was aiming at, Louise had been as frank as usual with him—that somewhat barbarous frankness, which took small note of the recipient's feelings. But after he had put a direct question, and followed it up with others, of which she too clearly saw the drift, she drew back, as though she were afraid of him. It was not alone the error of taste he committed, in delving in matters which he had sworn should never concern him; it was his manner of doing it that was so distasteful to her—his hints and inuendoes. She grew very white and still, and looked at him with eyes in which a nascent dislike was visible.

He saw it; but it was now too late. Day by day, his preoccupation with the man who had preceded him increased. The thought that continued to harass him was: if she had never known the other, all would now be different. With jealousy, his state of mind had only as yet, in common, a devouring curiosity and a morbid imagination, which allowed him to picture the two of them in situations he would once have blushed to think of. For the one thing that now mattered to him, what he would have given his life to know, and would probably never know, was concerned with the ultimate ratification of love. What had she had for the other that she could not give him?—that she wilfully refrained from giving him? For that she did this, and always had refused him part of herself, was now as plain to him as if it had been branded on her flesh. And the knowledge undermined their lives. If she was gentle and kind, he read into her words pity that she could give him no more; if she were cold and evasive, she was remembering, comparing; if she returned his kisses with her former warmth—well, the thoughts which in this case seized him were the most murderous of all.

His mental activity ground him down. But it was not all unhappiness; the beloved eyes and hands, the wilful hair, and pale, sweet mouth, could still stir him; and there came hours of wishless well-being, when his tired brain found rest. As the days went by, however, these grew rarer; it also seemed to him that he paid dearly for them, by being afterwards more miserable, by suffering in a more active way.

At times, he knew, he was anything but a pleasant companion. But he was losing the mastery over himself, and often a trifle was sufficient to start him off afresh on the dreary theme. Once, in a fit of hopelessness, he made her what amounted to reproaches for her past.

"But you knew!—everything!—I told you all," Louise expostulated, and there were tears in her eyes.

"I know you did. But Louise"—he hesitated, half contrite in advance, for what he was going to say—"it might have been better if you hadn't told me—everything, I mean. Yes, I believe it's better not to know."

She did not reply, as she might have done, that she had forewarned him, afraid of this. She looked away, so that she should not be obliged to see him.

Another day, when they were walking in the *Rosental,* she made him extremely unhappy by disagreeing with him.

" If one could just take a sponge and wipe the past out, like figures from a slate! " he said moodily.

But, jaded by his persistency, Louise would not admit it. " We should have nothing to remember."

" That's just it."

" But it belongs to us! " She was roused to protest by the under-meaning in his words. " It's as much a part of ourselves as our thoughts are—or our hands."

" One is glad to forget. You would be, Louise? You wouldn't care if your past were gone? Say you wouldn't."

But she only threw him a dark side-glance. As, however, he would not rest content, she flung out her hands with an impatient gesture. " How *can* you torment yourself so! If you insist on knowing, well, then, I wouldn't part with an hour of what's gone—not an hour! And you know it."

She caught at a few vivid leaves that had remained hanging on a bare branch, and carried them with her.

He took one she held out to him, looked at it without seeing it, and threw it away. " Tell me, just this once, something about your life before I knew you. Were you very happy?—or were you unhappy? Do you know, I once heard you say you had never known a moment's happiness?—yes, one summer night long ago, over in the *Nonne.* How I hoped then it was true! But I don't know. You've never told me anything—of all there must be to tell."

" What you may have chanced to hear, by eavesdropping, doesn't concern me now," Louise answered coldly. And then she shut her lips, and would say no more. She was wiser than she had been a week ago: she refused to hand her past over to him in order that he might smirch it with his thoughts.

But she could not understand him—understand the motives that made him want to unearth the past. If this were jealousy, it was a kind she did not know—a bloodless, bodiless kind, of which she had had no experience.

But it was not jealousy; it was only a craving for certainty in any guise, and the more surely Maurice felt that he would never gain it, the more tenaciously he strove. For certainty, that feeling of utter reliance in the loved one, which

sets the heart at rest and leaves the mind free for the affairs
of life, was what Louise had never given him; he had always
been obliged to fall back on supposition with regard to her,
equally at the height of their passion, and in that first arid
stretch of time, when it was forbidden him to touch her hand.
The real truth, the last-reaching truth about her, it would
not be his to know.   Soul would never be absorbed in soul;
not the most passionate embraces could bridge the gulf; to
their last kiss, they would remain separate beings, lonely and
alone.

As this went on, he came to hate the vapidities of the concerto in G major.   Mentally to be stretched on a kind of rack,
and, at the same time, to be forced to reiterate the empty
rhetoric of this music!   From this time forward, he could not
hear the name of Mendelssohn without a shiver of repugnance.
How he wished now, that he had been content with the bare
sincerity of Beethoven, who at least said no note more than he
had to say.

One day, towards the end of November, he was working
with even greater distaste than usual.   Finally, in exasperation,
he flapped the music to, shut the piano, and went out.   A
stroll along the muddy little railed-in river brought him to the
Pleissenburg, and from there he crossed the *Königsplatz* to
the *Brüderstrasse.*   He had not come out with the intention
of going to Louise, but, although it was barely four o'clock,
the afternoon was drawing in; an interminable evening had
to be got through.   He had been walking at haphazard, and
without relish; now his pace grew brisker.   Having reached
the house, he sprang nimbly up the stairs, and was about to
insert his key in the little door in the wall, when he was
arrested by a muffled sound of voices.   Louise was talking to
some one, and, at the noise he made outside, she raised her
voice—purposely, no doubt.   He could not hear what was being
said, but the second voice was a man's.   For a minute he stood,
with his key suspended, straining his ears; then, afraid of being
caught, he went downstairs again, where he hung about, between
stair and street-door, in order that anyone who came down
would be forced to pass him.   At the end of five minutes, however, his patience was spent: he remembered, too, that the person
might be as likely to go up as down.   He mounted the stairs
again, rang the bell, and had himself admitted by the landlady.

He thought she looked significantly at him as, with her usual pantomime of winks and signs, she whispered to him that a gentleman was with Fräulein—*ein. schöner junger Mann!* Maurice pushed her aside, and opened the sitting-room door. Two heads turned at his entrance.

On the sofa, beside Louise, sat Herries, the ruddy little student of medicine with whom she had danced so often at the ball. He sat there, smiling and dapper, balancing his hard round hat on his knee, and holding gloves in his hand.

Louise looked the more untidy by contrast: as usual, her hair was half uncoiled. Maurice saw this in a flash, saw also the look of annoyance that crossed her face at his unceremonious entry. She raised astonished eyebrows. Then, however, she shook hands with him.

"I think you know Mr. Herries."

Maurice bowed stiffly across the table; Herries replied in kind, without discommoding himself.

"How d'ye do? I believe we've met," he said carelessly.

As Maurice made no rejoinder, but remained standing in an uncompromising attitude, Herries turned to Louise again, and went on with what he had been saying. He was talking of England.

"I went back to Oxford after that," he continued. "I've diggings there, don't you know? An old chum of mine's a fellow of Magdalen. I was just in time for eights' week. A magnificent walk-over for our fellows. Ever seen the race? No? Oh, I say, that's too bad. You must come over for it, next year."

"Mr. Herries only returned from England a few days ago," explained Louise, and again raised warning brows. "Do sit down. There's a chair."

"Yes. I was over for the whole summer. Didn't work here at all, in fact," added Herries, once more letting his bright eyes snapshot the young man, who, on sitting down, laid his shabby felt hat in the middle of the table.

"But now you intend to stay, I think you said?" Louise threw in at random, after they had waited for Maurice to fill up the pause.

"Yes, for the winter semester, anyhow. And I've got to tumble to, with a vengeance. But I mean to have a good time all the same. Even though it's only Leipzig, one can have a jolly enough time."

Again there was silence. Louise flushed. "I suppose you're hard at work already?"

"Yes. Got started yesterday. Frogs, don't you know?—the effect of a rare poison on frogs."

This trivial exchange of words stung Maurice. Herries's manner seemed to him intolerably familiar, lacking in respect; and he kept telling himself, as he listened, that, on his returning from England, the fellow's first thought had been of her. He had not opened his lips since entering; he sat staring at them, forgetful of good manners; and, after a little, both began to feel ill at ease. Their eyes met for a moment in this sensation, and Herries cleared his throat.

"What did you do with yourself in summer?" he queried, and could not restrain a smile, at the fashion in which the other fellow was giving himself away. "You weren't in England at all, I think you said? We hoped we might meet there, don't you remember? Too bad that I had to go off without saying good-bye."

"No, I changed my mind and stayed here. But I shouldn't do it again. It was so hot."

"Must have been simply beastly."

Maurice jerked his arm; a vase which was standing at his elbow upset, and the water trickled to the floor. Neither offered to help him; he had to stoop and mop it up with his handkerchief.

For a few moments longer, the conversation was eked out. Then Herries rose. With her hand in his, he said earnestly: "Now you must be merciful and relent. I shan't give up hope. Any time in the next fortnight is time enough, remember. 'Pon my word, I've dreamt of those waltzes of ours ever since. And the floor at the *Prusse* is still better, don't you know? You won't have the heart not to come."

From under her lids, Louise shot a rapid glance at Maurice. He, too, had risen; he was standing stiff, pale, and solemn, visibly waiting only till Herries had gone, to make himself disagreeable. She smiled.

"Don't ask me to give an answer to-day. I'll let you know —will that do? A fortnight is such a long time. And then you've forgotten the chief thing. I must see if I have anything to wear."

"Oh, I say!... if that's all! Don't let that bother you. That black thing you had on last time was ripping—awfully jolly, don't you know?"

Louise laughed. "Well, perhaps," she said, as she opened the door.

"Good business!" responded Herries.

He nodded in Maurice's direction, and they went out of the room together. Maurice heard their voices in laughing rejoinder, heard them take leave of each other at the hall-door. After that there was a pause. Louise lingered, before returning, to open a letter that was lying on the hall-table; she also spoke to Fräulein Grünhut. When she did come back, all trace of animation had gone from her face. She busied herself at once with the flowers he had disarranged, and this done, ordered her hair before the hanging glass. Maurice followed her movements with a sarcastic smile.

Suddenly she turned and confronted him.

"Maurice! . . . for Heaven's sake, don't glare at me like that! If you've anything to say, please say it, and be done with it."

"You know well enough what I have to say." His voice was husky.

"Indeed, I don't."

"Well you ought to."

"Ought to?—No: there's a limit to everything! Take your hat off that table!—What did you mean by bursting into the room when you heard some one was here? And, as if that weren't enough—to let everybody see how much at home you are—your behaviour—your unbearable want of manners . . ." She stopped, and pressed her handkerchief to her lips.

"I believed you didn't care what people thought," he threw in, morosely defiant.

"That's a poor excuse for your rudeness."

"Well, at least tell me what that fool wanted here."

"Have you no ears? Couldn't you hear that he has just come back from England, and is calling on his friends?"

"Do you expect me to believe that?"

"Maurice!"

"Oh, he has always been after you—since that night. It's only because he wasn't here long enough . . . and his manner shows what he thinks of you . . . and what he means."

"What do *you* mean? Do you wish to say it's my doing that he came here to-day?— Don't you believe me?" she demanded, as he did not answer.

"And you in that half-dressed condition!"

"Could I dress before him? How abominable you are!"

He tried to explain. "Yes. Because . . . I hate the sight

of the fellow.—You didn't know he was coming, did you, or
you wouldn't have seen him?"

"Know he was coming!" She wrenched her hands away.
"Oh! . . ."

"Say you didn't!"

"Maurice!—Be jealous, if you must! But surely, surely
you don't believe——"

"Oh, don't ask me what I believe. I only know I won't
have that man hanging about. It was by a mere chance to-day
that I came round earlier; he might have been here for hours,
without my suspecting it. Who knows if you would have told
me either?—Would you have told me, Louise?"

"Oh, how can you be like this! What is the matter with
you?"

He put his arms round her, with the old cry. "I can't
bear you even to look at another man. For he's in love with
you, and has been, ever since you made him crazy by dancing
with him as you did."

With his hands on her shoulders, he rested his face on her
hair. "Promise me you won't see him again."

Wearily, Louise disengaged herself. "Oh there's always
something fresh to promise. I'm tired of it—of being hedged
in, and watched, and never trusted."

"Tired of me, you mean."

She looked bitterly at him. "There you are again!"

"Just this once—to set my mind at rest. Just this once,
Louise!—darling!"

But she was silent.

"Then you'll let him come here again?"

"How do I know?—But if I promised what you ask, I
should not be able to go with him to the *Hôtel de Prusse* on
the fifteenth."

"You mean to go to that dance?"

"Why not? Would there be any harm in my going?"

"Louise!"

"Maurice!" She mocked his tone, and laughed. "Oh,
go at once," she broke out the next moment, "and order
Grünhut never to let another visitor inside the door. Make
me promise never to cross the threshold alone—never to speak
to another mortal but yourself! Cut off every pleasure and
every chance of pleasure I have; and then you may be, but only
may be, content."

"You're trying how far you can go with me."

"Do you want me to tell you again that dancing is one of the things I love best? Not six months ago, you knew, and helped me to it yourself."

"Yes, *then,*" he answered. "Then I could refuse you nothing."

She laughed in an unfriendly way. He pressed her hand to his forehead. "You won't be so cruel, I know."

"You know more than I do."

"Do you realise what it means if you go?" In fancy, he was present, and saw her passed from one pair of arms to another.

"I realise nothing—but that I am very unhappy."

"Have I no influence over you any more—none at all?"

"Can't you come, too, then?—if you are afraid to let me out of your sight?"

"I? To see you——" He broke off with wrathful abruptness. "Thanks, I would rather be shot." But at the mingled anger and blankness of her face, he coloured. "Louise, put an end to all this. Marry me—now, at once!"

"Marry you? I? No, thank you. We're past that stage, I think.—Besides, are you so simple as to believe it would make any difference?"

"Oh, stop tormenting me. Come here!"—and he pulled her to him.

From this day forward, the direction of his thoughts was changed. The incident of Herries's visit, her refusal to promise what he asked, and, above all, the matter of the coming ball, with regard to which he could not get certainty from her: these things seemed to open up nightmare depths, to which he could see no bottom. Compared with them, the vague fears which had hitherto troubled him were only shadows, and like shadows faded away. He no longer sought out superfine reasons for their lack of happiness. The past was dead and gone; he could not alter jot or tittle of what had happened; he could only make the best of it. And so he ceased to brood over it, and gave himself up to the present. The future was a black, unknown quantity, but the present was his own. And he would cling to it—for who knew what the future held in store for him? In these days, he began to suspect that it was not in the nature of things for her always to remain satisfied with him; and, ever more daring, the horrid question reared its head: who will come after me? Another blind attraction only needed to seize her, and what, then, would become of

constancy and truth? If he had doubted her before, he was
now suspicious from a different cause, and in quite a different
way. The face of the trim little man who had sat beside
her, and smiled at her, was persistently present to him. He
did not question her further; but the poison worked the more
surely in secret; he never for an instant forgot; and jealousy, now wide awake, had at last a definite object to lay
hold of.

In his lucid moments, he knew that he was making her life
a burden to her. What wonder if she did, ultimately, turn
from him? But his evil moods were now beyond command.
He began to suspect deceit in her actions as well as in what
she said. The idea that this other, this smirking, wax-faced
man, might somehow steal her from him, hung over him like
a fog, obscuring his vision. It necessitated continued watchful-
ness on his part. And so he dogged her, mentally, and in
fact, until his own heart all but broke under the strain.

One afternoon they walked to Connewitz. It had rained
heavily during the night, and the unpaved roads were inch-
deep in mud. The sky was a level sheet of cloud, darker and
more forbidding in the east.

Their direction was Maurice's choice. Louise would have
liked better to keep to the town: for, though the streets, too,
were mud-bespattered, there would soon be lights, and the
reflection of lights in damp pavements. She yielded, however,
without even troubling to express her wish. But just because
of the dirt and naked ugliness which met her, at every turn,
she was voluble and excited; and an exaggerated hilarity seized
her at trifles. Maurice, who had left the house in a more
composed frame of mind than usual, gradually relapsed, at her
want of restraint, into silence. He suffered under her loose-
ness of tongue and laughter: her sallow, heavy-eyed face was
ill-adapted to such moods; below her feverish animation there
lurked, he was sure of it, a deadly melancholy. He had
always been rendered uneasy by her spurts of gaiety. Now,
in addition, he asked himself: what has happened to make her
like this?

Feeling his hostility, Louise grew quieter, and soon she,
too, was silent. Having gained his end, Maurice wished to
atone for it, and slipping his arm through hers, he took her
hand. For a few steps they walked on in this fashion. Then,
he received one of those sudden impressions which flash on us
from time to time, of having seen or done a certain thing

before. For a moment, he could not verify it; then he knew. Just in this way, arm in arm, hand in hand, had she come towards him with Schilsky, that very first day. It was no doubt a habit of hers. Like this, too, she would, in all probability, walk with the one who came after. And the picture of Herries, in the place he now occupied, was photographed on his brain.

He withdrew his arm, as if hers had burnt him: his mind was off again on its old round. But she, too, had to suffer for it. As he stood back to let her pass before him, on a dry strip of the path, his eye caught a yellow rose she was wearing at her belt. Till now he had seen it without seeing it.

"Why are you wearing that rose?"

Louise looked down from him to the flower and back again. "Why?—you know I like to wear flowers."

"Where did you get it?"

She foresaw what he was driving at, and did not reply.

"You were wearing a rose like that the first time I saw you. Do you remember?"

"How should I remember? It's so long ago."

"Where had you got that one from, then?"

She repeated the same words. "How should I know now?"

"But I know. It was from him—he had given it to you."

She raised her shoulders. "Perhaps."

"Perhaps? No. For certain."

"Well, and if so—was there anything strange in that?"

They walked a few paces without speaking. Then he asked: "Who has given you this one?"

"Maurice!" There was a note of warning in her voice. He heard it in vain. "Give it to me, Louise."

"No—let it be. It will wither soon enough where it is."

"Please give it to me," he urged, rendered the more determined by her refusal.

"I wish to keep it."

"And I mean to have it."

To avoid the threatening scene, she took the rose from her belt and gave it to him. He fingered it indecisively for a moment, then threw it over the bridge they were crossing, into the river. It struggled, filled with muddy water, and floated away.

In the next breath, however, he asked himself ruefully what he had gained by his action. She had given him the rose, and he had destroyed it; but he would never know how she had come by it, and what it had been to her.

He was incensed with himself and with her for the whole length of the *Schleussiger Weg*. Then the inevitable regret for his hastiness followed. He took her limply hanging hand and pressed it. But there was no responsive pressure on her part. Louise looked away from him, beyond the woods, as far as she could see, in the vain hope of there discovering some means of escape.

VIII

In descending one evening the broad stair of the Gewandhaus, and forced, by reason of the crowd, to pause on every step, Madeleine overheard the talk of two men behind her, one of whom, it seemed, had all the gossip of the place at his fingertips. From what she caught up greedily, as soon as Maurice's name was mentioned, she learnt a surprising piece of news. " A cat and dog life," was the phrase used by the speaker. As she afterwards picked her way through snow and slush, Madeleine confessed to herself that it was impossible to feel regret at what she had heard. Perhaps, after all, things would come right of themselves. In order to recover from his infatuation, to learn what Louise really was, it had only been necessary for Maurice to be constantly at her side.—Was it not Goethe who said that the way to cure a bad habit was to indulge it?

But a few days afterwards, her satisfaction was damped. Late one afternoon she had entered Seyffert's Café, to drink a cup of chocolate. At a table parallel with the one she chose, two fellow-students were playing draughts. Madeleine had only been there for a few minutes, when their talk, which went on unrestrainedly between the moves of the game, leapt, with a witticism, to the unlucky pair in whom she was interested. To her astonishment, she now heard Louise's name coupled with that of another man.

"Well, I never!" said the second of the two behind her. " I say, it's your move.—That's rough on Guest, isn't it?"

Madeleine turned in her chair and faced the man who had spoken.

"Excuse me, who is Herries?" she asked without ceremony.

In her own room that evening, she pondered long. It was one thing for the two to drift naturally apart; another for Maurice to see himself superseded. If this were true, jealousy, and nothing else, would be at the root of their disunion. Madeleine felt very unwilling to mix herself up in the affair: it would be like plunging two clean hands into dirty water. But then, you never could tell how a man would act in a case like this: the odds were ten to one he did something foolish.

And so she wrote to Maurice, making her summons imperative. This failing, she tried to waylay him going to or from his classes; but the only satisfaction she gained, was the knowledge of his irregularity: during the week she waited she did not once come face to face with him. Next, she looked round her for some common friend, and found that he had not an intimate left in all Leipzig. She wrote again, still more plainly, and again he ignored her letter.

One Saturday afternoon, she was walking along the crowded streets of the inner town. She had been to the *Motette,* in the *Thomaskirche,* and was now on her way home, carrying music from the library. The snow had melted to mud, and sleet was falling. Madeleine had no umbrella ; the collar of her cloak was turned up round her ears, and her small felt hat covered her head like an extinguisher.

On entering the *Peterstrasse,* she was jostled together with Dove. It was impossible to beat a retreat.

Dove seldom hurried. On this day, as on any other, he walked with a somewhat pompous emphasis through slush and stinging rain, holding his umbrella straight aloft over him, as he might have carried a banner. He was shocked to find Madeleine without one, at once took her under his, and loaded himself with her music—all with that air of matter-of-courseness, which invariably made her keen to decline his aid. Dove was radiant; he prospered as do only the happy few; and his satisfaction with himself, and with the world in general, was somehow expressed even through the medium of his long neck and gently sloping shoulders. He greeted Madeleine with an exaggerated pleasure, accompanying his words by the slow smile which sometimes set her wondering if he were not, perhaps, being inwardly satirical at the expense of other people, fooling them by means of his own foolishness. But, however this might be, the cynical feelings that took her in his presence, mounted once more; she knew his symptoms, and an excess of content was just as distasteful to her as gluttony, or wine-bibbing, or any other self-indulgence.

However, she checked the desire to snub him—to snub until she had succeeded in raising that impossible ire, which, she believed, *must* lurk somewhere in Dove—for, as she plodded along at his side, sheltered from the brunt of the weather, it occurred to her that here was some one whom she might tap on the subject of Maurice. She opened fire by congratulating her companion on his recent performance in an *Abendunterhaltung;* at the time, even she had been forced to admit it a creditable piece of work. Dove, who privately considered it epochmaking, was outwardly very modest. He could not refrain from letting fall that the old director had afterwards thanked him in person; but, in the next breath, he pointed out a slip he had made in a particular passage of the sonata. It had not, it was true, been observed, he believed, by anyone except Schwarz and himself; still it had caused him considerable annoyance; and he now related how, as far as he could judge, it had come about.

The current inquiries concerning the *Prüfungen* then passed between them.

"Poor old Schwarz!" said Madeleine. "We shall be few enough, this year. Tell me, what of Heinz? I haven't seen him for an age."

"I regret to say that Krafft is making an uncommon donkey of himself," said Dove. "He had another shocking row with Schwarz last week."

"Tch, tch, tch!" said Madeleine. "Heinz is a freak.— And Maurice Guest, what about him?"

"I haven't seen him lately."

"Indeed? How is that?"

"I'm not in the same class with him now. His hour has been changed."

"Has it indeed?" said Madeleine thoughtfully. This accounted for her having been unable to meet Maurice. "What's he playing, do you know?"

"The G major Mendelssohn, I understand;" and Dove looked at her out of the corner of his eye.

"How's he getting on with it?" she queried afresh, in the same indifferent tone.

"I really couldn't say. As I mentioned, he's in another class."

"Oh, but you must have heard!" said Madeleine. "It's no use putting me off," she added, with determination. "I want to find out about Maurice."

"And I fear I can't assist you. All I *have* chanced to hear —mere rumour, of course—is that . . . well, if Guest doesn't pull himself together, he won't play at all.—By the way, what did you think of James the other night, in the *Lisztverein?* "

31

"Oh, that his octaves were marvellous, of course!" said Madeleine tartly. "But I warn you," she continued, "it's of no use changing the subject, or pretending you don't know. I intend to speak of Maurice."

"Then it must be to some one else, Miss Madeleine, not to me."—Dove could never be induced to call her Madeleine, as her other friends did.

"And why, pray, are you to be the exception?"

"Because, as I've already mentioned, I don't see any more of Guest. He mixes in a different set now.—And as for me, well, my thoughts are occupied with, I trust, more profitable things."

"What? You have thoughts, too?"

"I hope you don't claim a monopoly of them?" said Dove, and smiled in his imperturbable way. As, however, Madeleine persisted, he grew grave. "It's not a pleasant subject. I should really rather not discuss it, Miss Madeleine."

"Oh, for Heaven's sake, don't let us play the prudish or sentimental!" cried Madeleine, in a burst of impatience. "Of course, it isn't pleasant. Do you think I should "—"bother with you," was on her tongue. She checked herself, and substituted—"trouble you about it, if it were? But Maurice was once a friend of ours—you don't deny it, I hope?" she threw in challengingly; for Dove muttered something to himself. "And I want to get at the truth about him. I'm sorrier than I can say, to hear, on all sides, what a fool he's making of himself."

Dove was suavely silent.

"Of course," continued Madeleine with a sarcastic inflection—"of course, I can't expect you to see it as I do. Men look at these things differently, I know. Possibly if I were a man, I, too, should stand by, with my hands in my pockets, and watch a friend butt his head against a stone wall—thinking it, indeed, rather good fun."

She had touched Dove on a tender spot. "I can assure you, Miss Madeleine," he said impressively, as they picked their steps across a dirty road—"I can assure you, you are mistaken. I think just as strictly in matters of this kind as you yourself.—But as to interfering in Guest's . . . in his private affairs, well, frankly, I shouldn't care to try it. He was always a curiously reserved fellow."

"Reserved—obstinate—pig-headed!—call it what you like," said Madeleine. "But don't imagine I'm asking you to interfere. I only want you to tell me, briefly and simply, what you know about him. And to make it easier for you, I'll begin by telling you what *I* know.—It's an old story, isn't it, that Maurice once supplanted some one else in a certain young woman's favour? Well, now I hear that he, in turn, is to be laid on the shelf.—Is that true, or isn't it?"

"Really, Miss Madeleine!—that's a very blunt way of putting it," said Dove uncomfortably.

"Oh, when a friend's at stake, I can't hum and haw," said Madeleine, who could never keep her temper with Dove for long. "I call a spade a spade, and rejoice to do it. What I ask you to tell me is, whether I've been correctly informed or not. Have you, too, heard Louise Dufrayer's name coupled with that of a man called Herries?"

But Dove was stubborn. "As far as I'm concerned, Miss Madeleine, the truth is, I've hardly exchanged a word with Guest since spring. Into his . . . friendship with Miss Dufrayer, I have never felt it my business to inquire. I believe—from hearsay—that he is much changed. And I feel convinced his *Prüfung* will be poor. Indeed, I'm not sure that he should not be warned off it altogether."

"Could that not be laid before him?"

"I should not care to undertake it."

There was nothing to be done with Dove; Madeleine felt that she was wasting her breath; and they walked across the broad centre of the *Rossplatz* in silence.

"Do you never think," she said, after a time, "how it would simplify life, if we were able to get above it for a bit, and see things without prejudice?—Here's a case now, where a little real fellowship and sympathy might work wonders. But no!—no interference!—that's the chief and only consideration."

It had stopped raining. Dove let down his umbrella, and carried it stiffly, at some distance from him, by reason of its dampness. "Believe me, Miss Madeleine," he said, as he emerged from beneath it. "Believe me, I make all allowance for your feelings, which do you credit. A woman's way of looking at these things is, thank God, humaner than ours. But it's a man's duty not to let his feelings run away with him.— I agree with you, that it's a shocking affair. But Guest went into it with his eyes open. And that he could do so—but there was always something a little . . . a little peculiar about Guest."

"I suppose there was. One can only be thankful, I suppose,

that he's more or less of an exception—among his own country-
men, I mean, of course. Englishmen are not, as a rule, given
to that kind of thing."

"Thank God, they're not!" said Dove with emotion.

"Well, our ways part here," said Madeleine, and halted.
As she took her music from him, she asked: "By the way,
when shall we be at liberty to congratulate you?"

It was not at all "by the way" to Dove. However, he only
smiled; for he had grown wiser, and no longer wore his
heart on his coat-sleeve. "You shall be one of the first to
hear, Miss Madeleine, when the news is made public."

"Thanks greatly. Good-bye.—Oh, no, stop a moment!"
cried Madeleine. It was more than she could bear to see him
turn away thus, beaming with self-content. "Stop a moment.
You won't mind my telling you, I'm sure, that I've been disappointed with you this afternoon. For I've always thought
of you as a saviour in the hour of need, don't you know?—
one does indulge in these fancy pictures of one's friends—a
strong man, helping with tact and example. And here you go,
toppling my picture over, without the least remorse.—Well,
you know your own business best, I suppose, but it's unkind
of you, all the same, to destroy an illusion. One has few enough
of them in this world.—Ta-ta!"

She laughed satirically, and turned on her heel, regardless
of the effect of her words.

But Dove was not offended; on the contrary, he felt rather
flattered. He did not, of course, care in the least about what
Madeleine called her illusions; but the mental portrait she
had drawn of him corresponded exactly to that attitude in
which he was fondest of contemplating himself. For it could
honestly be said that, hitherto, no one had ever applied to him
for aid in vain: he was always ready, both with his time and
with good advice. And the idea that, in the present instance, he
was being untrue to himself, in other words, that he was
letting an opportunity slip, ended by upsetting him altogether.

Until now, he had not regarded Maurice and Maurice's
doings from this point of view. By nature, Dove was opposed to excess of any kind; his was a clean, strong mind,
which caused him instinctively to draw back from everything,
in morals as in art, that passed a certain limit. Nothing on
earth would have persuaded him to discuss his quondam friend's
backsliding with Madeleine Wade; he was imbued with the
belief that such matters were unfit for virtuous women's

ears, and he applied his conviction indiscriminately. Now, however, the notion of Maurice as a poor erring sheep, waiting, as it were, to be saved—this idea was of undeniable attractiveness to Dove, and the more he revolved it, the more convinced he grew of its truth.

But he had reasons for hesitating. Having valiantly overcome his own disappointments, first in the case of Ephie, then of pretty Susie, he now, in his third suit, was on the brink of success. The object of his present attachment was a Scotch lady, no longer in her first youth, and several years older than himself, but of striking appearance, vivacious manners, and, if report spoke true, considerable fortune. Her appearance in Leipzig was due to the sudden burst of energy which often inspires a woman of the Scotch nation when she feels her youth escaping her. Miss MacCallum, who was abroad nominally to acquire the language, was accompanied by her aged father and mother; and it was with these two old people that it behoved Dove to ingratiate himself; for, according to the patriarchal habits of their race, the former still guided and determined their daughter's mode of life, as though she were thirteen instead of thirty. Dove was obliged to be of the utmost circumspection in his behaviour; for the old couple, uprooted violently from their native soil, lived in a mild but constant horror at the iniquity of foreign ways. They held the profession of music to be an unworthy one, and threw up their hands in dismay, at the number of young people here complacently devoting themselves to such a frivolous object. It was necessary for Dove to prove to them that a student of music might yet be a man of untarnished principles and blameless honour. And he did not find the task a hard one; the whole bent of his mind was towards sobriety. He frequented the American church with his new friends on Sunday afternoon; gave up skating on that day; went with the old gentleman to Motets and Passions; and eschewed the opera.

But now, his ambition had been insidiously roused, and day by day it grew stronger. If only the affair with Maurice had not been of so unsavoury a nature! Did he, Dove, become seriously involved, it might be difficult to prove to judges so severe as his future parents-in-law, that he had acted out of pure goodness of heart. For, that he would be embroiled, in other words, that he would have success in his mission, there was no manner of doubt in his mind—a conviction he shared with the generality of mankind: that it is only necessary for an offender's eyes to be opened to the enormity of his wrong-doing, for him to be reasonable and to renounce it.

While Dove hesitated thus, torn between his reputation on the one hand, his missionary zeal on the other; while he hesitated, an incident occurred, which acted as a kind of moral finger-post. In the piano-class one day, just as Dove was about to leave the room, Schwarz asked him if he were not a friend of Herr Guest's. The latter had been absent now from two lessons in succession. Was he ill? Did no one know what had happened to him? Dove made light of the friendship, but volunteered his services, and was bidden to make inquiries.

He went that afternoon.

Frau Krause looked a little gruffer than of old; and left him to find his own way to Maurice's room. In accordance with the new state of things, Dove knocked ceremoniously at the door. While his knuckles still touched the wood, it was flung open, and he stood face to face with Maurice. For a moment the latter did not seem to recognise his visitor; he had evidently been expecting some one else.

Then he repaired his tardiness, ceased to hold the door, and Dove entered, apologising for his intrusion.

"Just a moment. I won't detain you. As you were absent from the class all last week, Schwarz asked to-day if you were ill, and I said I would step round and see."

"Very good of you, I'm sure. Sit down," said Maurice. His face changed as he spoke; a look of relief and, at the same time, of disappointment flitted across it.

"Thanks. If I am not disturbing you," answered Dove. As he said these words, he threw a glance, the significance of which might have been grasped by a babe, at the piano. It had plainly not been opened that day.

Maurice understood. "No, I was not practising," he said. "But I have to go out shortly," and he looked at his watch.

"Quite so. Very good. I won't detain you," repeated Dove, and sat down on the proffered chair. "But not prac-tising? My dear fellow, how is that? Are you so far forward already that it isn't necessary? Or is it a fact that you are not feeling up to the mark?"

"Oh, I'm all right. I get my work over in the morning."

Now he, too, sat down, at the opposite side of the table. Clearing his throat, Dove gazed at the sinner before him. He began to see that his errand was not going to be an easy one; where no hint was taken, it was difficult to insert even the thinnest edge of the wedge. He resolved to use finesse; and, for several of the precious moments at his disposal, he talked, as if at random, of other things.

Maurice tapped the table. He kept his eyes fixed on Dove's face, as though he were drinking in his companion's solemn utterances. In reality, whole minutes passed without his knowing what was said. At Dove's knock, he had been certain that a message had come from Louise—at last. This was the night of the ball; and still she had given him no promise that she would not go. They had parted, the evening before, after a bitter quarrel; and he had left her, vowing that he would not return till she sent for him. He had waited the whole day, in vain, for a sign. What was Dove with his pompous twaddle to him? Every slight sound on the stairs or in the passage meant more. He was listening, listening, without cessation.

When he came back to himself, he heard Dove droning on, like a machine that has been wound up and cannot stop.

"Now I hope you won't mind my saying so," were the next words that pierced his brain. "You must not be offended at my telling you; but you are hardly fulfilling the expectations we, your friends, you know, had formed of you. My dear fellow, you really must pull yourself together, or February will find you still unprepared."

Maurice went a shade paler; he was clear, now, as to the object of Dove's visit. But he answered in an off-hand way. "Oh, there's time enough yet."

"No. That's a mistaken point of view, if I may say so," replied Dove in his blandest manner. "Time requires to be taken by the forelock, you know."

"Does it?" Maurice allowed the smile that was expected of him to cross his face.

"Most emphatically.—And we fellow-students of yours are not the only people who have noticed a certain—what shall I say?—a certain abatement of energy on your part. Schwarz sees it, too—or I am much mistaken."

"What?—he, too?" said Maurice, and pretended a mild surprise. For some seconds now, he had been mentally debating with himself whether he should not, there and then, show Dove the door. He decided against it. A "Damn your interference!" meant plain-speaking, on both sides; it meant a bandying of words; and more expenditure of strength than he had to spare for Dove. Once more he drew out and consulted his watch.

"Unfortunately, yes," said Dove, ignoring the hint. "I assume it, from something he let drop this afternoon. Now you know, your Mendelssohn ought to have been a brilliant piece of work—yes, the expression is not too strong. And it still must be. My dear Guest, what I came to say to you to-day—one, at any rate, of the reasons that brought me—was, that you must not allow your interest in what you are doing to flag at the eleventh hour."

Maurice laughed. "Oh, certainly not! Most awfully good of you to trouble."

"No trouble at all," Dove assured him. He flicked some dust from his trouser-knee before he spoke again. "I . . . er . . . that is, I had some talk the other day with Miss Wade."

"Indeed!" replied Maurice, and was now able accurately to gauge the motor origin of Dove's appearance. "How is she? How is Madeleine?"

"She was speaking of you, Guest. She would, I think, like to see you."

"Yes, I've rather neglected her lately, I'm afraid.—But when there's so much to do, you know . . ."

"It's a pity," said Dove, passing over the last words, and nodding his head sagaciously. "She's a staunch friend of yours, is Miss Madeleine. I think it wouldn't be too much to say she was feeling a little hurt at your neglect of her."

"Really? I had no idea so many people took an interest in me."

"That is just where you are mistaken," said Dove warmly. "We all do. And for that very reason, I said to myself, I will be spokesman for the rest: I'll go to him and tell him he must pull through, and do himself credit—and Schwarz, too. We are so few this year, you know."

"Yes, poor old man! He has got badly left."

"Yes. That was one reason. And then . . . but you assure me, don't you, that you will not take what I am going to say amiss?"

"Not in the least. It's awfully decent of you. But I'm sorry to say my time's up. And every minute is precious just now—as you know yourself."

He rose, and, for the third time, referred to his watch. After an ineffectual attempt to continue, Dove was also forced to rise, with the best part of his message unuttered. And Maurice hurried him, glum and crestfallen, to the door, for fear of the still worse tactlessness of which he might make himself guilty.

They groped in silence along the dark lobby. For the sake of parting with a friendly and neutral word, Maurice said, as he opened the door: "By the way, I hear we shall soon have to offer congratulations and good wishes."

To his surprise, Dove, who had already crossed the threshold, looked blank, and drew himself up.

"Indeed?" he said, and the tone was, for him, quite short. "I . . . the fact is . . . I've no idea what you refer to."

On re-entering his room, Maurice went back to the window, and taking up his former attitude, began to beat anew that tattoo on the panes, which had been his chief employment during the day. His eyes were sore with straining at the corner of the street, tired of looking at his watch to see how the time passed. He had steadfastly believed that Louise would yield in this matter, and, at the last, recall him in a burst of impulsive regret. But, as the day crawled by without a word from her, his confident conviction weakened; and, at the same time, his resolve not to go back till she sent for him, failed. He repeated, in memory, some of the bitter things they had said to each other, to see if he had not left himself a loophole of escape; but only with one half of his brain: the other was persistently occupied with the emptiness of the street below. When a clock struck half-past seven, he could bear the suspense no longer: he put on his hat and coat, and went out. He felt tired and unslept, and dragged along as if his body were a weight to him. A fine snow was falling, which froze into icicles on the beards of the passers-by, and on the glistening pavements. The distance had never seemed so long to him; it had also never seemed so short.

A faint and foolish hope still refused to be extinguished. But it went out directly he had unlocked the door; and he learned what he had come to learn, without the exchange of a word. The truth met him, that he should have been here hours ago, commanding, imploring; instead of which he had sat at home, nursing a futile and paltry pride.

The room was warm, and bright with extra candles. It was also in that state of confusion which accompanied an elaborate toilet on the part of Louise. Fully dressed, she stood before the console-glass, and arranged something in her hair. She did not turn at his entrance, but she raised her eyes and met his in the mirror, without pausing in what she was doing.

He looked over her shoulder at her reflected face. The cold steadiness, the open hostility of her look, took his strength away.

He sat down on the foot-end of the bed, and put his head in his hands. Minutes passed, and still he remained in this position. For what was the use of his speaking? Her mind was made up; nothing would move her now.

Then came the noise of wheels in the street below. Uncovering his eyes, Maurice looked at her again; and, as he did so, his feelings which, until now, had had something of the nature of a personal wound, gave place to others with the rush of a storm. She wore the same sparkling, low-cut dress as on the previous occasion; arms and shoulders were as ruthlessly bared to view. He remembered what he had heard said of her that night, and felt that his powers of endurance were at an end. With a stifled exclamation, he got up from the bed, and going past her, into the half of the room beyond the screen, caught up the first object that came to hand, and threw it to the floor. It was a Dresden-china figure, and broke to pieces.

Louise gave a cry, and came running out to see what he had done. "Are you mad? How dare you! . . . break my things."

She held a candle above her head, and by its light, he saw, in the skin of neck and shoulder, all the lines and folds that were formed by the raising of her arm. He now saw, too, that her hair was dressed in a different way, that her dark eyebrows had been made still darker, and that she was powdered. This discovery had a peculiar effect on him: it rendered it easier for him to say hard things to her; at the same time, it strengthened his determination not to let her go out of the house. Moving aimlessly about the room, he stumbled against a chair, and kicked it from him.

"A month ago, if some one had sworn to me that you would treat me as you are doing to-night, I should have laughed in his face," he said at last.

Louise had put the candle down, and was standing with her back to him. Taking up a pair of long, black gloves, she began to draw one over her hand. She did not look up at his words, but went on stroking the kid of the glove.

"You're only doing it to revenge yourself—I know that! But what have I done, that you should take less thought for my feelings than if I were a dog?"

Still she did not speak.

"You won't really go, Louise?—you won't have the heart to.—I say you shall not go! It will be the end—the end of everything!—if you leave the house to-night."

She pulled her dress from his hand. "You're out of your senses, I think. The end of everything! Because, for once, I choose to have some pleasure on my own account! Any other man would be glad to see the woman he professes to care for, enjoy herself. But you begrudge it to me. You say my pleasures shall only come through you—who have taken to making life a burden to me! Can't you understand that I'm glad to get away from you, and your ill-humours and mean, abominable jealousy. You're not my master. I'm not your slave." She tugged at a recalcitrant glove. "It is absurd," she went on a moment later. "All because I wish to go out alone for once.— But did I even want to? Why, if it means so much to you, couldn't you have bought a ticket and come too? But no! you wouldn't go yourself, and so I was not to go either. It's on a level with all your other behaviour."

"I go!" he cried. "To watch you the whole evening in that man's arms!—No, thank you! It's not good enough.—You, with your indecent style of dancing!"

She wheeled round, as if the insult had struck her; and for a moment faced him, with open lips. Then she thought better of it: she laughed derisively, with a wanton undertone, in order to hurt him.

"You would at least have had me under your own eyes."

As she spoke, she nodded to the old woman, who opened the door to say that the droschke waited below. A lace scarf was lying on the table; Louise twisted it mechanically round her head, and began to struggle with an evening cloak. Just as she had succeeded in getting it over her shoulders, Maurice took her by the arms and bent her backwards, so that the cloak fell to the floor.

"You shall not go!"

She stemmed her hands against him, and determinedly, yet with caution, pushed herself free.

"My dress—my hair! How dare you!"

"What do I care for your dress or your hair? You make me mad!"

"And what do I care whether you're mad or not? Take your hands away!"

"Louise! . . . for God's sake! . . . not with that man. At least, not with him. He has said infamous things of you. I never told you—yes, I heard him say—heard him compare you with . . . soiled goods he called you.—Louise! Louise!"

"Have you any more insults for me?"

"No, no more!" He leaned his back against the door. "Only this: if you leave this room to-night, it's the end."

She had picked up her cloak again. "The end!" she repeated, and looked contemptuously at him. "I should welcome it, if it were.—But you're wrong. The end, the real end, came long ago. The beginning was the end!—Open that door, and let me out!"

He heard her go along the hall, heard the front door shut behind her, and, after a pause, heard the deeper tone of the house door. The droschke drove away. After that, he stood at the window, looking out into the pitch-dark night. Behind him, the landlady set the room in order, and extinguished the additional candles.

When she had finished, and shut the door, Maurice faced the empty room. His eyes ranged slowly over it; and he made a vague gesture that signified nothing. A few steps took him to the writing-table, on which her muff was lying. He lifted it up, and a bunch of violets fell into his hand. They brought her before him as nothing else could have done. Beside the bed, he went down on his knees, and drawing her pillow to him, pressed it round his head.

The end, the end!—the beginning the end: there was truth in what she had said. Their love had had no stamina in it, no vital power. He was losing her, steadily and surely losing her, powerless to help it—rather it seemed as if some malignant spirit urged him to hasten on the crisis. Their thoughts seemed hopelessly at war.—And yet, how he loved her! He made himself no illusions about her now; he understood just what she was, and what she would always be; the many conflicting impulses of her nature lay bare to him. But he loved her, loved her: all the dead weight of his physical craving for her was on him again, confounding, overmastering. None the less, she had left him; she had no need for him; and the hours would come, oftener and oftener, when she could do without him, when, as now, she voluntarily sought the company of other men. The thought suffocated him; he rose to his feet, and hastened out of the house.

A little before one o'clock, he was stationed opposite the side-entrance to the *Hôtel de Prusse*. He had a long time to wait. As two o'clock approached, small batches of people emerged, at first at intervals, then more and more frequently. Among the last were Herries and Louise. Maurice remained standing in the shadow of some houses, until they had parted from their companions. He heard her voice above all the rest; it rang out clear and resonant, just as on that former occasion when she had drunk freely of champagne.

With many final words and false partings, she and Herries separated from the group, and turned to walk down the street. As they did so, Maurice sprang out from his hiding-place, and was suddenly in front of them, blocking their progress.

At his unexpected apparition, both started; and when he roughly took hold of her arm, Louise gave a short cry. Herries put out his hand, and smacked Maurice's down.

"What are you doing there? Take your hands off this lady, damn you!" he cried in broken German, not recognising Maurice, and believing that he had to deal with an ordinary *Nachtschwarmer.*

The savageness with which he was turned on, enlightened him. "Damn you!" retorted Maurice in English. "Take your hands off her yourself! She belongs to me—to me, do you hear?—and I intend to keep her."

"You drunken cur!" said Herries. He had instinctively allowed Louise to withdraw her arm; now he stood irresolute, uncertain how she would wish him to act. She had gone very pale; he believed she was afraid. "Isn't there a droschke anywhere?" he said, and looked angrily round. "I really can't see you exposed to this . . . this sort of thing, you know."

Louise answered hurriedly. "No, no. And please go! I shall be all right. I'm sorry.—I had enjoyed it so much. I will tell you another time, how much. Good night, and thank you. No . . . *please!* . . . yes, a delightful evening." Her words were almost inaudible.

"Delightful indeed!" said Herries with warmth. Then he stood aside, raised his hat, and let them pass.

Maurice had his hand on her wrist, and he dragged her after him, over the frozen pavements, far more quickly than she could in comfort go, hampered as she was by snow-boots and by her heavy cloak. But she followed him, allowed herself to be drawn, without protest. She felt strangely will-less. Only sometimes, when the thought of the indignity he had laid upon her came over her anew, did she whisper: "How dare you! . . . oh, how dare you!"

He did not look at her, or answer her, and all might have gone well, so oddly did this treatment affect her, had he only persisted in it. But the mere contact of her hand softened him towards her; her nearness worked on him as it never failed to do.

He was exhausted, too, mentally and physically, and at the thought that, for this night at least, his sufferings were over, he could have shed tears of relief. Slackening his pace, he began to speak, began to excuse and exculpate himself before ever she had blamed him, endeavouring to make her understand something of what he had gone through. In advance, and before she had expressed it, he sought to break down her spirit of animosity.

The longer he spoke, the harder she felt herself grow. He was at it again, back at his eternal self-justification. Oh, why, for this one evening at least, could he not have enforced his will, and have made her do what he wished, without explanation! But the one plain, simple way was the only way he never thought of taking. "I hate you and despise you! I shall never forgive you for your behaviour to-night!—never!" And now it was she who pressed forward, to get away from him.

He turned the key in the house-door. But before he could open the door, Louise, pushing in front of him, threw it back, entered the house, and, the next moment, the door banged in his face. He had just time to withdraw his hand. He heard her steps on the stair, mounting, growing fainter; he heard the door above open and shut.

For a second or two, he stood listening to these sounds. But when it dawned on him that she had shut him out, he pressed both hands against the wood of the heavy door, and tried to shake it open. He even beat his fist against it, and only desisted from this when his knuckles began to smart.

Then, on looking down, he saw that the key was still in the lock. He stared at it, stupidly, without understanding. But, yes —it was his own key; he himself had put it in. He took it out again, and holding it in his hand, looked at it, after the fashion of a drunken man, who does not recognise the object he holds. And even while he did this, he burst into a peal of laughter, which made him lean for support against the wall of the house. The noise he made sounded idiotic, sounded mad, in the quiet street; but he was unable to contain himself. She had left him the key—had left the key! Oh, what a fool he was!

His laughter died away. He opened the door, noiselessly, as he had learned by practice to do, and as noiselessly entered the vestibule and went up the stairs.

IX

SEVERAL versions of the contretemps with Herries were afloat immediately. All agreed in one point: Maurice Guest had been in an advanced stage of intoxication. A scuffle was said to have taken place in the deserted street; there had been tears, and prayers, and shrill accusing voices. In the version that reached Madeleine's ears, blows were mentioned. She stood aghast at the disclosures the story made, and at all these implied. Until now, Maurice had at least striven to preserve appearances. If once you became callous enough not to care what people said of you, you wilfully made of yourself a social outcast.

That same afternoon, as she was mounting the steps of the Conservatorium, she came face to face with Krafft. They had not met for weeks; and Madeleine remarked this, as they stood together. But she was not thinking very deeply of him or his affairs; and when she asked him if he would go across to her room, and wait for her there, she was following an impulse that had no connection with him. As usual, Krafft had nothing particular to do; and when she returned, half an hour later, she found him lying on her sofa, with his arms under his head, his knees crossed above him. The air of the room was grey with smoke; but, for once, Madeleine made no objection. Sitting down at the table, she looked meditatively at him. For some moments neither spoke.

But as Krafft drew out his case to take another cigarette, a tattered volume of Reclam's *Universal Library* fell from his pocket, and spread itself on the floor. Madeleine stooped and pieced it together.

"What have we here?—ah, your Bible!" she said sarcastically: it was a novel by a modern Danish poet, who died young. "You carry it about with you, I see."

"To-day I needed *Stimmung*. But don't say Bible; that's an error of taste. Say 'death-book.' One can study death in it, in all its forms."

"To give you *Stimmung!* I can't understand your love for the book, Heinz. It's morbid."

"Everything's morbid that the ordinary mortal doesn't wish

495

to be reminded of. Some day—if I don't turn stoker or acrobat beforehand, and give up peddling in the emotions—some day I shall write music to it. That would be a melodrama worth making."

"Morbid, Heinz, morbid!"

"All women are not of your opinion. I remember once hearing a woman say, had the author still lived, she would have pilgrimaged barefoot to see him."

"Oh, I dare say. There are women enough of that kind."

"Fools, of course?"

"Extravagant; unbalanced. The class of person that suffers from a diseased temperament.—But men can make fools of themselves, too. There are specimens enough here to start a museum with."

"Of which you, as *Normalmensch,* could be showman."

Madeleine pushed her chair back towards the head of the sofa, so that she came to sit out of the range of Krafft's eyes. "Talking of fools," she said slowly, "have you seen anything of Maurice Guest lately?"

Krafft lowered a spike of ash into the tray. "I have not."

"Yes; I heard he had got into a different hour," she said disconnectedly. As, however, Krafft remained impassive, she took the leap. "Is there—can nothing be done for him, Heinz?"

Here Krafft did just what she had expected him to do: rose on his elbow, and turned to look at her. But her face was inscrutable.

"Explain," he said, dropping back into his former position.

"Oh, explain!" she echoed, firing up at once. "I suppose if a fellow-mortal were on his way to the scaffold, you men would still ask for explanations. Listen to me. You're the only man here Maurice was at all friendly with—I shouldn't turn to you, you scoffer, you may be sure of it, if I knew of anyone else. He liked you; and at one time, what you said had a good deal of influence with him. It might still have. Go to him, Heinz, and talk straight to him. Make him think of his future, and of all the other things he has apparently forgotten.—You needn't laugh! You could do it well enough if you chose—if you weren't so hideously cynical.—Oh, don't laugh like that! You're loathsome when you do. And there's nothing natural about it."

But Krafft enjoyed himself undisturbed. "Not natural? It ought to be," he said when he could speak again. "Oh, you English, you English!—was there ever a people like you? Don't talk to me of men and women, Mada. Only an Englishwoman would look at the thing as you do. How you would love to reform and straitlace all us unregenerate youths! You've done your best for me—in vain!—and now it's Guest. Mada, you have the Puritan's watery fluid in your veins, and Cain's mark on your brow: the mark of the race that carries its Sundays, its language, its drinks, its dress, and its conventions with it, wherever it goes, and is surprised, and mildly shocked, if these things are not instantly adopted by the poor, purblind foreigner.— You are the missionaries of the world!"

"Oh, I've heard all that before. Some day, Heinz, you really must come to England and revise your impressions of us. However, I'm not going to let you shirk the subject. I will tell you this. I know the *milieu* Maurice Guest has sprung from, and I can judge, as you never can, how totally he is unfitting himself to return. The way he's going on—I hear on all sides that he'll never 'make his *Prüfung,*' now, and you yourself know his certificate won't be worth a straw."

"There's something fascinating, I admit," Krafft went on, "about a people of such a purely practical genius. And it follows, as a matter of course, that, being the extreme individualists you are, you should question the right of others to their particular mode of existence. For individualism of this type implies a training, a culture, a grand style, which it has taken centuries to attain—*we* have still centuries to go, before we get there.— If we ever do! For we are the artists among nations—waxen temperaments, formed to take on impressions, to be moulded this way and that, by our age, our epoch. You are the moralists, we are the . . ."

"The immoralists."

"If you like. In your vocabulary, that's a synonym for *Künstler.*"

"You make me ill, Heinz!"

"*Küss' die Hand!*" He was silent, following a smoke-ring with his eyes. "Seriously, Mada," he said after a moment— but there was no answering seriousness in his face, which mocked as usual. "Seriously, now, I suppose you wouldn't admit what this *Dressur,* this *hohe Schule* Guest is going through, might be of service to him in the end?"

"No, indeed, I wouldn't," she answered hotly. "You talk as if he were a circus-horse. Think of him now, and think of him as he was when he first came here. A good fellow—wasn't he? And full to the brim of plans and projects—ridiculous

enough, some of them—but the great thing is to be able to
make plans. As long as a man can do that, he's on the upward
grade.—And he had talent, you said so yourself, and unlimited
perseverance."

"Good God, Madeleine!" burst out Krafft. "That you
should have been in this place as long as you have, and still
remain so immaculate!—Surely you realise that something more
than talent and perseverance is necessary? One can have talent
as one has a hat . . . use it or not as one likes.—I tell you,
the mill Guest is going through may be his salvation—artisti-
cally."

"And morally?" asked Madeleine, not without bitterness.
"Must one give thanks then, if one's friend doesn't turn out a
genius?"

Krafft shrugged his shoulders. "As you take it. The artist
has as much to do with morality, as, let us say, your musical
festivals have to do with art.—And if his genius isn't strong
enough to float him, he goes under, *und damit basta!* The better
for art. There are bunglers enough.—But I'll tell you this,"
he rose on his elbow again, and spoke more warmly. "Since
I've seen what our friend is capable of; how he has allowed himself to be absorbed; since, in short, he has behaved in such a
highly un-British way—well, since then, I have some hope of
him. He seems open to impression.—And impressions are the
only things that matter to the artist."

"Oh, don't go on, please! I'm sick to death of the very words
art and artist."

"Cheer up, Mada! You've nothing of the kind in your
blood." He stretched himself and yawned. "Nor has he,
either, I believe. A face may deceive. And a clear head, and
unlimited perseverance, and intelligence, and ambition—none
of these things is enough. The Lord asks more of his chosen."

Madeleine clasped her hands behind her head, and tilted back
her chair.

"So you couldn't interfere, I see? Your artistic conscience
would forbid it."

"Why don't you do it yourself?" He scrutinised her face,
with a sarcastic smile.

"Oh, say it out! I know what you think."

"And am I not right?"

"No, you're not. How I hate the construction you put on
things! In your eyes, nothing is pure or disinterested. You can't
even imagine to yourself a friendship between a man and a

woman. Such a thing isn't known here—in your nation of artists. Your men are too inflammatory, and too self-sufficient, to want their calves fatted for any but the one sacrifice. Girls have their very kitchen-aprons tied on them with an under-meaning. And poor souls, who can blame them for submitting! What a fate is theirs, if they don't manage to catch a man! Gossip and needlework are only slow poison."

"Now you're spiteful. But I'll tell *you* something. Such friendships as you speak of are only possible where the woman is old—or ugly—or abnormal, in some way: a man-woman, or a clever woman, or some other freak of nature. Now, our women are, as a rule, sexually healthy. They know what they're here for, too, and are not ashamed of it. Also, they still have their share of physical attraction. While yours—good God! I wonder you manage to keep the breed going!"

"Stop, Heinz!" said Madeleine sternly. "You are illogical, and indecent; and you know there's a limit I don't choose to let you pass.—You're wrong, too. You've only to look about you, here, with unbiassed eyes, to see which race the prettiest girls belong to.—But never mind! You only launch out in this way that you may not be obliged to discuss Maurice Guest. I know you. I can read you like a book."

"You are not very old . . . or ugly . . . or abnormal, Mada."

She smiled in spite of herself. "And are we not friends, pray?"

"Something that way.—But in all you say about Guest, the impersonal note is wanting. You're jealous."

"I'm nothing of the sort!—But you'll at least allow me to resent seeing a friend of mine in the claws of this . . . this vampire?"

Krafft laughed. "Vampire is good!—A poor, distraught—"

"Spare your phrases, Heinz. She's bad through and through, and stupid into the bargain."

"Lulu stupid? *Ei, ei,* Mada! Your eyes are indeed askew. She has a touch of the other extreme—of genius."

"*Na!*—Well, if this is another of your manifestations of genius, then permit me to hate—no, to loathe it, in all its forms."

"*Ganz nach Belieben!* It's a privilege of your sex, you know. There never was a woman yet who didn't prefer a good, square talent."

"A crack this way, and it's madness; that, and the world

says genius. And some people have a peculiar gift for discovering it. Those who set themselves to it can find genius in a flea's jump."

" But has it never occurred to you, that the power of loving— that some women have a genius for loving?—No, why do I ask! For if I am a book, you are a poster—a placard."

" What a people you are for words! You make phrases about everything. That's a ridiculous thing to say. If every fickle woman——"

" Fickle woman! fickle fiddle-sticks! " he interrupted. " That's only a tag. The people whose business it is to decide these things—*die Herren Dichter*—are not agreed to this day whether it's man who's fickle or woman. In this mood it's one, in that, the other; and the silly world bleats it after them, like sheep."

" Well, if you wish me to put it more plainly: if what you say were true, vice would be condoned."

" Vice!! " he cried with derision, and sat up and faced her. " Vice!—my dear Mada!—sweet, innocent child! . . . No, no. A special talent is needed for that kind of thing; an unlimited capacity for suffering; an entire renunciation of what is commonly called happiness! You hold the good old Philistine opinions. You think, no doubt, of two lovers living together in delirious pleasure, in *Saus und Braus.*—Nothing could be false. A woman only needs to have the higher want in her nature, and the suffering is there, too. She's born gifted with the faculty. And a woman of the type we're speaking of, is as often as not the flower of her kind.—Or becomes it.—For see all she gains on her way: the mere passing from hand to hand; the intense impressionable nature; the process of being moulded —why, even the common prostitute gets a certain manly breadth of mind, such as you other women never arrive at. Each one who comes and goes leaves her something: an experience—a turn of thought—it may be only an intuition—which she has not had before."

" And the contamination? The soul? " cried Madeleine; two red spots had come out on her cheeks.

" As you understand it, such a woman has no soul, and doesn't need one. All she needs is tact and taste."

" You are the eternal scoffer."

" I never was more serious in my life.—But let us put it another way. What does a—what does any beautiful woman want with a soul, or brains, or morals, or whatever you choose to call it? Let her give thanks, night and day, that she is what

she is: one of the few perfect things on this imperfect earth. Let
her care for her beauty, and treasure it, and serve it. Time
enough when it is gone, to cultivate the soul—if, indeed, she
doesn't bury herself alive, as it's her duty to do, instead of decaying publicly. Mada! do you know a more disgusting, more
humiliating sight than the sagging of the skin on a neck that was
once like marble?—than a mouth visibly losing its form?—the
slender shoulders we have adored, broadening into massivity?—
all the fine spiritual delicacy of youth being touched to heavi-
ness?—all the barbarous cruelty, in short, with which, before
our eyes, time treats the woman who is no longer young.—No,
no! As long as she has her beauty, a woman is under no necessity to bolster up her conscience, or to be reasonable, or to think.
—Think? God forbid! There are plain women enough for
that. We don't ask our Lady of Milo to be witty for us, or to
solve us problems. Believe me, there is more thought, more
eloquence, in the corners of a beautiful mouth—the upward look
of two dark eyes—than in all women have said or done from
Sappho down. Spring, colour, light, music, perfume: they are
all to be found in the curves of a perfect throat or arm."

Madeleine's silence bristled with irony.

"And that," he went on, "was where the girl you are blas-
pheming had such exquisite tact. She knew this. Her instinct
taught her what was required of her. She would fall into an
attitude, and remain motionless in it, as if she knew the eye
must feast its full. Or if she did move, and speak—for she, too,
had hours of a desperate garrulity—then one was content, as
well. Her vitality was so intense that her whole body spoke
when her lips did; she would pass so rapidly from one position
to another that you had to shut your eyes, for fear that, out of
all this multitude, you would not be able to carry one away with
you.—If some of her ways of expressing herself in motion could
be caught and fixed, a sculptor's fame would be made.—A
painter's, if he could reproduce the trick she has of smiling entirely with her eyes and eyebrows.—And then her hands!—
Mada, I wonder you other women don't weep for envy of them.
She has only to raise them, to pass them over her forehead, or
to finger at her hair, and the world is hers.—Do you really think
a man asks soul of a woman with such eyes and hands as those?—
Good God, no! He worships her and adores her. There is only
one place for him, and that's on his knees before her."

"Well, really, Heinz!" said Madeleine, and the spots on
her cheeks burnt a dull red. "In imagination, do you know,

I'm carried just three years backwards? Do you remember that spring evening, when you came rushing in here to me? 'I've seen the most beautiful woman in the world, and I'm drunk with her.' And how I couldn't understand? For I thought her plain, just as I still do.—But then, if I remember aright, your admiration was by no means the platonic, artistic affair it . . . hm! . . . is now."

" It was not.—But now, you understand, Mada, that I think a man makes a good exchange of career, and success, and other such accidents of his material existence, for the right to touch these hands at will. The one thing necessary is, that he be fit for the post. I demand of him that he be a gourmand, a connoisseur in beauty. And it's here, mind you, that I have doubts of our friend.—Is it clear to you? "

" As clear as day, thanks. And you may be *quite* sure of me never applying to you for help again. I shall respect your principles."

" And mind you, I don't say Guest may not come out of the affair all right—enriched for the rest of his life."

" Very good. And now you may go. I regret that I ever bothered with you."

Krafft went across to where Madeleine was standing, put his hands on her two shoulders, and laid his head on his right arm, so that she, who was taller than he was, looked down on the roundnesses of his curly hair. " You're a good fellow, Mada —a good fellow! *Ja, ja*—who knows! If you had had just a little more of the *Ewigweibliche* about you! "

" Too much honour . . . But you don't expect English-women to join your harem, do you? "

" There would have been a certain repose in belonging to a woman of your type. But it's the charm—physical charm—we poor wretches can't do without."

" Upon my word, it's almost a declaration! " cried Madeleine, not unnettled. " Take my advice, Heinz. Hie you home, and marry the person you ought to. Take pity on the poor thing's constancy. Unless," she added, a moment later, with a sarcastic laugh, " since you're still so infatuated with Louise, you persuade her to transfer her favours to you. That would solve all difficulties in the most satisfactory way. She would have the variety that seems necessary to her existence; you could lie on your knees before her all day long; and our friend would be restored to sanity. Think it over, Heinz. It's a good idea."

"Do you think she'd have me?" he asked, as he shook himself into his coat.

"Heaven knows and Heaven only! Where Louise is concerned, nothing's impossible—I've always maintained it."

"Well, ta-ta!—You shall have early news, I promise you."

Madeleine heard him go down the stair, whistling the *Rose of Sharon*. But he could not have been half-way to the bottom, when he turned and came back. Holding her door ajar, he stuck a laughing face into the room.

"Upon my word, Mada, I congratulate you! It's a colossal idea."

But Madeleine had had enough of him. "I'm glad it pleases you. Now go, go! You've played the fool here long enough."

When he emerged from the house, Krafft had stopped whistling. He walked with his hands in his pockets, his felt hat pulled down over his eyes. At the corner, he was so lost in thought as to be unable to guide his feet: he stood and gazed at the pavement. Still on the same spot, he pushed his hat to the back of his head, and burst into such an eerie peal of laughter that some ladies, who were coming towards him, started back, and, picking up their skirts, went off the pavement, in order to avoid passing him too nearly.

The following afternoon, at an hour when Maurice was safely out of the way, Krafft climbed the stair to the house in the *Brüderstrasse.*

The landlady did not know him. Yes, Fräulein was at home, she said; but—— Krafft promptly entered, and himself closed the door. .

Outside Louise's room, he listened, with bent head. Having satisfied himself, he turned the handle of the door and went in.

Louise stood at the window, watching the snow fall. It had snowed uninterruptedly since early morning; out of the leaden sky, flake after flake fluttered down, whirled, spun, and became part of the fallen mass. At the opening of the door, she did not stir; for it would only be Maurice coming back to ask forgiveness; and she was too unspeakably tired to begin all over again.

Krafft stood and eyed her, from the crown of her rough head, to the bedraggled tail of the dressing-gown.

"*Grüss' Gott, Lulu!*"

At the sound of his voice, she jumped round with a scream.

"You, Heinz! *You!*"

The blood suffused her face a purplish red; her voice was

shrill with dismay; her eyes hung on the young man as though he were a returning spirit.

With an effort, she got the better of her first fright, and took a step towards him. "How *dare* you come into this room!"

Krafft hung his wet coat over the back of a chair, and wiped his face dry of the melted snow.

"No heroics, Lulu!"

But she could not contain herself. "Oh, how dare you! It's a mean, dishonourable trick—only you would do it!"

"Sit down and listen to what I have to say. It won't take long. And it's to your own advantage, I think, not to make a noise.—May I smoke?"

She obeyed, taking the nearest chair; for she had begun to tremble; her legs shook under her. But when he held out the case of cigarettes to her, she struck it, and the contents were spilled on the floor.

"Look here, Lulu," he said, and crossing his legs, he put one hand in his pocket, while with the other he made gestures suitable to his words. "I've not come here to-day to rake up old sores. Time has gone over them and healed them, and it's only your—*nebenbei gesagt,* extremely bad—conscience that makes you afraid of me. I'm not here for myself, but——"

"Heinz!" The cry escaped her against her will. "For him? You've come from him!"

He removed his cigarette and smiled. "Him? Which? Which of them do you mean?"

"Which?" It was another uncontrollable exclamation. Then the expression of almost savage joy that had lighted up her face, died out. "Oh, I know you! . . . know you and hate you, Heinz! I've never hated anyone as much as you."

"And a woman of your temperament hates uncommonly well.—No, all jokes aside,"—the word cut her; he saw this, and repeated it. "Joking apart, I've come to you to-day, merely to ask if you don't think your present little affair has gone far enough?"

She was as composed as he was. "What business is it of yours?"

"Oh, none. Except that the poor fool was once my friend."

She gave a daring laugh, full of suggestion.

But Krafft was not put out by it. "Don't do that again," he said. "It sounds ugly; and you have nothing to do with ugliness, you know. No, I repeat once more: this is not a personal matter."

"And you expect me to believe that?"

He shrugged his shoulders.

It was now she who smiled derisively. "Have you forgotten a certain evening in this room, three years ago?"

But he did not flinch. "Upon my word, if you are bold enough to recall that!—However, the reminder was unnecessary. Tell me now: aren't you about done with Guest?"

For still a moment, she fought to keep up her show of dignity. Then she broke down. "Heinz!—oh, I don't know! Oh, yes, yes, yes—a thousand times, yes! Oh, I'm so tired—I can't tell you how tired I am—of the very sight of him! I never wanted him, believe me, I didn't! He thrust himself on me. It was not my doing."

"Oh, come now! Tell that to some one else."

"Yes, I know: you only think the worst of me. But though I was weak, and yielded, anyone would have done the same. He gave me no peace.—But I've been punished out of all proportion to the little bit of happiness it brought me. There's no more miserable creature alive than I am."

"What interests me," continued Krafft, in a matter-of-fact tone, "is, how you came to choose so far afield from your particular type. It's well enough represented here."

She saw the folly of wasting herself upon him, and gave a deep sigh. Then, however, the same wild change as before came over her face. Stooping, she took his hand and fondled it.

"Heinz! Now that you're here, do one thing—only one—for me! Have pity on me! I've gone through so much—been so unhappy. Tell me—there's only one thing I want to know. Where is he? Will he *never* come back? For you know. You must know. You have seen him."

She had sunk to her knees; her head was bent over his hand; she laid her cheek against it. Krafft considered her thoughtfully; his eye dwelt with approval on the broad, slender shoulders, the lithe neck—all the sure grace of the crouching body.

"Will you do something for me, Lulu?"

"Anything!"

"Then let your hair down."

He himself drew out the pins and combs that held it, and the black mass fell, and lay in wide, generous waves round face and neck.

"That's the idea! Now go on."

Louise kissed his hand. "Tell me; you must know."

"But is it possible that still interests you?"

"Oh, no! My life depends on it, that's all. You are cruel and bad; but still I can speak to you—for months now, I haven't had a soul to speak to. Be kind to me this once, Heinz. I *can't* go on living without him. I haven't lived since he left me—not an hour!—Oh, you're my last hope!"

"You'll have plenty of hopes in your life yet."

"In those old days, you hated me, too. But don't bear malice now. There's nothing I won't do for you, if you tell me. I'll never speak to—never even think of you again."

"I'm not so long-suffering."

"Then you won't tell me?"

"I didn't say that."

She crushed his hand between hers. "Here's the chance you asked for—to save your friend! Oh, won't you understand?"

An inward satisfaction, of which only he himself knew the cause, warmed Krafft through, at seeing her prostrate before him. But as he continued to look at her, a thought crossed his mind, and quickly resolved, he laid his cigarette on the table, and put his hands, first on her head, amid the tempting confusion of her hair, which met them like a thick stuff pleasant to the touch, and from there to her shoulders, inclining her towards him. She looked up, and though her eyes were full of tears, her white face was alight in an instant with hope again, as he said: "Would you do something else for me if I told you?"

She strained back, so that she might see his face. "Heinz!— what is it?" And then, with a sudden gasp of comprehension: "Oh, if that's all!—I will never see Maurice Guest again."

"That's not it."

"What is it then?"

"Will you listen quietly?"

"Yes, yes." She ceased to draw back, let herself be held. But he felt her trembling.

He whispered a few words in her ear. Almost simultaneously she jerked her head away, and, turning a dark red, stared incredulously at him. Then she sprang to her feet.

"Oh, what a fool I am! To believe, for one instant, there was a human spot in you I could get at!—Take your hands away —take them off me! Because I've had no one to speak to for so long: because I know *you* could understand if you would— Oh, when a woman is down, anyone may hit her."

"Gently, gently!—You're too good for such phrases."

"I'm no different from other women. It's only you—with

your horrible thoughts of me. *You!* Why, you're no more to
me than the floor I stand on."

"And matters are simplified by that very fact.—I can give
you his address, Lulu."

"Go away! I may hurt you. I could kill you.—Go away!"

"And this," said Krafft, as he put on his coat again, "is how
a woman listens quietly. Well, Lulu, think it over. A word
at any time will bring me, if you change your mind."

One evening, about a week later, Maurice entered Seyffert's
Café. The heavy snowfall had been succeeded by a period of
thaw—of slush and gloom; and, on this particular night, a keen
wind had risen, making the streets seem doubly cheerless. It
was close on nine o'clock, and Seyffert's was crowded with its
usual guests—young people, who had escaped from more or less
dingy rooms to the warmth and light of the café, where the
yellow blinds were drawn against the inclement night. The
billiard table in the centre was never free; those players whose
turn had not yet come, or was over, stood round it, cigarette or
large black cigar in hand, and watched the game.

Maurice had difficulty in finding a seat. When he did, it
was at a table for two, in a corner. A youth who had already
eaten his supper, sat alone there, picking his teeth. Maurice
took the opposite chair, and made his evening meal with a
languid appetite. At the other side of the room was a large and
boisterous party, whose leader was Krafft—Krafft in his most
outrageous mood. Every other minute, his sallies evoked roars
of laughter. Maurice refrained from glancing in that direction.
When, however, his *vis-à-vis* got up and went away, he was
startled from his conning of the afternoon paper by seeing
Krafft before him. The latter, who carried his beer-mug in
his hand, took the vacated seat, nodded and smiled.

Maurice was on his guard at once; for it seemed to him that
they were being watched by the party Krafft had left. Putting
down the newspaper, he wished his friend good-evening.

"I've something to say to you," said Krafft without responding, and, having drained his glass, he clapped the lid to attract
the waiter's attention.

With the over-anxious readiness to oblige, which was becoming one of his most marked traits, and, in reality, cloaked a
deathly indifference, Maurice hung up his paper, and sat forward to listen. Crossing his arms on the table, Krafft began to
speak, meanwhile fixing his companion with his eye. Maurice

was at first too bewildered by what he heard to know to whom
the words referred. Then, the colour mounted to his face; the
nerves in his temples began to throb; and his hand moved along
the edge of the table, in search of something to which it could
hold fast.—It was the first time the name of Louise had been
mentioned between them—and in what a tone!

"Heinz!" he said at last; his voice seemed not to be his own.
"How dare you speak of Miss Dufrayer like that!"

"*Pardon!*" said Krafft; his flushed, transparent cheeks were
aglow, his limpid eyes shone like stars. "Do you mean Lulu?"

Maurice grew pale. "Mind what you're saying!"

Krafft took a gulp of beer. "Are you afraid of the truth?—
But just one word, and I'm done. You no doubt knew, as
every one else did, that Lulu was Schilsky's mistress. What you
didn't know, was this;" and now, without the least attempt at
palliation, without a single extenuating word, there fell from his
lips the quick and witty narration of an episode in which Louise
and he had played the chief parts. It was the keynote of their
relations to each other: the story, grossly told, of a woman's
unsatisfied fancy.

Before the pitiless details, not one of which was spared him,
were checked off, Maurice understood; half rising from his
chair, he struck Krafft a resounding blow in the face. He had
intended to hit the mouth, but, his hand remaining fully open,
caught on the cheek, and with such force that the delicate skin
instantly bore a white imprint of all five fingers.

Only the people in their immediate neighbourhood saw what
had happened; but these sprang up; a girl gave a nervous cry;
and in a minute, the further occupants of the room had gathered round them, the billiard-players with their cues in their
hands. Two waiters, napkin on arm, hastened up, and the
proprietor came out from an inner room, and rubbed his hands.

"*Meine Herren! Meine Herren!*"

Krafft had jumped to his feet; he was also unable to refrain
from putting his hand to his tingling face. Maurice, who was
very pale, stood staring, like a person in a trance, at the mark,
now deep red, which his fingers had left on his friend's cheek.
There was a solemn pause; all eyes were fixed on Krafft; and
the stillness was only broken by the proprietor's persuasive:
"*Meine Herren! Meine Herren!*"

In half a minute Krafft had collected himself. Turning, he
jauntily waved his hand to those pressing up behind; though one
side of his face still blazed and burned.

"Don't allow yourselves to be disturbed, gentlemen. The incident is closed—for the present, at least. My friend here was carried away by a momentary excitement. Kindly resume your seats, and act as if nothing had happened. I shall call him to account at my own convenience.—But just one moment, please!"

The last words were addressed to Maurice. Opening a note-book, Krafft tore out one of the little pages, and, with his customary indolence of movement, wrote something on it. Then he folded it through the middle, and across again, and gave it to Maurice.

Maurice took it, because there seemed nothing else for him to do; he also, for the same reason, took his coat and hat, which some one handed to him. He saw nothing of what went on—nothing but the five outspread marks, which had run together so slowly. He had, however, enough presence of mind to do what was evidently expected of him; and, in the hush that still prevailed, he left the café.

The wind sent a blast in his face. Round the corners of the streets, which it was briskly scavenging, it swept in boisterous gusts, which beat the gas-flames flat as soon as they reared themselves, and made them give a wavering, uncertain light. Not a soul was visible. But in the moment that he stood hesitating outside the brilliancy of the yellow blinds, the hubbub of voices burst forth again. He moved hastily away, and began to walk, to put distance between himself and the place. He did not shrink before the wind-scourged meadows, but fought his way forward, till he reached the woods. There he threw himself face downwards on the first bench he came to.

A smell of rotting and decay met his nostrils: as if, from the thousands of leaves, mouldering under the trees on which they had once hung, some invisible hand had set free thousands of odours, there mounted to him, as he lay, all that rich and humid earthiness that belongs to sunless places. And for a time, he was conscious of little else but this morbid fragrance.

An open brawl! He had struck a man in the face before a crowd of onlookers, and had as good as been ejected from their midst. From now on, he was an outcast from orderly society, was branded as one who was not wholly responsible for his actions—he, Maurice Guest, who had ever been so chary of committing himself. What made the matter seem still blacker, too, in his own eyes, was the fact of Krafft having once been his intimate, personal friend. Now, he could never even think

of him again, without, at the same time, seeing the mark of
his hand on Krafft's cheek. If the blow had remained invisible,
it might have been more easily forgotten; but he had seen it,
as it were, taken shape before him.—Or, had it only been returned, it would have helped to lessen the weight of his present
abasement—oh, he would have given all he had, to have felt a
return blow on his own face! Even the smallest loss of self-
control on the part of Krafft would have been enough. But the
latter was too proud to give himself away gratuitously: he
preferred to take his revenge in the more unconventional fashion
of leaving his friend to bear the ignominy alone.

Maurice lay stabbing himself with these and similar
thoughts. Only little by little did the tumult that had been
roused in him abate. Then, and just the more vividly for the
break in his memory, the gross words Krafft had said, came
back to him. Recalling them, he felt an intense bitterness against
Louise. She was the cause of all his sufferings; were it not for
her, he might still be leading a quiet, decent life. It was her
doing that he was compelled to part, bit by bit, with his self-
respect. Not once, in all the months they had been together,
had the smallest good come to him through her. Nothing but
misery.

Now, he had no further rest where he was. He must go
to her, and tax her with it, repeat what Krafft had said, to her
very face. She should suffer, too—and the foretasted anguish
and pleasure of hot recriminations dulled all other feelings in
him.

He rose, chilled to the bone from his exposure; one hand,
which had hung down over the bench, was ·wet and sticky
from grasping handfuls of dead leaves.

It was past eleven o'clock. Louise wakened with a start, and,
at the sight of his muddy, dishevelled dress, rose to her elbow.

"What is it? What's the matter? Where have you been?"

He stood at the foot of the bed, and looked at her. The
loose masses of her hair, which had come unplaited, arrested
his attention: he had never seemed to know before, how brutally black it was. With his eyes fixed on it, he repeated what
Krafft had ·told him.

Louise lay with the back of one hand on her forehead, and
watched him from under it. When he had finished, she said:
"So Heinz has raked up that old story again, has he?"

Maurice had expected—yes, what had he expected?—anger,
perhaps, or denial, or, it might be, vituperation; only not the

almost impartial composure with which she listened to him. For he had not spared her a word.

"Is that all you've got to say?" he cried, suffocated with doubt. "Then you . . . you admit it?"

"Admit it! Maurice! Are you crazy?—to wake me up for this! It happened *years* ago!"

His recoil of disgust was too marked to be ignored. Louise half sat up in bed again, supporting herself on one hand. Her nightgown was not buttoned; he saw to the waist a strip of the white skin beneath, saw, too, how a long black strand of her hair fell in and lay on it.

"You won't tell me you didn't know from the first there had been . . . something between Heinz and me?" she cried, roused to defend herself.—"And look here, Maurice, as he told you that, it's my turn now. I'll tell you why!" And sitting still more upright, she gave a reason which made him grasp the knob of the bed-post so fiercely that it came away in his hand. He threw it into a corner.

"Louise! . . . you! to take such words on your tongue! Is there no shame left in you?" His throat was dry and narrow.

"Shame! You only mean the need for concealment. Before you had got me, there was no talk of shame."

"Do you know what you're saying?"

"Oh, that's your eternal cry!" and, suddenly spurred to anger, she rose again. "I know—yes, I know! Do you think I'm a fool? Why must you alone be so innocent! Why should you alone not know that I was only jealous of a single person, and that was Krafft?"

Maurice turned away. In the comparative darkness behind the screen, he sat down on the sofa, put his arms on the table, and his head on his arms. He was exhausted, and found he must have slept as he sat; for when he lifted his head again, the hands of the clock had moved forward by several hours.

X

One morning towards the end of January, Krafft disappeared from Leipzig, and some days later, the body of Avery Hill was found in a secluded reach of the Pleisse, just below Connewitz. Some workmen, tramping townwards soon after dawn, noticed a strip of light stuff twisted round a snag, which projected slightly above the surface of the water. It proved to be the skirt of her dress, which had been caught and held fast. Ambulance and police were summoned, and the body was recovered and taken to the police-station.

The last of his friends to see Krafft was Madeleine, and the number of those interested in his departure, and in Avery's quick suicide, was so large that she several times had to repeat her lively account of the last visit he paid her. He had come in, one afternoon, and settling himself on the sofa, refused to be dislodged. As he was in one of his most ambiguous moods, she left him to himself, and went on with her work.

On rising to go, he had stood for a moment with his hands on her shoulders.

" Well, Mada, whatever happens, remember I was sorry you wouldn't have me."

" Oh, come now, Heinz, you never really asked me! "

It was snowing hard that night, a moist, soft snow that melted as it touched the ground, and Krafft borrowed her umbrella. As usual, however, he returned before he could have got half-way down the stairs, to say that he had changed his mind and would not take it.

" But you'll get wet through."

" I don't want your umbrella, I tell you.—Or have you two? "

" No; but I'm not going out.—Oh, well, leave it then. And may you reap a frightful rheumatism! "

As he went down, for the second time, he whistled the *Rose of Sharon*: she listened to it grow fainter in the distance; and that was the last she or anyone had heard of Krafft. The following morning, his landlady found a note on her kitchen-table, instructing her to keep his belongings for four weeks. If, by that time, they had not been claimed, she might sell them, and take the money obtained for herself. Only a few personal articles were missing, such as would be necessary for a hurried journey.—Of course, so Madeleine wound up the story, she had never expected Heinz to behave like a normal mortal, and to take leave of his friends in the ordinary way, and she was also grateful to him for not pilfering her umbrella, which was silver-topped. All the same, there was something indecent about his behaviour. It showed how little he had, at heart, cared for any of them. Only a person who thoroughly despised others, would treat them in this way, playing with them up to the last minute, as one plays with dolls or fools.

Avery Hill was laid out in a small room adjoining the police-station. It was evening before the business of identification was over. Various members of the American colony had to give evidence, and the services of the consul were called into play; for there were countless difficulties, formalities and cere-monies attached to this death by one's own hand in a foreign country. Before all the technical details were concluded, there were those who thought—and openly said so—that an in-tending suicide might cast a merciful thought on the survivors. Only Dove made no complaint. He had been one of the first to learn what had happened, and, in the days that followed, he ran to and fro, from one *Bureau* to another, receiving sig-natures, and witnessing them, bearing the whole brunt of surly Saxon officialdom on his own shoulders.

Twenty-four hours later, it had been arranged that the body should be buried in the *Johannisfriedhof,* and the consul was advised by cablegram to lay out the money for the funeral. Under the eyes of a police-officer and a young clerk from the consul's office, Madeleine, assisted by Miss Jensen, went through the dead girl's belongings, and packed them together.

Miss Jensen kept up, in a low voice, a running commentary on the falsity of men and the foolishness of women. But, at times, her natural kindness of heart asserted itself, to the con-fusion of her theories.

" Poor thing, poor young thing! " she murmured, gazing at a pair of well-patched boots which she held in her hand. " If only she had come to us!—and let us help her. "

" Help her? " echoed Madeleine in a testy way; she was one of those who thought that the dead girl might have shown more consideration for her friends, standing, as they did, imme-diately before their *Prüfungen.* " Could one help her ever hav-

ing set eyes on that attractive scoundrel?—And besides, it's easy
enough thinking afterwards, one might have been able to help,
to do this and that. It's a mistake. People don't want help;
and they don't give you a thank-you for offering it. All they
ask is to be let alone, to muddle and bungle their lives as they
like."

As they walked home together, Miss Jensen returned once
more to the subject of Krafft's failings.

" I've known many men," she said, " one more credulously
vain and stupid than another; for unless a man is engaged in
satisfying his brute instincts, he can be twisted round the finger
of *any* woman. But Mr. Krafft was the only one I've met,
who didn't appear to me to have a single good impulse."

The big woman's high-pitched voice grated on Madeleine.

" You're quite wrong there," she said more snappily than
before. " Heinz had as many good impulses as anyone else.
But he had reduced the concealing of them to a fine art. He
was never happier than when he had succeeded in giving a
totally false impression of himself. Take me for this, for that!
—just what I choose. Often it was as if he flung a bone
to a dog: there! that's good enough for you. No one knew
Heinz: each of us knew a little bit of him, and thought it was
all there was to know.—He never showed a good impulse: that
is as much as saying that he swarmed with them. And no
doubt he would have considered that, with regard to you, he
had been entirely successful. You have the idea of him he
meant you to have."

" He was never her lover," said Louise with a studied carelessness.

Maurice, to whom nothing was more offensive than the tone
of bravado in which she flaunted subjects of this nature, was
stung to retaliation.

" How do *you* know? "

" Well, if you wish to hear—from his own lips."

" Do you mean to say you've spoken to Heinz about things
of that kind?—discussed his relations with other women? "

" Do you need reminding that I knew Heinz before I had
ever heard of you? "

He turned away, too dispirited to cross words with her. The
events of the past week had closed over his head as two waves
close over a swimmer, cutting off light and air. Since the
night on which he had left his whilom friend the mark of his

spread fingers as a parting gift, he had ceased to care greatly about anything.

Compared with his pessimistic absorption in himself, Avery's suicide and Krafft's departure touched him lightly. For the girl, he had never cared. As soon, though, as he heard that Krafft had disappeared, he turned out his pockets for the scrap of paper Heinz had given him that evening in the café. But it threw no light on what had happened. It was merely an address, and, twist it as he would, Maurice could make no more of it than the words: *Klostergasse* 12. He resolved to go through the street of that name in the afternoon; but, when the time came, he forgot about it, and it was not till next morning that he carried out his intention. There was, however, nothing to be learned; number twelve was a gunsmith's shop, and at his hesitating inquiry, if anything were known there of a music-student called Krafft, the owner of the shop looked at him as if he were a lunatic, and answered rudely: was the Herr under the impression that the shop was an information *Bureau?*

Louise was dressed to go out. Pressed as to her destination, she said that she was going to see the body. Maurice sought in vain to dissuade her.

"It's a perverse thing to do," he cried. "You didn't care a fig for the girl when she was alive. But now she can't forbid it, you go and stare at her, out of nothing but curiosity."

"How do you know whether I cared for her or not?" Louise threw at him: she was tying on her veil before the glass. "Do you think I tell you everything?—And as for your 'perverse,' it's the same with all I ever do. You have made it your business always to find my wishes absurd." She took up her gloves and, holding them together, hit her muff with them. "In this case, it doesn't concern you in the least. I don't ask you to come. I want to go alone."

The more shattered and unsure he grew, the more self-assertive was she. There was an air of bravado in all she did, at this time—as in the matter of her determination to go to the dead-house—and she hurt him, with reckless cruelty, whenever a chance offered. Her pale mouth seemed only to open to say unkind things, and her eyes weighed him with an ironic contempt. To his jarred ears, her very laugh sounded less fine. At moments, she began almost to look ugly to him; but it was a dangerous ugliness, more seductive than her beauty had ever been. Then, he knew that she was not too good for him, nor he for her, nor either of them for the world they lived in.

They walked side by side to the mortuary. It was a very cold day, and Louise wore heavy furs, from which her face rose enticingly. The attention she attracted was to Maurice like gall to a wound.

There was not much difficulty in gaining admittance to the dead. A small coin changed hands, and a man in uniform opened the door.

The post-mortem examination had been held that day, and the body was swathed from head to foot in a white sheet. It lay on a long, projecting shelf, and a ticket was pinned on the wall at its head. On the opposite side of the room, on a similar shelf, was another shrouded figure—the body of a working-man, found that morning on the outskirts of the town, with an empty bottle which had contained carbolic acid by its side. The *Leichenfrau,* the public layer-out of the dead, told them this; it was she, too, who drew back the sheet from Avery's face in order that they might see it. She was a rosy, apple-cheeked woman, and her vivid colouring was thrown into relief by the long black cloak and the close-fitting, black poke-bonnet that she wore. Maurice, for whom the dead as such had no attraction, turned from his contemplation of the stark-stretched figure on the shelf, to watch the living woman. The exuberance of her vitality had something almost insultant, in the presence of these two rigid forms, from whose faces the colour had fled for ever. Her eyes were alert like those of a bird; her voice and movements were loud and bustling. In thought he compared her to a carrion-crow. It was this woman's calling to live on the dead; she hastened from house to house to cleanse poor, inanimate bodies, whose dignity had departed from them. He wondered idly whether she gloated over the announcements of fresh deaths, and mentally sped the dying. Did she talk of good seasons and of slack seasons, and look forward to the spread of contagious disease?—Well, at least, she throve on her trade, as a butcher thrives by continually handling meat.

Louise had eyes only for the face of the dead girl. She stood gazing at it, with a curious absorption, but without a spark of feeling. The *Leichenfrau,* having finished tying up a basket, crossed the room and joined her.

" *Eine schöne Leiche!* " she said, and nodded, appreciating the fact that a stranger should admire what was partly her own handiwork.

It was true; Avery's face looked as though it were modelled in wax. She had not been in the water for more than half an hour, had said the doctor, not long enough to be disfigured in any way. Only her hair remained dank and matted, and, although it was laid straight out over the bolster, it would probably never be quite dry again. No matter, continued the woman; on the morrow would come the barber, a good friend of hers, to dress it for the tomb; he would bring tongs and irons, and other heating-apparatus with him, and, for certain, would make a good job of it, so skilled was he: he had all the latest fashions in hair-dressing at his finger-ends. The face itself was as placid as it had been in life; the lids were firmly closed—no peeping or squinting here—and the lips met and rested on each other round and full. Seen like this, it now became evident that this face was one of those which are, all along, intended for death—intended, that is, to lie waxen and immobile, to show to best advantage. In life, there had been too marked a discrepancy between the extreme warmth of the girl's colouring and the extreme immobility of her expression. Now that the blood had, as it were, been drained away to the last drop, now that temples and nostrils had attained transparency, the fine texture of the skin and the beauty of the curves of lips and chin were visible to every eye. Only one hand, so the *Leichen-frau* babbled on, was convulsively closed, and could not be undone; and, as she spoke, she drew the sheet further down, and displayed the naked arm and hand: the long, fine fingers were clenched, the thumb inside the rest. Otherwise, Avery appeared to sleep, to sleep profoundly, with an intensity such as living sleep never attains to—the very epitome of repose. It seemed as if her eyelids were pressed down by some unseen force; and, in her presence, the feeling gained ground in one, that it was worth enduring much, to arrive at a rest of this kind at last.

"*Ja, ja,*" said the woman, and rearranged the covering. "It's a pleasure to handle such a pretty corpse. That one there, now,"—with her chin she pointed to the other figure, and made a face of disgust. "*Ein ekliger Kerl!* There was nothing to be done with him."

"Let me see what he's like," begged Louise.

"It's an ugly sight," said the woman. However, she pulled the sheet down, and so far that not only the face, but also a part of the hairy black breast was visible.

Louise shuddered, yet the very horror of the thing fascinated her, and she plied the woman with questions about the workings of the agonising poison that had been swallowed. After one hasty glance, Maurice had turned away, and now stood staring out of the high, barred window into a gloomy little courtyard, For him, the air of the room was hard to breathe, owing to the faint, yet unmistakable odour, which even the waxen figure of the girl had begun to exhale; and he marvelled how Louise, who was so sensitive, could endure it.

Outside, both drew long breaths of the cold, evening air, and Louise bought a bunch of violets, which she pressed to nose and mouth.

" Horrible, horrible! " she said, at the same time raising her shoulders in their heavy cape. " Oh, that man!—I shall never forget his face."

" What do you go to such places for? You have only yourself to thank for it." He, too, was aware that a needless and repellent memory had been added to their lives.

" Oh, everything's my own fault—I know that. You are never to blame for anything! "

" Did I ask you to go there?—did I? "

But she only laughed in reply, through and through hostile to him; and they walked for some distance in silence.

" Why are you going this way? " he asked suspiciously, when she turned into a street that led in the opposite direction to that which they should have taken.

" I'm not going home. I couldn't sit alone in the dark with that . . . that thing before my eyes."

" Who asked you to sit alone?—Where are you going? "

" I don't know . . . where I like."

" That's no answer."

"And if I don't choose to answer?—I don't want you. I want to be alone. I'm sick of your perpetual bad-temper, and your eternal self-righteousness."

He laughed, just as she had done. The sound enraged her.

" Oh, the dead at least are at peace! " she cried.

" Yes! . . . why don't you say it? You wish you were lying there—at peace from me! "

" Why should I say what you know so well? "

" Go and do it then!—who's hindering you? "

" For you?—kill myself for you? "

One word gave another; they pressed forward, in the falling dusk, like two distraught creatures, heedless of the notice they attracted, or of who should hear their bitter words. And because their gestures were, to some extent, regulated by the conventions of the street, because they could not face each other with flaming eyes, and throw out hands and arms to emphasise what they said, their words were all the more cruel. Louise made straight for home now; she escaped into the house, banging the door. Maurice strode down the street, in a tumult of resentment, vowing never to return.

Avery Hill was buried the following afternoon. Maurice went to the funeral, because, since he had seen the dead girl's body at the mortuary, he had been invaded by a kind of pity for her, lying alone at the mercy of barber and *Leichenfrau*. And so, towards three o'clock, he fought his way against a cutting wind to the *Johannisfriedhof*.

A mere handful of people stood round the grave. In addition to the English chaplain, and a couple of diggers, there were present Dove, two Americans, and a young clerk from the consul's office, who was happy to be associated, in any fashion, with the English residents. It was the coldest day of that winter. Over the earth swept a harsh, dry wind, which cut like the blade of a knife, and forced stinging tears from the eyes. This wind had dried the frozen surface of the ground to the impenetrability of iron; loose earth crumbled before it like powder. Grass and shrubs had shrivelled, blighted by its breath; the bare trees were sooty black against the sky. So intense was the prevailing sensation of icy dryness that it seemed as if the earth would never again know moisture. People's faces grew as wizened as the skins of old apples; throats and lungs were choked by the grey dust, which whirled through the streets, and made breathing an effort.

In the outlying cemetery it was still bleaker than in the shelter of the houses. Over this stretch of ground the wind swept as over the surface of a sea. The grave-diggers related the extraordinary difficulty they had had in digging the grave; the earth that had been thrown up lay cracked into huge, frozen lumps. These two men stood in the background while the service was going on, and stamped their feet and beat their hands, encased in monstrous woollen gloves, to keep the blood flowing. The English chaplain, a tall, cadaverous man, with sunken cheeks and a straw-coloured beard, had wound a red and white comforter over his surplice; the five young men pulled down the ear-flaps of their caps, and stood, with high-drawn shoulders. burrowing their hands in their pockets. The chaplain gabbled the few necessary prayers: they were inaudible to his hearers; for the rushing wind carried them straight over his shoulder into space. He was not more than a bare ten minutes over the service. Then the diggers came forward to lower the coffin. Owing to the stiffness of their hands, the ropes slid from their grasp, and the coffin fell forward into the hard yellow grave with a bump. The young men took the obligatory handfuls of earth, and struck the side of the coffin with them as gently as possible. With the last word still on his lips, the chaplain shut his book and fled; and the rest hastily dispersed. Maurice shook off the young clerk, who was murmuring unintelligible words of sympathy, and left the cemetery in the wake of the two Americans, for whom a droschke was in waiting to take them back to the town.

"Waal, I'm sort o' relieved that wasn't *my* funeral," he heard one of them say.

He walked at full speed to restore his famished circulation. When he was in the heart of the town again, he entered a café; and there he remained, with his elbows on the little marble table, letting the scene he had just come through pass once more before his mind. There had been something grotesquely indecent about the haste of every one concerned: the chaplain, gabbling like a parrot, out of regard for the safety of his own lungs; the hurry-skurry of the diggers, whose thoughts were no doubt running on the size of their gratuities; the openly expressed satisfaction of the few mourners, when they were free to hurry off again, as in hurry they had arrived. Not one present but had counted the minutes, at the expiry of which the dead girl would be consigned to her appointed hole. What an ending! All the talent, the incipient genius, that had been in her, thrust away with the greatest possible despatch, buried out of sight in the hideously hard, cold earth. Snuffed out like a candle, and with as little ceremony, was all the warm, complex life that had made up this one, throbbing bit of humanity: for what it had been, not a soul alive now cared. And what a night, too, for one's first night underground! Brr!—At the thought of it, he drank another cup of coffee, and a fiery, stirring liqueur. But the sense of depression clung to him, and, as he walked home, he regretted the impulse that had led him to attend the funeral. For all the melancholy of valediction was his. The dead girl was free—and he had a sudden vision of her, as she had lain in the mortuary, with the look of superhuman peace on her face. Over the head of this, he was sarcastic at his own expense. For though she *were* being treated like a piece of lumber, what did it matter to her? Beneath the screening lid, she continued to sleep, tranquil, undisturbed. On the other hand, how absurd it was that he, who had cared little for her in life, should in this wise constitute himself her only mourner! And, mentally and physically, he now jerked himself to rights, and even began to whistle, as he went, in an attempt to seem at harmony with himself. But the tune that rose to his lips was Krafft's song, *The Rose of Sharon,* and he straightway broke off, in disgust and confusion.

In his room, as soon as he had struck a match to light the lamp, he saw that a letter was lying on the table. By the gradual spread of the light, he made out that it bore an Austrian stamp, and directly he took it in his hand, he recognised the writing. Heinz!—it was from Heinz! He tore open the envelope with unsteady fingers; what could Heinz have to write to him about? Instinctively, he connected it in some way with the events of the afternoon. But it was a very brief note, covering hardly a page of the paper. Standing beside the lamp, Maurice held the sheet in the circle of light, and ran his eye over the few lines. He took them in, in a flash, that is to say, he read them automatically; but their sense did not penetrate his brain. He tried again, and still he could not grasp what they meant; still again, and slowly, word by word, till he could have repeated them by heart; but always without getting at their inner meaning. Then, however, and all of a sudden, as if some inner consciousness had understood them, and now gave bodily warning of it; suddenly, his knees began to shake, and he was forced to sit down. Sitting, he continued to stare at the page of writing before him, with contracted pupils. He commenced to read again, and even said the first line or two of the letter aloud, as if that might aid him. But the paper fell from his hand, and he gazed, instead, into the flame of the lamp, right into the inmost flame, till he was blind with it. His head fell forward, and lay on his hands, and on the rustling sheet of paper.

" God in Heaven! "

He heard himself say it, and was even conscious of the fact that, like every mortal in the throes of a strong emotion, he, too, called on God.

A long and profound silence ensued. It went on and on, persisted, was about to become eternal, when it was rudely broken by the sound of a child's cry. He raised his head. The walls swam round him: in spite of the coldness of the night and the fact that the room was unheated, he was clammy with perspiration. The skin of his face, too, had a peculiar, drawn feeling, as if it were a mask that was too tight for it. He shivered. Then his eye fell on the letter lying open on the table. Without a moment's hesitation, without waiting even to put the lamp out, he seized it, and went headlong from the house.

But he was strangely unequal to exertion. He felt a craving for stimulant, and entering a wine-shop, drank a couple of cognacs. His strength came back to him; people moved out of his way; he had energy enough to climb the stair, and to go through the business of unlocking the door.

At his abrupt entrance, Louise concealed something in a drawer, and turned the key on it. But Maurice was too self-absorbed to heed her action, or consciously to hear her exclamation at his haggard appearance. He shut the door, crossed to where she was standing, and, without speaking, pulled her nearer to the lamp. By its light, he scanned her face with a desperate eagerness.

"What is it? What's the matter?"

At the sound of her voice, the tension of the past hour relaxed. He let his head fall on her shoulder, and shut his eyes, swaying as she swayed beneath his weight.

"Forgive me! . . . forgive me!"

"You've been drinking, I think." But she held still under his grasp.

"Yes, I have. Louise! . . . tell me it's a horrible mistake. Help me, you *must* help me!"

"How can I help you, if you won't tell me what the matter is?" She believed him to be half drunk, and spoke as to a drunken person, without meaning much.

"Yes, yes . . . I will. Only give me time."

But he postponed beginning. Leaning more heavily on her, he pressed his lips to the stuff of her dress. He would have liked to sleep, just where he was; indeed, he was invaded by the desire to sleep, never again to unclose his eyes. But she grew restless, and tried to draw her shoulder away. Then he looked at her, and a feverish stream of words, half self-recriminative, half in self-defence, burst from his lips. But they had little to do with the matter in hand, and were incomprehensible to her. "It has been a terrible nightmare. And only you can drive it away." As he spoke, he looked, with a sudden suspicion, right into her eyes. But they neither faltered nor grew uneasy.

"It will turn out to be nothing, I know," she said coldly. "You're always devising some new way of tormenting me."

Her words roused him. Fumbling in his pocket, he drew from it Krafft's letter. "Is that nothing? Read it and tell me. I found it at home on my table."

Louise took it with unmoved indifference. But directly she saw whose handwriting it was, her face grew grave and attentive. She looked back from the envelope to him, to see what he was thinking, to learn how much he knew. In spite of his roughness there was a hungry, imploring look in his eyes, an appeal to her to put him out of misery, and in the way he desired. And, as always, before such a look, her own face hardened.

"Read it! What he dares to write to me!"

Slowly, as if it were impossible for her to hurry, she drew the sheet from the crumpled envelope and smoothed it out. As she did so, she half turned away. But not so far that he could not see the dark, disfiguring blood stain her neck and blotch her cheek—even her ear grew crimson. She read deliberately, lingering over each word, but the instant she had finished, she crushed the paper to a ball, and threw it to the other end of the room.

"The scoundrel!" she cried. "Oh, the scoundrel!" Clenching her two hands, she pressed them to her face.

Maurice did not say a word; he hardly dared to draw breath, for fear some sign of her guilt might escape him. Leaning against the table, he marked each tell-tale quiver of lip or eyelid.

"The blackguard!" she cried again, shaken by rage. "If I had him here, I'd strangle him with my own hands!"

He gloated over her anger. "Yes," he said in a low voice. "I, too . . . could kill him."

There was a pause, in which each followed out a possible means of revenge.

"Now you see," he said. "When I got home—when I found that—I thought I should go mad."

Reminded thus, of his share in the matter, Louise turned her head, and considered him. Her face was tense.

"Forgive me!" said Maurice, and held out his hands to her. She gave him another look of the same kind. "I forgive you? What for?"

"Because . . . since I got it, I've been thinking vile things."

"Oh, that!" She moved away, and gave a curt laugh, which

met him like a stab. But she had no consideration for him:
she had only room in her mind for Krafft's treachery. "I could
kill him," she said again. "Don't. . . . Leave me alone!"
—this to Maurice, who was trying to take her hand. "Don't
touch me!"

"Not touch you!—why not?" In an instant his softness
passed over into suspicion: it was like a dry pile that had waited
for the match. "I not touch you?" he repeated. "Do you
want to make me believe that what he says there is true?"

"Believe what you like."

"But that's just what I won't do. Turn here! Look me in
the face! Now tell me it's a lie."

She struggled to free her hands. "You hurt me, Maurice!
Let me go!"

"Be careful!—or I shall hurt you more than this. Now
answer me!"

"You!—with your ridiculous heroics! Be careful yourself!"

His grip of her grew tighter.

"For your precious peace of mind then—that you may not
be kept in suspense: what Heinz says there is—true!"

He did not at once grasp what she meant. He stood staring
stupidly at her, still clutching her hands. With a determined
effort, Louise wrenched them away.

"Don't you hear what I say? It's true—all true—every
word of it!"

At the cruel repetition, he went pale, and after that, seemed
to go on growing paler, until his face was like a sheet of paper.
A horrible silence ensued; neither dared to let go of the other's
eyes.

"My God!" he said at last. "My God!"

He sat down at the table, and buried his face in his
arms. Louise did not move; she stood waiting, her hands,
which were red and sore, pressed against her sides. And as
minutes passed, and he did not stir, she began in a vacant
way to count the ticks of the clock. If he did not speak
soon, did not go on with what had to come, and get it over,
she would be forced to scream. A scream was mounting in
her throat.

"When was it? . . . How? . . . Why?"

She made no answer.

He straightened himself, holding on to the table. "And if
that letter hadn't come, you wouldn't have told me?"

Again she did not reply. He sprang to his feet, interpreting her inability to bring forth a sound, as mere contemptuous defiance.

"*Why* did you tell me? Did I need to know?" he cried loudly, and, in the confines of the room, his voice had the force of a shout. As she still remained dumb, he leaned across the table and actually shouted at her. "Any more?—are there any more? He won't have been the only one. Tell me, I say! Good God! Don't you hear me?" The arteries in his temples were beating like two separate hearts. As nothing he said would make her open her lips, he snatched up her hands again, and dragged her a few steps forward—this, to prove to himself that he had at least bodily power over her. "How dare you stand there and say it's true! You brazen, shameless——!"

She thought he was going to strike her, and moved her head quickly to one side. The movement did not escape him; he was amazed at it, and horrified by it. "You're afraid of me, are you? You expect to be beaten, when you make a confession of that sort?" And as she kept her head bent, in suspense, he shouted: "Very well, you shall have something to be afraid of . . . you ——!" and lifting his hand, he struck her a blow on the shoulder. It was given with force, and she sank to the floor, where she lay in a heap, screening her face with her arm. The first taste of his greater strength was like the flavour of blood to a beast of prey. In her mind, she might defy him, physically he was her master; and he struck her again and again. But he did not wring any sound from her. She lay face downwards, and let the blows fall.

When his first onslaught of rage had spent itself, a glimmering of reason returned to him. He staggered to his feet, and looked down with horror at the prostrate figure. "My God, what am I doing?—what have I done?" A sudden fear swept through him that he had killed her.

But now, for the first time, she spoke. "It's true!" he heard her say.

At these words, the desire actually to kill her was so overwhelming that he moved precipitately away, and, in order not to see her, pressed his smarting hand to his eyes. But in the greater clearness of thought this shutting off of externals brought with it, the ultimate meaning of what she had done was revealed to him; he saw red through his closed lids, and, going back to her, he struck her anew. The knowledge that, under her dressing-gown, she had nothing on but a thin

nightgown, gave him pleasure; he felt each of the blows fall
full and hard on her firm flesh.

From time to time, she turned her face to cry: " It's true
. . . it is true! " deliberately inciting him to continue.

But the moment came when his arm sank powerless to his
side, when, if his life had depended on it, he could not have
struck another blow. With difficulty, he rose to his feet; and
such was the apathy that came over him, that it was all he
could do to drag himself to the sofa. Once there, he leaned
back and closed his eyes.

For half an hour or more, neither of them stirred. Then,
when she understood that he had done, that he was not coming
back to her, Louise pulled herself into a sitting position, and
from there to her feet. She could hardly stand; her head swam;
not an inch of her body but ached and stung. Her exaltation
had left her now; she began to feel sick, and, going over to
the bed, she fell heavily upon it.

Maurice heard her movements; but so incapable did he feel
of further effort that he remained sitting, with his eyes shut. A
new sound roused him: she was shivering, and with such violence that the bedstead was shaken. After a crucial struggle
with himself, he rose, and crossed the room. She was lying outside the bedclothes. He pulled off an eider-down quilt, and
spread it over her. As he did this, his arms were round her, all
the beloved body was in his grasp. When he had finished, he
did not remove them, but, kneeling down beside the bed, pressed
his face to the quilt, and to the warm body below.

And so the night wore away.

XI

THROUGHOUT February, and the greater part of March, the *Hauptprüfungen* were held in the Conservatorium: twice a week, from six to eight o'clock in the evening, the concert hall was crammed with an eager crowd. To these concerts, the outside public was admitted, the critics were invited, and the performances received notices in the newspapers; in short, the outgoing student was, for the first time, treated like a real debutant. Concerted music was accompanied by the full orchestra; the large gallery that ran round the hall was opened up; and the girls, whose eager faces hung over its edge, were more brightly decked than usual, in ribbons and laces. Some of those who stepped down the platform seemed thoroughly to relish their first taste of publicity; others, on the contrary, were awkward and abashed, and did not venture to notice the encouragement that greeted their entrance. There were players as composed as the most hardened virtuosi; others, again, who were overcome by stage-fright to such an extent that they barely escaped a total fiasco.

The success of the year was Dove, in his performance of Chopin's Concerto in E minor. Dove's unshakable self-possession was here of immense value to him. Not a note was missed, not a turn slurred; the runs and brilliant passage-work of the concerto left his fingers like showers of pearls; his touch had the necessary delicacy, and, in addition to this, his reading was quite a revelation to his friends in the matter of *temperament*. It is true that Schwarz prohibited any undignified display of the emotional side of Chopin; the interpretation had to be on classical lines; but even the most determined opponents of Schwarz's method were forced to acknowledge that Dove made no mean show of the poetic contents of the music. The master himself, in his imperturbable way—he chose to act as if, all along, he had had this surprise for people up his sleeve—the master was in transports. His stern face wore an almost genial expression; he smiled, and talked loudly, and, when the performance was over, hurried to and fro, full of importance, shaking hands and accepting congratulations, with a fine shade of reserve. Dove's fellow-pupils were enraptured for Schwarz's sake; for, undeniably, the master's numbers this year were poor, compared with those of other teachers. It behoved the remainder to make the most of this isolated triumph; they did so, and were entertained by Schwarz at a special dinner, where many healths were drunk.

Those who had "made their *Prüfung*," as the phrase ran, were, as a rule, glad to leave Leipzig when the ordeal was behind them. But Dove, who, on the day following his performance, when his name was to be read in the newspapers accompanied by various epithets of praise, had proposed and been accepted, and was this time returning to England a solemnly engaged man—Dove waited a week for his fiancée and her family, who had not been prepared for so sudden a move. He was the man of the hour. As a response to the flattering notices, he had called on all his critics, and been received by several; and he could hardly walk a street-length, without running the gauntlet of some belated congratulation. Schwarz had spoken seriously to him about prosecuting his studies for a further year, with the not impossible prospect of a performance in the Gewandhaus at the end of it; but Dove had laid before his master the reasons why this could not be: he was no longer a free man; there were now other wishes to be consulted in addition to his own. Besides, if the truth must be told, Dove had higher aims, and these led him imperatively back to England.

Madeleine was ready to leave a couple of days after her last performance. Her plans for the future were fixed and sure. She had long ago given up making adventurous schemes for storming America: that had merely been her contribution to the romance of the place. Now she was hastening away to spend the month of March in Paris; she was not due at the school to which she was returning till the end of April; and, in Paris, she intended to take a brief course of finishing lessons, to rub off what she called "German thoroughness." She, too, had made a highly successful exit, though without creating a furore like Dove. Since all she did was well done, it was not possible for her to be a surprise to anyone.

And finally, the rush she had lived in for weeks past, was over, the last afternoon had come, and, in its course, she went to the railway station to make arrangements about her luggage. On her way home, she entered Klemm's music-shop, where she stood, for a considerable time, taking leave of one and another. When she emerged again, the town had assumed that spectral look, which, towards evening, made the quaint old gabled streets so attractive.

For the first time, Madeleine felt something akin to regret at having to leave. She had enjoyed, and made the most of, her years of study; but she was now quite ready to advance, curious to attack the future, and to dominate that also. Still, the dusk on the familiar streets inclined her to feel sentimental. " This time to-morrow, I'll be hundreds of miles away," she said to herself, " and probably shall never see the old place again." As she walked, she looked back upon her residence there—already somewhat in the light of a remembrance—weighing what it had been worth to her. Part of it was intimately associated with Maurice Guest, and thus she recalled him, too. Of late he had passed out of her life; she had been too busy to think of him. Now, however, that she was at the end of this period, the fancy seized her to see him again; and she took a resolution which had, perhaps, been dormant in her for some time.

" I don't see why I shouldn't," she reasoned. " No one will know. And even if they do, I'm leaving, and it won't matter."

And so she pulled her hat further over her face, and brisked up her steps in the direction of the *Braustrasse*—a street which she disliked, and never entered if she could avoid it. If he had lived in a better neighbourhood, things might have gone better with him, she mused; for Madeleine was a staunch believer in the influence of surroundings, and could not, for instance, understand a person who lived in dirt and disorder having any but a dirty or disorderly mind. She went from door to door, scanning the numbers, with her head poked a little forward and to one side, like a bird's. As she ascended the stair, she raised her skirts, and her nostrils twitched displeased.

Frau Krause held the door open by an inch, and looked at Madeleine with distrust.

" No, he's not," she replied. " And what's more, I couldn't say, if you were to pay me, when he will be."

But Madeleine was not to be daunted by the arrogance of any landlady alive. " Why? Is he so irregular? " she asked. She had placed her foot in the opening of the door, and now, by a skilful movement, inserted herself bodily into the passage.

Frau Krause, baffled, could do no more than mumble a: " Well, if you like to wait! " and point out the room. She .followed Madeleine over the threshold, drying her hands on her apron.

" Are you a friend of his, may I ask? " she inquired.

" Why? What do you want to know for? Do you think

34

I'd be here if I weren't?" said Madeleine, looking her up and down.

"Why I want to know?" repeated Frau Krause, and tossed her head. "Why, because I think if Herr Guest has any friends left, they ought to know how he's going on—that's why, Fräulein!"

"How going on?" queried Madeleine with undisturbed coolness, and looked round her for a chair.

Throwing a cautious glance over her shoulder, Frau Krause said behind her hand: "It's my opinion there's a woman in the case."

"You don't need to whisper; your opinion is an open secret," answered Madeleine drily. "There *is* a woman, and there she sits, as you no doubt very well know." As she spoke, she pointed to a photograph of Louise, which stood on the lid of the piano.

"I thought as much," exclaimed the landlady. "I thought as much. And a bad, bold face it is, too."

"Now explain, please, what you mean by his goings on. Is he in debt to you?" Madeleine continued her interrogatory.

"Well, I can't just say that," replied the woman, with what seemed a spice of regret. "He's paid up pretty regular till now—though of course one never knows how long he'll keep on doing it. But it goes against my heart to see a young man, who might be one's own son, acting as he does. When he first came here, there wasn't a decenter young man anywhere than Herr Guest—if I had a complaint, it was that he was too much of a steady-goer. I used to tell him he ought to take more heed for his health, not to mention the ears of the people that had to live with him. He sat at that piano there all the blessed day. And now there isn't a lazier, more cantankerous fellow in the place. You can't please him anyhow. He never gives you a civil word. He doesn't work, he doesn't eat, and he's getting so thin that his clothes just hang on him."

"Is he drinking?" interrupted Madeleine in the same matter-of-fact way, with her eye on the main points of probable offence.

"Well, I can't just say that," answered Frau Krause. "Not but what it mightn't be better if he was. It's the ones as don't drink who are the hard ones to get on with, in my experience. Young gentlemen who like their liquor, are of the good-natured, easy-going sort. Now I once had a young fellow here——"

"But I don't see in the least what you've got to complain of!" said Madeleine. "He pays you for the room, and you no doubt have free use of it.—A very good bargain!"

She sat back and stared about her, while Frau Krause, recognising that she had met her match in this sharp-tongued young lady, curbed her temper, and launched out into the history of a former lodger.

It was a dingy room, long and narrow, with a single window. Against the door that led into an adjoining room, stood a high-backed, uninviting sofa, with a table in front of it. Between this and the window was the writing-bureau, a flat, man-high piece of furniture, with drawers and pigeon-holes, and a broad flap that let down for writing purposes. Against the opposite wall stood the neglected piano, and, towards the door, on both sides, were huddled bed, washstand, and the iron stove. Everything was of an extreme shabbiness: the stuffing was showing through holes in the sofa, the strips of carpet were worn threadbare. A couple of photographs and a few books were ranged in line on the bureau—that was all that had been done towards giving the place a homely air. It was like a room that had never properly been lived in.

While Madeleine sat thinking this, the sound of a key was heard in the front door, and Frau Krause, interrupted in her story, had just time to tap Madeleine on the arm, exclaim: "Here he is!" and dart out of the room. Not so promptly, however, but what Maurice saw where she came from. Madeleine heard them bandying words in the passage.

The door of the room was flung open, and Maurice, entering hotly, threw his hat on the table. He did not perceive his visitor till it was too late.

"Madeleine! You here!" he exclaimed in surprise and embarrassment. "I beg your pardon. I didn't see you," and he made haste to recover his hat.

"Yes, don't faint, it's I, Maurice.—But what's the matter? Why are you so angry with the person? Does she pry on you?"

"Pry!" he echoed, and his colour deepened. "Pry's not the word for it. She ransacks everything I have. I never come home but what I find she has overhauled something, though I've forbidden her to enter the room."

"Why don't you—or rather, why didn't you move? It's not much of a place, I'm sure."

"Move?" he repeated, in the same tone as before, and, as

he spoke, he looked incredulously at Madeleine. He had hung his coat and hat on a peg, and now came forward to the table. "Move?" he said again, and prolonged the word, as though the channel of thought it opened up was new to him.

"Good gracious, yes!—If one's not satisfied with one's rooms, one moves, that's all. There's nothing strange about it."

He murmured that the idea had never occurred to him, and was about to draw up a chair, when his eye caught a letter that was lying on the lowered flap of the bureau. In patent agitation, and without excusing himself, he seized it and tore it open. Madeleine saw his face darken. He read the letter through twice, from beginning to end, then tore it into a dozen pieces and scattered them on the shelf.

"No bad news, I hope?"

He turned his face to her; it was still contracted. "That depends on how you look at it, Madeleine," he said, and laughed in an unpleasant manner.

After this, he seemed to forget her again; he stood staring at the scraps of paper with a frown. For some minutes, she waited. Then she saw herself forced to recall him to the fact of her presence.

"Could you spare me a little attention now?" she asked. At her words, he jumped, and, with evident confusion, brought his wandering thoughts home. "I can't sit here for ever, you know," she added.

"I beg your pardon." He came up to the table, and took the chair he had previously had his hand on. "The fact is . . . I—— Can I do anything for you, Madeleine?"

"For me? Oh dear, no!—You are surprised to find me here, no doubt! But as I'm leaving to-morrow morning, I thought I'd run up and say good-bye to you—that's all. A case of Mohammed and the mountain, you see."

"Leaving? To-morrow?"

"Yes.—Goodness, there's nothing wonderful in that, is there? Most people do leave some time or other, you know."

His reply was inaudible. "It was very good of you to look me up," he threw in as an afterthought.

Madeleine, watching him, with a thin, sarcastic smile on her lips, had chanced to let her eyes stray to his hands, which he had laid on the table, and she continued to fix them, fascinated in spite of herself by the uncared-for condition of the nails. These were bitten, and broken, and dirty. Maurice, becoming aware of her intent gaze, looked down to see what it was at, hastily withdrew his hands, and hid them in his pockets.

"This is the first time I've been in your den, you know," she said abruptly. "Really, Maurice, you might have done better. I don't know how you've managed to put up with it so long."

"My dear Madeleine, do you think I could afford to live in a palace?"

"A palace?—absurd! You probably pay sixteen or seventeen marks for this hole. Well, I could have found you any number of better places for the same money—if you had come to me."

"You're very kind. But it has done me well enough."

"So it appears."

Sitting back, she looked round her, in the hope of picking up some neutral subject. "Are those your people?" she asked, and nodded at the photograph of a family-group, which stood on the top shelf of the bureau. "Three boys, are you not? You are like your mother," and she stared, with unfeigned curiosity, at the provincial figures, dressed out in their best coats and silks, and in heavy gold jewellery.

"Good God, Madeleine!" Maurice burst out at this, his loosely kept patience escaping him. "You didn't come here, I suppose, to remark on my family?"

"Well, I can't congratulate you on an improvement in your manners, since I saw you last."

"I am not aware of having changed."

"As well for you, perhaps. However, I'll tell you about myself, if it interests you." She had turned her cool, judicial gaze on him again; and now she set before him her projects for the future. But though he kept his eyes fastened on her face, she saw that he was not listening to what she said, or, at most, that he only half heard it; for, when she ceased to speak, he did not notice her silence.

She waited, curious to see what would come next, and presently he echoed, in his vague way: "Paris, did you say?— Really?"

"Yes—Paris: the capital of France.—I said that, and a good deal more, which I don't think you heard.—And now I won't take up your precious time any longer.—You've nothing new to tell me, I suppose? You still intend staying on here, and fighting out the problem of existence? Well, when you have starved satisfactorily in a garret, I hope some one will let me know. I'll come over for the funeral."

She rose, and began to button her jacket.

"And England has absolutely no chance? English music must continue to languish, without hope of reform?"

"How can you remember such rot! I was a terrible fool when I talked like that."

"I liked you better as a fool than I do now, with your acquired wisdom. And I won't go from here without offering you congratulations, hearty congratulations, on the muddle you've made of things."

"That's entirely my own affair."

"You may be thankful it is! Do you think anyone else would want the responsibility of it?"

She went out without a further word. But on the landing at the bottom of the first flight of stairs, she stood irresolute. She felt annoyed with herself that she had allowed an un-friendly tone to dominate their brief interview. This was probably the last time she would see him; the last chance she would have of telling him just what she thought of him. And viewed in that light, it seemed ridiculous to let any artificial delicacy of feeling stand in her way. She blew her nose vig-orously, and, not being used to indecision, turned as she did so, and began to ascend the stairs again. Brushing past Frau Krause, she reopened, without knocking, the door of Maurice's room.

He had moved the lamp from the table to the bureau, and at her entrance was bending over something that lay there, so engrossed that he did not at once raise his head.

"Good gracious! What are you doing?" escaped her in-voluntarily.

At this, he spun round, and, leaning back against the writing-table, tried to screen it from her eyes.

She regretted her impulsive curiosity, and did not press him. "Yes, it's me again," she said with determination. "And I suppose you'll want to accuse me of prying, too, like that female outside.—Look here: it's ludicrous for us who have been friends so long to part in this fashion. And I, for one, don't intend to do it. There's something I want to say before I go—you may be angry and offended if you like; I don't care"—for he frowned forbiddingly. "I'm no denser than other people; and I know just as well as every one else the wretched mess you've got yourself into—one would have to be blind and deaf, indeed, not to know.—Now, look here, Maurice! You once said to me, you may remember, that if you had a sister you'd like her to be something like me. Will you look on me as that sister for a little, and let me give you some sound advice? I told you I was going to Paris, and that I had a clear month there. Well, now, throw your things together and come with me. You haven't had a decent holiday since you've been here. You need freshening up.—Or if not Paris—Paris isn't a necessity—we'll go down by Munich and the Brenner to Italy, and I'll be cicerone. I'll act as banker, too, and you can regard it as a loan in the meantime, and pay me back when you're richer.—Now what do you say? Doesn't the plan tempt you?"

"What I say?" he echoed, and looked round him a little helplessly. "Why, Madeleine . . . It seems you are determined to run off with me. Once it was America, and now it's Italy or Paris."

"Come, say you'll consent, or at least consider it."

"My dear Madeleine! You are all that is good and kind. But you know you're only talking nonsense."

She did not answer him at once. "The thing is this," she said with some hesitation. "I wasn't quite honest in what I said to you a few minutes ago. I have the uncomfortable feeling that I am to a certain degree responsible, even to blame, for much of . . . what has happened here. And it isn't a pleasant feeling, Maurice."

"My dear girl!" he said again. "If it's any consolation to you to know it, I owe you the biggest debt of my life."

"Then you decline my proposal, do you?"

"You're the same good friend you always were. But you're making a mountain out of a molehill. What's all this fuss about? Merely because I haven't chosen to work my fingers to the bone, and wear my nerves to tatters over that old farce of a *Prüfung*. As for my choosing to stay here, instead of going home like the rest of you—well, that's a matter of taste, too. Some people—like our friend Dove—want affluence, and a fixed position in the provinces. Frankly, I don't. I'd rather scrape along here, as best I can. That's the whole matter in a nutshell, and it's nothing to make a to-do about. For though you think I'm a fool, and can't help telling me so—that, too, is a matter of opinion."

"Well, I don't intend to apologise for myself at this date, be sure of that! And now I'll go. For if you are resolved to hold me at arm's length, there's nothing more to be said.—No, stop a minute, though. Here's my address in England. If ever you should return to join us benighted ignorants, you might let me know. Or if you find you can't get on here—I mean if it's quite impossible—I have money, you know . . . and should be glad—at a proper percentage, of course," she added ironically.

"That's hardly likely to happen."

She laid the card on the table. "You never can tell.— Well, good-bye, then, and in spite of your obstinacy, I'll perhaps be able to do you a good turn yet, Maurice Guest."

As soon as he heard the front door close, he returned to his occupation of piecing together the bits of the letter. Ever since he had torn it up—throughout her visit—his brain had been struggling to recall its exact contents, and without success; for, owing to Madeleine's presence, he had read it hastily. Otherwise, what he had done to-day did not differ from his usual method of proceeding. This was not the first horrible unsigned letter he had received, and he could never prevail on himself to throw them in the fire, unopened. He read them through, two or three times, then, angered by their contents and by his own weakness, tore them to fragments. But the hints and aspersions they contained, remained imprinted on his mind. In this case, Madeleine's distracting appearance had enfeebled his memory, and he worked long and patiently until the sheet lay fitted together again before him. When he knew its contents by heart, he struck some matches, and watched the pieces curl and blacken.

Then he left the house.

Her room was in darkness. He stretched himself on the sofa to wait for her return.

The words of the letter danced like a writing of fire before him; he lay there and re-read them; but without anger. What they stated might be true, also it might not; he would never know. For these letters, which he was ashamed of himself for opening, and still more for remembering, had not been mentioned between them, but were added to that category of things they now tacitly agreed to avoid. In his heart, he knew that he cherished the present state of uncertainty; it was a twilight state, without crudities or sharp outlines; and it was still possible to drift and dream in it. Whereas if another terrible certainty, like the last, descended on him, he would be forced to marshal his energies, and to suffer afresh. It was better not to know. As long as definite knowledge failed him, he could give her the benefit of the doubt. And whether what the letters affirmed was true or not, hours came when she still belonged wholly to him. Whatever happened on her absences from him, as soon as the four walls of the room shut them in again, she was his; and each time she returned, a burning gratitude for the reprieve filled him anew.

But there was also another reason why he did not breathe a word to her of his suspicions, and that was the slow dread that was laming him—the dread of her contempt. She made no further attempt to drape it; and he had learned to writhe before it, to cringe and go softly. Weeks had passed now, since the night on which he had made his last stand against her—weeks of increasing torture. Just at first, incredible as it had seemed, his horrible treatment of her had brought about a slackening of the tension between them. The worst that could happen had happened, and he had survived it: he had not put an end either to himself or to her. On the contrary, he had accepted the fact—as he now saw that he would accept every fact concerning her, whether for good or evil. And matters having reached this point, a kind of lull ensued: for a few days they had even caught a glimpse again of the old happiness. But the pause was short-lived: it was like the ripples caused by a stone thrown into water, which continue just so long as the impetus lasts. Louise had been a little awed by his greater strength, when she had lain cowering on the ground before him. But not many days elapsed before her eyes were wide open with incredulous amazement. When she understood, as she soon did, that her shameless admission, and still more, his punishment of her for it, were not to be followed up by any new development; that, in place of subduing her mentally as well, he was going to be content to live on as they had been doing; that, in fact, he had already dropped back into the old state of things, before she was well aware of what was happening: then her passing mood of submission swept over into her old flamboyant contempt for him. The fact of his having beaten her became a weapon in her hands; and she used it unsparingly. To her taunts, he had no answer to make. For, the madness once passed, he could not conceive how he had been capable of such a thing; in his sane moments of dejection and self-distrust, he could not have raised his hand against her, though his life were at stake.

He had never been able to drag from her a single one of

the reasons that had led to her mad betrayal of him. On this point she was inflexible. In the course of that long night which he had spent on his knees by her bed, he had persecuted her to disclose her motive. But he might as well have spoken to the wind; his questioning elicited no reply. Again and again, he had upbraided her: "But you didn't care for Heinz! He was nothing to you!" and she neither assented nor gainsaid him. Once, however, she had broken in on him: "You believed bad of me long before there was any to believe. Now you have something to go on!" And still again, when the sluggish dawn was creeping in, she had suddenly turned her head: "But now you can go away. You're free to leave me. Nothing binds you to a woman like me—who can't be content with one man." Dizzy with fatigue, he had answered: "No—if you think that—if you did it just to be rid of me— you're mistaken!"

From this night on, they had never reverted to the subject again—which is not to say that his brain did not work furiously at it; the search for a clue, for the hidden motive, was now his eternal occupation. But to her he was silent, sheerly from the dread of again receiving the answer: take me as I am, or leave me! In hours such as the present, or in the agony of sleepless nights, these thoughts rent his brain. The question was such an involved one, and he never seemed to come any nearer a solution of it. Sometimes, he was actually tempted to believe what her words implied: that it had been wilfully done, with a view to getting rid of him. But against this, his reason protested; for, if the letter from Krafft had not arrived, he would have known nothing. He did not believe she would have told him—would there, indeed, have been any need for her to do so? Nothing was changed between them; she lived at his side, just as before; and Krafft was out of the way.—At other times, though, he asked himself if he were not a fool to be surprised at what had occurred. Had not all roads led here? Had he not, as she most truly said, for long harboured the unworthiest suspicions of her?—suspicions which were tantamount to an admission on his part that his love was no longer enough for her. To have done this, and afterwards to behave as if she had been guilty of an unpardonable crime, was illogical and unjust.—And yet again, there came moments when, in a barbarous clearness of vision, he seemed to get nearest to the truth. Under certain circumstances, so he now told himself, he would gladly and straightway have forgiven her. If she had been drawn, irresistibly, to another, by one of those sudden outbursts of passion before which she was incapable of remaining steadfast; if she had been attracted, like this, more than half unwilling, wholly humiliated, penitent in advance, yet powerless—then, oh then, how willingly he would have made allowance for her weakness! But Krafft, of all people!—Krafft, of whom she had spoken to him with derisive contempt!—this cold and calculated deception of him with some one who made not the least appeal to her!—Cold and calculated, did he say? No, far from it! What *could* it have been but the sensual caprice of a moment?—but a fleeting, manlike desire for the piquancy of change?

These and similar thoughts ran their whirling circles behind his closed eyes, as he lay in the waning twilight of the March evening, which still struggled with the light of the lamp. But they were hard pressed by the contents of the letter: on this night he foresaw that his fixed idea threatened to divide up into two branches—and he did not know whether to be glad or to regret it. But he admitted to himself that one of these days he would be forced to take measures for preserving his sanity, by somehow dragging the truth from her; better still, by following her on one of her evening absences, to discover for himself where she went, and whether what the anonymous writer asserted was true. If he could only have controlled his brain! The perpetually repeated circles it drove in —if these could once have been brought to a stop, all the rest of him infinitely preferred not to know.

Meanwhile, the shadows deepened, and his subconsciousness never ceased to listen, with an intentness which no whirligigs of thought could distract, for the sound of her step in the passage. When, at length, some short time after darkness had set in, he heard her at the door, he drew a long, sighing breath of relief, as if—though this was unavowed even to himself—he had been afraid he might listen in vain. And, as always, when the suspense was over, and she was under the same roof with him again, he was freed from so intolerable a weight that he was ready to endure whatever she might choose to put upon him, and for his part to make no demands.

Louise entered languidly; and so skilled had he grown at interpreting her moods that he knew from her very walk which of them she was in. He looked surreptitiously at her, and saw that she was wan and tired. It had been a mild, enervating day; her hair was blown rough about her face. He watched her before the mirror take off hat and veil, with slow, yet impatient fingers; watched her hands in her hair, which she did not trouble to rearrange, but only smoothed back on either side.

She had not, even in entering, cast a glance at him, and, recognising the rasped state of her nerves, he had the intent to be cautious. But his resolutions, however good, were not long proof against her over-emphasised neglect of his presence. Her wilful preoccupation with herself, and with inanimate objects, exasperated him. Everything was of more worth to her than he was, and she delighted to show it.

" Haven't you a word for me? Don't you see I'm here? " he asked at length.

Even now she did not look towards him as she answered: " Of course, I see you. But shall I speak next to the furniture of the room? "

" So!—That's what I am, is it?—A piece of your furniture! "

" Yes.—No, worse. Furniture is silent."

She was changing her walking-dress for the dressing-gown. This done, she dabbed powder on her face out of a small oval glass pot—a habit of hers to which he had never grown accustomed.

" Stop putting that stuff on your face! You know I hate it."

Her only answer was to dab anew, and so thickly that the powder was strewn over the front of her dress and the floor. The clothes she had taken off were flung on a chair; as she brushed past them, they fell to the ground. She did not stoop to pick them up, but pushed them out of the way with her foot. Sitting down in the rocking-chair, she closed her eyes, and spread her arms out along the arms of the chair.

He could not see her from where he lay, but she was within reach of him, and, after a brief, unhappy silence, he put out his hand and drew the chair towards him, urging it forward, inch by inch, until it was beside the sofa. Then he pulled her head down, so that it also lay on the cushion, and he could feel her hair against his.

" How you hate me! " he said in a low voice, and as though he were speaking to himself. Laying her hand on his forehead, he made of it a screen for his eyes. " Who could have foreseen this! " he said again, in the same toneless way.

Louise lay still, and did not speak.

"Why do you stay with me?" he went on, looking out from under her hand. "I often ask myself that. For you're free to come and go as you choose."

Her eyes opened at this, though he did not see it. "And I choose to stay here! How often am I to tell you that? Why do you come back on it to-night? I'm tired—tired."

"I know you are. I saw it as soon as you came in. It's been a tiring day, and you probably . . . walked too far."

With a jerk, she drew her hand out of his, and sat upright in her chair. Something, a mere tone, the slight pause, in his apparently harmless words, incensed her. "Too far, did I? —Oh, to-night at least, be honest! Why don't you ask me straight out where I have been?—and what I have done? Can't you, for once, be man enough to put an open question?"

"Nothing was further from my mind than to make implications. It's you who're so suspicious. Just as if you had a bad conscience—something really to conceal."

"Take care!—or I shall tell you—where I've been! And you might regret it."

"No. For God's sake!—no more confessions!"

She laughed, and lay back. But a moment later, she cried out: "Why don't you go away yourself? You know I loathe the sight of you; and yet you stick on here like . . . like a leech. Go away, oh, why can't you go away!"

"To-day, I might have taken you at your word."

At the mention of Madeleine's name, she pricked up her ears. "Oho!" she said, when he had finished his story. "So Madeleine pays you visits, does she?—the sainted Madeleine! You have her there, and me here.—A pretty state of things!"

"Hold your tongue! I'm not in the mood to-night to stand your gibes."

"But I'm in the mood to make them. And how is one to help it when one hears that that ineffable creature is no better than she ought to be?"

"Hold your tongue!" he cried again. "How dare you speak like that of the girl who has been such a good friend to me!"

"Friend!" she echoed. "What fools men are! She's in love with you, that's all, and always has been. But you were never man enough to know what it was she wanted—your friend!"

"Ah, you——!" The nervous strain of the afternoon

reached its climax. "You! Yes!—that's you all over! In your eyes nothing is good or pure. And you make everything you touch dirty. You're not fit to take a decent woman's name on your lips!"

She sprang up from her chair. "And that's my thanks!—for all I've done—all I've sacrificed 'for you. I'm not fit to take a decent woman's name on my lips! For shame, for shame! For who has made me what I am but you! Oh, what a fool I was, ever to let you cross this door! You!—a man who is content with other men's leavings. "

" It was the worst day's work you ever did in your life. Everything bad has come from that.—Why couldn't you have held back, and refused me? We might still have been decent, happy creatures, if you hadn't let your vile nature get the better of you. You wouldn't marry me—no, no! You prefer to take your pleasure in other ways.—A man at any cost, Madeleine said once, and God knows, I believe it was true!"

She struck him in the face. "Oh, you miserable scoundrel! You!—who never looked at me but with the one thought in your head. Oh, it's too much! Never, never while I live—I would rather die first.—shall you ever touch me again!"

She continued to weep, long after he had left her. Still crying, her handkerchief pressed to her eyes, her body shaken by her sobs, she moved blindly about the room, opening drawers and cupboards, and heaping up their contents on the bed. There was a limit to everything; she could bear her life with him no longer; and, with nerveless fingers, she strove to collect and pack her belongings, preparatory to going away.

XII

Easter fell early, and the Ninth Symphony had been performed in the Gewandhaus before March was fairly out. Now, both Conservatorium and Gewandhaus were closed, and the familiar haunts were empty.

Hitherto, Maurice had made shift to preserve appearances: at intervals, not too conspicuously far apart, he had gone backwards and forwards to his classes, keeping his head above water with a minimum of work. Now, however, there was no further need for deceiving people. Most of those who had been his fellow-students had left Leipzig; he could not put his finger on a single person remaining, with whom he had had a nearer acquaintance. No one was left to comment on what he did and how he lived. And this knowledge withdrew the last prop from his sense of propriety. He ceased to face the trouble that care for his person implied, just as he gave up raising the lid of the piano and making a needless pretence of work. Openly now, he took up his abode in the *Brüderstrasse,* where he spent the long, idle days stretched on the sofa, rolling cigarettes—in far greater numbers than he could smoke, and vacantly, yet with a kind of gusto, as if his fingers, so long accustomed to violent exercise, had a relish for the task. He was seldom free from headache; an iron ring, which it was impossible to loosen, bound his forehead. His disinclination to speech grew upon him, too; not only had he no thoughts that it was worth breaking the silence to express; the effort demanded by the forming of words was too great for him. His feeling of indifference—stupefying indifference—grew so strong that sometimes he felt it beyond his strength consciously to take in the shape of the objects about the room.

The days were eventless. He lay and watched her movements, which were spiritless and hurried, by turns, but now seldom marked by the gracious impulsiveness that had made up so large a part of her charm. He was content to live from hour to hour at her side; for that this was his last respite, he well knew. And the further the month advanced, the more tenaciously he clung. The one thought which now had force to rouse him was, that the day would come on which he would

see her face for the last time. The fact that she had given
herself to another, while yet belonging to him, ceased to
affect him displeasurably, as did also his fixed idea that she
was, at the present moment, deceiving him anew. His sole ob-
session was now a fear of the inevitable end. And it was this
fear which, at rare intervals, broke the taciturn dejection in
which he was sunk, by giving rise to appalling fits of violence.
But after a scene of this kind, he would half suffocate her
with remorse. And this, perhaps, worked destruction most
surely of all: the knowledge that, despite the ungovernable
aversion she felt for him, she could still tolerate his endear-
ments. Not once, as long as they had been together, had she
refused to be caressed.

But the impossibility of the life they were leading broke
over Louise at times, with the shock of an ice-cold wave.

"If you have any feeling left in you—if you have ever
cared for me in the least—go away now!" she wept. "Go
to the ends of the earth—only leave me!"

He was giddy with headache that day. "To whom? Who
is it you want now?"

One afternoon as he lay there, the landlady came in with a
telegram for him, which she said had been brought round by
one of Frau Krause's children—she tossed it on the table, as
she spoke, to express the contempt she felt for him. Several
minutes elapsed before he put out his hand for it, and then
he did so, because it required less energy to open it than to
leave it unopened. When he had read it, he gave a short laugh,
and threw it back on the table. Louise, who was in the other
part of the room, came out, half-dressed, to see what the matter was. She, too, laughed at its contents in her insolent way,
and, on passing the writing-table, pulled open the drawer where
she kept her money.

"There's enough for two. And you're no prouder in this,
I suppose, than in anything else."

The peremptory summons home, and the announcement that
no further allowance would be remitted, was not a surprise to
him; he had known all along that, sooner or later, he would
be thrown on his own resources. It had happened a little
earlier than he had expected—that was all. A week had still
to run till the end of the month.—That night, however, when
Louise was out, he meditated, in a desultory fashion, over the
likely and unlikely occupations to which he could turn his
hand.

A few days later, she came home one evening in a different
mood: for once, no cruel words crossed her lips. They sat
side by side on the sofa; and of such stuff was happiness now
made that he was content. Chancing to look up, he was dismayed to see that her eyes were full of tears, which, as he
watched, ran over and down her cheeks. He slid to his knees,
and laid his head in her lap.

She fell asleep early; for, no matter what happened, how
uneventful or how tragically exciting her day was, her faculty
for sleep remained unchanged. It was a brilliant night; in
the sky was a great, round, yellow moon, and the room was
lit up by it. The blind of the window facing the bed had not
been lowered; and a square patch of light fell across the bed.
He turned and looked at her, lying in it. Her face was towards
him; one arm was flung up above her head; the hand lay with
the palm exposed. Something in the look of the face, blanched
by the unreal light, made him recall the first time he had seen
it, and the impression it had then left on his mind. While
she played in Schwarz's room, she had turned and looked at him,
and it had seemed to him then, that some occult force had gone
out from the face, and struck home in him. And it had never
lessened. Strange, that so small a thing, hardly bigger than
one's two closed fists, should be able to exert such an influence
over one! For this face it was—the pale oval, in the dark setting, the exotic colouring, the heavy-lidded eyes—which held
him; it was this face which drew him surely back with a
vital nostalgia—a homesickness for the sight of her and the
touch of her—if he were too long absent. It had not been any
coincidence of temperament or sympathies—by rights, all the
rights of their different natures, they had not belonged together—any more than it had been a mere blind uprush of
sensual desire. And just as his feelings for her had had nothing
to do with reason, or with the practical conduct of his life,
so they had outlasted tenderness, faithfulness, respect. Whatever it was that held him, it lay deeper than these conventional
ideas of virtue. The power her face had over him was un-
diminished, though he now found it neither beautiful nor good;
though he knew the true meaning of each deeply graven line.
—This then was love?—this morbid possession by a woman's
face.

He laid his arm across his tired eyes, and, without waiting
to consider the question he had propounded, commenced to
follow out a new train of thought. No doubt, for each in-

35

dividual, there existed in one other mortal, some physical detail which he or she could find only in this particular person. It might be the veriest trifle. Some found it, it seemed, in the colour of an eye; some in the modulations of a voice, the _urve of a lip, the shape of a hand, the lines of a body in motion. Whatever it chanced to be, it was, in most cases, an insignificant characteristic, which, for others, simply did not exist, but which, to the one affected by it, made instant appeal, and just to that corner of the soul which had hitherto suffered aimlessly for the want of it—a suffering which nothing but this intonation, this particular smile, could allay. He himself had long since learnt what it was, about her face, that made a like appeal to him. It was her eyes. Not their size, or their dark brilliancy, but the manner of their setting: the spacious lid that fell from the high, wavy eyebrow, first sloping deeply inwards, then curving out again, over the eyeball; this, and the clean sweep of the broad, white lid, which, when lowered, gave the face an infantine look—a look of marble. He knew it was this; for, on the strength of a mere hinted resemblance, he had been unable to take his eyes off the face of another woman; the likeness in this detail had met his gaze with a kind of shock. But what a meaningless thing was life, when the way a lid drooped, or an eyebrow grew on a forehead, could make such havoc of your nerves! And more especially when, in the brain or soul that lay behind, no spiritual trait answered to the physical. —Well, that was for others to puzzle over, not for him. The strong man tore himself away while there was still time, or saved himself in an engrossing pursuit. He, having had neither strength nor saving occupation, had bartered all he had, and knowingly, for the beauty of this face. And as long as it existed for him, his home was beside it.

He turned restlessly. Disturbed in her dreams, Louise flung over on her other side.

" Eugen ! " she murmured. " Save me !—Here I am ! Oh, don't you see me ? "

He shook her by the arm. " Wake up ! "

She was startled and angry. " Won't you even let me sleep ? "

" Keep your dreams to yourself then ! "

There was a savage hatred in her look. " Oh, if I only could ! . . . if only my hands were strong enough !—I'd kill you ! "

" You've done your best."

" Yes. And I'm glad! Remember that, afterwards. I was glad! "

It had been a radiant April morning of breeze and sunshine, but towards midday, clouds gathered, and the sunlight was constantly intercepted. Maurice had had occasion to fetch something from his lodgings and was on his way back. The streets were thronged with people: business men, shop-assistants and students, returning to work from the restaurants in which they had dined. At a corner of the *Zeitzerstrasse*, a hand-cart had been overturned, and a crowd had gathered; for, no matter how busy people were, they had time to gape and stare; and they were now as eager as children to observe this incident, in the development of which a stout policeman was wordily authoritative. Maurice found that he had loitered with the rest, to watch the gathering up of the spilt wares, and to hear the ensuing altercation between hawker and policeman. On turning to walk on again, his eye was caught and held by the tall figure of a man who was going in the same direction as he, but at a brisk pace, and several yards in front of him. This person must have passed the group round the cart. Now, intervening heads and shoulders divided them, obstructing Maurice's view; still, signs were not wanting in him that his subliminal consciousness was beginning to recognise the man who walked ahead. There was something oddly familiar in the gait, in the droop of the shoulders, the nervous movement of the head, the aimless motion of the dangling hands and arms—briefly, in all the loosely hung body. And, besides this, the broad-brimmed felt hat . . . Good God! He stiffened, with a sudden start, and, in an instant, his entire attention was concentrated in an effort to see the colour of the hair under the hat. Was it red? He tried to strike out in lengthier steps, but the legs of the man in front were longer, and his own unruly. After a moment's indecision, however, he mastered them, and then, so afraid was he of the other passing out of sight, that he all but ran, and kept this pace up till he was close behind the man he followed. There he fell into a walk again, but a weak and difficult walk, for his heart was leaping in his chest. He had not been mistaken. The person close before him, so close that he could almost have touched him, was no other than Schilsky—the Schilsky of old, with the insolent, short-sighted eyes, and the loose, easy walk.

Maurice followed him—followed warily and yet unreflectingly—right down the long, populous street. Sometimes blindly,

too, for, when the street and all it contained swam before him,
he was obliged to shut his eyes. People looked with attention at
him; he caught a glimpse of himself in a barber's mirror, and
saw that his face had turned a greenish white. His mind was
set on one point. Arrived at the corner where the street ran
out into the *Königsplatz,* which turning would Schilsky take?
Would he go to the right, where lay the *Brüderstrasse,* or would
he take the lower street to the left? Until this question was
answered, it was impossible to decide what should be done next.
But first, there came a lengthy pause: Schilsky entered a music-
shop, and remained inside, leaning over the counter, for a quarter of an hour. Finally, however, the corner was reached. He
appeared to hesitate: for a moment it seemed as if he were
going straight on, which would mean fresh uncertainty. Then,
with a sudden outward fling of the hands, he went off to the
left, in the direction of the Gewandhaus.

Maurice did not follow him any further. He stood and
watched, until he could no longer see the swaying head. After
that he had a kind of collapse. He leaned up against the wall of
a house, and wiped the perspiration from his forehead. Passers-
by believed him to be drunk, and were either amused, or horrified, or saddened. He discovered, in truth, that his legs were
shaking as if with an ague, and, stumbling into a neighbouring
wine-shop, he drank brandy—not enough to stupefy him, only
to give back to his legs their missing strength.

To postpone her knowing! To hinder her from knowing at
any cost!—his blurred thoughts got no further than this. He
covered the ground at a mad pace, clinging fast to the belief
that he would find her, as he had left her, in bed. But his first
glimpse of her turned him cold. She was standing before the
glass, dressed to go out. This in itself was bad enough. Worse,
far worse, was it that she had put on, to-day, one of the light,
thin dresses she had worn the previous spring, and never since.
It was impossible to see her tricked out in this fashion, and
doubt her knowledge of the damning fact. He held it for
proved that she was dressed to leave him; and the sight of her,
refreshed and rejuvenated, gave the last thrust to his tottering
sense. He demanded with such savageness the meaning of her
adornment, that the indignant amazement with which she turned
on him was real, and not feigned.

" Take off that dress! You shan't go out of the house in it!—
Take it off! "

He raved, threatened, implored, always with icy fingers at

his heart. He knew that she knew; he would have taken his
oath on it; and he only had room in his brain for one thought:
to prevent her knowing. His rage spent itself on the light,
flowery dress. As nothing he said moved her, he set his foot
on the skirt, and tore it down from the waist. She struck
at him for this, then took another dress from the wardrobe—a
still lighter and gaudier one. They had never yet gone through
an hour such as that which followed. At its expiry, clothes and
furniture lay strewn about the room.

When Louise saw that he was not to be shaken off, that,
wherever she went on this day, he would go, too, she gave up
any plan she might have had, and followed where he led. This
was, as swiftly as possible, by the outlying road to the Connewitz woods. If he could but once get her there, they would be
safe from surprise. Once out there, in solitude, among the
screening trees, something, he did not yet know what, but something would—must—happen.

He dragged her relentlessly along. But until they got there!
His eyes grew stiff and giddy with looking before him, behind
him, on all sides. And never had she seemed to move so slowly;
never had she stared so brazenly about her, as on this afternoon.
With every step they took, certainty burned higher in him; the
thin, fixed smile that disfigured her lips said: do your worst;
do all you can; nothing will save you! He did not draw a
full breath till they were far out on the *Schleussiger Weg*.
Then he dropped her arm, and wiped his face.

The road was heavy with mud, from rains of the preceding
day. Louise, dragging at his side, was careless of it, and let
her long skirt trail behind her. He called her attention to it,
furiously, and this was the first time he had spoken since
leaving the house. But she did not even look down: she picked
out a part of the road that was still dirtier, where her feet sank
and stuck.

They crossed the bridge, and joined the wood-path. On one
of the first seats they came to, Louise dropped exhausted. Filled
with the idea of getting her into the heart of the woods, he was
ahead of her, urging the pace; and he had taken a further
step or two before he saw that she had remained behind. He
was forced to return.

"What are you sitting there for?" he turned on her, with
difficulty resisting the impulse to strike her full in her contemptuous white face.

She laughed — her terrible laugh, which made the nerves

twitch in his finger-tips. "Why does one usually sit down?"

"*One?*—You're not one! You're you!" Now he wished hundreds of listeners were in their neighbourhood, that the fierceness of his voice might carry to them.

"And you're a madman!"

"Yes, treat me like the dirt under your feet! But you can't deceive me.—Do you think I don't know why you're stopping here?"

She looked away from him, without replying.

"Do you think I don't know why you've decked yourself out like this?"

"For God's sake, stop harping on my dress!"

"Why you've bedizened yourself? . . . why you were going out? . . . why you've spied and gaped eternally from one side of the street to the other?"

As she only continued to look away, the desire seized him to say something so incisive that the implacability of her face would have to change, no matter to what. "I'll tell you then!" he shouted, and struck the palm of one hand with the back of the other, so that the bones in both bit and stung. "I'll tell you. You're waiting here . . . waiting, I say! But you'll wait to no purpose! For you've reckoned without me."

"Oh, very well, then, if it pleases you, I'm waiting. But you can at least say for what? For you perhaps?—for you to regain your senses?"

"Stop your damned sneering! Will you tell me you don't know who's—don't know he's here?"

Still she continued to overlook him. "He?—who?—what?" She flung the little words at him like stones. Yet, in the second that elapsed before his reply, a faint presentiment widened her eyes.

"You've got the audacity to ask that?" Flinging himself down on the seat, he put his hands in his pockets, and stretched out his legs. "Who but your precious Schilsky!—the man who knew how you ought to be treated . . . who gave you what you deserved!"

His first feeling was one of relief: the truth was out; there was an end to the torture of the past hour. But after this one flash of sensation, he ceased to consider himself. At his words Louise turned so white that he thought she was going to faint. She raised her hand to her throat, and held it there. She tried to say something, and could not utter a sound.

Her voice had left her. She turned her head and looked at him, in a strange, apprehensive way, with the eyes of a trapped animal.

"Eugen!—Eugen is here?" she said at last. "Here?—Do you know what you're saying?" Now that her voice had come, it was a little thin whisper, like the voice of a sick person. She pushed hat and hair, both suddenly become an intolerable weight, back from her forehead.

Still he was not warned. "Will you swear to me you didn't know?"

"I know? I swear?" Her voice was still a mere echo of itself. But now she rose, and standing at the end of the seat furthest from him, held on to the back of it. "I know?" she repeated, as if to herself. Then she drew a long breath, which quivered through her, and, with it, voice and emotion and the power of expression returned. "I know?" she cried with a startling loudness. "Good God, you fool, do you think I'd be here with you, if I had known?—if I had known!"

A foreboding of what he had done came to Maurice. "Take care!—take care what you say!"

She burst into a peal of hysterical laughter, which echoed through the woods.

"Take care!" he said again, and trembled.

"Of what?—of you, perhaps? *You!*"

"I may kill you yet."

"Oh, such as you don't kill!"

She lowered her veil, and stooped for her gloves. He looked up at her swift movement. There was a blueness round his lips.

"What are you going to do?"

She laughed.

"You're . . . you're going to him! Louise!—you are *not* going to him?"

"Oh, you poor, crazy fool, what made you tell me?"

"Stay here!" He caught her by the sleeve. But she shook his hand off as though it were a poisonous insect. "For God's sake, think what you're doing! Have a little mercy on me!"

"Have you ever had mercy on me?"

She took a few, quick steps away from the seat, then with an equally impulsive resolve, came back and confronted him.

"You talk to me of mercy?—you!—when nothing I could wish you would be bad enough for you?—Oh, I never thought it would be possible to hate anyone as I hate you—you mean-

souled, despicable dummy of a man!—Why couldn't you have
let me alone? I didn't care that much for you—not *that* much!
But you came, with your pretence of friendship, and your flattery, and your sympathy—it was all lies, every word of it! Do
you think what has happened to us would ever have happened if
you'd been a different kind of man?—But you have never had
a clean thought of me—never! Do you suppose I haven't known
what you were thinking and believing about me in these last
weeks?—those nights when I waited night after night to see a
light come back in his windows? Yes, and I let you believe it;
I wanted you to; I was glad you did—glad to see you suffer.
I wish you were dead!—Do you see that river? Go and throw
yourself into it. I'll stand here and watch you sink, and laugh
when I see you drowning.—Oh, I hate you—hate you! I shall
hate you to my last hour! "

She spat on the ground at his feet. Before he could raise his
head, she was gone.

He made an involuntary, but wholly uncertain, movement to
follow her, did not, however, carry it out, and sank back into
his former attitude. His cold hands were deep in his pockets,
his shoulders drawn up; and his face, drained of its blood, was
like the face of an old man. He had made no attempt to defend
himself, had sat mute, letting her vindictive words go over him,
inwardly admitting their truth. Now he closed his eyes, and
kept them shut, until the thudding of his heart grew less forcible. When he looked up again, his gaze met the muddy, sluggish water, into which she had dared him to throw himself. But
he did not even recall her taunt. He merely sat and stared at
the river, amazed at the way in which it had, as it were, detached itself from other objects. All at once it had acquired a
life of its own, and it was difficult to believe that it had ever
been an integral part of the landscape.

He remained sitting till the mists were breast-high. But
even when, after more than one start—for his legs were stiff
and numbed—he rose to go home, he did not realise what had
happened to him. He was only aware that night had fallen,
and that it would be better to get back in the direction of the
town.

The twinkling street-lamps did more than anything towards
rousing him. But they also made him long, with a sudden
vehemence, for some warm, brightly lighted interior, where it
would be possible to forget the night-haunted river. He sought
out an obscure café, and entering, called for brandy. On

this night, he was under no necessity to limit himself; and he sat, glowering at the table, and emptying his glass, until he had died a temporary, and charitable, death. The delicious sensation of sipping the brandy was his chief remembrance of these hours; but, also, like far-off, incorporate happenings, he was conscious, as the night deepened, of women's shrill and lively voices, and of the pressure of a woman's arms.

XIII

He wakened, the next morning, to strange surroundings. Half opening his eyes, he saw a strip of drab wall-paper, besprinkled with crude pink roses, and the black and gilt frame of an oblong mirror. He shut them again immediately, preferring to believe that he was still dreaming. Somewhere in the back of his head, a machine was working, with slow, steady throbs, which made his body vibrate as a screw does a steamer. He lay enduring it, and trying to sleep again, to its accompaniment. But just as he was on the point of dozing off, a noise in the room startled him, and made him wide awake. He was not alone. Something had fallen to the floor, and a voice exclaimed impatiently. Peering through his lids, he looked out beyond the wall which had first chained his attention. His eyes fell on the back of a woman, who was sitting in front of one of the windows, doing her hair. In her hand she held a pair of curling-tongs, and, before her, on the foot-end of the sofa, a hand-glass was propped up. Her hair was thick and blond. She wore a black silk chemise, which had slipped low on her plump shoulders ; a shabby striped petticoat was bound round her waist, and her naked feet were thrust into down-trodden, felt shoes. Maurice lay still, in order that she should not suspect his being awake. For a few minutes, there was silence ; then he was forced to sneeze, and at the sound the woman muttered something, and came to the side of the bed. A curl was imprisoned between the blades of the tongs, which she continued to hold aloft, in front of her forehead.

"*Na, Kleiner!* . . . had your sleep out?" she asked in a raucous voice. As Maurice did not reply, but closed his eyes again, blinded by the sunshine that poured into the room, she laughed, and made a sound like that with which one urges on a horse. "Don't feel up to much this morning . . . eh? *Herrje, Kleiner,* but you were tight!" and, at some remembrance of the preceding night, she chuckled to herself. "And now, I bet you, you feel as if you'd never be able to lift your head again. Just wait a jiffy! I'll get you something that'll revive you."

She waddled to the door and he heard her call: "*Johann, einen Schnaps!*"

Feet shuffled in the passage; she handed Maurice a glass of brandy.

"There you are!—that'll pull you together. Swallow it down," she said, as he hesitated. "You'll feel another man after it.—And now I'll do what I wouldn't do for every one—make you a coffee to wash down the nasty physic."

She laughed loudly at her own joke, and laid the curling-tongs aside. He watched her move about the room in search of spirit-lamp and coffee-mill. Beneath the drooping black chemise, her loose breasts swayed.

"Not that I've much time," she went on, as she ground the coffee. "It's gone a quarter to twelve already, and I like fresh air. I don't miss a minute of it.—So up you get! Here, dowse your head in this water."

Leaning against the table, Maurice drank the cup of black coffee, and considered his companion. No longer young, she was as coarsely haggard as are the generality of women of her class, scanned by cruel daylight. And while she could never have been numbered among the handsome ones of her profession, there was yet a certain kindliness in the smallish blue eyes, and in her jocose manner of treating him.

She, too, eyed him as he drank.

"*Sag' 'mal Kleiner*—will you come again?" she broke the silence.

"What's your name? he asked evasively, and put the cup down on the table.

"Oh . . . just ask for Luise," she said. On her tongue, the name had three long-drawn syllables, and there was a v before the i.

She was nettled by his laugh.

"What's wrong with it?" she asked. "*Geh', Kleiner, sei nett!*—won't you come again?"

"Perhaps."

'Well, ask for Luise, if you do. That's enough."

He turned to put on his coat. As he did so, a disagreeable thought crossed his mind; he coloured, and ran his hand through his pockets.

"I've no money."

"What?—rooked, are you? Well, it wasn't here, then. I'm an honest girl, I am!"

She came over to him, not exactly suspicious, still with a

slight diminution of friendliness in eyes and tone; and, as, if
there were room for a mistake on his part, herself went through
the likely pockets in turn.

" Not a heller! "

Her sharp little eyes travelled over him.

" That'd do."

She laid her hand on his scarf-pin. He took it out and gave
it to her. She stood on tip-toe, for she was dumpy, put her
arms round his neck, and gave him a hearty kiss.

" *Du gefällst mir!* " she said. " I like you. Kiss me, too,
can't you? "

He looked down on the plump, ungainly figure, and, without
feeling either satisfaction or repugnance, stooped and kissed the
befringed forehead.

" *Adieu, Kleiner!* Come again."

" *Adieu, Luise!* "

He was eyed—he felt it—from various rooms, the doors of
which stood ajar. The front door was wide open, and he left
it so. He descended the stairs with a sagging step. Half-way
down, he stopped short. He had spoken the truth when he
said that he was without money; every pfennig he possessed,
had been in his pocket the night before. Under these circumstances, he could undertake nothing. But, even while he
thought it, his hand sought his watch, which he carried chain-
less in a pocket of his vest. It was there, and as his fingers
closed on it, he proceeded on his way.

The day had again set in brilliantly; the shadows on roads
and pavements had real depth, and the outlines of the houses
were hard against a cloudless sky. He kept his eyes fixed on
the ground; for the crudeness of the light made them ache.

His feet bore him along the road they knew better than
any other. And until he had been in the *Brüderstrasse*, he
could not decide what was to come next. He dragged
along, with bowed head, and the distance seemed unending.
Even when he had turned the corner and was in the street
itself, he kept his head down, and only when he was opposite
the house, did he throw a quick glance upwards. His heart
gave a terrifying leap, then ceased to beat: when it began again,
it was at a mad gallop, which prevented him drawing breath.
All three windows stood wide open; the white window-curtains
hung out over the sills, and flapped languidly in the breeze.

He crossed the road with small steps, like a convalescent.
He pushed back the heavy house-door, and entered the vestibule,

which was cold and shadowy. Step by step, he climbed to the
first landing. The door of the flat was shut, but the little door
in the wall stood ajar, and he could see right into the room.

He leaned against the banisters, where the shadow was
deepest. Inside the room that had been his world, two charwomen rubbed and scoured, talking as they worked, in strident
tones. The heavy furniture had been pulled into the middle of
the floor, and shrouded in white coverings; chairs were laid on
the bed, with their legs in the air. There was no trace of anything that had belonged to Louise; all familiar objects had vanished. It was a strange, unnatural scene: he felt as one might
feel who, by means of some mysterious agency, found it possible
to be present at his own burial, while he was still alive.

One of the women began to beat the sofa; under cover of the
blows, which reverberated through the house, he slunk away.
But he did not get far: when he was recalled to himself by a
new noise in one of the upper storeys, he found that he was
standing on the bottom step of the stairs, holding fast to the
round gilt ball that surmounted the last post of the banisters.
He moved from there to the warmth of the house-door, and,
for some time before going out, stood sunning himself, a forlorn
figure, with eyes that blinked at the light. He felt very cold,
and weak to the point of faintness. This sensation reminded
him that he had had no solid food since noon the day before.
His first business was obviously to eat a meal. Fighting a growing dizziness, he trudged into the town, and, having pawned his
watch, went to a restaurant, and forced himself to swallow the
meal that was set before him—though there were moments when
it seemed incredible that it was actually he who plied knife and
fork. He would have been glad to linger for a time, after
eat ng, but the restaurant was crowded, and the waiter openly
impatient for him to be gone. As he rose, he saw the man
flicking the crumbs off the cloth, and setting the table anew;
some one was waiting to take his place.

When he emerged again into the thronged and slightly dusty
streets, his previous strong impression of the unreality of things
was upon him again. Now, however, it seemed as though some
submerged consciousness were at work in him. For, though he
was not aware of having reviewed his position, or of having cast
a plan of action, he knew at once what was to be done; and, as
before, his feet bore him, without bidding, where he had to go.

He retraced his steps, and half-way down the *Klostergasse,*
entered a gunsmith's shop. The owner, an elderly man in a

velvet cap and gold-rimmed spectacles, looked at him over the
tops of these, then said curtly, he could not oblige him.
What was more, he came out after him, and, standing in
the shop-door, watched him go down the street. At his refusal,
Maurice had hurriedly withdrawn: now, as he went, he was
troubled by the fact that the man's face was vaguely familiar to
him. For the length of a street-block, he endeavoured to recollect where he had seen the face before. And suddenly he knew:
it was this very shop he had once been in to inquire after Krafft,
and this was the same man who had then been so uncivil to him.
But as soon as he remembered, the knowledge ceased to interest
him.

Rendered cautious by his first experience, he went to another
neighbourhood, and having sought for some time, found a
smaller shop, in a side street. He had ready this time the fiction
of a friend and a commission. But a woman regretted wordily
that her husband had just stepped out; he would no doubt be
back again immediately; if the Herr would take a chair and wait
a little?—But the thought of waiting made him turn on his heel.
Finally, at his third attempt, a young lad gave him what he
desired, without demur; and, after he had known a quick fear
lest he should not have sufficient money for the purchase, the
matter was satisfactorily settled.

On returning to his room, he found a letter lying on the
table. He pounced upon it with a desperate hope. But it was
only the monthly bill for the hire of the piano.

In entering, he had made some noise, and Frau Krause was
in the room before he knew it. She was primed for an angry
scene. But he made short work of her complaints and accu-
sations.

" To-morrow! I'll have time for all that to-morrow."

He turned the key in the door, and sitting down before the
writing-table, commenced to go through drawers and pigeon-
holes. It had not been a habit of his to keep letters; but
nevertheless a certain number had accumulated, and these he
was averse to let fall into the hands of strangers. He performed
his work coolly, with a pedantic thoroughness. He had no
sympathy with those people, who, doing what he was about to
do, left ragged ends behind them. His mind had always inclined
to law and order. And so, having written a note authorising
Frau Krause to keep his books and clothes, in place of the out-
standing rent, he put a match to the fire which was laid in the
stove, and, on his knees before it, burnt all such personal trifles

as had value for himself alone. He postponed, to the last, even handling the small packet made up of the letters he had had from Louise. Then their turn came, too. Kneeling before the stove-door, he dropped them, one by one, into the flames. The last to burn was the first he had received—a mere hastily scrawled line, a twisted note, which opened as it blackened. *I must speak to you. Will you come to me this evening?* As he watched it shrivel, he had a vivid recollection of that long past day. He remembered how he had tried to shave, and how he had dressed himself in his best, only to fling back again into his working-clothes, annoyed with himself for even harbouring the thought. Yes; but that had always been his way: he had expended consideration and delicacy where none was necessary; he had seen her only as he wished to see her.—After this, the photographs. They were harder to burn; he was forced to tear them across, in two, three pieces. Even then, the flames licked slowly; he watched them creep up—over her dress, her hands, her face.

Afternoon had turned to evening. When, at length, everything was in order, he lay down on the sofa to wait for it to grow quite dark. But almost at once, as if his back had been eased of a load, he fell asleep. When he opened his eyes again, the lamp had burned low, and filled the room with a poisonous vapour. It was two o'clock. This was the time to go. But a boisterous wind had risen, and was blustering round the house. He said to himself that he would wait still a little longer, to see if it did not subside. In waiting, he slept again, heavily, as he had not done for many a night, and when he wakened next, a clock was striking four. He rose at once, and with his boots in his hand, crept out of the house.

Day was breaking; as he walked, a thin streak of grey in the east widened with extreme rapidity, and became a bank of pale grey light. He met an army of street-sweepers, indistinguishably male and female, returning from their work, their long brooms over their shoulders. It had rained a little, and the pavements were damp and shining. The wind had dropped to a mere morning breeze, which met him at street-corners. Before his mind's eye rose a vision of the coming day. He saw one of those early spring days of illimitable blue highness, and white, woofy clouds, which stand stationary where the earth meets the sky; the brightness of the sun makes the roads seem whiter and the grass greener, bringing out new tints and colours in everything it touches. Over it all would run this light, swift wind, bending the buds, and even, towards afternoon, throwing up a fine white dust.—And it was to the thought of the dust that his mind clung most tenaciously, as to some homely and familiar thing which he would never see again.

He had made straight for the well-known seat with the bosky background. Arrived at it, he went a few steps aside, into an open space among the undergrowth, which was now generously sprinkled with buds. The leaves that had fallen during the previous autumn made a carpet under his feet. Somewhere, in the distance, a band was playing: a body of soldiers was being marched out to exercise. He opened the case he was carrying, and laid it on the seat. He was not conscious of feeling afraid; if he had a fear, it was only lest, in his inexperience, he should do what he had to do, clumsily. In loosening the clothes at his neck, however, he perceived that his hand was shaking, and this made him aware that his heart also was beating unevenly. He stood and fumbled with his collar-stud, which he could not unfasten at once, and, while he was busied thus, the mists that blinded him fell away. He ceased, abruptly, to be the mere automaton that had moved and acted, without will of its own, for the past four-and-twenty hours. Standing there, with his fingers at his neck, he was pierced by a sudden lucid perception of what had happened. An intolerable spasm of remembrance gripped him. With a rush of bitterness, which was undiluted agony, all the shame and suffering of the past months swept over him once more, concentrated in a last supreme moment. And, as though this were not enough, while he still wrenched at his neck, tearing his shirt-collar in his desperation, her face rose before him—but not the face he had known and loved. He saw it as he had seen it for the last time, disfigured by hatred of him, horribly vindictive, as it had been when she spat on the ground at his feet. This vision gave him an unlooked-for jerk of courage. Without allowing himself another second in which to reason or reflect, he caught up the revolver from the seat, and pressed the cold little nozzle to his chest. Simultaneously he received a sharp blow, and heard the crack of a report—but far away . . . in the distance. He was on his back, without knowing how he had got there; straight overhead waved the bare branches of a tree; behind them, a grey morning cloud was sailing. For still the fraction of a second, he heard the familiar melody, to which the soldiers marched; and the branch swayed . . . swayed . . .

Then, as suddenly as the flame of a candle is puffed out by

the wind, his life went from him. His right hand twitched, made as if to open, closed again, and stiffened round the iron of the handle. His jaw fell, and, like an inner lid, a glazed film rose over his eyes, which for hours afterwards continued to stare, with an expression of horror and amaze, at the naked branches of the tree.

*   *   *   *   *

One midday, a couple of years later, a number of those who had formed the audience at one of the last rehearsals of the season, were gathered round the back entrance to the Gewandhaus. It was a fresh spring day, gusty and sunny by turns: sometimes, there came a puff of wind that drove every one's hand to his hat; at others, the broad square basked in an almost motionless sunshine. The small crowd lingered in order to see, at close quarters, the violinist who had played there that morning. Only a few of those present had known Schilsky personally; but one and all were curious to catch a glimpse of the quondam Leipzig student, who, it was whispered, would soon return to take up a leading position in the orchestra. Schilsky was now *Konzertmeister* in a large South German town ; but it was rather as a composer that his name had begun to burn on people's tongues. His new symphonic poem, *Über die letzten Dinge,* had drawn down on his head that mixture of extravagant laudation and abusive derision, which constitutes fame.

"Take a look at his wife, if she's there," said one American to another, who was standing beside him. " She studied here same time he did, and is said to have been very handsome. An English chap shot himself on her account."

"You don't say!" drawled his companion. "It's a queer thing, how common suicide's getting to be. You can't pick up a noospaper, nowadays, without finding some fool or other has blown his brains out."

"Look out!—here they come."

Behind the thick glass doors, Schilsky became visible. He was talking volubly to a Jewish-looking stranger in a fur-lined coat. His hat was pushed far back on his forehead; his face was flushed with elation; and, consciously unconscious of the waiting crowd, he gesticulated as he walked, throwing out the palms of his loosely dangling hands, and emphasising his words with restless movements of the head. He was respectfully greeted by those who had known him. A minute or two later came Louise.

At her side was a pianist with whom Schilsky had given a concert earlier in the week—a shabbily dressed young man, with a world of enthusiasm in his candid blue eyes. He, too, was talking with animation. But Louise had no attention for anyone but her husband.

"Well, not my taste . . . I must confess," laughed the man who had been severe on suicide. "Fine eyes, if you like—but give me something fresher."

She was wearing a long cloak. The door, in swinging to, caught an end of this, and hindered her progress. Both she and her companion stooped to free it; their hands met; and the bystanders saw the young man colour darkly over face and neck.

The others had got into one of the droschkes that waited in line beside the building. The dark stranger put an impatient head out of the window. The two behind quickened their steps; the young man helped Louise in, mounted himself, and slammed the door.

The driver gathered up the reins, cracked his whip, and the big-bodied droschke went swerving round the corner, clattering gutturally on the cobbled stone pavement.

The group of loiterers at the door dispersed.

THE END